Shcharansky

ALSO BY MARTIN GILBERT

VOLUMES OF THE BIOGRAPHY OF WINSTON S. CHURCHILL
III, The Challenge of War, 1914–1916 (*and documents*)
IV, The Stricken World, 1917–1922 (*and documents*)
V, The Prophet of Truth, 1922–1939 (*and documents*)
VI, Finest Hour, 1939–1941

ATLASES
Recent History Atlas, 1860–1960
British History Atlas
American History Atlas
Jewish History Atlas
First World War Atlas
Russian Imperial History Atlas
Soviet History Atlas
The Arab-Israeli Conflict: Its History in Maps
The Jews of Russia: Their History in Maps and Photographs
Jerusalem Illustrated History Atlas
Children's Illustrated Bible Atlas
The Jews of Arab Lands: Their History in Maps and Photographs
The Macmillan Atlas of the Holocaust

OTHER BOOKS
The Appeasers (*with Richard Gott*)
The European Powers, 1900–1945
The Roots of Appeasement
Sir Horace Rumbold: Portrait of a Diplomat
Churchill: A Photographic Portrait
Churchill's Political Philosophy
Auschwitz and the Allies
Exile and Return: The Struggle for Jewish Statehood
The Jews of Hope: The Plight of Soviet Jewry Today
Jerusalem: Rebirth of a City
The Holocaust

Shcharansky

HERO OF OUR TIME

Martin Gilbert , *1936-*

30203

THE JEWISH PUBLICATION SOCIETY OF AMERICA

ELISABETH SIFTON BOOKS
VIKING

ELISABETH SIFTON BOOKS · VIKING
Viking Penguin Inc.
40 West 23rd Street,
New York, New York 10010, U.S.A.

First American Edition
Published in 1986

LIBRARY OF CONGRESS CATALOGING IN PUBLICATION DATA
Gilbert, Martin, 1936–
Shcharansky, hero of our time.
Bibliography: p.
Includes index.
1. Shcharansky, Anatoly. 2. Jews—Soviet Union—
Biography. 3. Refuseniks—Biography. 4. Political
prisoners—Soviet Union—Biography. 5. Civil rights—
Soviet Union. 6. Israel—Emigration and immigration—
Biography. 7. Soviet Union—Emigration and immigration
—Biography. I. Title.
DS135.R95S494   1986   325′.247′095694 [B]   86-7773
ISBN 0-670-81418-0

Printed in the United States of America
by R. R. Donnelley & Sons, Harrisonburg, Virginia
Set in Bembo

This edition was published for the members
of the Jewish Publication Society of America
by arrangement with The Viking Press

Contents

List of Illustrations	vii
Acknowledgements	xi
Preface	xvii
1 From Donetsk to Moscow	1
2 The Awakening	13
3 Refusenik	23
4 Debates and Demonstrations	41
5 Marriage	45
6 Harassment, Hope and Hope Deceived	53
7 To Start Again	67
8 New Pressures, New Prisoners	73
9 Helsinki and Beyond	85
10 Lists	99
11 The Lottery of Refusal	103
12 Dangerous Times	123
13 Rejoicings, Beatings, Arrests	137
14 Culture and Repression	149
15 'Traders of Souls'	161
16 Accusations of Espionage	169
17 Arrest	187
18 Seeking to Build Up a Criminal Charge	193
19 Awaiting Trial	217
20 In Court	231
21 Road to Judgement	249
22 Judgement	267
23 Prisoner of Zion	277

24 Letters from Prison 293
25 'My Perpetual Optimism' 329
26 Suffering and Punishment 347
27 Hunger Strike 355
28 Letters, Alarms and Rumours 371
29 'Truly to Become a Free Person' 385
30 From the Urals to Jerusalem 405

Appendix 1: Prisoners of Zion 423
Appendix 2: Former Prisoners of Zion Still Refused Exit Visas 427
Appendix 3: Annual Emigration of Soviet Jews, 1951 to 1985 429
Bibliography 431
Maps 440
Index 443

List of Illustrations

Between pages 76–77

1 Shcharansky in reflective mood, Moscow 1976.
2 Boris Shcharansky in his Red Army uniform.
3 Tolya at kindergarten.
4 The two brothers, Tolya and Lyonya, in Donetsk.
5 Tolya with his mother, Ida Milgrom.
6 At the seaside.
7 Schoolboy.
8 A chess match at the seaside.
9 Shcharansky, junior chess champion of the Donetsk region.
10 The young student.
11 Rowing on the lake at Istra, near his parents' home.
12 Ida Milgrom and Boris Shcharansky.
13 A photograph of Shcharansky which Avital kept with her throughout the twelve years of their enforced separation.
14 Avital outside 10 Downing Street, London.
15 Arkhipova Street, Moscow.
16 At Moscow airport to say goodbye to Alexander Goldfarb.
17 Shcharansky, spokesman.
18 Eighteen refuseniks on 9 November 1976, following their release from detention.
19 Shcharansky after having been held in detention.

Between pages 204–205

20 Shcharansky with some of his closest refusenik friends.
21 Shcharansky in Moscow, under a map of Israel.
22 The Star of David sit-in and demonstration, Moscow, 25 October 1976.

23 Shcharansky, Alexander Lunts and Vladimir Slepak with two Israeli sportsmen, 21 September 1975.
24 Ina Rubin and Shcharansky.
25 Ida Nudel and Shcharansky entertaining American visitors.
26 Shcharansky, Leonid Volvovsky, Ida Nudel, Dina and Iosif Beilin and Enid Wurtman.
27 Vladimir Slepak, Shcharansky and Iosif Beilin.
28 The first night of Passover, 15 April 1976.
29 Shcharansky holding a photograph of Avital brought to him from Jerusalem.
30 Shcharansky at Tupik, November 1975, visiting Mark Nashpits in internal exile.
31 Refuseniks gather in a wood near Moscow to celebrate Israel Independence Day, 2 May 1976.
32 Ida Nudel and Sanya Lipavsky.
33 Shcharansky with Andrei Sakharov.
34 Shcharansky, Sakharov and Elena Bonner.
35 Shcharansky with Ludmila Alexeeva.
36 Reading a statement prepared for distribution in the West.
37 Slepak and Shcharansky, 13 March 1977, two days before Shcharansky's arrest.
38 Lefortovo prison, Moscow, where Shcharansky was held and interrogated for more than fifteen months.
39 Outside the courthouse, 14 July 1978, Shcharansky's mother hears that he has received a thirteen-year sentence.

Between pages 332–333

40 Ida Milgrom campaigning for her son.
41 Avital Shcharansky during her incessant quest for her husband's release.
42 Boris Shcharansky's grave.
43 Iosif Begun, three times Prisoner of Zion.
44 Ludmila Volvovsky and Ina Begun.
45 Anna Livshits and her father Vladimir in November 1985, less than two months before his arrest.
46 Roald Zelichenok and his wife Galina.
47 Ida Milgrom and Lev Ovsishcher.
48 A poster announcing a massive protest rally in London, 1983. The rally was later cancelled.
49 Leonid Shcharansky, in Moscow, under an Israeli flag.
50 Chistopol prison.

51 Avital in London with Margaret Thatcher.
52 Berlin, 11 February 1986, Shcharansky crosses the Glienicke
    Bridge between East Germany and West Berlin.
53 Ben Gurion airport, 11 February 1986. Shcharansky embraces
    the Israeli Prime Minister Shimon Peres.
54 Ben Gurion airport, 11 February 1986. Shcharansky sees one of
    his Western and former Moscow friends.
55 Moscow, 11 February 1986. Ida Milgrom learns of her son's
    release.
56 Jerusalem, 11 February 1986. Shcharansky at the Western
    ('Wailing') Wall.
57 Jerusalem, 12 February 1986. Avital and Natan Shcharansky
    on their balcony.
58 Jerusalem, 13 February 1986. Shcharansky meets the President
    of Israel, Chaim Herzog.

Acknowledgements

I would like to thank all those who helped me during two and a half years, between July 1983 and January 1986, to prepare this book – first and foremost Avital Shcharansky, to whom it was originally dedicated in the hope that she and her husband would be reunited in Israel as swiftly as possible.

Among those in Israel and the West who provided me with material and answered my many queries, hoping thereby to add one more voice to the campaign for Shcharansky's release, were his uncle Shamai Sharon, and several activist friends of his Moscow years who are now in Israel, among them Iosif Ahs, Dina and Iosif Beilin, Isaak Elkind, Eitan and Alexandra Finkelstein, Felix Kandel, Dr Alexander Lunts, Anatoly Malkin, Mark Nashpits, Ina Rubin, Lev Ulanovsky and Professor Alexander Voronel. Hillel Butman gave me his recollections of his contacts with Shcharansky in Vladimir prison.

I should also like to thank, among those who visited Shcharansky and his fellow Jewish activists in Moscow between 1972 and 1978, June Daniels, Alan Howard, Nora Levin, Irene Manekofsky, Ally Milder, Dr Lou Rosenblum, Alan Segal, Myrna Shinbaum, Zeesy Shnur, Connie and Joseph Smukler, and Enid Wurtman. Michael Sherbourne gave me the benefit of his own long telephonic association with Shcharansky and his Moscow colleagues. Thanks are due, for their help on specific points, to Stephen Clarke, Pamela Cohen, Rita Eker, Jerry Goodman, Nan Greifer, Judith Kleeman, Genya Intrator and Lynn Singer. Many others who helped me cannot, alas, be named. But their documents, recollections and advice were likewise invaluable.

For the photographs which I have selected I am grateful to Avital Shcharansky for those of Shcharansky's childhood and schoolboy years (photographs 2–13). I have also received photographs from several of Shcharansky's friends, among them Enid Wurtman (25, 26, 27, 32 and 34) and Mark Nashpits (30). Dina Beilina gave me important help in identifying the episodes and individuals in the photographs. Photographic material was also provided by the Associated Press (53, 54, 55 and 56), William Carlson of the *Cleveland Plain Dealer* (37), *Daily Telegraph* (back jacket), Granada Television (28), *Jewish Chronicle* (48), George T. Kruse (41), Popperfoto (52, 57 and 58), Len Rosenberg (46), Syndication International (40) and UPI/Bettman Newsphotos (39). The remaining photographs, as well as most of the documentation, are from the archives of the Contemporary Jewish Library (London), the Israel Public Council for Soviet Jewry (Tel Aviv), the National Conference on Soviet Jewry (New York), the Long Island Committee for Soviet Jewry (Long Island), the National Council for Soviet Jews of the United Kingdom and Ireland (London), Student Struggle for Soviet Jewry (New York), the Union of Councils for Soviet Jews (Washington) and the Women's Campaign for Soviet Jewry, 35s (London).

Those who helped me had only one aim: to add further strength to the world-wide campaign for Shcharansky's release. In piecing together the letters, appeals, reports and documents of the years 1973 to 1978, I followed the wish of Shcharansky's wife and friends that his part in the Jewish movement, and the story of the movement itself during the years when he was a part of it, should be told as fully and accurately as possible. Without the help and encouragement of the individuals and organisations named above, this could not have been done.

Dedicated

to Dr Iosif Begun, Prisoner of Zion
now serving a twelve-year sentence,
to his wife Ina
(whom I am proud to count among my friends),
to his fellow prisoners,
and to all former prisoners still refused their exit visas,
in the hope that they and their families
and all Soviet Jews who wish to do so
will be allowed to join
Anatoly Shcharansky
in Israel

Hence my affirmation – borrowed from the existentialists, and perceived by reason but not consciously – that freedom can neither be given nor taken away, since man *is* freedom, seems to me now as natural as life itself.

Anatoly Shcharansky, Chistopol prison, 1979

In this happiest day of our life I am not going to forget those whom I left in the camps, in prisons, who are still in exile or who still continue their struggle for the right to emigrate and for their human rights.

Anatoly Shcharansky, Israel, 1986

Preface

As I write these words, eighteen Jews are in prison or labour camp in the Soviet Union for their desire to live in Israel, and for their part in the struggle of their fellow Jews to obtain an exit visa. Among these prisoners, until February 1986, was Anatoly Shcharansky, who had been given a thirteen-year sentence: one of the longest sentences imposed on a Jew since the death of Stalin.

Had Shcharansky's efforts been those of a young Jew struggling alone for the purely personal goal of emigration to Israel, he would not have been sentenced to thirteen years in prison and labour camp. His achievement, for others his crime, was to have taken part in the struggle of those Soviet Jews who had been refused permission to leave the Soviet Union for Israel. It was an achievement which proved unacceptable to the Soviet State. Yet Shcharansky was never anti-Soviet. He never sought to change Soviet Communism, to bend it, or to break it. His sole aim was to depart for Israel. It was only after that aim had been denied him that he found himself acting as a spokesman for many of those who, like himself, had been refused an exit visa at that time.

In the immediate aftermath of the Bolshevik revolution of 1917, Soviet policymakers had reacted less harshly to Jewish hopes of living in a Jewish homeland. In 1924 Shcharansky's own uncle, then a young man of twenty-two, had been arrested in Odessa. His so-called crime, and that of many of his friends, was Zionist activity. His punishment, and theirs, was immediate expulsion from the Soviet Union. Together with two hundred other Jews who shared his aspirations, Shcharansky's uncle was put on board ship for Palestine. Such, fifty years before his nephew's imprisonment, was the Soviet punishment for Zionism: to be banished *to* Zion.

In 1977 Anatoly Shcharansky was arrested, and in 1978 he was tried and sentenced. His wife Avital, whom he had married in Moscow in 1974, and who at the time of his arrest had already been waiting for him in Jerusalem for nearly three years, became the centre and main force of a world-wide campaign on his behalf. In 1986, having served eight and a half years of his sentence, Shcharansky was released in an East–West spy swap, although he had never been a spy.

Shcharansky was innocent of the charges brought against him. The movement of which he was a part was not a subversive movement. The Jews who wished, as he did, and who still wish, to live in Israel are not motivated by hostility to the Soviet Union, but by a deep love of their Jewish heritage and of the State of Israel. Shcharansky's story is their story: the story of men and women who struggle, inside a closed and often harsh society, to preserve their ideals, to strengthen their Jewish identity, to further their goal of emigration to Israel, and to live with dignity despite harassment and the ever present threat of arrest and imprisonment.

This book was completed three weeks before Shcharansky's release, and at a moment when no Western observer imagined that such a release was possible. It brings together the story of a young Jewish hero and the courageous movement of which he was a part; and it is a call to the Soviet authorities to allow all those Soviet Jews who wish to do so to fulfil their destiny as Jews in the city to which they, like Shcharansky, have transformed the prayer 'Next Year in Jerusalem' to '*This* Year in Jerusalem'.

Martin Gilbert
Merton College
Oxford
12 February 1986

Shcharansky

1

From Donetsk to Moscow

Anatoly Shcharansky was born in the Soviet coal-mining city of Donetsk on 20 January 1948. Two months before he was born, the Soviet Union had voted in the United Nations in favour of the establishment of a Jewish State in Palestine. For Soviet Jews, however, 1948 was a bad year. Soviet Jewish heroism during nearly four years of war, and the slaughter of more than a million Soviet Jews by Nazi killing squads, had led, once the war was won, to no lessening of Soviet efforts to suppress Jewish culture, the Hebrew language or Jewish religious expression. These were the Stalin years, when Jewish fathers feared to tell their children of what it was to be a Jew.

Shcharansky's parents were both from Odessa, where his father Boris, born in 1904, had been educated at the Jewish Commercial School. Boris Shcharansky was one of four brothers. With their father, they often went to the Great Synagogue in Odessa, not only on the Jewish High Holydays and festivals, but also to hear some of the leading Jewish speakers of the time: the poet Chaim Nachman Bialik, the socialist Menachem Ussishkin and the Zionist Vladimir Jabotinsky. Boris Shcharansky's father often told his sons of how Jabotinsky had warned that although the Jews worked tirelessly for the culture of other nations, they had no future in those nations.

The family home in Odessa, Boris Shcharansky later recalled, was decorated with pictures of Palestine. In 1924, seven years after the Bolshevik revolution, his eldest brother Shamai was arrested by the Communist authorities as a member of a Zionist organisation, and, aged twenty-two, was put on board a boat for Palestine. Boris Shcharansky believed, however, as did many Soviet Jews at that time, that with the coming of Soviet Communism the Jewish predicament would be improved.

Shortly after his brother Shamai's expulsion, Boris began work in Odessa as a film scriptwriter. Later he worked in Baku. Several of the filmscripts which he wrote, on Jewish, Gypsy and adventure themes, were well known to Soviet audiences.

In 1932 Boris Shcharansky married Ida Milgrom. Born in Odessa in 1908, she had studied first music and then economics, graduating as an engineering economist. 'Her parents were teachers,' a friend remembered. 'Her home was very warm – lots of jokes. People liked to be invited there, and so did Boris.'

At the time of their marriage, Boris Shcharansky was twenty-eight and Ida Milgrom twenty-four. Boris became a journalist. Nine years later, following the German invasion of the Soviet Union, he volunteered to go to the front. Serving first as a military correspondent, he was later appointed political instructor in a heavy artillery regiment. At first he was shocked by the anti-Semitism which he encountered. Then, like all Soviet Jews, he was shattered to learn of the Nazi slaughter of Jewish men, women and children behind the German lines. The Jews were paying such a terrible price, he believed, that anti-Semitism would be impossible after the war; a common hatred of Nazism would unite Russian and Jew as had never before been possible. He therefore joined the Communist Party, convinced that, after the tragedy of the wartime slaughter, victory would bring in its wake a final improvement in the lot of Soviet Jews.

In 1945, as Nazi Germany faced defeat on all fronts, Boris Shcharansky reached Vienna with the Red Army. Then he returned to Odessa. When, however, he tried to get his job back on a newspaper in the city, he was told: 'We cannot accept you. Times have changed. We have more Jews than we need. Go to Donetsk and they will accept you.'

Living in Donetsk, and working as a journalist, Boris Shcharansky had no illusions about his future: twenty-eight years had passed since the revolution, his whole adult life. He and his wife had no reason to expect that either they, or any children they might have, would ever leave Russia. They were Jews by birth, by the designation 'Jew' inscribed in the 'nationality' section of their identity card, and by an inner knowledge of Jewish suffering, heritage and wandering: but the idea of being a Jew outside the Soviet Union, or in a future Jewish State, lay outside the realm of reality.

Boris Shcharansky and his wife had been childless for sixteen years. Then, in the summer of 1946, when Ida was thirty-eight, their son Leonid was born, their 'Lyonya'. Overjoyed to have had a child, and a son, the Shcharanskys decided that a daughter would complete their happiness. They had even chosen a name for her: Natalia. Then, one day in January 1948, as Ida Milgrom recalled thirty-one years later:

> Between midnight and one in the morning on the night of the nineteenth the persistent cry of a baby rang out and the doctor spoke: 'Mother, whom are you expecting?' 'A daughter,' I said, 'Natalia.'
> 'Well, I congratulate you, you have given birth to Anatoly. That's better than Natalia,' he said. 'Look, what a hero!'
> But I wasn't in a joking mood, my mood was heavy, and again – not a daughter, a son.
> But in the morning, when they brought him for me to nurse, I melted. He was such a charming creature: round-faced, light-haired, with puffy rosy lips. He sucked greedily, tired quickly, but didn't doze. He kept looking at me with such a bright gaze that it seemed as if we had known each other for a long time and that I had never been without him.

Tolya was, from his first days, a quiet child. 'He did not disturb his parents' and neighbours' peace at night,' Ida Milgrom wrote, 'he did not demand his parents' obligatory presence during the day, he ate well, and he amused himself.'

In the years following her son's arrest and imprisonment, Ida Milgrom often reflected on those early years. In May 1983, she set down her recollections in a letter to a friend in Israel: the State which had come into existence when her Tolya, her Tolik as she also called him, was four months old. Among her earliest recollections of her younger son's character was one which went back to the summer of 1948, to the party for Lyonya's second birthday. 'Tolya was five months old,' she wrote:

> The guests came. A big and very colourful ball was, among other gifts, presented to Lyonya, and Tolya reached out for it. The brothers began to play, but Tolya could not grab the ball by his short fingers and resorted to a ruse. When the ball was on the middle of the bed, he covered it with his plump body and would not get up any more. It was impossible to take it away from him, and Lyonya kept on screaming heartrendingly: 'It is my ball, give me the ball!' We, the grown-ups, wished to attract

Tolya with some dainty dish – with his beloved 'sucking' sweet (so Tolya called all caramels) – but we did not succeed. It turned out to be an easier task to tempt Lyonya with a glass of lemonade. And Tolya kept on playing the role of 'usurper' all evening through. Our guests had left already, Lyonya was put to bed, but the stubborn child fell asleep over his 'loot'.

★   ★   ★

The first year of Shcharansky's life in Donetsk was a year of trauma and danger for the Jews of Russia. On 13 January 1948, seven days before Shcharansky's birth, Solomon Mikhoels, Director of the Jewish Theatre in Moscow, and one of the best-known Soviet Jews of his generation, was murdered in Minsk. Mikhoels had been the head of an official and much-praised Jewish Anti-Fascist Committee which, in 1943, as the Red Army struggled against the German forces on the eastern front, travelled to Britain and the United States to explain the Soviet war effort to the Allies, and to enlist support and sympathy for the Soviet struggle for survival. The Anti-Fascist Committee had made an important contribution to the Soviet war effort in the West; now its most prominent member was dead: killed by the very State whose interests he had championed.

On 14 May 1948, when Shcharansky was less than four months old, the State of Israel was proclaimed in Tel Aviv. The Soviet Union at once recognised the new State as a sovereign member of the United Nations. At the same time, however, Soviet domestic propaganda denounced the new Israel. 'With the support of England and the United States,' one Soviet writer declared in August 1948, 'the bourgeois Jewish nationalists have attempted to transform Palestine into a purely Jewish State, without taking into consideration the interests and rights of the local population.' Soviet Jews, stated another writer, 'will never desire to exchange their Soviet homeland'.

On 16 October 1948 many thousands of Soviet Jews gathered outside the Moscow synagogue in Arkhipova Street to welcome Golda Meir, head of the new Israeli Legation in Moscow. It was the Jewish New Year, and there were emotional scenes of a shared heritage, despite the official hostility to all things Zionist. Among the cries from the crowd was one which echoed an age-long Jewish call, now given a renewed reality: *'Am Yisroel Chai!'* – 'The people of Israel lives!'

Just when Jewish feelings inside the Soviet Union were raised by the existence of a Jewish State, Stalin decided to crush them. Israel would continue to be recognised and even supported by the Soviet Union, but such recognition and support must be shown clearly to offer no hope to any Jewish national aspirations inside the Soviet borders.

In November 1948, the arrests began of hundreds of Soviet Jewish writers, artists, actors and musicians. These arrests continued throughout the early months of 1949. Almost every well-known Jew, who earlier had been a part of such Jewish cultural and literary life as had survived Stalin's purges in the 1930s, was arrested. Most were sentenced to ten years in forced labour camps, charged with three particular crimes: 'bourgeois nationalism', 'slandering the Soviet Union by spreading reports that there was anti-Semitism in Russia', and 'espionage on behalf of the Western Powers'. Most of them died in the camps.

Thus, during Shcharansky's childhood, accusations were being heard similar to those which, within thirty years, were to be levelled at Shcharansky himself.

On 10 December 1948, when Shcharansky was still less than a year old, the Soviet Union was a signatory to the Universal Declaration of Human Rights, a declaration stimulated by the wartime sufferings of Soviet citizens, including Jews, and millions of other victims of Nazism throughout Europe. This declaration, signed three years after the defeat of Nazi tyranny, established on international foundations the right of every individual 'to leave any country, including his own, and to return to his country'. This was a solemn pledge.

★   ★   ★

Each December, the Shcharansky family, like so many of the Soviet Union's three million Jews, celebrated the New Year: not the Jewish New Year of the autumn season, during which festival Anatoly was later to rejoice, but the former Christian, and since 1917 secular, celebration, when New Year trees are brought home and decorated and lit. 'In December 1948,' Shcharansky's mother has recounted, 'when Tolya was eleven months old, the first New Year tree appeared in our apartment. This event was joyful not only for children, but for their father too. It was he, their father, who brought the fir-tree, installed and decorated it. And in the evening, when the light was switched off, their father lit the candles and brought his favourites to the room – Lyonya being led by the hand

and Tolya riding on his father's shoulders. The child reached out to
the star crowning the tree, and pulled it. The frightened father freed
his hands, in order to hold the falling tree, and Tolya fell head first.'

Although Boris Shcharansky was not tall, the fall was such a
heavy one for the child that he lost consciousness. His father
fainted. His mother, frightened to see foam on her son's lips,
recalled 'rushing across the snow-drifts with the child, wrapped in a
big quilt, in my arms'. She remembered waving down a lorry,
'which stopped on the road, and the driver, who helped me to climb
into the cab, took us to the hospital.'

'We spent three days in the hospital under observation,' Ida later
wrote. 'No complications were detected. And when we were
leaving the hospital, the doctor on duty told us, laughing: "One can
become either an idiot or a genius after such a fall!"'

★   ★   ★

On 11 May 1949, the Soviet Union cast all three of its votes in the
United Nations to admit the State of Israel to the world organisation. The newly established Communist Government of Czechoslovakia was already selling Israel the guns, ammunition and
aircraft essential for its defence against the attacking armies of
Egypt, Syria, Transjordan and Iraq. Neither Soviet recognition of
the State of Israel as a Member State of the United Nations,
however, nor the presence in Moscow of an Israeli Legation, could
mask a growing Soviet hostility to all forms of Zionism, whether in
the Middle East, or inside Russia itself.

For the Shcharansky family in Donetsk, the anti-Zionist
campaign of 1949 was of no direct concern. Their lives revolved
upon the simplest of themes: two growing boys, their hard-
working mother and father, and two doting neighbours in their
crowded communal flat. That year, Lyonya entered kindergarten,
and Tolya was without his elder brother for most of the day. 'Tolya
did not like to play with toys in solitude,' his mother later wrote,
'and the toys were awaiting Lyonya's return from kindergarten.'
Instead of his brother's toys, Tolya turned to his father's books,
looking for the pictures and asking his father to tell him what they
meant. 'Afterwards,' his mother recalled, 'he retold their contents
to anybody who agreed to listen to him.'

Whenever Lyonya was punished by being made to stand in a
corner, he at once apologised, promising his parents: 'I shall not do
this any more,' resorting to tears if the apology failed, and soon

being allowed to leave the corner. Tolya, on the other hand, refused either repentance or tears, possessing, as his mother wrote, 'the striking confidence that he was right'. It was, she added, 'his own life-justice'.

In 1951, at the age of three, Tolya Shcharansky entered kindergarten. In the summer, to escape from the coal dust hovering about Donetsk, he was sent to a children's village with miners' children. There he was looked after by a young woman who was lodging with the Shcharanskys in Donetsk, 'Mamma Phenya' as she was known by the young boys.

While at the children's village Tolya fell ill. At first, neither his parents nor a doctor were summoned: the hospital and post office were six kilometres from the village. But after two nights during which the boy could not sleep because of fever, Mamma Phenya set off to the hospital on foot, carrying the sick child in her arms. 'A doctor in the hospital', Shcharansky's mother later wrote, 'advised us to crop Tolya's hair close and administer him aspirin. He could not diagnose the illness. When we came there, both Phenya and Tolya were unrecognisable: Phenya because of her agonising experience and nervousness, and Tolya, hollow-cheeked and nasal-voiced, without his golden hair, made a grim impression on us. All of us came back home on the same day and went to a doctor. There, after consultation with a neuropathologist, a paediatrician and a laryngologist, the diagnosis was determined – diphtheria.'

The illness was overcome; Tolya returned to Donetsk, and to his kindergarten. His father, who was frequently in charge of taking children home from the kindergarten, would often witness, as his wife recalled, 'a curious scene: Tolya was sitting in the centre of a room, with children from various age-groups surrounding him, telling them interesting episodes from his father's military experience, or the contents of the films, etc. He was always listened to with great interest and attention.' This 'streak of character', Tolya's mother added, 'he inherited from his father.'

When kindergarten was over for the day, Boris Shcharansky would often take his two boys to the cinema. 'Do you remember, Papa,' Shcharansky wrote to his father twenty-five years later, from prison, 'how you picked us up from kindergarten (ahead of time), took us to the films and retold their contents at home so we would fall asleep quickly? But you, Papa, fell asleep before we did. We'd shake you and shout, "Papa, don't wander! Keep on with the story!"'

Shcharansky's early days of school coincided with a moment of unprecedented alarm for the Jews of Russia, of whom the Shcharansky family was so small a fragment. On 11 July 1952, the trials began of twenty-four Jewish writers accused of 'espionage on behalf of foreign states', 'bourgeois nationalist activity' and 'anti-Soviet propaganda'. Twenty-three of the twenty-four Jews were sentenced to death and shot; the twenty-fourth, the only woman among them, was sentenced to twenty-five years in prison.

Nor was this to be the end of the torments of Soviet Jewry that year. On 29 November 1952 the Ukrainian *Pravda* reported the execution of three Jews in Kiev for 'economic' crimes: alleged 'speculation' in various items of clothing on a small scale. Two non-Jews who were accused of an identical 'speculation' alongside the three Jews in Kiev were not shot, however, but sent to prison.

Even worse dangers were in prospect; on 13 January 1953, a week before Tolya's fifth birthday, the Communist Party newspaper *Pravda* announced the arrest of a 'terrorist group' of 'criminal physicians', Jewish 'poisoner–doctors' who, 'under the leadership of American Intelligence', had planned at the behest of their 'American Zionist Overseers' the murder of the Soviet leadership. 'Foul Spies and Murderers in the Mask of Doctors and Professors', declared *Pravda*'s headline. Within weeks a renewed campaign was launched in the Soviet press against those three symbols of the anti-Communist conspiracy: cosmopolitanism, bourgeois nationalism and Zionism.

The Israeli Legation in Moscow was powerless to challenge these accusations. Within a month of the announcement of the 'Doctors' Plot', a small bomb, planted by unknown perpetrators, exploded outside the Soviet Legation in Tel Aviv. Two days later, on 13 February 1953, the Soviet Union broke off relations with Israel. Then, on March 5, Stalin died; and the rumoured anti-Jewish excesses, including the mass deportation of Jews to Siberia, did not come to pass. On April 4, only a month after Stalin's death, the Soviet Ministry of the Interior announced that the accusations against the doctors had been based on false testimony. By the end of the year, diplomatic relations between the Soviet Union and Israel were restored. In the coming two years, the Soviet Union supplied more than a third of Israel's needs in oil.

*   *   *

On 20 January 1954, in Donetsk, Anatoly Shcharansky celebrated his sixth birthday. As a present, his parents bought him a bicycle. It led to his first encounter with the Soviet police, the militia. Returning home for lunch one day, his mother recalled, 'I could not find Tolya at home, and there was no bicycle in our apartment either. Panic-stricken, I called my husband out of his work and we rushed to look for him. We found him at one of the local militia offices. He had been there for more than an hour, but the militia officials could not get any information from him about his address or his parents' place of work. He kept silence. But as soon as he saw his father, he asked him to take away his bicycle. The crippled bicycle was in the corner.'

Ida Milgrom's attention had been attracted to Tolya's right arm, 'which was hanging down lifelessly. I grabbed Tolya and rushed to the hospital with him. We came back home late, Tolya with plaster on his broken arm. In the evening Tolya told us that he had gone out on to the road on his bicycle, ignoring the driving regulations (he did not yet know them), and in a short time had found himself under the wheels of a motor-cycle. He had been brought to the militia office. But we did not manage to learn the reason for his stubborn silence at the militia office.'

In 1955 Anatoly Shcharansky left kindergarten for school. Whereas Lyonya was already a frequent victim of bad marks, with the resultant tears, for Tolya even bad marks led to no undue storms: 'no sufferings, no tears, no emotions', his mother noted. Both boys studied hard. 'Their conduct was not always perfect,' she wrote, 'but they were always cited as an example at parents' meetings at school.'

Tolya, from the age of eight, was playing chess. When he was twelve years old a chess problem which he had devised was published in the provincial newspaper of the Donbass region. For this the young Shcharansky even received a fee. Then, when he was fourteen, he won the title of City Champion in chess, and received his award at a public ceremony. 'He was so small,' one of his school friends later observed, 'it was impossible to see him.' Soon afterwards, Shcharansky became Province Champion in the Donbass chess competition. Local newspapers reported his prowess, reports which his father carefully cut out and pasted into albums. Chess had become Shcharansky's first love. 'I remember how much time, labour and love Tolya devoted to his passion,' his mother later wrote.

In 1964 Lyonya Shcharansky finished school in Donetsk, and

went to Moscow, to study at the Moscow Power Institute. Tolya remained at school in Donetsk.

Shcharansky's parents were afraid that, having had their two sons late in life, they might not have enough time to bring them up and to educate them. While trying to protect them from the anti-Jewish 'campaign against cosmopolitanism' of the early 1950s, and from the anti-Jewish atmosphere perpetuated by the death sentences meted out in the early 1960s for 'economic' crimes, they worked hard, as a family friend later remarked, 'to give their children everything – sport, the English language, theatre, books'. Twenty years later, Shcharansky recalled these early years in a letter from prison. 'I have had enough time and opportunity during the last three years', he wrote, 'to feel acutely how much my family gave me. One does not realise, during life's daily hustle, that all those values with which one is filled are given to one by one's parents, that they were filling me with them, as they might fill a cup. They were filling me with them then, not by words, but by the mere fact of their existence, their attitude to the world, the whole family atmosphere with its goodnaturedness, humour, optimism, vivid and kind interest in people and events, and by their constant readiness for danger.'

During their years in Donetsk, Shcharansky's parents had fought to protect him from what they called 'the danger'; from what, for the Jews of post-Stalin Russia, was the fear of an intensification of the anti-Semitism which had so marred, and scarred, earlier periods of Russian and Soviet life. Shcharansky's schooldays in Donetsk had coincided with frequent anti-Jewish trials and publications. Between July 1961 and March 1963, at a series of 'economic' trials, of just over a hundred defendants found guilty of 'speculation' in clothing, footwear or furs, and shot, at least sixty-eight were Jews. In an upsurge of anti-Semitic newspaper comment, many of the accused were said to have had a Zionist, a Jewish Social Democrat or a 'bourgeois–nationalist' past, or to have helped American and British spies to 'penetrate Soviet factories'.

In 1964, in Kishinev, the scene of the notorious pogrom of 1903, a booklet on *Contemporary Judaism and Zionism* stated: 'Judaism is the worst of all religions; pessimistic, nationalistic, anti-feminine and anti-popular.'

Western concern about the plight of the Jews in the Soviet Union was growing. On 15 September 1960, fifty scholars, writers, academicians and parliamentarians had gathered in Paris to make known their concern: Martin Buber was among the speakers, and support came from François Mauriac, Bertrand Russell, Reinhold Niebuhr and Albert Schweitzer. On 25 February 1963 a letter of protest from Bertrand Russell to Khrushchev, as well as the Soviet leader's reply, was published simultaneously in *Pravda* and *Izvestia*.

On 12 October 1963 a conference on the status of Soviet Jews, held in New York and sponsored by, among others, Martin Luther King, led to the establishment six months later of an American Jewish Conference on Soviet Jewry, to co-ordinate public concern throughout the United States. Six months later, on 27 April 1964, a group of young American Jews, all of them students, met at Columbia University to protest against the treatment of Jews in the Soviet Union. Four days later they organised a silent march to the Soviet Mission to the United Nations. With this march was born the Student Struggle for Soviet Jewry, one of whose leading spirits, Glenn Richter, was to devote the next two decades, and more, to the cause of Soviet Jewry.

In 1966 Anatoly Shcharansky reached the end of his school career, his academic success marked by the award of a coveted gold medal. The school medals and certificates were to be given out in the Donetsk theatre. 'We, Tolya's parents, attended the meeting,' his mother later wrote, 'and became the witness of genuine triumph, when Anatoly's name was called out.' Because of the alphabetical order, Shcharansky was named last. 'But he turned out to be the first person, and was rewarded with the applause of the audience and Praesidium. Tolya was in the last row of the theatre. On his way down to the Praesidium, he was accompanied by applause. One could hear the remarks from the people: "Look, here is Shcharansky!" and Tolya was pacing with his head proudly raised. He had then a dense head of hair, and, despite his small stature, he was producing a powerful impression. It was not only mine, his mother's, impression. Many friends and colleagues of mine told me the same.'

From Donetsk, where his portrait now hung on the school Board of Honour, and with his gold medal as a mark of achievement, Shcharansky travelled in 1966 to Moscow, where he enrolled as a student in the special mathematics school. He was eighteen years old.

In Moscow, Shcharansky was, as one of his fellow pupils later explained, 'an "A" student', who, on graduating from the mathematics school, gained a place at 'one of the most serious institutes' in the capital, the Moscow Physical–Technical Institute. There he began his graduate work, specialising in cybernetics.

During his years in Donetsk, Shcharansky had been untouched personally by anti-Semitism. But the moment was to come when the young assimilated Jew, now a brilliant student in Moscow, was to be confronted personally by that age-old curse. 'I was as Soviet as you could get,' Shcharansky later told an American journalist, 'but during a long hike in the Caucasus with my best friend he got angry with me about something and called me a "Yid". I think it was then that I decided this was no place for me.'

2

The Awakening

The five years which Shcharansky spent as a student in Moscow were years of ferment for the two and a half million Jews of the Soviet Union. In 1966 there was still an Israeli Legation in the Soviet capital, and Jews could and did listen to the music of visiting Israeli singers or applaud the team victories of Israeli sportsmen. But there was little chance, and little thought, of asking for an exit visa to go to Israel: the Soviet Union was not a country from which emigration was possible, for any group. The State of Israel was therefore a remote curiosity, the centre of Jewish national identity no doubt, but remote nevertheless from the personal aspirations of Jews living two thousand miles to the north.

Then, on 3 December 1966, in Paris, the Soviet Prime Minister, Alexei Kosygin, issued a formal declaration that Jews could, if they applied to do so, go to Israel to be reunited with members of their family. In that year, 2027 exit visas had been granted, and in 1967 1416 Soviet Jews were to receive their exit visas for Israel. This change in Soviet practice electrified Soviet Jewry, rousing hopes which had hitherto been impossible even to contemplate.

In June 1967, just as those hopes were spreading throughout the cities of the Soviet Union, the verbal threats which President Nasser had unleashed against Israel were transformed into actual military preparations, in which both Syria and Jordan joined, and the Jews of Moscow, like those throughout the world, watched with apprehension as the small State awaited the onslaught. Israel, endangered, struck first, destroying Egypt's air forces on the ground. Then the three Arab armies attacked. Radio Moscow, jubilant at the initial Arab successes in breaking across the 1949 ceasefire lines, announced the imminent destruction of the nineteen-year-old State.

This trumpeting of Israel's last hours of existence as a State released the hidden Jewishness and national pride of Russia's silent Jews. With each Moscow radio broadcast of another Arab victory, fear for Israel's existence turned into a passionate longing to be a part of the struggle: 'to die with my people', as one of Shcharansky's closest friends expressed it to me in Moscow sixteen years later.

'At first', as another of his friends wrote to me, 'it was the anguish at the thought that the Jews (I mean also Israel as an independent State) once again will be the victims.' Then, several days after Soviet Jewry's instant and instinctive identity with an apparently defeated brother, the truth became known. Israel had driven back the invading armies.

Israel's victory gave Soviet Jews a clear, indisputable reason to be proud of being Jewish. 'This feeling was so strong', yet another of Shcharansky's friends later told me, 'that it influenced the whole of Russia. Dirty jokes about Jews disappeared. Not that anti-Semitism disappeared, maybe it became even stronger, but now it was combined with some kind of respect.' Each and every Soviet Jew felt this pride, although there were still many who were afraid to speak of it openly, even to their wives or parents.

With pride in Israel came a deep desire to make a personal contribution to the life and future of the Jewish State: a desire which the Kosygin declaration of December 1966 seemed to bring within the bounds of reality. But no sooner had the Six Day War ended than the granting of exit visas came to a halt. All those who persisted in applying for exit visas were told that there was no chance of applications being granted as long as diplomatic relations with Israel, broken off in the war, were not restored.

The awakening of Soviet Jewry could not be reversed by a political decision not to issue any further exit visas, and in the aftermath of the Israeli victory there was an upsurge of activity. The small Hebrew language classes which had sprung up in the mid-1960s now burgeoned, even larger meetings now took place at the sites of the mass murder of Jews by the Nazis during the Second World War, private discussion groups exchanged information about Israeli life, and the applications for exit visas continued, with hundreds of Soviet Jews trying to find relatives in Israel from whom an invitation could be sent: the formal invitation without which no exit visa application could even be begun.

Shcharansky now, with so many tens of thousands of Soviet

Jews, embarked upon an exhilarating, and for many an ultimately satisfactory, voyage: the road to Jewish identity, and then to Israel. 'Everything he reached, he reached by himself,' commented one witness to Shcharansky's transformation. 'He had no Jewish tradition behind him. He decided everything for himself.' He also met Luba Yershkovich, a Jewish girl whose family was from Donetsk, and who was in Moscow studying music. It was she who in those early days encouraged him to look to Israel. Her father too, Anatoly Yershkovich, had always aspired to live in Israel.

Six months after the Six Day War, Shcharansky celebrated his twentieth birthday.

★   ★   ★

The Soviet Union had made no effort to restore diplomatic relations with Israel. The Israeli Legation in Moscow was closed and its diplomats withdrawn. But, beginning on a tiny scale in September 1967, and rising rapidly in the following four months, exit visas were granted to 379 Soviet citizens who had received the required formal 'invitation' from Israel, authenticated as it had to be by an Israeli notary, and sent openly in the post from Israel to the Soviet Union. Thousands of Soviet Jews now began to ask for these invitations, the first step in a long and complicated procedure for an exit visa: a procedure which included the requirement that one obtain the permission of one's parents to leave, and which also involved revealing to one's employer and local Party organisation the intention to leave, thus risking, and normally losing, one's job.

On 22 March 1968 Soviet Jews were surprised to read, in *Pravda*, the full text of a speech by the Polish Communist leader Wladyslaw Gomulka, according to whom there were many 'Jewish Polish citizens' who were not 'tied to Poland by feeling and reason but to the State of Israel'. Of these citizens Gomulka went on to say: 'They are certainly Jewish nationalists. Can one have a grudge against them for this? Only the same kind of a grudge as Communists have against all nationalists, no matter what their nationality is. I suppose that this category of Jews is going to leave our country sooner or later.' To those who considered Israel their 'homeland', Gomulka added, 'we are ready to give emigration passports.'

That *Pravda* should reproduce these remarks in full, and without hostile comment, seemed a hopeful sign. For many months Jews in Moscow spoke excitedly of 'the Gomulka variant'. At 230, the number of Jews actually allowed to leave the Soviet Union in 1968 was, however, lower than for any year during the previous six, almost the lowest since 1955.

The impossibility of all but a tiny fragment of exit visas being granted did not deter the awakening of Jewish national consciousness. In September 1968, at a memorial meeting at Babi Yar, the ravine in Kiev where more than thirty thousand Jews were massacred by the Nazis in a three-night orgy of killing in September 1941, Jews gathered in pious memorial. During the ceremony, the official Soviet speakers, while honouring the dead, also abused the State of Israel. Among the Jews present was a twenty-two-year-old student, Boris Kochubievsky. 'What's going on here?' he heard a man ask, to which a woman replied, 'Here the Germans killed a hundred thousand Jews.' 'That', commented the man, 'was not enough.' Boris Kochubievsky protested to the authorities. He had already applied to go to Israel and, to his surprise, on 28 November 1968 he received permission. Then, nine days later, he was arrested, held in prison for five months, and on 13 May 1969 brought to trial.

Kochubievsky was sentenced to three years in labour camp. In his final remarks to the court, he expressed his hope 'that no one else will share my fate because of his desire to go to Israel'.

The sentence on Kochubievsky – with whom, fourteen years later, I walked across the hills south of Jerusalem – did not inhibit the aspirations of those Soviet Jews for whom the survival of the State of Israel during the Six Day War had been such an inspiration. That October, while Shcharansky was at the start of his fourth year at the Moscow Physical–Technical Institute, several thousand Jews gathered in Arkhipova Street in Moscow, outside the Moscow synagogue. It was the eve of Simhat Torah, the Jewish festival of the Rejoicing of the Law. In a quarter-mile section of the narrow street, these Jews, most of them between the ages of eighteen and twenty-four, sang and danced in the cold drizzle until late into the night. Some sang Yiddish songs, others took up the refrains in Hebrew, the language of the Jewish State. Some of those in the crowd had pieces of paper on which they had written out such words as they knew in modern Hebrew; avidly, these words were swapped and spoken. One of the songs which was heard that night was a jingle mocking Soviet anti-Semitism.

When 1969 came to an end, it was clear that no substantial emigration was to be allowed. Three thousand Jews received their exit visas during that single year, the largest number in any year since the days of the revolution; but that number was in sharp contrast to the 34,000 who, in the sixteen months since September 1968, had asked for invitations from Israel. Under the statistics of 1969, it would take more than ten years before those 34,000 would be allowed out, and who could say how many tens, or even hundreds of thousands of other Jews might not wish to follow them, if the gates were to be opened more widely.

On 6 August 1969, eighteen Jewish families from the Soviet Republic of Georgia sent a letter to the United Nations Human Rights Commission. In their letter they wrote proudly of 'those who had handed down to us the tradition of struggle and faith' and ended with the appeal: 'Let us go to the land of our forefathers.' To the Israeli representative at the United Nations, Joseph Tekoah, these same Jewish families declared: 'The time of fear is over – the time of action has come!'

Shcharansky had not yet sought an invitation from Israel. Throughout the Soviet Union, however, Jews were beginning to demand the right to leave, or were becoming active in trying to learn about Jewish life, and about the State of Israel. In February 1970, in the town of Ryazan, four Jews from the city's Institute of Radio Technology were sent to labour camp for encouraging young Jews to seek the path of Jewishness and emigration, one of them, Yury Vudka, being sentenced to seven years. Today he lives in Israel.

In March 1970 several Soviet newspapers published articles claiming that Soviet Jews did not wish to emigrate. In answer, forty Jews wrote a letter, which was published abroad, stating that this was not true. Among the signatories was the forty-three-year-old Vladimir Slepak, the son of a devout Communist.

The protests against these articles were widespread. On 30 October 1970, the trial took place in Kishinev of two Jews, Yakov Suslensky and Iosif Mishener, schoolteachers from the town of Bendery, in the Soviet Republic of Moldavia. Their 'crime' was to have protested against one of the articles, this particular one in the Communist Party newspaper *Izvestia*, which maintained that no Soviet Jews wished to leave for Israel. Both men were found guilty of anti-Soviet slander. Suslensky was sentenced to seven years in labour camp and Mishener to six. Today, both of them live in Israel.

The number of exit visas fell during 1970, averaging less than eighty a month, and at the same time the number of Jews who had been refused an exit visa was growing. Among these 'refuseniks', as they had become known, was a small group who, seeing no hope of having their refusals reversed, decided to seize a twelve-seater aeroplane and fly it to Sweden. They were caught, and brought to trial in Leningrad. The main charge levelled against them was treason. Under Article 64–A of the Criminal Code of the Russian Republic, treason is punishable by death.

'All I wanted', one of the accused, Edward Kuznetsov, told the court, 'was to live in Israel.' But such protestations were to no avail. On 24 December 1970 the Leningrad sentences were made public. Two of the accused, Kuznetsov and Mark Dymshits, were sentenced to death, the rest to ten years and more in strict-regime labour camp. As the sentences were announced, their friends in the courtroom cried out: 'Hold on! We are with you! We are waiting for you! We shall be in Israel together!'

The news of the two Leningrad death sentences reached London at seven in the morning of 25 December 1970. A group of British Jews immediately gathered in protest, although it was Christmas Day, outside the Soviet Embassy. Among the protesters was Michael Sherbourne, a fifty-three-year-old schoolmaster who was soon to become an important link between the refuseniks and the West.

It was not only Jews in the West who were outraged by the harsh sentences. Outside the Supreme Court in Moscow, among several dozen Jews who gathered in protest, was Elena Bonner, a relative of Edward Kuznetsov. During the demonstration she met another of the protesters, Andrei Sakharov, a member of the Soviet Academy of Sciences and a non-Jew who, six weeks earlier, had been among the founders of the courageously named Soviet Committee on Human Rights, offering what it called 'creative help' to any Soviet citizens who might need a safeguard for their human rights, as defined by the Universal Declaration of Human Rights of 1948.

As Western protests grew, the two death sentences were commuted to fifteen years in prison and labour camp. Even these harsh sentences did not deter other Jews from continuing their public demands for exit visas, despite the fact that only 1044 Jews had been allowed out in 1970.

Two months after the Leningrad Trial, a conference was convened by the Israeli Government and Jewish community leaders from throughout the Western world. Opening in Brussels on 23 February 1971, and later known as 'Brussels One', the Conference called on the Soviet Government to give exit visas to any Jews who wished to go to Israel. Eight days before the conference opened, the Soviet news agency Tass had already condemned it as an 'anti-Soviet provocation'.

On 26 February 1971, while the Brussels Conference was still in session, twenty-four Jews marched to the Visa Office in Riga and demanded the right to leave. Their public protest, a rarity in the Soviet Union and an act of considerable courage, was followed two days later by a 'sit-in' outside the Supreme Soviet in Moscow by thirty Jews who, in the previous months, had been refused their exit visas. The Visa Office, more precisely the Department of Visas and Registration, known also by its Russian initials as OVIR, is a department of the Soviet Ministry of the Interior (MVD), and is responsible for the grant of exit visas: there is one in every Soviet city, with the central office in Moscow.

The Supreme Soviet protest of 28 February 1971 was followed within three weeks by a second trial, also held in Leningrad, which opened on May 11. Nine Jews were brought to trial, two of them accused of treason, including a young Hebrew teacher, Hillel Butman, who had been active in the growing emigration movement. Butman was sentenced to ten years' strict-regime labour camp. Then, on May 24, a third trial opened, this time in Riga. It was in Riga, the capital of the Latvian Republic, that many Jews had gathered each year at the wartime mass-murder pits at Rumbuli to remember the dead, and to renew their sense of Jewish identity.

One of the four Riga Jews accused was a twenty-three-year-old nurse, Ruth Alexandrovich. The charge against her was of distributing six copies of a small, privately prepared brochure 'For the Return of Soviet Jews to their Homeland', and fifteen copies of a second brochure, 'Your Native Tongue', on the Hebrew language. 'In the Soviet newspapers,' Ruth Alexandrovich told the court, 'they write with bias against Israel.' She had intended to correct that bias. 'In the Soviet Union there are no Jewish schools,' she added. Her advocacy of Hebrew was to fill that gap. She was sentenced to a year in labour camp.

On 20 May 1971, in a gesture of sympathy for the growing harassment of Jews, Academician Sakharov's Committee on Human Rights appealed in an open letter to the Supreme Soviet about the 'persecution of Jewish repatriates'. The 'only aim' of those on trial, the Committee added, was to 'protest against the unlawful refusals to give them visas for repatriation'.

In seeking 'repatriation' to Israel, the 2,150,707 Jews of the Soviet

census of 1970 were asking for similar rights to those which the
Soviet authorities were already recognising for the exit-visa applicants among the 1,846,317 Germans and 1,167,523 Poles of the
same Soviet census. The figure of 2,150,707 Jews in the census of
1970 was a minimum. Many other Jews by birth were not included:
Jewish women married to non-Jews, or the children of one Jewish
parent. Many such people, while not registered as Jews, and while
having 'Russian' rather than 'Jew' inserted in the nationality section
of their internal passport, felt nevertheless some affinity, even a
close affinity, to the growing Jewish consciousness: an affinity
which the Six Day War had powerfully enhanced.

The Jewish repatriation movement was not a dissident movement. The aim of the dissidents was to obtain inside the Soviet
Union those human rights already guaranteed by the Soviet Constitution. The aim of the Jews who called for repatriation was to
leave the Soviet Union. Had not the Jews of the world always
wandered? Did not the existence of the State of Israel since 1948
give them a place to go, from which they need wander no more?

The letter of 20 May 1971 not only supported the repatriation of
Soviet Jews to Israel. It also noted that the Soviet press presented
Zionism 'as a reactionary (almost fascist) political movement'. 'In
fact', the letter went on to explain, 'Zionism is no more than the
idea of Jewish statehood, and one can only admire the stubbornness
of an ancient and persecuted people which, in the face of very
difficult conditions, has revived a State that disappeared long ago. It
is precisely this revival, and the removal of the consequences of
dispersion that have been so tragic for the Jewish people, that is the
aim of Zionism.'

In December 1970 two Jews from Sverdlovsk, Yuly
Kosharovsky and Valery Kukui, had sent an open letter to the
Soviet President, Nikolai Podgorny, protesting against the death
sentence imposed upon Kuznetsov and Dymshits. On 16 June 1971
Kukui was brought to trial, charged with 'defaming the Soviet
State'. His sentence: three years in labour camp.

A second trial took place on 22 June 1971, of Raisa Palatnik, a
librarian. She was sentenced to two years in labour camp. In protest
against her sentence, thirty-five Jewish women in Britain, each of
whom was the same age as Raisa – thirty-five – formed a group,
known as the '35s', to campaign for her release. Having served her
sentence, Raisa Palatnik was allowed to go to Israel. The '35s'
remained in existence, active in seeking British public support for

the right of Soviet Jews to emigrate to Israel.

Also in June 1971, the American Jewish Conference on Soviet Jewry, which had been established in April 1964, was enlarged as the National Conference on Soviet Jewry, with its headquarters in New York, under an Executive Director, Jerry Goodman, assisted by Myrna Shinbaum, a cousin of Michael Sherbourne. Henceforth, in the United States, the National Conference on Soviet Jewry and the Union of Councils for Soviet Jews were both to publicise the information reaching them from inside the Soviet Union, and to seek American political support, particularly in the Senate and House of Representatives, for their respective campaigns on behalf of the prisoners and refuseniks.

A steady growth in the number of Jewish prisoners, abuse of Israel in the newspapers, denunciation of Zionism as fascism, and the continued rejection of applications to leave – such was the reality which confronted Soviet Jews in the summer of 1971. That summer Shcharansky visited his father, who had retired from journalism and was at a country rest house for Soviet journalists. During his visit he told his parents that he had just met a remarkable Jew, twenty-one years his senior, who twelve months earlier had applied to go to Israel and had been refused. This man was Vladimir Slepak, one of the signatories of the letter of March 1970.

Slepak had been born on 29 October 1927, the grandson of a teacher of Judaism. His father, Simon, had fought in the Red Army in 1919 against the anti-Bolshevik forces of Admiral Kolchak. A devout Communist, Simon Slepak was for many years one of the editors at the Soviet news agency Tass. He had named his son 'Vladimir' in honour of Vladimir Ilyich Lenin.

Following Slepak's first refusal, his apartment on Gorky Street, in the centre of Moscow, became a gathering place of Jews who, like him and his wife Masha, had been refused permission to leave the Soviet Union, or those who, like Masha Slepak's sister, were on the eve of a successful application.

Slepak and his friends were determined not to give up applying for an exit visa. They were not afraid of the repercussions of having asked to go to Israel, even when it meant, as it usually did, dismissal from one's profession. Nor did they act outside the framework of Soviet law. Their sole aim was to emigrate; not to play games with the authorities nor to provoke them, but to argue for the right to leave, and to obtain their exit visas. Entering this small, intense world of hope, activity and a sense of renewed Jewish identity,

Shcharansky quickly found in Slepak a friend and ally.

One remarkable factor gave the Jews who gathered in Slepak's apartment their cause for hope. The upsurge of applications for exit visas in 1971 and 1972 had been matched by a sudden and substantial increase in the number of visas granted, and in the number of Jews who were allowed to leave for Israel. In 1971 more than thirteen thousand were allowed to go. In 1972 the number of exit visas issued in the year was more than thirty thousand, among them Luba Yershkovich, Shcharansky's friend from the music academy.

★   ★   ★

The Moscow Physical–Technical Institute boasted one of the most highly regarded English courses in Moscow. It was arranged in three grades: beginners, continuation and advanced. Shcharansky entered the advanced section, and even there he did well. A student at the same Institute, Lev Ulanovsky, who came to know Shcharansky later, recalled his skills at English, his love of reading English books and listening to English on the radio.

In Moscow, in September 1971, a group of Jewish scientists, some of whom had already been refused their exit visas, decided to set up a private scientific seminar. Led by Professor Alexander Voronel, this seminar was to become a symbol of the determination of Soviet Jews not to allow 'refusal', and the isolation which normally followed it, to cut them off from their intellectual life and dignity. The first meeting of the seminar was held early in 1972.

3

Refusenik

On 17 April 1972, in Washington, the United States House of Representatives resolved that the President should 'request the Soviet Government that it permit its citizens to emigrate'. The President was Richard Nixon, who arrived in Moscow on May 22 on an official visit. Many Jews wrote to Nixon before his arrival appealing for help in obtaining an exit visa. One letter was signed by ninety-three Jews from Riga, another by fifty friends of those who had been imprisoned in the Leningrad and Riga Trials. During Nixon's visit almost every refusenik was detained, and Shcharansky's new friend, Vladimir Slepak, was among those sentenced to ten days in prison, charged with disturbing public order. No demonstrations had in fact taken place; all the arrests had been preventive, in anticipation of protests.

Angered by these arrests, and by the widespread harassment, a group of thirty wives and friends of those arrested or harassed wrote an open letter to the Soviet Prosecutor-General. The signatories included two women who were later to become close friends of Shcharansky, Ida Nudel and Dina Beilina.

Not only were these protests made openly, with signatures appended to them, but copies were sent to the growing number of Soviet Jewry campaigns overseas, including, in the United States, the National Conference on Soviet Jewry and the Union of Councils for Soviet Jews. Each protest was then published in the West, in campaign journals, in pamphlets, and in newspaper articles. Also made public in the West in the four months after Nixon's visit was the first list of Soviet Jews who wished to make contact with Jews in the West: the list was circulated in Israel by a recently constituted Action Committee of Newcomers from the Soviet Union. Containing more than a thousand names, it was the

first list to indicate the scale of the Jewish movement in Russia, and
to indicate also who spoke Hebrew, who had applied for Israeli
citizenship, and who had been refused an exit visa.

Also in Israel, a Scientists' Committee of the Israel Public
Council for Soviet Jewry held an emergency meeting, on 20 August
1972, to protest against the dismissal of refusenik scientists from
their professional work, and against their continued denial of an
exit visa. The main speaker was Professor Gershom Sholem, a
leading authority on Jewish mysticism who had emigrated from
Germany to Jerusalem in 1923. 'We are an experienced nation,' he
declared of the Jewish people, and he went on to ask: 'What has not
yet transpired between us and the world of nations? What poisoned
cup have we not already drunk?'

On 1 September 1972 this Scientists' Committee published the
first issue of what was to become, for a decade, a regular digest of
the fate of Soviet Jewry, the *News Bulletin*. One of its first reports
was of a demonstration by a group of Soviet Jews near the Lebanese
Embassy in Moscow, on September 6, to condemn the murder of
Israeli athletes by Arab terrorists at the Munich Olympics. Among
those who took part in this demonstration was Academician
Sakharov. As punishment, Sakharov and the demonstrators were
taken to the cells of a 'sobering-up place' used to keep drunks
overnight. 'These places', one former refusenik later reflected,
'were meant for a very low class of people. Sakharov was a very
prominent person. Years afterwards people used to say to me:
"When I met Sakharov in the sobering-up place," or "Sakharov
and I first met at the sobering-up place."'

One avenue of hope for all Soviet Jews who might wish to live in
Israel was glimpsed, albeit dimly, in November 1972, when talks
began in Helsinki between the governments of all thirty-three
European States, including the Soviet Union, together with the
Governments of Canada and the United States. These talks were to
lead eight months later to the establishment of a Conference on
Security and Co-operation in Europe. The intention, of the
preparatory talks and of the Conference, was to reach agreement on
questions both of security and of human rights. The principal
Soviet aim was to secure agreement on the 'inviolability of frontiers' – the frontiers established in 1945. For their part, the Western
States were eager to establish what they described as 'Respect for
human rights and fundamental freedom, including the freedom of
thought, conscience, religion and belief'. The Helsinki discussions,

which were to enter their 'working session' phase in Geneva in September 1973, took nearly three years before agreement was reached and a document was ready to be signed. But from the moment the preparatory talks started, Soviet Jews understood that what had begun in Helsinki could be of decisive importance for them, particularly as one Western aim was to secure Soviet agreement to 'reunification of families', and to 'facilitate' and 'expedite' the granting of exit visas to such families.

★   ★   ★

In order to be near their two sons in Moscow, Boris Shcharansky and his wife now moved to Istra, a village outside Moscow, known before the war by the name of its monastery, New Jerusalem. At Istra, the two Shcharansky sons would join their parents on Sundays, enjoying the quiet life of the countryside after the bustle of the capital. Their father was sixty-eight years old, and in poor health.

On 30 January 1973 a remarkable event took place in Moscow, the first session of a private seminar entitled 'Jewish history, culture and religion'. It had been organised by Professor Vitaly Rubin, a Jew, a refusenik, and an expert on China. The first talk was on Jewish mysticism, based on the writing of Gershom Sholem. It was given by Dmitri Segal, who later received his exit visa. The second talk was by Rubin himself, on James Michener's book *The Source*, an epic of the Jewish saga in the Land of Israel throughout the ages.

During the summer of 1972, Shcharansky had completed his studies at the Moscow Physical–Technical Institute. That autumn he began graduate work on the application of chess end-games as examples of 'making decisions in situations of conflict'. Then, in April 1973, he applied for an exit visa.

None of the work done at the Physical–Technical Institute was of a secret nature. Indeed, six of the students who had taken the same course as Shcharansky at the Institute subsequently left the Soviet Union. Four of them were Jews who received exit visas for Israel; the fifth was an Arab, returning home to the United Arab Republic. The sixth was an Armenian, Yury Yarim-Agaev, who later wrote to the Prosecutor-General of the Soviet Union, during Shcharansky's trial, of how, when Shcharansky told him, shortly after graduation from the Institute, that he had applied for an exit visa, 'I wished him all the best and thought it would be our last meeting. I really couldn't think of any reason to prevent him from emigrating: he had never been connected with any secret matters.'

In April 1973 an International Congress on Mathematics was held in Moscow. No Jewish mathematicians who had sought, and been refused, exit visas were given permission to submit papers. Shcharansky, himself a mathematician, though not yet a refusenik, decided to participate in a Jewish scientific seminar for the excluded mathematicians which was being held in the private apartment of Professor Alexander Lerner, its founder. The theme of Lerner's seminar was 'mathematical methods in biology and medicine'. At the same time, the other seminar for refusenik scientists, which had been organised by Professor Voronel, continued to meet, its theme being 'collective phenomena in physics'.

Professor Lerner, whose seminar Shcharansky now joined, was one of those who had protested publicly against the arrests during the Nixon visit. His Moscow apartment, like Slepak's, was a centre of warmth and enthusiasm for all refuseniks. The friendship between Lerner and Shcharansky was immediate and lasting. Twelve years later I was to sit in Lerner's apartment, underneath a portrait of Shcharansky which Lerner himself had painted. In those spring days in 1973, Lerner had already been 'in refusal' for a year and a half. He was also one of the thousand names on the list which had been prepared in Israel the previous autumn.

Shcharansky, his single application still unanswered, awaited his exit visa. It was common for several months to elapse between application and permission. Having heard nothing throughout the summer, in August Shcharansky obtained an interview with Lieutenant-Colonel Andrei Verein, the head of the Moscow bureau of the Visa Office. Verein told the young man that his application was 'legal and acceptable'. All seemed set for emigration by the year's end.

As the weeks passed without any positive reply, Shcharansky became impatient. It was then that he met Valery Kryzhak and Isaak Polhan, two young men who had already been refused permission to leave and who argued that the best way to obtain an exit visa was by public demonstration. A third demonstrator, Isaak Babel, was equally determined to be both seen and heard. Asked by a friend, Dr Alexander Lunts, whether it might not be sensible to postpone the demonstrations for a while as the KGB were getting 'unnerved' by them, Babel replied: 'Demonstrations should take place every two weeks. There are no hard times and no soft times.'

Babel continued to demonstrate. Today he, Kryzhak and Polhan live in Israel. They had already carried out two small demonstrations in 1972. The first was a demonstration by six refuseniks outside the *Izvestia* newspaper building in Moscow, with placards demanding exit visas; the second was the demonstration outside the Lebanese Embassy, to condemn the massacre of Israeli athletes at the Munich Olympic Games.

The refuseniks had started with only one aim: to have their refusal reversed, to receive their exit visa, and to leave the Soviet Union. But as more and more Jews were arrested, tried and sentenced, their concern for the prisoners grew, and they began to speak out on behalf of the prisoners.

Most of the debates long into the night were of how to leave, how to reverse a refusal. One of the refuseniks who sympathised most strongly with the need for public demonstrations in favour of exit visas was Ida Nudel, whose determination to leave the Soviet Union was intensified when her sister Ilana was given permission to go to Israel. All Ida's other relatives having been murdered by the Nazis, she was now alone. Another recent refusenik who favoured public demonstrations was Iosif Beilin, a young Jew from the former Polish city of Lvov.

This group also believed in the value of publicity on behalf of those Jews who had been refused their exit visas, or who were in trouble with the authorities. Iosif Beilin's wife Dina, who now lives with her husband in Jerusalem, later spoke of their efforts to obtain information about those who had been arrested, and to send it out of Russia. 'We worked very closely with foreign correspondents and with foreign tourists,' she recalled. 'We felt it was very important that news of the prisoners should be published immediately.'

One of the spokesmen for the group in its contacts with foreign journalists and tourists was Kyril Khenkin, a Soviet journalist who, having graduated between the wars from the Sorbonne, returned to Russia after the Spanish Civil War. After being refused an exit visa, he served as a link with Westerners and Western journalists in Moscow. When he received permission to leave at the end of 1972, Khenkin handed over this task to Alex Goldfarb; 'a very talented man', Dina Beilina remembered, 'he had lived in a very cultural family and received a good education. It was easy for him.' Goldfarb, too, had been refused permission to leave.

Scarcely had Goldfarb begun to act as spokesman for the little group, when another trial sent shock waves of worry through the

ranks of those Jews who were so desperate to leave Russia. On 29
March 1973 the trial began of a young Jew from Vinnitsa, Isak
Shkolnik, who nine months earlier had applied to go to Israel.
Before the trial began, Shkolnik was accused of being a British spy.
At his trial the accusation was changed; now he was alleged to have
been an Israeli spy, who had collected information in his head in
order to communicate it to officials in Israel once he had received an
exit visa. 'What do they want to punish him for?' his wife Feiga
wrote in a letter to the Soviet Prosecutor-General. 'For espionage
which did not and could not exist, or for too openly desiring to
leave for his historic homeland, Israel?'

Shkolnik was sentenced to seven years in labour camp. His wife
received her exit visa. In the West, every Soviet Jewry group,
including a recently established Lawyers Group of the National
Conference on Soviet Jewry, protested on his behalf, and in
Moscow, Ida Nudel worked tirelessly to try to help him.

The path of public protest was one which Shcharansky found
attractive: by the autumn of 1973 he was to be found in the
company of the small group of Jews in Moscow who did not fear to
be seen championing the rights of Soviet Jews to live in Israel. They
welcomed his presence but, as Iosif Beilin later recalled, 'he was
very quiet; he was very young.' It was not against Soviet law to
gather together in public with a small banner, even though the usual
response of the authorities was to seize the banner, within minutes,
and order the half dozen demonstrators to disperse. Although not
acting against the letter of Soviet law, this group was as familiar as
every Soviet citizen with the popular saying: 'The law is something
that can be turned and twisted, in whatever direction you wish.'

Nevertheless, exit visas continued to be granted, and on a scale
inconceivable a decade earlier. In 1972 more than thirty-one
thousand Soviet Jews had been allowed to leave for Israel, and the
figures for the first months of 1973 showed that even this substantial
total was likely to be exceeded. 'The vast majority of Soviet Jews',
wrote Shimon Peres, the Israeli Minister of Transport and Communication, in the *Jerusalem Post* on 11 May 1973, 'is by now totally
disenchanted with Russian Communism, and is in fact a Jewry *en
route* to Israel.'

★   ★   ★

On 6 October 1973, Syrian and Egyptian forces attacked Israel,
crossing the Suez Canal in the south and advancing across the

plateau of the Golan Heights in the north. From Moscow, on the following day, forty-five Moscow Jews sent a message of solidarity to the Government and people of Israel: 'We are with you at this critical hour.' The names of the signatories included Shcharansky's friends Professor Alexander Lerner, Vladimir Slepak, Dina Beilina and Ida Nudel.

That same day, in a telegram to the Israeli Prime Minister, Golda Meir, three former Red Army Colonels, Yefim Davidovich, Lev Ovsishcher and Nahum Alshansky, each of whom had been refused his exit visa, declared: 'Not for a moment do we doubt that victory will be ours. Long live the people of Israel.'

There were other protests, in which Jewish activists deviated for the first time from their established principle not to oppose Soviet policy openly; these Jews expressed their anger at the Soviet press and television hostility to Israel. More than a hundred Soviet Jews offered to give blood 'to the citizens of Israel who have been wounded in the war'.

On 13 October 1973, as the battle continued on the Golan Heights and in the Sinai Desert, hundreds of young Jews gathered outside the synagogue in Arkhipova Street in the severe cold of an early winter. Among them was Shcharansky. Another of those present, a girl of twenty-two, has described how 'we were in agony for news of the war. No one doubted Israel's strength, and we, the Jews of Moscow, considered ourselves citizens of our distant homeland.' The girl's brother, also a refusenik, was then serving a short prison sentence for having protested against the growing number of refusals. Preparing him a package of warm clothes, the girl smuggled a note inside it, written in Hebrew, telling him that Israeli forces were approaching Damascus.

The girl had no idea in which of several prisons in Moscow her brother was held. In search of advice, she went up to a group of young Jews who were holding a small demonstration on the steps of the synagogue. There, several of the Jews present tried to reassure her about her brother's imprisonment. As she listened to them, a young man came up to her. It was Shcharansky.

'He could see that I was afraid,' the girl remembered, 'and he tried to comfort me. He asked me all about myself, my work, my plans to go to Israel. He talked of all sorts of things other than prison and my brother.'

'I'm really called Natan,' Shcharansky told her. 'That's what I will be called in Israel. Are you thinking of going?' The young girl

was indeed thinking of going; Shcharansky commented 'that if I
wanted to go to Israel I must start studying Hebrew. I said, "Yes, I
want to study Hebrew."'

The young girl was Natalia Shtiglits. Later she chose the Hebrew
name Avital. She and the young man began to talk about Hebrew
classes. Shcharansky, cold and shivering from 'flu, spoke nevertheless with an animation which seemed to her remarkable. His
movements, glance and thoughts suggested freedom. Looking at
this enthusiastic young man for the first time, she later explained, 'I
thought, Israel is probably like him.' A few days later she went with
Shcharansky to her first Hebrew lesson. In order to be in the same
class as he, she pretended to be more advanced in the language than
she was; a fact he was later to recall with much amusement, in his
prison cell.

'What level are you on?' he had asked her. 'What about you?' she
countered. 'Well, I already know a thousand words: that's not bad.'

Suddenly feeling that the one thing in the world she wanted to do
was to study with this young man, Avital replied: 'That's it, I'm on
the same level.' 'Good,' replied Shcharansky, 'I'll ask my teacher
about you, but we study very seriously. You have to speak only
Hebrew.'

Their teacher, Micka Chlenov, was a virtuoso in many
languages. He was also even smaller than Shcharansky, who was
only five foot three. The two men often joked about how small they
both were. Once a week, the teacher, Shcharansky and the girl met
with some ten other pupils. Once a week they also joined a group of
all the teachers and all the classes in Moscow, often more than sixty
people, 'the most that was possible to come to a Moscow apartment', as Avital observed. If anyone spoke Russian not Hebrew,
'out he went.'

The impact on Shcharansky of this wise, cheerful teacher was
considerable. 'He made an atmosphere,' Avital later commented,
'always laughing, always smiling, a little bit like a clown. Whatever
he saw in Russian, on television or in the newspapers, he would
immediately translate it into Hebrew. In his lessons we would
pretend to be the Israeli Parliament each speaking for a different
point of view. In his lessons you felt you were no longer in Russia.'

For Jews in Russia to learn Hebrew was a tradition far older than
the refusenik movement, or the fifty-year struggle of Soviet Jewry
to retain its identity. Shcharansky's uncle Shamai, who had left
Odessa for Palestine in 1924, later told me of his own first memories

of childhood in 1906 and 1907: 'However much I search my memories I recall myself with a Hebrew book.'

Anatoly Shcharansky, choosing as his own Hebrew name the 'Natan' of one of his great-grandfathers, plunged into his Hebrew lessons with zeal, at the same time guiding Avital in her first steps in the language of the land in which they hoped soon to live.

In November 1973, however, within three months of Shcharansky's interview with Lieutenant-Colonel Verein, he learned that he had been refused an exit visa. When he pressed for a reason for this unexpected refusal, he was told that he had, after all, had 'access to classified materials'. This was not so: his thesis at the Faculty of Applied Mathematics, his only work, related to the programming of computers to play chess, and had no secret aspect.

Although he was now a refusenik, Shcharansky was fortunate in being able to remain at work in his area of expertise, having been accepted as a 'young specialist' at the Moscow Research Institute for Oil and Gas. There, he worked in his own field, that of automation computers. This Institute was classified as an 'open' institution, not involved in secret work.

A month after Shcharansky was refused his exit visa, Avital's brother was given permission to leave for Israel. As he was being driven away from Lod airport towards his first night in Israel, he heard on the car radio the news of the death of David Ben Gurion.

Had Shcharansky received his exit visa in November 1973, he would have been one of more than thirty-four thousand Jews to leave the Soviet Union that year, almost all of whom went to Israel. Neither his story nor his fate would have been of note, unless, in Israel, he had become a leading chess player or computer scientist. Instead of anonymity, obscurity, or both, he found himself propelled forward into a world of anguish and of struggle. By December 1973 there were more than two thousand Jews who had been refused exit visas, a small community with a common overriding aim: to receive permission to leave. Among them were several men and women whose lives were to be inextricably bound up with Shcharansky's in the following five years: Slepak himself, Dina and Iosif Beilin, Lev Ulanovsky, Professor Lerner, Alexander Lunts and Ida Nudel.

It was Ida Nudel who decided that one task which needed to be done, and which could be done, was to help the prisoners. With indefatigable energy and dedication, she kept in touch with them, travelled to see them in their places of internal exile, appealed to

Soviet officials about conditions in the prisons and camps, and
maintained links of comfort and concern with the prisoners' wives
and families. Her friends told her that such activity would prove
impossible. Ida Nudel persisted, carried it out, and also persuaded
many others to do whatever they could to help the prisoners
whenever an opportunity presented itself.

Entering this world of refuseniks and Jewish activists, Avital
quickly became used to the zeal of the KGB in 'blocking' the
apartment of someone whom they wished to frighten or to annoy,
filling the entrance way or corridor with stern-faced agents.
'Sometimes', she later recalled, 'the apartment owners and their
accidental guests would be "locked" in an apartment for several
days, while the agents stationed themselves in cars around the
corner, near the front door, in the elevator and near the apartment
door. They were like vultures waiting for their prey.'

On 8 November 1973 Avital celebrated her twenty-third birthday. 'I still don't know why my birthday attracted their attention,'
she later wrote of the KGB, 'but when the guests got ready to leave
after a noisy evening of wine, music and lively conversation, they
discovered KGB cars waiting for them at the entrance. Mattresses
were placed on the floor and all those for whom it was dangerous
had to stay for the night.' Avital's account continued:

> The morning was bleak and snowy, but the cars remained in
> their places. The agents had remained at their post all night,
> drinking vodka to warm up.
> My friends lounged about the room, some read, some wrote
> letters. Tolik offered to play chess with me. I didn't know much
> more than how to move the chess pieces; I didn't know that
> when he was still a child he was city champion and could now
> play fifteen games simultaneously with his eyes closed. In a
> word, he needed three moves.
> I remember every tiny detail and intonation of that morning.
> Then we said what we had been feeling for a long time: we
> needed each other.

The young couple decided to live together. Shcharansky rented a
small room in a two-storeyed detached house. Once a single family
had lived in it; now five families lived on the top floor alone, each
with one room, sharing a kitchen and a toilet. 'An ottoman which
had been knocked together out of boards', Avital remembered,
'took up a third of Tolik's living space. A large rug – a gift from his

parents – was spread on the floor; in the corner a small three-legged table was always piled high with books, papers, grammatical tables. Later, I covered this table with a red scarf that I bought in a Central Asian bazaar.'

Each morning, Shcharansky went out to work at his Institute. Avital remained in the room sitting on the ottoman, studying Hebrew, and avidly reading books about Israel which her Tolik had managed to get hold of. 'He called from work several times a day to make sure that everything was all right, and when he returned we greeted each other as if we had been separated for years.' In the evenings, Avital added, 'Tolik would talk to me for hours about Eretz Yisroel' – the Land of Israel – 'and I feared that a telephone call or outside noise would interrupt his story.'

As soon as the apartment was ready, Shcharansky invited his mother to Moscow to meet Avital. 'I waited for her tensely,' Avital later recalled, 'but Tolik joked and gently convinced me that we would get along very well. The doorbell rang. I saw a small, elderly woman, all wrapped up. She looked at me intently as she took off her large scarf. In a minute we were sitting on the ottoman and drinking tea with candy that she had brought us. I was attracted by her open smile, intelligent face and pleasing, slightly hoarse voice.' Mother and son, noted Avital, were 'remarkably alike: they had the same sharp wit and sense of humour, the same open, generous attitude towards life'. She added:

> I followed their discussion of family matters with amazement; I had not seen such frank trust between parents and children for a long time, especially in families where the children had decided to emigrate to Israel. This decision often frightened the parents, caused misunderstanding and tension and sometimes led to a familial break. Here it was entirely different; Tolik listened to his mother's advice on how to behave at work, reflected and then agreed with her.

Shcharansky told his mother and Avital of how, at work with the status of 'young specialist', he had been summoned to a meeting at which he had been condemned for his 'treachery' in applying to go to Israel. He had been made to stand, Avital explained, 'in the middle of a furious crowd of co-workers, each of whom tried to outshout the other in castigating him. These "simple Soviet citizens" tried to demonstrate the fact that they never had anything in common with this traitor. One girl got so worked up that she

called him a Zionist spy, and aggressor, who was going to Israel in
order to murder her Arab brothers (her husband served in the army
of one of the Arab countries).'

This was the first time, Avital noted, 'that Tolik was called a spy'.

The two women sat on the ottoman listening to the story. As
with all his accounts of life and troubles, Shcharansky filled it with
humour, and the three of them laughed together. 'The room was
warm and comfortable,' Avital recalled, 'and we were already well
acquainted.'

Shcharansky then told his mother their plans: they would marry;
Avital's brother would then, from Israel, send them an invitation;
they would receive permission and go to Israel. 'If we wanted to
look for some meaning in Tolik's visa problems,' Avital wrote, 'we
decided it was so that we could meet.'

That winter, Shcharansky and Avital went to Tallinn, the capital
of the Estonian Soviet Republic, and to Volokolamsk, to the west
of Moscow, near to where the Red Army had halted the German
forces during their most ferocious onslaught in 1941.

Ida Milgrom invited Avital to Istra, to meet Shcharansky's
father. On the following Saturday they took the train out of
Moscow. During the journey, Avital pressed Shcharansky to tell
her about his parents, his own childhood, his schooldays, and his
life until their meeting that October. 'Absorbed in the past,' she
remembered, 'I travelled to Tolya's parents' home in a place called
New Jerusalem after the local monastery and church; at this time of
year Christian pilgrims, mostly wrinkled old ladies in black,
flocked there. I felt as if I were going to visit very dear relatives. We
walked past the monastery woods along a snow-strewn path. Black
tree trunks protruded from huge snowdrifts. Clumps of snow fell
from the bare treetops to our feet; the crows cawed.' Avital's
account continued:

> This 'new' Jerusalem was so unlike our real one which we
> would finally get to someday. Closing our eyes, we could even
> imagine ourselves walking along the narrow, blindingly sunny
> Old Jerusalem streets, so familiar to us from postcards.
>
> Tolya's parents' home was a gift to me. Suddenly two homes
> entered my homeless life at the same time – ours in Moscow and
> his parents' in Istra. Everything there was suffused with kind-
> ness and humour. An atmosphere of trust and warmth
> prevailed.

When Tolya's father saw me he lit up. 'Finally the Shcharansky family will be tall.' (All the Shcharanskys are short; I'm very much the opposite.)

I loved to spend time at their home. We would go there to 'get warmed up' and to eat good food: we would also sit it out there when Tolik was being followed too brazenly.

★   ★   ★

On 23 November 1973 a court in Kiev sentenced Alexander Feldman to three and a half years in prison. The charge against him was 'malicious hooliganism', the false accusation of knocking a cake out of a woman's hand. His actual 'crime' was that he had repeatedly applied to the authorities in Kiev to let him go to Israel. Three days later, the *News Bulletin* of the Scientists' Committee of the Israel Public Council for Soviet Jewry published an appeal signed by twenty-one Moscow Jews, all of whom had been refused their exit visas. It was the first appeal published in the West of which Shcharansky was a signatory.

'We,' the appeal began, 'the Jews who have been fighting for a long time for emigration to Israel, have appealed to the Central Committee of the Communist Party of the Soviet Union and other Soviet authorities in connection with this matter. We did not receive any answer. In addition, we have been deprived of the right to work in accordance with our qualification, the right to inviolability of place of residence, the right to free existence.' The twenty-one signatories added: 'Let the authorities be silent about our absence of rights or claim the contrary. We ourselves have made another decision. As a sign of deprivation of our rights we will, when we find it necessary, wear the yellow Star of David as has always been done by our brethren under conditions of tyranny.'

The signatories of this appeal included Vladimir Slepak, Alexander Lunts, Vladimir Prestin, Pavel Abramovich, Victor Brailovsky, Zakhar Tesker, Dina and Iosif Beilin, Valery Kryzhak and Boris Tsitlionok, as well as Shcharansky.

That winter, Lev Ulanovsky decided to apply for an exit visa. Like Shcharansky, he was a graduate of the Moscow Physical–Technical Institute. 'I had suspicions', he later recalled, 'that the very fact that I had graduated from there could hinder my departure. I was told that Shcharansky, a refusenik, had graduated a year before me. I wanted to see him, to ask him what my chances might be. I came to the Oil and Gas Institute where he worked, and we walked along the street.'

Ulanovsky asked Shcharansky what his 'statistical' chances were of leaving. 'The statistics', Shcharansky replied, 'show that of the dozen people who graduated from our Institute and applied, a half have already been given their exit visas, so you see, the chances are about half and half.'

Ulanovsky told Shcharansky: 'I will probably apply in a few months. If I am refused, I will be quite ready to be active in my struggle for emigration.' The two men became friends: like Shcharansky, Ulanovsky spoke excellent English, and was to become a spokesman for the emigration movement. Like Shcharansky, he was to receive a refusal, but, after five years of waiting and reapplying, he was allowed to leave. From that moment, in Israel, he spoke affectionately of Shcharansky's kindness, his enthusiasm and his wisdom.

'Tolya was a young man who never sat still,' another of his friends now in Israel reflected with equal admiration. 'He never waited for someone else to do what he thought ought to be done.' One idea which Shcharansky had during his early months in refusal was to help people who were in the same position as he was to see how best to proceed with their applications to leave: he set out for them the different stages; showed them how to prepare the documents; explained the emigration process to them; showed them that it was not illegal, that it could be done according to Soviet law. Above all, he demonstrated that it was not so difficult 'to break the fear' of application.

Shcharansky's ideas were the product of a versatile mind. 'He never rested, he never spent five minutes resting,' Avital remembered. 'He was a very active man; he could work day and night.'

One of Shcharansky's closest friends, Dina Beilina, later reflected, as she and I sat in her home in Jerusalem: 'We did not expect to be refused. We expected to go. We were not fighters and not politicians. We became like a small community, and friends, and Shcharansky became one of our group.' Dina Beilina added: 'Vulnerability was to be alone, or to act alone: the band of brothers kept together, and acted together.'

*   *   *

Each Soviet Jew who was refused an exit visa had to work out what to do next. 'It was not possible to return to normal life,' Dina

Beilina later recalled. 'You were on a special list of "disloyal" people, you had no normal job, and even the people in the apartment block where you lived knew all about you.' Some, like Dina Beilina and Shcharansky, plunged into active work, protesting publicly at their exit-visa rejection and that of the other refuseniks. Others, particularly those who had been for many years active as scientists, strove to re-create in refusal the conditions whereby they could still study. In the late autumn of 1973 Professor Vitaly Rubin went so far as to hold a press conference to tell Western correspondents in Moscow about his cultural seminar. Among those who had already read papers at the seminar were many, like Mikhail Agursky who had spoken on anti-Semitism in Tsarist Russia, Dmitri Segal and Rubin himself, who were later to receive their exit visas. But that winter, the future was obscure for them personally, and seemed bleak for many, as the number of refuseniks grew.

For Shcharansky, with his humour and his optimism, the situation, though bleak, was never tragic; among the refuseniks, he was becoming a focal point of inspiration. The result was an increase in surveillance which had many serious and some comic repercussions. Avital later recalled how:

One winter night, when I was looking out of the window for Tolik, I suddenly heard an engine roar. I saw a black Volga slowly enter our snowy courtyard, pressing Tolya with its back fender. An hour or two later, another car just like it squeezed in the gateway and pressed against a refusenik who was coming to visit us. We couldn't understand how the cars would eventually get out. They remained under the window, so we knew that everything we would say could be overheard. We had no secrets, but we couldn't stand feeling like fish in an aquarium who were being stared at malevolently. All evening we were silent or communicated with paper and pencil.

When the KGB cars tried to leave in the morning, one got stuck in the snowdrifts, thereby locking the other in the courtyard. The roar of the engines woke up the neighbours. Sleepy and in a state of aroused curiosity, they poured into the yard, trying to find out what such luxurious cars were doing there. Our pursuers became enraged; without waiting to find out what happened, we got our things together and left for Istra.

Returning to Moscow, there was to be no let-up in the pressure. As
Avital wrote:

> Two days later, a young policeman dropped in on us, looked at
> us and our guests in confusion, demanded everyone's docu-
> ments and asked whose apartment it was. He kept looking at us
> curiously and finally couldn't contain himself:
> 'Who are all of you here?' he asked with the childish smirk of
> a conspirator.
> 'People,' Tolik answered mockingly.
> The policeman left and returned several hours later.
> 'I have been ordered to have you cleared out of the premises
> within twenty-four hours since you are not registered here. So
> get going,' he said harshly.
> In the morning, the neighbours began unceremoniously
> peeping in.

Shcharansky and Avital moved to another apartment in a house
nearby. Within a month the same incident had been repeated and
they moved again, to a room on the outskirts of Moscow. 'Here the
KGB left us in peace for a while,' Avital remembered. It was also an
apartment in which they had their own small kitchen, and could
prepare their food without the 'unfriendly scrutiny' of their
neighbours. Twice a week, their Hebrew class would meet in this
more secluded spot. 'In a period of six months', Avital later
recalled, 'many students went away, new ones replaced them, the
teacher changed, and quite often Russian words would be heard in
spite of the rules. But all of us valued these lessons greatly. I put
Tolya's declension tables on large coloured tablets and hung them
up in the kitchen. By this time I could already write some of the
Psalms of David in Hebrew, and we often sang them to Jewish
tunes.'

By the end of 1973, Western visitors to the Soviet Union had
become aware of the growing number of Jews who had been
refused exit visas, and of the plight of the prisoners. To those
Westerners whom they met, Soviet Jews such as Dina and Iosif
Beilin stressed the importance of such visits, of telephone calls, and
of Western campaigns of protest. The indignities of life as a
refusenik were also becoming clear. One Moscow refusenik, meeting a Philadelphia couple in November 1973, told them of how,
having lost his job as a radio electrical engineer when he applied to
go to Israel, he had worked as a loader in a bakery; but when he had

gone to collect his wages, he had been told by the supervisor: 'Go to collect your wages in Israel.' This refusenik was to become a close friend of Shcharansky; when I myself visited him in Moscow in August 1985 he was in his fourteenth year as a refusenik.

The Philadelphia couple also reported the last words of one of those whom they visited, a woman refusenik who, speaking on behalf of all her fellow refuseniks, begged: 'Remember us.'

In order to be 'remembered' and, as they believed, helped in their quest for an exit visa, a group of refuseniks decided that a priority in their lives was to try to alert Jews in the West to the seriousness of the refusenik situation: to pass on such details as they could gather about the most recent arrests, the harassments, and the growing number of exit visas refused. Sometimes this information was transmitted through those who had received their exit visas, sometimes it was given to visitors from the West, but as there was never any intention to hide it from the Soviet authorities, much of it was given on the open telephone. There were many important telephone links between the Jewish activists in the Soviet Union and Soviet Jewry campaigners in the United States, Canada, Britain and Western Europe; among them was the British schoolmaster, Michael Sherbourne, who had been among the protesters outside the Soviet Embassy in London after the first Leningrad Trial. Sherbourne's Russian was fluent, and his devotion to the refuseniks total. Since the late summer of 1972, he had spoken regularly on the telephone with Vladimir Slepak, Professor Lerner, Ida Nudel and Dina Beilina. It was during one of these telephone conversations that Sherbourne was introduced to Shcharansky. It was the beginning of a close telephonic friendship which was to last until Shcharansky's arrest three years later; a friendship of two men who had never met, who were separated in age by thirty years, but who struck up an instant intimacy, based upon common concerns and mutual trust.

Shcharansky's first telephone talk with Sherbourne took place in January 1974, within two months of the rejection of Shcharansky's application for an exit visa. 'He seemed', Sherbourne later observed, 'to enter the central group almost immediately, because of his personality.'

Shcharansky also entered, for the first time, the world of Jewish festivals and celebrations: those occasions for feasting and singing and recalling the events of Jewish history and the Jewish national struggle. At the centre of this historic struggle had been the Exodus

from Egypt, which, every Passover, was recounted in readings
from the Haggadah, the narrative of the Exodus, by Jews in every
corner of the globe, even in Moscow.

On 13 April 1974 Shcharansky and Avital celebrated the Passover
'in the company', as he recalled a year later, 'of Moscow's young
Hebrew teachers'. For him and Avital it was, he wrote, 'the first real
Passover in our life, with the reading of the Haggadah, and I
remember very well how meaningful for me sounded the words:
"In every generation a man should see himself as if he personally
came out of Egypt."'

Avital was also to remember that particular Passover prayer. 'For
us,' she said, 'this was not an obligation; it was our life.' But, she
added, 'beneath the windows, several black Volgas waited while
the KGB agents kept a surveillance. When we left, the doors
slammed, the agents sprawled in and the cars slowly trailed us.
Each agent knew precisely who was his "ward".'

4

Debates and Demonstrations

Throughout the summer, autumn and winter of 1973, refuseniks in Russia, and their supporters in the United States, had debated the wisdom of an amendment which had been introduced to the United States Trade Reform Act of 1972. The Act itself, which embodied the Soviet–American Trade Agreement of October of that year, had opened up the possibility of vastly increased trade between the United States and the Eastern-bloc countries. The amendment, sponsored by seventy-eight Senators headed by Henry M. Jackson, made these trade concessions conditional on 'respect for the right to emigrate'. On 14 September 1973 Academician Sakharov, in an open letter to the United States Congress, had urged support for the amendment on behalf of 'tens of thousands of citizens in the Soviet Union', including Jews 'who want to leave the country and who have been seeking to exercise that right for years and for decades at the cost of endless difficulty and humiliation'.

The 'Jackson Amendment', as it was known, had its origins in a proposal put forward by the National Conference on Soviet Jewry in September 1972 and subsequently pressed upon Senators and Congressmen through a specially opened Washington office of the National Conference. It was supported in the House of Representatives by a similar amendment, with Congressman Charles A. Vanik as the principal co-sponsor. The House of Representatives passed the amendment on 11 December 1973, by a vote of 319 to 80 – 'a clear and decisive result', as Jackson described it, urging the Senate to support it as decisively. One of those in Moscow who believed strongly that the Jackson Amendment could lead to an upsurge in exit visas was a refusenik, Alexander Lunts, with whom Shcharansky had formed a close friendship.

In the spring of 1974 four American Jews, among them Dr Louis

Rosenblum of the Union of Councils for Soviet Jews, visited
Moscow to find out to what extent Soviet Jews felt that the Jackson
Amendment would help them. On April 30 the four Americans
were invited by Lunts to his apartment. 'It was there', Lou
Rosenblum later recalled, 'that I met Anatoly Shcharansky. When
we first arrived in Moscow, I had asked Vladimir Slepak, Victor
Polsky, and Lunts to invite any of the informal associations of
individuals (formed, for example, around commonality of profession, age, or Hebrew language interest) that so wished to meet
and share their interests and concerns with me. So all during the
afternoon of April 30th there was a flow of people in and out of
Lunts's flat.'

Most if not all of the Jews who gathered to meet Dr Rosenblum
were already the object of surveillance by the Soviet authorities. 'A
seriocomic touch', he observed, 'was provided to the proceedings
by the KGB. Each Soviet Jew who came had rated two or more
"tails". Consequently, while we were meeting above, below a
convention of agents, similarly attired in dark business suits,
assembled a short distance from the entrance to the apartment
building.' It was then that Shcharansky arrived, with a group of
other younger refuseniks. 'Probably because of his superior English
speaking abilities,' Rosenblum reflected, 'he acted as translator for
his associates. He was quite reserved and did not interject himself
into the discussions – as well he might in his role of translator.' The
impression of Shcharansky which Rosenblum carried away with
him that spring day was of a 'pleasant, earnest, quiet young man –
more of a follower than leader'.

Shcharansky took no lead in the discussion of April 30, confining
himself to acting as interpreter. Lunts himself among the leaders,
Alex Goldfarb and Lev Ulanovsky among the younger men, were
those most actively supporting the Jackson Amendment:
Ulanovsky later recounted how Lunts and Goldfarb, from
Ulanovsky's apartment, used to take part in telephone conversations about the amendment with Jews in America.

On 15 May 1974, however, two weeks after the discussion in
Lunts's apartment at which Rosenblum had been present, the
debate over American trade and the conditions that would be
imposed on it was cruelly eclipsed, for the Jews of Moscow, by
the news that Arab terrorists had murdered twenty Israeli schoolchildren in the northern Israeli town of Ma'alot. All thought
of the Jackson Amendment was momentarily set aside, in sadness at

the slaughter and anger at the crime. It was decided, by those whose dream was to live in Israel, to hold a public protest at the massacre outside the Lebanese Embassy in Moscow: the first public show of support for Israel since the October War demonstration seven months earlier.

Among those present while the new demonstration was being organised was Avital Shtiglits, who later recalled how 'we sent telegrams to the Central Committee and the Mayor of Moscow telling them we were planning to demonstrate.' It was to be an open protest, with placards denouncing the massacre. About fifty Jews went to the demonstration, Avital remembered, 'and when we arrived we found about four hundred militiamen waiting.' The Jews hesitated in front of this symbol of Soviet control. But then, as one of the refuseniks present, Vitaly Rubin, later told his wife: 'Tolya suddenly jumped up and said, "Why are you waiting here? We can break the line without any fear", and forward he strode, little Tolya, and the others followed.'

It was Anatoly Shcharansky's first public act of leadership. As the confrontation continued, the officer in charge of the militia 'came over to us', Avital observed, 'and said, "I'm giving you one minute to leave."' The Jews refused to leave. The officer then ordered his men to seize the placards. The soldiers, 'like dogs', Avital recalled, 'started grabbing at the pamphlets. People were beaten and pushed and very soon I saw some vans arrive. I remember thinking they looked like the vans the Nazis had used as mobile gas chambers. We were put in the vans and taken to the building for alcoholics.'

Shcharansky and Avital found themselves pushed into a barred room crowded with fellow demonstrators. Among those whom they met for the first time in that inhospitable place of punishment was a Jew from Minsk, Colonel Lev Ovsishcher, who had first been refused his exit visa in 1970. 'In Yiddish', as Avital remembered ten years later, 'he told the story about how, at the Battle of Stalingrad, he had gone up in a small aeroplane to urge the Germans, through a megaphone, to surrender.'

Colonel Ovsishcher had been born in the Vitebsk region of western Russia in 1919. In 1941 he had become a pilot, then, as a member of the Communist Party, a political commissar. All his professional life was spent in uniform. 'I was in Berlin on 8 May 1945,' he told me in Minsk when we first met in 1983. Two years later we met again in Moscow: after fourteen years of waiting, stripped of his rank, his medals and his pension, he is still a refusenik.

Also outside the Lebanese Embassy that morning were Professor Alexander Lerner, two of whose children had been murdered by the Nazis near Vinnitsa in 1941, and Academician Sakharov, who four years earlier had been a founder member of the Soviet Committee on Human Rights. Not himself a Jew, Sakharov was now married to Elena Bonner, a Jewess, whose relative Edward Kuznetsov was then in the fourth year of the fifteen-year sentence imposed upon him at the Leningrad Trial.

Slepak, Lerner, Lunts and Rubin were among the senior figures of a Jewish movement which, by the very nature of Soviet society, could have no leaders and no organisation, only a cohesion of friendship and shared aims. Amid these remarkable personalities, Shcharansky, so small in stature, moved with all the assurance of an old-timer. Not all the activities were public demonstrations: each Monday, at seven in the evening, Professor Lerner opened his apartment to the seminar at which refusenik scientists discussed the use of mathematical methods in medicine and biology. The main theme of the seminar was the problem of creating an artificial heart. Lerner, whose daughter Sonia was given permission that year to go to Israel, was a scientist of distinction who had been awarded the title of Professor by the Soviet Academy of Sciences in 1955. Aged sixty-one in 1974, his one remaining wish was to live in Israel.

That year, as detente brought the Soviet Union and the United States closer together than at any time since the Stalin era, more than twenty thousand Jews were allowed to leave for Israel, an average of 1666 a month. At the same time, however, the number of those who had been refused an exit visa also grew, as did the number of prisoners.

On 29 May 1974 a Jewish doctor, Mikhail Shtern, a Communist for thirty-one years, was arrested in Vinnitsa. The charge against him was of 'bribe-taking and swindling'. His sons declared, however, that his 'real' crime was that he had refused to denounce their applications for an exit visa. Yet another prisoner now became the object of international concern.

There was concern too, among the refuseniks, about the fate of the Leningrad Trial prisoners. News of appalling labour-camp conditions had reached Moscow from one of those prisoners, Iosif Mendelevich; his account was to reach the West, and to be widely publicised by several British, European, American and Canadian groups active in drawing attention to the plight of Soviet Jews.

5

Marriage

In March 1974, at the 'Warsaw' cinema in Moscow, Shcharansky and Avital saw the film *Love Story*, based on the novel by Erich Segal. 'Do you remember how deeply moved I was?' Shcharansky later wrote to Avital. 'You were even surprised? I wasn't thinking then about the characters in the film at all. I was thinking only about us. For some reason, I was afraid, or, more precisely, I drove away the feeling that some kind of tragedy was awaiting us. Right then I decided to persuade you to submit your documents for emigration as soon as possible, without waiting for me to receive permission.'

Shcharansky now began to urge Avital to apply for an exit visa. 'I didn't want to apply,' she later explained, 'because I was afraid of what would happen to Anatoly.' But Shcharansky told her that she 'must' apply. He also asked her to stop going to demonstrations, as she later recalled, 'so instead I had to watch him at demonstrations. It was harder to stand and watch than being with the demonstrators. It was terrible to see him being beaten and arrested.' Avital's account, written five years later, continued: 'Even though I was afraid for Anatoly, I was sure he would be given permission to leave at any time – the following day or week. Many of our friends were given permission to leave at that time. I actually thought he would go to Israel first and that I would follow later. What could they do to me? I was a woman alone. So I asked permission.'

Avital waited for her permission, or refusal. She and Shcharansky decided to get married: he had applied again for his rejected exit visa, and they hoped to be able to leave as man and wife. But they were refused a civil marriage.

No wedding could take place, 'but', as Avital later explained, 'we were happy, so happy just to be together. We didn't worry about it too much. After a while we decided that if it was impossible to get

married in the Soviet Union, we would just wait until we arrived in
Israel and get married there. Then a friend said to me, "Why don't
you ask the synagogue to marry you?"'

Avital and her Tolya went to the Moscow synagogue. 'The rabbi
there was afraid,' Avital recalled. 'He said no, he could not help. It
would be a danger for the synagogue. He suggested we go to a
different city. I started going to synagogue, and one day I met an
old man – Girsh Manevich – a very religious man who was very
active there. We arranged to have a meeting with him.'

No such meeting took place. On 19 June 1974, the eve of
President Nixon's second visit to Moscow, eighteen Jews, some of
them activists, as they were now called, others Hebrew teachers,
were arrested, and held in prison for two weeks, until Nixon had
returned to the United States. Those arrested included Professor
Voronel, the founder of the first scientific seminar, his colleague
Professor Mark Azbel, Slepak and Shcharansky; two prominent
Hebrew teachers, Lev Kogan and Yuly Kosharovsky; three other
refuseniks, Alexander Goldfarb, Dr Victor Brailovsky, and Boris
Tsitlionok; and Zakhar Tesker, a young man who had been refused
permission to leave the Soviet Union because he had done his
military service – but not in a combatant or secret unit: he had been
an army footballer.

While Shcharansky and the other seventeen were held in prison,
Avital received a postcard inviting her to the Visa Office. There, on
her Tolya's seventh day in a prison cell, she was told that her request
for an exit visa had been granted. There was only one condition: she
must leave the Soviet Union within ten days. 'I said, "No, it is
impossible,"' she recounted, '"because I do not know where my
fiancé is. Please help me find him."'

Avital did not know what to do or which way to turn; in a
desperate attempt to see Shcharansky, she refused to pay for her exit
visa until she had seen him. On the following day, she returned to
the Visa Office, to seek more time. 'If you do not take this visa,'
they told her, 'you will stay in Russia for the rest of your life, and
you will have many problems.'

'I did not know what to do,' Avital later observed. 'Then
Anatoly's mother came to see me. We decided to hope for the best
and to take the visa.'

Avital went to see Girsh Manevich, the leading authority in
Moscow on Jewish matters, whom she had earlier befriended, to
ask him if he could arrange a Jewish wedding for them, under the

traditional chuppah, or canopy. 'I told Manevich that I had a visa to leave but that my fiancé was in prison. At first he said he could not arrange it. My fiancé was an activist, I wanted to go to Israel, and it would be dangerous for the Jewish community and the synagogue if they married us. I said, "OK, no is no."'

Manevich then said to her, 'Maybe you have a picture of your fiancé?' Looking at the picture, Manevich declared: 'It's Anatoly. I know him. He is such a brilliant man and I like him very much. Such a good Jew. I will try to do everything possible to help you.' Manevich added, 'You are very lucky. You will have a good husband.'

Manevich and Avital decided to arrange the marriage for July 4: her exit visa expired on the following day, when she would have to leave, or have the visa cancelled. She and Manevich met every day, so that he could teach her about the Jewish wedding ceremony. 'He was determined to arrange everything,' Avital remembered. She herself still had no idea whether her Tolya would be released in time for the wedding, 'but', she added, 'we went ahead with the plans.'

On 3 July 1974, two days before Avital's visa expired, one day before her wedding, if her Tolya could be found, Ida Milgrom came to her apartment to help with the final preparations. 'By that time,' Avital recalled, 'many of our friends had heard that I had received a visa and came to my flat to say "Shalom". They found it very strange that when I should have been preparing to leave I was sewing a new dress for myself.' Avital's account continued: 'I was not at all nervous. I felt very strong. People asked me, "Where is Anatoly?" and I told them he was in prison. They said, "What are you doing? How can you leave?" I just said, "It's all right. Don't worry. I know what I'm doing."' At last the wedding day arrived. 'Anatoly was still in prison,' Avital recalled, 'and I didn't know yet whether he would be released that day.' Early in the morning, Manevich came to the flat to make sure everything was in order. Under Jewish law, July 4 and July 5 were the last days on which a wedding could be held until the end of August: three weeks of mourning were about to begin, leading up to the commemoration of the destruction of the Temple by the Romans.

'Then I went out to phone friends to invite them to the wedding,' Avital recalled. 'When I got back, Anatoly was there.' At ten o'clock that morning, the KGB had told Shcharansky that he could leave his cell and go home. As he did not want to let them have the last word he said, 'No, I haven't finished my book.' And so he stayed in prison for another two hours until he had finished the book. 'Of course,' Avital later reflected, 'he didn't know that we were to be married that day or that I had received a visa and was leaving the following day.'

Tired, unshaven, Shcharansky returned home, to find that he was to be married that very day. He at once had a shower and hurried to the synagogue to complete the arrangements for the wedding. Several of his friends, who had also been released that day, hurried to join the couple, and at four in the afternoon the ceremony started. 'It was such a happy wedding,' Avital recalled. 'Afterwards, Manevich made a wonderful speech about the miracle of Jewish survival, about how miracles can happen if you really want them, if you really believe. And the Rabbi – who didn't know Anatoly was a refusenik – understood what was happening, because after the wedding ceremony we all started to sing Hebrew songs.'

Not only were there Jews at the wedding of Anatoly Shcharansky and Avital Shtiglits, but, as she later wrote, there was 'the KGB outside'. The wedding party went on 'until the middle of the night, singing and dancing the Israeli hora. It was a great celebration. I had learned about the wedding ceremony and because I knew a little about the religious part of the wedding it was like, you know, a window on Israel. We could feel Jewish life.'

In the days of waiting between her exit visa and her wedding, Avital had been assured that if she went to Israel 'quietly, with no fuss', her husband would be allowed to join her 'soon', within a matter of 'a few months'. Despite these assurances, Avital had been reluctant to leave. But Shcharansky convinced her that she should go. At six o'clock the next morning he drove with her to the airport. It was 5 July 1974, the last day on which her exit visa was valid. By noon she was airborne, flying first to Vienna, the staging post for all Soviet Jews who received their exit visas; and then on to Israel.

On 12 July 1974 Shcharansky sent his first letter to Avital:

My dear Natulya!

The first week of our separation has passed – that means one week less. This week was fast-moving yet tedious, anxious yet joyful. Now I feel such weariness that I don't seem to have the energy to make it home. After two stormy months, a lull has set in.

By the way, I'm beginning to 'lament' and this doesn't completely suit my mood. I'm tired, but at peace and for days on end somehow idiotically happy. I constantly feel that you and I did something beautiful which they can never take away from us.

I don't mean the chuppah itself, nor anything concrete, but simply our mutual feeling. I still don't have the strength to analyse and think things out, but there doesn't seem to be any need for it any more.

My dear, I write you a postcard every day and wait impatiently for news from you. . . . I want to see vividly how you live, what you see, what you think. I want to picture your meeting with Misha, and the group, your arrival in Tiberias, and Jerusalem.

After a whole series of postcards and letters, I haven't written anything for several days – I'm still waiting for some word from Vienna. But nothing has come, and this saddens me. I am constantly living on treasured memories, but I don't want our present life to be tied only to them and not to new prospects. I joyfully and jealously think how much every day means to you now, how quickly you will become immersed in that sunny, noisy, tense and so confusing world which we here call 'Artzenu', our Land. I don't want to miss out on these significant days of your life – why yours? – our life, and therefore, with great impatience, wait for the day when your letters start to come.

Avital now settled down in Jerusalem to await her husband, amid growing fears. But he was optimistic, and continued openly to demand the right to leave, not only for himself, but for all those Jews who, by the summer of 1974, had been refused an exit visa.

On 6 August 1974 Shcharansky sent his second letter to Avital. Jane and Jerry Stern were two American friends who had visited them both in Moscow.

My dear Natulya

How beautiful you are. Yesterday, I received your pictures, your letter and a letter from Jane and Jerry. Really, what would we do without such Jews?

Yesterday made it a month since you left. I remember when seven months passed after November 13, you had said, 'This is already a very long time.' But how little it is compared to one

month of separation! I miss you terribly. At the same time I am
glad you succeeded in breaking away from this dark life into the
bright sunlight. This alone represents a great victory for us. Of
course we shall soon be together. In September I plan to take
decisive steps to attract attention to our situation – keep this in
mind.

On August 20 Shcharansky sent Avital a third letter:

With your departure, time has changed completely. You have a
whole new absorbing life, but I am half with you and half in the
same rhythm, in the same old situation. One half drags the
other after it, and that other half bursts the shell and breaks out
of this banality. Every day is like a road marker; I strike against
each marker with my whole body, knock it down and move on
to the next. That's how I perceive time now.

That August, at the height of a Moscow summer, an American
Jew, Allan Meyerowitz, who was visiting the Soviet Union,
brought photographs of Avital in Jerusalem, which he had been
asked to take to Shcharansky. August was, and is, holiday time in
Moscow: for the refuseniks as well as for the mass of ordinary
Russians it is a time to go to the countryside, or to the Baltic or
Black Sea coasts. It is a time of empty apartments and hot, still
nights. That August, however, Shcharansky had not left Moscow
for somewhere cooler. 'His involvement with other Jews learning
how to conquer the Byzantine labyrinth of emigration procedures',
Meyerowitz later wrote, 'demanded that he stay in Moscow.'
    Meyerowitz gave Shcharansky the photographs of Avital. 'It was
not tears alone that streamed down Anatoly's face,' Meyerowitz
remembered. 'It was life itself – all the emotions which we humans
can feel in a flash overwhelmed him. There was so much tenderness
in his gaze, incredible anger along his lips.'
    Looking at the photographs of Avital, Shcharansky spoke to his
visitor of their earlier, and surviving, hopes. 'They shared the
dream of a normal life,' Meyerowitz recalled, 'a family and apartment along Israel's romantic coast, perhaps in Netanya or
Nahariya.'
    The two men spoke of Avital's exit visa. For her to have
remained in the Soviet Union, Shcharansky told his visitor, would
have been to forgo 'any chance' of their living in Israel. For her to
have refused her exit visa 'would have been a capitulation to a

Soviet system designed not to torture physically (though he assured me that physical measures were used at the right times), but slowly to make one weary, slowly to make one lose hope in emigration'.

It was the photographs of Avital smiling in Jerusalem that, as Meyerowitz observed, 'opened up an Anatoly who wanted to talk about Judaism and Israel. He wanted to speak its language, be reunited with a culture which in the Soviet Union was dead almost fifty years. He wanted to know what his birthright was, what the Soviets denied him access to. He wanted me to explain 3000 years of tradition in a night. He was a sponge for new insights, and proud that his wedding was performed by a Rabbi. It was one of the few Jewish ceremonies he ever attended. Judaism meant more to Anatoly than to any human being I had ever met.'

On becoming a refusenik, Shcharansky explained to Meyerowitz, 'you were gradually made to believe that you were persona non grata – no job, no apartment, no education for your children, no work papers, no record of schooling. You ceased to exist, were swallowed into the air.' But, Meyerowitz noted, if the Kremlin denied his existence, 'Anatoly would proclaim it in any way he could. Avital in Israel meant to Anatoly that no amount of Soviet psychological torture could destroy their dream. With Avital in the West, he had a real reason to live.'

Not only did Shcharansky protect himself from hopelessness by his faith that he would one day be with Avital in Israel, he also made incredible efforts to give hope to others who had been refused, and to join with those activists in Moscow who believed that it was important to alert Western Jewry to the plight of the Jews of Russia: first and foremost the prisoners, and then the refuseniks, some of whom had, by the autumn of 1974, been in refusal for more than four years.

The refuseniks were outcasts from Soviet society, but they were denied the opportunity to be a part of that other society, Israel, which would not only welcome them, but which, under its Law of Return, made legal provision for every Jew in the world who wished to live there to have the automatic right of entry and citizenship.

The energetic, caring Shcharansky also tried to help those Soviet Jews who did reach Israel. One of Avital's most poignant memories is of a telephone call which she was able to make to him. Shcharansky urged her – she was then studying Hebrew at a special centre for new immigrants – to seek out a family which had just arrived from Moscow, and to give them what assistance she could, to help them to find their feet.

'He never asked for anything for himself,' she later recalled. 'He was always concerned about other people. For this, there was nothing he would not do, or risk.'

6

Harassment, Hope
and Hope Deceived

Even as Shcharansky married his Avital, yet more Jews were being arrested in Moscow, to be detained for fifteen days behind prison bars. These new arrests had their origins two years earlier, when a group of Jewish scientists, who had been refused their exit visas and dismissed from their scientific establishments, decided to hold an international scientific conference, based upon the seminar led by Professor Alexander Voronel. This seminar had met many times since 1971, as a means of maintaining their scientific qualifications; now they had decided to invite Western scholars to join them in Moscow to exchange scientific information.

Such an international conference, declared two Soviet newspapers, *Trud* and *Sovietskaya Kultura*, was a 'provocation'. The Jewish scientist–refuseniks persevered. In June, all the foreign participants had been refused their visas to come to Moscow. Professor Lerner was forbidden for a while to leave his apartment, and Professor Voronel's apartment was searched, and material on the seminar confiscated.

The activists were not to be deterred by such pressure: that September, ten Moscow Jews joined together in a public protest against the refusal of the authorities to grant them exit visas. They too were arrested, and sentenced to fifteen days' preventive detention. The ten included Vladimir Davidov, Zakhar Tesker, Boris Tsitlionok, Iosif Beilin, Leonid Tsipin and Anatoly Shcharansky. Three Jews from Kishinev who had come to Moscow to join the demonstration were likewise sentenced to fifteen days, and sent back to Kishinev, where they had their sentence doubled. A short while later, on 29 September 1974, during the traditional memorial visit of Jews to the Nazi massacre site at Babi Yar, observers assaulted the Jews who had come to lay wreaths, and tore off the memorial ribbons from the wreaths themselves.

On 18 October 1974, three weeks after the incident at Babi Yar and two months before the Jackson Amendment was to be voted on in the Senate, Secretary of State Henry Kissinger made public the result of a series of discussions between American and Soviet representatives on the question of emigration from the Soviet Union. The Soviet Union had agreed, Kissinger wrote that day to Senator Jackson, that 'punitive actions' against individuals seeking to emigrate from the Soviet Union 'would be violations of Soviet laws and regulations', and would not therefore be permitted by the Soviet Government. 'In particular,' Kissinger told Jackson, 'this applied to various kinds of intimidation or reprisal, such as, for example, the firing of a person from his job, his demotion to tasks beneath his professional qualifications, and his subjection to public or other kinds of recrimination.'

Kissinger also told Jackson that, as a result of the agreement which had been reached, 'no unreasonable or unlawful impediments will be placed in the way of persons desiring to make application for emigration, such as interference with travel or communications necessary to complete an application, the withholding of necessary documentation and other obstacles including kinds frequently employed in the past.' In addition, applications for emigration would be 'processed' in the order in which they were made, 'including those previously filed, and on a non-discriminatory basis as regards the place of residence, race, religion, national origin and professional status of the applicant'. Concerning professional status, Kissinger added, 'we are informed that there are limitations on emigration under Soviet law in the case of individuals holding certain security clearances, but that such individuals who desire to emigrate will be informed of the date on which they may expect to become eligible for emigration.'

Not only was all this agreed to, but, as Kissinger told Jackson, it would be the American 'assumption' that, as a result of these promises, the rate of emigration from the Soviet Union 'would begin to rise promptly from the 1973 level and would continue to rise to correspond with the number of applicants'. These were substantial assurances. If adhered to, they would markedly improve the plight of the refuseniks.

Within a few days of the contents of Kissinger's letter to Jackson being known in Moscow, Alexander Lunts decided that he and a small group of activists should themselves travel to a number of towns in order to find out the opinion of Jews in the provinces about the Jackson Amendment, and the problems confronting Jews in the provinces who wished to emigrate. Lunts himself went to Derbent and Baku in the Caucasus. Shcharansky and Anatoly Malkin, a nineteen-year-old recent refusenik, went to Riga and Minsk. Another young activist, Vladimir Davidov, went to Sverdlovsk, and yet another to Kishinev. Iosif Beilin went to Lvov, his home town. Zakhar Tesker and Boris Tsitlionok went to Samarkand, Bukhara and Tashkent, in Soviet Central Asia. A ninth Jew, Leonid Tsipin, went to Kiev.

Unknown to the other eight, Tsipin, who had also taken part in the September demonstration, for which he had been given a fifteen-day sentence with the others, was a KGB informer. As a result of his involvement, four of the journeys, on which so much depended, were a disaster. Lunts and his wife Ludmila, reaching Derbent, were followed, as Lunts later recalled, 'by a regiment, including a couple of women and a dozen local KGB men', and, at the airport in Baku, were detained, searched and relieved of all their notes and notebooks. In Sverdlovsk, Vladimir Davidov was likewise detained, and his notes taken from him. The young man who had gone to Kishinev was severely beaten up, managed to visit several refuseniks, but was then arrested and sentenced to fifteen days' detention. Then he was given another ten days. For several weeks none of the activists in Moscow knew of his sentence, or where he was being held. 'We felt the KGB would do anything to him,' one of his friends later commented.

Shcharansky and Malkin flew from Moscow to Riga. There the local KGB followed them for a while, but, with the help of Valery Buiko, a refusenik who later received an exit visa, they managed to evade their pursuers. After two days in Riga, Shcharansky and Malkin took the night train to Minsk. Then, after a day in which they failed to meet anybody, they made contact with several refuseniks near the synagogue.

'We had found Jews in Minsk very frightened and living in complete isolation,' Shcharansky wrote in an open letter published in Israel six weeks later. 'We were the first people to visit them from Moscow in months.' The KGB, he reported, made life difficult even for Jews who received unsolicited invitations from Israel. 'One musician', he noted, 'was called before a committee and accused of being a fascist murderer of Arab children merely because he had received a letter from Israel. At that time he had not even decided whether to emigrate.'

Shcharansky went on to describe the atmosphere in Minsk as being 'particularly anti-Semitic', with a considerable amount of officially inspired literature and rumours against Jews. 'The worst thing is the KGB are making people sign pledges that they will have no contact with foreigners and will not try to go abroad,' he added. 'Even the women who sell brassières in the state department store have been made to sign. I cannot imagine what kind of State secrets they are supposed to have.'

On their second day in Minsk, Shcharansky and Malkin visited Yefim Davidovich, a former Colonel in the Red Army who, having applied to go to Israel, had been stripped of his officer's rank. 'I never saw so many KGB men as there were outside that house,' Shcharansky wrote. 'There must have been thirty of them. They followed us everywhere. Finally we were arrested at Minsk station when we were about to leave the city – and told we were wanted for questioning about a robbery.'

Shcharansky and Malkin were questioned for six hours, after which they were put on the night train to Moscow. 'It was 8 November 1974,' Malkin later recalled. 'It was my twentieth birthday.'

Shcharansky's removal from Minsk led to a brief reference to him in the *News Bulletin* of the Israel Public Council for Soviet Jewry. 'Minsk authorities detained young Moscow mathematician Anatoly Shcharansky', the bulletin reported, 'and confiscated his papers.'

Back in Moscow, Lunts and the other travellers met two leading American campaigners for Soviet Jewry, Irene Manekofsky, Vice-President of the Union of Councils for Soviet Jews, and Myrna Shinbaum, Associate Director of the National Conference on Soviet Jewry, who were visiting the Soviet capital. One of their tasks was to try to ascertain the whereabouts of the young man who had disappeared while visiting Kishinev.

'Three men came running to meet us,' Irene Manekofsky later recalled (her recollections were published in the United States *Congressional Record* on 20 July 1982), 'as we left the gargantuan Rossiya Hotel that cold November evening in 1974. We recognised them as three of the young, intense men we had met at the synagogue a day or two earlier. "We have located him," they exclaimed excitedly. "He is in prison in Kishinev. Now you can send your cable to the States."'

One of the three men, Irene Manekofsky remembered, was 'a short, balding, undistinguished looking man in his twenties.' He was 'immediately recognisable as the leader of the group', and invited her to an apartment, to hear, at her request, the story of the journey to the provincial towns. 'We sat late into the night and into the early hours of the morning,' she later wrote, 'sitting around the table with the ever present cups of Russian tea, tape recording the events of the trip,' and she went on to ask: 'Did it take us an hour, or perhaps an hour and a half? How long, we now try to recall, did it take us to become smitten with the charm, intelligence, wit, earnestness and leadership qualities of Anatoly Shcharansky? After listening to Tolya, as he was called by all who knew him, for hour after hour, watching his intense Jewish consciousness, his courage, his devil-may-care attitude about his own safety, he was no longer a small, undistinguished little man. To us, Tolya was nine feet tall, a giant of strength and determination, a man who knew what had to be done and did it.'

In talking about his journey to Minsk and Riga, Shcharansky revealed an aspect of his character which was already marking him out among his contemporaries: his fearlessness. 'When he was picked up and questioned on the trip', Irene Manekofsky recalled, 'he noticed that the KGB interrogator kept running back and forth to the telephone. "Do you have to rely on instructions from Moscow as to what you will do with me?" he chided. He told us how once the KGB had told him that he had been arrested twice and the third time he would go to prison. "This is already the third time," he quipped. Another time he related to us how he looked out of the window in his apartment and saw his KGB "tail" sitting in the car, drunk. He reported this to the KGB headquarters! This is unheard-of behaviour in the Soviet Union. But Tolya had a twinkle in his eye and a sense of humour to match.'

Shcharansky's 'favourite subject', Irene Manekofsky wrote, 'once we exhausted all of the details not only of the trip, but of the emigration movement in general, was his wife, Avital. How he loved her! He constantly talked about going to Israel to be reunited with her. He was proud of her. "I spoke to my Avital on the phone from Israel yesterday. Do you know, she now speaks Hebrew better than I do?"'

The urgent need, despite the break-up of four of the journeys, and the extremely worrying imprisonment of the young man in Kishinev, was to put as much information as possible into a form that would be communicated to the West. This work was at once begun in Lunts's apartment, in which, since Avital's departure from Moscow, Shcharansky had been lodging.

The many facts known to the activists in Moscow, including those gathered on the journeys, were put into the form of a letter, addressed to President Ford and dated 18 November 1974, five days before President Ford flew to the Soviet Far Eastern city of Vladivostok, for his first meeting with Leonid Brezhnev. The letter, signed by nine activists, including Shcharansky, was the first comprehensive account of the plight of those Jews who sought to leave the Soviet Union: of the applicants and of the refuseniks. Among the things which Lunts and his travellers had found out was that in some cases the local authorities had tried to get a document signed by the applicant declaring that he or she would 'never' try to leave the Soviet Union. This had happened to a young Jewish salesgirl in Minsk, 'who, today, out of fear of losing her job, signs the undertaking not to leave the country' and was as a result 'depriving herself of all possibility of emigrating for many years ahead.' The letter of November 18 went on to warn: 'Tomorrow similar forces may be disseminated throughout the entire country and hundreds of thousands of Jews will similarly sign, out of fear.'

The letter also explained the complexities of the documents which were needed before an exit visa application could be made: permission was needed in writing from a wife or a grandparent. If there were no grandparents, their death certificates had to be produced. 'Recently', the letter revealed, 'the authorities went to the absurd length of demanding certificates of death of parents who perished during the Second World War in the mass-slaughter camps of death of the Holocaust!' In Kishinev, as travellers to Moscow had reported, there were 'many scores of families who are unable to hand in their documents of applications for emigration because of this absurdity'.

The letter also drew attention to the financial burden of application – the money that had to be found for the obligatory renunciation of Soviet citizenship – and also to the fact that throughout the Soviet Union the applicant was normally thrown out of his profession the moment he applied for an exit visa, resulting in further financial hardship, even when the applicant found a low-paid job doing menial work, often at less than the official Soviet minimum wage: there were examples of this from Moscow, Lvov, Saratov and Minsk.

During a week of intense discussion, lasting late into the nights, this information had been put together in Moscow by those activists who felt most strongly that these facts ought to be made known in the West before the Jackson Amendment was debated in Congress. Among those who signed the letter of 18 November 1974 were Mikhail Agursky, Vladimir Davidov, Vitaly Rubin, Dina Beilina, Alexander Voronel and Lunts himself: all six were later to receive their exit visas, Voronel within three weeks. Three other Jews also signed the letter: Lerner, Slepak and Shcharansky. Eleven years later, Lerner and Slepak were still in the Soviet Union.

As soon as it was completed, the letter to President Ford was dictated over the open telephone in Russian to Michael Sherbourne. As translated and cyclostyled by him, it consisted of six closely typed pages, setting out the nature of the exit-visa application and refusenik problem, including harassment, loss of jobs, 'provocative arrest' and the cutting of telephone and postal communications. It also gave details of dozens of individual cases, drawn not only from Moscow, the home of each of the signatories, but from more than twenty other Soviet cities.

The letter of 18 November 1974 gave a disturbing picture of the scene as a whole: of the worsening situation for a growing number of Jews, despite the 100,000 exit visas granted in the previous four years.

The letter pointed out that during 1974 the Soviet Government had 'sharply reduced the number of permissions for emigration', in fact from 34,733 in 1973 to 20,376 so far in 1974, and it forecast a drop in future years as a result of what were described as an 'uninterruptedly increasing flood' of repression. The letter also spoke of how 1974 had 'brought to light a whole series of new types of harassment'. Using a number of direct quotations, the letter gave examples of the different reasons given for refusing an exit visa. Sometimes it was because of the classified work of a relative. Sometimes, as in the case of a Jew from Lvov, it was 'no near relatives in Israel', or, as was said to the unskilled Jewish labourers of Derbent who wished to go to Israel, 'there is nothing for you to do there.' Former military service had been given as a reason for refusal for Jews who had been demobilised in 1966 or 1967. Some refusals, such as that for the Moscow physicist Professor Benjamin Fain, were given as: 'possesses information useful to the Govern-

ment', but without any further explanation. In Odessa, many
refusals were given because 'not all the family are leaving'. Two
families in Riga had been told that they were refused because their
'nearest relatives' lived in the Soviet Union. A Moscow father of
two teenage children, Dimitri Ramm, was refused because of 'lack
of agreement of parents who are remaining'. Others were simply
told, 'permission cannot be granted at the present time', with no
further explanation.

An 'especially dangerous innovation', according to the letter,
were the refusals given because of residence in the so-called 'closed
towns' of the Soviet Union, among them Angarsk with a population of 300,000, Krasnoyarsk with 700,000 and Perm with 900,000.
The letter gave the names of Jews from these towns who had been
refused an exit visa.

With devastating detail, the letter gave a survey of the harassment
and trials of the previous year, as well as of the closing of the
international scientific seminar and the detention of its organisers.
Most of the events described were unknown in the West until the
letter arrived. Many related to young refuseniks whose plight
seemed most clearly to characterise the harshness of the situation,
and the worsening atmosphere. In June, in Kharkov, a nineteen-
year-old Jewish student, Alexander Slinin, had been expelled from
the university immediately after applying for the required 'character reference' needed by the Visa Office; straight after this, he had
been called up for military service. When he refused because it was
not necessary for university students to do such service, he was
arrested and sentenced to three years' imprisonment. In Moscow,
Anatoly Malkin had been expelled from the Institute of Steel and
Alloys immediately after handing in his emigration documents to
the Visa Office; in Krasnodar another Jewish student, Alexander
Silnitsky, was in a similar position; and there were further examples
of this 'conscription trap' in Riga, Tiraspol and other cities.

The letter also told of harassment and imprisonment: of Vladimir
Kislik, a doctor of technical sciences who had been forced to work
as a caretaker after he had applied to leave and had been beaten up on
the streets of Kiev by thugs who shouted at him: 'We'll show you,
filthy Jew beast . . .'; and of another refusenik, Alexander Feldman,
sentenced a year earlier to three and a half years in prison.

The letter of 18 November 1974 also gave examples of the search
and seizure of Jewish books: in Odessa on October 16, in Kiev on
October 21 and in Sverdlovsk on November 9. In Lvov, two small

Jewish prayer gatherings had been dispersed: following protests from religious groups in the United States these prayer groups had been reinstated, but only on condition 'that young Jews did not join them'. In Kiev a similar small prayer group, held in the home of ninety-two-year-old Ovsei Goldin, had been broken up, after being allowed to function for more than ten years. A prayer house in the Moscow suburb of Tomilino had likewise been closed down. In October, as Shcharansky had earlier reported, a Jewish musician in Minsk, Alexei Krivulin, who had received an invitation from Israel – the first and essential step on the way to applying for an exit visa – had been summoned to a meeting of the White Russian Dance Band of which he was a member, to be accused of being 'a fascist and a murderer of Arab children'.

The concluding paragraphs of the letter to President Ford stressed the isolation of the provinces from Moscow. It was an isolation which created 'a particularly suitable atmosphere' for reprisals. 'We only learned about Slinin a month after he was sentenced,' the letter explained. Knowing of this isolation, the authorities 'are taking unprecedented action to cut off contact between the activists in Moscow and the provinces', to ensure that, at the moment of the signature of the Jackson Amendment, 'there will be as few people as possible ready to take full advantage of their right to emigrate.'

The letter of 18 November 1974 reached Washington at a decisive moment in Soviet–American relations. Five days later, on 23 November 1974, Ford and Brezhnev met at Vladivostok. 'We have every right', Henry Kissinger told the Senate Finance Committee on December 3, 'to expect that the emigration rate will correspond to the number of applicants. If some of the current estimates about potential applicants are correct, this should lead to an increase in emigration.'

On 13 December 1974, ten days after Kissinger's remarks, Senator Jackson introduced his amendment in the Senate: amendment No. 2000 to the Trade Reform Act of 1972, praising the Kissinger 'compromise', as Kissinger's agreement with the Soviets had become known. 'I believe we have reached a fair and productive compromise,' Jackson declared. 'We have agreed upon an unprecedented measure to bring the blessings of liberty to those brave men and women who have asked only for the chance to find freedom in a new land.'

That same day, the Jackson Amendment was passed in the Senate by 88 votes to nil. Nor was that the end of the pressures on the

Soviet Union. Six days later, on 19 December 1974, Senator Adlai Stevenson successfully introduced another amendment to the Act, setting a strict upper limit on United States banking credits to the Soviet Union. The Soviet Government had been expecting a $1000 million credit. The Stevenson Amendment set $300 million as the upper limit, and this too was written into the amended Act.

As envisaged by Stevenson, the President could only increase the upper limit of these dollar credits with the approval of Congress. According to Stevenson, such approval would depend on Soviet 'moderation' in four specific matters: arms control, force-reduction talks, the Middle East and emigration.

Even as Shcharansky waited with all his fellow activists for news of the final passage of the Jackson Amendment, the plight of the prisoners worsened – a deterioration which led to immediate protest. On 3 December 1974 Academician Sakharov had issued a public appeal on behalf of Dr Mikhail Shtern of Vinnitsa, who had been held in prison without trial since May. 'If we remain silent today,' a Jewish activist told a visitor from Philadelphia, 'tomorrow will be too late.' On December 23, three weeks after Sakharov's protest, forty-five Moscow Jews filed into the reception hall of the Praesidium of the Supreme Soviet, a courageous act in itself, and, despite having been warned that submitting a petition would be considered a 'provocation', handed over a letter, signed by more than three hundred Jews, urging the release of all forty Prisoners of Zion (among them Iosif Mendelevich and Hillel Butman) and their emigration to Israel after their release. The petition was handed over to a clerk at the reception office by Alexander Lunts.

Jews from Riga and Kishinev, two of the cities visited earlier by the activists from Moscow, set off by train to join the protest, but were taken off before they could reach the capital. That same day, Jews in several cities began a forty-eight-hour hunger strike in protest against the continued imprisonment of the Jews who had been sentenced at the Leningrad Trials four years earlier.

In the week following the demonstration at the Praesidium and the hunger strike, Dr Shtern was brought to trial. One witness told the court that Shtern 'had, with premeditation, poisoned children – and was a spy for Israel'. When the sentence, eight years in labour camp, was announced on the last day of 1974, a shudder of fear swept through the refusenik movement. On the previous day, the Jackson Amendment had passed the House of Representatives, and on 3 January 1975, four days after Shtern's sentence, the amended Trade Reform Act was signed by President Ford, and passed into law. The Jackson and Stevenson Amendments were now binding legislative commitments, the Jackson Amendment ensuring that the Trade Reform Act of 1972 became the first specific United States legislation which made the fate of Soviet Jews an integral part of the laws of the United States.

The way now seemed clear for an immediate relaxation of pressures, and a reopening of the gates of emigration on a scale as comprehensive as anything for which the Moscow activists, Shcharansky among them, had ever asked or fought.

The Stevenson Amendment, with its conditional restrictions on credits, proved too much, however, for the Soviet authorities. As if to shatter the hopes of the refuseniks at the very moment when they were most raised up, on 10 January 1975 the Soviet Union cancelled the October 1972 Trade Agreement, seven days after the Jackson and Stevenson Amendments had been passed into law.

As a result of this cancellation, as one American expert, William Korey, noted, 'the Jackson Amendment to ease Soviet emigration practices no longer existed'.

'The annulment of the Trade Agreement between the USA and the USSR', Shcharansky and eight other Soviet Jews wrote in a letter to their friends in the West, 'has thrown us back at the moment when, it seemed, we were close to at least a partial solution of our problem, when hundreds of thousands of Soviet Jews started hoping for the possibility of unhindered emigration to Israel. Still, this does not discourage us. Like the Jewish people at all times we are firmly withstanding the blows of fate. We firmly believe in the idea of in-gathering of exiles and we believe in the support of all honest men, Jews and non-Jews, in their strength, influence and abilities to find new methods of struggle for our rights.' The other signatories were Lunts, Lerner, Slepak, Rubin, Dina Beilina, Deborah Samoilovich, Lev Ovsishcher and Yefim Davidovich.

Shcharansky, meanwhile, had received a further refusal from the Visa Office. On 25 December 1974 he wrote to Avital:

My dear Natulya

I want you to understand me: now, more than ever, I'm happy you are no longer living this depressing kind of life. Despite all that has happened to me, everything is immobile, and you can fall into despair, grow dull, and rot alive from this endless vortex. You offer me another life and I avidly grasp it.

Don't take the last reply from OVIR too much to heart, okay? Everything can change at any moment. And please don't think that I am simply sitting and waiting for the weather to change. Everything is more complicated now than before.

I am trying to use the means which is most effective at the given moment.

Natulya, my dear, do you remember that I often said (and believed) that the days spent here are not wasted, that this is a unique experience? I don't think so any more. Each day here is another stolen from us together. How I didn't appreciate time when we were together! It's a shame to think of how much time was lost, how much wasted on minutiae.

It is now six months since you left (and since our chuppah, Natulya, I congratulate you). Although I remember the days when we were together down to the minute, this half year is somehow one big jumble.

'Jacob worked seven years for Rachel but in his eyes they were like a few days because of his love for her' (Genesis 29:20). You see, I continue to read the Bible and see our life through it.

My beloved, my little sunshine, don't grieve and don't feel lonely on the Sabbath. Do everything that Jewish women do on that day, and I shall say the Friday night blessing over the wine as if we were greeting the Sabbath together. Tov?

'Tov' is the Hebrew word for 'good'. A few days later Shcharansky wrote again:

Natulya, my beloved!

I'm writing to you from the telegraph office. Two curious characters in hats are circling around me like sharks before an attack. And although I am not deprived of their company for a minute, I am alone now as never before. I haven't received anything from you; I am gradually losing not only the details, but the whole picture of your life; this is terrible and sad. I am counting very heavily on our conversation tomorrow.

'I have a thousand things to do now,' Shcharansky added. 'I'm tired, but live in the hope of relaxing soon with you. I embrace you warmly, I love you, I love you. Regards to everyone. Tolya '

More than six months had passed between Avital's departure and Shcharansky's new refusal. During that six-month period, more than ten thousand Jews had received their exit visas. For Avital in Jerusalem, as for Shcharansky in Moscow, the future was obscure and uncertain. Both were sustained by their love for each other, as every day that passed underlined the cruelty of their separation.

7

To Start Again

Disrupted though Shcharansky's visit to Minsk in November 1974 had been, it had put him in touch with two remarkable refuseniks, both former Red Army Colonels, Yefim Davidovich and Lev Ovsishcher. Both men, and the emigration movement in Minsk of which they were a part, were surrounded by an atmosphere of considerable hostility. It was in Minsk that a popular White Russian writer, Vladimir Begun (not a Jew, and no relation to the Moscow Hebrew teacher Iosif Begun), had warned his readers in the spring of 1974 that the Old Testament was 'an unsurpassed text of blood-thirstiness, hypocrisy, betrayal, perfidy, moral dissoluteness – all base human qualities'.

In protest against this, six Minsk refuseniks, including Davidovich and Ovsishcher, had written an open letter denouncing the 'torrent of lies and slander against the Jewish people'. Inside Russia, such protests were in vain. No one would publish them. Judaism, Radio Minsk insisted early in the following year, not only set Jews apart from other people, but was 'contrary to our Communist morality, the aims of our society, and the progress of modern life'. The protest by the six Minsk refuseniks did not remain a silent one, however: telephoned over the open line to Michael Sherbourne in London, it was at once circulated to all Western Jews active in the emigration campaign. 'We appeal to the millions of Soviet Russian intellectuals,' the six Minsk refuseniks wrote. 'We appeal to you to make a firm condemnation of the campaign of hounding an ancient people that stood at the cradle of modern civilisation.' Anti-Semitism was the 'worst enemy' not only of the Jewish people, they declared. 'It maims the souls of all who come in contact with it, whether they are the victims or the executioners.'

In Moscow, where the Jewish activists were as fearless as those of

Minsk in their determination not to remain silent witnesses of their
fate, Shcharansky continued to live and to work in Lunts's apartment. It was 'hard, daily work', Lunts later explained in conversation with me in Israel. 'At least eight or ten hours a day, meeting
people and contacting Western correspondents. It was also intensive work, because of our personal concerns. We wanted it done
very much.' Those concerns were, above all, for the young men
caught up in the 'conscription trap', young men whom Lunts and
Shcharansky knew in Moscow, or had met during their November
travels.

Lunts and Shcharansky were among that group of activists who
were convinced that public protests, and the rapid passing of
information overseas, were essential if Jewish emigration was to be
allowed to increase and the persecution stop. As Lunts expressed it,
'You cannot help a movement by silence.'

As well as taking part in demonstrations, the young Jewish
activists of Moscow learned Hebrew. Once a week they would
gather to speak Hebrew together, and only Hebrew. To avoid
being broken up by the authorities, the gatherings moved from one
apartment to another. On one occasion, as Anatoly Malkin later
recalled with irony, the gathering was held at Leonid Tsipin's
apartment. Frequently as many as fifty people gathered.
Shcharansky was nearly always present.

Sometimes the talk turned to the 'why' of refusal and the 'when'
of an exit visa. After one of the graduates of the Moscow Physical–
Technical Institute received his exit visa – thereby demonstrating
that the 'secret work' of the Institute was a fiction – there seemed no
reason why the other graduates, Shcharansky among them, should
not be allowed to leave. 'The feeling was that he would go out after
quite a short time,' Malkin remembered.

Meanwhile, however, in the aftermath of the Soviet rejection of
any linkage between trade and emigration, the number of Jews
refused exit visas continued to grow; all visitors to the refuseniks
found themselves caught up in the debate on the Jackson Amendment, which, following the Soviet Union's rejection of any conditions, was being denounced by Soviet officials as a device for
increasing tension between the Soviet Union and the United States.
On 3 February 1975 more than eighty Moscow activists,
Shcharansky among them, signed a letter to the *Baltimore Sun*,
describing the amendment 'not as an action of struggle against the
relaxation of tension', as that newspaper's Moscow correspondent

had claimed, 'but as an act directed towards the strengthening of relaxation, in giving it a human face'.

In their letter, the eighty activists noted that, thanks to 'this very support' from Senator Jackson and American public opinion, more than a hundred thousand Jews had left the Soviet Union for Israel in the previous five years; what mattered now was to continue the struggle on behalf of those 'thousands of Jews' who were still fighting 'for the realisation of their elementary rights to freedom and independence'.

There was no truth in describing the activists as seeking to increase tension between the superpowers; their aim was to leave the Soviet Union, not to embroil her in international tensions, nor to change the Soviet system. In February 1975 a refusenik scientist, Edward Trifonov, meeting Shcharansky for the first time, vividly remembered that Shcharansky's 'main aim was to emigrate to Israel'. Trifonov was later to receive his exit visa; today he is a Professor in Israel.

Two months had passed since the petition had been handed in at the Praesidium of the Supreme Soviet. As no reply had been made to it, nine of those who had been at the original protest decided to protest again.

'We had waited for the results of the Jackson Amendment,' Iosif Beilin later remarked. 'The KGB had said to us throughout January and February, "The Jackson Amendment won't help you." This demonstration was our answer.' It was to be the first demonstration by Jewish activists since the Soviet Government's rejection of the United States Trade Reform Act.

Iosif Beilin also recounted how, on the eve of the demonstration, Shcharansky had urged Anatoly Malkin not to participate, fearing that if Malkin were arrested the authorities would use it as a means of bringing charges against him. Since he had already received his army call-up papers, and had decided to ignore them, Malkin was particularly vulnerable. He knew that once he became a soldier he would be even less likely to receive an exit visa. He also knew that he had been sent his call-up papers only because, on becoming a refusenik, he had been forced to abandon his university studies, whose continuation had hitherto preserved him from military service. Shcharansky saw Malkin's danger, and did not wish him to court, or to risk, arrest.

On the morning of 24 February 1975 the nine protesters gathered near the Lenin Library: Iosif Beilin, Boris Tsitlionok and

Shcharansky among them. Also with them was a young dental student, Mark Nashpits, who had been refused an exit visa on the grounds that his father had defected when Mark was a small boy. In their hands were various banners. Also present were Alexander Lunts and Leonid Tsipin, who was not yet known to be an informer. An account of the brief protest was given two days later by Shcharansky, who wrote:

> A demonstration took place on 24 February 1975 on a landing at the top of the stairs in front of the Lenin Library in Moscow facing the reception hall of the Praesidium of the Supreme Soviet of the USSR. This site is some distance away from any footpath and is not near any place which is frequented by pedestrians. Moreover, it is impossible for vehicles to approach anywhere near it. The entrance to the Library itself is approximately thirty metres away from the site of the demonstration. In addition, on that particular day, the Library was in any case closed for cleaning.
>
> I raised my placard at 10.15 a.m. On it was written 'Visas for Israel instead of Prison'. I observed that the placards raised by the other demonstrators had either the same wording or 'Freedom for the Jewish Prisoners of Conscience' or 'Release the Jewish Prisoners of Conscience from camps and let them go to Israel'.

Shcharansky's account continued:

> I stood with my placard for not more than thirty seconds. At that point a number of individuals dressed in civilian clothing, who had been hiding, rushed towards us and tore up the placards. One of them twisted my arms behind my back in a most professional manner and dragged me into the library building. The same thing happened to the other demonstrators. None of us offered the slightest opposition and there was no shouting or cursing on the part of those detained. The entire demonstration lasted no more than thirty seconds and did not succeed in attracting the attention of any new observers apart from those who were already in the square or around it and who obviously were waiting to attack us.

Shcharansky and Beilin, Lunts and Tsipin were held for eight hours in the cell of a detention centre for drunks. Nashpits and Tsitlionok were put on a criminal charge of organising demonstrations. In Iosif Beilin's words: 'Tolya said to me, "You and I must go again to demonstrate: to show by our demonstration that Nashpits and Tsitlionok were *not* the organisers."' But, as Beilin wistfully remarked when he learned that the other three were unable to join them: 'Two people could hardly make a demonstration.'

On 31 March 1975, Mark Nashpits and Boris Tsitlionok were brought to trial, accused of 'violating public order' during the half-minute episode outside the Lenin Library. Both were sentenced to five years' exile in one of the most remote regions of Siberia.

That evening ninety-eight Soviet Jews, from nine cities, began a hunger strike in protest against the two sentences. The hunger strike ended on April 3 with a silent demonstration by seventeen Moscow Jews at the site where Nashpits and Tsitlionok had been arrested. The police took no action, and after fifteen minutes the participants dispersed: among them were Benjamin Fain, Ilya Essas and, risking arrest for evading military service, Anatoly Malkin. In a statement to the press explaining the reasons for the hunger strike they declared: 'Together with Boris Tsitlionok and Mark Nashpits we are repeating the words which we said more than three thousand years ago to Pharaoh: "Let my people go!"'

Nashpits and Tsitlionok appealed against their sentence, their appeal being heard in Moscow on 25 April 1975. Two American lawyers, Frank Winston and Richard Valerian, had come to the Soviet capital from the United States to do what they could to help. Shcharansky acted as their interpreter, taking them, as he himself was to say, 'from the lowest to the highest authority' to try to get permission for them to attend the trial – but to no avail. With Shcharansky were Vitaly and Ina Rubin. 'We both wanted to demonstrate our presence,' Ina Rubin recalled.

Among the American visitors to Moscow who were also on the steps outside the courthouse that April day was Harold Ticktin, a lawyer from Cleveland, Ohio. 'With Americans and Russian Jews mingling in the mild weather,' he reported, 'the occasion took on an almost festive air. At one point, Vitaly turned to me, pointing to the grim-looking guard and said: "I wonder what he's thinking, in this gloomy place, to hear so much laughter. He must think the world is being turned upside down."'

The humour that morning was short-lived. 'The mood', as Dina Beilina later explained, 'was one of nervousness.' The efforts of the two American lawyers, and Shcharansky's translations, were in vain: the five-year sentences on Nashpits and Tsitlionok were upheld.

Shcharansky's work for the prisoners was unremitting. But he never forgot his constant, waiting Avital. At the end of February she had managed to get a telephone call through to him from Jerusalem. 'We were really happy to speak to one another, after such a long interval in both letters and calls,' he wrote to Irene Manekofsky. 'We spoke a little Hebrew and I was glad to see that she spoke our language already much better than I. As far as I can understand, her absorption is making quick progress, she is getting now a systematic Jewish education and she accepts Israel's way of life as natural, as if she were a real sabra' – a native-born Israeli. Shcharansky added: 'You are sure to know the new dramatic circumstances of our life today. But we are not giving up, we try to look forward with optimism. Your support is a very important ground for this optimism. Best regards to all our friends, with all my heart, Anatoly.'

8

New Pressures,
New Prisoners

Between the arrest of Nashpits and Tsitlionok in March 1975 and their trial five weeks later, several Jewish activists received their exit visas, among them Mikhail Agursky, Vladimir Davidov and Alex Goldfarb. With Goldfarb's departure, the activists no longer had a spokesman. With his excellent English, Goldfarb had been a brilliant link between the activists and the growing number of visitors from the West. His contacts with Western journalists had been particularly valuable. Now another spokesman was needed, one who could speak in the presence of the others, and for them, when Western journalists came.

There were several suggestions for a successor to the fortunate Goldfarb. 'Lerner told me, "Maybe it can be Shcharansky,"' Dina Beilina later recalled. 'I laughed. He was a such a young man, so small, so quiet, so silent.'

One of those who recognised Shcharansky's talents was Ina Rubin, whose husband Vitaly had been much impressed by the young man's courage during the demonstration outside the Lebanese Embassy. Ina Rubin was convinced that Shcharansky would make a first-class spokesman. But she asked herself, as later in Jerusalem she asked me, would the young man, whose overriding dream was to join his Avital in Jerusalem, agree to take on such a demanding task? Dina Beilina later described, in a public statement issued in Moscow after Shcharansky's arrest, how, 'quiet, modest, of medium height, wearing a torn jacket in which he was arrested two years later, Anatoly said "I'll try."'

Shcharansky had been a refusenik for less than two years. He was twenty-seven years old. Two years of an exacting, unpredictable

challenge were about to begin; but no one could be sure that even
two years of public activity were in prospect. Perhaps, like Alex
Goldfarb whose work he was taking on, he would receive his exit
visa after a year or so; perhaps the Soviet authorities would be glad
to see this energetic new spokesman leave, just as, apparently, they
had been glad to let his two predecessors go.

In the very month that Shcharansky became one of the links
between the activists and the Western visitors to Moscow, the
pressures against the Jewish movement reached a climax. In March,
Shcharansky's friend Alexander Lunts was summoned unexpectedly to the KGB headquarters. There, during a two-hour interview, he was warned of possible criminal charges, on the basis of an
'unpublished' Supreme Soviet decree of 25 December 1972. This
decree, known as the 'law on warnings', made it a criminal offence
to disobey a warning, whatever that warning might be.

Lunts was told that charges would be levelled against him for
'causing harm' to the Soviet Union by supporting the Jackson
Amendment, as well as for 'collecting information about the
situation of the Jews in different towns of the USSR, with organising demonstrations, and meetings with foreigners'. Lunts was also
accused – he passed on this news to Western reporters by telephone
– of being 'paid from abroad' for his activities.

Several days after Lunts had been warned, Shcharansky himself
was summoned to the KGB, and, together with the police spy
Tsipin, still masquerading as a refusenik, was told that 'all the
necessary documents for starting criminal proceedings against
them in accordance with Article 70 had been prepared'. Article 70 of
the Criminal Code of the Russian Soviet Socialist Republic, with its
charge of anti-Soviet agitation and propaganda, has a maximum
sentence of seven years in prison followed by five years' internal
exile. Shcharansky was also told by the KGB that 'the West has lost
interest in the situation of the Jews in the USSR.' 'We'll do to you',
the KGB warned, 'what we did with your two friends. No one's
interested in you or these cases in the West. You are a candidate for
the next trial.'

Also warned about his activities, this time in the field of Jewish
culture, was another leading activist, Mark Azbel, who was told
that he faced a possible call-up for military service, at the age of
forty-three. 'I am absolutely sure', Azbel told Western correspondents on the telephone, 'this is connected with the whole
situation now of increased persecution.' A privately circulated

Jewish cultural journal, *Jews in the USSR*, to which Azbel was one of the contributors, was under pressure to close down. Several of Shcharansky's closest friends were involved in this journal, which was edited by Professor Voronel, who later received his exit visa. Among those who wrote for it were Benjamin Fain, Iosif Begun, and the poet, Felix Kandel: in an appeal to the West, they had urged public protest by writers, artists, scientists, and political, religious and social leaders, to prevent this magazine from closing down. It seemed that a major campaign was about to begin against every aspect of the refusenik movement.

★   ★   ★

In the West, and in Israel, Shcharansky was still not a well-known figure: he had after all been in refusal for less than two years, while Slepak, Lerner and others were approaching their fifth year of refusal. On 28 February 1975, however, the Israel Public Council for Soviet Jewry had published an appeal in its *News Bulletin No. 57*, under the heading: 'My name is Natasha'. The appeal began: 'My name is Natasha Shtiglits. I have been in Israel for nearly seven months, and am living in Jerusalem. My husband has been waiting for two years to emigrate.' Avital – as she was soon to call herself – also appealed on behalf of two other wives in Israel whose husbands were still in Moscow. She concluded: 'We are all young and have been married a short time.' She was twenty-four years old, the *Bulletin* told its readers. It was seven months since she had last seen her husband.

Another appeal on the same page as Avital's was from Ida Nudel's sister, Ilana Friedman, who was also living in Israel. Her appeal was headed: 'Please help me save my sister'.

★   ★   ★

During March 1975 Shcharansky wrote two letters to Avital. The first was dated March 15. In it, he addressed her in Hebrew as 'ishti' – my wife – and with the surname 'Sharon', the one used by his uncle Shamai, and which he himself wished to use once he was in Israel:

> My dear, my beloved,
>
> How much longer will fate try us? I'm sure you understand my mood. I have to think, decide and act in dramatic circumstances, full of confusion and uncertainty. But it is, of course,

easier for me than for others. After all, I have you. Because of you my life has definition, such depths, such refined perception and a feeling of fullness that I would not exchange it with anyone.

My dear, I beg you again and again, take care of yourself, do not allow yourself to grieve deeply, don't weep. You are living now for both of us, live calmly, fully and deeply, and when I come, you will share it with me.

Soon it will be Passover. Do you remember last Passover? Since then, you, Avital Sharon, crossed through Sinai, received the Torah and arrived in Jerusalem. I congratulate you, my dear 'ishti'. Although I am still in Egypt, we know that it is not for long.

Five days later, on 20 March 1975, Shcharansky wrote to Avital again, prefacing his letter with the Hebrew word for peace:

Shalom, my dear,

I haven't received a letter from you in a week, but I hope something will arrive before Passover. For those of us wandering over the Sinai, these are difficult days, but I have a basis for inner calm and optimism – you.

I, like many others, am helped by the conscious or, more often, unconscious feeling of historical optimism, a connection with Eretz Yisroel, which your teacher explained so well. This shouldn't sound like blasphemy, but for me this exists through you; you have turned this link into life itself for me.

Shcharansky was studying the Old Testament with one of his Hebrew teachers, Vladimir Shakhnovsky: trying to follow the traditional weekly readings which enable the Five Books of Moses to be read in full each calendar year. As he explained to Avital:

We read the Torah at Volodya Shakhnovsky's a few weeks behind the regular schedule. Now, during Passover, we are reading about the Exodus. I don't want to blaspheme and insist that it's more natural, but still it worked out very well, the dramatic events of our own Exodus and the celebration of Passover came at the same time.

In March 1975 Shcharansky was dismissed from his work at the Moscow Oil and Gas Institute. Following his dismissal, the

Shcharansky in reflective mood, Moscow, 1976.

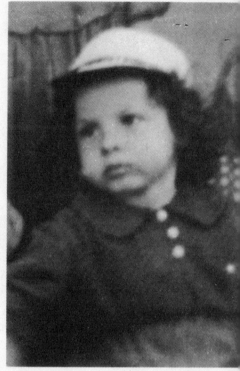

2 *Boris Shcharansky in his Red Army uniform during the Second World War.*

3 *Tolya at kindergarten.*

4 *The two brothers, Tolya and Lyonya, in Donetsk.*

5 *Tolya with his mother, Ida Milgrom.*

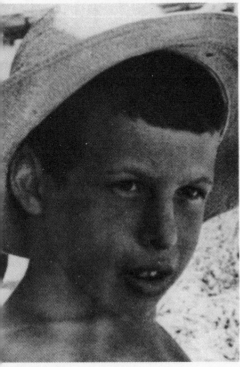

6 *At the seaside.*

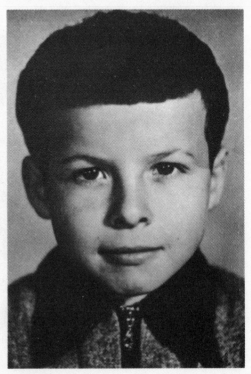

7 *Schoolboy.*

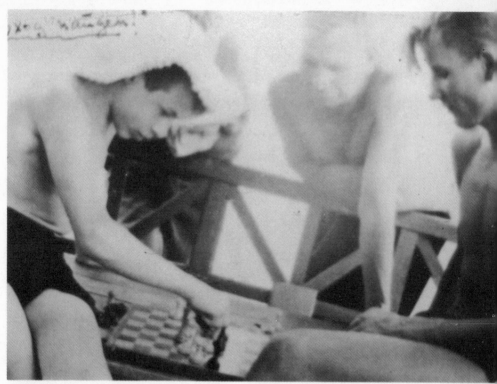

8 *A chess match at the seaside.*

9 *Shcharansky, junior chess champion of the Donetsk region.*

10 *The young student.*

11 *Rowing on the lake at Istra, near his parents' home outside Moscow.*

12 *Ida Milgrom and Boris Shcharansky.*

13 *A photograph of Shcharansky which Avital kept with her throughout the twelve years of their enforced separation.*

14 *Avital outside 10 Downing Street, London, during her unremitting campaign for her husband's release.*

15 *Arkhipova Street, Moscow, where Soviet Jews gathered each Saturday, and also at moments of crisis for Israel. It was here that Avital first met Shcharansky, during the October War of 1973.*

6 *At Moscow airport to say goodbye to Alexander Goldfarb, whom Shcharansky then succeeded as principal
translator and spokesman of the refusenik movement. Far left: Professor Alexander Lerner. On crutches: Goldfarb's
mother (subsequently refused an exit visa for more than a decade). Also in the group: Lev Ulanovsky (with domed head
and glasses), Vladimir Slepak (with bushy beard), Masha Slepak (in white sweater), Felix Kandel (with pointed
beard) and Shcharansky (in striped shirt). Far right (in cap): the Hebrew teacher Vladimir Shakhnovsky.*

7 *Shcharansky, spokesman; left Professor Benjamin Fain.*

18 Above   *Eighteen refuseniks on 9 November 1976,
following their release from fourteen days in detention,
together with the wives of Iosif Ahs and Boris
Chernobilsky, who were being kept in prison on a charge
of 'malicious hooliganism' following a demonstration.
Left to right (bottom row): Yakov Rakhlenko, Elena
Chernobilsky, Mikhaela Ahs, Zev Shakhnovsky,
Evgeny Yakir; (middle row): Anatoly Shcharansky,
Iosif Beilin, Igor Tufeld, Zakhar Tesker, Alexander
Gvinter; (top row): Leonid Tsipin (later revealed to be a
KGB informer), Mikhail Zelenny, Dmitri Shchiglik,
Victor Elistratov, Leonid Shabashov, Arkady Polishok,
Vladimir Slepak, Aron Gurevich, Isaak Elkind and
Mikhail Kremen.*

19 Left   *Shcharansky, unshaven, after having been
held in detention for forty-eight hours.*

Moscow authorities refused to recognise him as a Moscow resident. He was therefore obliged to live outside the city, in the township of Istra. Shcharansky tried to register as a private teacher of mathematics. The Finance Department of the township refused to register him, however, on the ground that all his students were living in Moscow.

To earn money, and to avoid the criminal charge of parasitism which could be levelled against any unemployed Soviet citizen, Shcharansky taught English, and physics, in private. His pupils included several Professors, among them Yury Orlov, a physicist who had been expelled from the Communist Party in 1956 for advocating 'democratic changes' in the Soviet political system, and who, in October 1973, had helped to establish the Moscow group of Amnesty International, together with Elena Bonner and Andrei Tverdokhlebov.

Shcharansky also did secretarial work for Academician Sakharov, acting as his interpreter when foreign visitors came to Moscow. With his vivid English style and enthusiastic grasp of the subjects under discussion, Shcharansky was a model among interpreters, going beyond mechanical translation to the mood and meaning of otherwise bland words.

Among the first visitors for whom Shcharansky acted as interpreter were several United States Senators and Congressmen, including Senator Christopher Dodd and Congressman Hamilton Fish Jr, who were in Moscow as part of a Senate and House Judiciary Committee mission to the Soviet Union. Another member of this mission was Joshua Eilberg, a Democratic Congressman from Pennsylvania. Shcharansky interpreted for the mission when they met the leading Jewish activists in Moscow, and also when they went to see Academician Sakharov. Later, Congressman Eilberg was to meet Avital in Jerusalem, and to speak movingly in the United States Congress of how 'only a cruel and inhuman policy keeps these two young people apart'.

*   *   *

The young couple remained, throughout this first year of their enforced separation, in correspondence. On 8 April 1975 Shcharansky wrote to Avital:

> After a long break, I have returned to reading regularly. I have read two good books in English: *The Source* and *Indestructible*

Jews, outstanding historical studies of our nation's path, its
role and function in the world, the reasons for its survival.
Perhaps these will help me in a small way to keep up with
you.

I had an interesting encounter recently. I was travelling on the
train from Istra, leafing through my four-language dictionary,
when suddenly an old man sitting across from me asked in
Hebrew with an excellent accent, 'Is that a Hebrew dictionary?'
We talked for a while in Hebrew; although he spoke so much
better than I, he was pleased to find a Hebrew-speaking companion. He told me he had a large Hebrew library at home and
had studied Hebrew literature for many years, having perfected
his knowledge of the language by listening to the Voice of Israel
broadcasts. Yet he was afraid to consider any contact with the
aliyah movement.

'Aliyah' is the Hebrew word for emigration to Israel: it means,
literally, a 'going up' to Jerusalem, the Holy City. Shcharansky's
letter continued:

When I told him who I was, he glanced around fearfully and sat
as if on hot coals. Funny? A man walks around lighting his way
with a match when there is a blazing bonfire next to him. But if
you think of how long and under what conditions he has carried
this lighted match, and that our first Hebrew teachers learned
from such old men, then you can't cease being amazed at the
ways of our survival.

In a further letter to Avital, Shcharansky referred to his friends
Mark Nashpits and Boris Tsitlionok:

Whatever we might have said to ourselves and others, the arrest
of Mark and Boris, and everything that followed it, initiated a
rather long and difficult period from which we are now fully
emerging. After their arrest, I spent a lot of time talking about
them with foreign journalists and lawyers and influential Congressmen. This produced some results: practically no meeting
between Americans and Russians in Moscow takes place
without the case of Mark and Boris being discussed.

Now they are in transit, which is the worst part. Boris is
being sent to the Krasnoyarsk Region and Mark to Chita. As
soon as I hear from them – around the second half of June – I'll
go to visit them.

On 27 May 1975 Anatoly Malkin, Shcharansky's companion on the journey to Minsk six months earlier, was arrested in Moscow and charged with avoiding military service. His defence was clear: had he not been expelled from his university for wanting to go to Israel, he would not be liable for military service; had he been granted his exit visa, the question of military service in the Soviet Union would never have arisen.

Shcharansky felt a special concern for his young friend, and sought to console him. 'If you go to prison early,' he said, 'you will get out early.' In those days, Malkin later reflected as we spoke together in Jerusalem, 'it really was so, it was better to go into prison and then be free, than not be free.' All Prisoners of Zion, at that time, received their exit visas once they had served their prison sentence.

Together with Dina Beilina, Shcharansky discussed Malkin's case with Sofia Kalistratova, a Moscow lawyer, not a Jewess, but well known for her defence of young Jews, and it was she who prepared Malkin's defence. Her line of argument was as follows: 'Why was this student expelled from university? For nothing. Why is he now being charged? Because he was called up to military service. But he was only called up to military service because he was expelled from the university.'

On 6 June 1975 nearly a hundred activists, including Shcharansky, addressed an appeal to all United States Senators and Congressmen on Malkin's behalf; the appeal, which had been drafted by Vitaly Rubin, was handed in to the American Embassy in Moscow.

Even as Malkin remained in prison awaiting trial, his friends, determined to alert the West to his, and to their own, worsening plight, prepared a second letter, which contained, like the letter to President Ford in November 1974, a comprehensive account of the plight of the refuseniks throughout the Soviet Union. Once more, the activists assembled the details of all that had happened to the refuseniks in the seven intervening months, and gave it to Senator Javits, who was then in Moscow, during a meeting with Javits and seven other United States Senators at the Rossiya Hotel.

The nineteen signatories of this letter of June 1975 pointed out that as soon as the Soviet authorities had rejected the 'almost accepted' Kissinger compromise, 'the pressure on Soviet Jews desiring to emigrate had increased' and 'its methods became more open'. Groundless refusals to grant emigration permits now acquired 'a bold, undisguised form'. The number of exit visas in 1974 had dropped by forty per cent from the figure for 1973. A press campaign had been launched 'slandering living conditions in Israel'. During the Passover festival, which began that year on 27 March 1975, police 'continually tried to drive away' those who had gathered near the Moscow synagogue, and even 'forced their way into the synagogue and tried to dictate the duration of the service'. Similar activities had been carried out in Kiev and Leningrad. On April 14, after 'numerous threats, interrogations and searches', a refusenik in Odessa, Lev Roitburd, his wife and three refusenik friends had been pilloried in the local evening newspaper.

Books on Judaism and Hebrew textbooks sent from the West were being confiscated by the authorities. Foreigners were not being allowed to bring in books in Hebrew, books about Israel, or books on Jewish history. Anti-Jewish feeling was being aroused in the Ukraine, Moldavia and White Russia by an anti-Semitic campaign, which found fertile ground where 'traditional anti-Semitism had always been strong'.

The letter of June 1975 pointed out that the number of refuseniks had been growing over the past six months, while 'the tempo of this growth has been increasing in comparison with the past.' It then examined in detail the reasons given for the most recent spate of refusals: 'so-called "security"' refusals had been given to activists like Lev Ulanovsky of Moscow and Leonid Levit of Tiraspol 'although they never had any contact with secret work'. Mark Freidman of Leningrad, who had worked as a dentist in the city's clinic for sailors, was also refused an exit visa on the ground that he was a 'possessor of secrets'. Other applicants had been refused because of 'lack of parents' consent', 'secrecy work of relatives in the USSR', 'those whom you want to join in Israel are too distant relatives', even 'there are instructions not to accept applications from single persons'. Three Jews, who had been demobilised seven years earlier, were rejected because of 'previous service in the army'. Two Jews in Kishinev were refused with the words 'emigration not considered advisable', and no further explanation of what this might mean.

Examples were given of the non-arrival of letters from overseas, including letters known to have been sent to Lunts and Rubin. It was stated that the disconnecting of telephones 'after conversations with overseas' had now become 'normal procedure' in Moscow, Leningrad, Minsk and Kiev. Invitations from Israel, which the Visa

Office made a prerequisite of all applications, were 'simply not being delivered to the addressees'. Jews who applied to leave were being thrown out of their places of work with even greater frequency than before. In May 1975, in Minsk, Colonel Yefim Davidovich, recipient of fifteen wartime orders and medals, had been demoted to the rank of private. The same had happened to Colonel Ovsishcher. 'The demotion of these officers', the letter of June 1975 declared, 'was not only an insult, but it was also an act which deprived them of their means of livelihood; they were deprived of their well-earned pensions.'

In a section on the conscription trap, it was pointed out that Anatoly Malkin was being held in prison, and that several other young Jews were expecting to be arrested at any moment, among them Alexander Silnitsky of Krasnodar and Boris Levitas of Kiev.

The letter of June 1975 also gave details of the trial of Nashpits and Tsitlionok, including the instructions which the police had given the 'witnesses': instructions which the other seven demonstrators had overheard while still in the cells. There were details also of the six-year labour-camp sentence imposed on Sender Levinson of Bendery on 27 May 1975: 'this was a rare case', the letter explained, 'of a Jew who wanted to emigrate to Israel being tried for having, in fact, violated Soviet law: Levinson sold clothing bought with money sent from overseas. But what had compelled him to do so? He, his pregnant wife and their child were left without any means of livelihood after he and his wife were dismissed from their jobs following their application for emigration to Israel. The verdict was also characteristic: six years of imprisonment in camps of strict regime.'

There were now forty-one Jewish prisoners, the letter pointed out, 'dispersed through twenty-seven camps in order to isolate each of them from any Jewish influence'. All were under pressure 'to renounce their intention to emigrate to Israel'. Punishment cells were used as 'an "education measure"'. Prisoners were deprived of their statutory visits by relatives, and were not allowed to study Hebrew or to receive Hebrew books. The conditions of those held in Vladimir prison, east of Moscow, including Butman, Suslensky and Mishener, was causing 'especial anxiety'.

The letter ended with details of the threats made recently against many activists, among them Alexander Lunts and Iosif Beilin in Moscow, Lev Roitburd in Odessa, Yefim Davidovich and Lev Ovsishcher in Minsk, and those who were involved in the scientific seminars among refuseniks – seminars which were the only way in which refusenik scientists could continue any form of scientific work. Professor Lerner had been 'called to the KGB several times', the letter noted, on account of the seminar on cybernetics which he had been holding in his apartment for the past two years. 'KGB officials told him that they could not reconcile themselves to the situation when a citizen of the USSR was engaging in scientific activities outside the framework of the Soviet institutions. They demanded that Professor Lerner should "close" his seminar.'

The authors of the letter of June 1975 pointed out 'that this summary is not, of course, a comprehensive one', but contained only 'examples of those methods which are used by the Soviet authorities in their struggle against the movement of Soviet Jews for emigration during the latest period'. The authors then signed their names, in alphabetical order, headed by Dina Beilina, Iosif Beilin and Yefim Davidovich. The other signatories included Alexander Lerner, Alexander Lunts, Ida Nudel, Lev Ovsishcher, Vitaly Rubin, Vladimir Slepak and Anatoly Shcharansky.

The letter of June 1975 was dictated over the telephone to Michael Sherbourne, who then distributed it to the Soviet Jewry campaigners in Britain, the United States and Western Europe. 'All recipients of copies of this statement', he wrote in a covering message, 'are requested to give it as much publicity as they can, and to try to ensure, where possible, that it is read by the leaders of the Western Governments.' These leaders were even then in the process of negotiating an agreement with the Soviet Union, under the framework of the Conference on Security and Co-operation in Europe, whereby the postwar frontiers of the Soviet Union would be given formal recognition. For its part, the Soviet Union would agree to a series of human rights provisions first laid down in 1948, in the Universal Declaration of Human Rights, including the right of every individual 'to leave any country, including his own, and to return to his country'. Shcharansky had been ten and a half months old when this original declaration was made; now, aged twenty-seven, those words which meant so much to every refusenik like himself were about to be enshrined in a solemn accord signed by the Soviet Union.

As these much publicised negotiations approached their last two weeks, it seemed to the activists in Moscow that it was more than ever important, certainly as important as it had been the previous November, to alert the world to the full extent of the pressures under which they lived, and, above all, to alert the world to the fate of the prisoners. To this end, on 15 June 1975 a group of Jewish activists in Leningrad and Moscow declared a one-day hunger strike. It was the fifth anniversary of the day on which, as they explained in their appeal to the West, 'the Soviet authorities launched a massive campaign against Soviet Jews', culminating in the Leningrad Trials. 'The people accused at those trials', the appeal read, 'were tried only for being Jews who wanted to live with their people in Israel, in their homeland.' Many were still held in 'extremely difficult conditions of detention'. 'We will never give up our desire', the signatories wrote, 'to bind our fate with the fate of the Jewish people in Israel.'

The Leningrad signatories of this appeal included Aba and Ida Taratuta, who, when I visited them recently, were in their twelfth year of refusal. The Moscow signatories included Yuly Kosharovsky, Pavel Abramovich, Vladimir Slepak and Vladimir Prestin, all still in refusal ten years later; Felix Kandel and Ilya Essas, now in Israel; and Shcharansky.

Nineteen Jews had signed the first letter of June 1975; twenty-eight had signed the second. All of them took risks in doing so, and accepted those risks.

9

Helsinki and Beyond

On 30 June 1975, a month before the expected signature of the Helsinki Agreement, seventeen refuseniks spent several hours with five United States Senators – Javits, Ribicoff, Humphrey, Scott, Percy and Matthias. Among the refuseniks were four Professors, Alexander Lunts, Benjamin Fain, Vitaly Rubin and Mark Azbel; Dr Victor Brailovsky; Ida Nudel; Dina Beilina; Lev Ovsishcher and Yefim Davidovich from Minsk; and Shcharansky. The refuseniks passed on their appreciation to Senator Jackson for his amendment, which they described to the Senators as 'an important cornerstone in their fight for emigration'.

Amid the debates which intensified on the eve of the Helsinki Agreement, Shcharansky's thoughts were in Jerusalem with his Avital. A year had passed since their marriage. Visitors, passing between Israel and the Soviet Union, brought news, photographs and messages. One such, in July 1975, was Senator James Buckley of New York, who, having visited Shcharansky in Moscow, promised Avital in Jerusalem 'to work for their reunification'. Buckley was one of fourteen Senators who visited Moscow that summer; on 2 July 1975, Lev Roitburd tried to fly from Odessa to Moscow to see them. He was at once arrested, and spent the rest of the month in prison, awaiting trial.

Returning to the United States on 5 July 1975, the fourteen Senators issued a statement in which they thanked the Soviet authorities for allowing them to meet the Jewish activists 'without interference'. The activists, who heard this statement broadcast over Voice of America, at once wrote to the Senators: 'Unfortunately, the first concrete result of this meeting was the arrest of Lev Roitburd.'

The case of Roitburd, the signatories added, 'is no exception in the practice of persecuting Soviet Jews fighting for their emigration to Israel. However, we hope that you will pay special attention to this case and will take steps expressing your opinion about it, as the incident took place during your stay in the USSR and was, most probably, connected with your visit there.'

The signatories of this letter included the four Professors, Rubin, Fain, Lerner and Azbel, as well as Dr Brailovsky and Dr Lunts, Ida Nudel and Dina Beilina, Lev Ovsishcher, Yefim Davidovich, Ilya Essas, Vladimir Prestin, Pavel Abramovich and Shcharansky.

On 30 July 1975 the third and final stage of the Conference on Security and Co-operation in Europe opened in Helsinki, with Leonid Brezhnev representing the Soviet Union, Gerald Ford the United States and Harold Wilson the United Kingdom. In all, thirty-five countries were represented: the United States, Canada, and all the countries of Europe except Albania. The so-called 'Basket Three' covered 'co-operation in humanitarian and other fields', agreeing to the reunification of divided families. Of central importance to all refuseniks was the sentence in the preamble that the participating States would act 'in conformity' with the Universal Declaration of Human Rights of 1948. Now, at the signing of the Helsinki Accords on 1 August 1975, the Soviet Union had endorsed, with all the solemnity of an international agreement, the right of every individual 'to leave any country, including his own, and to return to his country'. Avital Shcharansky, in Jerusalem, related how, shortly after the signing of the Helsinki Accords, she received 'an exuberant letter' from Shcharansky. 'They have signed an international agreement', he wrote, 'and it speaks exactly of us: of the reunification of families and of free emigration. Soon we will be together in Jerusalem.' Avital commented: 'Not only Anatoly but those around him were elated.'

Reflecting on Helsinki's impact on Shcharansky, his uncle Shamai said to me in Jerusalem in 1984, in his characteristically poetic style: 'He saw it as a second edition of the Ten Commandments. As the Russian proverb goes – I learned it at the age of ten – "What is written with the pen you cannot hew out with an axe." Once the agreement was written, no amount of oratory could change it. My nephew began to walk from meeting to meeting, saying to people: "Look at that! in black and white!"'

★   ★   ★

From the summer of 1975 until the early months of 1977, the influence of Shcharansky was felt throughout the Jewish movement. There were other leaders who likewise sustained the hope of those in refusal, championed their cause, or sought to spread Jewish knowledge in its widest aspect. In this last regard, Vladimir Slepak, Vitaly Rubin, Felix Kandel, Mark Azbel, Victor Brailovsky and Iosif Begun had emerged as leaders, with the magazine *Jews in the USSR* as a vehicle, openly circulated, with the names of its editors openly displayed. Alexander Lunts was still prominent in the fight for exit visas, while younger men, among them Vladimir Shakhnovsky, led a revival of Jewish religious practice. Hebrew teaching also continued, with Yuly Kosharovsky and Iosif Begun among the teachers.

The Jewish renaissance in Moscow took many forms, both religious and secular. Vitaly Rubin continued with his Jewish cultural seminar, where talks were given in Russian. As many as fifty people were sometimes present. Shcharansky, who attended the talks, was asked to give one himself. His subject was 'American Jewry', and he based it both on his personal contacts and on his reading, including the novels of Saul Bellow. 'It was a very good presentation,' Lev Ulanovsky recalled.

Shcharansky's knowledge of American Jewry was increasingly based not upon his reading, but upon personal acquaintance and long discussion. Among the American Jews who met him in Moscow were several distinguished writers and academics. One was Richard Pipes, a scholar of Soviet history.

According to one of the accusations levelled against Shcharansky two years later, Shcharansky had pressed upon Pipes 'the need to exert pressure upon the Soviet Union, and in particular, the expediency of blackmailing the Soviet Union with threats of curtailing the Soviet–American cultural and scientific relationship'. The accusation went on to allege that Professor Pipes gave Shcharansky specific instructions as to how to rouse 'national hatred' in the Soviet Union, informing him that 'influential circles in the United States see such national hatred as a powerful catalyst, furthering the erosion of Soviet society'.

It was a vulnerability of the Jewish emigration movement that it could always be charged with such absurdities; many Jews were afraid of what might be alleged against them, if they were to talk to foreign visitors. But it was the strength of the movement that there were always Jews, Shcharansky among them, who were prepared to meet foreigners, despite the risk, and to discuss with them the plight of the refuseniks, and the need for publicity in the West on

their behalf: a publicity which the activists believed could only be
beneficial for the mass of Soviet Jews who wished to leave, even if it
was clearly dangerous for the activists themselves, or certainly for
those among them whom the authorities chose to single out for
punishment.

The truth about Shcharansky's brief meeting with Professor
Pipes was prosaic. Pipes had been invited to the Soviet Union as the
guest of the Soviet Academy of Sciences, for the purpose of
undertaking research into Russian history. He met Shcharansky, on
the evening of 3 July 1975, at the home of Vitaly Rubin. As Pipes
stated on oath three years later, he had not known Shcharansky
before this meeting nor did he meet him 'in any manner whatsoever' after it. The occasion had been an 'informal reception'.
Pipes had arrived late. 'Several individuals still remained, among
them Anatoly Shcharansky. We did not enter into any discussion
other than ordinary social talk and the fact that his wife was in Israel
and that they had been separated immediately after the wedding.'
Pipes had told Shcharansky that he would be visiting Israel soon,
'and volunteered, if he so wished, to contact his wife there and
bring her his greetings. He gave me her telephone number. Politics
was never discussed.' This one meeting, Pipes added, was 'the only
encounter or communication I ever conducted with Anatoly
Shcharansky'.

As Shcharansky continued his liaison work, there were also
messages in the other direction. On 14 August 1975 Congressman
Robert F. Drinan, a Jesuit priest, reached Moscow, one of a number
of Congressmen who had come from the United States. With him
he brought several photographs of Avital, which had been given to
him by Myrna Shinbaum of the National Conference on Soviet
Jewry.

'Shcharansky was my guide and translator,' Drinan later
reported. 'We struck an instant friendship when I presented him
with a colour photo of his wife Avital, taken in the radiant sun of
Jerusalem.' Drinan also remembered 'the way Shcharansky was
shadowed by the KGB while he was my companion. It was
predictable that he would be apprehended: he was a natural leader.'
The community of Jews in Moscow who wished to emigrate,
Drinan added, 'depended on him in critical ways. He was creative
and resourceful in devising methods to dramatise the problems
facing Jews who wanted to leave, and he was close friends with Dr
Andrei Sakharov and other leaders in the dissident community.'

Shcharansky did not in fact 'dramatise' the problems of the refuseniks; these problems were dramatic enough without the need for anything more than explanation. This was Shcharansky's skill: to explain the details clearly, in excellent English, and in a manner which both convinced and commanded attention.

As an example of the 'dramatic' situation: six days before Drinan had reached Moscow yet another Jew had been tried and sentenced – Yakov Vinarov, aged twenty-one, from Kiev, who received a three-year labour-camp sentence for refusing to comply with a conscription notice. He had also renounced his Soviet citizenship.

During Drinan's visit, Shcharansky drove him to see Academician Sakharov and, as he always did at such meetings, acted as translator. Lev Ulanovsky, who also went with Shcharansky to see Sakharov on several occasions, later described, as he and I spoke together in Jerusalem, the attitude of the distinguished dissident scientist to the Jewish emigration movement. 'He defended all human rights,' Ulanovsky explained. 'He uses the word – not freedom, you can't pursue that in Russia – but human rights. In this capacity he always considered Jewish emigration one of the most important fields of human rights.'

Robert Drinan remained in Moscow for seven days. With Shcharansky always at his side, he met several leading activists, among them Professor Lerner, Alexander Lunts, Victor Brailovsky and Ida Nudel. Only Slepak was out of town that week. A highlight of Drinan's visit was a meeting with the head of the Visa Office for the entire Soviet Union, with whom Drinan raised the cases of five of the Moscow activists whom he had met 'who had been refused erroneously on security grounds'. The head of the Visa Office undertook 'to look into the case', and to give Drinan a report 'in a month or two'. Drinan was, however, to hear no more.

On August 17, while Drinan was still in Moscow, Lev Roitburd went on trial in Odessa. He was sentenced to two years in labour camp. Dina Beilina, who had gone to Odessa to attend Roitburd's trial, flew back on the following day to Moscow and, without even going to her apartment to change, hurried to see Drinan, and to tell him of the sentence.

Dina Beilina found Drinan outside the Moscow courthouse where Anatoly Malkin was to be tried that same day. Many refuseniks, including Shcharansky, had gathered at the courthouse, hoping to be present during the trial. None were allowed into the courtroom. Shcharansky was with Congressman Drinan, who also wanted to be present, and who asked for Shcharansky to be his interpreter. At that moment, however, a court official announced that the judge was ill, and the trial postponed. Three days later, Drinan's visa expired and he had to leave the Soviet Union; Malkin's trial was reconvened on 22 August 1975.

During the trial, Sofia Kalistratova spoke in Malkin's defence. 'She did a very good job,' Malkin later reflected, 'but Soviet trials have their own logic.' He added: 'I could have got two years, and I got three.'

A stream of Western visitors was now coming to Moscow to meet the refuseniks. Many of them met Shcharansky, whose zeal and humour remained with them as a lasting memory. June Daniels, from Iowa, spoke of Alexander Lunts's worry, on learning that he had received his exit visa, that 'Anatoly would now take the brunt.' On June Daniels's last day in Moscow, Shcharansky came to her hotel, 'insisting that I take pictures back to give to Avital'. When a Jewish visitor from Philadelphia, Connie Smukler, asked Shcharansky if he had any messages for her to convey, he replied: 'Just see Avital and tell her I love her.' To Connie Smukler's husband Joseph, Shcharansky was emphatic in his aim and goals. 'I don't want to be a hero,' he declared. 'I would rather not be in the movement at all. All I want is to go to Israel and join my wife.'

Another visitor to Moscow in the autumn of 1975 was a United States Congresswoman, Elizabeth Holtzman, who remembered three years later Shcharansky's 'personal courage, his pride in his Jewish heritage, and his sincere desire to emigrate'.

The Soviet press denounced these visitors. On 25 June 1975 an article in *Izvestia* listed 'pornographic magazines and postcards, playing cards with indecent backs packed together with openly anti-Soviet literature, vicious Zionist writings and religious literature', brought into the Soviet Union, it declared, 'under the guise of "spiritual food"'.

Such denunciations did not deter the visitors, for whom the Helsinki Agreement seemed to augur a reopening of the gates. Also in August 1975, Senator Patrick Leahy and Congresswoman Millicent Fenwick were in Moscow, together with Congressman Sidney Yates and the Speaker of the House of Representatives, Carl Albert. During their visit they met almost all the leading activists and heard Shcharansky interpret with such strength of feeling that they thought he was also the spokesman.

On her return to Washington, Congresswoman Fenwick introduced legislation to set up a Helsinki monitoring commission in the United States Congress. The legislation, sponsored by Senator Clifford Case of New Jersey, was enacted into law in the 94th Congress. The Chairman of the Commission was Congressman Dante Fascell, a Florida Democrat. Their task was to 'monitor compliance with the Helsinki Accords' and to report on breaches of the accords.

★　　　★　　　★

Shcharansky and his friends pressed upon all visiting Senators and Congressmen the need to publicise the plight of the refuseniks. In the atmosphere of Moscow, however, danger seemed to lurk in such a course, or so it seemed to visitors from the West, unaccustomed to Communism. 'When American visitors came,' Lev Ulanovsky explained, 'one of the first questions they would ask was: "Do you think that publicity about your case can *harm* you?" One of the main points Shcharansky always made, as did all activists, was that it would not only not harm, it would *help*.'

In 1975 the Jewish New Year began on September 6. On the following day Shcharansky was visited in Moscow by a Jewish woman from Omaha, Nebraska, Shirley Goldstein, Chairman of the Omaha Committee for Soviet Jewry. Shirley Goldstein had brought a tape recorder with her, and on it Shcharansky recorded, in English, 'a New Year's message'. Like all the statements quoted in these pages, whether written as this one by one man alone, or collectively, it was not intended as a clandestine or anonymous message, but was to be made known as widely as possible under the name, or names, of those who had prepared it. Shcharansky's Jewish New Year message read:

Shalom, dear friends

I am speaking to you on the very first day of the Jewish New Year. This year I have met with the same hope which I met the previous year and two years ago I met with the same hope that this year I will be in Jerusalem. B'shanah hazot b'Yerushalayim. I hope to join my wife at last, just as many of my friends hope to join their families, mothers, brothers, sisters, as all of us hope to join our people.

We are optimists in spite of the fact that the situation now is very dangerous. Only a few days ago, one of my close friends, a young Jew, Anatoly Malkin, was sentenced to three years in prison.

He was imprisoned because after he applied for a visa he was expelled from an institute and became eligible for the army and was called to serve, but refused and was sentenced to three years.

With this trial, the authorities want to frighten many young Jews who have the same choice: to go into the army and lose hope of emigrating to Israel for many years, perhaps ten or more years; or they can go to prison.

We know many young Jews who are now hiding from the authorities because they are also threatened with imprisonment. We know hundreds of young people who are afraid and who will agree to go into the army. We know thousands of people who suppress their desire to emigrate because they are afraid that they or their sons or their brothers will meet the same fate as Anatoly Malkin.

He was in fact a very courageous young man. But yesterday, in the evening, at the start of the Jewish New Year, I noticed so many other young Jewish people going to the synagogue, perhaps for the first time, and maybe against the desire of their parents.

They came to the synagogue to celebrate the Jewish New Year together with us and they were fighting with the police and with the trucks the police sent to prevent us from celebrating. They were getting their first lessons in Jewish life in the Soviet Union. Let us assure you that many of them will join our fight very soon.

Continuing, Shcharansky told his would-be trans-Atlantic listeners:

Malkin's trial wasn't the only one in recent days. In Odessa, Lev Roitburd was sentenced to two years in prison, only for his attempt to reach Moscow when he heard that American Senators were here. We Moscow Jews met them and he wanted to join us. The situation in the provinces is much worse, however, and he was warned by the KGB not to do it. When he tried he was caught, tried and sentenced to two years.

During recent days many Jewish families in Moscow got refusals to their emigration applications; they are now refuseniks. Many of the old refuseniks who have been waiting for two, three or even five years got refusals as well.

Dozens of people are taken in for interrogations, they are questioned about our scientific seminars, about our Jewish magazine. The authorities are trying to destroy all kinds of Jewish life here in the Soviet Union now. Surely it is a demonstration of the power of the authorities by which they try to frighten all of us.

Shcharansky's message continued:

Every time the Soviet Union undertakes new international obligations, such as the Helsinki Accords now, the authorities do their best to frighten all the people who can make use of them. First of all, they try to frighten the Jews, both those who are fighting for their right to live a Jewish life here and those seeking to emigrate to Israel. But it is not only a demonstration for us; it is surely a demonstration for you, our American Jewish brothers and sisters.

They want to show you that your help doesn't work, but I want to assure you that your support and your fight is the only reason for our survival. The very fact that we can continue our struggle now, the very fact that 100,000 Jews have emigrated and that emigration continues, the very fact that many young Jews can study Hebrew now, that we can hold our own scientific seminars, our very existence is only because of your support.

The authorities understand that our communications with you are very important to us. That is why they do their best to destroy them. For many months, we couldn't get one telephone conversation with Israel or one telephone conversation with America. We don't receive your letters and you don't receive ours.

The Soviet Union has undertaken some serious international obligations now and I'm sure that the pressure you can organise from America and from international organisations will work and will help us to communicate with you and to fight for our rights. I am sure that our firm determination to continue our fight, and your continued support are the two major things which will help Soviet Jewry to be saved.

I want to send best regards to all of our American friends from us, from those of us who are in Siberia like Mark Nashpits and Boris Tsitlionok, from those of us who are in prison, like Anatoly Malkin, Lev Roitburd and many others.

To all of you, to all of our Jewish brothers and sisters in

America, we hope that the day will come, we hope it will be in
the new Jewish year, when all of us will be able to meet in
Jerusalem – B'shanah hazot b'Yerushalayim. Shalom. L'hitraot
[This Year in Jerusalem. Peace be with you. See you soon].

Such was Shcharansky's Jewish New Year message, recorded on
tape, and brought to the West by Shirley Goldstein. It shows many
aspects of his character: his optimism, his concern for a fellow Jew
in trouble, his belief that the Helsinki Agreement would only help
Soviet Jews if they fought for their rights under it, and above all his
fight for all Jews who wished to leave, not just for himself. 'I don't
remember that he ever asked something for himself,' Dina Beilina
later recalled. 'He did not speak about himself; it was an element of
his character.'

                    ★   ★   ★

On 18 September 1975, twelve days after Shcharansky's personal
New Year message, the Praesidium of the Supreme Soviet, meeting in Moscow, ratified the Helsinki Final Act. That same day,
Shcharansky was one of thirty-three refuseniks who signed a 1500-
word open letter on what was called 'The Lessons of the Roitburd
and Malkin Trials'. This letter, dictated over the telephone to
Michael Sherbourne, translated by him, and circulated to Soviet
Jewry campaigners in the West on the following day, pointed out
that both trials had taken place after Leonid Brezhnev had signed
the Final Act in Helsinki.

The signatories of this open letter, the first to be prepared by the
refuseniks since the signing of the Helsinki Accords, included many
who were later to receive their exit visas: Vitaly Rubin, whose wife
Ina helped to type the letter, Benjamin Fain, Mark Azbel, Alexander Lunts, Felix Kandel and Lev Ulanovsky. It also included
others who, ten years later, had still been refused their exit visas,
among them the Hebrew teachers Yuly Kosharovsky and Vladimir
Shakhnovsky as well as Vladimir and Masha Slepak, and Iosif
Begun. At the age of forty-three, Begun – a refusenik since April
1971 – had emerged as a fine Hebrew teacher and a staunch
supporter of all those who wished to emigrate to Israel, or to learn
about Judaism.

Also signing the letter of 18 September 1975 was Dr Alexander
Lipavsky, known as Sanya, a forty-two-year-old Jewish doctor
whom Ida Nudel had befriended, and who was proving most

helpful to refuseniks in need of medical advice: among those he helped was Shcharansky, whom, sixteen months later, he was to betray.

Lev Ulanovsky, one of the organisers of this letter, later recalled how those who signed it came from several different groups: the scientists of *Jews in the USSR* and the cultural seminars, the religious group, the Hebrew teachers, and those who believed in public demonstrations. All were united in believing that it was essential to expose Soviet performance on Helsinki, and to demand compliance. 'Getting them all to sign was a major effort,' Ulanovsky reflected. 'Telephones could not be used, only taxis, and taxis were followed.'

The signatories of 18 September 1975 underlined the cruelty of the conscription trap, as it had been applied to Anatoly Malkin. 'Every family which includes young people between the ages of seventeen and thirty', they wrote, 'must be compelled to take into account the possibility of their being called to the army in the event of their submitting application for emigration. Therefore, it has become clear that even the threat alone of this possibility is holding back thousands of Soviet Jews from the attempt to apply for emigration.' This, the signatories declared, 'is one of the fundamental causes of the slowing down of emigration in the last year or so. There is every reason to assume that following this line to its most cruel conclusion, the Soviet Government intends to close down emigration completely in the next few years.'

The trials of Roitburd and Malkin indicated, the signatories stressed, 'that the Soviet Government is not only not fulfilling the obligations which it undertook at Helsinki, but has already, immediately after the signing of the Final Act in Helsinki, instituted further and new methods completely in opposition to those undertakings.' They went on to 'call upon all heads of Governments who signed the agreement in Helsinki to bear this fact in mind', hoping that the Governments who had signed the Helsinki Agreement 'will take the appropriate steps to induce the Soviet authorities to demonstrate not by words, but by their deeds, that they do not look upon the Helsinki Agreement as just another scrap of paper.'

Jews in the West strove to make the refusenik struggle known as widely as possible. On 10 October 1975 Jewish parliamentarians from throughout Europe, as well as Knesset members from Israel, gathered in Brussels to draw attention to the refuseniks' plight. Among the documents which they publicised was a letter received

from twenty-nine Soviet Jews, urging three things: the release of all
'Jewish Prisoners of Conscience', the implementation of the Helsinki Agreement and an end to the 'harassment and intimidation of
Jews who express their wish to reunite with their families', and the
stopping of 'groundless arbitrary refusals' so that those Jews 'who
are living for years as outcasts, deprived of means of subsistence,
and subject to constant public harassment', would be given permission to leave.

The signatories from Moscow were, in the order of signing,
Vitaly Rubin, Vladimir Slepak, Alexander Lerner, Anatoly
Shcharansky, Vladimir Shakhnovsky, Deborah Samoilovich,
Alexander Lunts, Dina Beilina and Ida Nudel. From Minsk, both
Lev Ovsishcher and Yefim Davidovich had signed. From Odessa,
Lev Roitburd's wife Lilia. From his place of exile in Siberia, Mark
Nashpits had signed, as had Boris Tsitlionok from his own Siberian
exile.

*   *   *

The refusenik community feared not only the repeated refusals to
which they were subjected, but anti-Semitic undertones in daily
life. During the autumn of 1975 they learned of a film, shown to a
select audience at the Moscow Documentary Film Centre, the
opening shot of which was a darkened screen and the crack of a
pistol shot, followed by a commentator's voice: 'That was how the
Jewess Fanya Kaplan tried to kill Lenin.' The film went on to depict
events in the Soviet Union for the past half-century. When a
sequence showed Hitler's tanks invading Russia the commentator
remarked: 'Jewish capital helped Hitler to power.' Stalin's rival
Trotsky, the founder of the Red Army, was referred to in the film
by his original Jewish name, Leon Bronstein. Whenever scenes of
deprivation, hunger or difficulty were shown, a prominent Jewish
leader also appeared on the screen. The film, entitled 'Secret and
Open Things', was being shown to Red Army groups, and in at
least one public cinema, the Znaniye, in Leningrad. In Minsk, both
Yefim Davidovich and Lev Ovsishcher protested against it.

There was a time, every year, when the Moscow refuseniks had a
moment of pure pleasure: the arrival of Israeli sportsmen for some
international sporting event. Although, since 1967, the Soviet
Union had had no diplomatic links with Israel, Israeli sportsmen
could still travel across the Iron Curtain for international competitions. To see 'those lovely sunburnt people', as a refusenik friend of

mine later described them, was to bring a touch of the land they could not see to those who were so desperate to see it. That September, an Israeli wrestling and weightlifting team was in Moscow. Unlike the international university competition of 1973, when police tried to prevent Moscow's Jews from entering the stadium to see the Israeli basketball team, all who wished to could watch the wrestlers and weightlifters. Shcharansky, however, could not at first see them, as he was so involved in trying to help Anatoly Malkin – Natan, or Natanchik, as he was known. But Shcharansky did see the sportsmen in the end, as he explained to Avital on 18 September 1975:

> Shalom, my dear,
>
> The Israeli weightlifters have been in Moscow for several days. A lot of people met them, but I couldn't since I was very busy with Natanchik's case. I was finally free yesterday evening and went to the Luzhniki Sports Complex. The situation was entirely different from that at the Universiad in 1973. We rooted for 'our' weightlifter as much as we could. It was difficult for him to compete with professionals – he is a clothes cutter from Tel Aviv who practises only once a week. Still he didn't do badly. Then he and the other Israelis came out to us and we chatted with them for two hours in Hebrew – I really don't know where the words came from. On Sunday, I'll probably go with them to the woods to observe Succoth. Our life is such that one day we meet with Israeli scientists and the next with weightlifters.

Shcharansky's letter continued, on a personal note:

> Last night I even dreamed that you came with some team to Moscow for a competition. Of course, we were together all the time, then suddenly we realised that you were late for the game (I don't even know which). You didn't want to go, but I said, 'You mustn't let your team down.' We hailed a taxi and raced over – and then I woke up.

The Jewish festival of Succoth, or Tabernacles, fell in 1975 on September 20. On the following day, Sunday, September 21, Shcharansky and Slepak were among more than a hundred Jews who joined the wrestlers and weightlifters in the woods near Moscow, to celebrate the festival, to talk and sing in Hebrew, and to dance Israeli dances. They were also photographed doing so by a KGB cameraman; but exuberance overcame caution. For Slepak and Shcharansky, as for all those milling about the birch trees, welcoming the Israelis was the natural thing to do.

Two weeks later their friend Andrei Sakharov was awarded the Nobel Peace Prize. He was at once denounced by the *Literaturnaya Gazeta* for supporting 'Nazi and fascist causes' and was compared to 'a laboratory rat manipulated by anti-Soviet forces'.

10

Lists

The importance of the Helsinki Accords was obvious to all refuseniks: here was a solemn agreement signed by the Soviet Union, some of whose clauses bore specifically on their struggle. Yet it was clear that the Soviet authorities did not intend to apply the Helsinki Accords to those Jews who had been refused exit visas, even to members of families who were divided between the Soviet Union and Israel.

A chance to stress the need for the application of the Helsinki Accords to the refuseniks came in October 1975, when Congressman Charles Vanik, co-sponsor of the Jackson–Vanik Amendment, visited Moscow. At a long meeting which Vanik held with Professor Lerner, Alexander Lunts, Victor Brailovsky, Vitaly Rubin and Iosif Beilin, it was Shcharansky who acted as interpreter. The group had one predominant message for Vanik: there were now 'some five hundred refusenik families in the same situation' and that the 'most important endeavour now was to fight for the principle of the right to leave'.

Five hundred seemed a staggering figure for the number of refusenik families, but it was borne out by a series of lists which the activists had been compiling for more than two years: lists of every family known to have been refused an exit visa. There were several methods of compiling these lists. As Dina Beilina explained, 'Much of the information came from Israel, from relatives and friends of the refuseniks who gave the names and details of the refusal in their letters from abroad; letters which arrived in the post.' Sometimes details of a refusal reached Moscow in a broadcast over Israel Radio, or other Western radio stations. Sometimes knowledge of a refused exit visa was acquired at the Visa Office in Moscow. 'We would go in turn to the Visa Office to gather statistics,' Lev Ulanovsky later noted. 'One went to the corridor outside the room in which refusals were given, a room of ill fate. We would sit and wait. Some people, as they came out, refused to give their name and address, or the date of their first application. They didn't want to be known as refuseniks. Others were willing to be listed.'

Among those who helped to compile the lists were Alexander Lunts, Anatoly Malkin and Leonid Tsipin, still not exposed as a KGB informer. 'In Moscow,' Malkin recalled, 'they gave you your refusal on a Monday. Tsipin and I went in every Monday. We asked people if they had been refused, and if so, why. Some people didn't want to give their names. But if they agreed to do so, we wrote it down.'

Thus a series of lists was compiled, typed out by Dina Beilina. After she had put the names in alphabetical order, city by city, each list was sent to the West. Their arrival made three things clear: that the number of Jews refused exit visas was growing; that the number of visas granted in 1975 would fall well below the figures for 1974; and that the 'reasons' given for refusals were as spurious as they had always been.

I have several of these lists in front of me as I write, their flimsy sheets giving name, date of birth, address, number of family members, and reason for refusal. Where the reason was given by the Visa Office as 'against the interest of the State' or 'State secrecy', it was in most cases a fiction. Those Jews who were really involved in any form of secret work were usually afraid to apply for an exit visa, knowing that they would be bound to receive a refusal, and were not willing to give up their careers for nothing. Sometimes, 'and only in order to show the absurdity of the reasons given by the Visa Office in refusing a visa', Dina Beilina remembered, 'did I write some explanation – for example, reason for refusal: "secrecy"; actual work: "nurse". I only gave the place of work of someone refused for secrecy when it would make it clear to anybody interested in our fate that this was an *absurd* reason for the refusal – for example, reason given by the Visa Office: "secrecy"; place of work of the applicant: "the Moscow circus".'

The lists made clear the scale of the problem, and the size of the growing long-term refusenik community. In the Moscow list, of 144 families, Vladimir Slepak was number three on the list, in refusal since 1970. Those in refusal since 1971 included both Vladimir Prestin and Pavel Abramovich, both of whom were active in Jewish cultural seminars, Iosif Begun and Yuly

Kosharovksy among the Hebrew teachers, as well as Ida Nudel, Boris Tsitlionok and Alexander Lerner.

The refuseniks listed for 1972 included the Hebrew teacher Vladimir Shakhnovsky, the sinologist Professor Vitaly Rubin, and two of the scientific seminar leaders, Professor Mark Azbel and Dr Victor Brailovsky. Refuseniks who had applied in 1973 included both Dr Alexander Lunts and, listed as number sixty-four, Anatoly Shcharansky. Against Shcharansky's name was the added notation that he had been refused on security grounds, and that his wife was in Israel.

Several of the lists were built up not by waiting in the corridor of the Visa Office, but from information brought to Moscow from distant cities, and collated in Lunts's apartment. One of the lists in front of me relates to Odessa, and has twenty-four names. The list for Kaunas has twenty-two names. One name each is given from the Lithuanian villages of Ponevezhys, Shauliai and Oshmiani. From Riga, fifty-five names are given; from Kiev, twenty-five; and from Lvov, thirteen. Of the three names listed from Bendery, two, Suslensky and Mishener, were Prisoners of Zion.

The lists covered every region of the Soviet Union: from the Siberian city of Novosibirsk, six; from the Ukrainian city of Vinnitsa, five; from the former Austro-Hungarian city of Chernovtsy, sixteen; from the White Russian capital of Minsk, seven, including Lev Ovsishcher and Yefim Davidovich; from the city of Perm, in the Urals, three; from Vilnius, the capital of the Lithuanian Republic, forty-three. Other towns included in the list were Beltsy, with five refusenik families; Tiraspol, with two; Tula, with three; the Georgian capital, Tbilisi, with four; the Ukrainian city of Kharkov, with seven; Derbent in the Caucasus, with seven; and Leningrad, with seventy-four. The Leningrad refuseniks in the list included seven prisoners, and three Hebrew teachers: Aba Taratuta, Isaak Kogan and Lev Furman.

In compiling these lists with such care, Lunts, Beilina and Ulanovsky, and the refuseniks themselves, who gave Lunts their names, were convinced that it was only by publicity in the West that the Soviet authorities could be made to open the gates in the East. The lists also gave a human face to the movement, enabling not statistics, but names and eventually photographs to be part of the Western campaign on their behalf. Giving the addresses made it possible for the refuseniks to be visited in their homes and to receive letters from Jews in the West.

Had any information in these lists been secret, Dina Beilina later commented, the Soviet authorities could have stopped both them and their compilers at any time since 1972. It was not the lists of refuseniks reaching the West that revealed whether a certain place of work was a place of alleged State secrets. It was the Soviet authorities, and they alone, who, whether such information was true or false, made it available each time they told an exit-visa applicant that 'State secrets' was the reason for a refusal. This was a reason which any refusenik could then pass on, and did pass on, to his friends or to the outside world: by letter, by telephone, or by word of mouth of those who did receive an exit visa.

The lists of the refuseniks, with the reasons for their refusal, circulated freely throughout the Soviet Union and abroad. No effort was made by the Soviet authorities to stop them. For five years, starting in 1972 before Shcharansky had become involved in the movement, these lists were an integral and open part of the struggle for exit visas. In 1977 they were to be used as part of the indictment against Shcharansky; but shortly before his trial, Dina Beilina, their compiler, was given her exit visa. Alexander Lunts, whose idea they had been, had been allowed to leave long before Shcharansky's arrest.

11

The Lottery of Refusal

In the first week of November 1975, Shcharansky, who was earning his living as a tutor in English and mathematics, made the longest journey of his life, travelling eastwards across Siberia to the town of Tupik, amid the vast forests of the taiga, where Mark Nashpits was in internal exile. The name of the place, 'Tupik', means 'dead-end' in Russian. From Tupik Shcharansky then travelled many further miles to Yeniseisk, where Boris Tsitlionok was serving his internal-exile term. Between the two towns, Shcharansky found time to write an account of his travels to Avital:

I am writing you this letter, postmarked from the distant city of Chita, almost at the other end of the USSR. I have just sent you a congratulatory telegram – I don't know whether it will reach you: it caused a big commotion. Right away I had to give up the idea of writing it in Hebrew, but it wasn't clear whether it would get to you in Russian. When I think that I can't be with you on your twenty-fifth birthday, I want to cry. I spent the last five days with Marik in Tupik. It really is a 'tupik'. It took five hours for Marik's aunt Musya and me to fly there from Chita on a small plane. Tupik is a regional centre, but in fact it is a small town (eight hundred people) in the taiga, inhabited mainly by hunters and those who serve them, teachers, doctors, etc.

Life there is, of course, very rough. Even now, at the beginning of November, the temperature in the daytime is −15 or −20° and at night −30. There are no water pipes; in the morning we dislodged a piece of ice from a barrel, and placed it in buckets on the stove. Marik learned how to stoke the stove deftly – the whole process from splitting the wood to heating up the hut took him no more than thirty minutes. I, too, learned this art by the end of my stay in Tupik. For me those were five days of rest, but five days are not five years!

Now I am leaving Musya and going to Borya. The shortage
of tickets and hotel rooms makes the trip very tiring. But we'll
be able to rest in Eretz. I only hope to find Borya in as good
shape as Marik.

The 'five days of rest' to which Shcharansky referred were indeed
restful for him, as compared with the pressures of Moscow and the
KGB; but internal exile, however much one might try to re-create
for oneself as 'normal' a life as possible, was a harsh and cruel
punishment. It was made easier, for Nashpits, by a present which
Shcharansky brought him: language tapes to enable him to learn
Hebrew and English. Ten years later, shortly after being given his
exit visa, Nashpits's first words to me, when we met in London,
were (in Hebrew): 'Do you speak Hebrew?'

Returning to Moscow, on 11 November 1975, Shcharansky sent
a postcard to Enid and Stuart Wurtman, with his greetings, in
English, for the Chanukkah festival. The postcard reached them in
the ordinary mail. 'I have heard', he wrote, 'that you in the USA
have a good tradition of joyful celebration of these holy days. We
haven't such a one here (or at least we have lost it), but surely the
meaning of Chanukkah is very actual for us today.' Shcharansky
added that, some days earlier, 'I turned back from Siberia, where I
attended Mark and Boris,' and his card ended: 'Thanks to all our
friends for their support.'

Writing that same day to Connie and Joe Smukler, Shcharansky
noted: 'My wife Avital is supposed to be in the USA on Chanukkah. I hope you'll like her. I also hope that on the next of the
holidays Avital and I will be able to see you in *our* apartment in
Jerusalem.'

Wherever Shcharansky was, Eretz Yisroel, the Land of Israel,
was always near to him in imagination, and spirit.

On 15 November 1975 Alexander Silnitsky, the student from
Krasnodar, was sentenced to two years in labour camp on the
charge of 'evading conscription'. He had only become 'liable' for
military service by the device of having been expelled from the
Krasnodar Polytechnic Institute when his family applied to go to
Israel. Silnitsky was the third young Jew to be sentenced in 1975 by
this device. Ironically, his great-grandfather Moshe Salman had
made the journey from Russia to Palestine in 1882, where he
became one of the founders of the Jewish village of Petah Tikvah:
gateway of hope.

Chanukkah, the Jewish Festival of Lights celebrating the triumph of the Maccabees over the Syrians, began in 1975 on November 29. One of the Western visitors to Moscow that day, a lawyer from London, later recalled going that evening with his wife and two other friends to the apartment of Vladimir Slepak. 'The door was opened by this little fellow in a polo-necked sweater. We were disappointed not to find Slepak at home. The little fellow invited us in. Within a few moments we were entranced. He delighted us with his stories, told us about his wife in Israel, of his own awakening as a Jew, of how he was doing translations for Sakharov, of how useful his English was, of how hopeful he was as a result of Helsinki, of how optimistic he was of following Avital to Jerusalem.'

As Shcharansky was speaking to the visitors, with an optimism which other visitors also noticed when talking to him that winter, Slepak returned. 'Why don't you come to a Chanukkah party?' he asked. The English visitors, four in all, were delighted. 'We found lots of people gathered at the party,' the lawyer recalled a decade later. 'Sixty or seventy people were crowded into the room. Vitaly Rubin was there. Alexander Lerner had written a poem on the Maccabees. There was a piano at one end of the room. Lerner read out his poem in Russian. Shcharansky stood by us, the four of us, and translated. As the party continued, he looked after us, and introduced us. He was a great spark, so confident, so young – and yet he looked so full of years and experience.'

On 2 December 1975 Shcharansky wrote another letter to Avital, whose photograph a visitor had just brought to Moscow. His letter was a brave affirmation of his frustration, and of his faith:

> Everyone was delighted with your large photograph, but my mother took it to Istra and won't give it up. She says that it decorates the apartment; so please send another one. Although maybe you shouldn't send one. Oh, how it's time for me to be there already. It is no longer a question of hope or faith, but simply my way of life: waiting for a visa, not even a visa, but simply a chance to meet you. When I was with Marik in Tupik and then Borya in that disgusting Yeniseisk, I imagined very clearly how we could manage in either place if I were exiled and you could come to me there. How much fuller that life would be than life without you in Moscow. Did we make a mistake? No, no, no. Destiny is letting us understand who we are and why we were given to each other.

Two years had passed since Shcharansky's first refusal, four
months since he had taken over the task of translator and spokesman. His optimism and his confidence impressed themselves on
strangers, and on those in the refusenik movement, whose tasks
seemed at times endless and even futile. On 24 December 1975, the
fifth anniversary of the conclusion of the Leningrad Trials, the
Moscow activists declared a Day of Solidarity with Jewish
prisoners. Thirty Jews, all of them refuseniks, went to the Supreme
Soviet, intent on holding a silent demonstration. They were not
allowed anywhere near the building. For ten minutes the group
stood in silence, surrounded by an equal number of police.

Shcharansky was not among them. Together with Victor
Brailovsky, Mark Azbel, Yuly Kosharovsky and Alexander Lunts,
he had been arrested by KGB agents as he tried to set off for the
demonstration and placed under house arrest. On the following day
those who were not under house arrest went to the Central
Committee building in protest. Their protest coincided with a
series of police raids on the houses of four more activists, Ilya Essas,
Pavel Abramovich, Vladimir Prestin and Iosif Begun. From each
house, the police confiscated books and articles on Jewish themes,
including, from Abramovich's home, Cecil Roth's *History of the
Jews*, a hand-copied version of Masada by Flavius Josephus, and a
history book by Simon Dubnov. Many personal letters were also
taken away, never to be returned.

The response of the activists to such pressures was to redouble
their own efforts. They were also determined not to allow violent
actions on their behalf, and protested vehemently, on 13 January
1976, against a Jewish extremist group which had placed a bomb at
the United Nations headquarters in New York. The extremists
claimed that they were acting on behalf of Soviet Jewry. 'We hereby
most vigorously condemn the attempted terroristic act,' the message began, and it went on to declare: 'the use of terroristic means in
a political struggle is morally contemptible. The use of such
methods is degrading oneself to the level of the terrorists who are
participating now in the meetings of the Security Council. We
believe that similar actions will only harm the cause of the Jewish
people in their homeland and Jews everywhere else.' Such acts of
violence were also harmful, the ten signatories warned, 'to the Jews
of the Soviet Union where they are using every chance to increase
oppression and anti-Semitic propaganda'.

This protest against the New York bomb was signed by Vitaly

Rubin, Alexander Lunts, Anatoly Shcharansky, Vladimir Slepak, Alexander Lerner, Dina and Iosif Beilin, Iosif Begun and Vladimir Shakhnovsky.

By the first weeks of 1976, it had become clear that the emigration figures for 1975 had seen a substantial decrease on those of the previous year: 13,363 as compared with 20,767 in 1974 and 34,733 in the peak year, 1973. On 21 January 1976, however, Alexander Lunts learned that he was to be given an exit visa. It was a moment of great joy not only for him, but for all his friends, none more so than Shcharansky. That day, Lunts signed one more appeal, addressed to the heads of the Italian and French Communist Parties. The four other signatories were Rubin, Lerner, Shcharansky and Slepak. All asked for the Western Communists to meet with refuseniks at the forthcoming 25th Communist Party Congress in Moscow. Human rights were again stressed: the five signatories, the appeal explained, 'have shown an interest in human rights in the USSR and in the fulfilment of the Helsinki Agreement.'

Concern for human rights did not interfere with Lunts's receiving permission to leave four weeks later – nor, in his turn, with Rubin's.

Throughout 1976, although weakened in some ways by the exit visas granted to some of the leaders – such as Lunts in January and Rubin in June – the band of brothers who constituted the leadership of the Jewish activists were more active than ever before: spurred into their activity by the plight of the long-term prisoners, by the fate of the eight new prisoners of 1975 – Nashpits, Tsitlionok, Levinson, Silnitsky, Roitburd, Malkin, Vinarov and Nisanova – by a growing anti-Semitic and anti-Zionist campaign in the Soviet press, and by the increased harassment of their own activities and attempts to isolate them from the rest of Soviet Jewry.

On 2 February 1976 a nine-page closely typed survey of these pressures was read over the telephone to Michael Sherbourne, to be translated by him and widely publicised in the West. It had eight signatures: eight people who had long been committed to publicity for the refusenik cause – Dina Beilina, Vladimir Slepak, Ida Nudel, Vitaly Rubin, Alexander Lunts (who left for Israel three days later), Eitan Finkelstein, Alexander Lerner and Anatoly Shcharansky.

The survey of 2 February 1976 was the third comprehensive account of the refusenik plight to have reached the West in fifteen months: like its predecessors of November 1974 and June 1975, it gave details of what it called the 'baseless refusals', pointing out at the same time the 'sharp increase' in such refusals. The survey also stressed that throughout the Soviet Union there was a 'widespread propaganda campaign' in the press accompanied by numerous threats against Jewish activists, and 'persecution even of the most modest initiatives of Jews directed towards a rebirth of Jewish national consciousness'.

This third survey, like its predecessors, gave considerable information about the most recent prisoners, including Yakov Vinarov, sentenced in August 1975 to three years in labour camp, Alexander Silnitsky, sentenced in December to two years, and Lidia Nisanova, a 'semi-literate' working woman with an eight-year-old daughter, sentenced to a year and a half in labour camp on 16 January 1976, six months after she had applied to go to Israel. There were details, too, of the harsh conditions inside prison and labour camp; and of discrimination against the Prisoners of Zion: Lev Roitburd had been deprived both of the right to buy food in the camp shop and of the right to receive a personal visit from his wife; three of the Leningrad Trial prisoners, Iosif Mendelevich, Vulf Zalmanson and Mark Dymshits, had throughout the second half of 1975 been denied their rights to receive parcels and visitors.

The survey of 2 February 1976 also gave many examples of harassment, the 'latest item' being the removal of Lev Ovsishcher from the train on which he was trying to go from Minsk to Moscow on 29 January 1976. To the long list of telephones cut 'because of conversations abroad' could be added 'the telephone of Mark Nashpits, in exile in the village of Tupik (Dead end!) 6500 kilometres from Moscow'. Nashpits, the survey noted, 'used to speak on this telephone to his relatives and friends in Moscow', and it remarked with wry humour: 'This must be the most easterly telephone cut in the USSR.'

Ten days after this third survey was telephoned to the West, Shcharansky was also a signatory of a message of gratitude to the United States Congress 'for the linkage of trade and emigration': a linkage, the message stated, responsible for the emigration 'of tens of thousands of Jews from the Soviet Union'. The message went on to stress that a 'further improvement' in the situation could only come about by 'specific' United States action and urged the need for continuing and strengthening the struggle for 'the right of free emigration'.

Fifty-seven Soviet Jews signed this message, including Lerner, Rubin, Slepak, Shcharansky, the Beilins, Azbel and Brailovsky. It was also signed by Ida Nudel, whose special concern had become the plight of the Prisoners of Zion; Lev Ulanovsky, who had become Shcharansky's helper in the matter of foreign press contacts; and Sanya Lipavsky, a newcomer to such public statements, and the man who, a year later, was publicly to accuse Rubin, Slepak, Lerner and Shcharansky of espionage.

The signatories of the message of 12 February 1976 spanned every branch of the refusal movement: religious leaders like Ilya Essas, Hebrew teachers like Yuly Kosharovsky and Iosif Begun, the two demoted Colonels from Minsk, Ovsishcher and Davidovich, and the Goldstein brothers from Tbilisi who, in refusal for more than four years, had become the targets of considerable local harassment.

The pace of protest and communication to the West had reached an apogee. On 16 February 1976, four days after this message signed by fifty-seven Jews had been telephoned to the West, more than seventy Jews went to the Central Committee building in protest against the ever growing number of refusals. 'We were ready to be arrested,' Ina Rubin remembered. 'We asked a lot of Western journalists to come, just for publicity.' To the surprise of the protesters, instead of being dispersed or arrested, they were asked by an official to choose six of their number to speak to the Deputy Head of the Communist Party Administration Section, Albert Ivanov, and the Director-General of the Visa Office, V. S. Obidin.

This was the first time in five years that any Soviet officials had agreed to see a group of activists. The six who were chosen to represent the seventy were Vladimir Slepak, Vitaly Rubin, Mark Azbel, Victor Brailovsky, Yuly Kosharovsky and Shcharansky. Entering the Central Committee building, they found themselves face to face with the very men who had the power to imprison them or let them leave the Soviet Union.

According to a transcript of the meeting which reached the West four months later, Ivanov began the discussion by insisting 'that 98.4 per cent of all Jews wishing to leave had already done so'. Regarding the remainder, 'refusals were issued mainly for regime considerations (secret information) or the material claims of parents or former wives demanding the payment of alimony'. An applicant, noted Slepak, 'is told about his refusal *after* the organisation has decided on his degree of secrecy, so why cannot he be told the degree and length of term of his refusal?' To this, Ivanov replied:

'No. The terms of "secrecy" will themselves remain secret. Things that were not secret yesterday might become secret today, and vice versa.' Were there 'any instructions, regulations, legal documents', asked Kosharovsky, 'anything at all laying down the terms of refusal of emigration permits for these reasons of secrecy?', to which Ivanov replied: 'There are no such instructions; nor will there be. Decisions are made individually.'

Turning to the reason of 'parental opposition' which was sometimes given for a refusal, Shcharansky asked if the Visa Office authorities would accept 'certified documents in cases where parents have had no contact with their children for some time and have no material claims on them?' To this Obidin answered in one word: 'No.'

The following altercation then occurred:

Shcharansky: Prior to this meeting we asked five hundred refusenik families the official reason for their refusals and more than half of them said the refusals were for reasons other than those named by you. Many received refusals because of past Army service. . . .

Ivanov: . . . the same as secrecy.

Shcharansky: Is it? For example, Zakhar Tesker of Moscow served in the army eight years ago, as a footballer. Some people have been refused because of the so-called security situation of relatives who do not intend to leave the USSR; more than twenty families of Jews from Derbent, with only primary education, have been refused because of 'inexpediency'. Matus Rabinovich from Krasnoyarsk, who has a daughter in Israel, was refused because he was told 'There is no "reunification of family" in your case.'

Ivanov (to Obidin): Do you know this case?

Obidin: Yes. Rabinovich has two daughters here and only one in Israel. The logical thing would be for her to return to the USSR and not vice versa.

Ivanov: Yes, of course.

Shcharansky pressed Obidin and Ivanov on the issue of the reasons for refusal; it was a subject on which he had made a considerable study. 'In many cases,' he told them, 'no reason at all was given for a refusal. One may assume that such strange refusals arise from the negligence or arbitrariness of local officials, but doesn't this show the need for an emigration law that would regulate the practice in such a way that arbitrary refusals wouldn't be possible?' To this Ivanov replied: 'I have explained already that every case is examined individually in accordance with the interests of the State. Truth is always concrete. It is impossible to draw up a law or an instruction on all the cases in life.'

The six Jews raised with Obidin and Ivanov the question of reunification of families, according to the Helsinki Accords, giving specific examples of refuseniks whose parents or children were already in Israel. They were told that all the cases which they had raised would be reviewed in six months' time.

Ivanov had given 'particularly harsh answers', Vitaly Rubin wrote in his diary, 'about the expulsion of students who have expressed their desire to emigrate to Israel from higher educational establishments, and their subsequent call-up for military service'. He had declared 'that once these young people had stated their wish to emigrate they lost their right to higher education, but their duty to serve in the army remained'. This approach, Rubin reflected, was 'completely contrary to the obligations undertaken by the Soviet side in Helsinki not to change the civil status of people who apply to emigrate'. The obligation was 'equally contradicted by Ivanov's declaration that the sacking of people who have requested to emigrate can be justified'. In essence, Rubin added, 'Ivanov's position was that people who want to emigrate must be stripped of their rights but that their duties remained.'

'I do not think that it was (or, more exact, can become) very useful,' Shcharansky wrote some weeks later, in English, of this meeting. 'Surely they spoke with us only because of their Congress,' he added, in a reference to the forthcoming Communist Party Congress, 'but we are not going to forget about our agreement to continue these discussions in a month, after they re-examine the cases of the refuseniks.'

As Shcharansky saw it, three main problems had been raised in the talks. These, he wrote, were:

(1) the absence of the emigrational law;
(2) the absence of the opportunity for the applicant to take part in the procedure of studying his case;
(3) the changing of the status of the applicant (such as losing his right for education with the simultaneous usage of his obligations to serve in the army as the punishment).

'I think it will be good', Shcharansky added, 'if these points will be mentioned to the Soviets on different levels as often as possible.

It can make the pressure more constructively.'

Despite the fact that they had been received and talked to, the group was not impressed; they knew that on the following day, when news of their meeting would have reached the West, the Second World Conference on Soviet Jewry would open in Brussels, where Soviet policy towards the Jews would be scrutinised and debated by 1200 delegates. During the conference the former Israeli Prime Minister, Golda Meir, herself born a subject of the Russian Tsar, declared amid stormy applause: 'I guarantee the rulers of Moscow, the Jews in the Soviet Union will be free!'

The Brussels Conference had before it a message signed by more than a hundred Soviet Jews, among them Ida Nudel, Victor Brailovsky, Vladimir Prestin, Vladimir Slepak and, from Leningrad, Aba Taratuta. Shcharansky, too, had signed. The Jews, they wrote, constituted a people 'with a single destiny and a single fate', existing as a people 'only as long as we choose to be one'. Each day, they declared, 'we re-create ourselves as a nation, because each day we make the decision to be one people and to remain Jews.' Each generation was confronted with the necessity of making that choice. 'It was this choice that formed the Jewish national character; it was this choice that preserved our people throughout the centuries.' Today the 'silent' generation of Soviet Jews had also to make that choice. 'On each individual Soviet Jew', the signatories wrote, 'will depend whether World Jewry tomorrow will number fifteen million persons or whether it will lose another two and a half million of its compatriots.' Today, the signatories avowed, there were 'not scores but hundreds of thousands' of Soviet Jews 'prepared to make the great choice: the choice between gradual disappearance into an alien culture, or national revival'.

The difficulties to be encountered once that choice was made were the subject of a remarkable letter sent from Moscow shortly after the Brussels Conference, and translated by Michael Sherbourne on 1 March 1976. Entitled 'The Labyrinth', it explained just how complicated a process it was to apply for an exit visa. Of the six compilers, Slepak, Lerner, Dina Beilina, Shcharansky, Edward Trifonov and Vitaly Rubin, three were themselves later to receive their exit visas by the arduous process which they described. Eight distinct phases were outlined:

(a) an invitation from relatives in Israel
(b) a declaration of your wish to leave

(c) a 'kharakteristika' (character reference) from your place of
     work
(d) permission from the parents of an applicant
(e) permission from a former wife or husband
(f) a certificate from your place of residence
(g) copies of certificates of birth, marriage, divorce, death of
     relatives, and educational diplomas
(h) a biography

The six activists then explained how difficult each of these stages
could be: time consuming, complicated, expensive and capable of
being negated on the mere whim of an institute head or a Visa Office
official. In answer to one applicant, they reported, an institute head
in Kiev, in refusing to give his required permission to an employee,
declared: 'I shall make you and your whole family rot here.'

Once a Jew was in refusal, the six activists explained, a series of
'repressions' could then descend upon him once he tried to 'struggle
against' his refusal. These 'repressions' included:

– phones disconnected during attempts to speak with relatives
   and friends abroad;
– correspondence detained and controlled;
– dismissal from work and expulsion from universities;
– persons followed and forbidden free movement within the
   country, such as trips to Moscow for applicants or trips to the
   provinces to find out the situation in small towns. In such
   cases people are often taken from the train;
– conscription or call-up for additional training. Here, the term
   of refusal increases because of 'secrecy';
– individuals interrogated for studying Hebrew, which is officially forbidden, and questioned and threatened with trial in
   connection with the publication of a journal in Russian on
   Jewish culture and traditions;
– people kept under house arrest or jailed during the visits of
   famous politicians to bar meetings;
– people dressed in civilian clothes beating Jews. The attackers
   are very well informed about their victims;
– children persecuted in school;
– court cases and repressions threatened and occasionally carried out. Lidia Nisanova of Derbent was warned that if she
   did not take back her documents from the Visa Office she
   would be arrested. On the basis of a completely fabricated
   case she was sentenced to one and a half years in labour camp.

'Unfortunately,' the authors of the document added, 'there are
many similar cases.'

While Shcharansky and the group around him struggled on
behalf of those who sought their exit visas, they and their friends
were fighting an equally determined battle to halt the growing
persecution of those connected with the privately circulated Jewish
cultural magazine, *Jews in the USSR*. On 12 March 1976 an appeal
on behalf of Jewish cultural life inside Russia was sent to the 25th
Party Congress by more than fifty activists, including Leonid
Volvovsky (a Hebrew teacher who in October 1985 was sentenced
to three years in labour camp), Benjamin Fain (who was shortly to
receive his exit visa), Ilya Essas (whose parents had just received an
exit visa, but who was not allowed to follow them for another nine
years), and three long-term refuseniks (who in 1986 were still in the
Soviet Union after fifteen years in refusal), Pavel Abramovich,
Yuly Kosharovsky and Vladimir Prestin. 'The Hebrew language',
they protested, 'has found itself under a secret ban.'

The Jews who studied Hebrew in the Soviet Union did so in
order to speak it not in the streets of Moscow, but in the streets of
Jerusalem. Each one of the signatories of this 'cultural' appeal was a
refusenik; each had sacrificed his career and comfort to try to go to
Israel. Beween them, and activists like Shcharansky, there was a
bond of common concern – the prisoners – and a common goal –
Israel. Shcharansky, as Avital later commented, 'would have liked
very much to sit and study, but he had to "run around" for
everybody'.

Among those whom Shcharansky met in Moscow in 1976 were
several leading American journalists, including David Shipler of
the *New York Times*, Peter Osnos of the *Washington Post*, Robert
Toth of the *Los Angeles Times* and Alfred Friendly of *Newsweek*.
Shcharansky and his friends spoke openly with the journalists and
met them without any attempt at subterfuge. On one occasion
Shcharansky and his friends met two American diplomats in
Moscow, Melvin Levitsky and Joseph Pressel. This meeting, like
those with the journalists, took place openly; it was indeed held in a
café on one of Moscow's busiest streets, without any attempt at
concealment. Nor, as was later to be alleged in court, was either
diplomat an agent of the Central Intelligence Agency: a decade
later, Levitsky was the United States Ambassador to Bulgaria.

★   ★   ★

On 10 March 1976 Michael Sherbourne reported again on a series of telephone conversations with Moscow and other Soviet cities, during which he had been given details of the conditions of certain prisoners, and of the cases of divided families and particular hardship. He also reported Slepak as saying that 'the "wave of emigration permits" was over, and that now things are tightening up again'.

Shcharansky was again in evidence by name in an open address to the 25th Congress of the Communist Party, setting out refusenik grievances about the 'arbitrary' refusals, and protesting against the long prison sentences: the other signatories included Fain, Abramovich, Prestin, Rubin and Kandel. The principal theme of their protest was to challenge the Soviet concept of 'secrecy' in the reiterated refusals, and to request a 'real' concept of secrecy such as would be 'accepted in the European countries'. There were 210 Jews refused permission for reasons of 'State security or secrecy', they pointed out. Most of those had either never had access to secret documents, as in the case of Felix Kandel, or their security clearance had ended eight or nine years earlier. A further 160 were refused because of service in the Soviet army: one of them, Lev Ovsishcher, had, they pointed out, been demobilised in 1961.

On 15 March 1976 the six Jewish activists who had been admitted to the Central Committee building in February received the reply to their requests. Not one of the eight cases which they had raised in connection with the 'divided families' pledge of the Helsinki Accords was to be allowed to leave. Among those refused were Lerner, Shcharansky, Rubin and Ulanovsky. 'It is a question of prestige,' Rubin remarked bitterly to a journalist from Philadelphia. 'The Soviet Government says nobody wants to leave because this is the happiest place in the world.'

By a bitter coincidence, eight days after this negative reply the Helsinki Final Act formally came into effect. From 23 March 1976 its terms were binding upon all its signatories. For the refuseniks, this last stage of the coming into force of the Final Act led to a renewed upsurge of protest. On March 30, Professor Lerner issued an open appeal stressing the 'absurdity' of the secrecy argument in his case.

On 23 March 1976, the day of the coming into force of the Helsinki Final Act, Millicent Fenwick had reintroduced to Congress her Bill 'to establish a commission to monitor compliance with the Helsinki Accords', telling the House of Representatives:

'No nation can now say that these considerations are internal affairs, out of bounds for the concern or comment of other nations. For the thirty-five nations which signed, they are matters of international agreement. The accords were signed and they must be honored. Detente must not be bought at the expense of such suffering and injustice.'

*   *   *

There were many refuseniks who had felt that once Alexander Lunts had received his exit visa, Shcharansky would receive one also. It was the time, as Shcharansky wrote to Irene Manekofsky, of 'our wonderful spring holidays' Purim and Passover. 'I've become much more impatient after Sasha's departure,' he added, 'and dream to celebrate at least one of these holidays with Avital.'

*   *   *

As a resident of Istra, his parents' village, Shcharansky could stay in Moscow only with friends, not in an apartment of his own. Following Alexander Lunts's departure, he needed somewhere new in which to sleep. One friend who gave him a space on the floor of the apartment in which she lodged was Lidia Voronina, a non-Jewish woman whose husband, Anatoly Reznik, one of Shcharansky's best friends, a Jew and a fellow mathematics student, had been given three days to leave the Soviet Union on the eve of the second Nixon visit. Lidia had been refused permission to join him, on the ground that she did not have her mother's permission to leave. Her mother, a life-long Communist, was a senior official at the Soviet Ministry of Justice.

Subsequently, despite her mother's high official status, Lidia Voronina joined in many of the refusenik appeals. Totally estranged from her parents, she was twice taken ill and had to go to hospital. Shcharansky took her food, gave her encouragement and, alarmed at her worsening condition, brought to her bedside Dr Sanya Lipavsky, who found that Lidia had been taking the wrong medicine.

As a result of Lipavsky's help, Lidia Voronina recovered, and Shcharansky continued to sleep on a mattress on the floor of her room. In the daytime, in order not to endanger her further, he used Slepak's apartment as his base: it was when calling on Slepak that most Western visitors first met him. On 29 March 1976 Lidia Voronina signed her first public protest: a letter signed by 113

Soviet Jews from fifteen cities, urging all 'people of goodwill' to help obtain an exit visa for Yefim Davidovich. The former Colonel had suffered three heart attacks, and yet was continuously being pilloried in the local press, interrogated and threatened with arrest. In January 1976 he had been accused by the Soviet news agency Tass of intending to 'renounce his Fatherland'. Davidovich had replied that 'he will not renounce his Fatherland, Israel, under duress; as to the other Fatherland, it has renounced itself.'

The appeal of the 113 Jews was outspoken. 'The actions against Davidovich', it declared, 'are premeditated and systematically attempted murder.' The 'energy and persistence' of the outside world would determine 'if Davidovich will see the land of his dreams'.

Among the signatories of this letter were Vitaly Rubin, Vladimir Slepak, Alexander Lerner, Dina and Iosif Beilin, Benjamin Fain, Lev Ulanovsky, Victor Brailovsky, Mark Azbel, Ida Nudel and Shcharansky, as well as Lev Ovsishcher from Minsk. Also signing were three other refuseniks, Eitan Finkelstein from Vilnius and the Goldstein brothers from Tbilisi, who were in their sixth year as refuseniks.

*   *   *

On 15 April 1976 a British television camera team, in Moscow to make a film about the refuseniks, was present in Professor Lerner's apartment to film the Passover celebration. More than sixty Jews had gathered for this Jewish 'Festival of Freedom', among them Masha and Vladimir Slepak, Dina and Iosif Beilin, and Shcharansky. The reading of the Haggadah, recounting the biblical story of the Exodus from Egypt, was done by Rabbi Joseph Ehrenkranz from Connecticut. As Ehrenkranz explained each passage in Hebrew, English and Yiddish, Professor Lerner translated it into Russian. 'This four-divisible, four-language repetition of the flaming words of the Haggadah', Dina Beilina wrote to a friend in the West, 'produced a tremendous impression.'

Laughter, enthusiasm, warmth and hope was the mood which the cameraman caught on film, as Lerner and his guests joined in the final prayer of the evening: 'Next Year in Jerusalem.'

Four days later, on 19 April 1976, Shcharansky was at Slepak's apartment when he was introduced to Nora Levin, Professor of Jewish History at Gratz College, Philadelphia, whose book *The Holocaust: The Destruction of European Jewry, 1933–1945*, had been

published in 1968. Nora Levin had brought to Moscow a taped
message from Avital. 'He was overjoyed to have it,' she remembered. 'He was ecstatic.'

Nora Levin also remembered how, during her visit, Slepak,
Shcharansky and the Beilins were very concerned about the 'alarm-
ing condition' of the Jewish prisoner, Alexander Feldman, who was
serving a three-and-a-half-year prison sentence in Kiev. 'He had
been attacked and bludgeoned with a shovel, and taken to hospital,
but no one knew his true condition.' Shcharansky urged pressure
on behalf of Feldman from the International Red Cross, and from
Amnesty International.

Nora Levin was also told about the 'sad situation' of Lidia
Nisanova, from Derbent, Georgia. 'Arrested and tried, accused of
"economic crimes", imprisoned for a year and a half in camp in the
northern Caucasus,' Nora Levin recounted, 'Lidia had come to
Moscow, made contact with some refuseniks, and on her return to
Derbent was arrested.' Her case seemed to Shcharansky to suggest
that the authorities wished, as Nora Levin wrote, 'to isolate
refuseniks from other Jews, and to isolate some refuseniks from
other refuseniks'.

On the following day, 20 April 1976, Nora Levin met
Shcharansky again. On their way to Vitaly Rubin's apartment, he
expressed his interest in a recently published book on the question
of Jewish political leverage in the United States, 'which he thought
must be vast', Nora Levin recalled, 'and which I explained was
vastly exaggerated'.

At Vitaly Rubin's apartment, Nora Levin learned that there were
some forty Jewish Prisoners of Conscience of whom the refuseniks
were aware. There may have been many more, she was told. One
serious problem, Shcharansky told her, was the Jews in small towns
'who are cut off and have few contacts'.

Nora Levin was never to forget her two conversations with
'Natan', as he called himself. A decade later, she wrote of how
'Natan was exceptionally exuberant, talkative and outgoing. He
seemed competent, fearless, and somehow invulnerable.'

Four days later, on 24 April 1976, Colonel Yefim Davidovich
died in Minsk. That same day, Shcharansky was among eighty-two
refuseniks who, in a public protest, declared that Davidovich had
been 'killed'; killed because he was a Jew and 'killed', they
explained, 'by the organs of the KGB'.

'Of course,' Dina Beilina later commented, 'the KGB did not kill

Davidovich directly; they killed him through persecution, rumours, interrogations, and threats of arrest. Even after his third heart attack they continued to interrogate him, and to make it clear that they would organise – even that they were actually organising – a false case against him. That is what we meant', Dina Beilina added, 'when we declared that he had been "killed" by the KGB.'

In their letter of 24 April 1976 the eighty-two signatories then addressed themselves to 'you noble-minded gentlemen in the West', as they called them, and went on to declare: 'Here it is, your reality, here it is, the spirit of Helsinki. Who will be the next victim? If the hangmen are not stopped today, then tomorrow many people won't be able to escape from their clutches.'

Among those who signed this protest were Davidovich's friend and fellow Colonel, Lev Ovsishcher, Victor Brailovsky, Vladimir Prestin and Ilya Essas, Academician Sakharov and his wife Elena Bonner. At Davidovich's funeral, four more of the signatories, Iosif Beilin, Eitan Finkelstein, Vitaly Rubin and Vladimir Slepak, together with Shcharansky, were the pall bearers. Each wore a blue-and-white sash, the Jewish national colours. The KGB was present, but took no action. Soon afterwards, Davidovich's widow and daughter received their exit visa. They were also given permission to take his body with them, and he was reburied on the Mount of Olives in Jerusalem.

★   ★   ★

From his new life in Israel, Alexander Lunts was active in trying to help the friends he had left behind. In a letter to Congressman Eilberg on 27 April 1976, he urged the Congressman to apply 'special methods of pressure' on the Soviet Union on behalf of Lerner, Slepak, Shcharansky and Ida Nudel, as well as three prisoners, Malkin, Nashpits and Alexander Sokiriansky, who was five years into an eight-year sentence. Of Shcharansky, Lunts wrote: 'the only possible reason for refusal was that his studies included a course in military science. Another student who took the same course at the same time was Lev Kogan. He applied after Shcharansky and yet has already received his permission and is now in Israel.'

The day of Lunts's letter was the day of Ida Nudel's forty-sixth birthday. Hundreds of telegrams were sent to her from the West. Not one of them arrived.

★   ★   ★

Shcharansky was now well known, respected and loved in the refusenik community. One of those who later recalled him was Robert Toth, Moscow correspondent of the *Los Angeles Times*, who described him as 'balding, short and stout, warm and brilliant'. Shcharansky said to him 'with typical assertiveness, but with a smile', Toth wrote, ' "If you are going to use my name, spell it correctly, S-h-c-h, not S-h, as you have it." ' Shcharansky laughed and added, 'It won't ever become a household name.'

Shcharansky's small stature was often a subject of humour. When Michael Sherbourne told him once over the telephone that someone had called him the Napoleon of the refusenik movement, he answered in a flash: 'Why? Because I am nearly bald? Or because I am so small?'

Shcharansky's wit, his optimism and his selflessness impressed themselves on all who knew him. During his first years in prison, one of his closest friends, the poet Felix Kandel, set down his recollections of those days in 1975 and 1976 when the two men had been so often together. Kandel, writing in Jerusalem, recalled:

> Here he is in front of us:
> Short, bald from his youth, with large forehead and plump lips, with white teeth and merry eyes.
> Short and bald from his youth – who'd be happy at this? He was. Who would have no complexes because of this? He had none. And people, surrounding him, felt the same way, too. He managed to win the heart of a beauty not without reason!
> Here he is in front of us: kind and gentle, calm and sensible, efficient and obliging.
> Tenacious mind, catching the meaning at once.
> Chess-player, counting many moves beforehand in his personal matters, work, life.
> Money is nothing to him, he needs nothing. 'I have one sweater already, what for the second one? One cannot put on two sweaters at once.'
> Clumsy in everyday life: breaking everything, spilling everything, overturning and losing everything. But not in his activities. Not in his work.
> Sweet-tooth.
> Clever, sensible, deprived of any aggression, Anatoly never acted under the influence of an impulse, or under the pressure of

someone's authority. He was always seeking to examine the situation and to make his own judgement. But as soon as he had come to some conclusion, he rejected the indifference and fear and was acting according to his conscience.

Here he is in front of us:

'I am hungry. Give me something to eat.'

Without impudence or ceremony, he came to his people, his friends. He ate – and hurried off, as urgent matters called him.

I wish God help you to have such a house, where one could knock without ceremony, at an inopportune time:

'I am hungry. Give me something to eat.'

I wish God help you to have such friends, who could knock at your door.

The Jew, who was anxious about Jews.

The Jew, who was anxious about non-Jews.

'When people are suffering, one must help them, without asking of their nationality.'

'It is in our traditions. In our blood.'

Here he is in front of us: an optimist, full of life, smiling from ear to ear.

Sure of himself and of other people. Concentrated on the hopes, not on the fear.

Reflecting on Shcharansky's optimism, Felix Kandel added that his friend had always considered 'the bad forecasts as temporary ones, the good forecasts – as eternal'.

12

Dangerous Times

On Sunday, 2 May 1976, the Jews of Moscow celebrated the twenty-eighth anniversary of Israel's independence. More than a hundred Jews, many of them with their children, went to a wood near Moscow; Shcharansky was among them. 'We read the declaration of Israel's Independence,' Dina Beilina wrote to a friend in the West, 'and sang "Hatikva", the Jewish anthem. Then we ate and drank, sang Hebrew songs, played football. It was a beautiful day.' That same day, the largest number of signatures on any message from Soviet Jews was sent by telephone to the New York Day of Solidarity with Soviet Jewry: 119 refuseniks signed, headed by Rubin, Brailovsky, Lerner, Azbel and Shcharansky, and including Slepak, the Beilins, Iosif Begun, Lidia Voronina and Leonid Volvovsky. Benjamin Bogomolny also signed. It was he whom the *Guinness Book of Records* described in 1985 as 'the most patient refusenik'; he had first been refused his exit visa in 1966.

The message of 2 May 1976 was one of thanks to the Jews of New York for helping to link Soviet–American trade to 'freedom of emigration'. As a result of this link, the signatories wrote, 'more than 120,000 people acquired their freedom.' The letter went on to warn, however, that conditions for the Jewish prisoners were calculated 'to destroy body and soul'. Refusals on the grounds of secrecy, the message urged, were a 'pretext'. Military service was being used as a 'tragic alternative'. The anti-Semitic campaign was gathering strength throughout the Soviet Union, reinforced by the 'absurd' United Nations vote in November 1975 equating Zionism with racism. The number of refuseniks was growing. The fate of individuals was being decided 'in an atmosphere of secret trials'.

'There are no human rights,' the message added, 'and there is no justice, as there was none in Pharaoh's reply to Moses: "I know not

your God and I will not let Israel go" (Exodus 5:2). The clauses of
the Final Act of the Helsinki Agreement have turned out to be but
empty words.'

The Helsinki Agreement was being ignored. In Washington, a
Bill was about to be presented in the Senate, introduced by Senator
Case, to establish a special commission to monitor the carrying out
of Helsinki. A similar Bill was before the House of Representatives,
as a result of the efforts of Millicent Fenwick, the Republican
Congresswoman from New Jersey who had visited the refuseniks
in Moscow the previous August. Among the outside organisations
pressing for such a commission were two which had mobilised
support throughout the United States: the National Conference on
Soviet Jewry, which helped formulate the monitor concept and
which on 4 May 1976 presented testimony at the hearings held on
Millicent Fenwick's Bill; and the Union of Councils for Soviet
Jews.

In the wake of the signing of the Helsinki Accords, Soviet Jews
experienced increased harassment: the invention of new accusations
of parasitism, dismissal from institutes of higher learning followed
by conscription into the Red Army, a fresh wave of refusals, and the
creation of yet more Prisoners of Zion. Given the previous lack of
legal basis with which to defend refuseniks and Prisoners of Zion,
Shcharansky now initiated the formation of a Moscow Public
Action group, also known as the Helsinki Watchdog group, to
'promote observance of the Helsinki Agreement'.

The Helsinki Agreement, with its preamble establishing the right
of the individual to leave his country at will, and its 'Basket Three'
stressing the right of divided families to be united, was, and remains
to this day, a central guarantee of the very rights and freedoms
sought by so many Soviet Jews. The Helsinki Watchdog group was
established on 12 May 1976. Its founders were honest and idealistic
Soviet citizens, headed by Yury Orlov, a leading non-Jewish
campaigner for human rights. Another of the non-Jews in the
original group was Ludmila Alexeeva, who was subsequently
allowed to leave the Soviet Union. Another human rights activist in
the group, Alexander Ginsburg, a baptised and devout Christian,
was Jewish on his mother's side, but had taken no part in the Jewish
emigration movement. Alongside the non-Jews were two Jewish
emigration activists, Shcharansky and Rubin.

Together, the members of the Helsinki Watchdog group worked
openly, and within the bounds of Soviet legislation, to further

human rights in the Soviet Union. Their aim was to bring to the
attention of the Soviet Government the wide gap between the
international agreement that the Soviet Union had so proudly
signed in Helsinki and the daily violations that were taking place.
To this end they gathered information of such violations and
forwarded lists of the glaring contraventions to the various relevant
governmental bodies inside the Soviet Union. When, as happened
in every instance, their submissions were met with silence, they
then openly disseminated this information to the thirty-five
countries which were co-signatories with the Soviet Union of the
Helsinki Accords.

Vitaly Rubin, who was present at the first meeting of the
Moscow group, noted in his diary on the following day: 'Yesterday
many people were present. First – a press conference. Yury Orlov
was half an hour late and an American press correspondent said: "If
Orlov is arrested it will be sensation No. 1." Shortly afterwards
Orlov appeared, and Tolya said: "The sensation did not take
place."'

In Jerusalem, Avital and her brother Michael followed with
concern each development in the refusenik situation. Shcharansky's
predecessor as spokesman, Alex Goldfarb, was worried about
Avital, and urged Enid Wurtman, whose husband was President of
the Union of Councils for Soviet Jews, to visit her in Israel. Enid
did so, felt an immediate bond of sympathy with her, and began to
gather support for Shcharansky in the United States. She was also
determined to visit Moscow once more, in order to bring
Shcharansky a personal report of Avital's life, and her hopes of a
speedy reunion.

★   ★   ★

In its May 1976 issue, the Soviet Yiddish-language magazine,
Sovietische Heimland, often an indicator of Soviet official policy
towards the Jews, published an article attacking the Jewish emigration movement, and mentioning specifically Lerner, Lunts, Slepak,
Finkelstein and Shcharansky. On May 31 the 100th session of the
refusenik scientific seminar took place in Professor Lerner's apartment. That same day, at the specific request of ten refuseniks, a
world-wide petition campaign on behalf of the refuseniks was
launched by the National Conference on Soviet Jewry in the United
States, which asked for the inclusion of 'native American minority
groups' and Church leaders among the signatories. Ten refuseniks

asked that their names be used in support of this petition: Dina Beilina, Slepak, Lerner, Rubin, Ovsishcher, Shcharansky, Isai Goldstein from Tbilisi, Ida Nudel, Vladimir Shakhnovsky and Eitan Finkelstein.

There was one group on whose behalf Shcharansky made particular efforts: more than a hundred families in the remote Russian village of Ilyinka who, early in the nineteenth century, had been converted to Judaism. Originally there had been three 'Jewish' villages; two had assimilated completely and the third, Ilyinka, was under official pressure to give up its Judaism. Several Ilyinka Jews had applied to go to Israel; one of them, Shmuel Matveev, had been imprisoned for a month during Passover 1975.

Shcharansky met several Ilyinka Jews at the Moscow synagogue. From them he learned that the local collective farm Chairman, V. Tarasov, was keeping back in his office 120 undelivered invitations. When asked about this by Matveev, Tarasov replied: 'We don't want you to go to the Zionists. We hate you.'

In June 1976 Shcharansky, Slepak and Dr Sanya Lipavsky set off from Moscow for Ilyinka to make contact with the Jews there, and to find out more about their struggle to emigrate. When they were within two miles of the village, the three men were arrested, searched, interrogated for two days, and then thrown out of the area. Shortly after their visit, the local newspaper asked of Shmuel Matveev: 'Who wants this man to leave Russia? Only the Zionists from Tel Aviv and the United States.'

Shcharansky and his friends had managed to find out that there were at least sixty refusenik families in Ilyinka: half the Jewish population. This fact was set out in a Helsinki Watchdog group report, sent to the Moscow authorities. When no reply was received, the report was sent to the West. A year later, the story of the Ilyinka Jews was published in the United States by Robert Toth, the Moscow correspondent of the Los Angeles Times.

The American journalists in Moscow frequently publicised the reports of the Helsinki Watchdog group. In the course of 1976, sixteen reports were prepared, and sent openly to the West. A further five were issued in the first six weeks of 1977. No member of the group made any attempt at concealment. Each report was signed by all those involved in preparing it, or willing to take responsibility for it. Shcharansky's name was on all twenty-one reports.

These Helsinki Watchdog group reports covered every aspect of human rights in the Soviet Union. One of them, entitled 'On the conditions of Prisoners of Conscience in custody' and dated 17 June 1976, stated that Prisoners of Conscience were exposed to 'physical and moral torments, genuine torture by means of hunger, in combination with hard physical labour'. There was a nine-page 'evaluation' of Helsinki, dated 22 July 1976, which stated that an analysis of various aspects of Soviet internal policy 'demonstrates that the Soviet Government does not intend to fulfil its internal obligations in Human Rights': among the prisoners mentioned in this report were three 'active members of the Jewish emigration movement', Lev Roitburd of Odessa, Yakov Vinarov of Kiev and Anatoly Malkin of Moscow. Another Jew mentioned in this report was Alexander Silnitsky of Krasnodar, who had been sentenced for refusing to serve in the army. 'He had been called up', the report noted, 'after applying to emigrate to Israel.'

A Helsinki Watchdog group report of 1 August 1976 dealt with the continuing harassment of former political prisoners. Another, dated 12 October 1976, was entitled 'On the abuse of psychiatric hospitals', and gave details of five political prisoners who were being subjected to psychiatric abuse. A further report, also issued on 12 October 1976, dealt with 'repressions in the Soviet Union' against Christian groups, including the Pentecostalists.

On 27 June 1976, a Helsinki Watchdog group report had dealt exclusively with the refusenik issue. Its subject was the Jews who had been refused permission to join their relatives in Israel. 'The Soviet violations of the Helsinki Accords are systematic rather than individual,' the report declared, and it went on to explain: 'Many Jewish families are known to have been denied their exit visas for many years. The number of such cases does not decrease, but rather increases.' The signing of the Helsinki Final Act in August 1975 'has not led to any change for the better'.

The report gave two examples of divided families. The first was that of Boris Levitas, refused permission since 1974 to join his parents, brother and sister in Israel. Levitas had been expelled from the Kiev Polytechnic Institute for 'anti-patriotism', but given no reason for his denial of an exit visa beyond being told that his departure from the Soviet Union would be 'non-expedient'.

The second case was that of Slepak's wife Masha, refused permission in March 1971 to accompany her seventy-year-old mother to Israel, and subsequently refused permission to join either her mother or her sister Henrietta, who had also been allowed to leave. 'We must add here', the Helsinki signatories wrote, 'that in their reluctance to allow the Slepak family to emigrate, the Soviet officials for more than six years have exposed the whole family, including the children, to many different kinds of repression, i.e. numerous arrests, dismissals from work, blackmail, disconnection of telephones, complete cessation of mail service.'

Another case dealt with by the Helsinki Watchdog group in this report was that of Yefim Davidovich, whose worsening health before his death it ascribed to the 'systematic persecutions brought about by the announcement of his desire to leave for Israel'. The report declared that the case of Davidovich was 'a gross violation' of two resolutions of the Helsinki Accords. 'Violated in this case', the report explained, 'was the part of the agreement according to which the submission of a request for an exit visa shall not lead to the change of the rights and responsibilities of the applicant (the change in Davidovich's status of retired Colonel was a direct result of his applying for an exit visa).' The Final Act also provided 'that requests coming from sick applicants shall receive a special consideration and their processing shall be accelerated'.

This report, sent to the Soviet authorities without eliciting a response, and then sent to the West, was signed by four of the Helsinki Watchdog group: Yury Orlov, Vitaly Rubin, Anatoly Shcharansky and Ludmila Alexeeva. An appendix listed seventy-seven divided families, among them Alexander Lerner, whose daughter Sonia was in Israel, Lev Ulanovsky separated from his father, Benjamin Bogomolny from his parents, and Shcharansky himself, now separated for two years from his Avital.

One year after this list of divided families was issued by the Helsinki Watchdog group as a public document, the journalist Robert Toth used it as the basis of an article in the *Los Angeles Times*. In an affidavit written in Israel in 1977, Lunts testified that it was he, Lunts 'and *not* Shcharansky who transmitted the list of refuseniks to the West'. Lunts added that this list 'had *already* been transmitted by him to the West when Robert Toth published an article containing a list of refuseniks', and he went on to stress that 'the publication by Toth of the list of refuseniks with divided families was *one year* after this list had already been compiled by Dina Beilina and published as a *public* document by the Helsinki Watchdog group.'

On 3 June 1976 Shcharansky sent the report on the divided families to Congresswoman Millicent Fenwick, together with a covering letter. The letter read:

Dear Mrs Fenwick,

I had the pleasure of meeting you and talking to you and Congressman Yates when you were in Moscow last summer as members of the group of American Congressmen. Since then, we have heard much about your permanent effort to stimulate United States public concern in the problem of human rights in Russia. No doubt the last steps of the Congress towards the creation of the Committee for monitoring the fulfillment of the Helsinki Agreement are of great importance.

You must have heard that the Public Action group for the implementation of the Helsinki Agreement in the USSR was established recently in Moscow. We attribute much importance to the creation of groups analogous to ours in the other countries.

Of course, to monitor the fulfillment of the Helsinki Agreement is the duty of governments. But humanitarian problems are of great concern for the people and surely independent public opinion can be the best judge of the real situation. Even more, free public opinion in the various countries can easily reach a common understanding of the statements of the third 'basket', where governments fail to do it.

I am sending you the first documents of our group. Hope to be in close contact with you in future.

Best regards to your colleagues.

Cordially yours,
Anatoly Shcharansky

Shcharansky was breaking no Soviet laws by involving himself in demands for the implementation of the Helsinki Agreement; nor was Vitaly Rubin, his Jewish colleague on the Helsinki Watchdog group. Indeed, on 4 June 1976 Vitaly and Ina Rubin learned that they were to be allowed to leave the Soviet Union. The granting of exit visas to two of his most active friends, first to Lunts and now to Rubin, raised fierce hopes for Shcharansky, which he set down at once in a letter to Avital:

My sunshine,

I have imagined our reunion and our life together in Eretz down to the smallest detail so many times that it seems as if we were already living together in our land. Since Sasha got his visa everyone is waiting for mine to come through. Two or three

times a day various people ask in amazement, 'You still don't
have permission?' Everyone is certain that it is literally a matter
of weeks or days. Now Vitaly Rubin is leaving; the two of us
represented the interests of the 'Zionists' in the group observing
the carrying out of the Helsinki Accords. And again everyone
tells me, 'You're next.' I try not to think about it and not to 'sit
on the suitcases', or else I could go crazy.

Vitaly and Ina Rubin prepared to leave Moscow for Jerusalem. On
the Helsinki Watchdog group, Rubin was replaced by Slepak.

On 14 June 1976, three days before the Rubins were due to leave
the Soviet Union, Shcharansky and Slepak appeared on British
television screens as spokesmen for the refuseniks. This was the
film which had been made in Moscow two months earlier by the
British television company, Granada. In this film, which was
entitled 'A Calculated Risk', Shcharansky was shown inside a
moving car, pointing out to the cameraman several of the sights of
'refusenik' Moscow, including the KGB headquarters to which so
many Jewish activists had been summoned in the past.

During the film, Shcharansky was asked if he ever regretted
taking a stand 'against the Soviet Government'. 'First of all,' he
replied, 'I want to say that [I am] not against the Soviet Government
but for my right to emigrate.' Did he regret his stand? he was asked.
'But I never regret,' he replied, 'though my life is much more
dramatic. But you see, now I live in peace with myself – an inner
peace, I mean. There is no constant irritation because of impossibility to say what you think: and to behave in such a way as you *do*
want is very important.'

Would he change his mind, Shcharansky was asked. 'No, never,
never,' he answered. And when did he expect to be allowed to leave
the Soviet Union? 'Who knows? I wait for visa for three years, and I
hope to get it as soon as possible. My wife is waiting for me.'

In the course of being filmed, Shcharansky declared: 'For three
years already I am fighting for my right to go to Israel.' Asked if the
dissidents were part of the same movement, Vladimir Slepak, who
was being filmed with Shcharansky, replied: 'We have a different
aim. We want to leave this country. They want to make this
country more democratic.' The Crimean Tatars, Slepak explained,
wanted to go back to the Crimea, to remain, that is, inside the
Soviet Union. As for the dissidents, 'They want to change *this*
country, to live in it. We want only to leave this country and to live

in *our* country: Israel.' Asked why so many Jews should want to leave, Shcharansky replied, 'They have no opportunity to fulfil their human rights as Jews.' As for Western Jewry, said Shcharansky, 'We feel their support.'

Some of the Granada film concerned a close friend of Academician Sakharov, Andrei Tverdokhlebov, a non-Jew, whose trial was taking place that day, and who was sentenced to five years' exile in a remote part of the Soviet Union. Shcharansky was knowledgeable about the general human rights situation, and therefore, while his first concern was Jewish emigration, in answer to questions from the television crew he spoke sympathetically of Tverdokhlebov, and of the struggle of the Germans living in the Soviet Union who wished to return to Germany, showing the cameraman the railings near the Central Committee building where fifteen or twenty Germans had chained themselves just over two years earlier – a 'brilliant demonstration', he called it. Shcharansky also spoke about Boris Levitas, one of the young Jews caught up in the conscription trap; Levitas appeared sitting with Shcharansky in the car, speaking, with Shcharansky as his interpreter, of his desire to join his parents in Israel.

There were shots also of Shcharansky and Slepak talking. 'After you spend two or three years in refusal losing all your human rights,' Shcharansky remarked, 'you are in a very desperate position.' And in ten years' time? he was asked. 'I am an optimist,' he replied. 'I hope this problem of emigration will be solved. I *do* want to hope.'

Alan Segal, the British film producer who was with Slepak and Shcharansky throughout the filming, later remarked of Shcharansky: 'He was smart as a whippet, the quickest learner I ever met. I would correct his English. He would absorb it straight away, and then think of something better.' At one point, Segal asked Shcharansky if he was not afraid that he would be arrested once the film was shown in the West. 'My dear chap,' Shcharansky replied, 'nothing will happen to me. This film will never leave the Soviet Union.'

The Granada film was shown throughout Britain on 14 June 1976. No immediate action was taken against Shcharansky or Slepak. Three days later, Vitaly and Ina Rubin were allowed to leave the Soviet Union for Israel. One of Shcharansky's closest friends and staunchest supporters, both on the Helsinki Watchdog group and in the wider emigration movement, was no longer at his side. But as soon as he reached Israel, Rubin, like Lunts before him, fought hard for those whom he had left behind. 'The world does not seem to understand', he told reporters at Ben Gurion airport, 'that the Soviet Jewish emigration movement is one of the most important events in contemporary history.' Rubin added that he would 'continue to serve as a watchdog to monitor Soviet compliance with human rights declarations'.

Following the showing of the Granada film, many activists believed that Shcharansky would be given permission to leave, to rid the Soviets of an articulate troublemaker. The first Soviet response was an article in the magazine *Novoye Vremya* entitled 'Ready for Everything if Paid and Doled'.

Not payment from outsiders, however, but pride in Israel, suffused the refusenik movement. On 4 July 1976 the dramatic Israeli rescue of Jewish hijack victims at Entebbe sent a thrill through the refusenik community. Shcharansky was in Moscow that day; a friend having gone to Istra for the summer, he had an apartment to himself. The day of the Entebbe rescue was the second anniversary of his marriage to Avital. On 8 July 1976 he wrote to her: 'For four days the Voice of America and other stations have been broadcasting the news about our boys' mission to Uganda. What an anniversary gift. My mood is excellent.'

The day of the Entebbe hijack rescue had also been the day of the United States bicentennial: the 200th anniversary of independence. That day Shcharansky sent President Ford a telegram of congratulation on the achievements of American democracy. Two years later, this telegram was to form part of the indictment against him. Why, he was asked, had he not referred in it to the 'realities' of life in America, to pornography and prostitution?

In the first week of August 1976, a fourteen-page document transmitted to Western Embassies in Moscow gave the first public statement of the Moscow Helsinki Watchdog group. One of the signatories, Vitaly Rubin, was already in Israel when the appeal was issued. Shcharansky had also signed it, and at a press conference which the Watchdog group gave in Moscow, to which the local Soviet press were as always invited, but never came, he told those Western journalists present that the most recent Soviet position on the reunification of families 'was to interpret the Helsinki undertaking not to assist Jewish emigration but to hinder it'. Shcharansky went on to explain that 'if a married man or woman applies to emigrate, and the parents remain in the Soviet Union, the authorities may refuse the application on the grounds that it is splitting up a family.'

At this press conference, Shcharansky pointed out that the Soviet authorities were allowing 'the occasional well-known refusenik to leave, but they are imposing more repressions than before Helsinki on persons outside Moscow.' He also mentioned the cutting off of refuseniks' telephones; the intercepting of letters and cables; and 'the case of Vladimir Slepak', who, on the occasion of his hunger strike in 1975, had been sent 4000 telegrams from the United States. 'He did not receive one,' Shcharansky told the reporters.

★　　　★　　　★

On 17 September 1976, Shcharansky joined seventy-two other Jews in sending a message to President Ford, and to the Democratic contender for the Presidency, Governor Jimmy Carter. In their message, the Jews asked that, 'as stated at the meeting of chiefs of State in Helsinki', the issue of human rights 'may become the most important test case for the sincerity of relations between the great powers'. The signatories continued: 'Under the pressure of international public opinion, the Soviet authorities were forced to release more than 130,000 Soviet Jews who wished to be reunited with their people; simultaneously, the Soviet authorities implemented an elaborate system of intimidation and reprisal against those who have wanted to leave and those who have attempted to take advantage of their right to leave.' The Soviet Union, added the signatories, 'does not fulfil the obligations it assumed in Helsinki with respect to human rights. Only prolonged and insistent pressure by international public opinion, starting with the American people and their leaders, can force the Soviet Union to honour its obligations.' The letter ended: 'There is no doubt that the life and fate of many people depend on your position of morality in international policy.'

The signatories of this letter included all the leading Jewish activists, Shcharansky among them. Also signing was Sanya Lipavsky, who, within four months, was to betray the movement and cast all its leaders into jeopardy.

★　　　★　　　★

For much of September 1976, Shcharansky and Dina Beilina worked alone in Moscow: the Lerners, the Slepaks and Ida Nudel having left for a holiday in southern Russia. 'Our main external problem is as follows,' Shcharansky explained on 22 September 1976 in a letter to Irene Manekofsky. 'The authorities continue their "counter-attack on Helsinki".' Some months earlier they had begun to give refusals 'on the grounds, with reference to the Helsinki Agreement, of *not* separating families'. In Kiev, Odessa and 'some other places', the authorities were 'simply refusing' to forward documents to the Visa Office, 'saying that they had received official instructions from the Ministry of the Interior not to forward the papers of those whose parents intend to remain here, even if the parents gave permission for their children to leave'. The officials said that this was done, Shcharansky added, 'in order to fulfil the Helsinki Declaration not to divide families'. His letter continued: 'I am sure that if there is not a strong reaction from the West against such an interpretation of Helsinki, this practice will be extended all over the country and new steps will be taken for "closing emigration", using Helsinki as the reason.'

Shcharansky ended his letter on a personal note. 'Do you hear from Avital?' he asked. 'She studies painting in Beer Sheva now.'

Like all activists and all refuseniks, Shcharansky was pinning many hopes on the forthcoming Helsinki review conference in Belgrade. All the signatory States would be present, under self-imposed scrutiny of their compliance or non-compliance with the Helsinki Final Act of 1975, including its human rights provisions. In his letter to Irene Manekofsky of 22 September 1976, Shcharansky sent his 'best regards' to the three members of the Congressional Helsinki Monitoring group, Congressman Yates, Congresswoman Fenwick and Senator Leahy. 'We'd like to know more about their activity and their plans,' Shcharansky wrote. 'We are sure that only close collaboration between independent, public opinions can help us to make from the Belgrade conference something more than usual lip service.'

★   ★   ★

On 29 September 1976 Soviet Jews made their now annual pilgrimage to the Nazi mass-murder site at Babi Yar, in Kiev. Three activists who sought to travel from Moscow to the memorial service, Iosif Ahs, Iosif Beilin and Iosif Begun, were detained when they reached Kiev station. Shcharansky was detained in Moscow. At the site itself, the authorities forbade the laying of any wreath with an inscription which referred specifically to the fact that the victims were Jews. But many Jews made their way to Babi

Yar, to pay their respects to the dead.

Shcharansky drew strength from the news of the gathering, and conveyed that strength to others: among them two American visitors who came to Moscow two weeks later, Connie Smukler and Enid Wurtman, to whom Shcharansky reported that 'hundreds of Jews' had gathered at Babi Yar. 'They were not refuseniks,' Shcharansky explained. 'They never applied to emigrate to Israel. They heard by radio that activists are threatened and unable to come to hold a memorial service at Babi Yar. So they came in our place; and stood in silence at Babi Yar.' This, Shcharansky told his two visitors, 'gives us hope, just as the fact that many people who are unknown secretly come to us and ask for literature about Jewish life and Jewish history and Israel – for any information to connect them with the Jewish people and restore their Jewish identities.'

Shcharansky's sense of humour, as well as of outrage, was stirred by his detention in Moscow as he tried to leave for Babi Yar. In a letter to Lunts in Israel, he described his conversation with a KGB agent during his detention. His letter was translated into English by Michael Sherbourne, then circulated among Soviet Jewry campaigners in the West. It read:

> The conversation was held in the spirit of 'detente'; there were cautious hints that they could compromise me after I came to Israel. Instead of the usual direct threats, there were complaints that it was difficult to reach an understanding with me as I immediately pass on everything to my English-speaking friends, etc. Then, he abruptly changed his tone and said: 'I warn you, if one word leaves this room, you will have only yourself to blame.' 'What are you talking about? I am too scared of your organisation to afford having mutual secrets with it. I am going to tell everything to everyone who will want to know,' said I.
>
> For some five to ten minutes he kept saying: 'No, I would like to tell you, but you should not tell it to anyone,' whereas I kept answering 'No, you should not tell me as I will pass it on to other people anyway, just let me get to the first telephone booth.' So, I did not find out the great secret of the KGB.

Shcharansky's letter continued:

> This ended his attempt to find a common language with me. He warned me that I was detained as I was suspected of resembling

a wanted criminal. I complained about the overt rudeness of the 'tails'. He denied their existence. However, when I went out to the street my 'tails' – menacing fellows who the day before had threatened 'to do me in' – were the essence of politeness and benevolence. When I reached a phone booth to telephone correspondents as I had promised, they gave me a handful of 2-kopeck pieces for the phone. Then I hailed a taxi, which they also entered, although two cars were following us. After unsuccessfully trying to get rid of them I said they would have to pay the fares. They only agreed to pay half. The entire next day I deliberately travelled by taxi and only paid half the fare, with the other half paid from the special envelope. Now I know what real 'detente' is all about.

News of the harassment at Babi Yar formed a part of a further message from Moscow, the fourth of the 'reviews' which had begun in November 1974. This one was dated 15 October 1976, and was signed by Lerner, Finkelstein, Shcharansky, Dina Beilina, Ida Nudel, Slepak and Lipavsky. Dictated over the telephone to Michael Sherbourne in London, it set out, as translated by him in twelve closely typed pages, the most recent pressures on Jews seeking to emigrate, the plight of the prisoners, and press attacks on individual refuseniks, among them Shcharansky, Slepak and Lerner, who had been accused in the Soviet press of being 'paid Zionist hired agents', 'recruiting agents for Israel' and 'slanderers and criminal elements'.

These were the strongest accusations yet levelled against any refusenik leaders.

13

Rejoicings, Beatings, Arrests

Shcharansky kept as closely in touch as possible with those Jews who visited him, and followed as best he could their personal fortunes. On 3 October 1976, having learned that one of his American visitors, Zeesy Schnur, had given birth to a daughter, Daniella, on the day before the Jewish New Year, he telegraphed from Moscow to Zeesy Schnur's apartment in Brooklyn. The telegram, which was in Hebrew, read (as transliterated by the Western Union): 'BRAHA LEJALDA SHEBAA BAROSH HASHANA MAZAL TOV VASHANA HAZOT BAJERUSHALAIM': 'Blessings to your daughter born on the New Year. Congratulations. This Year in Jerusalem.' The telegram was signed: 'Natan Shcharansky'.

★   ★   ★

Saturday night, 16 October 1976, marked the beginning of the Jewish festival of Simhat Torah, the Rejoicing of the Law. In Moscow that night the refuseniks put aside their fears and frustrations as the strength of Jewish identity surged forward. It was an identity which was reinforced for them by the support of Jews in the Western world. Shcharansky explained this when he spoke on the following day to his two visitors from Philadelphia, Connie Smukler and Enid Wurtman. On Simhat Torah, he explained to them, 'thousands of Jews gathered in the centre of Moscow in the very narrow street of Arkhipova, and they were dancing and singing, and there was a lot of joy. No one interfered. It was the piece of land in the centre of Moscow which Jews fought for themselves.' It was only possible to celebrate Simhat Torah 'so openly', Shcharansky added, 'because of the courage of so many Jews – many who are now in Israel – some who are still in prison – and also because of the strong support which you gave us all these years and are giving us today. You represent our hope for the future.'

To Enid Wurtman, who had befriended Avital, Shcharansky was full of questions. 'He was anxious to know if Avital was a good cook,' Enid Wurtman recalled, 'and wanted to know every detail of the Sabbath we shared with Avital and of every moment we were together.'

Seventeen refuseniks, among them Vladimir Slepak, Zakhar Tesker, Boris Chernobilsky and Iosif Ahs, decided to use the festival of the Rejoicing of the Law as the starting point for a series of sit-in demonstrations inside the Supreme Soviet building in the Kremlin. With them, on the morning of Sunday, October 17, they brought a letter demanding to know the reasons they had been refused exit visas, and asking to be told the prospective dates when such permission to leave would be given. They remained, waiting for an answer, throughout the day. Then, soon after the office closed at 5 p.m., the protesters, outnumbered by uniformed police, were driven off in three buses to some woods fifteen miles outside Moscow. There they were let out of the buses, and had to make their own way back to Moscow.

Among those waiting for them in Moscow were Connie Smukler and Enid Wurtman, who, in their notes written during their journey back to the United States, explained that the refuseniks were prepared to embark upon, and to persevere with, such a risky protest 'because there was no movement in their own situation. They felt that things "were dead" internally and abroad. They planned to continue demonstrating at the Praesidium of the Supreme Soviet until there were preventive arrests. They pledged that they would remain constantly present at the Supreme Soviet until their demands were met; to find out precisely in writing, how much longer they would have to wait for their visas and the reasons for the refusals.'

That night, Shcharansky's thoughts were with Avital, as Enid Wurtman and Connie Smukler offered to take her a cassette with a message from him. Two years and three months of enforced separation had begun to take their toll on Avital. That month she had managed to speak to Shcharansky on the telephone, but such conversations, so exciting to contemplate, are also difficult: terrible strains and fears emerge, impossible to assuage across the brief, fragile, tenuous connection, with its background noises, its constant crackles, and the ever-present worry of interruption, of a break in the connection. That night Shcharansky took the opportunity not only to tell her all his news, and to amuse her, but to try to set her mind at rest. Avital, concerned at the long separation, had even tried to return to Moscow in order to be with her husband and to demand, as an Israeli citizen, that her husband be allowed to return with her. Shcharansky said, in this taped message:

When I spoke to you, your sorrow and your hardship reinforced my exhaustion so thoroughly that everything seemed unbearable. My dear one, how can I calm you, how can I take away your tiredness, your pain? My dear, my beloved Natulenka. Better that I should tell you how I have been living recently.

The day before we talked to each other – that was Thursday – I gave a report on our operation in Entebbe, Uganda. It was given at Rubin's seminar in Felix Kandel's apartment. A very good man, Arkady Mai, now leads this seminar. About fifty people came and I was completely surprised. I didn't expect to give such an interesting report; I could see from people's faces that it held their attention, not so much because of what I said as the topic itself. After all, everyone knew everything and how it ended, except for some basic details.

I gathered all the material that had appeared in the Western press. The correspondents I know brought me copies of articles, a book, a radio interview transcript and other information about these Palestinian terrorists in other operations. I talked for three and a half hours instead of one and a half. All kinds of people were there from professors to fifteen-year-old kids. The whole time there was such silence and such suspense on their faces. When I finished there was such joy, as if everyone had just relived it all. Mark Zakharovich ran to kiss me, acting as if I were the very pilot who had landed the first aeroplane in Entebbe. This really was one of those moments when I felt that I had done a mitzvah, even though it was very easy, and pleasant work.

A 'mitzvah' is a good deed. Derived from the Hebrew verb 'to command' or 'to ordain', it constitutes a religious duty and meritorious act. By Jewish tradition there are 613 biblical commandments, 365 of which are prohibitions, and 248 positive mandates. Also according to Jewish tradition, while man should not anticipate any material recompense for performing a mitzvah, nevertheless 'One mitzvah brings another in its train'.

Shcharansky's letter continued with a reference to Avital's own plan to seek a visa to return to Russia in order to visit him. He wrote:

> My good mood continued, and then it was Simhat Torah when you commanded me to rejoice, and I tried to rejoice, but it was somehow very difficult. But then Enid and Connie arrived unexpectedly and we were together in the synagogue. Enid told me a little about the Sabbath you spent with them in Jerusalem and I felt that you were with me and it was good.
>
> I am speaking now in the Slepaks' back room. Do you remember we once studied Hebrew here?
>
> My friends from Odessa are arriving soon. They had some problems and want some advice. Then there are some people from a small town who are afraid of being seen, but very much want Jewish books and information on Israel. I am supposed to meet them and give them some things. Then Enid and Connie are leaving, and I shall go today to the municipal OVIR, perhaps today I can conclude my discussions on the municipal level. In a week there's an appointment at the All-Union OVIR – I'll go there with our applications. I found out that in the United States Senator Leahy had already gone to the Soviet Embassy with a request that your application to visit me be granted.
>
> I would like to talk to you in a leisurely way for the whole tape, to sit and simply talk, not about anything specific, and that's all. It's nice to think that in a few days you'll be able to listen and to send me another tape. Only please, as fast as possible.
>
> Today is October 19; in twenty-five days it will be our third anniversary. My God! How I would love to be with you, and perhaps I shall be with you yet. I think, if they'll let me go, they'll give me five days, and I won't ask for any more, it's enough. And three days – it's also enough. Only it should be soon.
>
> Enid asked how to help us. Yes, many people love us.
>
> Why are we so sad, my dear Natulenka? I want to tell you something cheerful, joyful. I remember how we went to that apartment to study Hebrew and you couldn't say a word, and how you tricked me before that, saying you knew so much in order to be in the same group with me, do you remember?
>
> And now you speak Hebrew so well I am embarrassed. Tomorrow I'm going again to Shakhnovsky to start studying

with him again. It's very important to study Hebrew; when I arrive, you'll be my translator. Here I am the translator for everyone and there you'll be mine.

An amusing incident occurred recently.

The tails were following me – the surveillance was intense and crude, with threats – in general it was 'jolly', you know that they even travelled with me in taxis and paid half without arguing, they were so afraid to let me out of their sight, and even then two of their cars were driving behind me.

In the midst of all this I receive a telegram – that is, Mama receives it in Istra. They are trying to put an urgent call through from Montreal. I can't get there, simply no time. With difficulty I transfer the call from Istra to the Central Telegraph building. I think, 'Well, it's urgent, I must appear. But I'm busy!' I appear with my tails, they give me the call and some people tell me, 'An entire school is listening to you in Montreal, would you like to say something to us?' I mumble a few sentences, am confused, then they say to me: 'We would like you to greet the Sabbath together with us now.' One girl tells something about herself, reads a prayer and lights candles. A boy says the blessing over the wine and bread, the kids sing something and dance. I am listening to all this and my tails are standing next to me and the place is full of people.

Then they say to me, 'Now we are all together, the whole school is listening to you, let's get up, Natan, and we'll sing "Hatikvah"!' Do you understand? And I get up, well, what can I do, and begin quietly to sing 'Hatikvah'. All the people in the telegraph office look at me as if I am an idiot.

Okay, we shall laugh some more sometime.

I often have the feeling that I want to sit down and write my memoirs – I feel so old, but fortunately this desire quickly passes.

It would be better to write humorous stories instead of memoirs. There is so much absurdity in this life.

I beg you not to despair, your mood is very important to me. Get this tape soon and send me an answer and let us soon be together.

In the centre of Moscow, Enid Wurtman and Connie Smukler were present at a special end-of-Sabbath 'Havdalah' service, which, because of the sit-in demonstrations, had been postponed from the Saturday night. Together with Shcharansky and many other refuseniks, they joined a visiting Rabbi from California in the prayers, the shaking of the spice box and the singing of Hebrew songs in honour of the departing Sabbath and of the week to come. Also present that night were Professor Lerner, Professor Naum Meiman, Ida Nudel, Dina and Iosif Beilin, and Vladimir Slepak.

'Locked arms with Soviet Jews,' Enid Wurtman noted a few days later in the diary of her visit, 'singing in the candlelight, symbolic of our solidarity with Soviet Jewry'. Eight years later Connie Smukler recalled: 'I still see Tolya's and Volodya Slepak's faces over the candle.'

On the morning of Monday, October 18, the seventeen refusenik demonstrators returned to the Supreme Soviet building. This time, they stitched the yellow Star of David to their clothing. Once more they entered the building and waited in the reception hall throughout the day. No move was made against them. Then, when the building closed at 5 p.m., they were seized once more, thrown into a bus, in which they were severely beaten, driven to a deserted area forty miles outside Moscow, and ordered off the bus. They refused, pointing out that it was illegal to bring people by force to a dark forest. Dragged off the bus, they lay down in front of it to try to prevent it from leaving. They were then kicked and beaten. Many of their assailants were drunk. One of the demonstrators, Zakhar Tesker, had his nose broken. Another, Iosif Ahs, was thrown into a ditch filled with water where he collapsed and almost drowned. The bus, meanwhile, drove off.

Although bruised and bleeding, the demonstrators who had been beaten up in the woods managed to return to Moscow that night by suburban trains. One by one they gathered in Slepak's apartment.

Angered by the beatings, the refuseniks at once called a press conference, that same night, to which they invited all foreign journalists in Moscow. Among those who came was David Shipler, Moscow correspondent of the *New York Times*. His report was published on page one of his paper on the following morning, under the headline: 'Moscow Jews Say They Were Beaten After a Visa Sit-In'. 'Their injuries were mostly bruises,' Shipler reported, 'although one man suffered a broken nose and another a black eye.' Shipler also quoted Zakhar Tesker's remark: 'They were beating us very professionally.' Under the heading 'Anti-Semitic Remarks Reported', Shipler cited one of the plainclothes policemen as saying: 'You Jews are one-third of the population of the world, and you want to occupy all of the world.'

So outraged was Felix Kandel that night, as he listened to accounts of the beatings in the forest, that he wrote a poem of protest. Within a week, that poem was published in Israel, for which, in due course, Kandel himself was to receive his exit visa. 'Hey, Jewish people!' the poem ended. 'Again, they're beating the Jews, Again and again. Who was not beaten up yet? Come out, it's YOUR turn!'

Throughout the night, Shcharansky and Dina Beilina were telephoning friends and visiting them. 'We did not ask people to come to the Supreme Soviet,' Dina Beilina later explained. 'We only informed them about the beatings. All of them understood that if we did not protest even more strongly, Soviet officials would in future beat us all the time.'

The Jewish spirit which bound the demonstrators with the wider Jewish world could not easily be quenched. Even as the protests continued, Zakhar Tesker's wife Rimma gave birth to a baby girl. She was given the name Geulah – 'redemption' – in the hope of her ultimate freedom. All three were later to receive their exit visas.

On Tuesday, October 19, the seventeen refuseniks went to the Supreme Soviet building for the third day running. This time forty more refuseniks joined them, each wearing a yellow Star of David. Among them were Shcharansky, Felix Kandel, the Beilins, Ida Nudel, Yuly and Inna Kosharovsky, Professor Fain and Professor Lerner. Once inside the Supreme Soviet building they were met, to their surprise, not by the usual hostile row of policemen, but by the Minister of the Interior, General Nikolai Shchelekhov, as well as by the head of the Moscow Visa Office, and several representatives of the KGB. Once more, the demonstrators were asked to join in a discussion.

'We demanded that those responsible for the beatings be punished,' Shcharansky told David Shipler. But their interlocutors refused to discuss the beatings in the wood of the previous evening, or to give any guarantees for the future. At this, three of the refuseniks, Slepak, Shcharansky and Boris Chernobilsky, stood up and left. The news of their walk-out was at once telephoned to London, where, on October 22, it appeared as the main overseas news item in *The Times*, with the headline: 'Soviet Jews walk out of meeting with Minister of Interior'.

From the Ministry of the Interior, the fifty-seven Jews walked through the Kremlin, past the Intourist Hotel and up Gorky Street: a unique demonstration in the history of Soviet Jewry. Despite jeering from many passers-by, they were allowed to complete their walk unhindered.

The demonstrations continued. On October 23, at the end of another all-day sit-in at the Supreme Soviet, twenty-nine Jews were taken to a 'sobering-up' station and warned against any further demonstrations. On October 25 the demonstrators gathered yet again, this time at the Central Committee building, again wearing the Star of David. The police moved in at once, and all the demonstrators were arrested. Sixteen of them, including Slepak, Felix Kandel, Yuly Kosharovsky, Vladimir Shakhnovsky, Iosif Beilin, Leonid Volvovsky, Isaak Elkind and Shcharansky, were accused of 'hooliganism' and sentenced to fifteen days' 'administrative arrest'. They were then taken to two different prisons outside Moscow, one at Zagorsk, the other at Serpukhov. Two of the demonstrators, Boris Chernobilsky and Iosif Ahs, were not sent to these distant prisons, but held in Moscow for interrogation.

The Jews arrested on 25 October 1976 constituted the largest number arrested since President Nixon's visit two years earlier. A week later, while the sixteen were still being held in prison, yet another demonstration was held outside the Supreme Soviet. Many of those who came were Jews who had hitherto been against demonstrations. These protesters, too, wore the yellow Star of David on their coats and jackets. At Dina Beilina's suggestion, evidence was taken by the demonstrators from all of those who had been beaten in the woods and were not in prison: a copy of this evidence was then taken to the Prosecutor-General's Office. 'It's not a bad idea,' Shcharansky said later to Dina Beilina, and then, laughing, 'You see, you did something without me!'

One of those arrested, Isaak Elkind, later recalled how, after a week in their respective cells, those arrested had been allowed into a yard for a brief period. Seeing Elkind for the first time in a week, Shcharansky began at once to discuss with him the book *The Six Day War*, written by Winston Churchill's son Randolph and Randolph's son Winston. Shcharansky pointed out to Elkind that, as reported by the Churchills, Israeli officers were the first to be killed in the tank battles of June 1967. They had been hit because they were in the most dangerous position on the tank. This, Shcharansky explained, was because it was the best position from which to observe enemy movements, and that by taking this position they thereby saved lives.

'We spoke about these officers,' Elkind told me in Toronto in

1983. 'They did what they did because it helped others': this is what had impressed Shcharansky. Elkind added, 'This was the character of the man: a small man, not a strong man, but with a good heart, and a good morality.'

Another of those who had been sentenced to fifteen days was a nineteen-year-old student, Igor Tufeld. He was Moscow's most recent refusenik, having received his first refusal only on October 18. When the sixteen were released they again called a press conference for Western journalists, and described the conditions of their imprisonment. Shcharansky reported that more than thirty prisoners had been forced to 'live like cattle' in a cell eighteen feet by twenty-seven feet, with iron bed-frames for only twenty-four prisoners.

Neither Boris Chernobilsky nor Iosif Ahs had been released after being interrogated. Now both were charged with 'malicious hooliganism', a charge carrying with it a maximum sentence of five years in prison.

★   ★   ★

In the West, campaigns on behalf of the refuseniks had gathered momentum. After the arrest of the Supreme Soviet demonstrators, telegrams of support had reached Moscow from both Governor Jimmy Carter and Senator Edward Kennedy. On 29 October 1976 I myself completed a small illustrated atlas, *The Jews of Russia: Their History in Maps and Photographs*, tracing the story of the Jews of Russia from the middle ages, through Tsarist times, to the demonstrations outside the Supreme Soviet, naming Slepak and Shcharansky as among those who had been arrested after the demonstrations, and focusing in its final maps, as the refuseniks themselves wished, on the Prisoners of Zion and the divided families. That same week in the United States, the Washington Committee for Soviet Jewry published a leaflet, *Marriage Refusenik Style: Wives 'Da', Husbands 'Nyet'*, giving case histories of seven divided families, Shcharansky's among them.

In Moscow, the refuseniks had a friend in Academician Sakharov, who, in a message to Israel Radio, spoke of his 'respect' for those Jews who had left the Soviet Union 'in order to build new lives in their modern–ancient homeland'. Sakharov added, with emotion in his voice: 'I feel a great sense of warmth towards these people.'

Concern about the fate of Boris Chernobilsky and Iosif Ahs now dominated the refuseniks, as possible five-year prison sentences loomed. On 3 November 1976 the two men's wives, Mikhaela Ahs and Elena Chernobilsky, appealed direct to Rosalyn Carter, whose husband had been elected President two days earlier, asking her to intervene 'before it is too late'. In Moscow, eight prominent activists formed a Public Action group to help the imprisoned men. Three of the eight members of the group, Mark Azbel, Benjamin Fain and Dina Beilina, were subsequently allowed to leave the Soviet Union; the other members were Victor Brailovsky, Naum Meiman, Alexander Lerner, Ida Nudel and Vladimir Prestin. On 4 November 1976 this group issued its first public appeal to Jews in the West, to Western lawyers, and to the United States Commission on Security and Co-operation in Europe, established to monitor the Helsinki Agreement. The appeal was also signed by Ludmila Alexeeva, one of the non-Jewish members of the unofficial Helsinki Watchdog group set up in Moscow that May. 'We are convinced', they wrote, 'that it is essential to start an immediate campaign to save these men.' Eminent Western lawyers should apply for visas to come to Moscow 'in the capacity of official defending lawyers' of the two men, who could be saved from prison only by 'timely and concentrated efforts'. Separate public statements on behalf of the two men were made by Alexander Lerner and Ida Nudel. As Lerner expressed it, those who were campaigning on their behalf should 'put aside all your concern about me and my family', in order to devote all possible effort to the new case. 'I ask all my friends to concentrate their attention on the fate of these two men', wrote Ida Nudel, 'to help them obtain their freedom.'

On 15 November 1976, to the amazement of their friends and campaigners, Chernobilsky and Ahs were released. 'It is unprecedented,' Shcharansky told the New York Times correspondent, David Shipler. 'I don't remember any precedent in our movement,' and this comment was published, with Shcharansky's name, in the New York Times of the following day. In the same newspaper report, Shipler quoted Slepak's opinion that the two men had been released because of 'pressure from the United States'.

The release of Chernobilsky and Ahs was a triumph for the protesters in Moscow, and for their supporters overseas. But whether it marked a turning point for the good was yet to be seen.

In a letter to a friend in the United States, Shcharansky pointed out that a fellow refusenik, Eitan Finkelstein, was a member of a small Lithuanian group which was being set up to monitor the Helsinki Accords. He also wrote about another refusenik, Isaak Elkind, who, with his wife and two children, had fallen on hard times:

> He is without work. He is a comparatively new refusenik (about half a year) and though he was on our list he never complained and we didn't realise how hard his position is. He was the thirteenth beaten in the forest and he was in the same prison that I was in, and from the talks with him I found out about his situation. In the past he finished the Judicial School of the Ministry of Interior and now the authorities hate him as he is from their system and it would be really difficult for him to get a visa.
>
> I think that as he is the only attorney among the refuseniks and as many lawyers abroad are ready to help us, it should be good to attract their attention to this case. I'll send all the needed additional information about him and his family soon.

Within nine months, Elkind was to receive his exit visa.

Shcharansky never tired of helping others, or of seeking support for those in need. Nor did he ever ask anything for himself. Once Dina Beilina received a packet of coloured pencils, for distribution to the Prisoners of Zion. 'I don't like to ask you,' said Shcharansky, 'but please could I have one?' It was to be a birthday gift for his brother's son. 'It was the only time he ever asked me for anything,' Dina Beilina remembered, 'and he asked for only a single pencil! I said, "Please, take them all. You can have as many as you like." But he said, "No, only one," and he was so happy.' 'Whatever money he had,' Dina Beilina added, 'he spent on taxis to visit people. He tried to be in so many places at the same time. He didn't even have a second sweater. He was in the same sweater all the time. He was even arrested in that sweater.'

Shcharansky had remained deeply attached to his parents. But being under such constant surveillance he was unwilling to endanger them by travelling to Istra. He would telephone them instead, calling them, affectionately, 'my old folk'.

That winter, Shcharansky wanted to visit Prisoner of Zion Anatoly Malkin at his place of work. But he was being followed wherever he went by so many KGB men that he decided not to go, not because of his own safety, which did not trouble him, but, as Malkin later explained, 'because he did not want to do *me* harm'.

The authorities now made a move against Shcharansky, which backfired. He was accused of living in Moscow without having a job: the much-feared 'parasitism' charge, a criminal offence. His friends at once rallied round, explaining that he was a tutor, Yury Orlov and Ludmila Alexeeva demonstrating to the authorities that Shcharansky was teaching them English, and Dina and Iosif Beilin establishing, to the satisfaction of the official investigators, that their young daughter was being taught mathematics by the alleged 'parasite'. Their testimony was both true and successful. In spite of the increasing pressure, Shcharansky remained as yet unmolested.

14

Culture and Repression

By November 1976 the surveillance of Shcharansky had become not only uninterrupted but, as Dina Beilina wrote nine months later, 'demonstrative'. She suggested to him that he write a letter of protest, but he declined, saying that there were others 'whose situation is worse'. There was no special need, Shcharansky insisted, either to draw attention to his personal case, or to divert attention from the needs of others.

Following Lunts's departure for Israel, Shcharansky now worked at Slepak's apartment. 'Many foreigners', Dina Beilina commented, 'had seen the KGB agents sleeping outside the door of Slepak's apartment.' In such circumstances, she wrote, it was absurd to accuse him, as then seemed likely, of espionage. 'Try to imagine', she wrote, 'a man who is being watched by agents; who lives in a bugged apartment; who lives in apartments which are searched without warrant or warning; who communicates only with others in a position similar to his – and you will see that under such conditions a spy cannot possibly exist.'

Most Soviet citizens, Dina Beilina added, were 'afraid even to walk up to people like Anatoly Shcharansky, to say nothing of talking to him about classified matters.' Nor was anybody ever accused of giving Shcharansky secret information, or of being the source of his information. 'It means', Dina Beilina later wrote, 'that if people did not give him secrets, he did not receive them. And not receiving them, there was no way in which he could have passed them on.' Everywhere Shcharansky went, on foot, by Metro or by taxi, two KGB men went with him, his perpetual 'tail'.

Shcharansky continued his work, despite the surveillance. On 16 November 1976 he received, in his capacity as a member of the Helsinki Watchdog group, an appeal from seven Jews in Soviet

Moldavia, on behalf of the small Jewish educational seminar, amateur theatre and Hebrew classes in the Moldavian capital of Kishinev, all of which had 'come up against not only the ill-will, but the direct opposition of the authorities, in spite of the fact', as the signatories stressed, 'that their efforts are in strict conformity with the Final Act of the Helsinki Conference', as well as with the Soviet Constitution. Since the end of October, the signatories added, two seminars, one on Jewish Art and the other on Bible Study, had been 'broken up'.

This appeal was given wide publicity in the West. So too was a memorandum by the Helsinki Watchdog group itself, signed by all ten members, including Sakharov's wife Elena Bonner, Yury Orlov, Ludmila Alexeeva, Slepak and Shcharansky, describing a search for 'anti-Soviet literature' which had taken place in Moscow on 16 November 1976 at the home of two Soviet lawyers, Konstantin Simis and his wife Dina Kaminskaya. 'Just several days before the November 16 search', the memorandum pointed out, Dina Kaminskaya had accepted the defence of Boris Chernobilsky, 'a participant in a demonstration for the right to emigrate to Israel'. The confiscation of books, notes and 'means of their professional work' was, the memorandum declared, 'a simultaneous violation of several articles of the Universal Declaration of Human Rights'.

The Helsinki Accords had become an embarrassment for the Soviet authorities, covering, as they did, many aspects of Soviet repression. To 'monitor' Helsinki in Moscow was to ensure that actions hitherto grudgingly accepted or too diverse to make much impact were both challenged and linked in a single framework: 'violation' of Helsinki.

The Jewish cultural movement was typical of those for whom, before Helsinki, there was no international legal framework. After Helsinki, any move against the Jewish seminars could be presented as a specific violation of Helsinki. For several months, preparations had been made for a three-day Jewish 'Cultural Symposium', to begin in Moscow in the last week of December 1976. The subjects to be discussed included 'Characteristics of Jewish national self-consciousness', 'Social, ethnic and language characteristics of Soviet Jewry', 'Soviet Jews are part of world history' and 'International and Soviet declarations and documents concerning national rights and culture'.

There were signs that the Cultural Symposium might be allowed to take place: on 17 November 1976, so Michael Sherbourne was told, and at once reported, fifty Jews had met in the apartment of the poet Felix Kandel for a lecture and discussion on the works of Ahad Ha'am and his influence on political and cultural aspects of contemporary Zionism. No action had been taken against them. Beginning six days later, however, on November 23, a series of searches was mounted in the apartments of nine of the thirteen organisers, including Benjamin Fain, Iosif Begun and Leonid Volvovsky. On November 24, ninety-two refuseniks, in a letter addressed 'to the Jewish communities of the world', declared that the searches 'were worked out and prepared on the basis of a long period of secret surveillance and bugging. They were directed against the Jews who openly stated about six months ago their intentions to discuss the present state and the perspectives for a Jewish cultural life in the USSR at a symposium that would take place in December, this year.'

The ninety-two Jews pointed out that the searches 'were conducted, as a rule, at night'. All material connected with the coming Cultural Symposium had been confiscated, including the papers to be presented and the programmes of the Symposium. Also confiscated were Hebrew textbooks, books on Jewish history, prayer books, and tape recordings of Jewish music. The letter to the Jews of the West continued: 'The blow was directed against the Jewish spiritual renaissance. We, Jews who were known only a short time ago as "The Jews of Silence", had decided for the first time for the last few decades to gather and to discuss our cultural problems. We were stimulated to this by the hopeful humanitarian clauses of the Helsinki Agreement that came as a result of the Helsinki Conference, initiated by the Soviet Union. Today we are witnessing another initiative of the Soviet authorities.'

Shcharansky did not sign this letter: like several of those who did sign it, he saw Jewish education, the Jewish cultural seminars and Hebrew studies, not as an end in themselves, but as what Dina Beilina later called 'a tool to reach the main goal: emigration to Israel'. 'Tolik and I believed', reflected Lev Ulanovsky nine years later, 'that drawing too much attention to the cultural seminars would weaken our main objective, emigration to Israel. We had to decide what it was we wanted to be asked for in international negotiations: it was a question of priorities.'

Among Shcharansky's friends who signed the appeal for the Cultural Symposium were Slepak, Lerner, Iosif Beilin, Felix Kandel, as well as Lev Ulanovsky himself. Also among the signatories were the two men for whose release Shcharansky had fought so hard in the previous month, Iosif Ahs and Boris Chernobilsky. That same day also, in a separate statement, Academician Sakharov spoke of the Cultural Symposium as 'an important precedent after decades of absence of free development of national culture', and appealed for international support.

The searches now gave way to interrogations. On 8 December 1976 four of the organisers of the Symposium were warned by the Deputy Minister of Culture, Vladimir Popov, that it should not take place. Two days later, these same four were called to the KGB headquarters and questioned for between six and eight hours each. 'Have you or your colleagues received recommendations or instructions from abroad?' they were asked. Other would-be participants were questioned on December 14. On the following day the Foreign Minister of Israel, Yigal Allon, stated in Israel's Parliament 'that the Soviet harassment of the Cultural Symposium was a violation of its own Constitution; that Israel cannot remain silent on the matter; and that the people of Israel and their Government salute the organisers of the Symposium, and also the Prisoners of Zion.' 'The Jewish people and the State of Israel will not be reconciled to persecutions of Jews by Soviet authorities,' Allon declared. 'There is not, nor can there be, any compromise between us and the USSR in this matter. No persecutions or arrests will deter Jews who want to learn their language and to transmit their Jewish heritage to their sons.'

It was decided to postpone the Symposium opening from December 19 to two days later, as December 19 was Leonid Brezhnev's birthday. The organisers did not want, they explained, to be appearing to celebrate that particular event by their meeting. On December 16, five days before the new date, four United States Congressmen who had been invited to participate in the Symposium were refused their visas, one of them being Dante Fascell, Chairman of the Congressional Helsinki monitoring committee. Michael Sherbourne actually received a visa, perhaps by bureaucratic error, but it was cancelled a day later. Then on December 21, on what should have been the first morning of the Symposium, all thirteen members of its organising committee were arrested. Professor Lerner was also taken into custody.

A press conference was quickly summoned, and to the Reuters correspondent and other foreign journalists present it was Shcharansky who gave the news of the arrests. Among the other

Jews at the press conference were Mark Azbel, Benjamin Fain and Pyotr Roitberg, each of whom subsequently received his exit visa.

With the thirteen Symposium leaders being held by the police, and the foreign guests not having been allowed into the Soviet Union because, according to the Soviet authorities, of 'lack of hotel accommodation', Shcharansky now emerged in an unfamiliar role. 'Because of the need for solidarity,' Lev Ulanovsky later recalled, 'we felt that we could not allow the KGB to triumph.' The Symposium was therefore carried out; a seminar of protest against the prevention of the Symposium. To an audience of about fifty, the replacement lecturers now spoke, first Sakharov and then Shcharansky. Papers written by participants who had been detained were then read out; one was on the small space allotted to the Jewish people in history courses in Soviet schools.

On 22 December 1976 a *New York Times* headline read: 'Organizers seized, Soviet Jews meet'. Shcharansky, himself held briefly by the police on the day of the *New York Times* report, told foreign journalists at a further press conference immediately after his release, and as police searches extended beyond the Symposium organisers: 'I think they might be using the Symposium as a pretext for a wider suppression.' Two days later all those who had been detained, or were under house arrest, were allowed to go free.

*　　*　　*

On 18 December 1976, three days before the Cultural Symposium was to have started, Shcharansky had been one of six signatories of a document, issued by the Moscow Watchdog group, on the Jews of Ilyinka. Their story showed, according to the document, that violations of the Helsinki Agreement 'are of a more obvious and gross character in little, unknown settlements'. In 1974 some Ilyinka Jews had been given visas to Israel; now their relatives were refused permission to join them, and the essential invitations from Israel were not being delivered. 'From the example of the treatment of the Jews of Ilyinka,' the document ended, 'we once again observe gross violation of the Helsinki Agreement, namely the reunification of families, freedom of communication, and decent treatment of the rights of minorities.'

This statement was widely circulated in the West. It had been preceded, on 2 December 1976, by six separate reports issued that day by the Helsinki Watchdog group, on different aspects of human rights and Jewish emigration. As a member of the group,

Shcharansky had been among the signatories of each of these six reports. One, entitled 'On Ukrainian Refugees', concerned twenty-five Ukrainian 'political prisoners' who were known to have renounced their Soviet citizenship, and seventeen Ukrainian families who had 'announced their intention' to live in the United States or Canada 'where many of their compatriots reside and where almost everyone desiring to leave the Ukraine has relatives'. A second of the reports of December 2 concerned four non-Jewish families who wished to emigrate, whose breadwinners had applied to the Helsinki Watchdog group for help. All four were working-class, among them a lathe operator from Odessa and a bus driver from Maikop. A third report concerned a non-Jewish woman who had gone on a fifty-day hunger strike after her permission to emigrate to Canada had been turned down. Enclosed with the report of her case was an account by Slepak of his visit to Leningrad to look into it.

A fourth report concerned the confiscation of material from the apartment of the two Moscow lawyers, Konstantin Simis and Dina Kaminskaya. Among Kaminskaya's clients, the report pointed out, were at various times several 'well-known fighters for civil rights in the USSR', including Vladimir Bukovsky, who, as a leading dissident and prisoner, was about to be expelled from the Soviet Union.

A fifth report on 2 December 1976 dealt with 'the fight to emigrate for religious reasons'. The sixth report, likewise signed by all the group, including Shcharansky, set out details of the Soviet performance of its human rights obligations. The report spoke of several non-Jewish issues, including people sent to prison for their religious beliefs, and people subjected to 'psychiatric repression'; it also noted that 'both on the question of free emigration and on the more frequent question of reunification of families, there have been no changes for the better.' The report added, of Jews who had applied to go to Israel: 'the number of those who we know have been turned down has even grown during the year.'

*   *   *

On 27 December 1976 the Helsinki Watchdog group issued another of its reports, in which it announced the formation of a similar Helsinki Watchdog group for Lithuania. This new group was headed by Victoras Piatkus, and included one refusenik, Eitan Finkelstein. On the following day, a further report of the Helsinki group gave details of the 'Christmas repression' of the Helsinki Watchdog group in the Ukraine. Shcharansky was among the signatories of both reports, as he was of one more on 7 January 1977, dealing with 'interrogations and other repressive acts' against members of the Helsinki Watchdog group, including searches in the apartments of Orlov, Ginsburg, Ludmila Alexeeva and Lidia Voronina; another on 10 January 1977, protesting at the action taken against the Jewish Cultural Symposium; and two reports on 14 January 1977, the first dealing with the dispersal of a Caucasian tribe, the Meskhetians, and the second with the problem of sick prisoners in labour camps, 'who need to be released urgently on account of ill-health'. At least three of the prisoners mentioned in the report were Jews: Leib Khnokh, Alexander Feldman and Dr Mikhail Shtern.

*　　　*　　　*

The increasing number of refuseniks, and the suppression of the Cultural Symposium, cast a pall of gloom over the refuseniks, and over the wider Jewish community, in the first days of 1977. But this did not lessen the willingness of the activists to protest on behalf of those who were in even worse trouble than themselves. Two letters at the beginning of 1977 were evidence of this continuing concern, and courage. The first, signed by eight Jews including Shcharansky, Dina and Iosif Beilin, and Ida Nudel, was to the Soviet Minister of Defence, Marshal Ustinov, and pleaded the case of those young Jews who, having applied to go to Israel, were then conscripted. 'A refusal to serve in the Soviet army on the part of a Jew who considers Israel as his Motherland and who desires to be reunited there with his people,' they wrote, 'this is not an evasion of military duty. It is an honest objection on the grounds of conscience. Similarly, respect for your own Soviet Constitution and for the military oath should compel you to renounce this practice as a means of pressure against Jews who wish to emigrate to Israel, and who are covered by the law on compulsory military service.'

The second letter, signed by eighteen Jews, among them Shcharansky, Yuly Kosharovsky, Iosif Begun, Leonid Volvovsky, Alexander Lerner and Dina and Iosif Beilin, was on behalf of an elderly Jewish couple from the Ural city of Sverdlovsk, Isaak and Dina Zlotver, who had been refused permission to join their son and daughter in Israel. Dina Zlotver, a retired physician, and her husband, who had left the Soviet army thirteen years earlier with the rank of Lieutenant-Colonel, were both suffering from cancer.

This letter was sent to all the Visa Offices of the Soviet Union, and to the Moscow Helsinki Watchdog group. 'We have seen in the past', it declared, 'what thick skins and strong nerves some of the bureaucrats filled with pseudo-authoritarian zeal could have. With what ease the use of these laws, in their opinion, contradicts the interests of the State. One could hardly expect from them any expression of humanism and love of mankind. We therefore appeal to you with a request to help the Zlotvers to become reunited with their children. We hope that your assistance will enable the parents and the children to be together again.'

This hope proved an illusion: the Zlotvers died in the Soviet Union, without ever receiving permission to leave.

The Soviet authorities had become disturbed by the work of the Helsinki Watchdog group, and, during the second week of January, carried out a number of searches in the apartments of three members of the group not specifically involved in the Jewish aspect of its work: Yury Orlov, Alexander Ginsburg and Ludmila Alexeeva. These searches led to an immediate protest by fourteen Soviet Jews who were involved exclusively in the Jewish desire to go to Israel: Professor Lerner, Professor Meiman, Ida Nudel, the Goldstein brothers from Tbilisi, Eitan Finkelstein from Vilnius, Lev Ovsishcher from Minsk, the poet Felix Kandel, three of the Cultural Symposium leaders, Mark Azbel, Victor Brailovsky and Vladimir Prestin, as well as Slepak and Shcharansky. By harassing the group 'which had taken responsibility for monitoring the Helsinki Agreement', these fourteen declared, the Soviet authorities 'are trying to rid themselves of this source which is revealing violations of decisions made at Helsinki and which were agreed upon by thirty-five nations, including the USSR and the United States'.

This message, telephoned from Moscow on 12 January 1977 'to the United States Congress, to the Jewish communities of the world, to people of goodwill everywhere', was circulated the same day throughout the United States by the Union of Councils for Soviet Jews and the National Conference on Soviet Jewry. 'Taking into account', the message ended, 'the noble activity of this group of leaders in the struggle for human rights, including the right of free emigration, WE APPEAL TO YOU TO USE YOUR INFLUENCE TO DEFEND THESE HONEST AND BRAVE PEOPLE FROM HARM IN THE FUTURE.'

These 'honest and brave people' included the two representatives of the Helsinki Watchdog group of the Jewish emigration movement, Slepak and Shcharansky who, on the following day, were among a number of Moscow Jews who spoke on the telephone to Congressman Andrew Young in Washington. Young was then United States Ambassador-Designate to the United Nations. The reason for the telephone call, which took place on the anniversary of the eve of Martin Luther King's birthday, was a briefing session for new members of Congress, sponsored by the Union of Councils for Soviet Jews. 'It is amazing', Andrew Young told Vladimir Slepak, 'that we can hear each other so well over such a long distance. Maybe our countries will be able to hear each other too, because of our friendship.' 'Thank you,' replied Slepak, who was then in his seventh year of refusal, 'I hope so, but it is not easy.'

During a second telephone link-up with the United States, between Slepak's Moscow apartment and the Rayburn building on Capitol Hill, Professor Lerner, Shcharansky and Dina Beilina each spoke to a number of Senators. During the call, Dina Beilina reported 'that on that very day, Amner Zavurov of Uzbekistan had been sentenced to three years in prison'. His 'crime' was that, having had his exit visa actually taken away from him after it had been issued, he had refused to take back his internal passport, the Soviet identity card. As two other Congressmen, Newton Steers, Republican, of Maryland, and William Brodhead, Democrat, of Michigan, came to the telephone, Dina Beilina also reported that the Moscow Helsinki Watchdog group was 'in serious danger', and that 'the KGB has been harassing the group's leader, Yury Orlov, as well as Alexander Ginsburg and Ludmila Alexeeva'. The Congressmen were also told that Slepak and Shcharansky were both members of the Watchdog group, which had sent out fourteen documents to the West 'detailing Soviet violations of Helsinki'.

It was not only by telephone to Washington, but by their own contacts in Moscow, that the activists alerted the West to the sentence imposed on Amner Zavurov. On the day of the telephone call, David Shipler sent a full account to the *New York Times*, which was published on the following day under the heading 'Uzbek Jew, Deprived of Passport, Gets 3 Years for Not Having One'. Shipler's was the most detailed report yet published in a major Western newspaper about an individual case of a Jewish prisoner.

*   *   *

For the Jews who were so cast down by being refused their exit visas, the Helsinki Watchdog group now appeared as a life-line. On

18 January 1977 twenty-eight Leningrad refuseniks appealed to it direct, on the question of the main reason for a refused exit visa, the alleged 'secret' work of the applicant. 'No comprehensive law or published set of instructions exist', they wrote, 'about leaving the USSR.' There was a set of instructions, they believed, but, they declared, it was 'a State secret'. Applications to leave were reviewed by a secret commission. Visa Office officials 'refer all complaints back to the place where a person works which, in turn, answers that it doesn't deal with emigration'. The result was a 'deliberately created, artificially closed circle, open to any kind of tyranny'.

The twenty-eight Leningrad Jews asked the Helsinki Watchdog group 'to determine what aspects and stages of work constitute "possessing secrets", whether a relative can be "tainted" with secrecy, and how long it takes for secrets to expire'.

It was the 'lack of defined standards for exit visas' which had led Moscow Jews to conduct their series of sit-ins at the Supreme Soviet the previous October. Now the refuseniks of Leningrad wanted their right to emigrate to become a part of Soviet public legislation according to 'international pacts and declarations' ratified by the Soviet Union. They could no longer tolerate, they said, although they were no longer surprised by, the Visa Office officials who said to them: 'Do you need to know the reasons for refusal? Well, invent them yourself.'

The impact of the Helsinki Agreement on the Jewish emigration movement had been profound. On 20 January 1977 an appeal to the heads of all governments who had been signatories at Helsinki was telephoned from Moscow to Michael Sherbourne in London. This new appeal was signed by a hundred Moscow Jews, twenty-five Leningrad Jews, twelve Jews from Riga, ten Jews from Minsk, and by Jews from nine other Soviet cities. The total number of signatories was larger than on any previous appeal: 163 in all.

The signatories pointed out that according to the Helsinki Agreement, as ratified and signed by the Soviet Union nine and a half months earlier, 'Every person has the right to leave any country, including his own, and to return to his country, and this right shall not be subject to any limitations other than those considered by law to be essential for the preservation of State security, public order, the protection and the health of the general population or the right to freedom of others.' These were the words of the Helsinki Accords. Refusals to grant permission to emigrate, which were given 'orally and without a time limit to the refusal, and without any legal basis', were thus, they wrote, 'a direct violation of both the spirit and the letter' of the Helsinki Agreement. A situation, they added, 'whereby would-be emigrants are brought to utter despair by being constantly refused, *quite illegally*, to be allowed to leave the country, for very many years, can no longer be tolerated'.

The appeal of 20 January 1977 ended: 'We emphatically insist that all those who are illegally prevented from leaving shall quickly be given permission to emigrate, or alternatively, that they be given in writing formal statements, giving the official legal reasons for refusing to allow them to emigrate, and stating the period of time that this refusal will stay in effect, in accordance with existing laws and regulations.'

Among the signatories of this appeal was Benjamin Bogomolny, in 1986, twenty years after first applying to leave, one of the longer-term refuseniks. Also signing were the Beilins, Lerner, Slepak and Ida Nudel. Shcharansky's name was there, as usual. From Tbilisi, the Goldstein brothers had signed, from Vilnius, Eitan Finkelstein, from Minsk, Lev Ovsishcher, and from Leningrad, Aba Taratuta and Lev Furman. Many recent refuseniks, Jews whose names were until then unknown in the West, also signed. A movement now existed, begun more than seven years earlier, which no harassment or cut-back in exit visas seemed able to shake, a Jewish national movement in a land where, fifteen years earlier, such a movement would have been judged utterly impossible.

Also signing this appeal was Dr Sanya Lipavsky.

★   ★   ★

On the day after the appeal of 20 January 1977, Lidia Voronina left the Soviet Union. She had received her exit visa a few weeks before. No one knew what such an exit visa might portend, or if 1977 would see Shcharansky too, and other of his friends, on the road to Jerusalem.

It was well known to the Soviet authorities that Lidia Voronina had for several years been among the main dissident supporters of the Pentecostalists. She had visited them in the Caucasus and in the Soviet Far East, had encouraged them to persevere in their struggle for their religious worship, and had made their plight known to Western journalists. Now, despite her mother's refusal to sign her application documents, she was being allowed out.

The question at once arose of where Shcharansky would now

lodge. The answer came from Sanya Lipavsky. 'Why don't we rent
an apartment together?' he said. But then Dina Beilina and her
husband intervened. It was a mistake, they said, to rent an apartment, as opposed to lodging somewhere informally and unof-
ficially. Only a few weeks earlier, Alexander Ginsburg had been
accused of having foreign currency in his apartment. 'If you rent
your own place,' Dina Beilina warned him, 'they can plant dollars
or marks on you, as they did with Ginsburg.'

Dina Beilina suggested that Shcharansky stay with her, or with
Slepak. 'If they "find" money in our apartments,' she said, 'then *we*
will be arrested, not you. We will be the hosts, you only our guest.
The blame will have to fall on us; and we can take it on our heads.'

Shcharansky bowed to the logic of Dina Beilina's request. From
21 January 1977 until January 30 he stayed with the Beilins. Then,
for the first two weeks of February, he lived with his parents in
Istra.

★   ★   ★

The Soviet authorities had allowed 14,261 Jews to leave the Soviet
Union in 1976. Since 1970, more than 150,000 Jews had been given
their exit visas. The Kremlin was ready to accept Jewish emigration
as a fact, and to allow a definite process for it; but a process which it
wanted to control. The contacts which the Jewish activists had with
the West threatened to take this control out of their hands, if it had
not already done so. The activists had been demanding emigration
openly and, since the Jackson Amendment of 1975, linking emigration with pressure from the United States. The Soviet authorities
would no longer allow this; they wanted to be the sole arbiters of
Jewish emigration, to say whether it would proceed, and if so at
what rate and on what terms. By the beginning of 1977 they had
decided to break the group which was insisting publicly what
should be done and how it should be done, on the basis of 'human
rights', 'Helsinki Accords' and 'Jewish national aspirations'. Such
reasons were unacceptable to the Soviet State.

15
'Traders of Souls'

At seven o'clock on the evening of 22 January 1977, Soviet television began the showing of a sixty-five-minute documentary film. The title was 'Traders of Souls', and the subject was Jewish emigration. The film was the first blow in an unusual, one-sided war against the Jewish activists, which was to culminate in a series of trials and imprisonments. It was also a crude and threatening answer to the Granada television film of the previous June and the Supreme Soviet demonstration of October.

In the opening scenes, the narrator expounded on the freedom and opportunity enjoyed by Jews in the Soviet Union. The camera then switched to Soviet emigration and customs offices, where applicants were met with broad smiles, treated politely and efficiently and had all their wishes granted. The viewers were then told that no less than 98.4 per cent of those who seek exit permits receive them. But what happened to these émigrés, the narrator went on to ask, once they reached Vienna? They were 'transported to the transit camp, and surrounded by armed guards behind barbed wire. There they wait for the selection – to be sent either to Rome or to Israel.' The moment Israel was mentioned, screeching jets were shown zooming across the screen, followed by close-ups of bandaged children. 'Israeli jets bomb peaceful Arab villagers,' the narrator explained. 'This is what Israel has brought to the Arab world.'

The film then turned its attention to Soviet Jews arriving in Israel, where, it asserted, they were forced to sign documents written in a foreign language which they do not understand, and thus unwittingly were put in financial bondage and undertook military obligations. 'The families who prior to their departure vowed that they would rather "eat earth" than return to Russia become disillusioned so quickly', the narrator said, 'that before long, they hound the thresholds of Soviet Embassies asking to be allowed to go back.' The fate of those Jews who opt for destinations other than Israel was not any brighter. Vienna slums, said by the narrator to be inhabited by former Soviet Jews, were shown on the screen, as were shots of the Rome flea markets where the neglected, impoverished Jews were 'reduced to selling Russian souvenirs, in order to try to eke out a living.'

The film then showed authentic film footage of Western demonstrations against Soviet immigration restrictions followed by what was claimed to be a Soviet television 'scoop' – a corpulent, caricature-like Jewish figure was shown at a particularly noisy protest meeting in London handing out what could easily be identified as five-pound sterling notes to each 'demonstrator'. This scene was immediately followed by sequences of explosions, wounded children and burning buildings, still photographs which some visiting Western viewers recognised as dating back to the 1948 Israeli War of Independence.

The film then returned to the Soviet Union, showing how all nationalities were treated with equality; there were the faces of smiling youngsters, followed by idyllic, rustic scenery. Why should Soviet Jews wish to leave all this, asked the narrator, and then gave his answer: because they are brainwashed by unscrupulous Western Zionists. The viewers were then taken to Moscow airport, where someone purporting to be an American tourist confessed to having attempted to smuggle anti-Soviet literature into the Soviet Union. He was said to have attempted to contact Soviet citizens with an eye to arranging a meeting between them and a United States Senator. He acted on the instructions of Zionist organisations, he told his questioners as the camera whirred, and he went on to say that he did not 'exclude the possibility that these organisations maintain clandestine ties with the CIA and do its bidding'.

The film then warned the Soviet viewers that the Zionists would 'stop at nothing' to further their propaganda. Shots were shown of Israeli athletes taking part in international competitions in Moscow. Meetings between sportsmen and Jewish activists were, the narrator declared, all part of the sinister Zionist plot, at which point the camera focused on the Israeli flag and the word 'Israel' on the athletes' uniforms. There was then a series of slow motion shots of Vladimir Slepak, the first activist to appear in the film. Slepak was shown embracing one of the Israeli athletes, as the narrator asked the viewers, 'How can it be that Zionist cadres were allowed to form inside the Soviet Union?' The narrator then answered his own question. These 'Zionist cadres', he declared, had been formed outside the Soviet Union. Shcharansky was also shown with the athletes, but not named.

A second activist was then mentioned by name, Iosif Begun, whose Moscow address was given to the viewers, and a photograph of a cheque for foreign currency, apparently made out to Begun, was flashed briefly on the screen. Next, a cheque made out to the Prisoner of Zion Boris Tsitlionok was shown, whereupon the names and addresses of other activists were flashed on the screen, Yuly Kosharovsky and Shcharansky among them. While these names and addresses were appearing, the narrator told the viewers that 'these people are all soldiers of Zionism within the Soviet Union and it is here that they carry out their subversive activities.' The camera crew then returned to Moscow airport where a number of departing families were interviewed, all of them reporting that they were leaving their elderly parents behind. The narrator then commented on 'the Zionist abuses of the Helsinki Accords' call for the reunification of families. What kind of reunification have we here, comrades? Parents remain here while children go to Israel.'

The next scenes were filmed inside a passenger aircraft. A family of Jews from Georgia, purportedly on its way to Israel, was shown gleefully singing Israeli songs. The narrator did not say when or how the next scenes were photographed, but explained that they were of the same family in Israel, now ragged, crushed and dejected, humming the saddest of tunes.

A letter said to have been written by a Soviet Jewish emigrant in America was then read out. The writer attested that he would be ready 'to get on his knees' to be permitted re-entry into the Soviet Union. But the narrator then told the viewers: 'he will not be forgiven and allowed back in.' In a final sequence, the Prisoners of Zion were presented as speculators, hooligans and drunks, after which the picture of the fat Jew handing out currency notes was flashed again on the screen.

The activists watched his film in horror. The showing of names and addresses, one activist reported to the West, 'can in a very real sense endanger the safety of the people involved'. As to the visual images, these, the activist declared, 'constituted a clear message of intimidation both to Jews and to non-Jewish dissenters'.

Shcharansky's immediate response to the film was to prepare a formal protest, which on 1 February 1977 he submitted to the People's Court of the Dzerzhinsky Region of Moscow. 'The idea of the film', he declared, 'was to discredit the Jews struggling for their right to emigrate to Israel and those representatives of the world public who support this struggle.' Of the scene in which Soviet Jews were shown meeting Israeli athletes, Shcharansky noted: 'At the time when close-ups of the faces of these Soviet Jews were shown on the screen the speaker claimed that the Israeli athletes, with whom these people were meeting, were not athletes at all, but Israeli spies. Many people who saw the film recognised me, many people recognised me in the street and therefore the text about the meeting between the "soldiers of Zionism" (this is what the film-makers called Soviet Jews fighting for their right to emigrate to Israel), and those whom the film-makers had called – without any proof – "agents of world Zionism and Western secret services" did not only insult my honour and dignity, but was also a slanderous accusation in connecting me with the Western secret services.'

Shcharansky then pointed out that, in order to 'illustrate' the activities of the so-called 'soldiers of Zionism', the film had mentioned a number of meetings between Soviet Jews and Western political leaders. 'In particular,' he wrote, 'it mentioned an allegedly illegal meeting with some American Congressmen headed by Sidney Yates that took place at a secret apartment. I was one of the participants in this meeting with American Congressmen that took place in the hotel "Sovietskaya" in the presence of representatives of the press.' The American Congressmen, Shcharansky added, 'had informed the Soviet Embassy in Washington beforehand about their intention to hold such a meeting'.

The showing of the film, Shcharansky declared, 'distributed information that did not correspond with reality and that constituted an insult to my civil honour and national dignity'; for that reason he wanted the court to secure a denial of the 'slanderous information', and for this denial to be issued 'in the same way by which the information was distributed'.

That the film had been endorsed at the highest level was clear, not only from the fact of its transmission at a peak viewing hour, but from the enthusiastic endorsement given to it on the day of transmission in a Soviet News Agency broadcast. Subsequent similar endorsements appeared in the Moscow evening newspaper *Viechernyaya Moskva*, the cultural magazine *Sovietskaya Kultura*, and in the two larger-circulation weeklies, *Nedelya* and *Ogonyok*. The article in *Ogonyok*, with a circulation of two million, was published on 29 January 1977, entitled: 'The Espionage Octopus of Zionism'.

On 2 February 1977, the four Jews whose names had been shown on the screen, Slepak, Begun, Kosharovsky and Shcharansky, sought permission of the civil court to bring an action against the State television company for 'insult to civil honour and national pride'. Twice more, on February 4 and February 17, they returned to the court, but, despite their protests, and in contravention of the Code of Procedure of the Soviet Civil Code, the court refused to accept their papers. Nor would it agree to put its refusal in writing, so that no further appeal was possible. Meanwhile, as Shcharansky told Michael Sherbourne over the telephone, 'My "tail" has become a "box"': the two KGB men who hitherto had followed him everywhere had been increased to four.

The accusations of the television film had been followed by a spate of newspaper allegations against the Jewish activists, and against Jews in general. On the day after the showing of the film, the newspaper *Izvestia* claimed that in many cases the invitations from Israel were 'forgeries', while the magazine *Ogonyok*, turning to an alleged historical fact, stated that in the years before the Second World War the 'Zionists' had conspired with the Nazis to set up a 'pro-Nazi' state in Palestine. The reason for the Israeli kidnapping and execution of Adolf Eichmann, according to *Ogonyok*, was to prevent him from revealing this shameful 'fact' to the world. 'It is like the times before a pogrom,' Shcharansky commented.

The first arrest to follow the showing of 'Traders of Souls' was not, however, of anyone mentioned in the film, or even of a Jewish emigration activist, but of a member of the Russian Orthodox Church, Alexander Ginsburg, one of the members of the Moscow Helsinki Watchdog group, who was arrested on 3 February 1977. A few days later Yury Orlov, head of the Helsinki monitors, was also arrested.

As soon as news of these two arrests reached Washington, twenty-nine Congressmen telegraphed in protest to Leonid Brezhnev. Having learned that Shcharansky was being followed 'by large numbers of KGB at all hours', they also protested in their telegram against the 'harassment' of other members of the Helsinki Watchdog group.

A statement signed by seventy-eight Jews from nine Soviet cities condemned the 'pogrom atmosphere' created by the film. Robert Toth, the Moscow correspondent of the *Los Angeles Times*, was told by one refusenik that young children who had never experienced anti-Semitism before were being called 'Yid' for the first time. 'There is always anti-Semitism among people in this country,' Shcharansky told Toth, 'and as a Jew you learn to sense it, but now it is at a very much higher level than normal.' Everyone in buses and the Metro was discussing the film and the articles, Shcharansky added. 'It smells of pogrom.'

Undeterred by the film or the harassment, more than sixty Moscow Jews staged a demonstration outside the Supreme Soviet on 21 February 1977, insisting that they be given written reasons explaining why they had been refused exit visas. Many of the demonstrators were 'veterans' of the October sit-ins. At the same time, similar protests took place in sixteen other Soviet cities, involving more than 160 Jews. 'We dare not become the forgotten men of emigration to Israel,' one activist reported to London by telephone, 'even if it means more of us being arrested. We have to take every action open to us within the law.'

A second sit-in took place on the following day. Once more, arrests were made. Shcharansky, who had returned from Istra to Moscow on 15 February 1977, to stay for five days at Slepak's apartment, had gone back to Istra on February 21, and there he stayed until the end of the month.

★ ★ ★

Much of the work which the activists did, their travels inside the Soviet Union and their messages to the West, concerned the fate of those who were under pressure, under arrest or in prison. It was for those who were in the most immediate danger, not for themselves, that they took the greatest risks and made the loudest noise. On 28 February 1977 Shcharansky was one of twenty-six signatories of a letter addressed to the 'Jewish communities throughout the world', on behalf of a former Professor of Physics, Naum Salansky, who had been deprived of any possibility of working in his profession since he had first been refused permission to emigrate to Israel, and had just been subjected to nine interrogations in the space of two months.

In their letter, the twenty-six signatories explained that Salansky was accused of preparing documents 'containing defamatory inventions' against the internal policies of the Soviet Union 'in regard to its attitude towards the national question of the Jewish population resident in the USSR'. Of Salansky himself, the signatories wrote: 'Not only is Naum Salansky an internationally well-known scientist and physicist. His childhood was spent in the ghetto of Kovno (now known as Kaunas), from where he emerged alive only by a miracle: a German officer prodded him under the ear with a bayonet! He was seven years old at the time, and since then he has been deaf in that ear. His mother, living in Israel, is suffering from cancer. He himself recently suffered a heart attack. All the norms of humanity and morality demand that he be allowed immediately to emigrate to Israel.'

The signatories of this letter, in addition to Shcharansky, included Begun, Kosharovsky and Slepak, the three other Jews named with him in the television film, as well as Ida Nudel, Dina Beilina, Felix Kandel, Leonid Volvovsky and Aba Taratuta. Salansky was later to receive his exit visa.

Three days after the letter on behalf of Salansky was sent to the West, Iosif Begun was arrested. The charge against him was 'parasitism'. In fact, as a letter from some of his friends in Moscow made clear, Begun, having been dismissed from his scientific work at the time of his application to go to Israel, had been dismissed again and again, on various pretexts, from the different labouring jobs he had subsequently obtained. Begun's repeated requests to be recognised for what he was, a Hebrew teacher, were denied.

The arrest of Begun boded ill for the Jewish activists, among whom he had long been both respected and loved. Shcharansky, that same week, decided to move back into Moscow. His private possessions had already been moved by Dr Lipavsky to the Moscow apartment which the doctor had mentioned earlier. It was now ready, apparently, to be lived in, complete with telephone. Lipavsky himself, however, was no longer in Moscow.

Shcharansky left Istra yet again, and moved into Lipavsky's empty and newly decorated room. There he stayed for three days, until 4 March 1977, a day that no refusenik then in the Soviet Union will ever forget. That day the Soviet Government newspaper *Izvestia* published a long letter, signed by Lipavsky, declaring that the Jewish activists with whom he had worked since 1972 were acting in the service of 'American Intelligence and anti-Soviet organisations abroad'. Lipavsky named four Jews: David Azbel, a former scientist–refusenik, and Vitaly Rubin, both of whom had earlier received their exit visas, and Alexander Lerner and Anatoly Shcharansky.

16

Accusations of Espionage

Lipavsky's letter of 4 March 1977 appeared in *Izvestia* addressed to the Praesidium of the Supreme Soviet of the USSR, to the United States Congress and to the United Nations Organisation. Its aim, Lipavsky wrote, was to 'open the eyes of those who are still deluded, who are being deceived by Western propaganda that shouts from the rooftops about the prosecution of "dissidents" in the USSR and which balloons the so-called question of human rights'. Starting in 1972, he wrote, 'I linked my destiny with persons who were denied exit visas for definite reasons based on existing legislation and who started loudly to speculate on the question of civil rights. Although these persons had different views on the forms and methods of their actions, they had a single platform and a single leader – American Intelligence and anti-Soviet organisations abroad.'

This was the crux of Lipavsky's charge. The rest of his letter was a description of how these 'persons' were directed. Through 'unofficial channels', he explained, 'they systematically received instructions, hostile literature and money'. Their activities were 'supervised' inside the Soviet Union by David Azbel, Alexander Lerner and Vitaly Rubin. 'Since I became a sort of secretary to V. Rubin and keeper of archives,' Lipavsky wrote, 'I was informed of all plans and intended actions which, as I understood later, were designed to damage the USSR's interests.'

By 1972, Lipavsky wrote, he had learnt that Azbel, Lerner and Rubin were 'closely connected with staff members of the Embassies of some foreign powers and correspondents accredited in Moscow'. The 'most stable' contacts had been with staff members of the American Embassy, as well as with American correspondents. At Rubin's apartment, and Lerner's, 'these foreigners

and also visiting emissaries of anti-Soviet centres' discussed and
made 'various recommendations' that were 'in their essence aimed
at distorting the problems of civil rights and human rights in the
USSR'. Lipavsky named three such 'emissaries': Joseph Smukler,
Noam Shudovsky and Irene Manekofsky. Although Lipavsky did
not say so, Smukler and Shudovsky were both members of the
Board of Governors of the National Conference on Soviet Jewry.
Shudovsky, who lived in New York, was one of those who made
frequent telephone calls from the United States to the refuseniks.

Hunger strikes staged by Rubin and Azbel were spurious: thinking 'most of all about their health', Lipavsky wrote, 'these
"martyrs" had regular meals, knowing in advance that the foreign
correspondents would not let them down.' Demonstrations 'in the
form of noisy spectacles of protest', Lipavsky added, 'that were
then presented by the Western press as a conflict between dissidents
and Soviet authorities, were staged in the same spirit, in collusion
with foreign correspondents'. The main task in all this 'was to
slander the Soviet system', to start 'a clamour about "the absence of
democratic freedom"', and to 'sow national discord'. The aim was
to 'incite emigration' from the Soviet Union with 'the intention of
undermining the mainstays of Soviet power'. The Cultural
Symposium had been typical of the 'provocative undertakings' to
such ends. Since these ideas had 'failed', however, to produce the
'desired result', there had been 'a substantial change in the direction
of the upper crust's activities. Being alarmed by the prospect of
declining interest in them by their foreign masters who have given
them considerable material aid, they decided to team up with the
so-called "Group for the Observation of the Fulfilment of the
Helsinki Accords", headed by Y. Orlov. V. Rubin was introduced
into the group and then A. Shcharansky.' This idea, Lipavsky
stated, had been presented by foreign correspondents as 'a step
towards the consolidation of persons struggling for "human
rights" in the USSR'.

Lipavsky then accused Alexander Lerner of proposing, in order
to 'whip up tension' between the Soviet Union and the United
States, 'to organise a secret collection of information about Soviet
defence institutions and enterprises, and under this pretext to
convince Western firms to stop supplying technical equipment to
the USSR'. After his 'departure' from the Soviet Union, Vitaly
Rubin 'was to hold relevant consultations on this question in the
United States and inform A. Lerner'.

In August 1976, according to Lipavsky, a letter had arrived from Rubin, through 'unofficial channels' via an American correspondent, requesting 'a quicker forwarding of this information, so as to start a campaign to put a ban on the sale of American equipment to the USSR. Although there were objections to collecting such information because this would be obvious espionage, A. Lerner, nevertheless, instructed A. Shcharansky and others to organise the collection of such information and its despatch abroad.'

Lipavsky's letter went on to describe how he himself had been introduced by Vitaly Rubin to Melvin Levitsky, a 'staff member' of the Central Intelligence Agency; how Levitsky has been angered when Lipavsky showed 'caution'; and how David Azbel, then in the United States, sent a letter with the 'pressing request' that he help Levitsky. The aim of all this, Lipavsky explained, was to try to obtain 'important defence information' from an old friend of his who was one of the 'top officials' at a research institute near Moscow.

Lipavsky went on to state that 'enemies of socialism' and of the Soviet Union were 'deliberately exploiting the so-called question of human rights in the interests of imperialism and world reaction'. He had seen for himself 'that adventurers and money-grubbers pose as champions of "human rights" with the prime aim of gaining publicity and securing regular earnings abroad by staging provocations and helping forces in the West'. Lipavsky's letter continued, with a reference to three leading activists, including Professor Mark Azbel:

> I was witness to constant infighting between A. Lunts, M. Azbel, and A. Lerner for leadership and distribution of means received from abroad. More and more I became convinced that the activities of these hangers-on were doing nothing but damage to the Soviet people and this could not but trouble me. I did not participate in the Second World War because I was a child at the time. I did not see the damage and the suffering spread by fascism throughout Europe. But I am sufficiently literate and have enough sense to appreciate the terrible losses suffered in that war by the peoples of the USSR, including people of Jewish nationality.
>
> Jews are perishing now, too. But this is happening not in the Soviet Union but in the deserts of the Middle East as a result of Israel's aggression. It is not in the Soviet Union but in foreign

countries that there live deceived Jewish families who hastened
to leave the USSR in search of the 'Promised Land' but who
found humiliation and fear of the morrow.

This, Lipavsky added, 'is not propaganda but the bitter truth'; it
came, not from newspaper or television reports, 'but through the
cries from the heart coming from distant countries about the
destinies of my former compatriots and friends, about how
"sweet" their life is'.

Lipavsky then called upon the Congress of the United States to
'investigate' why the Central Intelligence Agency served 'the foul
cause of fanning hatred among nations', and why 'it relies on
renegades, presenting them as heroes and martyrs.' His letter
ended: 'I publicly renounce my earlier application to leave the
USSR for Israel because I am convinced that the Soviet Union is my
only Motherland.'

★   ★   ★

Published with Lipavsky's letter was a commentary by two *Izvestia*
journalists. 'The publication of today's letter', they wrote, 'is one
more typical page in the dirty chronicle of American secret service
activity.' The writers added, in the one reference to Slepak in the
newspaper that day: 'At the various meetings which Lipavsky
always attended, table talk invariably included the working out of
anti-Soviet acts and instructions. Incidentally, at one of these
gatherings, a certain V. Slepak paid such warm attention to a lady
Vice-Consul from the USA, Allyn Nathanson, that his angry wife
roughly stuck her elbow into the ribs of that representative of
transatlantic power.' No doubt this ludicrous story was intended to
denigrate Slepak and to make fun of an American diplomat, as well
as giving a foretaste of Lipavsky's tales.

As was usual, *Izvestia* appeared on the streets of Moscow at two
o'clock that afternoon. At that very moment, the authorities carried
out searches in seven apartments, those of Lerner, Slepak,
Shcharansky, Ida Nudel, Boris Chernobilsky, Dina Beilina and
Michael Kremen. No one was arrested, however.

On the following morning all seven sent a statement to the West,
telephoned to Michael Sherbourne, and translated by him. The
accusations in Lipavsky's letter, they wrote, were 'reminiscent of
the anti-Jewish trials of the 1950s' recalling particularly 'the
notorious "Doctors' Plot"' of January 1953. The seven declared:

(1) *All* our activity over the past years has been directed *solely* towards obtaining for ourselves the possibility of emigrating from the USSR to Israel.

(2) We have strictly limited our activity so that everything we have done has been entirely within the framework of Soviet law.

(3) We have always informed Western public opinion and the Western press about our conditions and sufferings in *open* letters and declarations and in *open* telephone calls.

(4) We have *never* hidden from the Soviet authorities that we have kept the Western world aware of what we have been trying to achieve, in *open* conversations and letters through the post.

(5) What we have been doing *quite openly* not only has been in the interests of those Jews who wish to emigrate and go to Israel, but has been in the interests *of the Soviet people as a whole*, and in the interests of improving relations between the Soviet peoples and Government, and the governments and peoples of the Western world.

'With this new prospect', the seven added, 'of fresh anti-Jewish trials, based on completely false evidence, or, in fact, on *no evidence at all except lies*, we can only regret that the Soviet Union is returning to the days of the worst excesses of Stalin's time.'

Professor Lerner also issued a separate statement. He had been accused by Lipavsky, he said, of having directed the activities of people whose work was controlled by 'American Intelligence and anti-Soviet organisations abroad', from whom they, 'and hence I', received instructions, anti-Soviet literature and money. In response to these accusations, he was ready to confirm 'under oath' the following:

(1) I never was in any way connected with any intelligence bodies of foreign states, including the USA. I myself never collected and never entrusted anybody else to collect information containing military or State secrets.

(2) I never received any reward for my activity, neither from the CIA, nor from other foreign organisations.

(3) During the period of waiting for permission to emigrate, i.e. from the end of 1971, I met many foreigners: tourists, correspondents, scientists, diplomats and statesmen. But not one of them ever suggested that I collaborate with any foreign secret service or anti-Soviet organisations.

(4) All accusations against me and my friends are nothing but ill-intentioned aspersions.

One Western visitor who saw Shcharansky immediately after the publication of the Lipavsky letter was Bernard Dishler of Philadelphia. On return to the United States Dishler described the 'atmosphere of dread' which he had seen in the Moscow Jewish community that week. The Soviet Government 'have us like this', one activist had told him, placing his hands around his neck. The leading activists now feared, Dishler reported, that the Soviet Government was 'setting the stage for a new attack', this time putting Jews 'on trial for espionage'.

No one knew on whom the axe would fall. That Saturday, outside the Arkhipova Street synagogue, where normally so many refuseniks gathered, the street was empty.

Lipavsky's letter was not intended to stand alone. In distant Uzbekistan, Amner Zavurov's father Boris was summoned to the KGB and urged to put his name to a similar article that would be written for him. He was also asked to make contact with, and to incriminate, an American diplomat in Moscow, Joseph Pressel. 'If you tell us that Pressel is an anti-Soviet character,' Boris Zavurov was told, 'we will free Amner, and if you don't, we will arrest his brother Amnon.'

Boris Zavurov refused to emulate Lipavsky. Today, he and his sons are in Israel.

*   *   *

On 7 March 1977, three days after Lipavsky's letter had been published, Slepak and Shcharansky were invited to lunch at the apartment of Robert Toth, the Moscow correspondent of the *Los Angeles Times*. At the entrance to the building, however, they were stopped by four plainclothes agents and the policeman on duty outside the building. Toth, who was with them, protested that the two men were his guests. The agents then ordered the policeman to take away Shcharansky's internal passport – the identity card which Soviet citizens must carry at all times. Shcharansky protested, and the internal passport was returned to him, but only on condition that he and Slepak agreed to leave.

Robert Toth lunched alone. But he had already managed to discuss with them the issue which dominated all refusenik discussions that week: the reason for Lipavsky's letter. Clearly the letter enabled the Soviet authorities to move against Lerner, Slepak or Shcharansky as they pleased: as a document, it had advanced the battle against the refuseniks one major step beyond the television programme of six weeks earlier. As to Lipavsky himself, some activists felt that he had signed 'his' letter under severe pressure, perhaps out of fear for his own and his family's future. Its allegations were too fanciful, too neatly geared to a whole series of possible criminal charges, to be a spontaneous production.

Lipavsky may, argued some who had known him, have worked for several years as a genuine 'refusenik doctor'. He had signed many of the public protests. He had worked tirelessly to give medical attention to other refuseniks. He had attended to Professor Lerner and his wife when they were ill. When Yefim Davidovich had been taken ill at the beginning of 1976, he had travelled several times to Minsk to help him. Also in 1976, at Ida Nudel's request, he had visited Prisoner of Zion Alexander Slinin at his place of work, and helped him with a medical problem. He had repeatedly provided Michael Sherbourne with telephone numbers at which Sherbourne could reach meetings of Soviet Jews who had messages to convey. On 30 January 1977 he had told Sherbourne over the telephone that he himself had been dismissed from his work at a Moscow polyclinic, having turned down dozens of bribes to issue physical fitness certificates for driving licences. On 27 January 1977, Sherbourne reported, Lipavsky had been called in by the senior physician of the polyclinic 'who said he had three written complaints about him, specifically that he was working longer hours than the other doctors (!) which was unauthorised, and that he had been receiving telephone calls from abroad (!)'.

On 9 February 1977 Lipavsky had, according to his own account to the refuseniks, been prevented by the KGB from going by air to Uzbekistan to make contact with Amner Zavurov. As late as February 25, seven days before the *Izvestia* article was published, he had written letters to two United States Congressmen, Dante Fascell and Robert Drinan, asking them to help him to emigrate to Israel. Now he had disappeared; and his apartment, which he had once invited Shcharansky to share with him, was empty.

The activists now tried to recall all they knew about the man whose letter threatened them so directly. 'We must stress', Slepak told Robert Toth, 'that all we know came from Sanya himself.' He was born in Kiev in 1933. During the Second World War his family, like many other Jews in western Russia, was evacuated to Central Asia. He spent the war years in Tashkent, capital of Uzbekistan. After the war, the family returned to Kiev, 'but all their relatives were dead, so they returned to Tashkent, where Lipavsky went to medical school.' After working for some years as a doctor in Tashkent, he then went to the Institute for Neurosurgery in Moscow, where he received a Candidate of Science degree.

According to what Lipavsky had told his activist friends, he had been fired from the Institute of Neurosurgery 'because of anti-Semitism'. He had then taken a job in the northern port of Murmansk, rising to chief neurosurgeon for the Kola Peninsula, but said that he had again 'lost out' because of anti-Semitism. He then returned to Moscow as a doctor in the State Commission that conducts medical tests for those applying to become professional drivers: government chauffeurs, taxi drivers and ambulance drivers. He rose to become the Commission's chief doctor in 1972, when he first made contact with the Jewish activists. 'He came well recommended', Slepak told Toth, 'as a very good man and a very good doctor who could not yet apply to go to Israel because his father was in prison camp for economic crimes and would suffer.'

Lipavsky once hinted to the refuseniks that his father had been sentenced to death but that the sentence had been commuted to fifteen years. He still had time left to serve when, in early 1973, Lipavsky told the refuseniks that his father had been released because of ill-health. Then, early in 1974, Lipavsky announced that he had applied to emigrate, but had received a refusal on the grounds of 'secrecy', because his co-operative apartment, so he explained it, located an hour from Moscow, was close to several space research laboratories, including the cosmonaut training centre at Zvezdny Gorodok. 'I must have picked up secrets riding by on the commuter train each day,' Lipavsky used to joke. Later, however, he said that the refusal was due to his job in Murmansk, which had given him access to top-secret Soviet naval bases in the region where virtually all nuclear-missile submarines were serviced. He had performed surgery on 'high-ranking brass there', he said. As to his work at the Driving Commission, his application to emigrate had cost him the job as top doctor of the Commission, Lipavsky had explained, but he had been allowed to stay on as an ordinary doctor there. 'He was very inventive for us,' Shcharansky commented, 'using Commission telephones at the end of the day to

get calls from the West so we could pass out our press statements
and so forth.' Suspicion had begun to fall on Lipavsky in the second
week of February 1977, during a strange episode. As a result of his
sojourn in Tashkent, Lipavsky could speak Uzbek; he had therefore
agreed to go to Uzbekistan for the appeal of Amner Zavurov. But
he did not go. He telephoned none of the group for two days and
then said that he had been 'prevented from going by the KGB'.

'We had this strange feeling,' Shcharansky told Toth, 'but we just
thought he had lost his nerve and had gone home for a rest.' Then,
on 26 February 1977, Lipavsky disappeared. His landlady told
Shcharansky that he had been waiting impatiently for a telephone
call, but none came, and he left, saying he would return in half an
hour. Two days later, Shcharansky phoned Lipavsky's home,
where his old parents, his wife and seven-year-old son lived. 'His
wife said there was trouble with relatives in Tashkent and he had
had to leave for a week,' Shcharansky recalled. 'We were very
surprised because he had appointments set up – incoming phone
calls – but he was such a friendly guy, sweet, without an enemy,
and his wife said he would be back on the Saturday.' Then, on the
Friday, *Izvestia* published his letter.

In his article in the *Los Angeles Times*, Robert Toth speculated
that if Lipavsky had traded his father's freedom for becoming an
informant, whether voluntarily or under threat, it would mean that
he had been 'working for the KGB from the start'. If for money, he
could also have been a betrayer from the earliest days, 'or maybe it
occurred toward the end'. 'He had a car, you know,' Slepak told
Toth. 'Sanya had said he bought it with money his mother inherited
from her brother, who died rich in America. But then we heard
from friends who have friends among doctors in that driver
examination commission that his car was really bought with bribes
he took to pass people, and that he had deliberately given up his
speciality, neurosurgery, because there was lots more money to be
made through bribes at the commission.'

Several Americans who had met Lipavsky remembered his being
part of the 'inner circle' of leading refuseniks. In July 1975, Connie
and Joseph Smukler of Philadelphia were taken by Shcharansky to
the apartment of Dina and Iosif Beilin. In the apartment when they
arrived were Slepak, Lunts, Ida Nudel, the Beilins and Lipavsky.
Though 'relatively quiet', Connie Smukler later recalled, Lipavsky
took part in the discussions. It was probably as a result of that
meeting that Lipavsky had named Joseph Smukler as one of the

'visiting emissaries of anti-Soviet centres' in his letter to *Izvestia*.

The mystery about Lipavsky's motives, or how long he had been an informer, continued to concern and to puzzle his former friends. Shcharansky told Toth that in September 1977 Lipavsky 'went to someone in our movement and said he urgently needed 4000 roubles because his son in the army, a son from his first marriage, had struck an officer who called him a "Yid", and he was to be tried by a military court. Sanya said he could get to the officer if he had the money. We didn't have that kind of money but maybe a collection could be started, we said, but Sanya went away. When he came back he said all was okay.'

Shcharansky shrugged. 'Looking back, of course,' he told Toth, 'it was strange that he spent so much time in Moscow and not with his family, that he found us a room just when I needed to move from my old one, and all the other little things. But I would like to think', Shcharansky added sadly, 'that Sanya was not an informant all along, that he became one recently – not last week of course, but not very long ago.'

★   ★   ★

The ten days following the publication of Lipavsky's article were frightening ones for each of those who had been named in it. An eye-witness of those days was the poet Felix Kandel, who later wrote in his book *The Gates of our Exodus*:

> What had happened afterwards? What afterwards? Immediately after the article in the newspaper about 'Shcharansky the spy'?
>
> Psychological attack. Permanent pressure for ten days. Day and night. The car by the doorway. KGB agents by the door of the apartment. He was in the elevator, and they were there too. He was outside the synagogue, they were there, too, by his side. Five to eight men at once.
>
> Pressure. Insolent constant pressure, when one does not know, what will happen to one in a minute. When one is going out to the street, to the bakery or to buy a newspaper, putting on beforehand warm underclothes, taking a tooth-brush, a comb and other things which could be necessary in prison. Ten days. Demonstration of power and force. In order to shake, to drive out, to intimidate.
>
> Meanwhile he was studying Hebrew, visiting seminars, solving chess-problems, writing letters. His parents were visiting

him and were startled, when stumbling upon the agents by the door. He was soothing them. He was assuring them, that it is not terrible at all. Mere rubbish. The performance. And they believed him. They wanted to believe. They had to believe him because he was – their son. The tardy child. All the members of Shcharansky's family are optimists. It is hereditary. . . .

Ten days of permanent pressure. Ten days of expectations. Will they catch him or not? The pressure was enormous.

Now were they aspiring to break him. . . .

★   ★   ★

Lerner, Shcharansky and Slepak remained at liberty. But Shcharansky now reported that his 'box' of four KGB men had been increased to a 'cage' of eight. When he slept at Slepak's apartment on Gorky Street, these eight sat on the steps leading up to Slepak's door. When he went out to walk in the street, two KGB men preceded him, two followed him, while as many as four more walked on either side of him.

From Jerusalem, Vitaly Rubin issued a statement three days after Lipavsky's letter had been published, in which he declared:

> From the newspapers I know that I am being accused of being a CIA *agent*.
>
> I state *categorically* that the contents of the Lipavsky 'letter', where this accusation is made, are untrue.
>
> Lipavsky, together with other Jewish activists, met Mr Levitsky and some other members of the staff of the American Embassy, as well as foreign correspondents, in my home in Moscow. These meetings were not secret, had the character of normal friendly contact, and had nothing to do with any spy activity.
>
> I participated in these conversations and know this for certain.
>
> We knew that the KGB hated these meetings, especially after the creation of the Helsinki Watchdog group.
>
> If the so-called 'letter' of Lipavsky is not a fraud, to force Lipavsky to sign such a document, the KGB had to apply to him exceptional means of pressure.

The 'trumped-up story', Rubin added, served three aims: 'to compromise Jewish activists and dissidents as American spies', to stop friendly contacts between Soviet citizens and foreign correspondents 'and to undermine the trust between foreign newsmen and Soviet citizens', and to 'intimidate Jews who are in contact with Jewish activists'.

Three days after issuing this statement, Rubin spoke at a press conference in Jerusalem, commenting that the Lipavsky letter 'was an absurd document that showed the poverty of fantasy of the KGB scriptwriters'. Another speaker, Avital's brother Michael, noted that the punishment for people found guilty of crimes such as Lipavsky described 'ranges from ten years' imprisonment to death'. The aim of the Soviet authorities, declared Alexander Lunts, was to 'destroy the whole Jewish emigration movement by frightening everyone from requesting visas'.

Avital Shcharansky also spoke. She was 'close to desperation', she said, but strengthened by knowing that her husband had not given up 'his struggle to reach the Jewish homeland'.

Other speakers at the Jerusalem press conference were Slepak's mother-in-law and Lerner's daughter: both 'worried aloud', the *Jerusalem Post* reported, 'about their relatives' poor health and the danger that they would break down in the face of Soviet pressure'.

On the following day, 11 March 1977, in Moscow, the television film 'Traders of Souls' was broadcast again. Photographs showing Slepak and Shcharansky embracing Israeli sportsmen in Moscow were enlarged and held on the screen for several seconds.

The day after this showing of 'Traders of Souls' was a Saturday. That afternoon Shcharansky went to Arkhipova Street, near the synagogue. His 'cage', of course, went with him. While he was in Arkhipova Street he met Iosif Ahs, the young man against whose arrest he had fought so strongly five months earlier. 'I asked him,' Ahs later remembered, ' "Tolik, what will happen? How do you feel?" He replied: "Iosif, I am ready for ten years." '

Iosif Ahs commented: 'He said it very sweetly. He understood everything. He understood the meaning of the Lipavsky letter.' Ahs added: 'He was very quiet. He even smiled.'

On 13 March 1977, Vitaly Rubin managed to put a telephone call through to Moscow from Jerusalem, and to speak to both Shcharansky and Lerner. 'They said there had been no new developments,' Rubin wrote in his diary. 'As usual eight people were following Tolya. The two were in fine spirit – what magnificent people. I told Tolya about Natasha, that in the next few days she would be leaving with her brother Misha for the USA, and that powerful forces are fighting on their behalf and that a campaign is

developing in the USA. When I told Tolya that I think that with
every day the danger of their arrest decreases he answered: "I think
so too. It's even a pity, since we have prepared so well for it." "You
still haven't lost your sense of humour," I said. "What do you
think! We laugh all the time!" he answered.'

'In a month or so,' Rubin believed, the Soviet authorities 'will let
them out, writing (possibly even announcing through Tass) that
the Soviet Government has decided to show its humanitarianism.'
Perhaps, Rubin wrote, the Soviet authorities would even announce
that they were 'letting them out to go to their masters'.

On 13 March 1977, Slepak and Shcharansky received two visitors
from Ohio, Darrell Holland and William Carlson. Both men were
journalists on the Cleveland *Plain Dealer*. Shcharansky told them
that after Avital had left Moscow he had received letters from her
'but that now these have stopped coming'. He was certain that she
still wrote to him 'but that the Government confiscates her letters'.

Asked by the two journalists why some refuseniks were willing
'to endanger their lives' to leave the Soviet Union, Shcharansky and
Slepak replied that they wanted to be 'free men, free to practise their
Judaism, to educate their children and to escape from the anti-
Semitism of Russia'. Shcharansky told the journalists: 'We have
burned all the bridges behind us here and we are like a bicycle rider
on a tightwire. We can't go back and we can't stop or we will fall
off.' Reminded by the journalists that the Soviet rejection of their
visa applications and their 'personal rebellion' could produce persecution that 'could be tantamount to pushing them off the wire',
Shcharansky replied: 'We must go ahead because we want our
children and our friends to be free.' 'We prefer this life to our
previous life in this country and we believe that we have the most
free life in Russia because we are doing what we believe in.'

Slepak and Shcharansky pointed out to their two American
visitors that most of the Jews who had been refused permission to
go to Israel were scientists, doctors, lawyers and teachers. 'The
Government tells us it does not want to prepare specialists in Russia
to work in Israel,' they said, 'but we are fighting for our human
rights and we cannot be content to live under the repression we
experience here.'

To the two American journalists, as to all visitors, Shcharansky
had spoken openly of his concern for 'human rights', believing that
Jewish immigration to Israel was an integral part of those rights. As
he waited in Slepak's apartment, however, he knew the dangers

which such outspokenness entailed. The 'cage' of KGB men at the bottom of the stairwell was proof of that, if anyone needed visible proof. For the Soviet authorities, the very words 'human rights' were anathema, let alone such well-publicised activities in support of them. 'Mr Slepak and Mr Shcharansky', noted Peter Reddaway in *The Times*, 'have been under heavy pressure for some time as they belong to Dr Yury Orlov's group monitoring Soviet observance of the Helsinki agreements.' All outside observers feared some imminent Soviet action against the two Jews; Lipavsky's article was still only nine days old.

That day, Shcharansky wrote a letter to Avital in Jerusalem. 'My darling wife,' he began, 'A whole week has passed since I embarked on my new "spying career", and I am beginning to get used to my "lofty position", to the ever present bodyguard at the door, to life without material things or papers (practically all my documents have been confiscated), but I am determined to write this letter to you.' The letter continued:

> On the first night after the *Izvestia* article appeared, when I had to readjust myself to a new life and a new scale of time, it became clear to me as never before how dreadful and without meaning my life would be without you. But remembering everything, I felt that I regretted only one thing – and this regret was so strong it brought tears to my eyes – that we have no children.
>
> But now I have become somewhat calmer and my mind is more at rest, and I am sure that we soon will have some, don't you think so?
>
> I am living with the Slepaks. My 'tails' are living just outside the door. They have 'taken root' on the landing outside and are stuck close by. My 'bodyguards' have completely shaken the imagination of our friends. In the morning, remembering the night before and the cars, the ring of 'tails' around us in the street, the 'Watchmen' by the doors and in the elevator, they have decided that the only fitting resemblance to this is Bulgakov's *The Master and Margarita*. This is the picture of our life today. Mama is holding up reasonably well, but I'm waiting with horror for the tension to relax when I'm sure that the reaction will set in. But Papa is taking it very badly. He doesn't sleep; he has heart pains, his blood pressure has jumped right up, and I'm afraid he may not be able to stand the strain of his situation.

You are all working well for us there, but there is nothing more we can do here. Now there is no other way out for us. Soon we shall be together. I kiss you, my beloved.

Natan Sharon, your husband

The Master and Margarita by Mikhail Bulgakov was one of Shcharansky's favourite books, a satirical, nightmare fantasy, surrealistic and Kafka-esque, describing the post-revolutionary period when intellectuals were constantly under suspicion, dogged by the secret police.

The atmosphere around the activists had become surrealistic. 'Fifty of us went to a friend's apartment,' Dina Beilina remembered, 'together with the KGB. Anatoly was to speak to Avital. The line got through, but Avital was not there. He was crushed.' Avital had in fact flown from Israel to Switzerland. Then, over the line to Michael Sherbourne in London, Dina Beilina dictated a statement beginning 'Brothers in arms . . . .'. She was allowed to do so without interruption.

This new collective letter was signed by 250 Jews, the largest number ever to have signed such an appeal. It was addressed to the Israeli Parliament and to 'all Jewish communities throughout the world', and began: 'Brothers in arms throughout many centuries of battle for our existence and of much suffering, we appeal to you at one of the most dramatic moments, perhaps one of the major turning points in the history of the Jews of Russia. Our history is one never ending web of humiliation, aggression, pogroms. Across the lives of our grandparents was smeared like a black thunder-cloud the infamous Beilis trial. Across the days of our fathers hung the awful nightmare of the notorious arrests of the so-called "Doctors' Plot". And now in our times there has burst upon us the preparations for a new trial – a trial of Jewish "spies" recalling the notorious trial of the so-called "spy and traitor" Dreyfus.'

The signatories reminded the Jews of the rest of the world of a three-year sentence recently imposed on Amner Zavurov in Uzbekistan, the arrest of Iosif Begun in Moscow, the 'case in preparation' against Dr Salansky in Vilnius, 'and now the monstrous accusations in the columns of the newspaper *Izvestia*'. The letter ended:

On the surface, only a small part of the erupting volcano can now be seen. All the rest is as yet inside, hidden, concealed from view. What is being cooked up down there in the depths is as yet unknown to us, but we shall no doubt very soon feel it and experience the full effect of the depths of the anti-Jewish prejudice being stirred up ready to vomit forth from the mouth of the volcano. Today it is an accusation of spying and treason in the newspaper, and from there it is not far to a dreadful trial. And already all around us we can hear the echoes and the murmurs of this anti-Jewish feeling in the streets, and shops, the buses, the Metro, the schools where our children are pupils.

Yesterday it was only the refuseniks under threat, today it is every Jew in the Soviet Union who is a potential victim for sacrifice. In this serious and dangerous moment in our lives we want you to know that no treachery, no threats, no slander, no libel can intimidate us. We shall continue with the fight for our freedom because we know that you are with us. We shall do everything in our power to restore and maintain the honour and dignity of our people. AM YISROEL CHAI! THE PEOPLE OF ISRAEL LIVES!

The signatories of this emotional, frightened, unbowed appeal were all of those who, over the past years, had been in the forefront of the Jewish struggle to go to Israel, among them Mark Azbel, Felix Kandel, Dina Beilina, Iosif Ahs, Eitan Finkelstein, Zakhar Tesker and Benjamin Fain, each of whom was subsequently to receive an exit visa, and Victor Brailovsky, Ida Nudel, Boris Chernobilsky, Lev Ovsishcher, Isai and Grigory Goldstein from Tbilisi, Vladimir Prestin, Yuly and Inna Kosharovsky, and Vladimir and Masha Slepak, all of whom, eight years after those traumatic, dangerous days, are still refused permission to leave the Soviet Union.

That night, a second message was dictated to Michael Sherbourne. It was addressed to the Israeli Parliament and signed by Lerner, Slepak and Shcharansky, the three most under threat in Lipavsky's article. The message read:

Brothers,

The recent dramatic events in Moscow and the Soviet Union generally testify to the readiness of the Soviet authorities to go to almost any extreme lengths in order to suppress the growing national renaissance of the Jews of Russia. They are now continuing the campaign of anti-Jewish trials of Beilis, Dreyfus and the so-called 'doctor–poisoners' of 1953.

The Jews of Russia once again have been feeling that over their heads there hangs the sword of Damocles of repressions, persecutions and pogroms. The situation is such that we feel exactly like hostages in the hands of terrorists who acknowledge no laws, national or international, and who are ready to take extreme measures at any moment.

However, we have faith in the solidarity of the Jewish people – our people – and we believe that truth and justice will prevail.

*   *   *

On 14 March 1977 Avital, who had reached Geneva, managed to put a telephone call through to her husband. 'He shouted down the phone', she recounted three days later, 'that KGB men were surrounding all the Jewish activists in Moscow and making life very difficult for them there.'

That evening, as Felix Kandel later recalled, Shcharansky tried to relax: 'he switched on the radio, listening to music. The soft chair. Tea and sweets. Silence and peace. "I am settled down," he said. Ten days had passed. "They'll hardly grab me now."'

Shcharansky spent that night in Slepak's apartment. Then, on the morning of 15 March 1977, the Soviet authorities unexpectedly announced the release of Dr Mikhail Shtern, the sixty-year-old doctor from Vinnitsa who still had five and a half years to serve of his eight-year labour-camp sentence. Shtern's release, declared the Soviet news agency Tass, was a 'humane act' in the light of Shtern's age.

'I think that they will now arrest someone else instead of Shtern,' was Shcharansky's first comment to two Western journalists who were with him in Slepak's apartment when he heard the news of Shtern's release. They had raised a glass together to celebrate the good news.

The two journalists, Harold D. Piper of the *Baltimore Sun* and David Satter, an American who worked with the *Financial Times* in London, asked Shcharansky what it was like 'to be followed so intensively'. Instead of replying with some statement of indignation, which was never his style, Shcharansky said he would give them an illustration. He would simply go out and be followed, and the correspondents could come along and watch. So all three, together with Slepak and Felix Kandel, put on their coats and went to the elevator. 'These KGB operations', Shcharansky explained, 'had a certain etiquette of their own'. First, one agent would enter the elevator, then Shcharansky, then another KGB man. This was what happened, the two Western correspondents piling in behind Shcharansky and, amid the crush of KGB men, leaving no room for Slepak, who had to walk down: in fact, he ran down.

When Shcharansky, Kandel, the two journalists and the two KGB men reached the ground floor, yet more KGB agents were waiting. The two journalists and Kandel were thrust to one side. Shcharansky, pushed sharply from behind, was forced 'by adroit hands', as Felix Kandel observed, into a waiting car.

A few moments later, Slepak, reaching the bottom of the stairwell, emerged into the street. 'Where's Tolya?' he asked. Tolya, he was told by the troubled onlookers, had been driven away.

17

Arrest

The first news of Shcharansky's arrest to reach the West was in a telegram sent by his friends in Moscow late on the evening of 15 March 1977. 'Greatest fears realised,' it read. 'Shcharansky arrested. Now at Lefortovo prison, Moscow. Family informed KGB investigating Shcharansky for crimes against State. Help please!'

That help was not long in coming. On 17 March 1977 Avital Shcharansky flew from Switzerland to London to campaign for her husband's release. 'Wife fights for Jew held by KGB' was the headline in *The Times* on the following morning. Avital's brother Michael Shtiglits, who accompanied her on her journeyings, tried to deliver a letter of protest to the Soviet Embassy, but the Embassy refused to accept it, a Second Secretary telling him: 'Your brother-in-law is guilty of serious crimes against the State.'

Avital had been in Geneva when she heard the news of her husband's arrest. Later she remembered thinking to herself: 'Now it begins. I must be strong.'

On the day that Avital flew to London, sixteen United States Senators and Congressmen wrote to President Carter, asking him to use his 'good offices' to help Shcharansky 'in any way you deem appropriate'. Among the signatories were five of those who had met Shcharansky in Moscow: Senator Patrick Leahy, Congressmen Philip Burton, Robert Drinan and Joshua Eilberg, and Congresswoman Millicent Fenwick.

In Washington, Irene Manekofsky sought to alert the White House and the State Department to Shcharansky's plight. 'We are all dying a thousand deaths over Tolya,' she wrote to Michael Sherbourne, Alexander Lunts and Vitaly Rubin on 19 March 1977. 'It is just unacceptable to me and to all his friends that he will go to

prison for ten years, or more. And what will happen with Lerner
and Slepak? It is the impossible thing that has happened and I cannot
accept it.'

From London, Avital flew on to the United States. There, on 23
March 1977, she was present at a press conference held at the offices
of the Greater New York Conference on Soviet Jewry. 'My
husband is in a lot of serious trouble,' she said. 'Everything he has
done was because he wants to leave Russia, because he wants Jews
to leave Russia.' With Avital at this press conference were two other
wives whose husbands were still in the Soviet Union, Jeanette
Mager and Esther Lazaris.

In Washington, Irene Manekofsky sent President Carter an
appeal from several of Shcharansky's friends in Israel, including
Alexander Lunts, Vitaly Rubin and Shcharansky's predecessor as
spokesman, Alexander Goldfarb. In New York, Lynn Singer,
President of the Long Island Committee for Soviet Jewry, took
Avital to see the Secretary General of the United Nations, Kurt
Waldheim, and the United States Ambassador to the United
Nations, Andrew Young.

Secretary of State Cyrus R. Vance was about to go to Moscow.
On the eve of the visit, Academician Sakharov gave a press
conference in Moscow, in which he declared that if President Carter
was 'really serious' about his human rights campaign, 'he must come
to the support of Anatoly Shcharansky'. Any 'hesitation', Sakharov
added, 'will have very tragic consequences'. Commented the *Wall
Street Journal* on 25 March 1977, 'President Carter should make it
publicly clear that whatever deals may be struck, the US recognizes
the especially disturbing undertones of the Shcharansky arrest.'

While in Moscow, Cyrus Vance did raise the question of
Shcharansky, but not in a direct form. 'During his visit to Moscow
in March,' a State Department official informed Lynn Singer six
months later, 'Secretary Vance emphasized to Soviet officials our
interest in the resolution of a large number of cases of Soviet Jews
refused exit visas for Israel.' The official added that a list of several
hundred names, given to the State Department by the National
Conference on Soviet Jewry, and 'including Mr Shcharansky's,
was submitted to the Soviet Government'.

          ★   ★   ★

On Gorky Street, Slepak remained unmolested. Lerner, too,
accused in the Lipavsky letter of being the main conduit for

espionage, remained at liberty. Also still at liberty were Dina and Iosif Beilin, and the others whose apartments had been searched and materials seized. Of the Jewish activists only Shcharansky and Begun were in prison cells. Of the human rights activists, Orlov and Ginsburg were likewise behind bars.

On 22 March 1977, exactly a week after Shcharansky's arrest, his parents, Boris Shcharansky and Ida Milgrom, were called in to Moscow for interrogation. That same day their apartment in Istra was searched. A week later, Ida Milgrom returned to Moscow to demand an explanation of why her son had been arrested.

Neither of Shcharansky's parents, nor his brother, had yet applied for exit visas. He had tried, therefore, not to involve them in any way in his activities. 'He was very careful,' Dina Beilina explained. 'If he was followed, he did not go to their place.' But from the first day of Shcharansky's arrest, his brother Leonid had gone to see Shcharansky's friends in Moscow, to say that he, and his wife, 'would participate in whatever was needed'.

Leonid's wife Raya had never been involved with the struggle for Jewish emigration. Like Leonid, she stood outside the circles in which her brother-in-law had been so active. When Shcharansky was arrested, however, she remarked to a friend: 'I know Anatoly well. If he is arrested, there is something wrong with the world.' Later, when her friends at work learned by chance that she was Shcharansky's sister-in-law, they were indignant. But she said to them, simply: 'Ah, yes, he wants to go to Israel, he is not a criminal.'

Ida Milgrom and Leonid now travelled into Moscow every week, to demand access to Shcharansky, or at least to be told what the charge against him was to be. Shcharansky's friends in Moscow were likewise tireless in support of him. So too were many friends and groups outside the Soviet Union. On 30 March 1977 Stuart Wurtman, former President of the Union of Councils for Soviet Jews, published a thank-you note from Professor Lerner, Ida Nudel, Vladimir Slepak, Dina and Iosif Beilin, Iosif Ahs, Mikhail Mager and others, to those non-Jews who had previously spoken so strongly on behalf of the refuseniks.

The signatories also wrote about Shcharansky. 'We are all indebted to him', they declared, 'for the service he has given to the cause of human rights. For the past two years, he has been one of the primary spokesmen for this cause in the world, perhaps even helping to set the stage for the growing interest in this subject now.' Of their and Shcharansky's efforts 'to reunite our families and our people', the signatories added, 'we will never give up.'

Shcharansky had struggled first and foremost for his rights as a Jew, and for the rights of all Soviet Jews, to go to Israel. He deserved, the refuseniks declared, 'the support of all people – Jews and non-Jews – since he was of enormous help and inspiration to all nationalities, including the Germans and Pentecostal Christians, in their desire to regain their human rights.' He was also, they pointed out, 'the inspiration and initiator' of the Helsinki Watchdog group.

One of Shcharansky's colleagues on the Moscow Watchdog group had been Ludmila Alexeeva. She had received her exit visa.

On 31 March 1977, Ida Milgrom was told by an official of the Investigations Department of Lefortovo prison, V. I. Volodin, that her son had committed 'especially dangerous crimes against the State', that the investigation would take 'a long time', and that she would be told nothing further until the investigation was completed. When she asked Volodin if she could visit her son in prison, he said no.

★   ★   ★

On 13 April 1977 Dr Mikhail Shtern, having been released from prison on the day of Shcharansky's arrest, arrived in Holland. Two days later, with Avital present, Congressman Robert Drinan, who had agreed to serve as American Chairman of an International Committee for the release of Anatoly Shcharansky, held a press conference in Washingon. On 18 April 1977, the many Jews in Moscow who had banded together at the time of his arrest to campaign for his release now sent an appeal to the West, urging all those Western scientists, artists, religious leaders and academics who had hitherto campaigned for Shtern to join the struggle for Shcharansky's release. 'We were about to rejoice,' they wrote, 'following the report of Dr Shtern's release, when the news about another arrest was received. This time the victim was Anatoly Shcharansky, a Jew, a fighter for human rights, whom the authorities have been denying for the last three years his right to emigrate to Israel.' In Lipavsky's *Izvestia* article, they pointed out, Shcharansky had been accused of spying for the United States, and they added: 'We know Shcharansky well and are convinced that these charges are false. We are convinced that the authorities are resorting to such charges to exert pressure on President Jimmy

Carter to stop the international campaign for human rights, in order to discredit the Jewish emigration movement and to halt emigration from the USSR.'

The letter of 18 April 1977 went on to warn that the 'Shcharansky case' had started 'against the background of a sharp increase in "anti-Zionist" propaganda in the media: articles in newspapers and magazines and films on this subject slanderously charging crimes committed by the Zionists, about "Zionist genocide" and about the "international Zionist plot"'. Rumours were circulating around Moscow 'claiming that an explosion in the Moscow underground in January and a fire in the Rossiya Hotel in February were acts committed by the Zionists. Thousands of lectures on the same subject are being read in different organisations and enterprises.' This was creating 'an explosive situation'; the Shcharansky case was acquiring 'an especially grim meaning in this context'.

The signatories of the letter were 'convinced', as they wrote in their appeal, 'that if all people of goodwill would speak out in Shcharansky's defence, that if voices – such as yours – would speak out in defence of law and justice, truth will prevail'.

This appeal was addressed not only to those who had earlier campaigned for Shtern, but to the United States Congress, the British and Canadian Parliaments, and the Permanent Secretariat of the Helsinki Conference. It was signed by more than twenty-five Jews, among them Eitan Finkelstein, Benjamin Fain, Mark Azbel, Dina and Iosif Beilin and Iosif Ahs, all of whom later received their exit visas, and by Professor Lerner, Vladimir Slepak, Victor Brailovsky, Vladimir Prestin, Pavel Abramovich, Lev Ovsishcher, and the Goldstein brothers, all, in the spring of 1986, still in the Soviet Union.

On 22 April 1977 a Soviet news agency commentator, in a broadcast to the West, declared that Shcharansky was to be charged under Article 64 of the Russian Republic's Criminal Code. Under this article, the maximum penalty was death. According to the Soviet commentator, he was to be accused of being a part 'of a group of Jews who intended to collect information about secret organisations'. Eight days later, the charge under Article 64 was confirmed in a letter from Prosecutor Ilyukhin to Ida Milgrom. It was Ilyukhin who was supervising the investigations in the case.

Article 64, treason, was the worst of all possible charges. Shcharansky's closest friends, Slepak, Lerner, Ida Nudel and Dina Beilina, immediately sent a further appeal to the West on his behalf.

'Anatoly is in the greatest danger at this moment,' they wrote, 'and needs the strongest and widest possible support from everyone in the West.' Not only was Shcharansky 'a consistent and active campaigner' for Jewish emigration to Israel, and 'a dedicated supporter of the rebirth of Jewish awareness and culture', but, they wrote, 'he was also active on Professor Orlov's Committee for monitoring the Helsinki Agreement. His courage earns him respect and support.'

18

Seeking to Build Up
a Criminal Charge

On 6 May 1977, at a press conference organised by the editorial board of *Izvestia*, Sanya Lipavsky reiterated the charges in his letter to *Izvestia* in March, repeatedly mentioning by name Rubin, Lunts, Azbel, Slepak and Lerner as well as Orlov and Alexeeva. The formation of the Helsinki Watchdog group he carefully ascribed to 'Y. Orlov with the participation of V. Rubin'. It was 'Rubin and his closest friend D. Azbel', Lipavsky added, 'who did everything to draw me into the network of the American secret service'. In a message from Peter Osnos of the *Washington Post*, 'an assignment' had been given to Rubin, to 'gather information about government enterprises' at which the refuseniks worked. Lipavsky then told the press conference: 'Discussing the aforementioned letter to Rubin, I said bluntly to Lerner: "But this is a crime." Yet he remained silent and declined to answer. Later I learned that he ordered Shcharansky and others to organise the acquisition of that information and send it abroad.'

On 10 May 1977, four days after this press conference, the KGB began its interrogation of Jewish activists. The first to be brought to the Lefortovo prison for questioning was Professor Mark Azbel, who was interrogated that day for eight hours. The name of Azbel's interrogator was Sharudillo, in front of whom Azbel saw a file headed: 'Contact with the CIA'. Azbel was then interrogated in connection with 'his contact with Shcharansky'.

Dr Victor Brailovsky was brought in for questioning on May 11. 'I can arrest you immediately as we did with Shcharansky,' he was told by KGB investigator Solovchenko. 'Your activities and support of the Helsinki Agreement give me this possibility. I do not believe that there exist people who are not afraid of pain. I do not believe that there exist people who are not afraid of torture. I do not believe that there are people who are not afraid of death. You are a sick person, and I assure you you will not survive more than two years in our camp, while you'll be sentenced to at least seven years.' Courageously, Brailovsky refused to be a false witness against Shcharansky, arguing that he had not been given any information about the case, and had been asked 'incriminating questions'.

Most of those questioned were asked to sign a paper saying that they would not tell anybody what questions they had been asked. When Professor Benjamin Fain was asked at his first interrogation, on May 12, to sign such a paper, he refused.

During this first interrogation, Fain was first threatened with imprisonment, then promised an exit visa if he 'co-operated with the interrogators'. That night, as the activists discussed the interrogations so far, it was clear that the main line of questioning concerned a group invented by the interrogators, which they referred to as the 'Moscow Aliyah', or 'Moscow Emigration to Israel' group. 'We activists knew Soviet law well,' Dina Beilina later recalled, 'and we never organised any groups: it was the Soviet dream to provoke us into doing so.'

On 12 May 1977, in a telephone conversation with Moscow, Michael Sherbourne (whom the Soviet news agency Tass in a statement that week had created a lord) was given the text of twelve questions which had already been put to both Professor Azbel and Professor Fain, seeking to link Shcharansky and the imaginary group. 'Aliyah' is the concept of wishing to go to Israel: the KGB wished to make out that it was the name of an actual group.

Q: What did he do in the 'Moscow Aliyah'?
Q: What did he do inside the group?
Q: When was the 'Aliyah' organised?
Q: What role did he play in the organisation of this group?
Q: What was his relationship with the members of this 'Aliyah'?
Q: With whom was he acquainted and what relationship existed between them, what sort of rapport did they have?
Q: What documents did the 'Aliyah' issue?
Q: Where were these documents sent – to the governments of which capitalist countries were they addressed?

Q: What documents did he himself write?

Q: Did he know any foreigners and who were they?

Q: What was his relationship with foreigners?

Q: What do you know about letters and appeals sent to the governments of capitalist countries which will be used for bourgeois propaganda?

The Moscow activists were certain from these questions, as they told Sherbourne that night, that 'this case affects us all'. They were now 'convinced' that the authorities were going to take 'large-scale measures' to break up the Jewish emigration movement, by giving it the spurious organisational framework of the 'Moscow Aliyah'. Shcharansky would be used as a means to link people and cities into a single, and then crushable, entity, and to connect the Jewish movement with the CIA: to portray it as an anti-Soviet fifth column. 'When did he first appear among you?' Fain had been asked. 'Who and what is he? What sort of a man is he?'

★　　　★　　　★

Ida Milgrom was still refused permission to see Shcharansky. In a 'petition of complaint' which she sent to the Prosecutor of Moscow on 12 May 1977, she asked to be allowed to visit her son, both 'so that we can together choose a lawyer' and also in order 'to be convinced that the prejudiced attitude of those who are conducting the investigation is not adversely affecting my son's condition in prison'. She received no reply.

★　　　★　　　★

Throughout the period of Shcharansky's imprisonment without trial, his father had suffered enormously. A sensitive man, he had fought bravely for the four years of war on the eastern front against Nazi Germany, for the ideals of truth and justice – ideals with which he later imbued his sons. Now his ideals lay shattered about him as he gazed in disbelief at the incomprehensible, unfounded allegations levelled by the State against his own son. He was taken physically ill and, bedridden after the second in a series of heart attacks, he told Dina Beilina he was thinking of getting up: 'You see, Dina, I think I should go to the Party Central Committee and give back my Party Card and give back all my medals. I think I should protest too.'

Dina Beilina and Ida Milgrom, realising how ill he was, dissuaded him. 'One day we may need your actions,' they said, 'but not now. All the world is active now.'

Boris Shcharansky was seventy-three years old.

*   *   *

On 17 May 1977 the Moscow evening newspaper, *Viechernyaya Moskva*, revealed another informer in the activist ranks: Leonid Tsipin. In the Moscow Visa Office, the newspaper explained, it had been 'permitted' to read Tsipin's statement, 'cancelling his previously submitted request for emigration to Israel', and asking that this statement 'be shown to the editorial board of some newspaper so that I should be able to tell publicly, so that all should hear, about my fall and my enlightenment and about the people who, calling themselves "fighters" for human rights, are in reality provocateurs and adventurists and about their protectors and leaders abroad.'

Tsipin made no reference to Shcharansky, although he did speak of his own visits to Kiev and Kharkov, one of the fact-finding journeys in November 1973 of which he and Shcharansky had been a part. On that occasion, Tsipin said, Lunts had told him to hurry, as information 'was expected at a definite date'.

Since 1971, Tsipin declared, he had carried out 'instructions' received from Victor Polsky, an activist who had subsequently received his exit visa, though Tsipin did not say so, and Slepak. Their goals, he said, and those of the movement of which he found himself a part 'were not determined by us. Our activity was directed and financed by the anti-Soviet foreign organisations, including the Zionist ones. They did not rely very much on our initiative. Plans were simply worked out for us. We were supposed to prepare provocative "actions", that is, to arrange noisy scenes, that would arouse the necessary, that is anti-Soviet, reaction in the West, and also to select, or more exactly, to fabricate slanderous information.' As 'pretext' for all this, Tsipin added, 'we were supposed to report the refusals for permission to emigrate to Israel obtained by individual citizens of Jewish nationality. Any justified refusal had to be presented at all cost as arbitrariness on the part of the authorities and as an infringement of human rights. This tendentious information was transmitted by us to certain foreign correspondents, and also to the workers of certain Embassies.'

Tsipin then told of the 'expensive gifts' received from the Jewish Agency, the National Conference on Soviet Jewry, and 'all sorts of foreign "committees" and "funds"', and he went on to mock 'all these "fighters for human rights", A. Lunts, A. Lerner, V. Slepak and others' who were concerned most of all 'with their own pockets and the publicity in the West, which was supposed to bring them dividends in the future'. Tsipin also said of the various 'representatives of the foreign anti-Soviet centres' whom he had met: 'To unite young people of Jewish nationality, that is what they wanted from us.' For this purpose, he added, 'we tried to organise so-called circles for the study of Hebrew.' He himself had been an instructor 'in one of such circles', where 'we did not teach Hebrew as much as we made agitation for emigration to Israel and spoke about the "life of paradise in the Promised Land" in accordance with what was written in the textbooks received illegally.'

Tsipin spoke of 'special instructions' to collect information on the themes of 'the absence of rights of Jews in the USSR' and of 'the violation of human rights'. Such material had been 'demanded from us by representatives of various anti-Soviet organisations who visited us from time to time in the guise of tourists'. Among those mentioned by name by Tsipin were four of those who had been particularly close to Shcharansky: two former Presidents of the Union of Councils for Soviet Jews, Inez Weisman and Irene Manekofsky, as well as Lou Rosenblum and Michael Sherbourne. But Tsipin made no reference to Shcharansky.

'International Zionism,' Tsipin declared, 'like any manifestation of racism, like Nazism, is alien and hostile to all Soviet people, including Soviet Jews.'

At the very moment when Tsipin's statement of 17 May 1977 added yet another set of accusations to those first broached by Lipavsky two months earlier, the Jewish activists in Moscow were worried about the efforts being made in the West, no doubt inspired by the KGB, to question whether Shcharansky's case really was 'at all Jewish'. These doubts, explained twenty-one of Shcharansky's friends in a message addressed 'to all people interested in justice and peace', and transmitted in a telephone call to Michael Sherbourne late that same night, May 17, 'are due to the fact' that Shcharansky was a member of the Helsinki Watchdog group in Moscow, 'which extended his activity beyond the scope of Jewish emigration into the sphere of human rights in the USSR'. The signatories, including three, Mark Azbel, Victor Brailovsky and Benjamin Fain, who had already been interrogated in the Shcharansky case, went on to state that in their view, 'Interrelation between the Jewish emigration and the general human rights movement in the USSR has a versatile character. We realise that the Jewish problem in the USSR stands very much apart and has its own specific aspects. *However, we cannot imagine these two movements to be absolutely separated* – there are a number of problems, such as support of Prisoners of Conscience, legal problems, scientific contacts, which require co-operation of the Jewish movement and the movement for human rights.'

In the case of Shcharansky, the signatories pointed out, he had always been portrayed, as in a photographic close-up in the television film 'Traders of Souls', as a 'soldier of Zionism'. Four times he had been sentenced to fifteen days' detention 'for his Jewish activity'. The accusations against him of 'grave crimes against the State' were intended 'to discredit just the Jewish movement'.

The signatories who thus so emphatically stood behind Shcharansky for the sake, as they wrote, 'of emigration from the Soviet Union to Israel, and of the future of all Soviet Jewry', included Yuly Kosharovsky, who had also been denounced as a 'soldier of Zionism' in the television film, Ida Nudel, Alexander Lerner, Vladimir Slepak, Felix Kandel, Dina Beilina, and the young religious leader, Ilya Essas. Eight days later, on 25 May 1977, Dina Beilina began to dictate a similar statement over the telephone to Michael Sherbourne, but the line was cut after the first minutes. 'Whereas until now', Dina Beilina had said before the line was cut, 'it was a question of limiting the extent of Jewish emigration and of slowing down its onward march, now they are undertaking attempts to annihilate entirely the whole movement,' and this, she declared, 'is causing us special concern'.

On 23 May 1977, Granada television broadcast a sequel to its film 'A Calculated Risk'. The second film, entitled 'The Man Who Went Too Far', showed scenes from Avital's campaign on Shcharansky's behalf, including a hunger strike which she had carried out outside the Soviet Embassy in London. This second film was immediately made a further part of the indictment against Shcharansky, who was told by his interrogators that Soviet Ambassadors throughout Western Europe had reported back to Moscow on the 'bad influence of the film'.

Under Soviet legal procedure, Shcharansky had the right to see the evidence being used against him. He therefore insisted on seeing both films. Seeing Avital on the screen, learning from the film of her activities on his behalf, and realising the extent of the concern of the outside world was an enormous morale boost to him.

Mischievously, he told the interrogators: 'I do not see it very well', and insisted that they show it to him 'once more'. Reluctantly, they did so, and had then to run it through a third time, as again he insisted that he still could not see it clearly. 'I saw it all the day,' he later recalled. 'I was thankful to think that I could see the face of my wife and my friends after such isolation.' Asked by his interrogators whether he had helped in the compilation of the first of the two films, Shcharansky replied: 'Yes, of course I did help. I think it did a good job. It is on human rights.'

On 31 May 1977, a member of the Helsinki Watchdog group, Malva Landa, one of nine members of the group now under arrest, was sentenced to two years in labour camp. The charge against her was that her carelessness had caused a fire in her apartment.

On the following day, 1 June 1977, the Hebrew teacher Iosif Begun, who had been held in prison since before Shcharansky's arrest, was sentenced to two years' Siberian exile. The charge against him was 'parasitism'. The fact that he was a regular teacher of Hebrew had not been allowed as proof of legitimate employment.

Also on June 1, Ida Milgrom received a letter from the Prosecutor's Office informing her that her son was to be charged with treason. One of the activities on which this charge was based, she was told, was 'rendering aid to a foreign State in carrying out hostile activity'. No mention was made in the letter of two of the other treasonable activities covered by Article 64–A: espionage, and passing State or military secrets to another country.

It was Sakharov's wife, Elena Bonner, who passed on the news of Shcharansky's charge to Western correspondents in Moscow. The accusation of treason, David Shipler telephoned at once to the *New York Times*, 'represents the severest attack in years against the advocates of an open society, and it dramatizes a growing campaign by the KGB – the secret police – to discredit and eliminate dissidents by linking them to the United States Central Intelligence Agency.' Of Shcharansky himself, Shipler wrote: 'His role was important to the dissident movement, for he provided a key link between Jews seeking emigration and Russians and others wanting to stay and liberalize the society. Furthermore, he was a consummate public relations man, fluent in English and scrupulously accurate with his facts, who acted as a spokesman to the Western press on behalf of Jewish activists.'

The interrogations in Shcharansky's case continued. On 11 June 1977 the *Los Angeles Times* Moscow correspondent, Robert Toth, who had earlier been seized by the Soviet authorities in a Moscow street, was questioned about his meetings with the refuseniks, and about Shcharansky's part in these meetings. Toth was questioned twice again, on June 14 and June 15, before being expelled from the Soviet Union.

On 13 June 1977, as the full impact of the charge against Shcharansky began to be felt in Washington, President Carter held a press conference at the White House, in which he declared: 'I have enquired deeply within the State Department and within the CIA as to whether or not Mr Shcharansky has ever had any known relationship in a subversive way or otherwise with the CIA. The answer is no.' Carter added: 'We have double-checked this and I have been hesitant to make that public announcement, but now I am completely convinced that contrary to the allegations that have been reported in the press, Mr Shcharansky has never had any sort of relationship to our knowledge with the CIA.'

Shcharansky's 'only purpose', Robert Toth told a meeting of the National Conference on Soviet Jewry on his return to the United States, 'was to get out, and help other Jews get out, of the Soviet Union', and he added: 'All this nonsense about espionage is just a lot of boloney.'

On 15 June 1977 Ida Milgrom asked one of the best Soviet lawyers in political cases, Dina Kaminskaya, if she would undertake her son's defence. Kaminskaya agreed to do so, provided that the Moscow College of Soviet Advocates were in agreement. Ida Milgrom then wrote a letter to the Deputy President of the College, Advocate Sklyarsky, which, accompanied by Dina Beilina, she handed to him, asking permission for Kaminskaya to take on the case. In reply, the Moscow College of Advocates advised Kaminskaya to hand back all her cases: she was, in effect, expelled from the College. Within six months, she and her husband, himself an outspoken figure, had been expelled from the Soviet Union.

From Moscow, on 8 July 1977, one of the most moving letters of all was sent to the West on Shcharansky's behalf. It was signed by the leading human rights activists of the Soviet Union, including Sakharov and his wife Elena Bonner. The letter read:

He appeared about five years ago among those Moscow Jews who were waiting for repatriation. Invariably filled with benevolence and concern for others and at the same time full of life and energy, Anatoly Shcharansky became quickly a universal favourite. There is no point in enumerating the stages of his fight with bureaucratic abuse of authority, of his struggle for his own repatriation, and of his support for his friends. The whole history of Jewish emigration in recent years was pierced through by his personality like a laser beam. With time his interests broadened organically and he became one of the initiators of the creation of the Public Group for Fulfilment of the Helsinki Agreement in the Soviet Union.

Until the moment when he was arrested, without any warrant for arrest, when he was physically grabbed at the entrance to an apartment building before the disbelieving eyes of foreign correspondents immediately following a press conference which they had held, Anatoly gave all his strength and all of his ability to helping other people. He demanded not only the right of emigration – he insisted on the fundamental natural human rights. He helped all who are suffering, including the persecuted members of the religious communities of Baptists and Pentecostalists.

Anatoly placed himself in a determined fashion among others whenever the feeling of risk arose. Intelligent, brave, endowed with a lively mind and with the gift of being able to approach people, and with a fluent command of English, Anatoly became necessary to people. Strict in his morals, he never allowed himself to tolerate anything dishonourable, and the authorities knew this. They knew this and therefore they did not simply take reprisal against him – they first had to slander him.

We who know him are convinced of his innocence. But the desire to take the most savage of reprisals against him who was disturbing their peace can only triumph if the voice of public opinion both here and abroad does not cry out persistently loud and clear. We call upon you to defend Anatoly Shcharansky. Turn around you people! Speak! Write! Demand! Shout!

To the President of France, Valéry Giscard d'Estaing, Ida Milgrom wrote on July 15: 'I, the mother of Anatoly Shcharansky, appeal to you and request your help for my son. He is young and has only just started really to live. But he wanted to remain a Jew, and he wanted to live with his people in his own country.' Ida Milgrom added: 'Long years of waiting for permission to be allowed to emigrate after being given an entirely unreasonable refusal, forced separation from his wife and now – prison – this has been his fate and now perhaps he will be deprived for ever from being allowed to see his beloved Israel. I hope that you will not allow such a cruel savage punishment to be inflicted upon an innocent person.'

On the day of Ida Milgrom's letter to the French President, another appeal was addressed to him by twenty-three of Shcharansky's friends. 'As a Frenchman,' they wrote, 'you can be proud of the fact that at that critical time when the honour of France was clouded over by the shadow of the disgraceful Dreyfus trial, there were brave people who selflessly stood up for justice, and defended the life and honour of an innocent man, and thus deprived the anti-Semites of official support from the national Courts of Justice. We are sure that you will not stand aside and remain indifferent when, in the Soviet Union, another, even more glaring injustice is in the making, when an absurd accusation of the most serious of crimes is being used in order to take reprisal against a noble and irreproachably honourable man.'

The signatories of this appeal included Professors Lerner, Fain and Meiman, as well as Vladimir Slepak, Dina and Iosif Beilin, Vladimir Shakhnovsky, Felix Kandel, Vladimir Prestin and Pavel Abramovich from Moscow, the Goldstein brothers from Tbilisi, Lev Ovsishcher from Minsk, Eitan Finkelstein from Vilnius and Aba Taratuta from Leningrad.

Eitan Finkelstein also wrote a letter, over his own signature, to the Soviet authorities. 'Being both a refusenik and an activist,' he wrote, 'Shcharansky was under the constant surveillance of the KGB, and therefore he could not possibly have established contacts with individuals with any knowledge of Government secrets.' Finkelstein added: 'I hereby testify that in all his activities Anatoly Shcharansky did nothing that was not simultaneously done by other individuals, all of whom face no accusations.'

Slepak, Lerner, Arkady Mai, Vladimir Shakhnovsky, Felix Kandel, Lev Ulanovsky, Zakhar Tesker, Dina Beilina, Victor Brailovsky and Ida Nudel all added their voices to Shcharansky's defence, issuing public statements on his behalf. 'The accusation of conspiratorial actions with selfish motivation', wrote Lerner, 'is in direct conflict with Anatoly Shcharansky's moral values. His high moral qualities are undoubted because of his phenomenal modesty, unselfishness, complete honesty, strong moral views, and his faithfulness to his wife, from whom he parted in 1974.'

In his statement, Lev Ulanovsky wrote of Shcharansky's 'readiness to help others, and his endless charm'. Dina Beilina likewise wrote of her friend's character: 'Brilliant, and having perfect command of English, Shcharansky helped us write complaints about the lawlessness with which the emigration matters are being treated. His presentations at the seminars in Dr Lerner's apartment were outstanding and we shall ever remember his report about the Entebbe raid – a report that ended with an ovation.'

Felix Kandel, in writing of Shcharansky's character, described him in his statement that week as 'a man who is perfectly honest, sincere, truthful; a man who is noble; a man able to control his emotions and his actions; a man of great intelligence and analytic abilities; a man who is frank, who can say to others what he thinks of them; a man who thinks on the social scale, a man for whom personal problems form a unity with social ones; a man who is a fighter, for whom the struggle is not an obsession or a desire, but a reasonable analysed necessity; a man who is unselfish, who will never sacrifice his principles for the sake of any benefit.'

Victor Brailovsky, in another written statement issued on Shcharansky's behalf, made a point which several others also made, that the accusations were aimed 'not only against Shcharansky, but also against all Jewish activists in the USSR'. Shcharansky had been selected, wrote Ida Nudel, 'because of his youth, as well as the reputation of a champion of free Jewish emigration from the Soviet Union that he had gained in the Western world', and she added, in her inimitable way: 'Today we, the Jews of the Soviet Union, are accused of espionage, for the single reason that the accusation of killing Christian babies would sound ridiculous in this country of atheists.'

From Moscow, Dina Beilina managed to telephone a forceful appeal to London, which was at once sent on to Israel. There, it was read at a vigil at the Western, or Wailing, Wall. 'Brothers and Sisters', it began, 'the Shcharansky case is neither a mistake nor a political stunt, as some have been hoping until recently. It is one further stage in an escalation of hate. It is a threat of death for one, it is a threat of deprivation of freedom for hundreds, it is a threat of demoralisation and the loss of the remnants of national dignity for millions of Soviet Jews.'

'I can testify from personal knowledge', Vitaly Rubin stated in Jerusalem on 17 July 1977, 'that Shcharansky was dedicated solely to protecting the human rights of his fellow men and he was active both in the movement of Jews seeking to emigrate to Israel as well as others in the Soviet Union who sought human rights for themselves in that country. Shcharansky was open – not secret – in all of his activities and I know personally that when he met with foreign correspondents it was done in a completely open and legal manner.' Such contacts, Rubin pointed out, were 'protected and guaranteed by the provisions of the Helsinki Final Act and other international treaties'.

From inside the Soviet Union, the public protests on Shcharansky's behalf continued to reach the West. On 27 July 1977, in a telephone message transmitted through Michael Sherbourne, twenty of Shcharansky's friends spoke of the need 'to fulfil the Helsinki Agreement in its entirety', not only its security aspects but also its humanitarian obligations. 'The right to emigrate', they declared, 'gives the Jews of the USSR the possibility to be united with their people in their historic Motherland.' The message continued:

> Thousands of Jews continue to be kept back in the USSR, Jews who are trying to apply to emigrate, among them families living in the dismal state of being 'refusenik' for six or seven or more years. These people, as a rule, are deprived of the possibility of working and are then persecuted for 'leading a parasitic way of life'. The most active of them are made to undergo judicial repression on the basis of false accusations. At present there are in fact in prisons more than thirty Jews whose only crime is their desire to emigrate to Israel. They have committed no other crime.
>
> The most glaring example of persecution of a Jewish activist is the arrest of Anatoly Shcharansky and the preparation against him of an absurd accusation of High Treason on the basis of a lying denunciation from an agent provocateur.

The Helsinki Final Act was shortly to be reviewed at a conference in Belgrade. The twenty signatories of the appeal of 27 July 1977 'begged' that the Belgrade Conference include on its agenda 'the question of violations by the USSR of the Helsinki Final Act in the sections referring to emigration policy'. Of the signatories of this letter, Benjamin Fain, Dina and Iosif Beilin and Eitan Finkelstein were later to receive their exit visas: but eight years later, Alexander Lerner, Ida Nudel, Vladimir Slepak, Arkady Mai, Vladimir

20 Above   *Shcharansky with some of his closest refusenik friends. Left to right: Professor Vitaly Rubin, Vladimir Slepak, Lev Ovsishcher, Riva Feldman, Iosif Beilin (behind Shcharansky's head), Dina Beilina, Ida Nudel and Professor Alexander Lerner.*

21 Left   *Shcharansky in Moscow, under a map of Israel.*

22 Below   *The Star of David sit-in and demonstration, Moscow, 25 October 1976.*

23 Above *Shcharansky, Alexander Lunts and (far right) Vladimir Slepak, with two Israeli sportsmen in a wood near Moscow on 21 September 1975. This meeting was later to form part of the public denunciation of Shcharansky.*

24 Left *Ina Rubin and Shcharansky.*

25 Below *Ida Nudel (far left) and Shcharansky entertaining American visitors: Connie Smukler, Enid Wurtman, and Mrs Jules Lippert.*

26 *Five refuseniks and one visitor: Shcharansky, Leonid Volvovsky (sentenced in 1985 to three years in labour camp), Ida Nudel (in 1986 still a refusenik and forbidden to return to her apartment in Moscow), Dina and Iosif Beilin (now in Jerusalem), and Enid Wurtman (also now in Jerusalem).*

27 *Three refusenik friends in 1976: Vladimir Slepak, Shcharansky and Iosif Beilin. Only Slepak was still in Moscow ten years later, after more than fifteen years as a refusenik, four of them in Siberian exile.*

28 *The first night of Passover, 15 April 1976. An American Rabbi, Joseph Ehrenkranz, conducts the service. To his right, the Slepaks; to his left, Shcharansky.*

29 *Shcharansky in Moscow, holding a photograph of Avital brought to him from Jerusalem by one of his many Western visitors.*

30 Shcharansky at Tupik, eastern Siberia, in November
1975, visiting his friend Mark Nashpits, then in internal
exile. After nearly twenty years as a refusenik, Nashpits
was allowed to go to Israel a few months before
Shcharansky's release.

31 Moscow, 2 May 1976. Refuseniks gather in a wood
near Moscow to celebrate Israel Independence Day. Next
to Shcharansky, reading a prayer, is Professor Edward
Trifonov, who subsequently received his exit visa.

32 Ida Nudel and Sanya Lipavsky, the 'refusenik' doctor who was to betray both the movement and Shcharansky, in
March 1977.

33 *Shcharansky in Moscow with Academician Andrei Sakharov.*

34 *Shcharansky, Sakharov and Sakharov's wife Elena Bonner.*

35 *Shcharansky with Ludmila Alexeeva, a fellow member of the unofficial Helsinki Watchdog group. Alexeeva was later allowed to leave the Soviet Union.*

36 *Reading a statement prepared for distribution in the West. In the background, Masha Slepak.*

37 *Slepak and Shcharansky photographed in Slepak's apartment on 13 March 1977, two days before Shcharansky was arrested when leaving the apartment.*

38 *The front entrance to Lefortovo prison, Moscow, where Shcharansky was held and interrogated for more than fifteen months.*

39 *Outside a Moscow courthouse, on 14 July 1978, Shcharansky's mother, Ida Milgrom, hears that he has received a thirteen-year sentence. With her is her son Leonid.*

Shakhnovsky, Lev Ovsishcher from Minsk, the Goldstein brothers in Tbilisi and Aba Taratuta in Leningrad were still waiting.

In a moving petition to Leonid Brezhnev a few weeks later, eighteen refuseniks, among them Lev Ovsishcher, wrote of how Shcharansky 'is suffering only because he insisted on his unquestionable right to emigrate to Israel and because he helped others to obtain their rights'.

Even as Shcharansky awaited trial, the Soviet authorities granted exit visas to Mark Azbel and Benjamin Fain, two of those who had so frequently signed declarations with him, or protested on his behalf. Two former Prisoners of Zion were also given their exit visas, and arrived in Israel: Alexander Feldman and Yakov Vinarov. Also reaching Israel in July 1977 was Mikhail Mager of Vinnitsa, on behalf of whose divided family Shcharansky had once protested. Exit visas were also granted that month to Elena Bonner's children.

These exit visas were impressive, and intended to be so, as Soviet and American delegates prepared to go to Belgrade in October, for the first of the Helsinki review conferences. Less publicised than the exit visas was the arrest of a non-Jew, Victoras Pyatkus, a member of the Lithuanian Helsinki monitors.

In Moscow, the interrogators continued to try to build up a case against Shcharansky, and from Moscow they moved on to at least thirteen other Soviet cities, including Minsk, Riga, Odessa, Vilnius and Leningrad. Anatoly Malkin was questioned in his labour camp at Alexandrov Gai by Major Martemyanov, who had also carried out some of the Moscow interrogations. 'I signed nothing,' Malkin later recalled. 'He asked me about the Minsk visit and the Riga visit of November 1974. I was questioned for two days.' Iosif Ahs, another of those whom Shcharansky had helped, was likewise questioned, but said nothing and signed nothing. In the remote Uzbek city of Dushanbe, about ten refuseniks were interrogated, none of whom had ever met Shcharansky. How, they were asked, did the information about them reach the West? In Saratov a refusenik by the name of Iosif Shraiber was questioned. Shraiber, too, had never met Shcharansky. 'Don't be surprised,' the interrogator told him. 'This is an all-Union undertaking.' The whole Soviet Union was to be scoured for a Jewish emigration movement. In Kharkov, Vladimir Pevzner, who had also never met Shcharansky, was asked about the ways through which information concerning him had reached the West. Three other Kharkov Jews, whose names, like Pevzner's, had appeared on the Lunts–Beilina list of refuseniks from Kharkov, were asked: 'How did your lists of refuseniks reach *Moscow* and the West?' In Odessa, Lev Roitburd was asked how his name had got 'into the list of divided families'. In Kiev, Vladimir Kislik, whose beating-up had once been publicised in the West, was questioned for three days, the first session lasting twelve hours, mostly about those collective letters in which his name had appeared.

In Riga, the questions were about the way in which the lists of Riga refuseniks had reached Moscow. In Leningrad, six refuseniks were questioned about their signing of collective letters. Eitan Finkelstein, interrogated in Vilnius, was told that in a short time he would join 'your pal Shcharansky'. Outraged by being asked to 'confirm' Shcharansky's guilt, Finkelstein handed a statement to his interrogators which began: 'I hereby declare that I refuse to co-operate with the investigation in the case of Anatoly Shcharansky because it is being conducted in contradiction to the Constitution of the USSR. Gravest violations of the norms of Soviet legislation are being committed in the course of the investigation.'

None of those questioned gave evidence against Shcharansky: all insisted that he was a man of the highest standards of honesty and decency. Leonid Volvovsky wrote on the bottom of his interrogation sheet: 'I would like Shcharansky to know, when he sees this, that the Motherland remembers him and prays for him; it prays that the Almighty will strengthen his spirit and mind.'

During one of the interrogations in Minsk, the following exchange took place: 'Who attended Colonel Davidovich's funeral?' 'Why are you asking this question?' 'Secret information might have been passed to foreigners on a train.'

Those interrogated were also shown several documents, and asked to comment on them. These documents included the letter written on behalf of the refuseniks who had been beaten in the woods, the statement on the fifth anniversary of the Leningrad Trials, the protest by many refuseniks outraged by the film 'Traders of Souls', the letter to the French and Italian Communist Parties, and the Moscow Watchdog group document about the reunification of divided families.

Interrogated for eight hours, one of Shcharansky's friends, Iosif Ahs, was then asked to sign the protocol of what he had said. Exhausted though he was by the questioning, he saw at once that what he was being asked to sign was not what he had said. It looked, he later recalled, as if it 'had been prepared long before-hand'. He therefore wrote on the protocol itself a strong protest against the misrepresentation.

'For the first time,' Dina Beilina reflected, 'people came from different cities to give us copies of their testimonies. They were afraid, not of being arrested, but of being used by the KGB against an innocent man. The KGB tried to frighten people from one side by threatening them with arrest, and tried from the other side to tempt them, by promising them exit visas.' The KGB did not expect, Dina Beilina added, 'such resistance from simple people. Finally, in the trial, they were able to use only their own collaborators.'

From those who were interrogated, and refused to sign the undertaking not to reveal what they were asked, it has been possible to list the principal questions which, throughout the summer and autumn of 1977, were asked of Jewish activists and refuseniks throughout the Soviet Union. The most frequent questions were:

> Are you acquainted with Shcharansky? Who introduced you to him and where? What are Shcharansky's first and patronymic names? Who are his parents and where do they live? Is Shcharansky registered as living in Moscow? Have you ever been to his home? Has he been to yours? What is his speciality? Where did he work lately? What were his financial resources? Who is his wife? What is her first name? Where is she now?

> What was the last place at which Shcharansky worked? From what college did he graduate? Did he receive postal money orders, certificates, currency or parcels? What do you know about his friends? What are his relations with them? How is his mental health? (This question was asked late in the investigations.)

> When did Shcharansky apply to emigrate and what induced him to do so?

> Which of the collective letters were written by Shcharansky, given by Shcharansky to you to sign? Did Shcharansky sign letters for you, on your request or without informing you about this?

> Which appeals did Shcharansky write to international bodies, to Soviet organisations, to the governments of bourgeois countries? Which of them were used by bourgeois propaganda? Which of them were written together with you?

What was the aim of these documents? How did they get to the West? Were you present at Shcharansky's telephone conversations?

What do you know about Shcharansky's criminal activities, and when did he tread his criminal path? What do you know about the foreigners who met him, especially the correspondents and diplomats? Were you present at Shcharansky's meetings with them?

Did Shcharansky introduce you to foreigners, to 'useful' people? Did he help you to write applications, claims? Did he see you with Soviet officials? Where did the meetings with foreigners take place?

What did you tell Shcharansky about your last job which was the reason that your exit visa was refused? What do you know about Shcharansky collecting information about refuseniks and among refuseniks?

What do you know about so-called demonstrations and press conferences held by refuseniks? What was Shcharansky's role in these?

Other questions frequently asked were:

How did Shcharansky induce the Jackson Amendment? Do you know that the adoption of this discriminating amendment greatly damaged Soviet–American relations? Did you know that the list of refuseniks was used by Jackson to secure his amendment?

How did the list of refuseniks from your town get to Moscow? How did it get from Moscow to the West?

What are your feelings concerning the articles from *Izvestia* and *Viechernyaya Moskva*? (The letters of Lipavsky and Tsipin and the commentaries, as well as the follow-up anti-Zionist article.)

Did you take part in the press conference concerned with the assault in the forest (October 1976)? What role did Shcharansky play in such press conferences?

What sort of activities did Shcharansky engage in in the 'Aliyah movement'? (The person questioned was asked to define Aliyah. The question was then reformulated: What sort of activities did Shcharansky engage in among the refuseniks?)

Which foreigners did Shcharansky come in contact with?

Did Shcharansky help the person questioned in the realisation of his desire to emigrate to Israel? Did he help write letters and appeals to the Soviet as well as other authorities? Did he follow people to their meetings with Soviet officials?

Have you signed any documents passed around among the refuseniks; if so, have you seen Shcharansky's signature on such documents? Did Shcharansky show or ask you to sign any documents?

What do you know about the filming of the British documentary 'A Calculated Risk' and the participation of Shcharansky in it?

How did Shcharansky send information abroad? Had the person questioned ever witnessed any phone conversations or meetings involving Shcharansky and foreign correspondents or tourists?

What did Shcharansky do at the meetings with Senators and Congressmen? Where did these meetings take place? What was discussed?

What do you know about the Helsinki Watchdog group? When was it organised? What was Shcharansky's role? Which of the documents written by the group have you seen? Which of them was written by Shcharansky? How did your name get on to the list of divided families?

Had Shcharansky participated in a particular demonstration? What was the nature of his participation? What do you know about Shcharansky's contacts with the CIA?

*   *   *

Following Ida Milgrom's failure to obtain the legal services of Dina Kaminskaya, she and Dina Beilina approached more than thirty other lawyers. 'Honest lawyers refused to take the case,' Dina Beilina later recalled. 'They did not want to participate in a show trial and thus give a false impression that justice was being done.' Some, as Dina Beilina explained, said: 'We don't want to participate in this case because we cannot help Shcharansky; his fate was predicted in the official newspaper *Izvestia*; and all that will happen is that we will be thrown out of the College of Advocates: particularly if we defend his Zionist beliefs.'

There were also lawyers whom Ida Milgrom and Dina Beilina approached who, having earlier participated as defence lawyers in political trials, had lost the special clearance to act in any case involving secrecy.

Only a single lawyer agreed to take the case. 'And by chance',

Dina Beilina remembered, 'we learned that he had received a special order from the authorities to take his case.' This lawyer suggested that Shcharansky plead guilty to the charges, in which case the defence would put in a plea for leniency. Ida, insisting that her son was innocent, rejected any such suggestion.

'In Moscow,' wrote Michael Sherbourne on 28 June 1977, 'in his tiny cell, or in the forbidding atmosphere of the interrogation room in the Lefortovo, Shcharansky has no lawyer.' In this letter, which he circulated to Soviet Jewry campaigners in Britain, Sherbourne pointed out that while Orlov, the head of the Helsinki monitors, was to be charged under an article of the criminal code which had a maximum penalty of twelve years, Shcharansky faced a maximum penalty of death. He was 'on trial for his life', Sherbourne wrote, 'because he is a Jewish leader . . .'.

Shcharansky had not been arrested, Sherbourne wrote, because of his association with the dissidents. He was in Lefortovo 'because he is a leader of those Jews who stand up to be counted as JEWS'. This was indeed true. None of the non-Jewish members of the Helsinki Watchdog group was interrogated in the Shcharansky case. Not one was asked to give evidence against him. Jews alone would have been his accusers, if the interrogators had achieved their aims.

On 5 August 1977 Lev Ovsishcher was summoned for questioning in Minsk. In his late fifties, a man without guile, single-minded in his desire to live in Israel, he had no intention of making life easier for himself by lying about Shcharansky. However much the interrogators might pride themselves on their ability to get answers which even the most experienced of those under interrogation had not wished to give, they were unable to deflect Ovsishcher from the truth. His interlocutor was Major Skalov:

> Question: Do you know Shcharansky? Where did you meet, when and under what circumstances? How would you describe him as a man?
>
> Answer: I cannot give you an exact date, I don't remember. We met many times, including twice in Minsk. He can be characterised as a sincere person who wants to emigrate to Israel and live there; this is something he has persistently tried to achieve over the last few years.
>
> Question: Describe the meetings with American Senators and Congressmen, and was Anatoly Shcharansky there?

Answer: At the first meeting Shcharansky acted as interpreter. He only spoke about how we could be helped to achieve our wish to leave for our homeland in Israel.

Question: What do you know about Shcharansky's links with the CIA?

Answer: I know nothing about any links between Shcharansky and the CIA. The first I heard about it was Lipavsky's letter in *Izvestia* on 4 March 1977. This article struck me as barely coherent, and Lipavsky as not being the man he passed and passes himself off as.

Major Skalov's questioning of Ovsishcher continued:

Question: What do you know about Shcharansky's links with American and other Zionist organisations?

Answer: I don't know anything about any links between Shcharansky and Zionist organisations. We, who have been refused for many years the right to leave for Israel, are visited by our Western friends as tourists. None of us, including Shcharansky, ever consider asking them about their political beliefs or whether they belong to any Zionist or Communist organisation. This does not concern any of us. It is enough for us that they are friends.

Question: What do you know about Shcharansky's links with foreign correspondents?

Answer: I don't know what you mean by links with foreign correspondents, therefore I don't know what to answer. If meetings with foreign correspondents are called links, then I don't know what to answer. Clearly, the Soviet organs should draw up a special regulation defining whether one can meet with foreign correspondents or not, and in what circumstances meetings are permitted and when they are not, and hence one could consider 'links' those which are not permitted.

At this point Major Skalov asked Ovsishcher about a list of refuseniks, which the Major produced:

Question: How was this list drawn up? Who compiled it? What aim did they have in mind in compiling it?

Answer: I do not understand what this list has got to do with the accusation that Shcharansky was involved in espionage. There is nothing secret in this list, and therefore I don't think that it has got anything to do with the case.

The Major then told Ovsishcher 'that since an expert had judged the list secret' he could be accused of giving 'false evidence'.

> *Answer*: The expert can consider this list anything he likes, including a secret, but I don't think that it contains any secrets. Moreover, your threat that I could be accused of giving false evidence is an attempt to force me to give the desired answer under threat of criminal action. I will definitely put that in the statement.

The investigator next showed Ovsishcher a large number of photocopies with the texts of collective letters sent to the West: to the Senate, the Congress, the American people, and the President. These letters, in the Major's words, were 'found during a search'. All the letters were unsigned. Apparently, Ovsishcher noted, they were drafts. They were certainly not photocopies of the originals.

> *Question*: What role did Shcharansky play in drafting and distributing these letters? How were these letters transferred to the West? What channels were used?
> *Answer*: Firstly, I don't know what these letters have got to do with the Shcharansky case, and secondly, in general I doubt whether these letters were really drafted and therefore they are not evidence: anything which isn't signed cannot be used in an espionage case. They are only evidence that there is no evidence in the case against Shcharansky.

Major Skalov tried to convince Ovsishcher that the lists were photocopies of originals and that he, the investigator, would vouch for their accuracy.

> *Answer*: Your protestations that these are really copies do not convince me at all and are no proof whatsoever. All so-called 'photocopies' can be put to one side without answer.

The Major produced the text of the press communiqué about the film 'Traders of Souls'.

> *Question*: What relationship did Shcharansky have with this communiqué?
> *Answer*: Please explain to me what connection this communiqué has with a case of betraying the Motherland. Possibly,

if you can convince me that such a link exists, I will answer you. But for now I don't know what you want from me with such a question.

Major Skalov told Ovsishcher that the investigation was 'trying to find its way', and that it was clearer to him, the investigator, what questions were relevant.

> *Answer*: I read the text and agreed with it, but I don't understand what the connection is with the charge.
> *Question*: What do you know about the film made and edited abroad with Shcharansky's assistance?
> *Answer*: Nothing.

The interrogator then showed Ovsishcher something which he described as 'instructions' about what to do if 'the so-called refuseniks' leave the Soviet Union so that there would be 'links'. All this was written on a third of a page. Ovsishcher answered, in reference to these 'instructions':

> Explain to me, what is this crudely written document? What is it and how can one answer questions about these scribbles that you call 'instructions'? Perhaps it is a provocative piece of paper which someone specially threw up so that someone would be falsely accused? I, for example, don't know what it is. I think that no one could say anything about that piece of paper; it's not worth it.

Major Skalov said nothing: and this document too was put aside. He then showed Ovsishcher a retyped printed report by Reuters on the situation of Jewish emigration from Minsk and Riga, and said that Reuters had made this report 'on the basis of materials Shcharansky collected when visiting these towns'.

> *Answer*: Once again the same thing: what is the connection between this report and espionage? If I understood I would possibly know what to answer. And in general you should ask the editor or a Reuters correspondent this question. The report, apparently, has been typed by the KGB from a radio broadcast and signed by someone unknown. In general I have my doubts about whether there was such a report.

A copy of the Israeli paper *Nasha Strana* (Our Country) was

produced, with an article about the situation concerning the
emigration of Jews from the Soviet Union.

> *Question*: What did Shcharansky have to do with this article?
> *Answer*: I don't know. You should go to Israel with this
> question and meet the paper's editor. He knows better than I.

Major Skalov then showed Ovsishcher a postcard from Maria
Davidovich, the widow of Yefim Davidovich, who was then in
Israel. The postcard had been sent to Maria Davidovich's sister
Anya, who was still in Minsk, and read: 'Anya, don't go again to
LP; we are getting fed up with him here.' The investigator then
asked Ovsishcher who Maria Davidovich had in mind in using the
initials 'LP' and 'Did Shcharansky have anything to do with it?'

> *Answer*: The postcard is addressed to a certain Anya. You ask
> her. I have no intention of talking about the gossip in
> somebody's personal letters.

The interrogation was over. It had proved impossible to undermine
Ovsishcher's straightforwardness. Shcharansky's friends who had
still to be interrogated were struck by the older man's courage, and
gained strength from it.

★   ★   ★

In the West, concern about Shcharansky led, on 23 August 1977, to
a hearing in the Swedish Parliament. A Judge presided, and Avital
Shcharansky spoke a few words on her husband's behalf. The idea
of the hearing was that of a Swedish parliamentarian, Rune
Torwald, who had visited Moscow a month earlier, and had heard
from Shcharansky's friends of the case being built up against him.

On 28 September 1977 the Kiev evening newspaper, *Vechirni
Kiev*, published an article by Saul Raslin, a Jew who had hitherto
posed as a refusenik. According to Raslin, the Soviet press had
already 'brought out many facts which testify to the participation of
the CIA in the activity of the Zionist activists. It was these very facts
which helped me to come to my senses and stop. And I decided to
speak about the activity of a group of "refuseniks" in Kiev.' Many
refuseniks came to see these visitors from abroad, Raslin wrote, and
he added:

A large part of the visitors came from the United States,

although we knew that Israel would also get the information we gave. But Israeli Zionists themselves also penetrate into the Soviet Union under different pretexts. Thus, in May of last year, the European championship in judo was held in Kiev at the Hall of Sport. The Israeli team consisted of one sportsman and his trainer, Alius Gelad, who had come to the Soviet Union in 1957 as – a singer in an Israeli chorus. Regarding his current 'passion', Gelad himself told the story in the apartment of one of the 'refuseniks', having introduced himself as an officer in the Israeli Intelligence services. Trying to get useful information, he assured those present that they could talk candidly with him.

Raslin's article, like Lipavsky's six months earlier, was not only a farrago of nonsense, but also a clear warning, both that accusations of the most serious sort were being prepared, and that there were a few individuals who had been infiltrated into the refusenik movement several years earlier specifically to make them.

*   *   *

While Shcharansky awaited trial, his friends sent him many books. Almost all of them were confiscated. One of the books which did reach him was an Agatha Christie novel in Hebrew. Later, Shcharansky told his brother: 'Agatha Christie died in good time. If she knew what I was doing with her book she would die a second time. I used it to improve my Hebrew!' A second book which reached him was a book on mathematical logic for beginners. This he used to remarkable effect, building up before each interrogation a logic tree of questions and answers, which was designed to discover some indication of the progress and nature of the wider investigation from the questions which he was being asked and from the anticipated sequence of questioning. To question the questioners: that became his aim.

In the period leading up to his trial, Shcharansky was interrogated three hundred times: often several times a day. His sharpness in his own counter-questioning was remarkable for someone who had neither the texts of the Criminal Code and its commentaries, nor any legal representation to help him. At one point the investigator declared, as Shcharansky later told his brother, that he must be in some contact with the outside world. His cell was repeatedly searched, and eventually he was moved to the punishment cell in Lefortovo. 'They simply did not understand how he was able to cross-examine them,' one of his friends later commented, while he himself later remarked laughingly to his mother: 'I knew I was clever. But I did not know I was *so* clever!'

As month followed month at Lefortovo, Shcharansky decided to try to make prison life, and the interrogations, more bearable by returning as best he could to the Hebrew studies which had been broken off so precipitately by his arrest. As he later wrote to Avital:

> I set myself the task of reviewing my entire stock of words. During approximately two months, I persistently recalled every word which I could somehow snatch from my memory. The total turned out to be fairly considerable – approximately two thousand words. Then I tried to bring all these words into my active vocabulary. To do this I began (and continue) to translate everything that I heard and read. Not word by word, only the general sense. Of course, this sometimes dragged out my conversations with the interrogator, but in return I clearly attained something: in any case, I read and understood those few articles in Hebrew which were among the documents of the case. Of course there is no one to check me, but I nevertheless feel much more confident in our language than I did before.

There were times when Shcharansky was deliberately deceived by his interrogators. He was told that Lev Ulanovsky and Victor Brailovsky were in the same prison and had given testimony against him. This was untrue. He was also told that his father had died, another lie; the interrogators knew how worried he was about his father's health. Neither of these lies shook his resolve, however, to assert his innocence. At one point he was even offered an exit visa if he would point a finger of guilt at the other leading activists. He refused to do so: he was innocent of any crime against the Soviet State, and so were they. Courageously, from the total isolation of a prison cell, Shcharansky betrayed neither himself, nor his friends, nor the Jewish dream to live in Israel.

19

Awaiting Trial

Though Shcharansky had been held in prison for six and a half months without trial, the Jewish movement remained as fearless as before in demanding its rights. With the opening of the Helsinki review conference in Belgrade imminent, seventy-five Moscow and Leningrad Jews sent the Soviet leader, Leonid Brezhnev, a suggested amendment to the new Soviet Constitution which would have radically altered official practice with regard to emigration procedure. The amendment would have abolished receipt of an invitation from Israel as a requirement for exit application, required the exact definition of the reasons for a refusal and its term of effectivity, established an appeal procedure, ensured that the military service of a young applicant would not be used to delay his exit after demobilisation, barred the drafting of an applicant who had asked to renounce his Soviet citizenship, and forbidden the dismissal or demotion of an applicant. The group also appealed to the Belgrade Conference participants, outlining these proposals and asking the Conference to support them.

The Helsinki review conference opened in Belgrade on 4 October 1977. That day Ida Milgrom appealed to the Conference, 'to those of you who are gathered to discuss the most basic humanitarian questions, Peace, Human Rights, etc.', to free her son and grant him the right to join his wife in Israel. 'He is not a criminal,' she wrote.

In Moscow, twenty-eight Jewish activists were put under house arrest for the duration of the Conference. Michael Sherbourne's wife Muriel, in Moscow that week, learned that on 6 October 1977 Ida Milgrom had been to the Prosecutor's Office to ask to see her son, and to do so in the presence of a lawyer. She was told that because of her association with 'bad friends', the refuseniks, she could not do so. The refuseniks, Muriel Sherbourne wrote on her return to London, 'feel their future depends on the outcome of this case'. Ida Milgrom was under considerable pressure. If she gave up her association with these 'bad people', she was told, her son's future could be much improved. Ida Milgrom refused to be coerced. 'My son's friends *cannot* be bad people,' she replied.

Established at the instigation of the National Conference on Soviet Jewry, on 20 October 1977 an Ad Hoc Commission on Justice for Anatoly Shcharansky held a public hearing in Washington, under the Chairmanship of William J. McGill, President of Columbia University. Among the members of the Commission were Senator Frank Church, and Chesterfield Smith, a former President of the American Bar Association. The hearing was held in the Democratic Caucus Room on Capitol Hill. Two experts on civil liberties served as co-counsels of the Commission: Alan Dershowitz of Harvard University and Jack Greenberg, director of the Legal Defence and Education Fund of the National Association for the Advancement of Coloured People. The aim of the hearing was to gather evidence which would constitute a legal brief for Shcharansky's defence.

Among those giving evidence was Avital, who denounced the charges against her husband as 'absurd', noting 'that it was inconceivable for a Soviet refusenik who was constantly followed by members of the KGB twenty-four hours a day to become a foreign agent'. Another speaker was Isaak Elkind, the former refusenik lawyer whom Shcharansky had once befriended and helped, who attested to Shcharansky's 'highest moral character' and to the fact that 'all his activities in the Jewish emigration movement were legal under Soviet and international law'. Alfred Friendly Jr, *Newsweek* correspondent in Moscow from 1974 to 1976, who had known Shcharansky well, stated: 'Shcharansky's only crime was to speak the truth and, worst of all, in English'.

The Soviet authorities, stung by these assertions of Shcharansky's innocence, now sought to blacken his name by personal accusations. 'During the past three years,' declared Moscow journalist Viktor Vladimirov in an English-language broadcast on 28 October 1977, 'Anatoly Shcharansky changed wives three times. The second of them, Natalia Shtiglits, who now is appearing at various gatherings as Shcharansky's disconsolate wife, ought to know that her husband initially intended to leave for Israel at the invitation of his "fiancée", Yershkovich, for whom he professed passionate love to the Visas and Registration department here. When Shtiglits herself went to Israel, he did not grieve long over this loss. Natalia Shtiglits was promptly replaced as Shcharansky's wife by a Lidia Voronina. These', declared Vladimirov, 'are facts, and no amount of slanderous hullabaloo can refute them.'

'At first,' Dina Beilina later recalled, 'the Soviet authorities said that Tolya was not married at all. Then they said that he had been married three times. We decided to argue, but it was so funny that we laughed.'

In his broadcast, Vladimirov went on to say that Shcharansky was 'a traitor to his Motherland' and would be punished 'with all the strictness of Soviet law in keeping with its letter and spirit'.

On 29 October 1977, Vladimir Slepak celebrated his fiftieth birthday. He had been a refusenik for seven and a half years. That day he telephoned his father, seeking a reconciliation. 'Who is speaking?' asked the old man. 'Your son.' 'I have no son.' 'Then who am I?' 'An enemy of the people.'

On 16 November 1977 Ida Milgrom was called for interrogation to the Lefortovo prison, and asked, by Investigator Gorbunov, to be a witness in the charge of treason against her son. She not only refused to be a witness, but wrote a letter of complaint to the Prosecutor-General, Rudenko, declaring that 'at the beginning of the investigation, seven months ago, Investigator Volodin informed me that my son was a criminal and will be punished'; that her son, Anatoly Shcharansky, was called a criminal a number of times in the reports of the official Soviet press; that many of the refuseniks questioned as witnesses in the Shcharansky case are being 'subjected to pressure' by being forced to testify, or threatened with the denial of an exit visa for refusal to testify, or even having their actual testimony altered; that Investigator Gorbunov had also tried to alter her testimony, and in so doing had tried 'to use a mother in order to defame her son', and to 'confirm through my lips the dirty slander that had been stated in a Tass report'; that she was refused the right to consult her son about engaging a lawyer, quite apart from being refused any right even to visit her son; that she was refused the right to include her letter of complaint in the protocol of the interrogation recorded by Investigator Gorbunov.

This was a courageous complaint from a woman of sixty-nine. Three days later, to a visitor whom she met in Slepak's apartment and who asked her to say something about her son, Ida Milgrom pointed to a map of Israel on the wall and declared: 'Photograph the State of Israel and say, in the name of Anatoly, that his heart is there.'

This same visitor returned to Slepak's apartment on 21 November 1977 to say goodbye to Shcharansky's friends. He found them 'glued to the radio'. They were listening to the Egyptian President, Anwar Sadat, addressing the Israeli Parliament. 'A strange fate,' commented Iosif Beilin to the visitor, 'Sadat, the big enemy, comes to Jerusalem and speaks of peace with Menachem Begin, and we, 2500 refuseniks, are still rotting here, in the hell of hatred.'

Nine of Shcharansky's friends were summoned for questioning to the Lefortovo prison on 25 November 1977. Masha Slepak and Professor Meiman, who were among those summoned, were too ill to go. Those who went, including Vladimir Slepak, Alexander Lerner, Ida Nudel and the Beilins, refused to confirm in any way Shcharansky's guilt, or to sign the protocol of their interrogation, lest it be used in some way to incriminate him. Dina Beilina went so far as to write a formal complaint to the Prosecutor-General, pointing out that her interrogator 'did not want from me a true testimony of an objective witness for the defence, but tried to obtain only accusatory testimony'.

On 1 December 1977 Dina Beilina submitted a formal written statement to the court, in the course of which she declared that she knew Shcharansky well 'and count him among the best people I have met in life. I know that with his moral qualities he could not have committed a criminal act, nor even the least offence.' All his actions since he had first been refused his exit visa had been 'exclusively according to the law and constitution of the USSR.'

The first aim of the accusations against Shcharansky, Dina Beilina wrote, was not to ascertain any criminal act by Shcharansky, but 'to frighten Jews who wish to emigrate to Israel'. The second aim was the wish of the authorities 'to avenge themselves on the known activist Anatoly Shcharansky, who was not only fighting for his emigration, but helped all others who were deprived lawlessly of their right to do so.'

Dina Beilina went on to point out that the investigation was not being conducted in an 'objective' manner:

(a) Shcharansky was called a criminal before his arrest. In the newspaper *Izvestia* it was stated that he can expect to be punished. He was called a criminal in the commentaries of the official Tass. It was stated there that he can expect a punishment with all the severity of the law. He is called all the time a criminal, even during the investigation, including mine.

(b) Before his arrest Shcharansky was subjected to pressure – he was followed for many months demonstratively – I can bear witness to that. Now he is still under pressure: he is isolated for more than eight months, is under the threat of terrible punishment and is left without juridical help, which is contrary to the law.

Dina Beilina's statement was never submitted to the court, despite her wishes. But with the period of investigation extended, in what was both an unprecedented and, as the activists insisted, unlawful way, the interrogations also continued. On 12 December 1977 Boris Tsitlionok was called for interrogation in Krasnoyarsk, and threatened with two to six years in a Siberian labour camp if he did not 'co-operate' in giving testimony.

None of those who had been interrogated gave false testimony. None was prepared to invent the required stories, of a spy ring, of instructions from abroad, or of agents sent to them with specific, disruptive or disloyal requests. At one point in his incarceration Shcharansky was told: 'If you co-operate with us, you will receive a short prison term, and you will be living with your wife very soon.' He replied: 'I am happy I can live in peace with my conscience.'

In London, on 8 December 1977, an International Committee for the release of Anatoly Shcharansky heard evidence not only from Avital, but from Felix Kandel, who had received his exit visa four weeks earlier, and from Dina Kaminskaya, who had just been expelled from the Soviet Union. 'On the basis of all we have heard', the Committee concluded, 'we must hope that justice will be done which will satisfy public conscience.'

*   *   *

On 15 December 1977 Ida Milgrom was called again to Lefortovo prison, to be told that although her son had now been held in prison for the maximum nine months laid down by Soviet criminal procedure, the Praesidium of the Supreme Soviet had 'extended the investigation for another six months'. No such extension was provided for in any written law. Nor had Shcharansky been allowed to see his parents or a lawyer since his arrest nine months earlier. 'I do not know what the situation is in the bourgeois legal procedure,' Ida Milgrom wrote to the *Literaturnaya Gazeta* in the third week of December, 'but during my bitter experience of the last nine months, I have met with facts that show the tendentiousness of the Investigator and the Prosecutor, and the restriction of the right of defence in our circumstances.' The extension of the period of her son's detention 'for a period exceeding that determined by the law' was, she considered, 'a criminal punishment imposed without a trial'.

Ida Milgrom's letter was never published by the *Literaturnaya Gazeta*, but, as an open letter, was published outside the Soviet Union.

★   ★   ★

Throughout the Soviet Union, Jewish activists were determined to speak up for Shcharansky. On 17 December 1977 eighty-seven Jews, from Moscow, Kiev, Minsk and Leningrad, signed a petition pointing out that Soviet law allowed only nine months' imprisonment without trial. That period had now passed. 'We demand his immediate discharge,' they wrote, 'in accordance with Soviet laws.' A week later, in Moscow, forty Jews held a memorial vigil on the steps of the Lenin Library to mark the seventh anniversary of the first Leningrad Trial; they then issued a statement in which they demanded 'the release of all the Prisoners of Conscience from prisons, exile and camps, the stopping of the so-called "Shcharansky affair" and the cessation of persecution of Jewish activists'. The list of the signatures began with some of Shcharansky's most outspoken friends: Ida Nudel, Alexander and Judith Lerner, Vladimir Slepak, and Dina and Iosif Beilin.

Western protests about Shcharansky's arrest led to a Soviet news agency statement on 22 December 1977 describing American appeals for Shcharansky's release as 'nothing but another attempt, under the hypocritical pretext of "concern for human rights", to intervene in the internal affairs of the USSR'.

Four days later, on 27 December 1977, the Association of American Law Schools began its annual conference in Atlanta, Georgia. During the conference an unofficial 'human rights' meeting was called into session by Dean Peter Liacouras and Professor Burton Caine, both of Temple University Law School, in Philadelphia. Both men had just returned from Moscow, where they had met Soviet legal and judicial officials, and had expressed their concern over Shcharansky's case. At this conference, the Deans of seventy-two law schools throughout the United States joined by more than a hundred Professors issued a statement in which they 'deplored' the Soviet actions in the Shcharansky case as 'counter' to the rule of law and minimum standards of justice.

On the following day, 28 December 1977, *Literaturnaya Gazeta* denounced those who sought to 'lecture the Soviet people on how to live in their own house': the Soviet Union would not allow anyone 'to cast doubt on its right to manage its internal affairs without prompting and moralising maxims by preachers from across the ocean'.

Slepak and Dina Beilina also made a private protest, together with four other friends of Shcharansky, when they went on 17 January 1978 to the Chief Prosecutor's Office. There, they were received by the Assistant Prosecutor-General, Tsibulnik. The six Jews protested against the prison conditions under which Shcharansky was being held. 'It is good for him', Tsibulnik declared, 'that he is in Lefortovo prison. Otherwise it would be worse for him. Ours is the best prison in the Soviet Union.' 'You mean he won't be released?' asked the four friends, at which Tsibulnik merely laughed.

Returning to her apartment, Dina Beilina spoke on the telephone to Michael Sherbourne, to report on what Tsibulnik had said about the extension of the period of Shcharansky's imprisonment without trial. A part of the discussion with the Assistant Prosecutor-General had included the following altercation:

Refuseniks: In the Constitution, the law states that all are equal before the law. The Constitution states that no one should be punished without trial, that during the time of preliminary investigation, the maximum time for which a person can be held is nine months. So if all are equal before the law, including Shcharansky, if no one can be punished without a proper trial, then he, too, should not be punished because he is imprisoned, under guard, in solitary, without visits from relatives, without legal aid. He should not be held in such conditions. He should be released before his trial, if one is to be held.

Tsibulnik: The Supreme Soviet is the supreme legislative organ, and therefore can issue any such decree or instructions.

Refuseniks: Does the Supreme Soviet have authority to issue a decree to allow for a man to be shot in execution without a trial?

Tsibulnik: You have not understood me. It could be entirely in

Shcharansky's interests and entirely possible that the investigation is completely in his own interests.

On 20 January 1978 Shcharansky, still held incommunicado in
the Lefortovo prison after more than ten months, reached his
thirtieth birthday. A week later, in Washington, Boris Ponomarev,
the head of a ten-member delegation from the Supreme Soviet, was
asked at a news conference to comment on the case. 'This is the
internal business of the Soviet Union,' he replied. He then went on
to say that in international practice, as well as under the 1975
Helsinki Accords on East–West co-operation, 'it is not appropriate
to allow interference in the internal affairs' of other countries. He
added that Shcharansky had been 'brought to court for serious
offences' and would be permitted a lawyer and a trial. Senator Javits
of New York, who had met Shcharansky in Moscow in 1976,
interrupted Ponomarev to say that 'the United States' interest in
persons like Shcharansky, charged with a crime or disadvantaged
because they want to emigrate, is a matter deeply vexing to our
country.' Also in Washington, the National Conference on Soviet
Jewry had sponsored a Congressional Wives Committee for Soviet
Jewry, chaired by Helen Jackson, the wife of Senator Jackson. More
than forty wives of Senators and Congressmen gathered that day in
Washington to greet Avital.

The Shcharansky case was raised again later that day by Senator
Jackson, at a dinner given by the Coalition for a Democratic
Majority at which Avital was a guest. Jackson declared: 'We have
filled this room tonight to say to the Soviet Prosecutor: "Stop this
ridiculous attempt to accuse Anatoly Shcharansky of spying. Let
this brave and long-suffering young man leave and join his wife."'

The accusation of treason, reiterated for so many months, made
many uninformed observers wonder whether there might not be
some truth in it after all, despite President Carter's denial. 'Please
believe me,' Lynn Singer, President of the Long Island Committee
for Soviet Jewry, wrote to her local Nassau County Executive,
'there is not a word of truth in this accusation. Anatoly, since 1974,
has been trying to join his wife of one day, in Israel.' As a result of
Lynn Singer's efforts, a grove of trees was planted on the lawn of
the Nassau County Court Building, 'The Anatoly Shcharansky
Justice Garden'. It was the first such dedication.

Long Island was in the news again two weeks later, when the
United Press International reported that Shcharansky was to be

exchanged for Robert Thompson, a Long Islander imprisoned in the United States since 1965, with a thirty-year sentence. He had been found guilty of spying for the Soviet Union. The other Soviet prisoner said to be about to be exchanged in the same 'deal' was Edward Kuznetsov, one of the Leningrad Trial prisoners. The exchange was also to include an Israeli pilot shot down over Mozambique in 1977, and a group of Chilean Communists imprisoned in Chile since 1973.

No such exchange took place. Meanwhile, on 23 February 1978, Ida Milgrom was told that an official lawyer had been appointed to represent her son. Her name was Silva Dubrovskaya, a sixty-eight-year-old woman who did not appear on the list of working Soviet lawyers. At the same time, Ida Milgrom was told that the investigation against her son under Article 64–A, treason, had been completed.

On 7 March 1978 there was a further bizarre twist in the Shcharansky saga when it was confirmed in Washington that not Shcharansky, but Lipavsky, had worked briefly for the Central Intelligence Agency. For a period of nine months in 1975, it appeared, he had provided American Intelligence with information on the Soviet scientific community. According to a report in the *New York Times* on the following day, American Intelligence sources explained that Lipavsky 'had taken the initiative in approaching American diplomats with an offer to supply information about the science community'. According to these sources, 'there was a debate at the time about the value of using such a person who could have been an agent provocateur.' It was eventually decided that, in view of the limited sources on the Soviet scientific world, 'it was worth taking the risk.' The sources went on to say that the CIA had dropped Dr Lipavsky when strong doubts arose about his 'value'.

Commenting on these revelations, Eugene Gold, the Chairman of the New York-based National Conference on Soviet Jewry, said that it now appeared that Lipavsky had volunteered his services for the CIA 'as an agent of the Soviet secret police and for the purpose of implicating Soviet Jews actively engaged in the legal struggle to emigrate'.

One of those who had befriended Lipavsky in Moscow was the *Washington Post* correspondent there, Peter Osnos, who was now back in Washington. Osnos wrote of Lipavsky in the *Washington Post* on 10 March 1978: 'the CIA ultimately dropped him, sources

say, because it doubted his reliability. Naturally, the agency never
warned anyone else.'

In the West, Avital Shcharansky began a tour of university
campuses across the United States, sponsored by the Union of
Councils for Soviet Jews, and the Student Struggle for Soviet
Jewry. It was her fifth such journey through the United States, in
her struggle for her husband's release.

On 13 March 1978, two of Shcharansky's most devoted and
outspoken supporters, Dina and Iosif Beilin, were suddenly told
that they could leave Russia. Nine days later, they were on their
way to Israel. The rule among the refuseniks is: if you receive your
exit visa, go. Perhaps no couple have felt the pain of leaving more
than did Dina and Iosif Beilin; Shcharansky and Dina had been
together at so many dramatic moments. Dina it was who had typed
out the lists of the refuseniks, for which Shcharansky had been
indicted. It was also she who had explained to Robert Toth that the
so-called 'State secrecy' refusals had nothing to do with secrecy.
Her declaration in Shcharansky's defence submitted the previous
December had been one of the most outspoken.

★   ★   ★

On 15 March 1978 Shcharansky had been held in prison for a year
without trial. Nor had he been allowed to see his mother or brother.
In the United States Congress, a special debate was held to mark the
anniversary; several Senators and Congressmen who had met
Shcharansky in 1975 and 1976 appealed for his release. That same
day, the Congressional Wives Committee for Soviet Jewry peti-
tioned the Soviet authorities to allow Shcharansky to 'fulfil his
dream to join his wife in Israel'. In Moscow, Shcharansky's friends
declared a twenty-four-hour fast as a 'mark of solidarity' with him,
and sent out an appeal 'to all honest people' which ended: 'Save an
innocent man! Save Anatoly Shcharansky!'

More than a hundred Jews signed this appeal, a number
reminiscent of the appeals which Shcharansky himself had signed in
the past. The signatories were from many cities, among them fifty-
seven from Moscow, twenty from Leningrad, eight from Kiev, six
from Kharkov and six from Minsk.

On 16 March 1978 Ida Milgrom was shown a note from her son,
the first communication she had been allowed from him in a year.
The note declared his 'categoric refusal' to accept a State-appointed
lawyer. Then she heard no more from him. The interrogation of his

friends had ceased. No one knew when, or if, a trial would begin. In urging the Union of Councils for Soviet Jews to be prepared to launch a massive campaign once the trial began, Morey Shapira, who was later to be the Union's President, wrote: 'I really hope that I'm 100 per cent wrong on this and that Shcharansky will never come to trial at all.'

An American expert on the Soviet Jewry issue, William Korey, reported on 10 April 1978 that 'considerable speculation' had arisen in the United States 'over the possibility that a seemingly doomed Shcharansky, awaiting the execution of the harshest penalty, might either be deported or exchanged for one or more prisoners in other countries. The one thing that can be said on the basis of hard evidence, though,' Korey added, 'is that the Shcharansky case could prove most unfortunate for all concerned.'

On 19 May 1978, while Shcharansky was still being held in prison without trial, Yury Orlov, head of the Helsinki Watchdog group, was convicted of 'anti-Soviet agitation' and sentenced to a total of twelve years' 'deprivation of liberty', seven in prison to be followed by five in internal exile. This was ominous news for those who still hoped, against hope, that Shcharansky might be released.

On 1 June 1978, the Jews of Moscow announced a public demonstration by women and children who had been refused their exit visas. The demonstration was at once forbidden by the authorities. Ida Nudel, determined to make some demonstration, displayed a small banner on her balcony. Decorated with a Star of David, it read: 'KGB, GIVE ME MY VISA'.

Ida Nudel was arrested and, on 21 June 1978, brought to trial. The charge: 'Malicious hooliganism'. Her sentence: four years in exile, in remote Siberia. She was forty-seven years old. Among the statements that had been submitted to the court were several from Ida Nudel's neighbours, demanding that she be punished. 'If it were in my power,' one witness informed the court, 'I would have suggested the harshest measure of punishment, as such people should not be pitied; they put to shame our people and our State.'

Only one eye-witness was not summoned to testify. He was a Jew, Abram Nizhnikov, who had submitted an affidavit to the court, telling how, from his balcony, he had heard the crowd shouting: 'Jews are rioting,' 'There is no Hitler to stop them,' 'There is no Stalin to stop them.' These cries, Nizhnikov reported, were being made in the presence of a number of militiamen who did nothing to prevent them.

On the day of Ida Nudel's 'hooliganism', Vladimir Slepak had also carried out what was described by the authorities as a 'window demonstration'. Because of the intended public protest that day by refusenik women and children Slepak, like Ida Nudel, had been confined for the day to his apartment. He too had displayed a banner on his balcony, decorated with a Star of David, and asking: 'LET US GO TO OUR SON IN ISRAEL'. Eight months earlier, his son Alexander had been granted an exit visa.

Like Ida Nudel, Slepak was arrested, and then charged with 'malicious hooliganism'. At his trial, held like hers on 21 June 1978, no relatives, friends or foreign correspondents were allowed into the courtroom. His sentence was five years' exile, in a remote Siberian village not far from the Chinese border.

Vladimir Slepak and Ida Nudel were sent to Siberia. Dina and Iosif Beilin were already in Jerusalem. By reason of exit visas or exile, four of Shcharansky's closest friends were no longer in Moscow.

On Friday 7 July 1978, sixteen days after Slepak and Ida Nudel had been sentenced, it was announced in Moscow that Shcharansky's trial would begin in three days' time. Ida Milgrom at once sent a telegram to Leonid Brezhnev, stating that this was the first she had heard of the trial, and 'expressed fear', as David Shipler reported to the *New York Times*, that the trial would be held in secret. 'Some Western analysts', Shipler reported, 'believe that after a trial, Moscow might be willing to expel Mr Shcharansky from the country as part of an exchange involving two Russians arrested on espionage charges in the United States and now awaiting trial.' This was the second time Shcharansky had been the 'beneficiary' of such rumours: but then, as before, they were without foundation.

To be tried on the same day as Shcharansky, but in a courtroom at Kaluga, a hundred miles south of Moscow, was Alexander Ginsburg, a member, with Shcharansky, of the Helsinki Watchdog group who, like Shcharansky, had been held in prison without trial for more than sixteen months. In protest against the two trials, Secretary of State Cyrus Vance announced the cancellation of two United States Government missions to Moscow. His own arms limitation talks in Geneva, however, due to begin two days after the start of the trials, would go on. From the Prime Minister's Office in Jerusalem came an appeal, on 10 July 1978, 'to all Governments and Parliaments and people of goodwill in the free world to begin, without delay, to work for the rescue and release of Anatoly Shcharansky'.

'For Russians who have hoped for a liberalized society', David Shipler reported from Moscow on 9 July 1978, 'for Soviet Jews who have struggled against a historical anti-Semitism and fought for the right to emigrate, for Americans who have sought closer ties between the two great powers, the Soviet Government's decision to try Mr Shcharansky for treason darkens the future.' For 'other Russians', Shipler added, 'who have nurtured a corrosive anger at dissidents and Jewish activists for smearing their Motherland and invoking pressure from the West against their country, the decision represents overdue revenge, a reassertion of tough internal leadership sorely missed since Stalin's days.'

If Shcharansky were to be convicted, Shipler added, 'as he must be, given the precedent of past political trials – and after he is sentenced, perhaps to death or to many years in prison, nothing will be the same.' All who then protested against their refusal as Shcharansky did 'will have been put on notice', Shipler warned, 'that the State considers them traitors, that no amount of Western publicity or high-level American pleading can save them'.

Shcharansky was ready for his ordeal. 'When I was put on trial after months of complete isolation,' he later recalled, 'I was inspired by the behaviour of people who had gone through the same experience and remained the way they were before. They hadn't given in or given up, and that gave me hope.' Shcharansky added that he had also gained strength 'from the pages of our Jewish history', above all from the story of Judah Maccabee, military leader of the Jewish revolt against Syria more than two thousand years ago. 'The fact', he said, 'that there is a history of resistance always helps.'

20

In Court

The trial of Anatoly Shcharansky began in a courtroom in Moscow at ten o'clock in the morning of Monday, 10 July 1978. Ida Milgrom and Leonid Shcharansky had asked to be present throughout. They were told that they would only be allowed in after the first break. Ida Milgrom was later refused permission to attend, however. Nor were any Western observers or journalists allowed to be present.

When Leonid Shcharansky was eventually allowed in, accompanied by two police officers, he was taken to the first row, six feet away from his brother. They smiled at each other. 'You've got too fat,' quipped Anatoly, his first words to anyone who knew him since he had been seized in the stairwell of Slepak's apartment sixteen months earlier.

The opening session began with a statement by the Chairman of the court, Judge P. P. Lukanov, who declared that Shcharansky's mother had been given sufficient time from December 1977 to June 1978 to choose a defence lawyer, but, he claimed, she had not chosen one. Leonid Shcharansky then intervened to say that this did not answer the question at all, but, ignoring this intervention, the Chairman stated that in the absence of a choice by Ida Milgrom the court had appointed Silva Dubrovskaya as defence counsel. Shcharansky, he added, had refused to accept her services.

The Judge then asked Prosecutor Pavel Nikolaevich Solonin, who was the senior deputy to Prosecutor-General Rudenko, whether Shcharansky could defend himself. Solonin said he had no objection. The court also had no objection. At this point Silva Dubrovskaya left the courtroom.

Under Soviet law, no accused person can be sentenced to death unless he has been defended by a lawyer. The Prosecutor-General's agreement to the departure of Silva Dubrovskaya meant that Shcharansky was not to be sentenced to death. Shcharansky realised this at once, as did his brother.

Solonin then asked that all the judicial matters connected with the central accusation of espionage, interrogation of witnesses, the conclusions of the experts, and the presentation of documents should be conducted in a closed session of the court. Shcharansky, speaking for the first time as his own legal representative, declared that he was 'emphatically opposed' to the trial being conducted in a closed court. In the materials of the case, he said, there was not one single secret document. There was no official rubber stamp indicating secrecy on any of the testimony of witnesses, conclusion of the experts, or documents. Therefore, a closed session of the court was not in any way applicable.

Replying to Shcharansky, the Judge declared that the court in its administrative session had already decided in advance to conduct the judicial investigation into the charge of espionage in closed court. By doing this, it forbade all reference in open session of the court to the testimony of witnesses, the conclusion of the experts, and documents connected in any way with the accusation of espionage.

Shcharansky persistently maintained that there was nothing secret either in the indictment or in the materials of the case; the court sessions should therefore be open, not closed. The Judge refused to accept these statements. The preliminary court investigation, he said, had already decided that these sessions should be closed.

The closed session of the court would take place on the following day.

Shcharansky, acting as best he could in his own defence, then stated that during the sixteen months he had been held in detention, he had not been permitted to find out the opinion of his relatives. Only today he had been told his mother would not be in court. Leonid, realising that his brother had been told that Ida Milgrom had not come to court of her own free will, called out that their mother was indeed standing outside the courthouse, but had been refused entry. As a result of this intervention, Leonid was moved from the front of the court to the back row on the Judge's instructions.

Shcharansky then told the court that at the end of the preliminary investigation he had submitted a document of forty pages, includ-

ing the calling of certain witnesses and the presentation to the court
of a number of material documents. He said that whereas the
prosecution had apparently had time in the course of four days to
read fifty-one volumes (of several thousand pages in all) prepared
by the KGB as the documentary basis for the case, it had refused to
accept any of the statements made in his forty pages. 'I have no
further petitions other than those I previously submitted,' he said.
He then expressed surprise that in the short period of four days,
during which the case documents had been available to the prosecution and to himself, the prosecution had managed to make themselves completely acquainted with all fifty-one volumes.

The Judge asked the Prosecutor his opinion. He could answer the
question only after ten minutes, the Prosecutor said. There was a
break. After fifteen minutes, the Prosecutor said he was prepared to
accept six submissions from the accused from the forty pages.
These included: the Lipavsky statement; a report that had appeared
in the foreign press that Lipavsky had worked as a CIA agent; a
report in the foreign press about Robert Toth; and a statement by
Leonid Volvovsky. The court retired to consider these issues.

Upon resumption, the Prosecutor stated that the accused was
being charged under Article 64, section A, of the Criminal Code,
'Treason', and Article 70, part one, 'Anti-Soviet agitation and
propaganda'. These charges came under two headings, he
explained: (a) letters to foreign correspondents and abroad; (b)
telegrams and meetings with American Senators. The accusation
stated that as a result of Shcharansky's activities the Jackson
Amendment had been accepted by the United States Congress, and
had done considerable material harm to the Soviet Union. The
accusation further stated that Shcharansky had slandered the Soviet
Union by spreading accusations of anti-Semitism against the Soviet
State; this included the making of a propaganda film, 'filmed
illegally, with commentary added by Michael Sherbourne'. Part of
this film was confiscated at customs and would be presented to the
court as material evidence. This was the British television film 'A
Calculated Risk'.

The Prosecutor continued with a further accusation that
Shcharansky had held meetings with the American historian
Richard Pipes in the Hotel Sovietskaya in Moscow, and that Pipes
had given him instructions on how to carry out propaganda
and anti-Soviet work. Zionist activities were carried out at
meetings with Zionist emissaries who came in the guise of tourists,

members of delegations and officials.

The first part of the accusation was devoted to the anti-Soviet activity under Article 70. The second part, spying, under Article 64–A, consisted first of the collection and collation of a list of 1300 refuseniks. Reference was made to Robert Toth's article about these lists, in which he had stated, according to the Prosecutor, that, by giving the place of work of those refused exit visas on grounds of 'secrecy', the lists had revealed where secret work was being done. The reverse was in fact true: almost all those refused on grounds of secret work, like Shcharansky himself, had worked in institutions and enterprises where no secret work at all had been involved. It was only these non-secret work places that were mentioned in the lists. In any case, Toth's article, which had stressed the absurdity of the 'secrecy' argument, had been the result, not of a briefing by Shcharansky, who was now accused of it, but, as the Soviet authorities well knew, of a briefing by Dina Beilina, who had been given her exit visa four months earlier, and was already in Jerusalem.

According to the Prosecutor, there was a possibility that Toth's former secretary, Popova, would be brought in as a witness, as well as Zakharov, the janitor of the compound where foreign correspondents live. Zakharov, the court was told, had found a list of refuseniks in Shcharansky's handwriting. (No such handwritten lists had ever existed. Dina Beilina had prepared her lists on tape, and then typed them out. Only a few phrases were written out by hand. Nor had Dina Beilina ever given the lists to Robert Toth, in any form. 'He simply never asked for them!' she later pointed out.)

A woman, Konina, would be called as a witness: the landlady of the apartment occupied by Shcharansky when he had lodged briefly at Lipavsky's new apartment. It was also charged that the former Moscow Jewish activist Vitaly Rubin, now living in Jerusalem, had sent a letter to Shcharansky via Lipavsky giving details of how and when to collect and hand over espionage material. No such letter had ever been sent. (Shcharansky later commented to his brother that the letter allegedly from Rubin, which had been shown to him during the interrogation, had been addressed to Lipavsky. It contained a phrase, Shcharansky reflected, which, if it had been in an actual letter, he would not have missed, requesting 'the gathering of certain information'. Before being shown this phrase during the interrogation, Shcharansky told his brother, he had never seen such a phrase in any letter from anyone in Israel.)

The Prosecutor then told the court that a woman by the name of Panchenkova would be called as a witness, from whom 'a list had been confiscated'. (Again, this was a fabrication. This confiscated material was not lists of refuseniks, but some philosophical articles written by Lidia Voronina.)

Another point of the accusation was the assembling and disseminating of the Helsinki Watchdog group's documents. All the documents they had collected were considered to be 'slanderous' to the Soviet Union and would be brought and presented to the court as evidence. This material, the Prosecutor declared, had served as the basis for programmes which had been broadcast by radio stations hostile to the Soviet Union, such as the Voice of America, Radio Free Europe, Radio Liberty and the BBC.

The formal indictment was then read, basically a repetition of what had been stated in court by the Prosecutor.

Shcharansky, who spoke next, accepted and recognised that the documents were factual. He agreed that many of the documents were what had been written, and that he was part-author of them. He denied the accusation that they fell in any way under Article 64–A, spying. He was then asked whether he admitted his guilt. He denied it completely, stating that the accusations were 'absurd'.

Shcharansky then told the court that he had been held in solitary isolation for nearly sixteen months. Now the authorities were attempting to close the court 'to continue his isolation'. Just as in the investigation, when he had refused to give testimony about individual documents and personalities while without proper legal representation, so he would refuse to do so during the trial. Only if the trial was to be an open one would he be willing to discuss these documents in detail. Although he accepted responsibility for the documents as a whole, he was not prepared to give evidence on individual documents taken separately.

None of the Helsinki Watchdog group documents were in any way slanderous, Shcharansky declared. In regard to Soviet policy on emigration and the lack of Jewish culture, they were entirely factual.

A discussion then began between the Prosecutor and Shcharansky regarding the lack of Jewish culture in the Soviet Union. Shcharansky pointed out that there were two Jewish languages, Yiddish and Hebrew, but that there was no possibility of studying either in the Soviet Union. He could name at least ten Hebrew teachers who were deprived by the authorities of the

possibility of teaching. In the so-called 'Jewish Autonomous
Region' of Birobidjan, in the Soviet Far East, there was not one
school in which Yiddish was taught; the 'present policy of nationalism which is spreading in the Soviet Union', he said, 'is a reversion
to the times of Stalin'.

As evidence of anti-Semitism, Shcharansky wished to present to
the court the book by Vladimir Begun, *The Creeping Counter-
Revolution*, which could be compared, he said, to the pre-First
World War forgery, *The Protocols of the Learned Elders of Zion*. The
contents of Vladimir Begun's book, Shcharansky pointed out,
were 'almost identical' to several anti-Semitic books published in
Russia in Tsarist times, and in Nazi Germany. He was refused
permission to submit Begun's book to the court.

Commenting on the accusations of Zionist activity and contact
with Zionist emissaries, Shcharansky said he wished to point out
'that there is a growing Jewish national movement, and that every
nation goes through a stage of development of its national growth,
and that now Zionism is a manifestation of the growth of Jewish
nationalism'. It was 'a fact', he said, 'that there is a Jewish State.'

Shcharansky reminded the court that during the Second World
War a Jewish Anti-Fascist Committee had been formed in the
Soviet Union, which had been 'very successful in assembling a
great deal of material help in the form of millions of dollars from the
American and other Jewish communities'. When these Jews had
collected money from abroad, there had been no objection to their
contacts with foreign Jews, 'but now any connection with them is
considered interference in the Soviet Union's internal affairs'.
'Connections today', he said, 'are considered subversive; before,
they were considered beneficial.'

Shcharansky went on to point out that the Jackson Amendment
had been discussed by Congress as early as 1972, before he was even
involved in the Jewish movement in the Soviet Union, or had even
applied to emigrate. With regard to his contacts with the Senators,
not only was this 'not a subversive activity', he stated, but on the
contrary, he had adopted 'a position of compromise, a moderate,
halfway position', and what he had done could have been 'beneficial
to the Soviet Union'. It was not his responsibility, but that of
the Soviet Government, that Soviet–American relations had
deteriorated.

With regard to collective statements signed by a number of
people, Shcharansky, who had been accused of falsifying the

signatures, explained that where the signatures seemed to be written by one hand, they had first been collected from different people from various towns, and then the statement had been rewritten by hand. The signatures obviously appeared in the hand of the person who had written the fair copy of the statement.

The Prosecutor then asked Shcharansky about his visit to the village of Ilyinka. Shcharansky replied that he had not visited the village because he had been detained by police before he managed to get there. He expressed surprise at the Prosecutor's remarks that no one in Ilyinka wished for an exit visa, declaring that 'a large number of people there wish to emigrate'. The four witnesses brought to the court from Ilyinka were those who stated they did not wish to leave. But no witnesses had been brought from those large numbers of families who wanted exit visas: at least seventy of about 120 families.

Shcharansky then told the court that he wished to give evidence about certain people who had been treated for mental 'illness'. The Prosecutor said it was 'undiplomatic' to produce evidence about sick persons; it was 'contrary to decency and sensibility'. On the contrary, Shcharansky insisted, it was possible to discuss this, and he named Leonid Plyushch as an example. He said there were people who, for example, were accused of suffering from 'megalomania' and others who suffered from 'emigration mania' and other similar 'illnesses'.

Next came questions about Jewish prisoners. The Prosecutor asked Shcharansky how he obtained his information about their 'bad conditions' and where he got documentation from. He, the Prosecutor, had 'exactly opposite information from documents'. Shcharansky retorted that the Prosecutor's documents could hardly be called objective since they came from the very Soviet organisations and institutions which kept the prisoners in dreadful conditions. His knowledge came from former prisoners and from relatives of present prisoners. In addition, he had personal experience, having been in a punishment cell for two days. The Prosecutor asked him why he had been placed there. Shcharansky replied that the discussion was not about 'why', but about the conditions in the punishment cells.

The discussion turned to Anatoly Malkin. The Prosecutor said, 'You refer to his being called to the army as "victimisation", whereas it is one's duty to serve in the army.' Shcharansky replied that, on the contrary, Malkin had been expelled from the institute where he had been studying, thus making him subject to the draft, as soon as he had applied to emigrate to Israel.

Shcharansky told the court that he had discussed Malkin's case with Albert Ivanov, an official of the Central Committee, and that Ivanov had said that expulsions and drafts 'as a policy' would be continued. Shcharansky asked that Ivanov be called as a witness. This was refused.

Reference was then made to Shcharansky's personal letters and statements, and to the article by Robert Toth, on the Jews of Ilyinka. The Prosecutor asked Shcharansky why there were press conferences at which the only journalists present were Western ones. Shcharansky replied that all correspondents had been invited, even Soviet ones. On one occasion, they had invited a representative of the Novosty News Agency, who had not come. Similarly, representatives of the Eastern-bloc press had been invited, but none had ever appeared. Representatives of the Italian Communist paper *Unità* and the French Communist Party paper *L'Humanité* were invited. One had never replied; the other asked that he be sent the information in the post.

A discussion followed about Shcharansky's marital status. The court said it considered him single; Shcharansky said he had had a Jewish religious wedding. The validity of this religious marriage was questioned, and a theological debate ensued. The Prosecutor maintained that there was another witness, the Rabbi of the Moscow synagogue, Jacob Fishman, who had declared and would give evidence that since the marriage had not taken place in the synagogue, it was not valid. (A Jewish religious wedding need not occur in a synagogue; many do not.)

Next, the Prosecutor declared that since Natasha Shtiglits, Shcharansky's wife, had a Russian mother, she could not have had a religious wedding. Nor, he added, did she have a ritual immersion before her marriage.

To refute these various religious points, Shcharansky sought to call as a witness Girsh Manevich, the authority on Jewish religious law who had helped them to get married in 1974. Manevich had already written a letter to Brezhnev on these various points, but the court refused to call Manevich as a witness. Shcharansky declared that under any circumstances his marriage and marital status was a personal matter, which did not come under the court's jurisdiction.

The matter of Shcharansky's work was then brought up. For

three years after receiving his degree, he said, he had worked at the
Institute of Oil and Gas, then for three years as an English teacher.
Asked why he had not paid taxes on his earnings as a teacher,
Shcharansky replied that he had tried to pay taxes, but the authorities did not permit him to be registered as a teacher. The Prosecutor
retorted that a 'real Soviet man' would have found a way of paying
taxes.

Shcharansky was asked about helping people to emigrate who
happened not to have relatives abroad; was this not a deception of
the authorities? Shcharansky replied that in fact it was the system
which encouraged this situation by insisting that those wishing to
emigrate may only go where there are 'close relatives' in Israel, thus
depriving them of the rights recognised by the United Nations
Universal Declaration on Human Rights.

The Prosecutor then asked Shcharansky why, when he sent a
telegram of congratulations to the President of the United States on
the 200th anniversary of the Declaration of Independence, referring
to the great achievements of democracy in the United States, he did
not refer at the same time to pornography, the millions of unemployed, prostitution, and so forth. Shcharansky replied that he was
'fully aware' of the many negative aspects that exist in Western
states, but these facts are reported in Western newspapers, whereas
negative conditions in the Soviet Union are never reported in the
Soviet press.

There was another aspect to this charge of not mentioning
unemployment and prostitution in his telegram: at the very
moment when Shcharansky had sent his congratulations to
President Ford, the Chairman of the Praesidium of the Supreme
Soviet of the Soviet Union, Nikolai Podgorny, had also sent a
congratulatory telegram to President Ford. It too made no mention
of unemployment, prostitution, or any other negative aspect of
American life. Instead, it spoke of the need for 'mutual respect,
equality, and a striving for mutual understanding and co-operation'
between the Soviet Union and the United States. A distinguished
Canadian lawyer, Irwin Cotler, who later acted for Avital, has
commented: 'The conclusion is inescapable. If the Soviet Union
wishes to use a congratulatory letter sent by Anatoly Shcharansky
as evidence to support a charge of anti-Soviet slander against
Shcharansky, then, having regard to the Soviet principle of equality
before the law and the courts, they must use the Podgorny letter as
evidence to support a charge of anti-Soviet slander against

Podgorny, if not the other members of the Praesidium, including
Brezhnev.'

★   ★   ★

The first day's court proceedings were over. An American visitor
who was in Moscow that day wrote in a letter to a friend of the
'tension in the air outside the courtroom', where about fifty Jews,
all activists, had gathered at the barrier which blocked off the
alleyway leading to the courthouse. There, surrounded by policemen and plainclothesmen, they had stood from ten in the morning
until six in the evening. 'The refuseniks are extremely nervous,' this
American visitor wrote, 'because they don't know what is indict-
able and what is not. Many people were doing what Anatoly was
doing before he was arrested.' She added: 'People were scared to
show up.' Hence the fifty, compared with well over a hundred who
went by train to Kaluga each day for Ginsburg's trial.

The refuseniks knew exactly what the charges and accusations
were. Their fears arose from several causes: that their legal activity
would henceforth be declared illegal, that the sentence on
Shcharansky would constitute a terrible precedent for the whole
movement and all its leaders, that it would signal danger for each of
them; and they were afraid, above all, for Shcharansky himself.

Among those at the barrier at the entrance to the alleyway was
Ida Milgrom. Speaking to David Shipler of the *New York Times*,
she remarked of Shcharansky's father: 'He knows his son is not a
criminal, that he is an honest man.' Each morning, Ida Milgrom
was to come to the court and each morning she was to be refused
access.

On the morning of 11 July 1978, in an attempt to answer the
previous day's allegations that Shcharansky had not been properly
married to Avital according to Jewish law, Girsh Manevich sent a
telegram to the Chairman of the court, asking to be called as a
defence witness. 'I wish to confirm', he declared in his telegram,
'that Anatoly Shcharansky and his wife Natalia (Avital) were duly
married according to the rites of the Jewish religion, and that their
marriage is recognised by Jewish and civil authorities throughout
the world.' Manevich received no reply. Nor was he invited to give
evidence.

The court was in session throughout Tuesday, July 11, but it was
a secret session which even Leonid Shcharansky was not allowed to
attend. Nor was anyone allowed to gather outside the courthouse,

the whole street being sealed off. Among those giving evidence during this closed session was Sanya Lipavsky.

The session was secret, not because any 'secrets' were revealed, but because it was clear from the long months of interrogation that a trial held entirely in open session would reveal nothing treasonable, and thus destroy the whole purpose of the trial. Shcharansky later told his mother and brother that Lipavsky's evidence was almost identical to his *Izvestia* article of March 1977. The other 'secret' witnesses, Tsipin, Raslin and Riabsky, had likewise spoken only of generalities and absurdities.

Riabsky had not been a refusenik, and was indeed a member of the Communist Party. Somewhat to the surprise of the refuseniks, he had openly invited Richard Pipes to visit his apartment. Ina Rubin, thinking it strange that someone who was a Party member and not a refusenik should have invited home a foreigner whom he had not met before, had told her husband that she was suspicious of him. Immediately afterwards, Riabsky had telephoned Rubin to say that he was 'afraid' to invite Pipes to his home. From that moment it had been obvious to the refuseniks that the KGB monitors had overheard Ina Rubin's remark (in her private apartment) and had at once alerted Riabsky to his 'mistake'.

On Wednesday, 12 July 1978, the morning session was again declared a closed one. Ida Milgrom and Leonid Shcharansky were again refused admittance. For the afternoon session, however, Leonid Shcharansky was allowed into the court. Two KGB men sat on either side of him, but he was permitted to take notes. 'Compared to the first day of the trial,' he noted, 'today's sitting was strained and nervy. Anatoly looked tired and drained. Nevertheless, he held himself with confidence and restraint, occasionally smiling at me.'

Shcharansky had realised, during the two closed sessions, that he was not to be allowed to answer in open court a series of spurious and trivial charges. No wonder he looked 'tired and drained': nearly sixteen months had passed since he had last been able to converse with his friends, to breathe fresh air, to eat normal food: sixteen months during which he had been under threat of sentence of death.

The first two witnesses to be called during this afternoon session were Sukhachevskaya, a doctor from Vladimir prison, and a medical orderly from one of the Perm region labour camps. They claimed that conditions in the prisons were normal with full medical services, and that the temperature in the punishment cells varied from 18 to 24°C. Dr Sukhachevskaya said that the food 'was, of course, not caviar, neither the black nor the red variety', but it was 'sufficient and of good quality'.

Another prosecution witness was Pyotr Adamsky from Vilnius. He too had posed for several years as a refusenik, receiving publicity in the West for his plight, but now he spoke as an enemy of the movement into which he had been welcomed.

The next witness was Sonya Davidovich, the daughter of the late Yefim Davidovich of Minsk. In December 1977 she and her mother, a non-Jew, had returned from Israel. For some time she stood in the witness stand and said nothing at all; the Judge several times spoke to her, telling her to begin testifying. She then said she would answer questions but would not speak of her own accord. In reply to questions, she said she did not know Shcharansky but had seen him twice. The Prosecutor asked her such questions as 'What are the conditions of life like in Israel?' She said she would only speak to the essence of the matter, and that her life in Israel was quite irrelevant to this case. The Prosecutor asked her several more questions, but she did not answer.

The Judge then began to read aloud the evidence which Sonya Davidovich had given at the preliminary investigation; at this preliminary investigation, he said, both wife and daughter had testified that emigration to Israel had not been the desire or intention of the late Colonel, but that 'the whole family had become victims of Zionism'. The Judge now read from evidence presented at the preliminary investigation stating how bad life was in Israel. The Prosecutor had asked, 'Why did you come back from Israel?' The answer had read: 'Only when we were in a foreign country did we realise what we had lost and left behind.'

The Prosecutor now referred to a letter signed by about sixty Jewish activists after Davidovich's death. Was writing such a letter a moral thing to do without consulting the family, he asked Sonya Davidovich. No, she said. The questioning continued:

Prosecutor: Shcharansky and all those who signed the letter maintained that your father's death was due to the Soviet authorities. What is your opinion of that?

Sonya: That is their opinion and I cannot answer this question, but I know that my father repeatedly asked for a visa to Israel.

Sonya Davidovich then agreed to answer Shcharansky's questions:

Shcharansky: Have you read your father's book, *The Way of Jews in the Red Army*, in other words, about the Jewish national question?
Sonya: No, I didn't read it in Israel.
Shcharansky: I didn't ask if you read it in Israel, but had you read it at all?
Sonya: Yes.
Shcharansky: Do you think your father was honest in writing this book? [The Judge refused to allow this question to be put.]
Shcharansky: Did I, Shcharansky, influence your father in his desire to go to Israel? [Sonya Davidovich refused to answer.]

Other questions put by Shcharansky were either refused by the Judge, or the witness refused to answer. There was then a break from 2.10 to 4.10 p.m.

When the session resumed, the witness was Irina Musinchina, a neighbour of Sanya Lipavsky.

Prosecutor: Who visited Shcharansky?
Witness: Five or six times the foreign correspondent Robert Toth.
Prosecutor: What did Shcharansky give Toth?
Witness: Once I saw him give Toth forty pages.
Judge: Did you see what was written on the pages?
Witness: No.

The Judge reminded the witness that at the preliminary investigation she had described what was written, but she did not confirm this evidence.

Prosecutor: Had Shcharansky ever been to Robert Toth's apartment?
Witness: I don't know.
Prosecutor: Had Shcharansky arranged meetings with Toth by telephone?
Witness: We have no telephone in our apartment.
Prosecutor: How did he arrange these meetings?
Witness: I don't know.
Prosecutor: Describe the character of Shcharansky.
Witness: He seemed to be well brought up, well educated, well mannered, cultured, modest, but careless about his dress.
Prosecutor: Who else came to see him?
Witness: Some religious people.

Prosecutor: What did they talk about?
Witness: I don't know.
Prosecutor: Weren't you curious?
Witness: No, I'm not a curious person.

The next witness was Abramov, deputy chief of the personnel department of a food-canning factory in Derbent. He referred to an anti-Zionist meeting in 1974. Lists were then read out of those leaving the Soviet Union; the Prosecutor referred to them as 'traitors to the Motherland'.

The Prosecutor asked Abramov to comment on the allegations that the Soviet Union had no Jewish culture. He replied that from 7.00 to 7.40 on the local radio there is a programme in the Tat language, the language of the local 'mountain' Jews. The Prosecutor asked Shcharansky if he had ever been to Derbent. No, Shcharansky said, but his friends had. Shcharansky then began his questioning of the witness:

Shcharansky: Do you know how many Jews had left Derbent? [The Judge refused to let the question be put.]
Shcharansky: Does anyone know Hebrew in Derbent? [Again, question disallowed.]
Shcharansky: Do you attend the synagogue? [Question disallowed. There was general laughter in court.]

The next witness was Riabsky.

Judge: What do you know about the collection by Shcharansky and Vitaly Rubin of information and passing it to the West?

The witness spoke mainly about Rubin, referring to him as a poor-quality scientist, and describing Shcharansky as an 'organiser of provocative actions aimed at denigrating Soviet emigration policies'. In particular, he had organised an 'illegal meeting' with United States Senators. Riabsky then said that Richard Pipes had come to the Soviet Union with specific instructions to act as a Zionist emissary. Dr Pipes, he said, was a personal friend of President Carter's National Security Adviser, the 'anti-Soviet' Dr Brzezinski.

Riabsky referred to Shcharansky as a leader of 'Aliyah'. He said that as a result of the activities of Shcharansky, Soviet–American relations were unable to move from a dead point. Pipes had subsequently spoken about the formation of the Helsinki Watch-dog group just before the Helsinki Conference.

Shcharansky: Is it not true that the Helsinki Agreement was signed in 1975 and the meeting with Pipes was in 1976?
Witness: Pipes came for the express purpose of discussing family reunification.

The next witness was a man called Platonov, from Leningrad. He told the court that he did not understand his role in the Shcharansky case because they did not know each other. He then gave his testimony; it did not deal at all with Shcharansky but with Alexander Ginsburg, and another dissident, Yury Galanskov, who had died in a Soviet labour camp. Platonov referred to conditions in the camp.

Apparently, this witness was to have been called in the Ginsburg trial in Kaluga, but had mistakenly been brought by police to the Shcharansky trial.

The next witness was Leonid Tsipin, once Shcharansky's colleague in the preparation of petitions and demonstrations.

Judge: What do you know about Shcharansky's anti-Soviet activities?
Tsipin: Shcharansky was the author of many letters calling for the adoption of the Jackson Amendment and he organised a letter in support of Anatoly Malkin.

The appeal on Malkin's behalf had actually been written by Vitaly Rubin, who had subsequently received his exit visa. But as with every reference in court to a collective letter, Shcharansky was portrayed as its organiser and only begetter, and no reference made to others who had been at the centre of such activities, yet who had been given their exit visas and were now in Israel.

Tsipin then spoke about the meetings with American Senators, who had talked, he said, about 'compromise'. Shcharansky, however, Tsipin declared, had 'adopted a much tougher line'. In one letter to the Senators, Tsipin added, there had been a call for the release of the 'Prisoners of Zion', but these persons 'were merely hooligans correctly convicted of having committed criminal actions'. Shcharansky, said Tsipin, knew all the foreign correspondents and diplomats 'from whom the smell of anti-Sovietism exudes'.

Tsipin described the United States Embassy personnel in

Moscow, Melvin Levitsky and Joseph Pressel, as 'CIA agents', which they were not. Sometimes, Tsipin declared, their meetings with Shcharansky in a café in one of Moscow's streets took 'the atmosphere of conspiracy'. Shcharansky was 'often on duty' at the Visa Office in Moscow to interview and take details from new refuseniks, and the list of refuseniks and the information about them was 'transferred' to Senator Henry Jackson. There was, Tsipin said, a special list of very active refuseniks. At the Moscow Synagogue on Saturdays, he would often be asked when Shcharansky would be coming.

Tsipin then referred to Odessa and other cities where there were trials of, as he called them, 'Jewish nationalists' who were accused of hooliganism, and to visits by leading Jewish activists to members of the Central Committee of the Communist Party of the Soviet Union. He also described a letter to the central committees of the Communist Parties of France and Italy immediately prior to the 25th Party Congress in Moscow; by sending this, he said, Shcharansky was obviously trying to put the French and Italian Communist leaders in an embarrassing situation, and to get them to speak from the platform during the Congress and to have them criticise both there and in other parts of the world the attitude of the Soviet authorities and Soviet emigration policies.

Tsipin continued his evidence by describing how Shcharansky had acted as a link between Professor Sakharov's group and the Jewish refusenik movement. Shcharansky had read 'forbidden books', including 'provocative books in English', he said. Tsipin then referred to interviews conducted with refuseniks in the reception room of the Supreme Soviet, and to the interviews held with the Minister of the Interior Nikolai Shchelekhov.

Shcharansky: Did you ever take part in what you call meetings of conspirators in the campaign?
Tsipin: No, I never took part in them, but I know about them from other people.
Shcharansky: Where is the café?
Tsipin: On Kutuzovsky Prospect, just near the building where foreign correspondents live.

This was one of the most public places in Moscow, and under continual surveillance.

The next witness was Dr Sanya Lipavsky. The Judge asked him what he knew about the making of the film, 'A Calculated Risk'.

Lipavsky answered in great detail which, he said, he had learned from other people, adding that special emissaries of Zionist organisations came in two groups, separately and secretly, 'to make this anti-Soviet film illegally and smuggle it out illegally'.

Lipavsky told the court that after the screening on Soviet television of the film 'Traders of Souls', Shcharansky and other refuseniks sought in court to take a libel action against the producers of the film because, they said, they were afraid of a mob lynching Jews in the streets of Moscow now that their faces were known to the citizens of the Soviet Union.

Lipavsky then looked Shcharansky straight in the eye and said emphatically: 'How can we, the Soviet Jews who do not want to emigrate, live here after all you have done?' Was Lipavsky suggesting, Shcharansky asked, that after the trial 'there will be an increase in anti-Semitism in the Soviet Union?'

Throughout the day's proceedings, Leonid noted, 'Anatoly was often halted in mid-speech as they kept interrupting him, the hall resounding with laughter. Sometimes the Judge for no apparent reason overruled his questions. But when the witnesses Riabsky, Tsipin and Lipavsky fell silent, the Judge did not hurry them but patiently waited for them to continue. Instead, he sympathetically asked them whether they had anything more to say and supportively asked them leading questions. When Anatoly asked the witnesses questions, immediately after the answer the Judge demanded of Anatoly irritably, "Have you finished?" In this way the Judge further charged an already tense situation.'

Towards the end of the session, and in answer to a question from the Judge, Lipavsky, using the same words as Tsipin, referred to letters addressed to the French and Italian Communist Parties. He then referred to letters addressed to the Jewish community of America about the two prisoners, Lev Roitburd of Odessa and Anatoly Malkin of Moscow. Shcharansky, he added, spoke extensively at the Helsinki Watchdog group about separated families.

Lipavsky went on to allege that Shcharansky aimed 'to change the existing state and social order in the Soviet Union'; he then embarked upon an historical account of the defence of the Soviet Union and how it had defeated all attempts to undermine Soviet society; he spoke of the Allied 'intervention' of 1917 and how it had failed, and of attempts in the 1920s and by Hitler which had also failed.

Again looking straight at Shcharansky, Lipavsky asked him:

'How could you, with your brilliant analytical mind, believe you could succeed when so many others at so many other times have failed?'

Lipavsky also spoke a great deal about the visit to the village of Ilyinka. Robert Toth had intended to join them, he said. He referred to letters regarding the Jackson Amendment.

Shcharansky: Had you ever seen me writing these letters or signing them?
Lipavsky: No.
Shcharansky: Then how can you testify about my connection with these documents?

The Judge refused to allow the question to be answered.

Lipavsky next spoke about Vitaly Rubin passing on 'espionage assignments' to Shcharansky. George Krimsky of the Associated Press and Peter Osnos of the *Washington Post* were also mentioned in this connection.

The court then adjourned until the following day: the day on which judgement was to be delivered.

★   ★   ★

Speaking to French and West German television correspondents on 12 July 1978, President Carter condemned Shcharansky's trial, and that of Orlov, as 'an attack on every human being who lives in the world who believes in basic freedom and is willing to speak for those freedoms or fight for them'. Avital Shcharansky was in Geneva that week, as the American Secretary of State Cyrus Vance and the Soviet Foreign Minister Andrei Gromyko began talks on a new Strategic Arms Limitation Treaty. 'I will ask Mr Vance to address Gromyko,' she said, 'and demand the immediate liberation of my husband and that he be sent to me.' Avital added: 'All his troubles have come because he is a Jew and wanted to emigrate. He always fought openly, he has done nothing against Soviet law. And now he is in criminal hands.'

21

Road to Judgement

The fourth day of Shcharansky's trial opened at ten in the morning of Thursday, 13 July 1978. Two witnesses were expected in the courtroom that morning, both from Ilyinka, but they failed to appear. The Judge asked the Prosecutor's opinion about the non-appearance of these two witnesses; he answered that they could do without them. The Judge then asked Shcharansky whether he had any objections. 'By virtue of my position,' Shcharansky answered, 'it makes absolutely no difference to me.'

The court moved on to discuss the evidence submitted by the Prosecutor on the charge of treason. Eight documents of specific episodes were submitted by the Prosecutor in connection with this charge – documents which the Judge was to declare in his summing-up were evidence of 'concrete criminal activities'. The first document in the charge of treason was an appeal to the United States Senate about the Jackson Amendment, dated July 1974, as well as what the Judge was later to describe as a 'hostile' review, composed with Shcharansky's 'assistance' and passed in November 1974 through the American Embassy in Moscow. This review contained, according to the Judge, 'aspersions' about the activities of the Soviet Union. 'In the same month,' the Prosecutor alleged, Shcharansky 'also sent this review to several Senators and Congressmen'.

This first accusation pointed out that the appeal of July 1974 and the review of November 1974 were 'in connection with the fact' that in December 1974 the United States Congress approved an amendment to the Trade Law 'which made the allocation of credit to Socialist countries' dependent upon the opportunity given to the United States 'to interfere in their internal affairs'. In the appeal of July 1974 this amendment, 'which damaged the political and economic interests of the USSR', had been called an 'important achievement', and of 'invaluable support' to those who were seeking to obtain exit visas.

The second document presented by the Prosecutor as proof of treason was the appeal beginning 'Dear Brothers' written at the end of 1974. Shcharansky, it was alleged, had taken part in the 'preparation and forwarding' of this document to the West. It was an 'anti-Soviet' document in which, the Judge later concluded, Shcharansky 'slandered the Soviet Government's activities in connection with the position on the terms of trade with the United States'. ('There were a lot of letters beginning with the words "Dear Brothers . . ."', Shcharansky later remarked to Leonid during one of his brother's rare prison visits, 'but, by an irony of fate, this precise letter in the accusation had never been passed on to anybody.')

The third document was 'The Lessons of the Roitburd and Malkin Trial', given to foreign correspondents in Moscow on 17 September 1975, together with two letters which Shcharansky and others 'composed and sent abroad', addressed to United States Senators and Congressmen, 'in which he slanderously announced "the persecution and harassment of those who wanted to emigrate" and urged the Senators and Congressmen to interfere in the internal affairs of the Soviet Union'.

The fourth document was a letter to United States Senators concerning the Jackson Amendment. This document, the Prosecutor alleged, had been compiled at the request of the Senators. This Shcharansky denied.

The fifth document was an eleven-page statement by Sanya Lipavsky, listing all the materials which Lipavsky had given the KGB from the room in which he had, as he expressed it, 'cohabited' with Shcharansky. In reply to this document, Shcharansky told the court that he had 'simply never seen any of this material before'.

The sixth document was a deposition by Lipavsky, a modification of his *Izvestia* article. In it he made no reference to Shcharansky, but only to his own links with the CIA. This was not however made clear in the court.

The seventh document was a questionnaire about the Jewish emigration movement, which the Prosecutor alleged had been sent through the diplomatic post to be given to Shcharansky. The name of the Embassy involved was not mentioned. Shcharansky told the court that he had first seen this document during the investigation.

The eighth and final document for the treason charge was a

protest note sent from the Soviet Ministry of Foreign Affairs to the
United States Embassy in Moscow, protesting against Robert
Toth's meeting in a Moscow street with Valery Petukhov, a man
posing as a dissident, who had offered him material on parapsychology. Shcharansky told the court that he was sorry not to
have been able to cross-examine Petukhov about this meeting, a
request he had made several times during the investigation.

★   ★   ★

For the charge of 'anti-Soviet agitation and propaganda', fifteen
documents were submitted by the prosecution. The first was the
appeal to the Communist Parties of France and Italy, dated February 1976, alleging, in the words of the prosecution, 'that citizens
of Jewish origin in the USSR are exposed to harassment and
discrimination'.

Commenting on this when his brother visited him in prison a
year later, Shcharansky expressed his opinion that had the leaders of
the French and Italian Communist Parties 'responded in some way'
to this appeal, it would not have been part of the accusation. 'It was
precisely their silence', Shcharansky remarked, 'and the reluctance
of the Communist newspaper correspondents to meet with the
activists, that untied the hands of the authorities. So little had
been required of the French and Italian Communist leaders,'
Shcharansky added. 'They should not have kept silent.'

The second document in the anti-Soviet charge was the British
television film 'A Calculated Risk' which, according to the Prosecutor, 'contained slanderous declarations about the "difficult situation" of minorities in the USSR'.

The third document was the declaration about the death of Yefim
Davidovich on 24 April 1976. This had been signed by eighty-two
refuseniks. Its text was not read out to the court.

The fourth document on the anti-Soviet charge was the Helsinki
Watchdog group report dated 17 June 1976, about prisoners in
camps. In this 'so-called "document"', the Prosecutor pointed out,
Shcharansky, 'together with his accomplices Orlov and Ginsburg',
had 'slanderously declared' that people serving sentences in the
Soviet Union were exposed to 'physical and moral torment, and
real torture, by means of starvation combined with hard physical
labour'. (Reflecting on this charge in a conversation with his
brother some years later, during a brief prison meeting,
Shcharansky commented that, arising out of his own experiences

and observations since his trial, he could now make 'a considerably more sharply worded document'.)

The fifth document was a set of other reports issued by the Helsinki Watchdog group. These reports, said the Judge in his summing up, were 'defamatory'; Shcharansky, in his defence, stated that he 'did not consider them defamatory'. The text of the documents was not read out in court.

The sixth document was one of the Helsinki Watchdog group reports, dated 1 August 1976, on the situation of former political prisoners in the Soviet Union, in which, the prosecution alleged, and the Judge considered proven, 'Shcharansky, together with Orlov, Ginsburg and other persons, slanderously states that the fate of nearly all former "political prisoners" is the further imposition by the Soviet authorities of "severe discriminatory measures" not stipulated by law which are considered by the former prisoners to be an "extension of the punishment for their conviction".' (Speaking to his brother during a later prison visit, Shcharansky commented that neither this, nor the previous two documents, had been read out in the courtroom, either during its open or during its closed sessions.)

The seventh document was an appeal to the Supreme Soviet and to the United States Congress. Here was another document which, though referred to in the court, was not quoted from in any way.

The eighth document was a report of 22 July 1976 on the abuse of psychiatry, a second similar report of 12 September 1976 and a 'so-called' press conference held on 1 October 1976, when, with Orlov and Ginsburg, Shcharansky had, in the words of the Prosecutor, 'repeated slanderous concoctions about the internal policy of the Soviet Government'.

The ninth document in the 'anti-Soviet' charge was an appeal to the Jewish communities of the United States. Again, it was not read out to the court, in either open or closed session.

The tenth document was a Helsinki Watchdog group report, dated 28 December 1976, about 'arrests for religious reasons', and information about what the Prosecutor called 'the so-called "Christmas repressions" against the group which had been set up in the Ukraine to monitor the carrying out of the Helsinki Agreement'. The testimony of witnesses and the results of an examination of materials collected during searches in the homes of three members of the group, M. Tykhyi, P. Rudenko and A. Bordnik, 'disproved the allegations in the document of the Soviet Union's "absolute neglect" of its international obligations', but did reveal, the court was told, information about 'certain illegal activities' by representatives of foreign governments 'in respect to those mentioned in these documents'. What these 'illegal activities' were was not stated.

The eleventh document was a Helsinki Watchdog group report, dated 2 December 1976, about Ukrainians who were said to have been 'refused their application to leave the USSR'. Examination of the records of the Visa Office, the Judge noted in his conclusions, showed that those mentioned in this document had never applied to the Soviet authorities to leave the Soviet Union.

The twelfth document, also from the Helsinki Watchdog group, and likewise dated 2 December 1976, was about the emigration of workers for economic reasons. The court was told that one of those mentioned in this document was involved in a 'criminal case'. The salary certificates of these Jews had been examined, proving that the document contained 'hostile fabrications'.

The thirteenth document, origin unspecified, was about 'the right to choose the country in which to live'.

The fourteenth document was a declaration concerning the Soviet television film 'Traders of Souls'. After the film had been shown, the offices of Moscow Central Television had allegedly been 'inundated' with anti-Semitic comments. The declaration had protested against this.

The fifteenth document was a financial certificate, submitted at the Prosecutor's request from the Soviet Foreign Despatch and Trade Organisation 'Vneshposyltorg', testifying about foreign currency which had been received in Shcharansky's name. The certificate showed a number of remittances for a total of between two and three hundred United States dollars, dating from 1973 and 1974. When asked by the Prosecutor for his opinion of these remittances, Shcharansky replied: 'It's all the same to me.'

*   *   *

'The atmosphere worsened from day to day', Leonid Shcharansky noted. 'It was worst on the fourth day.' At one moment a heckler in the courtroom called out: 'People like this should be hanged!'

On 14 July 1978 at 11.15 a.m., the British television film 'A Calculated Risk' was shown to the court. During the film there was heckling from those present, who called out, as Leonid Shcharansky noted: 'Agent provocateur!', 'No one supports those who want to leave!', 'Spider!', and so on. After the film had been shown, Shcharansky declared that the court's translation was full of mistakes and that the text of the film had been distorted by the official translation.

The court then adjourned for half an hour.

The next session of the court began at 12.45, when the Prosecutor asked Shcharansky whether he knew that these pictures would be shown in the West. Shcharansky reminded the Prosecutor that during the preliminary investigation he had stated that his appearance in the film 'was a normal interview for general use'.

There then followed questions about the figure of 10,000 Germans who had been allowed to leave the Soviet Union. Where did this figure come from? Shcharansky was asked. He replied: 'I had earlier requested that official information about the departure of those of German nationality should be made available for this case, but this had been refused me. However, such information does exist.' The Prosecutor asked: 'Where did you get the information about the poor situation of Germans in Central Asia?', to which Shcharansky replied: 'I made no such statement. This is an incorrect translation. The presenter's words have been attributed to me.'

The Prosecutor asked that the letter written from Israel by Yefim Davidovich's wife and daughter should be considered in this case. (It was not clear, however, what this letter contained; the only letter of the Davidovich family mentioned earlier was said to have been critical of life in Jerusalem, but without any reference to Shcharansky.) Shcharansky did not object. The Prosecutor then requested that certain carbon paper should also be considered as material evidence. Expert opinion had pronounced that the imprint of part of the lists of refuseniks found by a concierge on 15 April 1977, in the courtyard of a building where foreign reporters lived, was still on the carbon. Shcharansky declared that he had first seen the lists and the carbon paper only during the investigation. It was true, he said, that the carbon showed traces of a text, but he had first seen this text, he repeated, only during the investigation.

At one o'clock the Judge declared that the judicial investigation was over. He then allowed an hour and a half for the Prosecutor and the Defendant to prepare their concluding speeches. At 2.20 that afternoon, Solonin began his closing speech.

He started by charting the historical development of the Soviet Union. All privilege had been abolished, all paths were open, there was a free health service, people were given good housing, welfare was steadily increasing, and there was a policy of peace. 'What can capitalism offer? Capitalism has never provided anything like this and never will be able to.'

'Our path, admittedly, has never been an easy one,' Solonin continued, 'we have constantly had to defend ourselves. More than once the capitalists have entertained ideas of crushing us. But our country has not been crushed.' Lenin had argued that any revolution is only 'worth its salt' when it can defend itself. But the capitalists kept trying to interfere in Soviet internal affairs, 'just as they are trying to do now, with their secret service, spying and sabotage, which includes ideological sabotage'. Solonin added: 'Our country's successes have engendered panic in the imperialist camp. Hence they rain down waves of lies on us. They blacken the Soviet system. They involve various Zionist organisations, anti-Soviet centres, and also such provocative radio stations as Radio Liberty and Radio Free Europe in their anti-Soviet intrigues.' To this end various anti-Soviet operations were 'fabricated' under the code names of 'Solzhenitsyn', the 'Sakharov Affair', the 'Defence of Soviet Jews', and the 'Human Rights' campaign.

It was 'pertinent', said the Prosecutor, to put the question: 'And what is the human rights situation in America?', and he went on to tell the court that the American public was 'not even acquainted' with the Final Act of the Helsinki Agreement. The aim of the campaign was to divert attention away from the economic situation in capitalist countries, away from the 'flouting of rights' in the world of capital. He was sure that the capitalist countries 'would also revile the essence of this trial', and he added: 'Some insects release a smelly substance for defence; this is the way that dissidents behave. They voluntarily serve as tools of the enemy.' They were 'brigands of the pen'. As was known, 'we do not try people for their beliefs but for breaking the law. And anti-Soviet activity does conflict with the law.'

The Prosecutor now spoke in glowing terms of the opportunities open to Soviet citizens. It was not preordained, he said, that Shcharansky would come up before a court. All paths had been open to him. He had had the chance to avail himself of socialist rights, and he had used them. He had received free higher education, and he had the right to work. But instead, he had set out on the path of 'illegal behaviour, ideological error, and political thoughtlessness. Many were hooked by this bait.' As had been stated on the previous day, 'a critical individualism' had appeared in

Shcharansky. He was a product 'of processing by the imperialist diversionary service'. He wanted to be at the centre of things: he considered himself a generator of ideas, and aspired to be exceptional.

'What did he mainly do at work?' asked Solonin, and he went on to answer his own question: 'He studied Hebrew. From 1975 he did not participate in socially useful labour. As the witness Tsipin said, "In daily life Anatoly Shcharansky was slovenly and morally unstable," and hence he found himself in the company of Ginsburg, Orlov, and Alexeeva.' At first, Solonin declared, Shcharansky had been assigned 'a modest role as a so-called "sound effects man", i.e. people involved in various provocative actions, controlled from abroad'. He had been noticed, however, 'and they began to give him more difficult tasks, including the gathering of secret information.' He had established contact with well-known Western correspondents, 'and he collected secret information.'

Solonin's speech for the prosecution continued: 'It goes without saying that we are for friendship. Many tourists come from abroad, among them scholars and writers, and we greet them with Soviet hospitality. But in this case we are talking about conspiratorial meetings at which State secrets were betrayed. These emissaries of various rank from abroad gave instructions and little sops, inflamed national feelings, and incited them towards an illusory homeland so that they would go there and make themselves at home on land seized from the Arabs. This is the cause of the crimes committed by Shcharansky. His hostility has been established in all clarity in the course of the trial.'

Shcharansky, declared Solonin, had acted to undermine the Soviet Union's military power, was engaged in espionage and harboured 'treacherous schemes'. He had met with foreign correspondents, diplomats and 'Zionist emissaries' from abroad. On their instructions, he had provided them with defamatory material. Reactionary circles had used these materials for anti-Soviet purposes. Between 1974 and 1976 he had personally prepared and passed on to various States 'not less than seventeen documents' of a defamatory character. They included direct calls and incitements to intensify the pressure on the Soviet Union in order to make the Soviet authorities feel the short-sightedness of their position. An example of this was the appeal to the American people and the United States Congress. 'This appeal was slanderous and a fabrication.'

In 1974 the Jackson Amendment had been adopted. At the end of 1974 Shcharansky had taken part in drafting the message 'Dear Brothers . . .'. At the end of 1975 Lunts, Rubin and others had sent the document 'We appeal to you. . . '. On 12 January 1976 Shcharansky had sent a letter of support at the request of the mover of the Jackson Amendment. In early 1976 he had sent a survey report on the emigration policy of the Soviet Union to the Zionist congress in Brussels 'in order to put pressure on the Soviet Union'. He had constantly organised 'conspiratorial meetings with various activists from abroad', at which he had spoken 'about the need to put pressure on the Soviet Union'. His activities 'soon came to be appreciated by the Western secret services and Zionist organisations'. The numerous letters of support addressed to him 'illustrate this.'

Solonin went on to describe the friendship of the peoples of the Soviet Union, a multi-national country in which the many nationalities lived in harmony. In speaking about anti-Semitism in the Soviet Union, Shcharansky, he said, had tried to slander the 'internationalist nature' of the Soviet Union. The 'overwhelming majority' of Jews did not want to leave, and they were 'building socialism'. As an example, Solonin cited several Jews from Derbent who had no desire to leave, and who condemned those who did.

The Public Prosecutor explained that 'Tsarist Russia really was a prison-house of peoples. Jews were deprived of rights.' He added: 'With us, as is known, chauvinism is against the law.' He then read out several articles from the Soviet Constitution which spoke of 'the equality of all peoples', and cited an article by Leonid Brezhnev on the national question. The Jewish question, he declared, had been 'definitely solved' in the Soviet Union: there was no anti-Semitism 'and there cannot be any'. The meaning of Soviet society was 'encapsulated in the fraternity of the peoples of the Soviet Union'. There were 2,151,000 Jews in the Soviet Union, less than one per cent of the total population. It was in the Soviet Union that Jews for the first time were granted the right of self-determination. A Jewish autonomous region had been created, 'but the majority prefer to stay in the cities'. Jews took part in all walks of life: '25,000 are deputies in regional Soviets; they comprise 5.7 per cent of scientific workers, 50 per cent of journalists; and 6.7 per cent of lawyers are Jews'; 379,000 Jews had been awarded with decorations and medals; out of every 100,000 students 311 were Jewish, 'and

they make up the highest percentage in higher education establishments (68,700).'

This idyllic picture of the situation of Jews in the Soviet Union
was more than idealised; it was a distortion of the reality, in which
there were no Jewish schools, where the Hebrew language could
not be learned except privately, where Jewish religious worship
was strictly curtailed, where anti-Semitic feeling was widespread,
and where a love of Israel, and a desire to live in Israel, were
denounced as treason.

The Prosecutor then spoke with equal distortion about Israel
itself. It was, he said, a country 'with little culture'. The process of
nation-forming there was not yet completed. Students 'are taught
in English and use English textbooks'. Shcharansky had 'no right to
raise his hand against the Soviet Union. Our country saved the Jews
from extermination during the war. Shcharansky's attempt to
establish American control over Soviet policy has been a complete
failure.' Shcharansky had stated that 150,000 Jews have left. 'This
means, they can emigrate after all?' the Prosecutor asked. A
proportion of the population of the Soviet Union were not allowed
to leave 'because of considerations of security', the Prosecutor
continued, 'or when moral questions are involved, i.e. when old
parents or young children are left behind, and so on'. But if a person
was refused, the decision was reviewed every six months. The
Prosecutor cited several examples of Jews 'departing for a distant
uncle and leaving a sick mother behind'. The picture was clear.
'Why doesn't Shcharansky shout about this?' Solonin asked, and
answered, derisively, 'Because he is an active assistant of Western
Zionist organisations.' Emigration, Solonin added, was used 'as a
means of boosting Israel's population'. But 300,000 people had left
Israel. After the Yom Kippur War 'months of mourning' had been
declared when Golda Meir announced 'We are few.'

All this was a mockery of the reality. 'We are few' had referred to
Israel's three million Jews as compared to the eighty million Arabs
in the States surrounding Israel. The 'proportion' of Jews not
allowed to leave for real security considerations was, as the Lunts–
Beilina lists had made clear, a tiny proportion of the whole
refusenik body. The six-monthly review which Solonin mentioned
was hardly ever a positive one; on this basis, even Shcharansky had
been unsuccessfully reviewed at least seven times.

The Prosecutor went on to challenge Shcharansky's 'claim' that
the decline in the number of those who wanted to leave the Soviet

Union was due to 'repression'. In fact, he said, the number of applications to leave had fallen 'because life in Israel is bad'. The *New York Times* 'in particular' had written about this. The Prosecutor cited the letter of a Soviet Jew who said he wanted to return from Israel 'because he had never been surrounded by so many swindlers'. There was laughter in court at this.

Turning from the specific allegations against Shcharansky, the Prosecutor ranged over a wide propaganda field, regaling the court with a gratuitous and largely spurious attack on the West in general, and on Israel in particular, including a series of unfounded allegations of no relevance to the charges. The United Nations, he said, had condemned Israel and equated Zionism with racism. Israel lived on gifts, he said, and spent sixty per cent of its income on defence. Spiritually, Israel was in a 'dead end'. Culturally it was 'in a mess'. He again quoted Golda Meir: 'It is with pain that I consider what they would think in Russia if they knew how bad it is in Israel.'

As for Shcharansky's 'treacherous activities', the Prosecutor cited Tsipin's deposition on the influence which Shcharansky had exerted on the Jackson Amendment. Allegedly, Shcharansky himself had told Tsipin about this. Tsipin had spoken of the close contacts between Shcharansky and several Western correspondents through whom he had passed information to the West. Shcharansky had 'deliberately acted against the Soviet Union's military might'. In 1976, from letters sent by Rubin to Shcharansky, it was clear that 'the latter had passed over information on 1300 people and about the location of 200 enterprises'. He had 'collected, processed and stored these lists and through various channels, observing the rules of conspiracy, transferred them to the West'.

No letters had been sent from Vitaly Rubin to Shcharansky, only a single letter from Ina Rubin to Lipavsky: and this letter contained no reference to passing over 'information'. As for 'the rules of conspiracy', as was true of all the documents signed by Shcharansky, the material sent by Jewish activists to the West had been sent openly, without any attempt at secrecy, signed with the names of the signatories, and published with those names.

The letter to Lipavsky from Ina Rubin, which Ina Rubin had sent to Moscow through the *Washington Post* correspondent Peter Osnos, was an answer to Lipavsky's request as a 'refusenik' to find somebody in the United States who would adopt his family and campaign for them. Ina Rubin's letter reported that progress was

being made through a Rabbi at Columbia University, and asked
Lipavsky various personal questions about himself in connection
with the hoped-for adoption. None of this was mentioned in the
court, where the authorship of the 'Rubin' letter was transferred
to Vitaly Rubin, its addressee changed from Lipavsky to
Shcharansky, and its contents turned from personal help to
espionage.

The Prosecutor then declared that 'it had been proved' that in the
autumn of 1976 Lerner, Shcharansky and Lipavsky had received 'a
secret letter from the CIA through the diplomatic bag'. Lipavsky
had given a copy of the letter to the KGB. The back of the letter
'stated what was to be done'. It was 'addressed to Shcharansky'.
The typist Zaplyaeva had typed the lists of the 1300 refuseniks 'and
she had given an enormous amount of proof about this'. (Leonid
Shcharansky later noted that this lady had been moved into the flat
where the Rubins had lived, and he added, of her connection with
the activists with whom he was now associated, 'She had typed
nothing for us.') The Prosecutor went on to say that Shcharansky
had 'passed the lists to the West', that Robert Toth 'had shown an
interest in military establishments', and that Shcharansky 'was
acquainted with him'.

Once more the Lunts–Beilina lists were being used to condemn
Shcharansky, even though there was nothing illegal in them, nor
any breach of secrecy. As to Zaplyaeva, who had rented a room in
the communal apartment with the Rubins throughout their time in
Moscow, and had frequently tried to join in their meetings with
foreigners, after the Rubins had left for Israel she had received an
apartment of her own in a fashionable part of Moscow: 'an obvious
KGB agent', Dina Beilina later reflected.

In connection with these lists typed by Zaplyaeva, the court was
told that on 15 April 1977, a month after Shcharansky's arrest, in
the yard of the house where foreign correspondents live in
Moscow, at 14 Kutuzovsky Prospect, the janitor, Zakharov, had
found in a rubbish bin lists of Jewish names, and, correctly sensing
their importance, promptly turned them in to the KGB. Thus the
'secret intelligence information that Shcharansky regularly supplied to the West until his very arrest, observing every measure of
caution and conspiracy', as *Izvestia* reported on 15 July 1978, was
discovered in a rubbish bin at the right time in the right place, in the
yard of the house where Robert Toth lived.

The lists which Zakharov had found turned out to be machine

copies of typed lists. It was established, the Prosecutor declared, that the typing was done by Zaplyaeva. The KGB was in possession of the lists and had included them in the Shcharansky case record.

In answer to this line of argument, Shcharansky told the court that he had never had any typing done for him by Zaplyaeva. She had been given typing to do by Lipavsky, and it was to Lipavsky alone that she had returned the work done. To Shcharansky's surprise, his statements were confirmed by Zaplyaeva's own testimony to the court, given in closed session. The Government Prosecutor made no objections to her testimony, or to Shcharansky's statement, even though they refuted one of the basic charges in the indictment.

Thus it was Lipavsky who had ordered typed copies of certain prepared lists of refuseniks from Zaplyaeva, and it was he who received from her the original lists and the typewritten copies. One of the copies had been included in the Shcharansky case record. No one knows where any of the other copies are. The question, Shcharansky's friends asked in a letter from Moscow immediately after his sentence, was: 'Where are the original handwritten lists? Lipavsky said he turned all his materials in to the KGB. Why, then, did the original lists not figure in the trial? The conclusion we can draw is that the original lists prove that Shcharansky had nothing to do with them.'

Of course, Shcharansky's friends added, 'there was a simple way of examining the lists objectively. The 1300 persons listed could give exhaustive testimony. During the preliminary investigation, some 200 Jewish refuseniks all over the USSR were called in to testify in court. The witnesses accepted by the court were Lipavsky and his ilk: Riabsky, Tsipin, Raslin and Adamsky.'

★   ★   ★

After a twenty-minute break, the Prosecutor continued his speech, telling the court that Shcharansky had acted 'to undermine and weaken Soviet power', and had carried out a policy 'of anti-Soviet provocation'. He had distributed defamatory documents. In his numerous letters to his 'confederates' he had distorted the real situation of religion in the Soviet Union. 'All of this is a foul lie: no one threatens our Soviet freedoms. They are stipulated in Article 52 of the Constitution. We have no laws against religion and we only try people for concrete infringements of the law.' Soviet legislation did not forbid teaching children religion, only the forcible teaching of religion. It was for breaking the law.

This was not strictly true, the law on religion being so vaguely worded that it was (and is) impossible to teach religion to children without breaking the law, whether by 'forcible' teaching or by ordinary teaching.

The Prosecutor now used his speech against Shcharansky as a foil for a series of falsifications and flights of fantasy. In the Soviet Union, he said, there were 'eighteen religious establishments and there were Judaic schools'. The religious institutions were allowed to practise their faith, and this they did. The 'leader' of what the Prosecutor called 'the United States church', Robert Marshall, 'had given a positive evaluation of the situation of religion in the Soviet Union, and the well-known boxer Muhammad Ali, who had visited the Soviet Union not long ago, had declared that as far as religion was concerned there was no problem.'

'Our legislation on religious belief is the most humanitarian and the most democratic in the world,' the Prosecutor declared, and he went on to denounce Israel for having 'a dominant religion'. The Sabbath was not a holiday 'but a doleful minute of silence which lasts a whole day'. The Sabbath, however, 'does not prevent Israel bombing the Lebanese'. No Shcharansky had the right 'to deny our superiority'. In tones of mounting anger, the Prosecutor went on to say that Shcharansky 'accuses Soviet psychiatrists, for example, of using psychiatry for judicial purposes. This is a crude lie. The State indictment officially declares that such cases are impossible.' The humanism of Soviet doctors was well known. Soviet power was not the passive observer 'but the active friend of those in difficulties'. Psychiatry was not a punishment. Only an 'ignoramus' could claim that a psychiatric hospital was a prison. Shcharansky's activity had been 'anti-humanitarian'; it involved 'dragging in sick people for anti-Soviet purposes'.

Here again, the Prosecutor had embarked upon a fiction, using it as a peg on which to describe the 'poor state' of the medical services in capitalist countries: '600,000 people in Britain are waiting for operations'; forty per cent of the sick in the United States could not receive medical help. He then went on to speak about the poor medical facilities in the territories occupied by Israel.

'Shcharansky, Ginsburg and Orlov talk about the camps,' the Prosecutor continued. 'Shcharansky spreads these slanders for anti-Soviet purposes.' Labour in the camps was not 'forced', he insisted, and the food there was 'average.' Witnesses from Vladimir prison, and from the Mordovian camp, had testified to this. 'The American criminologist Ford made favourable comments about our camps,' the Prosecutor added, and he went on to declare, as a point of criticism, that neurosurgery was practised in the United States, while in Israel there was 'torture of prisoners, the tearing out of nails, and so on'. A 'Swiss delegation' visiting Israel was cited in support of these allegations. If Shcharansky 'really and honestly cared about human rights', the Prosecutor told the court, 'then he would direct his protests against the United States and Israel'. In the Soviet Union such treatment of prisoners was strictly punished. 'Our prisoners have rights enjoyed by the prisoners of no other country. And it is the Soviet Union which has called on the whole world to respect human rights.'

Israel, the United States and Britain: each in its turn was presented by the Prosecutor as the wrongdoer. Only the Soviet Union emerged in Solonin's speech as a paragon: yet none of the documents of which Shcharansky had been signatory, which dealt with the plight of the refuseniks, and in particular of the Prisoners of Zion, was read out to the court, or cited by the Prosecutor.

The Prosecutor then told the court that the State indictment declared Shcharansky guilty. There were cries of 'Correct!' and applause in court. Shcharansky's guilt was proven 'by all the factual materials considered during the trial'. For a 'correct understanding', the Prosecutor added, 'we must take into account that Shcharansky has a subjectively hostile mentality', testified to by Tsipin's, Lipavsky's and Riabsky's evidence, and by 'the numerous letters about the Jackson Amendment, and the close links with foreign correspondents and diplomats who had a hostile bias directed into anti-Soviet activity, as Shcharansky well knew'.

Solonin went on to stress that Shcharansky was being tried not for his views, but for breaking the law. 'Critical views are found in any newspaper or journal,' he said, 'but people like Shcharansky, Ginsburg and Orlov do not criticise, but conduct themselves from an anti-Soviet position'. The criminal nature of his activities had been 'patiently explained' to Shcharansky, but this had not helped, so he then had to be 'isolated'. Only isolation had put an end to Anatoly Shcharansky's anti-Soviet activities.

The Prosecutor told the court that the charge against Shcharansky was that 'with absolutely clear forethought' his activities were designed 'to disrupt and weaken the military might of the Soviet Union'. All measures to warn him had been taken. Now measures of criminal responsibility would have to be taken. Bearing in mind that Shcharansky had not repented, 'it would only be just to apply to him the strictest punishment.'

Solonin then demanded, on behalf of the State, a sentence of fifteen years: three in prison and twelve in a special-regime labour camp, the harshest type of camp. Shcharansky, he said, deserved 'the highest possible sentence', but, 'taking into account that he was a young man,' he asked for only fifteen years.

According to Soviet law, the maximum prison term under Article 64–A was fifteen years, while under Article 70 it was seven years. Shcharansky therefore faced, if not death, a possible total of twenty-two years' deprivation of freedom.

★   ★   ★

Shcharansky now spoke in his own defence. Before doing so, he pointed out that he had been forbidden to make any reference to documents or testimony presented in the closed sessions of the trial. He was therefore unable to defend himself against the main accusation of espionage. He wished, however, to draw the special attention of the court to the fact that the testimony of the chief witness for the prosecution, Lipavsky, which had been heard in closed session of the court, was 'particularly distorted, confused and mendacious'. As he, Anatoly Shcharansky, did not have the right to refute this testimony, nor to make any reference to any of the testimonies made or documents read out in closed session, the whole trial was in effect a closed trial.

Shcharansky argued that the court should either have given permission for matters heard in closed session to be discussed during the time allotted to the hearing of the oral argument, in open court, or should have allocated a special time during the closed sessions specifically for oral argument on the accusation of espionage. They had adopted neither course.

Shcharansky then told the court:

> I understand that to defend myself in a semi-closed trial such as this is a hopeless case from the very beginning, all the more so here since I was declared guilty by *Izvestia* a full year and a half before this trial took place, and even before the case was opened and the investigation begun. My social activities were transformed by the editors of this newspaper and by my accusers to anti-social deeds and anti-State activities. My open efforts to

produce information of a non-secret character, available to all, were transformed into espionage.

I have no doubt that this court will carry out the instructions given it, and support the request of the prosecutor in the sentencing.

In the contemporary world, there are various systems. But this does not cover the full extent of the activities and lives of the people inhabiting this earth. Each nation has its own period of renaissance, and Russia also passed through such a time. The history of the Jewish people differs from that of all other nations in that for 2000 years it had no home of its own, no statehood, and no soil of its own on which to blossom. In spite of this, the Jewish people has preserved its identity and continued to exist and flourish in exile.

Continuing, Shcharansky declared:

One hundred years ago the modern Zionist movement came into being as a real force and developed a meaning for the whole scattered Jewish people. At the end of the last century, the world witnessed the disgraceful Dreyfus trial in France. A spectator at this trial – which can better be described as civil execution – was the assimilated Jew Theodor Herzl. After this, political Zionism was born.

In creating and carrying out the Bolshevik Revolution and for the first years of Soviet power, many Jews took part in the creation of the USSR and were responsible for bringing it to its position of eminence today as a great world power. There were many attempts to assimilate the Jews, but they were never successful. The 'Black Years' of 1948 to 1953 were the most difficult in the history of the Jews of the USSR, culminating in the so-called 'Doctors' Plot' hatched by Stalin. It was then that the central Government began to expand its insidious campaign against the Jews. At this time, there appeared numbers of people who expressed a desire to emigrate. Naturally, before long, each of them found himself in prisons or labour camps and most perished there. In the 1960s, this movement for emigration was reborn, and as a result 150,000 Jews so far have emigrated.

How can this be explained? Is it merely a result of provocation by the American secret service? Did it not previously exist? No. This is a historical process. The Jews began to search for an identity and express themselves not in assimilation but in emigration and in yearning to reach their ancient and now newly reborn Motherland fighting for its existence in a world still hostile to it, a world which is prepared to forget the Holocaust when six million of our people were brutally done to death, a world which has found it hard to accept the fact that the Jewish people will not disappear from the face of the earth.

'Our reborn State of Israel in which we take such pride', Shcharansky told the court, 'will continue to flourish and be an example for the other nations of this earth. I am proud to be a part of this movement of renaissance.'

The court then adjourned until the following and final day.

22

Judgement

On the morning of Friday, 14 July 1978, the court reconvened for its final session. The session opened with Shcharansky completing the remarks which he had begun on the previous afternoon. His remaining words were dignified and outspoken, a tribute to his strength of character, and to his innocence:

In March and April, during the interrogation, the chief investigators warned me that in the position I have taken during the investigation, and held to here in court, I would be threatened with execution by firing squad, or at least fifteen years. If I would agree to co-operate with the investigation to destroy the Jewish emigration movement, they promised me early freedom and a quick reunion with my wife.

Five years ago I submitted my application for exit to Israel. Now I am further than ever from my dream. It would seem to be cause for regret. But it is absolutely otherwise. I am happy. I am happy that I lived honestly, in peace with my conscience. I never compromised my soul, even under the threat of death.

I am happy that I helped people. I am proud that I knew and worked with such honest, brave and courageous people as Sakharov, Orlov, Ginsburg, who are carrying on the traditions of the Russian intelligentsia. I am fortunate to have been witness to the process of the liberation of Jews from the USSR.

I hope that the absurd accusation against me and the entire Jewish emigration movement will not hinder the liberation of my people. My near ones and friends know how I wanted to exchange activity in the emigration movement for a life with my wife Avital in Israel.

For more than 2000 years the Jewish people, my people, have been dispersed. But wherever they are, wherever Jews are found, each year they have repeated, 'Next year in Jerusalem.' Now, when I am further than ever from my people, from Avital, facing many arduous years of imprisonment, I say, turning to my people, my Avital: *Next Year in Jerusalem!* And I turn to you, the court, who were required to confirm a predetermined sentence: to you I have nothing to say.

Following Shcharansky's statement, the time had come for the Judge's summing-up, and for the verdict. As well as citing the twenty-three documents and sets of materials mentioned by the Prosecutor in presenting the case against Shcharansky on the previous day, the Judge now referred to others. First, he said, there was a 'review' prepared by 'Shcharansky and others' and given to 'a group of American Senators' in May 1975, 'in which he continued to press Western countries to interfere in the internal affairs of the USSR, trying to justify this interference by declaring "the presence of an anti-Semitic campaign with fascist tendencies"' in the Soviet Union; a trend which was written of in such a way as to suggest that it was supported by 'central authorities'. Similar 'calls and fabrications', the Judge declared, had been 'placed in other documents' by Shcharansky; documents which had been 'passed to a group of American Congressmen in August 1975 at a secret meeting in the Sovietskaya Hotel'.

Leonid Shcharansky later noted, after a meeting with his brother in prison: 'It was precisely to defend himself against this accusation or aspersion – the words "the presence of an anti-Semitic campaign of fascist tendencies" were attributed to him – that Tolya applied for Vladimir Begun's book *The Creeping Counter-Revolution* to be added to his file. But he was refused the request.'

As to 'secret' meetings in the Sovietskaya Hotel, Shcharansky and his friends knew all too well that no privacy, let alone secrecy, could be expected in a hotel in which so many foreigners stayed, and where the KGB itself had offices.

The Judge declared that in July 1975 Shcharansky had met 'confidentially' with 'American Government adviser' Richard Pipes at Vitaly Rubin's apartment, 'and had declared again the need to exert pressure on the USSR, and in particular the expediency of blackmailing the USSR with the threat of curtailing the Soviet–American cultural and scientific relationship'. The Judge also alleged that Shcharansky had received from Pipes 'concrete recommendations' concerning the methods of 'stirring up' anti-Soviet activity inside the Soviet Union, in particular 'of rousing national hatred' which, according to the Judge's version of what Pipes had said, 'influential circles in the USA see as a powerful catalyst, furthering the erosion of Soviet society'.

Also referred to, in addition to the principal documents on which the charges were based, were what the Judge called 'two reviews with hostile contents', one dated 2 February 1976 and the other 17 September 1976, 'calling on the statesmen of the USA', as the Judge characterised them, 'to force the USSR by means of prolonged consecutive pressure to discharge its "as if" broken obligations in the sphere of human rights'. Then, at the end of 1976, Shcharansky, 'together with others', had, the Judge alleged, 'composed and sent abroad, through the representatives of the capitalist States, a letter calling for the retention of Jackson's discriminatory amendment, as a means of intervention in the internal affairs of the Soviet Union'.

Of these documents, the survey of 2 February 1976 had also been signed by, among others, Dina Beilina, Vitaly Rubin and Alexander Lunts, each of whom had been given an exit visa: not something that was likely if the document had been a criminal one. The message of 17 September 1976 had been signed by seventy-three Jews, many of whom were subsequently to receive their exit visas, including Lev Ulanovsky. Had either document been in any way injurious to the Soviet State, its many signatories could long before have been punished: not only 'could' but presumably 'should' have been. But no action whatsoever had been taken against them, nor against the signatories of the appeal in support of the Jackson Amendment.

The accusation against Shcharansky continued: 'Aspiring to compromise the democratic essence of the Soviet State, its national policy and to undermine the confidence in it in the world arena, Shcharansky conducted anti-Soviet agitation and propaganda: he, personally, and through his accomplices also prepared materials with slanderous concoctions, and was sending them abroad by means of the post, through foreigners, and through other channels, with the purpose of their active utilisation by anti-Soviet centres and organs of bourgeois propaganda, and for the realisation of actions of ideological sabotage against the USSR.'

As evidence of this, the accusation cited at this point a document dated 24 December 1976 entitled 'On the prosecution of Soviet citizens of Jewish origin'.

Another document mentioned at this moment in the judgement

was one dated 5 February 1975 about the 'strict limitation on the admittance of Jews to Institutes of Higher Learning and other jobs' and about the anti-Semitic campaign' – a campaign, the Judge noted, which was described in the document 'as if conducted in the press, at lectures and at meetings'.

After citing these documents, the Judge declared: 'The court considers the guilt of Shcharansky to be proven, (a) in episodes connected with helping foreign states to conduct their hostile activity against the USSR and (b) in episodes connected with conducting anti-Soviet propaganda and agitation'.

This was not the end, however, of the documentation which the Judge wished to bring forward. The next item in his speech was the testimonies of Lipavsky, Tsipin, Riabsky and Raslin, all of whom showed, he said, 'that Shcharansky, together with others, over a long period of time, was systematically compiling, keeping with the purpose of spreading, and actually spreading through foreigners among a wide circle, materials containing slanderous concoctions, defaming the USSR'.

No reference had earlier been made in open court to Saul Raslin. He was from Kiev, where he had been a frequent informer against refuseniks. He had also written an article in the Kiev evening newspaper *Viecherny Kiev* almost identical in its accusations to the articles by Lipavsky and Tsipin in Moscow. (Of Riabsky, Shcharansky later commented to Leonid: 'I met him at Vitaly Rubin's. Once Rubin even said to me, "Look, here is a Party member, but he is not afraid to come here."')

Continuing his summing-up, the Judge spoke of the evidence of the witness Popova, Robert Toth's secretary. According to Popova, Shcharansky had informed Toth 'of the results of his visit to the settlement at Ilyinka'. Noting that Toth had published an article containing this information in the *Los Angeles Times*, under the headline, 'Soviet Jews survive in desolate spot', the Judge declared that this article was 'indicative' of Shcharansky's visit to Ilyinka.

Of Popova, the view of Shcharansky's friends was 'that she had clearly been planted by the KGB'.

The next item referred to by the Judge was the letters, visiting cards, photographs, gramophone records and notebooks 'from which one can realise the extent of Shcharansky's close contacts with a wide circle of foreigners and the opportunity he had to use those foreigners for forwarding anti-Soviet materials to the West'. There were also documents, the Judge noted, bearing on the stay in the Soviet Union of those foreigners 'with whom Shcharansky was continually connected', and on the 'actively hostile' attitude towards the Soviet Union of certain mass-circulation newspapers 'whose correspondents were staying in Moscow, and were closely connected with Shcharansky'. Lipavsky, Tsipin, Orlov, Ginsburg and Riabsky had 'identified' these foreigners 'who were connected with the accused': the Judge referred specifically to the records of these identifications.

Lipavsky and other 'witnesses', none of them Shcharansky's close friends and none of them refuseniks, were then cited as having been present when 'Shcharansky and others' delivered information to foreigners over the telephone – information, said the Judge, 'containing slanderous fabrications about the Soviet State and its social system'. (Shcharansky later noted that the witnesses other than Lipavsky did not confirm at the closed session the testimonies which they had given during the preliminary investigation, and that, despite much brow-beating by the Judge during the closed session, they declared 'that they had not heard anything' said during the telephone calls about secret installations or factories; 'only people's names had been mentioned, not places'.)

The Judge then referred to 'certain materials at the court's disposal' which, although he did not specify what the material was, 'indicated that the wide distribution of all the documents mentioned so far and their active utilisation was done on the initiative of the accused 'in order to conduct ideological sabotage against the USSR by such foreign anti-Soviet centres or organs of bourgeois propaganda as the *Chronicle Press*, the Continent publishing house, the Samizdat Archives in Munich, the publicity house of the Russian émigré organisation, Radio Liberty, the "German Wave" radio band, the BBC, Radio Israel and others'.

The Judge then stressed that the various documents which he had cited, with their 'slanderous materials', had been published by the official Helsinki Commission and by the United States Congress, as well as broadcast by the British television company Granada as a result of its 'illegal shooting' in Moscow. The showing of the film in court, the Judge pointed out, had made clear its 'hostile commentaries'. (Shcharansky later told his brother that no documents were produced in connection with these alleged 'slanderous materials', and that as to the film 'A Calculated Risk', 'no attempt was made to prove its defamatory nature'.)

The Judge then turned to the 'proof' of the 'slanderous character' of the information contained in the documents 'manufactured and spread by Shcharansky'. The first proof came from those prisoners of whom it had been alleged that their ill-health required their immediate discharge from prison or labour camp. The testimonies of the prisoners themselves, said the Judge, 'disproved the accused's concoctions' about the conditions of their custody, and showed that there was no reason for discharging them 'in connection with the state of their health'.

As to the proof that there were no divided families in Russia, the 'examination of the exit visas' of those who had applied to leave the Soviet Union was proof that at least seven of those mentioned in the divided-families document 'had already left the USSR or received permission to emigrate at the moment of the composing of the document by the accused'. Those who had been refused permission to leave had been refused 'for valid reasons', either because 'they live with their families in the Soviet Union or because they do not have any relations whatsoever abroad'. (Shcharansky later commented to his brother: 'As these reviews were compiled over a considerable period of time, it was only natural that by the time of their publication some people had already received their permission to emigrate.')

Despite the Judge's attempt to minimise this issue, all seventy-seven families listed in the Watchdog group document were genuine cases of divided families. Some of them were families where the children were in Israel while the parents remained in the Soviet Union, as in the case of Professor Lerner. Others were families where the husbands were in the Soviet Union while the wives were in Israel, as in Shcharansky's own case.

As to the claim in another of the documents submitted to the court, that there were prisoners in the Soviet Union who had been sentenced 'for their political, national or religious beliefs', this, said the Judge, was 'convincingly' disproved by an examination of the archives of the 'criminal cases of Tverdokhlebov, Roitburd, Malkin, Vinarov and others who were condemned for various normal offences', and by an examination of the personal files of other prisoners who were still serving their sentences.

There was also proof, the Judge added, in connection with certain prisoners who had completed their sentences, 'confirming the lawfulness and validity of the punitive measures' still being taken against them, contrary to the allegations in another of the documents in the charge.

The Judge then turned to the document alleging the misuse of psychiatry. The records of one 'criminal case' and other medical files 'confirm', he said, 'that the application of compulsory measures of a medical character is exercised in accordance with the existing legislation, and that only those who really suffer from mental diseases have been sent to psychiatric hospitals'.

The Judge naturally made no reference to the Soviet Union having been condemned by the World Psychiatric Association in May 1976 for what the Association had described as 'systematic abuse' of psychiatry, and for refusing to change its practice.

Referring to the 'allegations' about 'the people in Ilyinka', the Judge declared that an examination of the village, a discussion held there, 'and other evidence' showed that there had been 'no violations of the legal rights of the people in Ilyinka'. (To his brother, Shcharansky later remarked: 'By the by, there was nobody from Ilyinka present at the trial.' Nor did the Judge read out from the document itself, which clearly detailed the refusals of the Soviet authorities to allow the Ilyinka Jews not only to emigrate to Israel, but to join members of their families already there.)

Another of the documents submitted to the court had told of 'new arrests' for religious activity. The Judge commented that some of the people mentioned 'were really charged and validly sentenced for their various criminal offences', others had not been arrested or sentenced 'at the moment of this document's circulation'.

The Judge now declared as 'groundless' what he called 'Shcharansky's claim that he was not pursuing criminal objectives, but following only his wish to draw the attention of world public opinion to the problems connected with emigration from the USSR'. He then set out the 'proof' of Shcharansky's 'hostile attitude towards the Soviet State and its social system, and the aim of his activities, which were directed at causing damage to the independence and military strength of the USSR, with the purpose also of undermining Soviet power'. The 'proof' of this was seven-fold. First, the 'facts' of Shcharansky's participation and forwarding of the documents cited. Second, his 'ignoring of precautionary warnings'. Third, his regular connections with the correspondents of foreign newspapers 'whose attitude towards the Soviet Union was hostile' and with foreign 'organisations and emissaries whose anti-Soviet undermining activities Shcharansky was well aware of'. Fourth, the testimony of Lipavsky, Riabsky and Raslin that the 'real aim' of Shcharansky and his 'accomplices' was the 'fight against the system' existing in the Soviet Union – activity 'inspired and financed through the officials of the United States Embassy in Moscow by interested political and bourgeois workers in the West, jointly with anti-Soviet and Zionist centres'.

The fifth 'proof', stated the Judge, was that the 'area of interests' of various foreign emissaries and newspaper correspondents, and the type of information they asked for, 'points directly to their clear connection with the American secret services and the centres of ideological sabotage'. Sixth, there was the 'material evidence' of what the Judge called the 'letters of instructions' from representatives of the capitalist States 'containing recommendations about the concrete forms and methods of conducting hostile activity in the USSR'. These letters had been brought into the Soviet Union 'illegally', by 'various ways, including diplomatic channels'. (No such letters existed.)

The seventh and final 'proof' was, said the Judge, those documents 'which prove the fact that, after Shcharansky abandoned decent work, he was in receipt of money, parcels and other material support from abroad, which stimulated him and facilitated the realisation of his criminal design'. Articles 64–A and 70 of the Criminal Code covered exactly Shcharansky's 'active' role 'in helping foreign States to conduct their horrible activity against the USSR, in forwarding information which gave away state secrets of the USSR, and also in conducting anti-Soviet agitation and propaganda'.

The Judge now declared Shcharansky guilty. 'Acting to the detriment of the independence and military strength of the USSR during years 1974 to 1977', Shcharansky had, he said, 'systematically helped foreign States in conducting their hostile activity against the USSR. From 1976 to his arrest, he was also engaged in espionage and anti-Soviet propaganda and agitation in order to weaken and undermine Soviet power.'

This was the third reference to Shcharansky being involved with the 'military strength' of the Soviet Union. Yet no single document cited to the court, and none of the witnesses so carefully rehearsed, had made any mention whatsoever of military secrets or military enquiries. This too, however, now became a part of the charge against him.

In order to fulfil 'his treacherous intentions', the Judge continued,

Shcharansky had 'established and maintained criminal connections with a number of diplomats, correspondents and other representatives of the capitalist States in the USSR, including both those who collaborated with Intelligence services and the emissaries of Zionist organisations and foreign anti-Soviet centres, who came to the USSR in the guise of tourists'. On his own initiative, and on 'the instructions of those persons', Shcharansky had supplied them systematically with materials 'hostile to the USSR, and also took part in composing them'. In these materials, the Judge declared, Shcharansky had called upon the Governments 'of certain foreign States, first and foremost the United States Government, to exert constant pressure upon the USSR, under the guise of the care of "human rights", in order to change its foreign and internal policy'. On Shcharansky's 'initiative', the Judge added, 'these materials were actively used by reactionary circles of the capitalist States in conducting their hostile activity against the USSR, and he was perfectly aware of this.'

The Judge now gave his verdict: thirteen years' deprivation of liberty, three in prison and ten in strict-regime labour camp. The sixteen months during which Shcharansky had already been held in prison would count towards this total. Release would come in March 1990, when he would be forty-two.

*   *   *

Outside the courtroom, behind the barrier at the end of the alleyway, Ida Milgrom had once more stood in the street throughout the day. With her, reported David Shipler to the *New York Times*, were 'about 150 dissidents, a score of correspondents and some 75 uniformed and plainclothes policemen'.

While the trial was still proceeding, Ida Milgrom had read out to those assembled an open letter to President Carter: 'All the difficult days of the trial,' she read, 'I have been standing in front of the iron barriers, in front of a thick wall of KGB men and militiamen, hoping to see my child, at least from far away. All these days I have heard your sincere, authoritative voice in defence of innocent men. Would you accept, Mr President, our deep, heartfelt gratitude.'

As soon as Ida Milgrom had read out the text of her letter to President Carter, Academician Sakharov, who was also present, told the assembled crowd: 'What is happening now is pure sadism, a mockery of a mother's feelings.'

According to Soviet law, no one could be barred from entering a court for the sentencing at the end of a trial, 'let alone a mother!' as Dina Beilina later remarked. But Ida Milgrom received no answer to her request, and the guards at the barricade continued to refuse to let her past.

As the afternoon wore on, David Shipler reported, Ida Milgrom again walked to the barricades to ask the guards that she be allowed in during the sentencing, just to catch a glimpse, perhaps her last, of her son. She waited for an answer. 'Suddenly and without warning,' Shipler wrote, 'a khaki-colored prison van evidently carrying Mr Shcharansky wheeled out of the courthouse and drove away.'

Ida Milgrom covered her face and screamed. The crowd, realising that it must have been Shcharansky in the van, shouted in unison 'Tolya! Tolya!'

'You're not people, you're fascists,' Sakharov declared angrily to the policemen, while Ida Milgrom, as Shipler saw, 'grey and broken, wept and staggered away as arms reached out to hold and comfort her'.

Moments later, Leonid Shcharansky walked out through the barricades into the waiting crowd. 'Thirteen years,' he said as loudly as he could. Watching this scene, David Shipler noted that Leonid Shcharansky was 'shaking and could hardly speak'. After Leonid's wife Raya had pushed through the crowd and grabbed his arm to steady him, Leonid read out to the crowd his verbatim notes of Shcharansky's final statement.

The crowd listened in silence, deeply moved by Shcharansky's faith and courage. Then, as they were ordered to disperse they broke into song: the Jewish and Israeli anthem 'Hatikvah' – Hope.

23

Prisoner of Zion

On 14 July 1978, the day on which Shcharansky was sentenced, three other Soviet courts issued verdicts of guilty. In one, Alexander Ginsburg was sentenced to eight years' severe-regime labour camp. In another, the head of the Lithuanian Helsinki Watchdog group, Viktoras Piatkus, was sentenced to three years in prison, to be followed by seven in labour camp and a further five in internal exile. In a third verdict that same day, a Soviet citizen named as A. N. Filatov, and said to have been an 'agent of a foreign Intelligence service', was sentenced to death.

Linking the sentences against Shcharansky and Filatov with a single commentary, on 15 July 1978 the Communist Party newspaper, *Pravda*, published an editorial entitled 'Their Just Deserts'. The editorial began: 'Two trials were held in Moscow last week, whose early stages have already been described in the Soviet press. The Military Collegium of the Soviet Supreme Court tried the criminal activities of the agent of a foreign Intelligence service A. N. Filatov. The judicial collegium of criminal cases of the Russian Soviet Federative Socialist Republic Supreme Court tried the criminal case against A. B. Shcharansky who was accused of betraying the Motherland through espionage, assisting a foreign power in its hostile activities against the USSR, and conducting anti-Soviet agitation and propaganda.' The editorial continued: 'Sentences were passed in both cases on July 14. The criminals, traitors to the Motherland and spies, received their just deserts. Filatov was sentenced to be shot, and Shcharansky to thirteen years.'

Pravda then told its readers that over the course of a few days the higher Soviet judicial bodies had 'studied, considered, and evaluated dozens upon dozens of volumes of criminal cases, much substantive evidence, the conclusions of experts, and heard the testimony of witnesses'. All the facts gathered in the course of these judicial investigations had proved 'the same thing: during those days there sat in the dock not simply deluded victims or people who had accidentally gone off the rails. The Soviet courts were trying criminals who perfectly well knew what they were doing.'

The *Pravda* article then described how 'espionage equipment, gold, foreign currency, and so on', had been found in Filatov's flat, and that he had been 'caught at the scene of the crime' while carrying out a spying mission. Filatov's trial by the Military Collegium had been a completely closed one.

Outside the Soviet Union no one knew anything about Filatov, either before or after his trial. Indeed, many Western newspapers and Sovietologists expressed doubts whether such a person existed at all and whether there had been a trial. Nevertheless, news about the 'spy' Filatov and his death sentence was published in the Soviet press simultaneously with news about Shcharansky's trial, about which the whole world was aware.

The purpose of such a 'combined' revelation of sensational material was clear. As Boris Shcharansky commented a few days later: 'By combining in one report the trial of the experienced spy Filatov and the case of the Jewish activist Shcharansky neither the KGB nor Soviet journalists invented anything new. They were the faithful successors of their teachers Yagoda, Yezhov and Beria, who, in concocting their open trials of "enemies of the people", put well-known people on the same benches as inveterate scoundrels who were allegedly involved in the same "case".' This was done, Boris Shcharansky added, 'so that the "straightforward Soviet man", either hearing or reading the evidence of these scoundrels in the papers, would more easily believe in the guilt of the honest people sitting next to them'.

Even in this 'scummish tactic', Boris Shcharansky added, 'the secret police were not original; the innovator in this respect was the Roman governor of Judaea, Pontius Pilate, who ordered the crucifixion of two robbers next to Jesus on Golgotha. But over these two thousand years mankind had become a bit wiser. Yagoda's, Yezhov's and Beria's weapons had noticeably rusted, and one would have to be an absolute cretin to use them now.'

On 15 July 1978 the Moscow, Lithuanian and Georgian Helsinki

Watchdog groups issued a collective protest against the trials of Shcharansky, Filatov, Ginsburg and Piatkus. The signatories of this report included Elena Bonner, Sofia Kalistratova, Malva Landa, Naum Meiman, as well as Eitan Finkelstein from Vilnius and Isai Goldstein from Tbilisi. Each trial, they declared, had its own 'special targets', Shcharansky's being intended 'to foster a hysterical atmosphere of spy mania around the struggle for the right to emigration, and to intimidate its participants, especially Jews, with extreme measures of punishment'.

The Helsinki Watchdog group also noted that Soviet press, radio and television 'linked Shcharansky's trial to that of Filatov, accused of espionage and sentenced to be shot. Filatov, however, has no connection either to Shcharansky or to the human rights movement.' The Watchdog group protest continued:

> The severity of the espionage charges against Shcharansky is untenable in the face of the absurd and vague evidence against him. In general, the episodes incriminating him are not illegal. The court paid undue attention to such trivial questions as, for example, whether or not Shcharansky's marriage is valid under Judaic law. The two main episodes incriminating Shcharansky in espionage were his compiling a list of 'refuseniks' – people who have long been attempting to emigrate and have been refused permission – and sending this list abroad, and a certain secret questionnaire, of which Shcharansky learned only after his arrest.
>
> The accusation against Shcharansky is based entirely on the evidence of the provocateurs Lipavsky and Tsipin. Their false testimony the court held to be more convincing than the reliable public statements by President Carter that Shcharansky had no connection at all with the CIA. In his speech, the Prosecutor could not present any proof of the crimes attributed to Shcharansky. The court repeatedly mentioned that Shcharansky had met with foreign correspondents, American Senators, Congressmen, and other prominent people – all absolutely legal meetings. The attempt to use such meetings for these charges completely contradicts both the letter and the spirit of the Helsinki Final Act.

The Helsinki Watchdog group's combined report of 15 July 1978 ended its section on Shcharansky's trial with an historical comparison. 'Shcharansky's trial', it declared, 'is a contemporary version of the Dreyfus trial. The difference is that Dreyfus had real possibilities for defence, something which Shcharansky completely lacks. More than anything, Shcharansky's criminal trial is a blow at the emigration movement, especially the Jewish part of this movement; it is also yet another attempt to discredit the Jewish people as a whole.'

In the aftermath of Shcharansky's sentence, the parallels with the Dreyfus case were also mentioned by Shcharansky's father, and by Jean Ellenstein, a member of the Communist Party of France, who noted in *Paris Match* that in the Dreyfus case 'an official personage, a Cabinet Minister, stated even before the end of the investigation: "I am convinced of his guilt." In the Shcharansky case his mother was told right at the beginning that her son was a "dangerous criminal" and that he would be severely punished.' In the Dreyfus case the 'excellent character reference' given by the Prefecture was withdrawn. In the Shcharansky case 'all the character references of witnesses who attested that he was an honest and modest person' were never admitted in evidence. In both trials, 'provocateurs were employed who, instead of evidence, repeated various pieces of rumour and gossip.'

But there were also substantial differences, Jean Ellenstein pointed out. While the French press and public opinion 'literally poured out a stream of articles and speeches which finally led to a review and ultimately to the vindication of Dreyfus, in the Soviet Union, as usual, "moral and political unity" ruled: the press said what it was told to say, and the public did not openly talk about the case. Furthermore, the illegal actions of the authorities against Anatoly Shcharansky, and through him his relations, continued.'

One of those who was not fooled by the simultaneous sentencing of Filatov and Shcharansky was David Shipler who, in a despatch from Moscow on 16 July 1978, stated that Shcharansky's thirteen-year sentence 'was based on a condemnation of activities that for years were a normal part of the Jewish emigration movement's efforts to publicise its position', activities for which dozens of others 'have gone unpunished'.

The aim of the Soviet authorities in staging the trial and finding Shcharansky guilty, wrote Zeev Ben-Shlomo in the London *Jewish Chronicle* on 21 July 1978, was 'to intimidate and demoralise the Jewish emigration movement', just as their aim in Alexander Ginsburg's trial was 'to clamp down on the human rights movement'.

On 24 July 1978 Shcharansky's portrait was on the front cover of *Time*, under the disintegrating letters of the word 'Detente'. That same day his photograph was on the front cover of *Newsweek*. An article in *Newsweek* by Professor Alan Dershowitz of Harvard proclaimed Shcharansky's innocence with the words: 'He was the voice of the Jewish refuseniks – those whose requests to emigrate from the Soviet Union had not been granted – to the outside world. His every act was out in the open: it was his purpose to let Soviet authorities know that his voice – the articulate translation of thousands of other refusenik voices – was being listened to abroad. He did nothing in secret: that was neither his method nor his purpose.'

Tirelessly, always hoping that her next effort would be the successful one, Avital Shcharansky travelled the Western world on behalf of her husband, speaking to students, churchmen, community leaders, diplomats and statesmen. As she did so, two French lawyers, Allan Rappoport and Maître Jacoby, as well as Alan Dershowitz and a Canadian attorney, Irwin Cotler, put their legal expertise at her disposal.

Among the charges brought against Shcharansky had been his allegedly 'secret' meetings with visiting American Senators and Congressmen, including one with eight Senators at the Rossiya Hotel. 'There was no secret about this meeting,' Senator Ribicoff told the Senate on 26 July 1978. 'It had been planned even before we left Washington. The Soviet authorities knew in advance that the meeting would take place. It was held in the lobby of the hotel "Rossiya". There was no secret either about the fact of the meeting or about what would be discussed.' To Shcharansky himself, all eight Senators wrote in an open letter on 26 July 1978: 'The use of such an open meeting, which took place three years ago, as evidence of your criminal behaviour is tragic and illegal.' They added: 'We continue to insist that the Soviet authorities review their actions in the case against you and permit you to emigrate from the Soviet Union.'

In August 1978 Irwin Cotler prepared for Avital an appeal, addressed to Prosecutor-General Rudenko, setting out, with a vast apparatus of legal knowledge and personal affidavits, the facts of Shcharansky's case. Cotler's appeal concluded that the charge of treason was 'clearly as invalid in law as it is unfounded in fact'. He also submitted that the charge of anti-Soviet slander and agitation was 'unfounded in fact and invalid in law', and that Rudenko, as

Prosecutor-General, 'should protest the substantial violations of law and procedure, to the end that the judgement be vacated according to law'.

*   *   *

Among those in prison at Vladimir when Shcharansky arrived in July 1978 was Iosif Mendelevich, one of the first Leningrad Trial prisoners, who later recalled:

> Inessa, the warden, woke us up a few hours before reveille: 'They brought Shcharansky.'
>
> *Iosif*: 'Where is he?'
>
> *Inessa*: 'Sitting in a transit cell. He is very pale, very weak. No food has been given to him, and he's been held this way all night.'
>
> *Iosif*: 'I'll send him some food, Inessa. Can you pass it to him?'
>
> *Inessa*: 'No, I can't as there are other guards downstairs.'
>
> *Iosif*: 'Even at least a package of tobacco?' She understood that I wanted to put a note inside it.
>
> *Inessa*: 'I said that I can't.'

'At this point', Mendelevich noted, 'our conversation terminated. I ran to the toilet in order to notify the lower floor by tapping on the toilet pipes. Gayduk, a Ukrainian national who was in solitary at that time, answered me. "I can't contact the transit cell. It's isolated from the other cells on this floor."' Thus it was, Mendelevich added, 'that I was not successful in contacting Anatoly, despite the fact that it was important to pass on information to him about the prison'.

Contact was eventually made between Shcharansky and Mendelevich, and also with another of the other Leningrad Trial prisoners, Hillel Butman. The messages were passed in Hebrew, on slips of paper inside books borrowed from the camp library. In one such message, Shcharansky described a protest by Moscow refuseniks on behalf of the Leningrad Trial prisoners.

When one or other prisoner was in the exercise yard, there was sometimes the chance of a brief snatch of conversation over the wall, even though neither prisoner could see the other. Mendelevich described one such 'conversation':

> *Iosif*: 'Anatoly – do you know how to get additional food?'

'No,' Anatoly laughed.

Iosif: 'But you were involved in politics! You established contacts with people.'

Anatoly: 'But, I'm not a businessman.'

'His Hebrew is excellent,' Mendelevich noted. During the thirty minutes allotted each day to exercise, he added, Shcharansky would 'spend his time singing in Hebrew'.

On another occasion Hillel Butman managed to speak with, though also not to see, Shcharansky, who put him in the picture as to the Moscow activist scene: 'a sort of "Who's Who in Moscow"', Butman later told me. For talking to another prisoner, Shcharansky was sentenced to ten days in a punishment cell.

In October 1978 Shcharansky, Butman and Mendelevich were moved from Vladimir prison to a prison at Chistopol. Vladimir was a city frequently visited by Western tourists. Chistopol, much further to the east, in the Tatar Republic, was in a region closed to foreigners. The train journey from Vladimir to Chistopol gave Butman an unexpected chance: neither he nor Mendelevich had yet seen Shcharansky. Now, in the train, when Shcharansky was being brought back under escort from the officers' toilet, 'the wise guy Hillel', as Mendelevich later recalled, 'twisted his body around in such a way that he could see him. Hillel said: "He's short, at the most 1 metre 60."'

On 13 October 1978 Shcharansky arrived in Chistopol. Two days later he wrote to his mother and father, his brother and sister-in-law, and Avital:

15 October 1978

Greetings my dear Mama, Papa, Lyonya, Raya, shalom my beloved Natulya!

It has been two days since I acquired a new address. There is no need to get particularly upset about it – so far it has not produced any essential changes in my situation.

My dears, I beg you again and again, take care of yourselves and your health with all your might, try as much as possible not to live in that state of daily anxiety and tension which I sense from Mama's letters. You have lived such a long, hard and good life, and I dream that you will spend the last decades of your life in the warmth and joy which you so justly deserve, among your loving children and many grandchildren. But to

do this you have to think more about your health and worry less
about mine. I want to tell you once more, my dear old folks,
that I do not simply love you, but I am very deeply grateful to
you for all that you gave me and all that you taught me. It is
amazing what one must go through in order to understand such
simple things.

After a personal message to Avital, Shcharansky continued:

During this whole time I have received only two of your letters
– the first ones from Canada. And for a very long time I haven't
received anything. I dream of seeing your drawings. Sketch me
something or someone – Michael or Dina or Ilana with Ariel in
her arms or simply some scene from our Israeli life.

I would like to hear something about Jane and Jerry, Michael,
the Shudovskys, Joshua and Gladys, the Manekofskys and
many, many others whom I have often thought about all this
time. I won't list them all lest anyone be insulted. It's simply
impossible to name them all. Of course it's hard for you to write
about everyone – let others also write.

Ilana Ben-Joseph was the woman with whom Avital was living in
Jerusalem; Ariel was Ilana's son; Jane and Jerry Stern, like Noam
Shudovsky and his wife, were Soviet Jewry campaigners in New
York; Joshua and Gladys were Congressman Eilberg and his
wife.

Early in October 1978, Avital's brother Michael had celebrated
his thirtieth birthday in Jerusalem. 'Give him my congratulations,'
Shcharansky wrote in a message for Avital, 'and tell him that on
that day I drank an extra mug of tea to his health.' As for himself, he
added: 'Still, in spite of my very limited opportunities I try all the
time to study some Hebrew. These studies have contributed to my
general health and mood during all this time.'

Shcharansky's November and December letters were likewise
written to his whole family:

14 November 1978

Greetings, my dear beloved ones,

I promised to write to you on the 10th of the month, but there
was a delay: they returned my letter with the explanation that I

have the right to only one letter per month but in fact I write two, one to my parents and the other to my wife, who receives it via my parents. They ordered me to write either to my parents, not addressing my wife, or to my wife at her address, not mentioning my parents. To tell the truth, my first reaction was not to write any other letter but to try and get the one I had written sent, but then I thought that this could lead to new serious agitation for everyone because of the absence of a letter from me and I decided to try to meet this condition. There's no sense in writing to Natashenka's address since I have received *nothing* from her (except for the first two letters from Canada three months ago), although I know from your letters that she writes to me every day. I am therefore writing to you and I hope that you and Natashenka can fill this letter with those words and feelings which I cannot express through no fault of mine.

I am sure that Natulya will be able to fill up this letter with the bond which exists between us always and which can't be broken.

10 December 1978

Greetings, my dear beloved ones!

Unfortunately, I am writing to you again without knowing whether you received my previous letter of November.

I want to inform you right away that I shall not be able to meet with you earlier than the beginning of August 1979, since I have been deprived of my February meeting.

In my new place in Chistopol, I have completely mastered my dual role of observer–participant; the critical view of the former helps the latter to live and the energy of the latter sustains the former. I have been in this situation almost uninterruptedly for the past twenty months and have succeeded in coping with it. The unbelievable sixteen-month-long tension which in my past life I experienced only for a few minutes at a time has long since left me. Although my present life appears monotonous, grey and wretched on the surface, it would be full of internal energy and movement were it not for my constant anguish and sorrow about you and for you, my dears. I can't help thinking that my beloved Natasha must spend so many of her best days, months and years in waiting, that you, my dear old folks, may simply not have the strength. I am particularly upset about Mama, the constant tension and anxiety in which she is living are clear from her letters. Mama, I beg you, you must force yourself to live not 'from letter to letter' as you yourself write, but moderately and calmly. Otherwise even your strength won't suffice for long. I beg you again and again, my dears, guard your health, and keep yourself in hand, don't get nervous because of each unpleasantness, of which, of course, there could still be many.

Shcharansky remained in prison at Chistopol. In Jerusalem, Avital expressed her faith that it would not be for long. 'If he remains in prison,' she told a newspaper reporter on 2 March 1979, 'it would be a great injustice. And I do not believe there is such injustice in the world.'

An insight into Shcharansky's character is revealed by one particular recollection of both Mendelevich and Butman. Both were convinced that Shcharansky would be released before they would, and therefore gave him, orally, a mass of information about their predicament which they hoped he would pass on as soon as he was out. He accepted their confidence in him, and made considerable efforts to remember everything they told him. He, however, whose release they confidently expected before theirs, said nothing about his own situation and sought nothing from them should they reach Moscow or the West before him, which both of them did.

On 13 April 1979 Hillel Butman was released. Shcharansky and Mendelevich remained at Chistopol.

Despite her repeated requests, no copy of the final judgement on Shcharansky had been given to Ida Milgrom. Without this document, however, no appeal could be made on her son's behalf. On 7 May 1979 George P. Fletcher, Professor of Law at the University of California, Los Angeles, and an expert on Soviet criminal law, held a long conversation on this issue with Chief Justice A. K. Orlov of the Supreme Court of the Russian Republic. 'Although Justice Orlov was cordial,' Professor Fletcher wrote in a report on the conversation, 'he took a firm stand against the family's or anyone else's receiving a copy of the judgement. Even if the family should now obtain the services of a Moscow lawyer, the lawyer could at most read the judgement.' Orlov went on to tell Fletcher, quite openly, that Soviet officials did not want the judgement 'to fall into Western hands'.

In the few letters that he was able to send his mother, Shcharansky wrote of severe headaches and pain in his eyes. But he did not want her to worry unduly. 'You should not think from my letter that my spirits are low,' he wrote in June 1979. 'My optimism, and my conviction that I did what I had to do, remain the same.'

★   ★   ★

The work of the Jewish activists continued unabated. On 17 November 1978 a review of the 'current state of the Soviet Jewish emigration movement' was handed to a group of United States Senators in Moscow. All but one of its twelve authors had been friends of Shcharansky, among them Alexander Lerner and Lev Ovsishcher. At the same time, a detailed statement urging a renewal of the Jackson Amendment in any further Soviet–American trade agreement was prepared and signed by more than a hundred refuseniks, 'without Shcharansky being there!' as Dina Beilina wrily recalled.

During 1979, Lev Ulanovsky was among those who prepared a report on the discrimination against Jews who applied to go to university. The report, like those for which Shcharansky had been accused, was widely publicised in the West.

The year 1979 was also the year of the largest number of exit visas granted to Soviet Jews: more than 50,000 Jews were allowed to leave. On 12 July 1979, during the first anniversary of Shcharansky's trial, Congressman Drinan, who had become Chairman of the International Committee for Shcharansky's release, published an open letter in the Washington Post. 'When I am desperate about the state of your failing health,' wrote Drinan, 'I think that the US Senate should declare that the SALT Treaty will not even be brought up until you are liberated. In more sanguine, reflective moments I am heartened by the knowledge that 50,000 Soviet Jews will be able to emigrate from the USSR this year. You did this, Anatoly, more than any other human being.'

The campaigns on Shcharansky's behalf were well organised and well intentioned. But the leverage they wanted the United States to apply for his release went beyond the realm of practical politics. 'If the Kremlin wants the trade status of most-favored nation,' Drinan added in the open letter, 'why can't they release you as an act of good faith? Why doesn't our Government insist that we will not yield on this point until you are allowed to join Avital in Israel?'

On 6 August 1979 Ida Milgrom and Leonid were allowed to visit Shcharansky in Chistopol prison. When the visit was over, Ida

Milgrom sent an account of it to Avital:

> On August 5, at three o'clock in the afternoon, Lyonya and I
> took off from Domodedovo airport and at five o'clock we were
> already in Kazan. But the last plane to Chistopol had left
> already, the last steamboat had already sailed too, and we had
> one final opportunity – the tickets, the very last two tickets, for
> the steamboat sailing at seven o'clock in the evening. So we
> were sailing along the Volga and Kama until four o'clock on the
> following morning.
>
> On August 6, at five o'clock in the morning, we found
> ourselves in the territory of Chistopol prison. It was a prison
> like all prisons. There was a two-storey building with barred
> windows and iron gates, located inside a yard. The wicket in
> these gates is opened only after you ring the bell. Lyonya rang it
> and learnt that we would have to wait until the Chief came at
> eight o'clock.
>
> We sat down on a comfortable bench under a leafy tree,
> putting down our bags and briefcase. We hoped that we might
> be able to hand something over to Tolya. The waiting was
> tedious. There was no living soul in the yard, only silence and
> peace. Lyonya walked from time to time along the side of the
> building, tapping on the fence, and clicking his tongue from
> disappointment. Then a horse and cart appeared at the gates. A
> prisoner was escorting this cart, on which was a rusty tank,
> filled with who knows what.
>
> At this time the prison yard became alive. People of the
> lowest ranks appeared. Prisoners were taken to work, and we
> were sorry that we could not somehow capture this picturesque
> scene.
>
> We did not succeed in our attempts to get something to eat,
> since in the so-called 'stall' one could buy only vinegar.
> Lyonya's attempts to get something to eat were interrupted
> when a certain Colonel appeared, and we guessed that he might
> be the Chief of the prison himself, Malofeev 'personally'.
>
> Lyonya was right. The man introduced himself as Malofeev
> and confirmed that we would have to wait. Afterwards I
> applied to another officer, asking him how long we must wait,
> and got the same indefinite answer.
>
> We waited. During this long waiting by the iron gates, I had a
> painful foreboding, which reminded me of my condition when
> I waited for the dreadful sentence, standing behind the iron
> fence by the court-building in Moscow in July 1978.

Then we were ordered to put down all our belongings.
Tolenka was already waiting for us in the room to our right.
Our escort showed us the entrance, behind a glass barrier. In
front of this barrier, on the outer side, were two chairs, for me
and for Lyonya.

Two witnesses sat down to our right. They were present
throughout our meeting, but did not disturb us and did not
interrupt us.

The situation was very quiet. But my and Lyonya's inner
condition was very uneasy.

Thin, pale, with an unlikely thin nose and big eyes, Tolya
was unrecognisable. He started to talk. His voice was so
familiar, so dear! Addressing Lyonya, he said: 'What is the
matter with Mama? She has changed very much, hasn't she?'
And I was smiling at him. I even laughed in order not to burst
into sobs. I was joking, making fun of my old age, trying to
attract him (and myself) away from the grim impression.

Tolenka took the initiative. He warned us that he could only
answer questions concerning his health for a maximum of
twenty minutes. And he started immediately to describe his
feelings, minutely and clearly, and he drew our attention to
what we had to obtain.

He reacted very vividly to the information we gave him, and
demanded more information about you, Natashenka. He asked
us to pass you his love, his constant feeling of contact with you,
despite the fact that almost none of your letters and telegrams
had been delivered to him, with rare exceptions. Those letters
which were delivered were limited to the greetings and the
'finale' part only. Nevertheless, he realises how you feel, he is
always next to you, he is very happy that you are constantly
next to him too.

Tolya expressed a lively interest in all his friends, both here
and there. He asked everybody to write to him – maybe some
letters will get through. Tolya told us a lot about the substance
of his case. Lyonya took some notes for himself.

Tolenka informed us of certain articles in the Soviet press
which he wanted us to pay attention to, and recommended us to
read.

In comic tones he told us that when he was taken from
Vladimir prison, his black prisoner's costume with its inscription across the chest 'Shcharansky', was taken off and he had to
put on the overalls he was wearing at our meeting. He said it

was a pity he had to part with that costume, it was an unusual one, and besides, he had had to pay a lot of money for it – twenty-five roubles.

When the time for our meeting was over, I asked him if I could kiss him. He smiled his broad smile and asked: 'Unlike Carter kissed Brezhnev?' He kissed me, and then moved backwards, trying to face us. Then he lifted his hand, and doubled it into a fist; his last greeting to us.

'Witnesses' hurriedly blocked the door from our vision, and let us go out only after Tolya had been taken away.

Afterwards we had a conversation with the Chief of the prison, then another conversation in the Department of Internal Affairs in Kazan. Then more applications and complaints, again and again.

But you know about these matters, my dear girl. We hope for happiness, together with you, and believe it will come in the nearest future.

Shalom, my dear, my beloved girl,

Ida Milgrom

In a telephone call to Avital on 8 August 1979, Ida Milgrom said that during the visit her son 'appeared to be distraught and had difficulty in speaking coherently'. He had told his mother, so she reported to Avital, that he could not read at all, 'since, after trying to read for ten minutes, his pains are so intense that he has to lie down, but it is forbidden for prisoners to lie down during the day in the cell'. If he tried to do so, 'several guards immediately come in, pounce upon him and threaten him with punishment cell for trying to lie down and this is why the first visit due to his family was cancelled.'

Ida Milgrom also told Avital that the Prison Commandant had insisted that all this was 'not his concern'. If a prisoner was ill, 'a doctor will say so. If not, he is healthy (although no doctor has seen him), i.e. he must not lie down, he must not complain, etc.'

Shcharansky also told his mother, as she reported to Avital, that he was 'delighted' to learn that some of the Prisoners of Zion had reached the end of their sentences and been released, and that 'more Jews are leaving and more are applying'. Because of this, 'he felt that his sacrifice was not in vain.' He also sent regards to all his friends in the Soviet Union and abroad 'and said that, although his pains were increasing, and his eyesight was now so bad, he felt that his suffering might be helping other Jews'.

This report, passed on by Avital, was broadcast over the World Service of the BBC on 9 August 1979.

Ida Milgrom's visit brought important news to Chistopol, which Shcharansky was able to pass on to Mendelevich. Several of the Leningrad Trial prisoners had been released, including Kuznetsov and Dymshits, who had been exchanged for two Soviet spies held in the West. Mendelevich also noted Ida Milgrom's message that this was accomplished 'in the framework of the arms limitation agreements between Carter and Brezhnev, and Brezhnev promised that after the American Senate ratifies the current Strategic Arms Limitation Talks, then they will release him (Anatoly) and release you (Iosif) and Ida Nudel. . . .' The date of ratification, Shcharansky told Mendelevich, was expected to be 25 November 1979. A few weeks later, however, the prisoners learned that the Strategic Arms Limitation Talks had broken down.

On 12 October 1979 Shcharansky managed to throw a note for Mendelevich into the rubbish bin outside his cell. The note reported that a hunger strike of all political prisoners was to begin on the following day, in protest against the non-delivery of letters. 'It's bad timing,' was Shcharansky's laconic comment. 'Just yesterday was Yom Kippur' – the Jewish day of fasting – 'and now to fast again? Is there any point in doing that?'

On two occasions at Chistopol, Mendelevich later recalled, Shcharansky managed to call out in English to a prisoner in a cell opposite his. He was on both occasions sentenced to solitary confinement.

'The method the KGB uses against prisoners is to isolate them fully from the outside world,' Shcharansky himself later explained. 'What was so terrible about this isolation was that it often led a prisoner to begin compromising himself morally because he had been cut off from the system of values he would normally live by.'

Shcharansky was determined not to let this happen at Chistopol. He therefore strove to create the kind of mutual respect among his fellow prisoners that he had earlier sought to create between Soviet human rights activists and the Jewish emigration movement. As he later reflected:

The Soviet authorities hate any kind of solidarity among independent-minded people. In prison this becomes even clearer than it is in ordinary life. Prisoners are forbidden to write collective letters of protest. You are punished if you write to the authorities on behalf of another prisoner – say a sick man who is not getting medical attention. The authorities say, 'Look, your letters don't help.' And they are right logically. But there exists another, inner logic: the prisoner who writes such a letter may not save his neighbour in the next cell, but he saves his own soul.

Acts such as writing protest letters were a crucial element in Shcharansky's struggle for survival. But the punishments were also severe. After his release he was to recall 'real torture by hunger': 1500 calories one day followed by only 900 calories the next, for as many as forty consecutive days. Shcharansky was not without resources of his own, however. In solitary confinement he would counter the loneliness and isolation by singing as loudly as he could each of the Hebrew songs that he knew by heart. 'How astounded were the prison guards', he commented, 'when they put me in an isolation cell and almost all the days I was singing.'

Shcharansky also drew on his youthful skill at chess. 'I spent a lot of time analysing chess problems,' he later recalled. 'Of course, I can play the game in my head without a board. That really helped me keep in psychological control.'

He was also helped by the occasional mistakes of his captors. On one occasion he was given a Soviet propaganda publication linking Jewish activist groups in the West to the Central Intelligence Agency, and trying to show how desperately unhappy Soviet Jews were once they reached the West. But the publication contained among its illustrations a facsimile of a letter from President Reagan to Avital. 'I could read what the President said about me to my wife,' Shcharansky recalled. It was a moment of joy long to be savoured: proof that he was not forgotten either by Avital or by the world with which she was clearly in contact at the highest level.

24

Letters from Prison

Following his meeting with his mother on 6 August 1979, Shcharansky was allowed to write her one letter a month, according to Soviet prison regulations. Because he found it so difficult to read or write for more than ten minutes at a time, he decided to write his letters in diary form, a few paragraphs each day. The first extended letter was begun on 8 August 1979, and continued until 9 September 1979. The second was begun ten days later, and continued until 9 October 1979:

8 August 1979

My dear Mama, Papa, Lyonya . . . and my darling – I've got to stop – I was about to mention Natulya. For a moment I'd forgotten that I'm forbidden to speak directly to her in my letters.

I'll write my letter day by day in small portions, as you asked me. In this way, it won't be too much strain for my sight. Frankly, this type of letter writing isn't to my taste. I always disliked writing diaries.

Today is August 8. As was to be expected, I have mixed feelings after the meeting with you. On one hand, it was a great and joyous experience to see you through the glass window and to talk with you. But on the other hand, I reproach myself not to have asked you more questions about my friends, to have forgotten to mention a lot of things. Worst of all, we spoke so little about Natashenka. On reflection, our meeting seems to me now to have been a moment of lost opportunities. But you know I am an optimist, and thus I always find a way to console myself.

Let me give you an example: it could have happened that our meeting had not taken place at all or that it had been less informative for all of us. In any case, I hope that you'll give my best regards to all my friends whose names I didn't have time to mention. As for Natulya, I'm not going to make particular statements. For me it's enough to think of her. Then I feel real happiness, and I know that she feels the same.

9 August 1979

Since we discussed the question of the mail, I'll limit myself to a brief enumeration. As usual, Mama holds the marksmanship lead in letter-bombarding. Between July 10 and August 6, I received from her twelve (!) letters, and only one of hers failed to hit the target. Her letter which arrived here July 13 was confiscated, as well as her July 17 telegram. But I received her telegram that confirmed the receipt of my letter.

Mama has not only picked up a really cosmic speed in writing letters, but has also improved their legibility and contributed to their successful arrival, in contrast to Lyonya. Mama, if this type of sport is not too exhausting for you, please go on bombarding me!

As for legibility, Papa's letters hold first place. Not a single word has been crossed out [that is, censored]. His letters are as vivid and ingenious as his retelling of films. When Lyonya and I were in kindergarten, he used to retell us various films and we enjoyed it greatly. Do you remember, Papa, how you picked us up from kindergarten (ahead of time), took us to the films and retold their contents at home so we would fall asleep quickly? But you, Papa, fell asleep before we did! We'd shake you and shout, 'Papa, don't wander! Keep on with the story!' I long for you, Papa, and even for your 'shortcomings'. Mama and Lyonya told me that you felt much better. I hope that's the case. It's a pity I don't have your photo.

10 August 1979

Now let's switch to another topic, the 'Chronicle of Current Events' after our meeting.

The next day the doctor (a lady) arrived, an oculist from Kazan. She listened to me carefully, and wrote down all my symptoms. She checked my vision with the chart and my eye pressure. She concluded that everything was all right with my eyes. She told me, no it's more correct to say that she concluded, that there is nothing wrong with the eyes themselves and that I'm simply suffering from eye strain. She prescribed eyeglasses. As she explained it, these glasses are not for improving the eyesight but rather to 'relieve eye strain'. In her opinion, if I use them everything will quickly cure itself, which I hope to God will all come true. In the near future I hope they'll send me the glasses and I'll get used to them. Anyway, I've decided to hold off on the letter [of protest] to Moscow, the one I told you about at our meeting, until I get the results from 'experience'.

Today I finally received one of the long-awaited books, *The Art of Programming*, volume II, by Knut. I hope to get the rest in the near future. Anyway, if everything turns out okay with my eyesight and with the books, then living or existence will become easier and more pleasant.

11 August 1979

Your promised photo still hasn't arrived. Did you put it in a letter or just hand it to someone to pass on to me?

Anyway, I was rather lucky. During my arrest they took away all my things, including my folder with the photos. After examination, most of the photos were returned to me, and now I have the pleasure of admiring most of my 'accomplices': Haskell and Audrey [Lookstein, of New York], Connie and Joe [Smukler, of Philadelphia], Roy and June [Daniels, of Iowa] with their children, Jane [Stern] with Natasha and Misha [Avital's brother] with the sign 'For Senators Only' . . . all the 'athletes' in the woods, etc. And from Natulya's photos one can make a whole album. I've laid them out in chronological order according to the month and year, from Istra to the Dead Sea. When I look at them my eyes even stop hurting.

As far as I can remember, we didn't once have our photo taken together, Natulya and I; only once at Joyce's there was a photo taken. Did it come out I'd like to know? When Natasha was going away Lena's mother warned us, 'Don't have your picture taken; it's bad luck. You'll never meet again.' We listened to her. But it's time to meet again, don't you think?

And yet another daring personage, Jenny, Bob [Toth]'s nine-year-old daughter, risked being photographed with me not too long before our separation. But Victor Ivanovich [Volodin, the Investigator preparing the trial against Shcharansky] liked that photo so much I couldn't resist giving it to him. Among the shots in my collection is one of Levka Kogan standing with his mother and with his friend. On the photo in Natasha's handwriting is this caption: 'Levka is going on an excursion to *jail*.

He didn't care for flowers on the windowsill, white curtains, five-course dinners, etc.' Almost all the photos of my colleagues are bright and colourful, and they decorate my cell better than flowers, better than white curtains and other bourgeois delights.

12 August 1979

I'm writing in bits and pieces. Because of this I don't have a complete letter but rather something not quite formed, something that flows and flows, like a jellyfish. The diary genre isn't my style, anyway, and even the circumstances for diary keeping aren't right. There are really few events that happen here, and there's hardly any point in writing down inner feelings.

When Natulya was with me on Kavalski Street she, being the economical, pennypinching type, would throw loose change into some kind of trunk or box, behind a book on a shelf, or under the rug – fifty kopecks and even 'silver' roubles. And then when your brain was bursting, trying to figure out where the money for the next two or three days would come from, she would 'find' her stash, and this was truly a joyous find! So if suddenly lacking in enough emotion, I have only to dig into my memory and invariably I come up against a scene or even a phrase from the past, which quickly binds me with Natasha, just like the one I thought of now.

13 August 1979

So far, your letters from Kazan haven't reached me. I decided to hold off on my letter for just one day in the hope of getting yours. I'll finish tomorrow. I still haven't got any glasses because in Chistopol there still aren't any frames for the glasses. I'll have to wait.

If in the first months after Lefortovo I completely 'swallowed' all printed things fresh, then if I now hardly slide over the pages, not only because of my eyes, so I sometimes stumble on anything that arouses my curiosity. For example Yevseev's article from *International Life*, no. 8, where in part there are several curious remarks about the events of March 1977, or that interesting article about parapsychology and its application in May 3's *Pravda*.

Anyway, I now read very little. In the mornings it's about ten to fifteen minutes. I learn seven to ten new words in Hebrew [he was allowed a Hebrew–Russian dictionary], as a rule, always about the same theme, and throughout the day amuse myself with the thought that I'm turning in all directions and that I try to adjust better. And to this diversion I add another, Knut's book on programming. In it are small problems which challenge me. Having read several pages of the text – I try not to prolong the reading, just ten to fifteen minutes is my limit – I take a certain problem and try to solve it in my head. In the evening, I give myself ten minutes to test myself on paper on everything I had amused myself with throughout the day, and for twenty minutes I write this letter.

Well, it's not very intellectually fulfilling or time-consuming, but what can you do? There is only one hope, and that's that the situation with my eyes will improve. Of course, I don't forget my love of poetry. Regularly, I repeat aloud my favourites, like Lermontov.

14 August 1979

Your letters sent from Kazan still haven't arrived, and so I decided not to wait any more. Anyway, if I wait longer, it may happen that I won't be able to write you a letter in August. So I'm coming to the 'final' section. I'll begin with you: How are Raya and Sasha? How are you all going to live in September? Are you again together at Lubertsy? I ask all of you once again to tell me news of mother's and father's health. Why are there no changes with aunt and cousin? We must hope that they'll be in the 50,000 grouping [meaning 1979's Jewish emigration]. Are A.J. and Judith Abramovna [Alexander Lerner and wife] as active as usual, or have they allowed themselves to rest? And how is the jolly company, my chief, Malva [Landa], Lyusya [Elena Bonner] and the others? My regards to them. Are they continuing their seminars and if so where?

I hope mother doesn't forget to pass on my regards to Roman and Garik [Superfin]. To Volodya [Slepak], Ida [Nudel], and Iosif [Begun].

Please write me a detailed and pertinent letter about Natasha and her life today. Of course this depends only on Natasha and her friends, so this request is principally addressed to them. And if only you add a few words about today's life in Israel, my eyes will hold out for this.

I kiss, kiss all of you and Natulya, my dears.

15 August 1979

PS   I risked holding off sending this for one day and I was right. Today I received three of your letters. I also received word that Lyonya's letter from Moscow was confiscated.

I kiss all of you,

Tolya

27 August 1979

My dear ones:

I'm aware of your request to begin writing letters well in advance lest I should overstrain my eyesight.

I'm beginning with my health. Unfortunately, my eyesight has not improved. The acute pain in the temple which I mentioned during our meeting has lessened to a considerable degree. But another kind of pain has developed, in the frontal lobe. It's felt constantly, and increases when I read. This pain intensifies as soon as I lie down on my left side. When I turn to my right side, it disappears. While reading, I'm tormented by a burning feeling below my eyes. This pain stays with me longer than it did previously. I'm giving you such a detailed description so that (1) Mama shouldn't reproach me for hiding the true situation, (2) in this way you'll be able to inform the specialists you consult about my symptoms. Perhaps that will help them diagnose my disease.

I've not yet received my eyeglasses because new frames aren't available in Chistopol. On August 23 I applied for glasses in written form. This petition was sent by me to Strusov. I also wrote to Romanov. I asked him to send me the glasses he has got for me as soon as possible, and if the glasses do not improve my condition, that will become evident in two or three days, to send me to the hospital for a check-up to diagnose the disease.

Except for my eyesight, my health condition can be regarded as good. I keep on exercising in gymnastics. In the courtyard when I'm allowed out I use the time for jogging. Every day I do a total distance of two and a half to three kilometres. I could jog even more but then I become bored. Last May, I could hardly run 500–600 metres.

28 August 1979

I got the glasses from Romanov (I'm wearing them while writing to you). I'm not used to them, but it seems to me that I feel better by wearing them. Without them I see everything

around me very well. They examined my eyesight twice and
came to the conclusion that I can see 100 per cent. When
wearing the glasses I don't see well. I have the impression that I
see everything through a mist. When I try to read and keep a
book or copybook at a normal distance it seems to be okay. I
don't feel so much pain in the eyes. Today I read for about
twenty minutes, then I went over the letters again which I
received yesterday, and I feel rather good. Of course, the pain in
the temple is still with me, the burning feeling below the eyes
and the bags under my eyes have not disappeared. But the pain
does not increase as rapidly as before. Tonight when the mail is
brought in I'll go on testing my eyesight. But now I have to
interrupt this letter; I'm afraid of overdoing it.

29 August 1979

My enthusiastic mood which I had experienced because of the
glasses has decreased to a certain extent, but I don't want to
jump to conclusions. Let's wait and see.

Now let's turn to the letters that arrived yesterday. From Lev
Petrovich [Ovsishcher]'s 'adapted' [censored] letter I learned
that his daughter has already left. I remember Sofia
Kalistratova's words in February 1977: 'We live in strange
times. We're happy when friends depart.' I think that also in
Lev Petrovich's case he should be happy to say farewell to his
children. My best regards to the people from Minsk. I hope
they will be able to join their children in the near future (and this
wish refers too to many other families).

Papa, you're really smart! You described your wedding day
fifty years ago. As always, you demonstrated your highly
skilful approach to writing letters within the framework of
what you are permitted to write. No single word has been
crossed out. Your fifty years' work experience in the press has
helped you. My dear parents! Once more let me congratulate
you on your golden anniversary. I wish to be able to celebrate
your 100th anniversary, but I'd better be a realist. So I wish that
you'll celebrate your 75th anniversary. In the next twenty-five
years you'll have plenty of time for educating Natulya's children and maybe grandchildren. But for the time being, just
relax!

As in Papa's letter, I have to turn to another subject, from
marriage to death. From your letter I learned of Uncle Noah's
passing. I never met him. I heard of him for the first time a year

ago. Natulya mentioned him in a letter. She wrote that he lived in Canada and had a large family there. As far as I understand they helped Natulya a lot. While reading her and your letters, I felt even from a distance the warmth and care extended to her by Uncle Noah and his 'clan'. I had hoped to have the opportunity in the near future to show him my gratitude for everything he has done. I'm so saddened to learn that I won't be able to do it.

30 August 1979

For the last three days I haven't received any letters. Neither did I receive a telegram confirming the delivery of my letter to you. Today two more letters were confiscated, from Vladimir Khnokh [Leningrad] and Vitya Elistratov [Moscow]. [Three lines censored] Yesterday I got your parcel. Everything was there except the syrup-filled sweets and the tablets. What can be done!? There were less than thirty grams of them. Both pairs of socks fit me. Thanks a lot.

7 September 1979

As you can see, I've interrupted writing for quite a while. I didn't write because I felt that my diary sounds like that of a sick and nervous, over-anxious man who listens to the beating of his heart and whose mood depends on changing impressions. If one gives way to such weakness one runs the risk of growing old very soon.

Here's the situation: on the one hand, reading and writing has become less painful, but on the other this relief is deceptive since pain does not disappear but is kept down temporarily. By using the glasses, it has become even more difficult to regulate the optimal reading time. Let me explain. Previously I interrupted reading and writing for two days. In this way I tried to avoid the effect of overstrain. Then I decided to read not more than thirty to forty minutes in intervals of three to four hours. Altogether I read two or two and a half hours a day. By practising this type of reading, I experienced only a slight burning feeling below my eyes.

But the relief did not last long. Two days later, all the symptoms and painful sensations I told you about during our meeting reappeared. I stopped reading for two days. After such an interruption I could read again for one to one and a half hours. I didn't experience acute pain while reading, contrary to reading without the glasses. But only a few hours later – that is, the following morning after having read the evening before – I again have heavy headaches and acute pain in my eyes. Of course, under these conditions, I'm not able to read or write.

At the moment, using my glasses, I can read for about fifteen to twenty minutes in the morning and evening without increasing pain. As you can see, the glasses are not much help. Most important is the lack of any diagnosis. Without this no effective treatment can be begun. On September 10 I'll write again to Romanov to inform him of the results of my experiences with the glasses. I'm going to ask him again for a check-up at the hospital. It's absolutely necessary to find out the true reason.

The summer has passed very quickly. Now the sun is not to be seen. In the morning when I'm allowed to exercise the temperature is 7–8°C [45°F]. But I don't shiver as I did in the spring. Probably it's the result of my physical training. I keep on jogging and jumping. Every day I pour cold water on myself, and in this way I feel rather good. You see, I did give you a full report on my health. In my next letter I'll give you additional information. If you would, write to me of Natashenka in great detail. Though you speak with her on the phone every week I have very little information about her. I haven't had letters from her for ages. From Mama's letter I learned that Natulya is again going on a trip, but there are no details. [Two lines censored]

8 September 1979

Yesterday I was informed that Lyonya's letter had been confiscated. I'm sorry that my brother is not in his best shape. I hope he'll try hard to become a good team player again and regain his previous good shape.

I learned of the tragic events in the Poltinnikov family from J.A. [Judith Lerner]'s letter. [Dr Irma Poltinnikov and her daughter Dr Victoria Poltinnikov, long-term Novosibirsk refuseniks, had been driven to paranoia by their many years of suffering. When they received exit visas to rejoin the other daughter in Israel in early 1979, they thought it was merely another KGB provocation. Failing to persuade his wife and daughter, the husband, Dr Isaac Poltinnikov, left for Israel. Irma and Victoria locked themselves into their apartment. Irma starved to death; Victoria hanged herself.] This is horrible, especially because these events [the paranoia] started several years ago and many people could have been aware of this tragic development. And nobody could do anything! Only permission could have saved the situation, but it came too late.

Anxious about his mother's health, Shcharanky tried, on that 8 September 1979, to write with deceptive optimism about his own:

I'd like to stress again that I'm going to send a petition to Romanov and insist on a check-up at the hospital for a diagnosis. The local physician does not understand the nature of my disease. He told me that he is not a specialist and thus could not do more than rely on the ophthalmologist's orders. But he was not given any orders. I was given glasses (+0.5) and that's it. After I had been examined by the ophthalmologist on August 7 there were no new analyses or examinations. Of course, another treatment could be okayed at the local level. But does it make any sense, since two previous courses of that treatment didn't have any effect?

I don't know my weight, but you should not worry because of my growing thin. My cellmate has lost about 25 kilos [55 lb]. He thinks it's quite okay. Why should we have an unnecessary burden? [Two lines censored]

At present I'm studying the conjugation of verbs of the type 'ayin-ayin' where the letters of the root coincide. In this connection, I remember my first Hebrew teacher, Micka, who once declared that we would sooner or later reach that point in our studies. Now I've reached it. Besides, I remembered Micka [Chlenov] because of another development. I mentioned previously that I had taken out several magazine subscriptions for my cellmate (not everybody is as rich as I am), and we've been receiving *Soviet Ethnography*. Since I had to save my 'eye energy' I didn't intend to read the magazine, but just turn the pages. Suddenly, I came across an article titled 'The Whale Alley' that had been discovered by Micka. I remembered that one of the participants of the expedition (autumn 1976) had told me about Micka's discovery, but I had thought it was exaggerated. You see, I was wrong. Please give him my best regards. Tell him that everybody I know in the Tatar Republic is interested in his work aimed at the renaissance of the ancient Eskimo civilisation and all other 'endangered civilisations'. I'd be happy to hear from him. My warm feelings towards him have two reasons: (1) his lessons were a good pretext for meeting Natulya (we needed this pretext only for the first two or three weeks), (2) Micka is obviously my only male acquaintance shorter than I am. That is, of course, extremely comforting for my self-esteem.

The next section of this letter was dated 9 September 1979:

The destinies of people could be compared with gear wheels that move and help move others. There are so many examples of this among our friends and relatives. We can trace the same pattern in my and Natulya's lives over several years. The same holds true for you, my dear parents – for several decades, for a whole generation and even for our people in the course of many centuries. The wisdom and experience reveal themselves in our individual lives. Some people achieve their goals very fast. They don't even have time to reflect on what has happened and how surprising it is. But that's not the most important issue. . . .

Of course I could depict here large and small gear wheels and their role. I could even describe a whole set of gear wheels, but I'm afraid to bore you with such mechanical analogies, and that would evoke the association with 'people as tiny screws' [a reference to Stalin's speech at the end of the Second World War in which he compared the efforts of Soviet citizens to the functions of 'tiny screws']. But I hope you'll understand me properly. By trying to explain his conjectures regarding the connection between electricity and magnetism, Maxwell 'filled' the surrounding world (the ether) with 'gear wheels' and transmission systems. In this way, he arrived at all his formulas. Maxwell's formula has proved to be valid, but his 'gear wheels' are forgotten now because they're not needed any more. Now we've got used to the concept of an electromagnetic field. I'm writing about this because I can't write about everything [a reference to the censorship].

You see, I was going to write a few words to Natulya on the significance of October 13, but I arrived at Maxwell's theories. That's Papa's heredity. Like him, I tend to discuss free topics. But contrary to Papa, I can't retell the content of a film. Such a talent was not given to me by the inner laws of my life. But I don't think the lack of this talent will impoverish me, right?

Now I'm going to switch to the traditional ending of my letters, 'quesions without replies'. My first one thousand questions are –

(1) Give me all details of my darling Natulya's life.

(2) Give me all details of my darling Natulya's life.

(3) Give me all details of my darling Natulya's life. . . .

After having answered my thousand questions, please start answering my other queries: your health, Papa and Mama, Sasha's studies, Raya's and Lyosha's work, our relatives and friends in Moscow, Siberia, Israel, the USA, Canada and England. I await your letters impatiently. Now I'm going to give some relief to my eyes, at least for two days. They need it badly. I kiss all of you.

Love,
Tolya

19 September 1979

My dear ones,

Now it's time to start writing a new letter. There are no changes in my eyesight and thus I'll write this letter in small parts.

I'll answer Mama's questions about my health tomorrow. She asked me on what items I had spent 300 roubles. They were subscriptions, food and books. The books have not yet arrived, and it won't be easy to get them. Now they're still being examined for some mysterious reasons. But I don't lose the hope of receiving them.

Once more, Shcharansky was trying to put his mother's mind at rest, desperate as he was about her health. In reality, he had two roubles to spend on poor-quality margarine and bread in the camp canteen.

Shcharansky's letter of September 19 continued:

The information on your other daughter-in-law [Avital] aroused many questions (more questions than answers were given). Why was her trip postponed? Whom was she supposed to meet at the airport? What was she doing in Yamit? I don't have any claim on not being informed. I fully understand that you also lack information because of communication diffi-culties. But about life in Moscow you could have written more details. Perhaps the confiscated letters or the illegible [that is, censored] lines contained just this information. But Mama's attempt in the September 9 letter to retell Natasha's letter of August 8 was a failure.

What about Raya's job and Sasha's studies? What are the

prospects of Boris and Marik? [Boris Tsitlionok and Mark Nashpits, released prisoners awaiting exit visas]. Has Lyova [Lev Ulanovsky] already left? How are Alexander Jakovlevich [Lerner], Volodya [Slepak], Ida [Nudel], etc.? Is Alik in good health? And that of Andrei Dimitrievich [Sakharov]? Please write about all those things in a simple and direct way, avoiding all that could be interpreted as [two lines censored].

Your celebrating the Jewish New Year was much more amusing than you imagined. Evidently, Papa, you have not studied well enough the calendar sent to you by Natulya. It seems, Papa, there was little use in teaching you in the cheder [a Jewish religious school]. Of course, seventy years have already passed, and you have forgotten everything. I've a suggestion, Papa. If it isn't too difficult and boring to you, please describe to me (if there aren't other concrete things to write about) the genealogy and history of our family (as far as you can remember, of course). I'm interested in the genealogy of yours and Mama's families. Maybe I'll be able to understand the structure and place of the 'clans' discovered by Natulya, those new relatives of ours. This topic is too complex to be dealt with in one or two letters. But why should we hurry? You can write on this topic in five, ten or fifteen letters. Of course, you shouldn't do it to the detriment of your health, your daily regime and your professional activity.

The postcard which was enclosed in Chana Aronovna [Elinson]'s letter was received. Past experience shows it's better to write like Rimma Yakir [Moscow activist], directly on Israeli postcards. Then I can enjoy the wonderful landscapes of our country.

20 September 1979

Today I'm going to tell you about my health. There are no changes in comparison with the period which I described in my previous letter. As promised, I forwarded a petition to Romanov on September 10. I asked to be sent to a hospital where my disease can be diagnosed.

The next day, they began taking medical tests, among them a general blood test. The X-rays of my skull were taken. The results are not yet known to me. I guess that you are in a better position to learn of it than I. In any case, no diagnosis has been made. It's quite possible they'll come to the same conclusion –

'practically in normal health', though my eyes 'hold another opinion' [seven lines censored].

Shcharansky still tried to put his mother's mind at rest about his health; but here, where he had clearly gone on to say something about the pains and problems with his eyes, the camp censor had done the protection for him. His letter of September 20 continued:

I agree with the doctors that my pain is not of organic origin, since my daily gymnastic exercises and jogging do not increase the pain, but on the contrary, lessen it to a certain degree. My experience has convinced me that the 'aspirin therapy' which I underwent in the spring was not a success. If there's no urgent need, one should not get accustomed to the use of drugs. Health should be recovered in a natural way – by gymnastic exercises, cold water, etc.

It was a pleasure to eat Raya's biscuits [two words censored]. We enjoyed also the homemade cake (Baumkuchen) which was sent to my cellmate. To make this cake one takes a lot of eggs and it's usually eaten [two words censored] on holidays and other festive occasions, such as weddings. The last time we ate the Baumkuchen it was sent to my neighbour on the occasion of a wedding [two words censored]. This time, there was no particular event in honour of which he got the cake. So I felt free to associate the eating of my portion with your 50th wedding anniversary and the fifth anniversary of my wedding with Natulya.

21 September 1979

In just a few hours, the Jewish New Year will begin. I've just received several letters, among them yours (enclosed were Natashenka's congratulations). It's good that this letter has come just in time. Although it was sent out a month ago, Natasha wrote her greetings about this evening. I have a feeling just as if I were together with her, celebrating the holiday. Mama, your attempts to justify yourself and Papa for having celebrated New Year at the incorrect time are unnecessary. It was much fun for me, but it didn't influence me. You know, I have reliable information on these matters [possibly referring to fellow prisoner Iosif Mendelevich, a religious Jew].

Today I received Alla Begun's abbreviated [that is, censored] greetings and a New Year greeting from Dimitry Shchiglik

[Moscow activist]. Besides, I got letters fom Boris [Tsitlionok] and Marik [Nashpits], two in one envelope. Give my best regards to all. I hope that Boris and Marik won't stay too long in Moscow [that is, will be able to emigrate]. There was no news from Ida [Nudel] for a very long time, let alone from Volodya [Slepak]. In one of his letters, Volodya mentioned his new neighbour, Sasha Podrabinek [a Jewish dissident banished to Siberia for sending to the West information on psychiatric repression in the USSR].

I'm finishing today's letter. The holiday will begin shortly. Next year in Jerusalem – together with Natasha and you, my dear ones.

26 September 1979

A letter from the deputy medical department chief of the Tatar Republic was read to me. According to him there is no reason for sending me for a medical examination at the hospital. He came to this conclusion after consulting a specialist on September 17. It turned out that my presumption (concerning the aim of a previous medical exam) was correct. I try to get used to my 'eye situation' when my eyesight is temporarily impaired. But it is impossible for me to reconcile myself to the lack of a diagnosis. Because of that I'm deprived of proper treatment. I can only hope that my disease will perhaps go away in the distant future.

27 September 1979

Today I'm in high spirits since I haven't received your letters for more than a week. Why am I so glad about it? To understand my mood, we have to turn to the theory of probability. As you've probably noticed, I'm usually given correspondence in batches. There's an 80 per cent chance of getting batches of mail on one and the same day. I don't take into account the probability of getting two batches at once. That happens rather rarely, usually on holidays, as last week on the occasion of the Jewish New Year. Now we are expecting no holidays. If I get my batch, let's say on Tuesday, then I can't expect anything more to come for the following days of the week. Taking into consideration only those weeks when I receive only one a week, the diagram of density of the probability of getting letters on specific days looks like this –

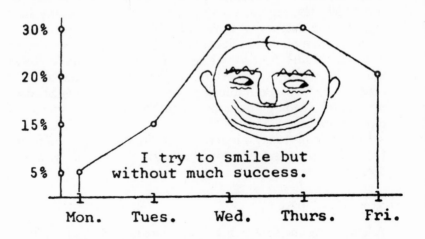

The diagram shows that the probability of getting a letter on Thursday equals 30 per cent, on Friday 20 per cent, etc. And if I didn't receive your letter by Thursday, as it happened this week, it means that I'll get it today or tomorrow with chances divided in proportion $3/2 = 60\%/40\%$, where these 60 per cent are related to this day (today). It's very easy to compute. If you find it rather difficult to follow, ask one of your older sons [former prisoners] to explain it to you.

If I don't receive a letter today, I'll get it tomorrow. My mood will be even better. The probability of receiving letters on Friday will increase up to 44 per cent (the highest point during the week). You see, the theory of probability has a direct involvement with improving one's health and mood. I'm writing you all this, my dear ones, to convince you to consult your older sons. You should know that you can't get my letter every single day. There exists only an increased probability of receiving one the next day.

28 September 1979

Yesterday was a really successful day. First, the theory of probability turned out to be correct in my case. I received my portion of letters. Second, my request has been granted, and I was brought several books from the Chistopol book store: a French–Russian dictionary, *Constructive Mathematical Logic From the Classical Point of View* (I tried to order it from Kazan and Moscow, but all my efforts had been in vain), and some other books. In my situation, this is a real treasure. I can't even decide which to read first, and I only hope my eyesight won't be a hindrance.

I received New Year's greetings from Lyusya [Elena Bonner] and Andrei Dimitrievich [Sakharov], from Arik Rakhlenko, from the Shvartsman family and from Lova Ulanovsky [Moscow refuseniks]. I was given Mama's letters. I'll start reading them today. In the third one, of September 20, there are at least some details of Natashenka's life. Dear Mama, please continue your efforts in this direction.

For the first time, I was trying out eye exercises. It seems to me that it works. Of course, I'm not able to follow all the directions. Let me give you an example: we don't have any diffused daylight here, or even undiffused daylight. We have, rather, electric light. I usually wear dark glasses (except for the occasions when I read and write). I do my eye exercises (except for the first two) wearing dark glasses. [Three lines censored] There is another problem: I can reach with my hand not three or four vertebrae, but five or six. So I'm not sure how to act: on the one hand, I have enough time for all my exercises, but on the other, I'm not so sure it's necessary to do all of them. It could happen that I'd be in the same situation as the well-known character in literature who washed his neck, but the bride didn't come.

1 October 1979

Today(!) I received Lyonya's New Year telegram in which he voices his hope that he'll at last succeed in hitting the goal. This hope came true. The goalie was able to intercept the kick and keep it for some time. A funny symmetry resulted. Mama and Papa's greetings were given to me nine days ahead of time, but Lyonya's and Raya's delayed by nine days. If we add this up and divide in half, we get the exact New Year date. That's extremely convenient.

I'm continuing my exercises. I think it's good for my eyes. Perhaps I'll switch from twice a day to four times a day.

5 October 1979

Mathematical statistics are quite reliable. This week, I again received my letters on a Thursday. Yesterday, I was given two letters from Mama and a greeting card from Lyova Furman from Leningrad [the city's leading unofficial Hebrew teacher].

The informative part of the card is not perceivable [that is, censored], but the greetings are intact. Thank God for that!

In Mama's letter of September 23 there were two photos – one of Papa and the other hers. Of course, it was nice to see again that Papa was doing fine at the age of sixty and even more – descending into a mine. But why didn't Papa send me a recent photo? There shouldn't be any problem with that. We have a whole photo lab at home. But perhaps Papa can't prepare a picture now because of bad health?

I learned in the same letter that you didn't go to Moscow for the New Year, despite your previous intention. That arouses my suspicion that the true reason for not sending a recent shot of Papa is his health. Despite the fact that in my childhood everybody spoke of my family resemblance to Papa, I'm becoming now similar to Mama – everything that happens is a cause of anxiety over your health.

I feel rather good. I think that the eye exercises you sent me are effective. I do them three or four times a day (the water exercise only in the morning). Now I can read two and a half to three hours a day, of course, with breaks. I can read for thirty or forty minutes straight, if I take breaks of several hours.

6 October 1979

As previously, my reading and writing result in redness and a burning feeling below my eyes and other unpleasant sensations, but now it only occasionally turns into headaches. Maybe my self-treatment and physical treatment will be the most effective means as was already the case with my fever [four lines censored].

Mama would like to know what happened to her letter of September 6 in which she mentioned Liuda. I didn't receive it. Apparently it's the same letter of whose confiscation I was informed on September 12. Mama's effort to inform me of that letter's contents was without result. Best regards to Edik [Kuznetsov], Leib [Khnokh] and Natasha's other new friends, in particular to those whose names I was not able to understand. [Fifteen lines censored]

Mama's second letter, that of September 26, contained a very pleasant addition, Natasha's postcard which was carefully cleansed of many [one line censored]. Nevertheless I learned that Natasha is aided by the practical experience of Ariel, Jonathan and Chanka [the children of Ilana Ben-Joseph]. I hope soon enough she'll be able to use this experience.

Is Lena in good health? Mama mentions two letters [two to three words censored] in which she retold Natashenka's letters [two lines censored].

Shcharansky's thoughts were, as always, much with Avital, whose twenty-ninth birthday was to be on 6 November 1979. In pondering her incessant journeys on his behalf, he was reminded of one of the most popular Russian children's stories, *The Little Frog Who Travelled A Lot*, writing to his mother:

7 October 1979

It's high time to start conveying congratulations to you. A true festival of birthdays is coming up: on November 2 Sasha will celebrate his, Mama's and Natasha's birthdays are on November 6 and Papa's on November 7. What a great range of age differences – from Sasha's eight years to Papa's seventy-five years! (The age of the ladies should not be mentioned, of course!) There's no use in repeating my good wishes to all of you; I have written about it many, many times. It's only a pity that we're wasting so much time which we cannot share with each other. All those years were such a precious experience for us (at least for me). It seems to me I would not have been able to realise the true significance of our family in my life. By celebrating our family anniversaries there are several round numbers: Papa's 75th birthday, Mama's 70th birthday, Papa and Mama's 50th anniversary. Papa, Natasha wrote in her postcard that you deserve an award for good health. Now that's the most important thing, isn't it?

Sashka, how are you getting along with your language studies? And what about the language in which we communicated six or seven years ago? Do you remember it? What are you reading now? Isn't it boring to learn at school? You are really quite grown up now. It shouldn't be difficult for you to write a few lines to me telling me about yourself. Perhaps you could draw something funny and send it to me? I really liked the gnome you drew.

There's no need to ask you to convey my greetings to Natasha on the 6th. But where will she be on that day, my restless traveller, my little frog? I'm unable to keep pace with her, especially taking into consideration the present mail service. In this regard she's better off than I. She always knows exactly where I am. After meeting Gilya [Hillel Butman] she can easily figure out what I'm supposed to do at any given moment.

Dear Papa, on the occasion of your 75th anniversary, I'll try to amuse you. Take volume 23 of the *Great Soviet Encyclopaedia* (the edition published in 1953). On page 567 you'll find an article on the eighteenth-century Russian inventor Kryakutny who built a thermal energy balloon fifty-two years before the Montgolfier brothers succeeded in it. Lyonya and I often came across this name in our school books and in other books we read in our childhood at a time when the priority of Russian serfs in science and technique was a favoured topic.

But in issue no. 3 of this year's *Russkaya Literatura* there's an interesting article by L. Ya. Reznikov, 'The Immortal Sulakadzev', which tells about numerous forgeries by really outstanding falsification of 'old manuscripts'. In particular, the author mentions the myth created of Kryakutny, who really didn't exist at all. It's interesting to learn that Sulakadzev's swindles were already denounced in the nineteenth century. L. Ya. Reznikov indicates that Sulakadzev, after several decades of oblivion, was revitalised in the '50s when the hunt for all kinds of first-timers was in vogue. It should be stressed that the mythical Kryakutny is not mentioned any more in the third edition of the Encyclopaedia. Thus truth becomes evident sooner or later, even if it's hidden in 'old manuscripts'. Why should we be afraid of today's manuscripts?

9 October 1979

Yesterday I was told of the confiscation of two letters [one line censored]; one from Judith Abramovna [Lerner] and the other, you can guess – from Lyonya. I hope that Judith's attempt to use Aesopian language is a temporary one. I really don't know what to suggest to my brother. Try to change your handwriting or last name, or mail the letters not from Moscow but with the aid of other people, let us say, from Siberia. Don't leave your fingerprints on the paper. Your conversation with me can disappear in this way.

Yesterday I was given Mama's letter of September 28 which was written after a phone conversation with Natulya [ten lines censored]. Your attempt, Mama, to tell me the text of Psalm 27 was a complete failure, and therefore I'm not able to fulfil Rabbi Kook [of Jerusalem]'s recommendation.

There was a unique event yesterday. At last, I was given

twenty-eight books ordered at various times. They're on mathematics, literature, etc. Some of them were sent twice. I didn't know my order was going to be delivered so I ordered the same book twice. All day long we sorted out and looked through the books to decide what was going to be left in the cell and what was to be sent to the storeroom. One is not allowed to have many books in the cell. One can change them from time to time.

Because of this activity I overstrained my eyes and felt a rather intense pain. But even that was proof of an improvement: (1) this pain didn't turn into headaches, (2) already by this morning I was able to sit down to finish this letter. Previously I would have had, after such a strain, to 'relax' for several days [two lines censored]. I do eye exercises regularly, three or four times a day. If there are additional exercises, please send them to me [four lines censored]. Such a good combination – I have less trouble with my eyes and I have enough books to read. But I won't strain my eyes.

So I'm going to finish this letter. I won't read or write any more today. I'll start reading tomorrow. Probably I'll begin with *Artificial Intelligence* by Hunt.

After having read this letter I'm rather critical of its contents. The diary form and the limited number of topics contribute to the repetition of one and the same theme: how's my eyesight? What did I receive and what not? Reading my letter, one has the impression that I am totally subject to the rhythm of prison life, but fortunately this is not the case. I hope that [two to three lines censored] next letter will bear witness of my feelings, thoughts and words.

Let me once more convey my best congratulations to Natashenka, Papa, Mama and Sasha on their birthdays. Best greetings to all our friends. I kiss and embrace you all, my dear ones,

Tolya

★ ★ ★

On 28 September 1979 Ida Milgrom spoke on the telephone to Genya Intrator, head of the Canadian Committee for Soviet Jewry. The telephone conversation was conducted in the Toronto home of Stan Solomon, one of twenty-eight relatives of Shcharansky who lived in Toronto. It was Stan Solomon's uncle Noah, Shcharansky's father's cousin, who had recently died, and of whom Shcharansky had written in one of his letters to his mother.

Ida Milgrom spoke briefly, in Yiddish, to Solomon's wife Debbie. 'Tell her', Ida Milgrom then asked Genya Intrator in Russian, 'that we are filled with gratitude and emotion for everything the family is doing for us.' As for Boris Shcharansky, Ida Milgrom added, 'he is feeling much better now, he is sitting right beside me and smiling.' Her husband, though Ida Milgrom did not say so, was gravely ill, the victim of a series of severe heart attacks.

★   ★   ★

In October 1979 Shcharansky's friend and fellow-spokesman, Lev Ulanovsky, received his exit visa, and flew to Israel. That same month, my own atlas, *The Jews of Russia: Their History in Maps and Photographs*, was reissued in Jerusalem. The preface to the new edition, which gave details of the sentences on Shcharansky, Slepak and Ida Nudel, ended: 'I should like to dedicate this edition of the Atlas to Shcharansky, Slepak and Ida Nudel, whose courage in adversity reflects the noblest aspects of the long and often tragic story of Russian Jewry.'

On 17 December 1979 the *New York Times* published a report from David Shipler, recently appointed its Jerusalem correspondent, which threw new light on the origins of Dr Lipavsky's letter to *Izvestia* in March 1977. A recent émigré from the Soviet Union to Israel by the name of Boris Kamenetsky had just disclosed, wrote Shipler, how in mid-1962, when Kamenetsky was senior assistant to the Chief Prosecutor of Uzbekistan, Lipavsky had approached him and offered to 'inform on everybody' if his father, then facing a death sentence for economic crimes, were to be spared. Six months later, during a chance meeting in the street, Lipavsky had again approached Kamenetsky and had begun to tell him, according to the latter's recollection, 'of his work for the KGB . . .'.

As 1979 came to an end, Shcharansky wrote two more letters, both of which reached his mother. The first was dated 20 November 1979:

Greetings my dear ones,

I can easily imagine how much worry and anxiety were caused for Mama and you all once again by yet another break in correspondence. I also understand your disappointment when instead of a regular detailed letter you receive this note. But in all of this, of course, I am not the one to blame. As usual, I had prepared a long and detailed letter of about thirty pages for you. However, it was first returned to me to correct, and then, after I'd done so in general, was returned again.

It is now evening. After some hesitation I decided not to waste any more time and send you some information about the questions that you are most concerned about. I am not writing you a long letter not only (and not so much) because of my eyes, but above all to avoid another confiscation and thus increase your anxiety and worries. I'll write and send you the next letter as usual, on December 10, and warn you in advance to be prepared for possible delays, since I don't intend giving up my rights of giving you details about how I feel, my mood, and about the correspondence that I've received, or not, as the case may be. Send me a telegram at once telling me that you have received this letter.

Above all I want to warn you not to come for the next meeting since I've been deprived of it. We'll now meet, I hope, not later than April in the Zone [that is, after his transfer from prison to labour camp], for a personal meeting. Could you please find out beforehand what the rules and regulations are concerning this? There is the problem, certainly, of the civilian things which you still didn't manage to take with you. There is no question of my being able to bring them with me: I wouldn't be able to lift them, especially now that books have appeared. I'm planning to talk to the authorities about this in the near future.

My eyes: having received, though with great delay, Mama's telegram on October 23 about the forthcoming medical check-up, I immediately put in a request to Romanov. There was no answer, but a few days ago, on November 16, three doctors arrived from Kazan and examined me; an optician, a therapeutist, and a surgeon who only came along for the ride. The result: they think that it is nothing more than a question of 'tiredness of the eye muscles'. They affirmed that eye exercises would be useful, which I'm doing, and they even suggested something else: to narrow and expand the pupils while looking at a certain spot. Apart from that, they decided to renew the B12 and B1 vitamin injections.

That's everything for the time being. But the main thing, of course, is that over the last month and a half I've noticed a definite improvement. Even though *all* the symptoms about which I complained to you remain, those terrible eye and head aches which came when I read or wrote have gone. As a result it is now possible for me during the day (with breaks of course) to read for three to four hours, which makes things a whole lot easier. The improvement is certainly connected with the exercises that you sent me, which I'm doing vigorously. I must say, though, that the eye exercises from the second part evoke (as opposed to the first seven) a marked tiredness of the eyes and I only do them once a day, in the morning. A ray of sunshine in my eyes in my circumstances can only occur in my dreams, but is it worth wasting time which I could devote to Natasha, yourselves, and many friends on trivia?

Naturally, I devote almost all my available eye energy on books. Thanks to them time has passed much faster. I've almost completely stopped reading newspapers. Occasionally, though, interesting articles even appear there, as, for example, in no. 41 of *Novoye Vremya*. (Incidentally, I get it and some others in English, and from the New Year I'll try to read it in French as well.)

There's yet another disappointment for Mama. I tried, after overcoming a certain inner resistance, to fulfil your request and send you a lock of hair as a charm. But nothing came of that: the authorities absolutely correctly consider that their responsibilities do not include the encouragement of superstition, prejudice and remnants of the past among certain undeveloped citizens. So you'll have to wait at least until a personal meeting.

The post: since at present I don't have any earlier letters, or even drafts, on me with details about the confiscated letters, I'll have to be not only brief but also not quite accurate. Fortunately, I have all the letters that I've received so I can list them all. Today, the 20th, they informed me about the confiscation of Lyonya's letter. As far as I recall they confiscated another of his letters in this 'report period', and it's been a few months since I've received a letter from him. I spend my time signing for them. (Lyonya, it's really not very funny – put a stop to your 'conditional' jokes. Rewrite them properly, and we'll see if they get to me if your name is on the envelope.)

Apart from that, during the 'report period' it seems that two of Mama's letters were confiscated, and three other letters, one from an unknown person. As citizen Gogol said on such occasions, 'It's a rare bird that can fly to the centre of the Dnieper.' It seems that there were other confiscations, but at the moment I can't remember them.

Well, we'll now move on to more cheerful news. The most remarkable event for many months was without doubt the arrival of Natasha's two letters from Israel(!!), sent, respectively, on August 15 and 23. They were in Moscow on September 4, and by November 11 I had them in my hands. In my 'prematurely deceased' letter I described my reaction in detail to these letters and joyfully responded to the discussion which Natasha began with me in them. I will not try to repeat all of that now, of course. But that is nothing terrible for Natasha and myself with our stable relations and constant contact. I'll only say that in the letters my dear fashion-conscious wife described how she wandered around Yamit dressed as a Bedouin. And today, the 20th, I received Natulya's telegram of November 15 from Jerusalem, and a photo of Avital together with her well-groomed little brother in Papa's letter of November 13 with Mama's postscript. All of this was certainly excellent compensation for the disappointment caused by my letter.

Shcharansky then gave his mother details of the letters and postcards which he had received in October and November, including a letter from Judith Lerner, a postcard from Avital sent through Moscow, and a telegram from his mother with greetings for the Jewish festival of Simhat Torah. His letter continued:

There was a drawing by Sasha in one of Mama's letters. I tried to send him my self-portrait but unfortunately this outstanding piece of art was lost together with the letter. In another letter there were some snaps of my old friends (Jane, Jerry, June, Ellen) and new relatives (Anit and parents). Greetings to them all. I'm looking forward to more photos.

Clever Papa! His letters pass through the censorship like a knife through butter, without a single scratch. I enjoy reading the chronicle of our family life.

As in all his letters, Shcharansky asked many questions about the health and whereabouts of his friends. He was concerned, in this letter, about Judith Lerner's health (she was to die in Moscow in 1983 without ever receiving an exit visa). He was always remembering, too, the birthdays of his friends, and asking his mother to send them greetings. And he wrote with sympathy of the 'old refuseniks', those like Prestin, Abramovich, Kosharovsky and Lerner, who were now in their eighth and ninth years of refusal. At the same time, commenting on the general upsurge of exit visas that

year, he asked: 'Will they achieve the 50,000 mark?'
Shcharansky's letter continued:

Oh yes, yet another greeting, for Jerry and Jane and their son
Michael on his wedding. In general let Natasha pass on my
greetings to our many relatives and friends whom she sees
nowadays. I often remember many of them for one reason or
another. Also don't forget Professor Cotler, who was kind
enough to pass on greetings to me from the 'Magnificent Seven'
of old acquaintances. Of course I send them my reciprocal
greetings, gratitude and best wishes. Time is running out, and I
have to end since I want to send this short message tomorrow
morning. I hope that my next letter will avoid the fate of the
last. A big kiss to you all and my dear and loved Natulya. Look
after your health, and everything will be okay.

Goodnight,
Tolya

PS   Greetings for Chanukkah, even though I still don't know
exactly when it begins.

Shcharansky's second letter at the end of that year was dated
9 December 1979:

Greetings my dear and loved ones,
I don't know what to do. Today is December 9. I promised
you in the last letter, or more accurately in its last posted
variant, to write on the 10th, but I didn't know that my run of
'post office bad luck' would dog me for so long. [Eight lines
censored] They informed me that this letter was sent on
November 26 with the number 202. However, I still don't
know whether you received it or whether it was lost.
Moreover, throughout the recent 'epistolatory' period, i.e.
since November 21, I have received only two letters: from
Judith Abramovna [Lerner], and from Mama the massage
exercises. Therefore I don't know what I should do: whether to
wait for the post, or to repeat the contents of the last letter. In a
word, I decided not to break my vow and wait hopefully from
one day to the next for a telegram from you about the arrival of
my last letter and any other correspondence. In any case, I'll try
to receive it. And meanwhile I'll report on the recent spell of
duty.

First, about my health. If you didn't receive my last letter then I repeat that my eyes are much better. Certainly, things are still far from normal and in these circumstances that's probably unattainable. But for the last month or two I can allow myself, when possible, to read and write for four or five hours a day (with breaks, of course). The improvement is undoubtedly connected with the exercises that mother sent which I'm doing successfully. . . .

I do the eye exercises about three to four times a day. One in the morning together with a water massage. I do the second series of breathing exercises once, sometimes twice, and as a rule in the morning before the usual gymnastics. It seems to me to be a very useful thing. But I must admit that I'm doing them in a far from thorough way. I only breathe in and out about thirty-five to forty times in each of the three positions instead of the recommended minimum of fifty. And not because of my heart: it soon gets used to it. But this stomach movement itself was very unusual for me and the muscles involved get tired very quickly. I'm gradually stepping up the load, however. But I still haven't got to the third series, self-massage. I first want to master the breathing exercises. What's the hurry? But I'll probably begin them in the next few days. Moreover, emboldened by the support of the doctors from Kazan I repeated the exercises that I did in February. In a word, this is no life, but solid exercise.

It amazes me how one can find time, with all of this, to read. In general I was very happy to bury myself in books, and I have once again become interested in questions that concerned me ten years ago (such as simulating chess games, and so on). True, I have no ambitious plans in this respect. But that's probably for the best. Now I am really only satisfying my curiosity and am not trying with the aid of science to escape from questions that life itself poses. But in any case it is not impossible in the Zone, with the right to two letters a month, that I will with time develop the theme. True, my attempts in this respect have not been all that successful. Thus, in the last letter, enthused by Mama's message about her knowledge of mathematical statistics, I continued my 'research' into the role of 'chance' in our correspondence by applying the methodology of testing statistical hypotheses. Alas, I immediately had to reject all of its formulas and calculations, and then the letter completely disappeared without trace.

In that letter, incidentally, I described the likeable robot
Sheiki (described in particular by Hunt in his book *Artificial
Intelligence*), which was built at Stanford University. I wrote to
you about him because his life on the surface strongly resembles
my own. 'Sheiki', writes Hunt, 'moves on its own by com-
mands given in simplified English in a modified environment.
His whole outer world consists of a series of rooms, doors,
boxes, windows, and light sources.' One only has to change all
these nouns from the plural to the singular to make his external
world my own. But, certainly, the similarity soon ends. I can
easily 'widen' my physical world: transfer, for instance, my
accommodation to the alley during a walk, going backwards
and forwards 500–600 times; transform the bed at will – into a
sports' court or into a study; and I can even easily turn the
boring bread [one word censored] into a nicer crispbread
(thankfully, the radiators work very well) and with a certain
play of the imagination (associations are what the poor Sheiki
lacks completely) they can remind me of those 'toasts' which
Natasha cooked in a hurry a few hours before our wedding, and
at the same time also of our walks together near Volokolamsk.
(For some reason I've been thinking a lot about them recently.)
And when you lose yourself in books then it can seem that you
are back in the student hostel. And in some respects it is even
more convenient: for instance, you don't have to dash down to
the canteen and stand in a queue for supper – the food is brought
directly to your room!

Hence my affirmation – borrowed from the existentialists,
and perceived by reason but not consciously – that freedom can
neither be given nor taken away, since man *is* freedom, seems to
me now as natural as life itself. It is not accidental, of course,
that I met Natasha only after I left life to enter the realm of
freedom as a conscious necessity. Incidentally, I think that I
wrote to you about this a few months ago. But I think that you
will understand me correctly. My inner state, Natulya and
everyone, is associated with this and it is this that for many
years has given me a constant sense of joy, relief and confidence.

The post: apart from the exercises I received from mother a
letter (of November 14) with several exceedingly pleasant
enclosures: a postcard from Natulya and two photos of friends
with Sasha's comments. Natasha promises you a 'warm letter'
with details of her trip: it would be nice if at least some details
reached me of her, as usual, hectic life. The views themselves of

Jerusalem – in my circumstances all of this gives me many pleasant moments.

I understand completely Mama's complaints about the frequent changes of weather in Moscow. Here also all sorts of strange things are happening: at one moment it's unusually warm, at another windy, ice, snow, rain, all at the same time. But now, it seems, winter has at last come into its own. I'd like to think that it won't be as harsh as it was last year, when the temperature fell to −47°C. And how are things with you? Are Mama's headaches still continuing because of the weather? How is Papa? I'm all right. True, I haven't run around the courtyard for a long time: if it's not wet, it's slippery, but I try to make up for it by skating along the ice track and energetic exercises in the cell in the mornings. I'm still dousing myself in cold water.

Mama mentions the things. Not long ago they suggested that I draw up a list of things which are to be sent. They promised to do so in the near future. [One page censored] In truth, my life here is some sort of oasis of calm in comparison with what's going on around you. Certainly, I can understand Judith Abramovna's disappointment that she won't be able to meet her nephews. But does not such a fate, my dear old ones, threaten you? Is it not time for you to take up study? Your objections are obvious: old age, sclerosis. But does not Papa still retain some of the higher Jewish education that he obtained at the Odessa Jewish School? Even if he thinks that he has forgotten everything, once he starts reading any simple textbook he'll soon discover that that is not the case. Was Alexander Jakovlevich [Lerner]'s portrait of Mama a success?

My plan worked. It's now December 11, evening, and I've just received six of your letters and a postcard from Mama, a note from Marek [Nashpits] and Bora [Tsitlionok], your telegram about the arrival of my letter. [Five lines censored] Now at least I know that the letter got to you and that I don't need to repeat myself (to some extent I've already done so, but that's no disaster). It's a pity that I've still not got your letters in answer to mine, so there's no dialogue. Certainly, I was very happy to receive your letter, Natashenka's two photos. . . .

Once more, Shcharansky then turned to questions about his family and friends, before continuing:

Tomorrow I will answer in detail all your questions, and the

morning after I'll send the letter off (or, more accurately, I'll
have it sent off). And meanwhile I'll once again answer Mama's
main question. I feel perfectly all right, perhaps for the first time
in many months. The headaches are rare (no more frequent than
when free), I have completely forgotten about the shivers, my
heart hardly ever hurts, and my eyes no longer stop me reading
for about five hours a day. I am strengthening them (my eyes)
and looking after them with Mama's exercises and I'm certain
that if the circumstances change they'll be perfectly all right.
My general feeling is now excellent. So it's now your turn,
Mama and Papa, and I very much beg you not to fall ill. So,
then, good night, till tomorrow.

It's December 12, good morning. I've already done my
exercises, had breakfast, been for a walk, and am now getting
down to yesterday's post. Rather like a sanatorium? It's a pity
that the package holiday is coming to an end. I am looking with
pleasure at the photo from Mama's letter of November 18.
Natulya there is altogether thin. Could it be because of the trial?
On the other hand, right up to the trial I put on weight, and only
afterwards began to lose the extra pounds. [Seven lines cen-
sored] Yesterday they gave me Raya's letter of the 18th and
Sasha's (apparently of the 24th).

Sashenka, thanks for your letter and drawing. I sent you my
self-portrait so that you wouldn't forget me. But I don't know
whether you received it or not. But your portrait of me is rather
better. You will certainly be the first artist from the
Shcharansky family. And how is your English? You know it's
very useful to be able to speak a language that the grown-ups
don't know. Your dad and myself often used to speak in
English when we were young when the parents were around
(uncle Bora and aunty Ida), and they didn't understand anything – that was fun. You still don't have a brother for some
reason, but to make up for that you can speak to Daddy in secret
even when Mummy is about. Imagine what fun that would be?
Raechka, if you don't like the sound of that, then hurry up. The
Shcharanskys after all pick up languages very easily. Thank you
for your greetings from your relatives. Give my greetings also
to your big, friendly family. I won't name them all in order not
to get confused. I received a short letter from Arik Rakhlenko
together with the latest greetings from Bora [Tsitlionok].
Thank heavens that at last Bora's Odyssey is over. Let's hope
that everything won't start anew for Marik [Nashpits]. . . .

Papa, in your letter of November 29 you continue (and by the look of it finish) your short piece about your family. I hope that he hasn't forgotten that he still has to write about Mama's relatives. There it seems to me that the family links are particularly complicated and if you carefully unravel them one could well find that you yourself are a cousin at first remove. But I feel that with Mama's help Papa will get to grips with all of these genealogical intricacies. And his pen, as you can see, is still sharp: despite his seventy-five years, Papa's sporting condition is such that all his blows still hit their target (touch wood). Papa dear, how are you feeling? Be very careful, I beg of you. What is the medicine that you are taking? What illness is it for? Incidentally, Mama makes you go for a walk after meals. And [one word censored] who knows something about medicine says that after food one should have a lie-down for at least fifteen or twenty minutes. 'He who lies down after meals is the greatest lazybones', as the [one word censored] saying goes [two lines censored].

Three letters arrived from Mama yesterday, of November 18, 24, 28, and the postcard of the 29th. I am very worried about the obvious deterioration in Mama's health (though she only refers to it in passing but I've got used to reading [one word censored]). Perhaps, Mama, it would be an idea if you took up a less active lifestyle for a time? Mama refers to Ida's letter and her advice. I also think that you should prepare for spring in advance, contact the relevant organisation, and discover the regulations. The regular series of exercises arrived with Mama's letter of the 24th. I must admit that I'm mastering them much more slowly than Mama sends them. But I will ultimately get to grips with them all since they help me a lot. However, I have such [one line illegible] is beyond the eye treatment [illegible]. Moreover, it's not quite clear to me how one is supposed to combine all of these uncoordinated parts: is there some sort of rule for doing them (for example, first the eye exercises, the breathing, and then massage)? Does one have to do all of the exercises or as you go on to the more complicated ones can you stop doing the earlier ones? It seems to me that if I did all the exercises which Mama sent me, and not only once at that, then twenty-four hours a day would hardly be enough.

Shcharansky went on to ask about family and friends, and about Avital's current travels in the United States. 'I'd love to know how her trip went,' he asked his mother, and added, addressing his brother:

Lyusenka, my dear Lyusenka, why do you disappoint me so? You don't need to worry about me so. After all, I'm not a Zen Buddhist (I don't know how to sit with my legs crossed under me), but I easily pick up feelings sent over a distance by people close to me. And you? If you can also do this, then I say to you a thousand times: 'You are absolutely calm. Healthy. Everything will be all right.' Relax, obey these words and calm yourself. After all, you have much strength, optimism, energy, which, it seems to me, you don't even suspect that you have. Don't forget for a moment that you have friends who need you and who will be with you always however much our lives might change.

Chanukkah will be beginning at the end of the week: I send greetings to Natulya, yourselves, and all of our friends for this marvellous holiday. Among Natulina's postcards returned to me by the investigators there is the following one: she is sitting with Misha in an airport waiting for a plane – before her first journey across the ocean exactly four years ago. They planned to light the Chanukkah candles in the plane itself. And where will Natulya be celebrating Chanukkah this time?

And yet another association with December and the approaching New Year. Does Natulya remember the old, worn, ink-stained, thin book, the second part of the Jewish history for schoolchildren which wandered about with us from flat to flat? It was published, I think, in Vilnius, for the junior classes of Jewish schools. I took it with me and read it on the way to Tallinn during our new year 'honeymoon' journey. Later on all sorts of courses about our history passed through my hands – fat ones and thin ones, short ones and long ones, in Russian and in English, for schools and for teach-yourself work. Books came and, naturally, they went, but this one, useless, creased, even coverless and missing a few pages, in one way or another stayed with us as part of the family. And thanks to that, naturally, it ended up in the hands of the investigator, and it is now with me in the [illegible]. It's dear to me not as a source of information, but as a constant reminder of our past: very close and very far. Perhaps it is even a good thing that the book is for junior pupils since that is exactly how I feel when faced with our history. Natashenka has far outstripped me in this respect. Every time I dip into this book, a lot of involuntary associations arise. Incidentally, don't think that I am comparing myself with the great Rabbis Hillel and Akiva. But when reading about Rabbi Hillel I can't help remembering how not a little snow fell on Natasha and myself when we tried to enter our school. And are not the many years of patience and fortitude of my beloved Avital similar to those of Rachel? I remember when for the first time I heard the story of Rabbi Akiva and Rachel, I couldn't help thinking: what a beautiful story. The part about separation at the time seemed so improbable [illegible] that I couldn't take them for real. But life itself finds its own correctives, and makes the impossible possible, and turns tales into reality.

And so, I had come to the end, and at that moment they brought me yet four more of Mama's letters: of November 15, 19, 22 and 26 [nine lines censored]. Amazing Israeli landscapes from Sasha's album with notes from Sasha and Natashenka. Natulya is right, Sasha really is a genuine artist. What absolutely beautiful photos. There are no new questions in the letters themselves, therefore I won't add anything to this letter. It's a pity that I still didn't find out what exactly Debbie asked to pass on to me. Incidentally, it's not difficult to guess. Greetings to them all and Genya [Intrator]. Does Genya often call you? Greetings to our American relatives. How are Lyusya and Andrei Dimitrievich [Sakharov]? Give them and other friends greetings for the New Year. . . . I await your letters and answers to the questions in the last letter. Yes, I nearly forgot, my best wishes to Sasha Lunts for his birthday. Incidentally, Papa writes that one of the branches of our family bore the surname Lunts. Perhaps we are related to them? That would be amusing. Incidentally, that would be easy to check: do you remember that Sasha's American relatives sent him a detailed genealogical tree listing the families over several centuries? But that's all, I'm finishing. Even my much more healthy eyes insist on that.

Greetings to all my friends, acquaintances and those far away.

I give you all a big kiss, and my beloved Avital,

Tolya

It's raining again.

★   ★   ★

In the autumn of 1979, rumours of Shcharansky's ill-health had perturbed his friends in the West. There were those who feared that he was dying. In order to counter these rumours and fears, three Soviet doctors examined Shcharansky.

Their report was published by the Soviet authorities on 19 November 1979. It read: 'Factual: weight – 52 kilograms, skin – clean and of normal colour, elastic, turgor – adequate. Visible mucous membranes are of normal colour and clear. Tongue – clear and moist. The heart tones are distinct, no murmurs, within normal bounds. Blood pressure – 125/65, pulse rate – 64, strong and tense, rarely missing a beat. Abdomen – soft and painless. Liver and spleen – not enlargled, peristalsis – good. Urogenital system – no deviations from the normal. Physiological functions – normal. In no need of hospital treatment.'

There was no way in which such a confident report would be tested. The Soviet authorities were determined that the world should feel that Shcharansky was well. For Ida Milgrom in Moscow and Avital in Jerusalem, however, it was a cruel rebuff to their hopes that he would be admitted to hospital.

That month, Avital Shcharansky published a book entitled *Next Year in Jerusalem*. 'Again, I am starting on my travels in order to knock on all doors, to try all possibilities,' she wrote. 'And I appeal to you, my readers. You were with me during Tolik's trial. You sent telegrams of protest; you went out to demonstrations; you prayed for us; you supported us with your participation. You prevented a terrible reprisal against the Jews of Russia. Thanks to you my husband remained alive. Each of you can do a lot. Together we are strong. I beg you, my readers: Help us!'

At Chistopol, Shcharansky and Mendelevich had still not met. One winter night there was such a heavy fall of snow that, for the morning exercise, prisoners had to walk knee-high in snow. They asked for shovels to clear the snow but the authorities refused. Shcharansky therefore asked to be taken back to his cell. 'Just at that moment,' Mendelevich later recalled, 'they took me out to walk! We met in the courtyard. I recognised him immediately from the pictures Ida Nudel sent me in 1975.' Mendelevich added: 'But how he has changed! His face is grey, his cheekbones protrude – and only the eyes glow, with warmth and goodness shining from them.' Mendelevich remembered their brief first conversation together at Chistopol, and their subsequent efforts to maintain contact:

'Anatoly!'

'Iosif!'

The guards were taken aback momentarily but immediately caught our hands, and separated us.

We were not punished following this incident because it was the 'fault' of the guards. They were supposed to prevent meetings between prisoners. But they couldn't sever the ties between us. It's impossible to plug up all the holes; our experience was not less rich than theirs. Daily in my passing Shcharansky's cell I would bless him with 'Shalom' while turning to the guard. The guard didn't understand.

Guard: 'Huh. What?'

Iosif: 'Nothing. Nothing.'

A similar opportunity was presented during the exercise period. In the door of my exercise yard was a crack. Toward the end of the walking time I would bring my eye close to the crack in order to gaze at Anatoly while he was passing.

Iosif: 'Shalom. I received letters today from Israel.'

Anatoly: 'I haven't received any mail for a month now.'

Guard: 'Stop the conversations. We will punish you.'

★   ★   ★

In an attempt to draw world attention to her husband's plight, Avital Shcharansky set off from Jerusalem once more, travelling in the summer of 1979 to Paris, Toronto and Madrid, where the second of the Helsinki review conferences was in session. Her mood was one of subdued optimism. 'She had hoped that her husband might be released at the time of the Olympics, when the Russians might have been expected to offer a few concessions,' wrote Miriam Chinsky after an interview with Avital in Toronto.

One hope was that Shcharansky might now be exchanged for someone of importance to the Soviet Government. That April, Alexander Ginsburg, who had been sentenced to eight years on the same day as Shcharansky, and who had been one of his colleagues in the Moscow Helsinki Watchdog group, was exchanged after serving less than three years of his sentence.

25

'My Perpetual Optimism'

On 20 January 1980 Shcharansky's friends gathered in Moscow to celebrate, in his absence, his thirty-first birthday. Professor Lerner made his apartment the scene of the meeting. All were particularly pleased that Boris Shcharansky was coming into Moscow to join the celebrations.

'Ida Milgrom was already there,' one guest later recalled, 'and Boris Shcharansky was expected to come on his own. It was already getting late and he did not come yet and we all began to worry what could happen to him. Finally, Lerner and Ida Milgrom went to the street, to the public phone since Lerner's phone had been long before disconnected, to call some friends to ask them if they knew something about Boris Shcharansky; and hospitals, if necessary. After several unsuccessful attempts they learnt finally that Boris Shcharansky had died of a stroke on his way to the party, in the trolley-bus.'

'We were afraid', the guest noted, 'that something awful would happen to Ida Milgrom and the Lerners – they were barely alive, stricken with grief.'

In Jerusalem that night, Alexander Lunts was also giving a small party to celebrate Shcharansky's birthday, as well as his own. Avital was present, also Enid and Stuart Wurtman, who had emigrated to Israel from the United States, and David Shipler. As the party began, Lunts told them that in Moscow he and Shcharansky would have celebrated their birthdays together. While he was speaking, Avital was called to the telephone. It was someone in Moscow on the line, to tell her that Boris Shcharansky was dead.

That night, Ida Milgrom sent a telegram to Chistopol prison, to tell her Tolya of his father's death. Shcharansky at once telegraphed to his mother: 'I am with you.' That same day, at Chistopol,

Shcharansky received a telegram from Avital in Jerusalem. It too read: 'I am with you.'

When the news of his father's death reached Shcharansky in Chistopol, Iosif Mendelevich was in the cell opposite. They had worked out a means of talking, quietly, by singing what appeared to be snatches of Jewish prayers and psalms. That night, Mendelevich later wrote, 'in the chilling loneliness of my cell, I sang':

> *Iosif*: 'Do you hear?'
> *Anatoly*: 'Yes, Iosif, I hear.'
> *Iosif*: 'Shabbat Shalom Anatoly.'
> Instead of responding 'Shabbat Shalom' I heard:
> *Anatoly*: 'My father died the day before yesterday.'
> *Iosif*: 'Bad tidings.'
> I had predicted it from inside my flesh. How could I help?
> Give encouragement? Day and night I couldn't find solace. My
> grieving friend is near me, but I can't help him. Finally, an idea
> springs into my head. I'm beginning feverishly to prepare for
> the next day's walk. I'm writing the word of the Kaddish, the
> prayer for the dead, rolling the paper into a little ball the size of a
> pea, wrapping it in a thick piece of paper, and begin to practise
> throwing it in my cell.
> I fear the ball is too big and won't penetrate through the
> fencing above the exercise yard. At which angle and from what
> distance must I throw it?
> After I have practised for a long time and found the right
> method, I wait for the morning. The walk begins. I tap the wall
> of the exercise yard. Anatoly responds.
> *Iosif*: 'Be ready to receive.'
> The task is difficult. The guard stands above my head all the
> time, goes away for a few moments, and immediately comes
> back. I follow his movements surreptitiously. The moment he
> turns his back, I throw the ball, but it hits the fence and falls
> back. The guard returns. It's snowing and he doesn't spot the
> small ball. I snatch the ball the moment the guard goes away
> again, and try once again to throw it. Again – I'm not success-
> ful; I don't hit one target. Here one needs a real marksman.
> The walk is over. I return to my cell, and I have no wish to
> continue to live. I'm such a failure. I can't even help my friend!
> The next day I put a different plan into action. In the wall of
> the exercise yard near the ground there is a tiny hole, in which it

is possible to insert the refill of a fountain pen. I put one refill into another and connect a string to the second refill. The note is connected to the end of the string. I call Anatoly by tapping and attempt to explain the principle to him.

Iosif: 'I'm putting the refill in, you grab the end and pull it towards you.'

But he has difficulty in finding the location on the other side; he asks 'Where is it? Where exactly?' The walk is over.

Failed again! Nightmare. Tomorrow, I'll try again the previous method. During the subsequent attempt I succeed in making it fly over to the other side.

Anatoly: 'It got here.' There are no words more pleasing to one's ear. 'It's here!' 'It's here!'

It's here! It's here! What happiness. Now he can say Kaddish. Thus we found a way to keep in touch.

Later, when Shcharansky was able to write to his mother, he wrote of the effect on him of his father's death:

It is difficult for me to begin this letter, even though many days have gone by since the black evening I received your telegram telling me that Papa had died. It was a terrible shock. As it hurts to touch an open wound, so it pains me to recall my memories of Papa, which span most of my life. Right from my childhood, which was so full of Papa. I remember those wonderful winter days, my birthdays. During the first sixteen months of our separation, I kept thinking about our last meeting, at Volodya Slepak's home on 13 March, the evening I was arrested. Papa tried to comfort you; how much he needed comforting himself. I was harrowed by the fear that the meeting at Volodya's was the last one. Later, the uncertainty vanished. I saw Leonid, then you. I began to receive letters from Papa. I was, of course, very worried about Papa; I was worried, but I was also confident. As it turned out, that evening at Volodya's was indeed the last time. It's as though I spent a long time on a fragile, swaying bridge. I was almost across; I had only to stretch out my hand. But it was too late.

By law, Shcharansky should have seen his father in Lefortovo prison after the trial. This visit had been cancelled by the authorities, who knew exactly how much Shcharansky worried about his father. His letter continued:

Mama dear, I beg you to take care of yourself. There is only one way to do that – learn not to fray your nerves and waste your mental energy, whatever the cause. Stop living from letter to letter. There will almost certainly be more interference with your correspondence. Maybe there will be no more meetings. But it is essential to do things quietly, not to get nervy, not to grieve, not to fill yourself with fears. Look after your health, rest regularly. This is the only way we can hope for better days. I ask you to learn this, Mama, before it is too late. Don't forget that you are 'the captain of the family ship' as Papa was so fond of saying, and a captain must be more than wise and strong – a captain must be quiet and serene. The fortunes and the spirit of the entire crew depend on it.

The day after I received your telegram telling me of Papa's death I decided, in his memory, to read and study all hundred and fifty Psalms of David (in Hebrew). This is what I do from morning till evening. I stop only to eat, take walks, do eye exercises, and glance at the newspapers. What does this give me? First of all, it is quite tiring, it leaves me almost no energy for black thoughts and painful memories. Secondly, this study is very useful to me in several ways – learning the language is filling an enormous gap in my basic Jewish education. Thirdly – and this seems to be the main thing – as I read these verses, my thoughts return to Papa, to you, to Avital, to the past and the future, to the fate of our close and more distant family – but in a more general, spiritual way. Gradually, my feeling of great loss and sorrow changes to one of bright hopes. I am denied the right to visit Papa's grave but when, in the future, I hear these wonderful verses, these lines that encompass the lives of all the Jews in Israel, and not only there, I shall remember Papa. It will be as if I had erected a memorial stone to him in my heart, and he will be with me all the days of my life.

In my telegram to you, I put 'I am with you.' The same day I received a telegram from Avital in Jerusalem, in which I read, 'I am with you.' This is certainly not a coincidence. Yes, I know and feel that we are together constantly, everywhere – our missing family, and friends far and near – and this gives me the strength to retain my perpetual optimism, which I received as a legacy from Papa.

★   ★   ★

On 22 January 1980, two days after Boris Shcharansky's death, Academician Sakharov was taken to the Prosecutor's Office in

Right Ida Milgrom,
Moscow, campaigned
~~tire~~lessly for her son for
~~eig~~ht years.

Below Avital
~~S~~charansky pausing
~~for~~ a moment during her
~~ow~~n incessant quest for
~~her~~ husband's release.
~~Am~~ong those whom she
~~me~~t during her long
~~sea~~rch for justice were
~~Pr~~esident Reagan,
~~Fr~~ançois Mitterand and
~~M~~argaret Thatcher.

Below right
~~Bo~~ris Shcharansky's
~~gra~~ve just outside
~~M~~oscow. Below the six-
~~po~~inted Star of David,
~~his~~ name and dates, is
~~wr~~itten in Hebrew
~~let~~tering: 'His soul will
~~rep~~ose in goodness and
~~his~~ seed will inherit the
~~la~~nd'.

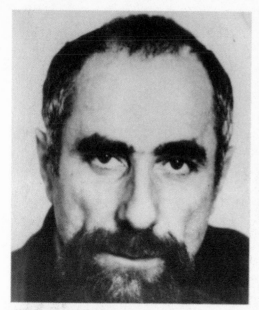

44 *Ludmila Volvovsky and Ina Begun, two of the wi[ves]
who, in Moscow, fight for their husbands' release from
prison and labour camp.*

43 Above *Iosif Begun, three times Prisoner
of Zion, whose third sentence, in 1983, was
twelve years in prison and labour camp.*

45 Right *Anna Livshits (aged ten) and her father
Vladimir, photographed in Leningrad in November
1985, less than two months before his arrest on
unspecified charges.*

46 Below *Roald Zelichenok, sentenced in August
1985 to three years in labour camp for his part in the
Jewish emigration movement, and his wife Galina,
almost totally blind, who, in Leningrad, campaigns for
his release.*

Ida Milgrom and Lev Ovsishcher. Among the interrogations conducted after Shcharansky's arrest in 1977, that of ...ishcher revealed the strength and courage of an elderly refusenik, and helped substantially to weaken the case ...nst Shcharansky. Ovsishcher, who in 1985 married Lev Ulanovsky's mother Tatiana, was in 1986 still not ...wed to leave the Soviet Union to join his daughter in the West or his son-in-law in Israel.

A poster announcing a massive protest rally in ...don in 1983. The rally was cancelled following ...iet-inspired suggestions that a three-month period of ...tern campaign 'quiet' would result in Shcharansky's ...ase. It did not do so.

49 *Leonid Shcharansky, in Moscow, under an Israeli flag.*

50 *Chistopol prison.*

51 *Avital in London with Margaret Thatcher.*

Berlin, 11 February 1986. Shcharansky crosses the Glienicke Bridge between East Germany and West Berlin on ~~way~~ way to Frankfurt, Ben Gurion airport and (by nightfall) Jerusalem. With him is Richard Burt, United States ~~bassador~~ ambassador to Bonn, one of those involved in the negotiations which led to Shcharansky's release.

53 Left   *Ben Gurion airport, 11 Febru[ary]*
1986. Shcharansky embraces the Prime
Minister of Israel, Shimon Peres.

54 Below   *Ben Gurion airport,*
11 February 1986. Shcharansky sees one [of]
his many Western and former Moscow
friends of a decade earlier who had gather[ed]
in their hundreds to greet him.

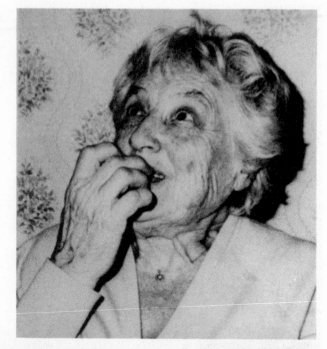

*Right   Moscow, 11 February 1986.
...Milgrom learns of her son's release
...prison and his arrival in Israel.*

*Below   Jerusalem, 11 February
...Shcharansky at the Western (or
...ling') Wall, holding the Book of
...ms which he had kept with him in
...n and labour camp.*

57 Left *Jerusalem,
12 February 1986. Avital an[
Natan Shcharansky on their
balcony.*

58 Below *Jerusalem,
13 February 1986. Shcharan[
holds on to Avital's sleeve as [
meets the President of Israel,
Chaim Herzog. Shcharansk[
had been born in the Soviet
Union in the same year as the
creation of the State of Israel.*

Moscow and shown a Decree of the Praesidium of the Supreme Soviet, stripping him of all his State honours. He was also told that he was to be banished to the city of Gorky, 250 miles east of Moscow: a city officially closed to foreigners. Sakharov was given two hours to leave Moscow: that afternoon he and Elena Bonner flew eastwards to begin their internal banishment. On the following day, undeterred by his punishment, Sakharov authorised the inclusion of his signature on a statement by the remaining members of the Moscow Helsinki Watchdog group, condemning the Soviet Government 'for suppressing the independence of Afghanistan'.

In Chistopol, Shcharansky and Mendelevich now managed to maintain contact. It was a source of strength for both of them, amid the harsh conditions and enforced isolation. Mendelevich later noted down some of their snatches of conversation, themselves contrary to the strict prison rules.

> *Anatoly*: 'Iosif, can you send me the 27th Psalm from the book of Psalms? Avital wrote me that the Rabbis contend that you should read it daily.'
>
> I copy down the section for him, and the next day successfully pass it over the fence.
>
> And, thus, despite my weakness, my heart is strengthened with the possibility of helping my fellow man whose situation is worse than mine. On Sabbath I sing to him: 'What are you doing today?' And he sings back to me: 'I have a Passover Haggadah. I'm reading it. It helps me to learn the language. I already know the Psalms that are found there. It strengthens my soul because I learn from the faith and heroism of King David.'
>
> What a wonderful man. And he is held in this stinking prison! I answer him in song: 'David, King of Israel Lives and Exists!'
>
> *Guard*: 'Mendelevich. Stop talking with Shcharansky!'
>
> *Iosif*: 'I'm not talking. I'm singing.'
>
> *Guard*: 'In prison, it's forbidden to sing.'

By faith and humour, the prisoners were able to maintain their morale, and through the Psalms, and the order of service for the Passover, to retain their links with the Jewish world from which they were now so ruthlessly cut off.

★   ★   ★

On 15 March 1980, the third anniversary of Shcharansky's arrest, Avital appealed from Jerusalem to 'all who cared' to 'continue to fight with renewed strength' to free her husband, and all other Prisoners of Zion in the Soviet Union. That same day, from Istra, Ida Milgrom appealed to Leonid Brezhnev, listing what she described as 'numerous violations' of Soviet law in her son's case. 'Even prior to my son's arrest,' she wrote, 'and prior to the presentation of charges against him, he was accused of spying by the official press. "No one can be adjudged guilty of a crime . . . except by the sentence of a court" states Article 160 of the Soviet Constitution. "A defendant is guaranteed the right to legal assistance" states Article 158 of the Constitution. My son was deprived of this inherent right not only during the investigation but during the trial as well. "No one can be punished as a criminal . . . except by the sentence of a court" states Article 160 of the Constitution. My son was subjected – in a blatant violation of the law – to a seven-month imprisonment in addition to the nine months of imprisonment stipulated by the Soviet law. Thus, another article of the Constitution of the USSR, Article 34 that guarantees the equality of all citizens before the law, was also violated.'

'In addition,' Ida Milgrom wrote, 'my son was deprived of the very elementary right of engaging a lawyer of his choice to act in his defence and he was not allowed to defend himself in court against the main charge – espionage.' Both the Supreme Court of the Soviet Union and the Supreme Court of the Russian Republic have indicated that 'preventing a defendant who does not have a lawyer from defending himself at the trial is a grave violation of the right of the defendant to receive defence and it serves as an unconditional ground for an obligatory repeal of the verdict' (Article 345 of the Code of Civil Procedure of the RSFSR). This very condition was especially noted by the Decree No. 5 of the Plenary Session of the Supreme Court of the USSR on 16 June 1978, i.e. only one month before the beginning of Anatoly's trial. It was as if his trial was conducted in order to show that there were written laws and unwritten laws and that he, Shcharansky, was tried according to the unwritten ones.'

Ida Milgrom also pointed out that she had received no answer to her requests to start an appeal against the verdict. All those to whom she had written in connection with an appeal 'preferred to remain silent'. Her letter continued: 'One asks why was such a number of grave violations of the law necessary? Who needed it? Justice? Then it is not justice, but judicial reprisal! The State? But was not the law created in order to protect the interests of the citizens and thus to protect the interests of the State? My son is innocent! Both the interrogators and the prosecutors and the judges know that. An innocent man cannot be convicted other than by violating the law and this is why there were so many violations of the law in this unjust case. I repeat: my son is innocent! He is a victim of a political game, a political hostage. At the same time, he is kept in prison – for nothing!'

On the day of his mother's letter, 15 March 1980, Shcharansky was transferred, having spent three years in prison, to labour camp at Perm, for the second, ten-year phase of his sentence. By law, Ida Milgrom was now entitled to spend three days with him in the labour-camp Zone. The visit took place in April. Half of Moscow's refuseniks had clubbed together in order to enable her to take him the choicest delicacies. As soon as she was back in Moscow, Ida Milgrom sent an account of it to Avital:

My dear Natashenka,

Four of us went there together – I, Lyonya, Andrei and Vitya Ladyzhensky [family friends]. We were loaded to overflowing, since we had counted upon a three-day meeting. And, despite past experience, we hoped to give Tolya a parcel. The way was long, unknown, languishing. However, owing to the care of the friends who were attending me, the journey by train turned out to be rather comfortable. We were in a separate compartment, had various food, and well-chosen books (by the by, Andrei and Vitya read them aloud in turn). We were laughing, joking, we looked forward to a prolonged meeting, and because of this, the two nights and a day which we spent in the train were not tiresome at all. On the contrary, the physical and moral strain, which we had felt during the process of preparations for the trip ceased, and I even felt myself ready for any of the surprises you, darling, warned me about during our telephone talk before this journey (from Edik [Kuznetsov]'s experience – do you remember? – that the date can be cancelled at the last moment).

On April 25, at twelve o'clock Moscow time (two o'clock Ural time) we detrained at Chusovskaya station. From there we had to go further, but had no idea by what transport, or when it would be possible. We were lucky, since we managed to come to an agreement with a driver, got into his car and set out. We weren't certain if we would reach our final destination in this car

– the road was so bad: mud, pits and bumps – and, indeed, once
we were finally in the area, we found that it was absolutely
impassable by car. We got out, paid the driver and stood at the
crossroads, surrounded with our trunks, bags, rucksacks and
coats. But fortune smiled upon us again. The driver of a lorry
which was passing by promised to unload his lorry somewhere
and come back afterwards and take us to the ultimate end: the
'35th Zone'.

We waited anxiously for him, but not in vain: he came back.
My friends lifted me up (no light burden it was!) seated me into
the cab, put our things into the back and climbed into the back
themselves, and the heavy lorry took us on, negotiating the
rough road. The sombre views I watched through the dirty
windscreen of the cab, impassable mud under the heavy lorry's
wheels and the compassionate glances of the driver, who did
not dare, obviously, to ask me a certain question, were all
causing the feeling of inner anxiety. As we approached the
labour-camp Zone, my heart started sinking and, as if it had
stopped beating, suddenly started to beat quickly. I was
frightened. If I am able to reach the place, will I have time to
look at him?

We arrived at the place, finally climbed out of the lorry.
Lyonya went to clear up the situation while the other three of
us waited in impatient expectation among our knapsacks.
Somebody came and looked over us. Somebody asked us if we
had come for a specific visit. Somebody looked smilingly at us.
Somebody else cast scornful glances at us. It was hard for me, so
much so that finally the expectation turned out so unbearable
for me that after thirty or forty minutes I left my two friends to
watch over our 'load' and went myself towards the door of the
building behind which Lyonya had disappeared.

I met Lyonya in the corridor. He was already on his way to
call me, after his visit to the head of the 'Institution'. Finally here
we are, in the study of the officer on duty and there I learnt,
from Lyonya's conversation with this man, that the visit will
take place! The burden fell down from my shoulders, everything around me suddenly became light and bright, and even
Lenin's glance, whose portrait was on the opposite wall,
became kind and tender. I joined animatedly in the conversation with the officer.

I was listening to some warning words, but my mind was
perceiving only one thing: I'll see Tolya. We'll be together

soon, now. But suddenly I heard that permission for the visit was given for one day only. I ran (!) from the study and directed my way to the Chief's office. I managed with difficulty to 'subdue' the secretary, and even from the threshold I started to prove my right for a three-day visit. Finally, I was begging the Chief, appealing to his filial and paternal feelings. I demanded again, if not a three-day visit, then a two-day visit at least.

But I realised, felt already, that he, the Chief of the Institution, was restricted, unfree himself! Not lifting up his eyes, not looking at me, he promised me that he would return to this question tomorrow. And at the same time he ordered the Captain who was present there to allow the visit for one day.

Lyonya came in. We kept on repeating again and again some words about 'rights', insisting upon something, demanding, begging. But our applications were already in the Captain's hands and we left the Chief's, Major Osin's, study.

The room for the visit had been prepared. Andrei and Vitya helped bring our belongings to the building where the visit had to take place. Afterwards they had to go back to Chusovskaya station, where there was some kind of hotel, as it was impossible for them to stay for the night inside the Zone.

We agreed that if the length of the visit is prolonged, they will depart (I was still not losing the hope!) and if the visit is not to be prolonged, they will come to the Zone by 4 o'clock on the next day. We said goodbye to each other. They left and we stayed, to wait for a signal. We waited for a long time, looked around and were very nervous. We wished to imagine where we would be called to, where Tolya would come from. The picture around us was so unattractive. There were very few people. Representatives of administration, of both sexes, appeared from time to time. A prisoner approached us and flung a remark at us: 'The room is being prepared for you,' lit a cigarette and pocketed a pack of cigarettes which Lyonya offered him. He left. And we were still waiting.

We came into the 'Zone' at 4.15. At 6.45 we were led to the room where the visit had to take place. The preparations for the meeting continued until 7.15. A 'he' was 'working' with Lyonya, a 'she' – with me. [Ida Milgrom and Leonid were being thoroughly searched.] Then there was the checking of what we had brought with us, a thorough examination of all the products both from the inside and outside. When everything was examined and sorted out we were ordered to 'vanish' from the sphere of vision. Tolya had been led to us under escort. He was also searched beforehand, and his clothes were changed completely. We could meet him only after he had been brought beyond the iron door which led to the visiting room. The distance from this iron door to the door of the kitchen where we were 'sheltering' was about two metres. I got over this distance in one jump, before the fixed time, and hugged Tolya in my arms in the presence of all three escorts. I set him free only after he, making himself free of my embraces, said calmly: 'Mama, we have three days ahead, we shall have enough time to kiss each other and to talk to each other.'

And here it began! On learning that the visit was allowed for one day only, he became indignant, reproached us with having agreed to it and expressed his protest to the Captain in a very sharp form. It was, he declared, an unprecedented case. The three-day visit is due after three years of imprisonment. And the Chief of the Institution had let us know beforehand that if we came before April 27 then the visit would be three days long, without fail, etc.

Tolya was so anxious, and so angry with us, that I felt myself a criminal and lost my head absolutely. I started to soothe him, telling him that perhaps tomorrow we'll get the permission for one day more, that the Chief had promised me. Tolya gave a laugh and said: 'Tomorrow you'll not manage to find here anybody from the administration. It is all over, one cannot count upon that. Have no doubts.' It happened exactly as he said.

The escorts left, the latticed iron doors closed with a bang, the iron bar of the outer padlock clicked and we remained, the three of us, in the locked 'apartment' consisting of two small rooms, with two beds and bedding, a small table and ashtray in each room: a big kitchen with an electric kitchen-range, a sideboard filled with kitchen utensils, dishes and plates, and a small refrigerator, a table, and three or four stools. There was also a separate lavatory with all necessary utensils: buckets, rags and brooms.

We could make contact with the outer world through the soldier on duty (either a Tatar or Bashkir). His name was Alik. He was handing me my own sleeping pills and powders, bringing bread from a stall and kept on answering my questions concerning the whereabouts of the Chief or officers: 'Nobody is here.' It was a lie. Both the Chief and the officer-on-duty were there.

After no more than two or three minutes of the first 'shock' connected with news about the visit's shortening, Tolenka, addressing me and Lyonya, said: 'It is all over now, no illusions. We shall not have more than one day. I know their "promises" only too well. Let us establish the strict order of our time. It is 7.25 now. There are 24 hours at our disposal. Sleep is cancelled. We'll keep awake during all these 24 hours and talk about ourselves, our friends, and above all inform me as minutely as you can about my Natulenka.'

The dishes and plates with the most varied of foods which we had brought with us were placed on the table: black and red caviar, vegetables – fresh spring onions, green cucumbers, fresh green parsley and fennel – everything for salad (even sunflower-seed oil in a small bottle, which Raya packed despite my objections), dried fruits, oranges, lemons, larded meat, meat croquettes, boiled chicken, grilled chicken, eggs, in order to cook his beloved omelette, juices, sweets, homemade pastry-strudel, which Raya baked specially for him, coffee, condensed milk, tea and a lot of other things.

Tolya looked at all this and said sadly: 'You see, they did not let me know beforehand about your visit, and I am full with balanda': the name which prisoners give to prison-food.

Our telegram informing him that we were coming on the 25th was not delivered to him.

The first turn to speak was given to Tolya. He wished to tell us the contents of the judgement, which he had learnt by heart. It took a lot of time and so, at Lyonya's suggestion, we decided to dwell on separate points, which seemed to be of the greatest importance.

Tolya then returned to the period before the trial. He told us that as soon as he found himself in the elevator on March 15, he realised by the nervousness of KGB men surrounding him that there would be no return. At the beginning he was taken to Moscow City Investigation Department. Investigator Galkin talked to him there. He confronted Tolya not as a person under investigation, but as a criminal, whose crime was already proved. He shouted and raged. Tolya snubbed him and thus put him even more beside himself.

On the next day Tolya was sent to Lefortovo. There his first confrontation was with the Chief of the prison, Petrenko, who

was removed shortly afterwards, and then with Povarenkov. I
know this fellow only too well and will remember him forever.
I think that in competition with the most frantic fascists, he
would be the winner.

Tolya imparted to us many interesting and bitter things
about the investigation period. He could not of course tell us
everything, because of the shortage of time. And we could not
remember everything he told us.

I hope very much that the hour will come when we, together,
will learn everything from him personally. And I hope too that
it will happen in our native land, in the circle of relatives and
friends, beloved and kind people.

I'll dwell on one interesting fact. We knew about it, partially,
and you did too, Natulenka. Gardner's book of problems in
mathematical logic suggested to Tolya an idea on the possibility
of playing 'games' with the investigation: there were some
problems in reflex logic in the book. These problems and his
studies of chess-game formalisation suggested this idea to him.

'If I sat with them at the chess-board I would win, undoubtedly. What are all my mathematics worth, if they can't help me
at this difficult time? I have to try.' And one day he started 'the
game'. Before each interrogation Tolya made a 'tree of aims' – a
'logic tree'. It gave him moral satisfaction and brought fruits at
the same time. Becoming certain that Shcharansky had some
contacts with the 'open air', the investigators began themselves
to tell him what was really going on in the 'open air'. It helped
Tolya not to wander in the dark, and to get, very often, the
relevant information, although with some delay. By the by,
eighteen investigators interrogated Tolya.

Tolya told us that the Investigators, driven to despair by his
unyielding, uncompromising stance and steadfastness, and
losing hope of breaking him morally, were giving orders to the
administration of the prison to put him to physical tortures –
and at once Tolya was put into a cold and damp punishment
cell, where streams of cold water were flowing down the walls.
At the beginning you feel a terrible cold there. In two to three
hours a strong fever begins, and towards the end of the
punishment period (eight to ten hours) convulsions of the
extremities start. Tolya's legs had been jerking up with such
force that it was impossible to hold them. Immediately after this
he was called to the interrogation. The Investigator expressed
to him most sympathetically his indignation at the prison

authorities. The Investigator assured Tolya that 'as soon as he learnt that Anatoly Borisovich was put into the punishment cell, he demanded to stop these disgraceful things immediately,' etc.

So, playing hypocrites and expressing their 'anger' with the prison authorities, the Investigators expected to achieve a 'co-operation', 'splitting', but they did not succeed. Each time, another Investigator started everything from the beginning, but Tolya continued his 'game'.

We were listening to Tolya very attentively and tried to feed him from time to time. As he was not hungry and we were frightened of overloading his stomach, we gave him only fruits and juices during the first hours. Lyonya was peeling oranges continuously and giving Tolya orange sections, or sugared lemon ones, and Tolya washed them down with juice.

Finally the moment came when Tolya asked for 'real food'. He could not decide for a long time what menu he would like to choose. At Raya's insistence we had taken two pieces of fresh meat with us in a special bag. I fried this meat for Tolenka, made a fresh salad, gave him a sandwich with black and red caviar for a titbit, poured him some juice and the splendid supper was ready.

But Tolya was consuming everything somewhat absent-mindedly, and Lyonya and I got the impression that he didn't notice any difference between the 'balanda' he had eaten some hours ago, and the delicatessen, which we were serving him in this unusual restaurant of the 35th Zone of Perm camps.

Tolya continuously interrupted his story, asking about those friends whose fate he greatly worried about. The Investigators had constantly speculated with their names, presenting them as 'exposers'.

We did not sit at the table for long. After a short while we sat down on a bed, and there, embracing each other, we talked, asked and answered questions, and looked at each other attentively.

Tolenka noticed that Lyonya had put on weight and that Mama had grown old but, in comparison with the impression he'd got during our meeting in Chistopol, I was looking better now, in his opinion.

We were recalling Papa, and Tolik was interested to know if it would be possible to take his remains to Israel. He told us that he often recalls Papa's marvellous tales about his childhood and his family, and he regretted that his father had not written down the details of this period.

Tolenka was angry with us that we do not inform him sufficiently about you, my dear. He wanted to know more than we know. He commended me for my initiative in retelling to him your letters to me. He asked me to keep up this practice. He also dreams about your future big family, as you do. He hopes and believes that both of you will be together. He realises that it could happen earlier, but in connection with the international situation one needs time, patience and will. The last one – will – both of you have and it gives you the strength.

'I regret nothing,' said Tolya, 'and if now, when I have the experience of the passed ordeal, I were to find myself in the same situation again, I would keep on struggling for the freedom of our people, for the right of each person to be free. But I am grieving for all of you, for you, Mama, and for my beloved, dear Natashenka. What a hard life fell to your lot!' He kept on returning to this very often.

Natashenka! My dear! I assured him that we are proud of him, that we are full of hopes for future happiness and that it gives us strength. And that despite all difficulties we are happy. It is true, isn't it, my dear girl? I was not lying to him – confirm this for me, and everything will be easier for me.

Staying at his side on the bed, I kept checking his pulse. He has cardiac arrhythmia and I am constantly worrying about it. He noticed what I was doing, smiled, kissed me and said that he does not feel arrhythmia at all. He never felt it, although he had it. At one time the doctors said that he has dynamic cardiac arrhythmia and it is impossible to cure it, but that it doesn't hinder living.

Tolenka told me, and several times repeated it, that the condition of his eyes is absolutely normal now, and he can work, read, write for many hours at a time. But now he needs more to breathe fresh air, to see the sun and the daylight. He walks after work (in the Zone), reads only newspapers for the time being, sees a film on Sunday, usually. He works as the pupil of a carpenter. Before our meeting he worked zealously, but now, in connection with the shortening of our visit, he will revise his attitude towards the work. He told us about his transportation from Chistopol to the camp, several interesting episodes, what preparations had taken place in the Zone before he arrived here (he was told about them afterwards), and a lot of other things. It is impossible to put them all in one letter.

I'll dwell now on the description of his appearance. He looks better in comparison with what we had seen in Chistopol. There was not that terrible paleness and heavy look. The bags under his eyes have diminished considerably, and the eyes' redness has vanished completely. But no, he is still unrecognisable! Even the oval of his face is changed. It is quite understandable. Before his arrest he weighed about 62–65 kilograms (his height is 159–160 centimetres, I can't recall precisely) – too much, obviously. Now, after he put on three kilograms in the camp, he weighs 51 kilograms. Before his deportation from Chistopol he weighed 48 kilograms. Naturally he has changed externally. His nose has become quite sharp, his cheeks sunken, his forehead wrinkled. And all this has affected the expression of his face. One can feel his ribs, he has no belly (and this fact makes him glad) and his general physical condition is fine. He kept on going to the mirror and discovered that he could not recognise himself from three weeks ago, so he has changed for the better. 'It is a pity the bags under the eyes did not vanish completely,' he told us.

All in all, his complexion is good and that is an extremely important and positive factor. Do you agree with me?

Our meeting was taking place under the slogan 'Let us make the most of our time!' And because of this everything we did, we did watching the alarm-clock.

Each thirty to forty minutes Tolenka announced 'so many hours and minutes have passed, and so many hours remain.'

Everything was going on in this way until seven o'clock in the evening of April 26. Our date had to be finished at 7.25 and these last minutes we spent looking each minute at the clock, to be certain that we still had twenty-five minutes more.

But suddenly we heard the clanging of iron – the iron doors and locks were opened – and heavy steps. The same people, the Captain, two escorts and Alik were standing in front of us. 'The visit is over,' we heard. 'Sorry,' objected Tolya. 'There are still twenty-five minutes at our disposal, leave us alone.'

The Captain showed us his watch: 7.25. And our alarm-clock was still showing 7.00. The clock had stopped and we had not even noticed it. It was useless to argue, our time was over. Tolya was taken away. Lyonya and I were looking at each other in embarrassment. Suddenly I remembered that we had not said goodbye to each other. Violating again the fixed prison orders, I

rushed to the barred iron doors and began to demand hysteri-
cally that they bring Tolya back, to give me the opportunity to
embrace him, to say goodbye to him.

Lyonya was soothing me, keeping me back, but I continued
screaming. Tolya was brought back. We embraced him, smiled
upon each other, and repeated again and again the same words:
'Be healthy, be healthy, see you soon!'

Tolya was taken away. We stood behind the iron partition
with our arms uplifted. Going away, he looked back, lifted up
his thin arm too, smiling his wide, kind smile, not taking his
kind, clever eyes off us.

He was taken away to the left, to captivity.

How long will it last? Shall I meet you again, my son, my
pain, my pride, my love? Shall I see you again? – these were my
thoughts at these moments.

After Tolya was taken away, we were kept there for no less
than half an hour. And again control, warnings. The Captain
told us that I can forward to Tolya through him the things we
had asked about in our application. I gave him the electric
shaving set, slippers, scarf and woollen socks. We had prepared
woollen underclothes also, but the Captain refused to take more
than four things. I passed him also two pictures of you and two
pictures of Boris Moyseevich in his coffin. Before we left, the
Captain warned us that these things will be counted as the parcel
which we could send him afterwards. I grieved, as we had
hoped to send him this parcel immediately after our returning.
Nevertheless, despite all warnings, we are planning to send him
a parcel at the end of the month. We want to put there three tins
of caviar, a track-suit and a light cap (Tolya asked us to send him
these things, except caviar). All the parcels which we had sent
Tolya earlier are rotting at the store-house. He will be able to
receive them only after he has been discharged.

I have already covered a lot of paper with writing, but did not
tell you even a small particle of what he asked me to tell you,
Natulenka (even when he was silent). He told me that even
during the most difficult minutes of his life, during all these
three years, he was not alone for a minute. You were with him
constantly. He demanded of me to give him a detailed account
of you, and I was helpless, since I do not know actually how are
you looking, what are you doing concretely, who are your
closest friends. Tolya had a lot of requests for me in connection
with you, my darling. I had to report to him on all his friends,

on all sorts of people I know and do not know. I had to give him the fullest information about you, my girl, and I came empty-handed. What could I tell him about his beloved wife?

One can learn by one's own mistakes and now, taking into account my mistakes, I am appealing to you and to everybody near you: do write me everything about my dear girl. Write me everything you see, feel and know! Friends! Do you hear me?

Natashenka! You must not feel so upset over the headlines of the articles which appeared in the press after our visit to Tolya. It is time to get accustomed to foreign correspondents' style. We heard here quite often things we had not told them, and we have stopped reacting painfully to such misunderstandings. In any case, we think that their wording is even better for our reality here than the account we gave ourselves.

And I wish to tell you that never ever any one of us thought that you and the friends surrounding you struggle for Tolya insufficiently. We are certain that you are doing even impossible things, that all your life is directed to saving Tolya. We believe it, we are sure of it. And Tolya is sure also that your efforts, and the goodwill of many people, will give him his freedom back. Tolya realises perfectly that events on a world-scale are affecting his term and he is ready to wait. He is optimistic, cheerful and full of hopes, as well as we are.

God will help us to meet each other in Jerusalem as soon as possible.

Many kisses, take care of yourself, my dear. Your Tolya begs you to do it.

                                        Ida Petrovna

26

Suffering and Punishment

While he was in labour camp at Perm, Shcharansky suffered as much as, if not more than, he had in prison. The steel workshop in which he worked as a welder was a place of noise and heat and blinding light. His dizziness, severe headaches and blurred vision persisted: his mother and brother had again been shocked by his appearance during their visit of 5 September 1980.

On 23 September 1980 Shcharansky collapsed in the steel workshop and was taken to the prison hospital. Three days later, while still feeling dizzy, and with his eyes still painful, he was sent back to his welding. Then, on 18 October 1980, without explanation, he was taken from the steel workshop to a place of work so dangerous that every prisoner tried to avoid it: to fix and strengthen the barbed wire around the camp. 'At any minute', a friend of his later commented, 'you can be shot and then it will be said you were "shot while attempting to escape". As it is well known beforehand that political prisoners will refuse such a task, it means that the Camp Commandant had received an order to organise a provocation against Tolya.'

Refusing to work on the wire, Shcharansky was sentenced to fifteen days' solitary confinement in the labour-camp prison.

On 18 November 1980, Shcharansky was ordered to report to a new job, cleaning toilets, a job which meant an improvement in his daily food rations. But he again refused to report to work, arguing, as was indeed the case, that an elderly prisoner, who relied on this job for the few extra rations it merited, would be dismissed.

Once more, his refusal to work led to a fifteen-day sentence in solitary confinement.

On 3 December 1980, at the beginning of the Jewish festival of Chanukkah, and just out of the punishment cell, Shcharansky lit the first of the traditional Chanukkah candles, having made them himself out of little pieces of wax. This small act of memorial greatly agitated the guards who ordered him to put out the candles immediately. He refused, on the grounds that it was his duty and privilege as a Jew to perform the customs of his people. Again he was sent to the punishment cell. In addition, a book of Psalms, a present from Avital, and his Jewish calendar were confiscated. After repeated requests that these items be returned, he was promised that he would get them back. A short time later, he was informed that his case had been discussed with the KGB and orders had been issued not to return his belongings.

Following this incident, Shcharansky was characterised 'a disciplinary problem' and sentenced to six months in the camp prison, where conditions were considerably harder than in the camp. There, he had considerable trouble with his back, and also hurt his hand.

As details of Shcharansky's move to the camp prison reached Avital in Jerusalem, she redoubled her already substantial efforts to secure his release, travelling to Madrid for yet another review meeting of the Helsinki Agreement, and to the United States.

Shcharansky began his six-month sentence in the labour-camp prison on 13 January 1981, a week before his thirty-third birthday. Throughout his confinement in this inner prison, he continued to demand his book of Psalms, writing to the authorities to point out that there was no Soviet law laying down conditions for having prayer books. He was informed in reply that 'Soviet Russia is really at war against religion' and that his punishment was in line with this.

Replying, Shcharansky pointed out that according to Soviet law, each individual has freedom of religion and freedom of conviction. He began to strike in protest, and was sentenced to fifteen days in the punishment cell in addition to the six months in the inner prison. When he finished his fifteen days, he again demanded that his book of Psalms be returned to him, and refused to work until he received it. In reprisal, he was thrown into isolation for another fifteen days.

In all, Shcharansky spent 185 days in a punishment cell, 75 of them consecutively. During this period, he suffered from near starvation; in one incident, he was barely able to inform a fellow prisoner that he was on the verge of collapse before he lost consciousness. Since food was provided only every other day in the punishment cell, and this was not a food day, Shcharansky was given only an injection to sustain him, but no additional food. After four days in this condition, he was taken to the camp hospital and received emergency treatment.

Shcharansky stayed in the prison hospital for thirty-three days. He was then returned directly to the punishment cell. From there he had to go to an 'open' trial, at which there were a Judge, a Prosecutor, two prosecution witnesses and the defendant.

The prison trial lasted for five minutes. Two charges were levelled against him: that he had 'not yet confessed' to the espionage charges of his trial three years earlier, which indicated 'poor education', and that he had been a 'bad influence' on other prisoners in the camp.

Shcharansky, forced to act once more in his own defence, replied that it was indeed true that he had never pleaded guilty to the accusations for which he was being punished. As to being a bad influence on other prisoners, this he said was impossible, as most of his time in the camp had been spent in solitary confinement.

The trial had lasted five minutes. Shcharansky was sentenced to be sent back to Chistopol prison for a prison term of three years. Taken from labour camp in January 1981, he then returned to Chistopol, where, on arrival, he was sentenced to two months in a punishment cell, for the 'crime' of having been sent back to prison.

From his cell at Chistopol, Shcharansky persevered in his efforts to write a letter to his mother. Dated 4 February 1981, it read:

My dear Mama – Shalom,   With God's help

This is my third attempt to write you a letter; I want to hope that it will be more successful than the two previous attempts. They have just announced to me that my second letter to you has been confiscated. It was short compared to the first letter, which was about twenty-five pages long; but as you see its fate was the same. I can very easily imagine your anxiety due to my prolonged silence, so therefore do not be surprised that this letter is so short, I just want to be sure that it will arrive.

I will limit myself to only the most concrete information. Again, I have to sadden my mother, that from now you will not receive two letters a month from me, as was the case up till now. From now on it will be the opposite – one letter every two months. It will remain so for at least six months, so this letter today will be for both January and February.

In my effort to compensate you for the limitations imposed on me, I wrote twenty-five pages in my first letter, which to my sorrow did not arrive. Now I will again avert to another sad subject – the letters that I receive from you. Last month ten letters out of fourteen were confiscated, four letters from you, Mama, and two additional telegrams wishing me a Happy Birthday.

In your last letter you wrote about it being a year after Papa's passing away. How did you solve the problem about a stone on Papa's grave? As you see, your flow of letters has really dried up. Mama, you are waiting in vain for a meeting in the spring; all the meetings for 1981 have been cancelled. In December I sent you only one letter; a second letter to Avital I did not manage to send. It is a shame, since I will not have another opportunity like that in the near future.

Mama, as you have probably already noticed, I only refer to you, and not to other relations or friends, not even to Avital. This is because they warned me that I must only refer to the person to whom the letter is addressed.

In addition to this I have understood that according to the law the use of humour is also undesirable. It is possible that in this letter I appear sadder than I really am. In reality, in spite of the perversity of my fate, I certainly do not feel bad. For this there are two reasons. The first, my health is all right, the hand has healed, the back does not worry me any more, and I have no more headaches.

In the mornings I exercise intensively. The second reason is that now I have better conditions for reading and studying. There is reading material, I receive journals and I have found something interesting in philosophy.

I promise you, Mama, that letters like this, so short and dry won't happen again. I just decided that, now, the important thing is that you should know that I am alive and well.

March is already approaching and then I will try to write at greater length. With Avital there will not now be communication by letter. I hope you will understand me correctly. I do not ask after anybody and I do not tell you about anybody (so there will not be even the slightest clue). I do not even send my regards to anybody.

Yours,
Natan

Shcharansky also wrote a letter, in March 1981, to Leonid

Brezhnev, telling the Soviet leader that because, according to a decision of the 26th Congress of the Communist Party that February, religion was allowed in the Soviet Union, he wanted his book of Psalms returned.

In his letter to Brezhnev, Shcharansky described himself as a member of the Helsinki Watchdog group. For this reason, his letter was confiscated by the prison authorities, who told him that no such group existed. Shcharansky replied that as he was tried and punished for belonging to this very group, it must therefore exist.

On 19 February 1981 Iosif Mendelevich had arrived in Jerusalem, released after ten years of his twelve-year sentence. The excitement in Israel was intense: as if a sealed gate had been miraculously opened. A man who had been in the same prison as Shcharansky was in the Land of Israel.

The account which Mendelevich gave of conditions at Vladimir and Chistopol made it clear that Shcharansky was being held in conditions of the utmost severity. After describing the meagre food ration and its poor quality, and the total isolation, Mendelevich declared: 'One's body is constantly aching, one feels completely broken.' He added: 'I felt then that if I continued to follow this pattern, I would deteriorate completely, and lose my humanity entirely. I had to summon up all my spiritual powers to struggle against all the currents that were attempting to overpower me, to cause me to sink into the mire.'

Edward Kuznetsov, one of the two Leningrad Trial prisoners who had originally been sentenced to death but were later given prison sentences, had also been released. On 20 March 1981, in an article in the *Jerusalem Post*, he wrote about Shcharansky. 'Even Western citizens,' he pointed out, 'if they are in trouble with the KGB even over some trifle, will instantly weaken in spirit; confessions to fantastically devious crimes, published in the Soviet press, radiate despair and fear. All the more so with Soviet citizens. But Anatoly Shcharansky has carried himself with amazing courage.' Although the espionage charges against him were 'clearly trumped up', Kuznetsov added, 'Shcharansky could have played along with the prosecution in order to lighten his inevitable punishment. This he refused to do: he refused to lie in order to please the KGB, for, apart from anything else, he did not want to hurt a movement of which he had been a part.'

The 'struggle to free Shcharansky', Kuznetsov wrote:

is not just a struggle for the freedom of one more political prisoner (tomorrow they will arrest a hundred, a thousand, as many as it takes, in his stead, and there will not be enough hard currency around to ransom them all).

Primarily, it is a struggle to have the very concept of political prisoners eliminated forever.

★   ★   ★

On 28 May 1981, as part of her unceasing quest to help her husband, Avital Shcharansky met President Reagan in the White House. With her was Iosif Mendelevich. Avital's visit was part of a journey which she was carrying out with the help of the National Conference on Soviet Jewry to attract public and government attention to her husband's plight. Had the meeting with Reagan made her more hopeful? she was asked. 'Yes,' she replied.

Throughout the Soviet Union the trials of Jewish activists continued. On 26 May 1981 Vladimir Kislik had been sentenced to three years in labour camp. Five and a half months later, on 13 November 1981, Alexander Paritsky, a teacher of Jewish studies to refuseniks in Kharkov, was also sentenced to three years in labour camp.

In August 1981 Shcharansky was transferred from the punishment cells at Chistopol to the ordinary cells. There he was put to work knitting shopping bags: his quota was one bag an hour. If he were to fulfil his quota, he would receive two roubles a month to spend at the prison canteen to supplement his rations. But his health was not good enough to keep up such a rate of work; he could manage only one bag every four hours.

From May to August 1981, Ida Milgrom received no letter from her son. In September, she was afraid he had died in a punishment cell. That same month she received a letter from him. He had frequently been in solitary confinement. 'For a long time', he told her, 'my only contact with living beings has been with a bird on the window-sill and the insects in my cell.'

On 1 November 1981, in New York City, a flight of steps opposite the United Nations building was named the 'Shcharansky Steps' at a ceremony sponsored by the Greater New York Conference on Soviet Jewry, the Student Struggle for Soviet Jewry, and the Mayor of New York, Edward Koch.

That winter, Ida Milgrom was allowed her second visit to her son in three years. She was seventy-four years old. Together with

Leonid, she made the long journey, including a five-hour walk along a frozen river. She reached the prison on 4 January 1982. There, she and Leonid were received by the Prison Commandant, Captain Romanov, who told them that the meeting with Shcharansky which was due that day had been cancelled because he had refused to end a hunger strike. Romanov added that he had seen Shcharansky on the previous day, when he had tried to convince him to stop his hunger strike, but Shcharansky had said that as long as he was prevented from having contact with the outside world, he would not stop. Ida Milgrom was informed that her son was being force-fed every three days. She said she would not leave Chistopol until she was allowed to see him. But her tenacity was in vain; permission to see him was refused. 'The repression is continuing,' she wrote on January 7, after her return to Moscow, 'the humiliation is growing. They want to break my son physically and morally.' She went on to ask, in a desperate plea: 'Is there any way that this world can prevent the destruction of an innocent victim of arbitrary cruelty?'

The world to which Ida Milgrom appealed had no answer. Protest marches, diplomatic encounters, letters to the newspapers, the skill of intermediaries: all failed. Yet the campaigns, the efforts and the struggle continued throughout the Western world.

On 12 April 1982 Ida Milgrom returned to Chistopol. Once more she was forbidden to see her son. Once more she protested to the Prison Commandant, not only that she could not see her son, but that she had received neither the January nor February letters which all prisoners are allowed to write. These two letters, Romanov told her, had been confiscated 'and destroyed by the censors' because they contained 'secret information', but when her son had been 'given the opportunity' to change the content of his February letter in order to meet the censorship requirements of the prison, he had refused to do so, and, for this, was being punished. He was also being punished for failing to complete his daily work task of making eight potato sacks. He had only managed to make a single sack. For these offences, he had been given three months' solitary confinement, of which he still had a month and a half to serve.

Knowing of her son's previous ill-health due to prison conditions, Ida Milgrom asked the Commandant whether the failure to complete the potato sacks might not have been as a result of his continued deteriorating health. The prison officials present denied this, telling her: 'He is healthy.'

On 15 April 1982 Ida Milgrom went to Kazan, where she met the regional Director of the Administration of Prisons. Again she asked about her son's condition, and again was given the same information: he was in solitary confinement, and he was well.

Ida Milgrom was granted an interview in Moscow on 24 May 1982 with Colonel Sokolov, the assistant to the Director of the Central Organisation of Soviet Prisons. At this meeting she demanded the 'normalisation of correspondence' and the right of 'a visit by relatives'. She was told that her son had not been 'deprived of a visit'. She therefore returned yet again to Chistopol, on 5 July 1982, but once more she was refused permission to see her son. This July meeting, she was told, 'had been cancelled in January'.

'The conditions of my son's imprisonment', Ida Milgrom wrote to the Minister for Internal Affairs, General Shchelekhov, at the beginning of August 1982, 'are accompanied by incessant cruelty and never-ending torture. The cutting of all contacts for Anatoly with the outside world is the very latest of these tortures. I ask you, sir, is my son still alive?'

27

Hunger Strike

The holiest day in the Jewish calendar, the Day of Atonement, fell in 1982 on September 27. That day, Shcharansky sent a telegram to his mother, informing her that he had begun a hunger strike at Chistopol prison in protest against not being allowed to send or to receive his statutory monthly letters. As soon as the news was known in the West, thirty former Prisoners of Zion appealed from Jerusalem to 'people of goodwill' throughout the world 'to rise up as one soul and protest'. Shcharansky's life work 'is of paramount importance to us, because we love him as a close friend and as a human being'. Among the signatures were Ruth Alexandrovich, Mark Dymshits, Hillel Butman, Iosif Mendelevich and Edward Kuznetsov, some of the first prisoners of the 1970s; and also Sender Levinson, Alexander Silnitsky, Iosif Mishener, Yakov Vinarov, Anatoly Malkin, Boris Tsitlionok, Yakov Suslensky and Lev Roitburd, for each of whom Shcharansky had, in the past, been an outspoken champion.

In Moscow, Ida Milgrom sent a telegram of protest on 27 September 1982 to the head of the Central Organisation of Soviet Prisons; and on the following day she went to see him. On the evening of September 30, she described the meeting to Avital when they spoke on the telephone. These were Ida Milgrom's words:

> Yesterday I was at the GUITU [the Central Organisation of Soviet Prisons]. I requested a meeting with Sokolov but was told that he would be on holiday until after the November holidays. I could meet with a less senior official.
>
> In the presence of two GUITU officials, Kazantsev and Bychkov, I made a declaration, accusing this department, holding them responsible for all that has happened and may happen. They had continuously failed to respond to my

constant appeals over the past ten months.

I charged them with having tortured me and Anatoly in prison over the past ten months, because for ten months they have blocked all correspondence between us by withholding Anatoly's letters.

I asked them to form a special commission that would go to the prison, talk to Anatoly and prison officials, to find out why they withhold his letters.

Not one of their answers to me was to the point. Bychkov kept repeating the same things: 'Why is it that other prisoners are working? They do not disobey the prison regime, they even earn money and send it to their mothers – your son systematically violates the regime.'

I answered: 'I am at present not interested in other prisoners, but in my son. Until now, I was not even interested in why you are punishing my son. I pose one question to you – why have you illegally withheld his letters? Show me in writing where it is stated that it is legal to deprive one of one's right to correspondence with relatives for violating the regime.'

Bychkov was silent.

I said: 'Your silence supports my claim that this is not legal. I wish to issue a protest and demand not a bureaucratic answer but an objective investigation.'

Again he talked about violating the regime.

I said: 'My son was in a terrible physical state when he started this hunger strike. Now he is deteriorating physically, and this is only because you have driven him to it. It is clear that this can only lead to catastrophe, and you will be guilty.'

Kazantsev replied: 'He will not achieve anything by this strike. Nothing will change. And as to what you say about him dying, he will not die because we have started to force-feed him.'

The officials then spoke of how Shcharansky had violated the camp rules. Ida Milgrom stated that she was 'not interested' in that. She then asked them: 'I want to know why my son is deprived of correspondence, but I can see that I will not receive a decent answer from this office.' Receiving no reply, she demanded confirmation that Shcharansky was indeed holding a hunger strike. Her report of the conversation continued:

Kazantsev then asked: 'Generally speaking, how do you know that he has started a hunger strike?'

Ida Milgrom: 'That is my business. And tell me, Mr Kazantsev, what answer can you give me as to why I have not yet
received an answer to a telegram which I sent to your Ministry
of Internal Affairs on 27 September 1982?'

After this, Ida Milgrom told Avital, she felt the meeting had not
been successful and left the office.

As Ida Milgrom fought to see, and to save, her son, the Moscow
Helsinki Watchdog group issued its final report, 'Document 195'.
Signed by the last three members of the group, Professor Meiman,
Elena Bonner and Sofia Kalistratova, it pointed out that sixteen
members of the group were in labour camp or internal exile, among
them their founder, Yury Orlov, and two of the representatives of
the Jewish emigration movement, Shcharansky and Slepak. 'In
these circumstances', the report concluded, 'the group cannot fulfil
the duties it assumed, and under the pressure of the authorities is
obliged to terminate its work.'

Concern for Shcharansky was growing. On 31 October 1982 a
letter was published in the Western press from Andrei Sakharov,
written from his place of internal exile at Gorky. Addressed to Pope
John Paul II, to the French President François Mitterand and to the
Italian Communist Party leader Enrico Berlinguer, it urged all
three men 'to help save the life of Anatoly Shcharansky'. That same
week, the President of Italy, Sandro Pertini, sent a letter to Leonid
Brezhnev on Shcharansky's behalf.

Shcharansky remained on hunger strike throughout October,
November and December 1982. He continued to be refused
permission to write to his mother, or to receive visits from her as
laid down in the prison regulations. 'One can only hope that the
Soviets will relent,' wrote the *Wall Street Journal* on 11 October
1982, 'and Mr Shcharansky will be saved. But what can be said
about the leadership of a country that uses such cruel methods to
keep people from leaving?'

Avi Weiss, an American Rabbi active in the campaign for
Shcharansky's release, later commented that it was during
Shcharansky's hunger strike that people in the West began to
identify more widely with his struggle. It 'struck the imagination of
Jews and non-Jews all over the world,' he said. 'People began to ask
themselves: "Didn't I, in the Western world, who had the opportunity to protest, also have a duty to speak out?"'

During a protest meeting in Stockholm, Avital Shcharansky had put herself inside a cage. Weiss later recalled 'the impact on American opinion of these physically separated yet twin souls who were obviously so much together.'

On 19 November 1982 Ida Milgrom returned to Chistopol, but she was once again refused permission to see her son. For ten days she remained there, offering, if she were allowed to see him, to persuade him to end his hunger strike. Her offer was rejected. No letters were to be allowed, and the hunger strike could go on.

Shcharansky's hunger strike showed the world how determined he was, and how strong. Seeing this, the campaign on his behalf gathered a new momentum. In London, the Foreign Office summoned the Soviet Ambassador in order to express the British Government's displeasure. In Holland, to which Avital made several visits, the Dutch Parliament treated his case as seriously as if he had been a Dutch national. As a result of public concern in France, even the French Communist Party leader, Georges Marchais, wrote a letter of protest on his behalf, one of hundreds of such appeals from statesmen, scientists, writers and academics.

Enormous pressure from people of goodwill, and large protest demonstrations, showed the extent of public concern. In the *International Herald Tribune*, Anthony Lewis, addressing himself to Brezhnev's successor, Yury Andropov, warned that if Shcharansky were to die in prison, 'the consequences for Soviet–US relations would be severe', because even those Americans 'who think superpower understandings are urgent would despair of the chance for useful negotiation with such a government'. The 'converse', Lewis wrote, was also true: 'A Soviet decision to release Mr Shcharansky would be a dramatic sign that the new leadership is pragmatic and wants to do diplomatic business.'

To counter these protests and appeals, Soviet broadcasts, newspaper articles and books gave an uncompromising picture of Shcharansky's guilt. 'It was proved in court', wrote Avtandil Rukhadze in his booklet *Jews in the USSR* at the end of 1982, 'that Anatoly Shcharansky and his accomplices sought to undermine the defence capacity of the USSR.' All Prisoners of Zion, Rukhadze concluded, 'the moment they lose their propaganda halo and appear in their true colours, are swindlers, embezzlers, extortionists, bribe-takers, profiteers, intriguers, common and state criminals. These people have nothing in common with the overwhelming majority of Soviet Jews who are honest workers and patriots.'

On 29 November 1982 Shcharansky was nominated for the

Nobel Peace Prize by a California Congresswoman, Barbara
Boxer. A month later, on December 30, the distinguished physicist
Edward Teller wrote in the *Christian Science Monitor*: 'Andropov's
decision regarding Anatoly Shcharansky could become a most
important first signal.' He went on to explain: 'As long as
Shcharansky remains imprisoned, he serves as an example of the
absence of freedom and dignity inside the Soviet system. As a
martyr, he has the greatest possible influence throughout the
world. There can be little doubt that free people everywhere would
be grateful for the release of this exceptional man of courage.'
    Ida Milgrom now returned yet again to Chistopol. But on 14
January 1983 the Prison Commandant refused to allow her to meet
her son. During this conversation, a KGB officer by the name of
Galkin was present. He told Ida Milgrom: 'Try to re-establish
contact, by all means send a letter to Anatoly through us and you
will get an answer.' Galkin and the Commandant suggested that the
letter include a request from Ida Milgrom for an end to the hunger
strike. Moreover, they told her, as soon as he stopped his hunger
strike, correspondence would be re-established.
    Ida Milgrom wrote her son a letter, setting out in detail how
'everybody in the whole world' was worried about him, and
fighting for his release. Galkin and the Commandant refused to
accept this letter. Ida Milgrom then wrote a very short second letter
in which she expressed her concern about his health and hoped to
re-establish contact with him.
    Two hours later the prison authorities brought Ida Milgrom a
letter from her son. There were only nineteen lines to the letter, six
of which were crossed out by Galkin in front of Ida Milgrom. She
refused to accept this letter and decided to leave. They managed to
convince her, however, that if she read the letter nothing would
change, that 'nothing bad would happen'. In the first uncensored
section of the letter, Shcharansky began:

> Dear Mamochka,
>
>   I know how much anxiety and pain you and Natulya have
> had over the past year, and it was because of my concern for
> your peace of mind that I took this extreme step. If I receive
> confirmation that you got my note, I'll end this hunger strike.

The next five and a half lines of Shcharansky's letter were crossed
out by Galkin. In what remained of the letter he wrote that his

health had become much worse, and obliquely stated that he required immediate hospitalisation. 'My condition', he wrote, 'is a little worse than it was in September 1981 but I hope that it will improve as it did then.' That was the occasion when, after being in a punishment cell for 185 days, he had been found unconscious on the floor and then kept in hospital for 33 days.

The Prison Commandant and the KGB representative then demanded that Ida Milgrom send her son confirmation that she had received his note. She replied that as a third of it had been crossed out she could not tell her son that she had received it. The Commandant and Galkin discussed Ida Milgrom's answer for two hours, after which she agreed to write a short message to her son to say that she hoped 'that contact would be re-established'. She then went to the city of Kazan, where, on 17 January 1983, she talked with the head of the Medical Department of the Ministry of Internal Affairs of the Tatar Republic. Her son was in a critical condition, she said, and she went on to demand his immediate hospitalisation. The head of the medical administration told her, however, that Shcharansky was continuing his hunger strike, and for this reason no instructions for hospitalisation could be given. Ida Milgrom returned to Moscow.

Shcharansky had in fact stopped his hunger strike on 14 January 1983, after 110 days, and on the very day his mother was at Chistopol talking to the Prison Commandant. She returned to Moscow, however, not knowing that this was so: another cruel device by the authorities to make her suffer.

Thursday, 20 January 1983, was Shcharansky's thirty-fifth birthday. 'A decision by the new Soviet leadership to release your husband and allow him to join you in Israel', the British Prime Minister, Margaret Thatcher, wrote to Avital, 'would be not only a humanitarian gesture, but also a step towards better East–West relations. I earnestly hope that they will now take this step.' Yitzhak Navon, the President of Israel, who was then in New York, appealed directly to the Secretary-General of the United Nations, Perez d'Cuellar, to intervene with the Soviet authorities to allow Shcharansky 'at least to receive mail and visits from relatives'. This, Navon added, was 'a simple humanitarian request with no political implications'. D'Cuellar promised to 'do his best'.

Many Western statesmen and politicians protested on Shcharansky's behalf. Avital Shcharansky, and many leading campaigners for Soviet Jewry, were in Madrid for the Helsinki

Final Act review conference which had been in session since 1981.
As if in answer to them, on 21 January 1983, Andropov sent a
personal message to the French Communist leader, Georges
Marchais. Shcharansky was no longer on hunger strike, Andropov
reported, his health was 'satisfactory' and his life 'is not in danger'.

In his letter to Marchais, Andropov explained that Soviet law did
not 'exclude the possibility of reducing the punishment following
an appeal', but such a possibility would depend upon 'the behaviour
of the accused', and was, he warned, 'not helped by a vociferous
campaign of pressure from outside. On the contrary, it is hindered.'

On 23 January 1983, in San Francisco, an International Tribunal
of Inquiry was called 'to inquire into the imprisonment of Anatoly
Shcharansky and his mistreatment by the Soviet Government'. The
case for Shcharansky was presented by Professor Alan Dershowitz
and Professor Irwin Cotler. In its conclusion, the Tribunal found
'unimpeachable evidence of Mr Shcharansky's innocence',
evidence, it said, 'which should be shared with the world'.

On the following day, Granada television showed another film
about Shcharansky, entitled 'A Difficult Prisoner', during which
Iosif Mendelevich recalled, of his brief meetings with Shcharansky
in prison: 'He was yellow with the yellowness of an old prisoner.
When he spoke he was shaking with an excitement which was real
physical exhaustion.'

On 4 February 1983, Shcharansky's mother was summoned to
the KGB headquarters and told that the Soviet Union was being
'damaged' by the international outcry over her son. At the same
time, she was told, her son was 'well', and she should cease to
agitate herself and the world over his condition. She was then
seventy-five years old.

Shcharansky was still not allowed to see any members of his
family. But the Soviet authorities did give way, as they had not
done hitherto, by allowing him to correspond with his mother.

★   ★   ★

On 7 February 1983 Shcharansky was allowed to write his first
letter since November 1981. It read:

My dear ones,
    I've just learned that I've been allowed to write a new letter to
replace the confiscated one written in January. In the previous

letter I wrote in detail about my health during the first ten days
after having ended my hunger strike. So I'm writing without
delay because I can imagine how anxious Mama and Natasha
are to get news. I'll try to be brief; in this way the letter has
better chances of reaching you.

First, Mama, I'm going to calm you. I ceased the hunger
strike as I promised you on the evening of January 14 after
having received your second note. Second, almost all my
troubles which I mentioned in my note have disappeared. My
blood pressure has stabilised and has gone back to normal. My
dizziness has disappeared. Thanks to my diet, I have almost
gained back my usual weight, now almost the same as before
my fast. I don't feel cold any more. I walk [in the prison exercise
yard]. In short, my physical improvement has led to a number
of positive emotions. I enjoy fresh air, snow, the sun; my body
needs it. It's a kind of triumph of physical existence.

Everything would be okay if there weren't one detail. I'm
sorry to say that it's my heart. There are frequent changes of my
pulse and arrhythmia that reflect my general physical situation.
When I lie down I don't have heart trouble; only when I stand
up. Therefore, I have to be very careful. Maybe this is not only a
result of the hunger strike but a temporary, secondary effect of
my quick recovery. I was gaining weight extremely fast, and it
might be that my heart wasn't able to adjust to the new
situation.

In your note, Mama, you wrote that on the anniversary of
Papa's death you'd visit his grave. I'd decided in advance to
observe the anniversary of his death according to the Jewish
calendar by reading Psalms. According to my calculations, the
anniversary would be on January 15, and I had to start my
preparations on January 14 in the evening. I'd actually begun on
the morning of the 14th.

All these months, there has been a photo of Natasha in front
of me, taken by Papa in Istra. On January 14, I took out Papa's
photo of himself in his war uniform which he sent me not long
before his death. I also took out a photo of Lyonya and Mama.
Then I began thinking about which Psalms I should read after
Kaddish because I realised that I wouldn't have enough strength
to read all. But at that moment, I couldn't imagine what kind of
day it would be.

On the evening of the 14th I realised that I was wrong, hat it
wasn't the proper date. I therefore made a new decision to

observe the anniversary of his death and to celebrate the receipt
of Mama's note over the course of two days. That corresponds
more to Jewish tradition. For many centuries, Jews who lived in
the Diaspora observed two days of a holiday because they were
afraid they might have made a mistake in the proper date.

Maybe, Mama, it's strange to you that I mention the anniversary of Papa's death together with joyful days, holidays. But
since the Psalms of King David helped me to overcome fear in
Chistopol and my strong pain and sufferings because of Papa's
death, I feel a special kind of sadness, gratitude and hope. I often
remember Papa, but these memories are filled not only with
grief but with joy because of King David's Psalms.

There are such wonderful memories that Papa left. He was
such a kind man, selfless and wise at the same time, and if there
were some moments which I wouldn't like to remember,
they're related to my own behaviour. Unintentionally, I inflicted offence on him, and I exploited his forgetfulness and
kindness. Only rarely did Papa show some outburst of anger,
but it disappeared very quickly.

It's very strange that I think now of instances in our family's
life when I was unfair to Papa. But I don't think of the times I
was unfair to you, Mama. Surely there were many such times,
and there will come a time when I'll remember them. My dear
Mama. I pray for your health and I hope so much that God will
give you the strength and health to meet me, and to live
together with me and Natasha in one big family. But I don't
know what awaits me and all of us. Therefore, I ask you to
forgive me for all the instances when I was unfair to you,
Mama.

In my happy and interesting life were two important and
very happy events. The first wasn't a matter of choice. You'll
agree, Lyonya, that we both were very lucky to have been born
in this family and have these parents. The second was my
meeting up with Avital.

But I'm not going to write a postal substitute for my
thoughts and emotions for Natasha. The information which
reaches me about Avital is very sparse, but from Mama's
postcards I learned that she spent a whole day with Uncle
Syoma [Anatoly's father's brother, Shamai] and helped him to
work on his will. I would like to meet Uncle Syoma so much to
listen to his stories about his wife, about Odessa, about Papa
and the family. I can't forgive myself that I didn't really care

enough for all those unique stories that Papa told us about his childhood and about Odessa in the early 1920s.

Now I have received from Books by Mail [the Soviet mail order house] a textbook on Arabic. It's extremely interesting to me to learn this language. Because of my sclerosis which I mentioned in a 1981 letter I'm not able to learn vocabulary by heart, and I'm just reading the book. Some Arabic words become engraved in my memory. The awareness of our common language roots, of Arabs and Jews, increases the feeling of sadness because of the difficult road to peace between our peoples.

I think of you, all my dear ones, of all our friends and relatives, distant and near. Best regards to everyone who doesn't forget me. Love to all of you, and to my beloved Avital.

Tolya

Shamai Sharon, Shcharansky's uncle, was a working man with few possessions. At the age of eighty, he had gone to Jerusalem from New York to be with Avital, who gave him what help she could. His 'will' was a touching tribute to his faith that Avital and her husband would one day be united.

On 20 February 1983 the official Soviet news agency Tass issued a statement concerning a possible review of Shcharansky's sentence, based on two conditions: his 'behaviour' in prison and an end to 'noisy propaganda campaigns'. This statement was reported in the *Jewish Chronicle* under the headline 'Shcharansky release hint'. On the day after the Tass statement, a leading British Jew wrote to the Soviet Jewry activists who had planned a march on Shcharansky's behalf: 'I wonder whether, in view of the discussions that are going on at a high level, it would be worthwhile, for a period of perhaps three months, to put no public and publicised pressure for his release on the Soviet Government.' The march was cancelled.

On February 23 Shcharansky wrote his second letter since ending his hunger strike:

My dear ones,

I'd hoped that I'd receive at least one letter from you in exchange for the one from me. But the month and the February limit are coming to an end, your worries increase, and I can't wait any longer.

There's no need to devote much time to my health in this letter. Although the process of recovery isn't as fast as I might have wished, still it's recovery. My heart works with more confidence, and there's less pain in my chest. I've started light exercises, but so far this kind of exercise compared to that broadcast over the radio is like a ride in a bus to Riza lake contrasted with reaching the peak of Everest. But still progress is noticeable.

I've undergone a one-month treatment, and now after a brief interval I've been prescribed an additional series of ATP shots for the strengthening of the myocardium. This is a good medicine; it helped me in 1981. My blood pressure is normal, and I don't have any dizziness. I'm in an optimistic mood. Mama, I don't understand your reproaches. I have never tried to conceal my physical condition from my doctors. I always describe my condition to them in detail. According to my friends, I look even a little thinner and younger than half a year ago. Maybe they just want to please me?

I feel much older now. During the past year, I've undergone several steps towards ageing. Here are the most noticeable ones: Step (1) I've stopped reading articles on politics. I spend about 5–10 minutes reading the political pages in *New Times* (in English), 15 minutes on *USA Magazine*, 20–30 minutes on economics, politics and ideology. Step (2) I've stopped reading the sixteenth page of *Literaturnaya Gazeta*; its humour isn't funny. Step (3) I've started reading the articles and listening to the radio programmes on health and ways of strengthening it.

The most pleasure I get is from reading about the harm of nicotine and alcohol. Once you begin finding out about those fond of liquor and nicotine shortening their lives, you begin to feel that your own life becomes longer. This has a better effect than any of the medicines.

In my last letter and note to Mama, I was talking about the losses which I experienced during the past months, but I didn't say anything about my gains. No matter how strange it sounds I had some acquisitions, too. First, during the hunger strike, I had few headache attacks, three times in 110 days, while before I had them once in seven to ten days. Secondly, I feel less pain in my eyes, and most amazingly, for the first time in the past years my memory has improved. Two years ago I complained about having progressive sclerosis. There was a time when I'd look up the same word in a dictionary (English or Hebrew) several times a day, and still forget it in two or three hours. Last autumn, when I started to read much more than before, I noticed that I could retain in my memory a greater amount.

Still, my memory now is far from what it was in 1977–8 [in Lefortovo prison before his trial]. Maybe this wonderful improvement in my memory can be explained by the fact that I've had a chance to read wonderful books during the past months, such as a collection of poems by Anna Akhmatova. I haven't read so many beautiful poems for quite a while. Of course, I didn't try to memorize anything. I'm not used to this; besides, I wasn't in the right condition. But I was amazed when I found out that several months later I could suddenly recall some of the lines.

There is, for example, a poem, not the most noticeable and profound, from this collection, 'May Snow'. There's a reference to the Psalms of King David in its epigraph –

Transparent shroud falls upon the fresh turf
And melts unnoticeably.
The cruel cold spring kills the full buds
And the sight of early death is so appalling
That I cannot look at God's world.
I feel in me the sadness which
King David has bestowed upon
The millennia in a truly royal way.

Why did these lines charm me so much? The description of spring and late snow? Is it because of the fact that at the time I read it a postcard with a picture of Jerusalem under snow, sent by Rimma was lying here in the cell? Or was it because it reminded me of the snowy winter of 1973–4 when Natulya and I went to Tallinn, Istra and Volokolamsk? Or was it because of the two last lines?

I had a chance to experience that lavishness of King David's gift myself, as you remember. But please don't get the wrong idea that I'm sad because of this quote from Akhmatova. As white light which passes through multicoloured glass and afterwards still retains different parts of its spectrum – so are the good books which single out now the sweet sadness of recollection, now the joy of recognition, now disturbing hope.

Today is Purim, and of course I celebrate this holiday in my own way. On such days it seems easier to take trips in time and space. By a journey in space I mean a kind of imagining what my dear ones in Moscow, Jerusalem and other places are doing that very moment. By a journey in time I mean establishing a link between the present and ancient times when Purim came into existence.

I remember how Natulya and I celebrated Purim, and I also think of Purim 1977, the last one before my arrest.

My best wishes for Passover to Natulya, you and to all my friends and relatives. I'd like to quote those words which I wrote to Natashenka in connection with another holiday. Last Chanukkah, I lit candles all eight nights. It was a real Chanukkah light produced by a tiny piece of paraffin. Every night I had to cut it even into smaller pieces. I was afraid it wouldn't last for eight nights. But when the eighth night came, all eight tiny candles were burning, burning as bright as on the first night. These eight candles are like the past eight years of our lives. They symbolise such a dear and difficult happiness and an extraordinary experience. For those eight years I am infinitely grateful to He who 'set us in the land of the living; He keeps our feet from stumbling. For Thou hast put us to the proof and refined us like silver' (Psalms 66:9–10). That's what I wanted to express. [This is known as the Psalm of Deliverance.]

This letter has become unusual, but perhaps it's for the better. The lighter the load, the greater the speed.

I'm still worried about Mama's health, since I haven't received any news from you. I'm anxious to hear about Natulya, Lyonya, Raya, Sashka, Liuda and all our friends and relatives.

On Friday, I received a parcel. Thank you so much, but there were five or six times fewer stamps than I'd asked for to enable me to order books by mail. They won't suffice for more than four to six weeks. But that's, of course, a trifle. It was a correct decision of yours not to replace the sweets with warm clothes; I wouldn't need them now.

I embrace and kiss my dear Avital and all of you. Best regards to all our friends, near and far.

Tolya

PS It's already evening. Tomorrow morning I have to hand over this letter for postal delivery [and censorship]. But just now I received an unexpected Purim gift – a postcard from Lyonya and two postcards and a letter from Mama. It was your first response to my January letter [confiscated and rewritten in early February]. So I'll add a few words about my heart since Mama asked.

I feel an arrhythmia of my heart. The intervals between the heartbeats remind me of a combination of random numbers. There's a permanent feeling of uneasiness, of pain in my chest. This pain has become weaker, although it takes time.

There's another strange thing happening to me. When I lie down on my back or right side, but not on my left, my chest pain and the arrhythmia eventually disappear. My pulse becomes regular and normal. But when I get up or make some energetic movements the pain starts again. Several weeks ago, I had extremely unpleasant sensations when trying to get into a vertical position. I felt an unpleasant noise in my ears as if I were boarding a plane or plunging into water. I got dizzy and my heart rate slowed.

That happened mostly in the morning, not evening. Now, after having undergone treatment, these phenomena have disappeared. At present, the dizziness, noise in ears, etc., happen to me only when doing energetic exercises or walking fast and for a long time. And even these unpleasant sensations have become much weaker.

I want to emphasise that I'm optimistic and hope for full physical recovery, but aware that it will take a rather long period of time.

It's time to finish this letter and go to bed. Love to all of you and Natulya. Good night.

★   ★   ★

More than a thousand delegates were preparing to go to Jerusalem from all over the world for the 'Brussels Three' Conference on Soviet Jewry. As the Conference drew near, the British Prime Minister, Margaret Thatcher, wrote to its organisers: 'The Government deplores the present plight of Soviet Jewry and the drastic cutback in emigration from the Soviet Union. Soviet persecution of those who seek to exercise fundamental rights such as the freedom of movement and the freedom to profess and practise their faith is an affront to basic human values, and violates the provisions of the International Covenant on Civil and Political Rights and the Helsinki Final Act. The Soviet failure to honour their human rights commitments has cast a dark shadow over international life and has further weakened international trust and confidence.'

For three consecutive years the number of exit visas granted to Soviet Jews had fallen, and fallen sharply, from 21,471 in 1980, to 9475 in 1981, to 2638 in 1982. The figure for 1982 was the lowest since the opening of the gates eleven years earlier.

28

Letters, Alarms and Rumours

On 22 March 1983 Shcharansky wrote again to his mother, but the letter was not allowed to be delivered. He kept a copy of it, however, and was to incorporate it in his next letter a month later. The letter read:

My beloved ones,

Thank God yesterday I received your telegram of your receipt of my February letter. Nevertheless there arose new doubts and questions: Why doesn't it mention your health? Why isn't there a single word about Natasha? But after receiving your telegram I calmed down a bit. I can only guess why it took so much time to forward my letter to you.

Mother's letters are filled with questions about my health and my heart, so I'll begin with that. Although I haven't lost my optimism, I feel that the road to recovery will not be as short and straightforward as I would have hoped. In the first ten days of March, I had an unexpected turn for the worse. Suddenly, the pains in the area of my heart became worse and I felt an overwhelming weakness. In a number of instances my blood pressure dropped severely and I needed injections of camphor and cardiamine.

Because of my lack of medical knowledge and experience I was very concerned. I was quite happy when an electrocardiogram did not confirm my suspicions. The doctors told me that there were no signs of an infarct [heart attack] or of a condition preliminary to a heart attack. According to the doctors, the only significant difference between this cardiogram and that taken at the end of 1977 or beginning of 1978 was the predominance of extrasystoles, i.e. more frequent irregularities of the heartbeat.

Still, the cardiac pains and my general weakness, a feeling of heaviness in my head and in my legs when I sit or stand, have forced me to refrain from my daily walking and from the light exercises I had been doing [a complex system of exercises for the vegetative vascular system published in *Sovietskaya Rossiya* on 24 February 1983]. I'd be interested in receiving expert opinion about these exercises.

In practice, I've been spending between twenty-one and twenty-two hours daily lying down, and after seven or eight days my condition improved considerably. The doctor has recommended that I resume my walking, that I move and breathe the fresh air outside [in the prison yard]. I'd be happy to follow this advice. My body longs for movement and my muscles for exertion. However, as soon as I renewed my walks the pains in my chest got stronger again. These last few days I've again stopped walking, although I'm not totally bedridden.

I'm now drinking a herbal tea, Valerian tincture and Leonurus tincture, to alleviate my chest pains. I'm also taking Novocain tablets to improve my heart functions. The pains in my chest have still not diminished although they've become bearable. The doctors say that my pulse and heartbeat have improved, that my pulse has become stronger. I feel they're right. Today they started giving me carboxylase injections again.

I can't give Mama accurate answers about my pulse because there are too many fluctuations in the course of the day. I can only give a general description of my condition. When I'm lying down, my heartbeat and pulse are usually (but not always) normal and deep, about 80 beats per minute. As soon as I sit up or even move in a reclining position, my heartbeat begins to show irregularities, often at every second beat.

If I sit motionless for a long time, my heartbeat returns to normal (again not always). I don't understand the principle behind this. But my heart condition is disturbed at the slightest effort – even taking a few steps. My heart seems to react to the slightest movement.

Still, at least one can no longer call me thin. I'm eating as before, better than I've eaten in a long time when I had to observe my diet. I move around extremely little, less than ever before. Recently, I noticed that the food given to me does not arouse a strong desire to eat it immediately. Because of my hunger strike, a greedy desire for food tormented me during the last two months. This greediness did not depend on the degree of satiation. Since I ate bit by bit, my nutrition process got extended for the whole day. I had the feeling as if my body had created a kind of camel hump where food reserves could be stored (only food, not liquid).

I was already afraid that I had become a glutton (according to Dante, gluttony is a grave sin). But a few days ago I was saved from this sin. I'm enclosing a clipping from yesterday's *Sovietskaya Rossiya*, 'A Grandmother Lifting Weights', so that you, Mama, should realise that if you take care of your health your whole life is before you.

Having checked Mama's questions regarding my health, I have to add that no tests, except electrocardiograms, have been taken. Evidently, there's no necessity to do it. I do not object to being hospitalised. I don't understand, Mama, why you had the impression that I objected to hospitalisation. I told them that it's okay to get the necessary treatment on the spot. If hospitalisation should be necessary, it's all right with me.

My physical condition doesn't prevent me from reading, writing or conversing, but I have to keep within limits in every respect, e.g. sitting too long at the table tires me out, and walking increases my pains in the chest. I cannot lie on my left side because then my heart troubles me.

I agree with you, Mama, and the doctors that my recovery depends mainly on my nerves. The less I think of my pain, the better I feel. I'm writing so much about this only because of all your questions. I started today doing those exercises for better heart functions that you sent me. At present, it's rather difficult to do because I began only five days ago. But I'll keep on doing them. Perhaps you could send me a complete description of respiratory exercises, physical self-massage, etc. I'll try out everything.

I think I've written quite enough about my health. After having mailed my February letter, I got your Purim telegram, seven letters and five postcards, most written by Mama. There were two postcards from Lyonya, one about his work and the other about his moustache. Yesterday I learned that Rimma Yakir's letter was confiscated. We're both less lucky this year than last. Rimma's and Lyusya's letters were nice exceptions against the background of total silence. Their letters make me happy and convey their optimism to me.

You ask about my reading. Last year, I read mainly periodicals, particularly during my 110 days of fasting. I read a vast range of magazines and books. Among the novels worth mentioning was the fascinating *Two Bundles of Letters* by Davydov. The topic of this novel contains many interesting associations. I also read in *Philosophical Issues* 'The Phenomenological Theory of Time and its Subjective Interpretation'. The author shows transitions from objective time to time as a subjective reality and to a kind of momentary time consciousness, and further from consciousness to a kind of emotional experience of time. In my present situation, it was not at all difficult to understand these ideas of time transition. But many years ago it would have taken much longer to understand the essence of this phenomenological theory.

But life's fussiness was a certain obstacle. This year, I succeeded in subscribing to almost everything I was interested in. I spend relatively little time now reading periodicals.

Now there's a completely changed situation, one I haven't experienced in many, many years. I don't have to wait for an interesting book, but just the opposite – interesting books wait to be read by me. A few days ago, I started reading *Islam* by the well-known French Arabist Mosse. I had to postpone this reading because there was an opportunity to read – for a couple of days – a rather rare edition of Rilke's poems. Next in turn is an English edition of *Dubliners* by Joyce. It was sent to me by Books by Mail. I was also promised a reader in old Chinese philosophy and a number of other fascinating books, among them an Arabic textbook (it's high time for me to renew my Arabic studies).

But I'm in no hurry. I'm waiting for the moment when there's an improvement in my health. Not long ago, I read a three-volume treatise by Gumilyev of Leningrad University, *Ethnogenesis*. He has created an interesting theory of the nature, origin, development and ruin of the 'ethnos' which is regarded by him not as a condition but as a process. According to him, the ethnos is neither an amorphous condition nor a social category nor a unity based on a common language, common territory, economy, etc. It is a system of certain behaviour stereotypes of moral norms, etc. Ethnogenesis is therefore an integral part of Nature herself.

This process that took its origin from such representatives as Moses or Mohammed united people into a new ethnos. In expounding his theory, Gumilyev makes use of a vast historic material. He thinks in grand categories. Ethnosphere is only one of the frameworks (or structural systems) of the earth. I think his ideas are between science and art. There's a lack of strict scientific thinking. But does there exist any other form of discovering a new reality that has not yet been penetrated by the human mind?

Regarding 'ethnos', I remember another book I received a year and a half ago, *The Inhabitants of the World*, an ethnographic handbook by Solomon Ilyich Drucker, which I often consult. His tables showing the ethnic structure of a country are based on the principle of linguistic relationship of the corresponding peoples.

No wonder a number of complications arose in regard to the classification of Jews, who aren't regarded – as is well known – as a nation. The author relates Jews living in Israel to the Semitic group of peoples, since their common language is Hebrew. But the Jews of Europe and America are related by him to the Germanic group because of their language, Yiddish. According to this classification, Natasha belongs to the Semitic group, but I'm a pure Aryan. I'm afraid that my Orthodox wife could be confused by such a 'mixed marriage'. [Anatoly draws a cartoon of a smiling face entitled 'I am smiling'.]

When I was drawing my self-portrait, I remembered that you hadn't sent me any photos of Natasha for a long time. Don't you have any new photos of my darling Avital, of yourself and our friends? When our regular correspondence is restored, you might try to send me some.

Yesterday, I read the following words in a letter by Rainer Maria Rilke (*Letters to a Young Poet*, letter of 1904): 'We have already had to rethink so many of our concepts of motion, we will also gradually learn to realise that that which we call destiny goes forth from within people, not from without into them. Only because so many have not absorbed their destinies and transmuted them within themselves while they were living in them, have they not recognised what has gone forth out of them; it was so strange to them that, in their bewildered fright, they thought it must only just then have entered into them, for they swear never before to have found anything like it in themselves.'

Avital and I have chosen our destiny quite consciously and we were mastering it when it was in the profundity of our inner selves. Our destiny became our life.

As I learned from your letters, your phone conversations

with Natasha have intensified. Unfortunately, this hasn't affected the extent of my information about Natulya so far. Those
were legendary times when I used to get her letters through
Mama or Mama was sending them to me together with her own
letters, as well as letters I'd receive directly from Israel. If I were
unable to take these letters in my hands and reread them, I
would probably not have believed my own memory.

But fortunately, not only my memory is with me, not only
old letters and photos are with me, but our remarkable past, our
exciting integral present and our future. It's particularly easy
and pleasant to think about this during these spring days, just
before Passover, when my body is again being saturated with
health, when warmth is in the air and hope fills the heart. Love
to all of you and to my dear Avital. Best regards to all our
friends and relatives.

Tolya

Shcharansky's next letter from Chistopol was sent on 20 April
1983:

My dear ones,

There are really no limits to human longing. For over a year,
it was my dream to find out if my letters to you were sent out on
a certain date and under a certain number. My recent letters
have passed through the Chistopol barrier three times, like
horses trained to jump over obstacles. Three times I've heard
those wonderful words filling me with life and energy, like a
cup of strong tea, like an unexpected visit to the prison store!
But despite my joy, that isn't enough for me now. I would like
this letter to be forwarded to you without delay. I'd be happy to
receive your answer before writing you again. I'd like to start
the day without the nagging question, 'Will there be any news
or not?'

Today I received your telegram affirming the receipt of my
letter. But your telegram didn't comfort me. An uneasy
thought crossed my mind, 'Maybe some misfortune has happened at home.' And if everything is all right at home, how
long have you been waiting for my letter? And then I start
worrying, 'Perhaps the late delivery of my letter has led to the
worsening of Mama's health or Natasha's mood?' For twenty
days I waited for your telegram affirming the receipt of my
letter written in February.

As for my March letter, the situation has become still worse. Twenty-four days ago my letter to you was mailed, but I haven't had any telegram yet. Your postcards and letters are, of course, a comfort. But simultaneously I'm worried by the question I ask myself: 'Why is the distance from Moscow to Chistopol three, four, five times shorter than that from Chistopol to Moscow?'

Literaturnaya Gazeta carried an article, 'Marked by Atom', dealing with the delivery of letters on time. Mailing a letter to a certain place, the correspondents keep vigilant watch on its movements as if they were physicians or physicists observing the movement of an atom. I don't know what kind of radioactive tracers are contained in my letters and what kind of 'radiation' causes such delaying effect.

Have you received my March letter? Will you get it? Perhaps it got lost, as happened in 1981. Then you received instead of my letter an apology from the Ministry of Communications and financial compensation for a registered letter.

The deadline for my April letter will soon pass. I can't wait longer. Now I have to act in the same way I did two years ago, to rewrite my March letter, then add information related to April. I won't worry at least about the first half of the letter, since it has already undergone censorship and has been okayed.

Now I'm starting to rewrite my letter of March 22.

Having written out the full text of his earlier letter, Shcharansky continued with his letter of 20 April 1983:

My life, that is my health, which is still my main concern, constantly undergoes ups and downs. I'm healthy for two, three, four days, then sick for one or two days. By 'healthy', I mean that I feel well enough to walk slowly for an hour during the exercise period, plus thirty minutes in the evening in my cell. The rest of the time I divide between sitting and lying down. I read, converse and work. My chest doesn't hurt and only aches slightly. It seems to me then that I'm on the verge of recovery. But then, all I have to do is attempt even the mildest exercises, sit-ups, for example or something similar, and my heart makes its presence felt most vehemently.

By 'sick' I mean that my chest hurts the entire day. I sometimes feel as if there's an open wound in my heart which my left arm aggravates with its every motion. I have no strength to walk. I'm bedridden all day, my head is heavy, and I feel a general weakness.

Still, my blood pressure is more or less normal. My pulse isn't bad, certainly much better than it was. Very often it's regular, without extrasystoles. Yet as before, the pulse note is disturbed by the slightest movement. My treatment is finished for the time being. In the course of a little over two months, I've been given fifty injections – ten of vitamin C, ten of Duplex, ten of carboxylase, ten of ATP and another ten of carboxylase. In addition, I've been given a series of Novocain tablets, plus several series, all in all 100 tablets at intervals.

Besides that, I still drink Valerian tincture and Leonurus tincture. The series of exercises that Mama sent me for my heart is intended for fifteen days. I completed it, and only then realised that I did it all wrong. A second copy of these exercises arrived with instructions that they're to be performed while reclining on one's right side. I'd been doing them in a sitting position, so I had to start all over again. I'm finishing them now. Have there been results? In terms of arrhythmia, my heart seems to have improved, but I can't say whether this is due to the exercises, the medications or the combination of the two.

Two things worry me. First, the constant and inexplicable fluctuation in my condition from health to sickness and back again. Second, my inability to begin even the lightest exercise. Any exercise immediately has an effect on my condition, bringing me from health to sickness. I think that after completing the series of exercises for my heart I'll begin a series of Chinese exercises that Mama sent me. Frankly speaking, I'm quite tired of being sick. My body is still gaining weight, or rather overweight. But it remains weak and demands more exercise. The doctor says this will pass. It's a matter of time. There's no organic damage and the problem is related to the vegetative nervous system. One must have faith and wait.

As far as the mail's concerned, I've received seven letters from Mama and four postcards after my March letter. These include a letter and postcard from Donetsk. One of Mama's letters was confiscated. Two postcards came from Lyonya. One contains scepticism about a possible meeting, and I share this scepticism. The other tells about the birth of Lena [Israeli friend]'s child. While sending congratulations to Lena and Venya, I think sadly that it won't be easy for Natasha and me to catch up, but this will have to be done; we have no choice.

Last year there was a long and at times vehement discussion in *Literaturnaya Gazeta* about popular and mass culture. Articles by Lev Askhinsky and Andrei Bitov [contemporary writers] made themselves noticed. There were no platitudes in Bitov's article and it contained a number of interesting and precise thoughts. I can say that I feel the notion of progress redeemed by a phrase of his, 'the ethical element in the idea of progress can be found in the fact of the refusal to see man as a robot.'

Immortal values are immortal because there's no need to create them; one can just live with them. The faith in the effectiveness of progress, as well as in the effectiveness of tradition, like any faith, can endow anyone with enormous energy produced by the interrelation of epochs. It can bring firmness to every step you take.

I recently read *My Pushkin* by Marina Tsvetaeva [Russian émigré author who committed suicide after returning to the Soviet Union in the early 1940s]. With all her sincerity, the fire and passion of her love and enmity, she writes about herself, about the world where she lives and to which she says farewell: 'Because when you love, you always say farewell.' In my opinion, her words contain profound and eternal truth. One feels like clinging to each moment of precious hours, days and years; the joy each of these moments brings is closely inter-related with the feeling of sadness one experiences at parting with them. But her phrase is followed by another, 'you love truly only when you say farewell.' One can feel here that a fundamental truth about life is conveyed, blended with the truth of one particular moment, the moment of parting.

One phrase in her text has frightened me, 'there are books which have so much life-blood in them that you become afraid that they will change while you put them aside, like the river which changes while you live, and the book too lived like the river; it lived and is gone. No one has ever entered into the same river twice, but has there been anyone who has entered into the same book twice?'

No doubt I've already told you how indispensable to me were the books from a remarkable library in Lefortovo in 1977–8. Years ago, numerous books had been read in a rush, amid other activities, in order to fill some invisible but mandatory 'credits' of one's education. What was gathered from such a reading of Homer or Virgil, for example, was enough to make one understand the classical metaphors. I thought then that real literature began around the eighteenth century. Before then, there were just Shakespeare, Dante and two or three others.

But suddenly, time changed its pace. There was nowhere to rush to. I had an opportunity and an obligation to think things over and weigh them carefully without rushing, to analyse and sum things up. I had to say farewell to many things, and perhaps to everything. And I found out that this new time scale, the silent space, was much better suited for conversations with 'familiar strangers' – Homer, Sophocles, Aristophanes, Virgil, Cervantes, Rabelais and many others. Having found out that the library carried practically nothing by my favourites, Chekhov, Dostoevsky and Western writers, I decided, okay, I'll fill the gaps in my education and will turn to the forgotten plots. During the first days and weeks I was making my way through the dust of ages. It was an attempt to escape from my place and time, at least for a while. I was making my way with difficulty, studying the silent life and silent literary tradition from a great distance, which meant that I stayed where I was.

The breakthrough happened somewhat accidentally. I was reading a comedy by Aristophanes in which one of the characters tells another something like, 'Ah, you have a Corinthian vase – you're a traitor.' Corinth was then at war with Athens, where Aristophanes lived. Having read this, I started to laugh, and suddenly became aware of the closeness between people separated by twenty-five centuries. The contact was established. The naturalness of the feelings and actions of classical characters, their clarity untroubled by centuries of reflections, was all in tune with the condition I was in.

Don Quixote is a dreamer who enjoys life to the fullest, in contrast to the dull players of the dull minor parts. He towers not only over them but over his author as well. Socrates, too. It seemed as if all these authors and characters hurried towards me from different books, countries and centuries as though to help me, saying: 'You see, in reality there's nothing new in this world of ours, but how many wonderful things there are for whose sake it's worth living, and it would be a pity to die.'

At that time, I was given advice to read thoroughly the Criminal Code. I wasn't in a hurry to do so. When I had to become my own attorney I seemed to have felt the insufficiency of my knowledge of the law. But there's no doubt that reading Xenophon's book about Socrates gives me much more than the study of any kinds of codes.

Something else happened. While reading, I became an observer once again. The time of action described in a book became interconnected with Lefortovo of 1977. These books and I had already our own past which was common to us. This both united me with the characters of the books and deprived me of my former spontaneous and free reaction. Formerly, I was on familiar terms with Socrates, but not out of pride – in the face of death everybody is equal. Now, I've become a tiny 'dot' again. Again I realised the immensity of Socrates, his significance and readiness to move through millennia to bring help to others in the same way as he once came to help me. That's why I wrote to you that one can't read the same book twice.

It's time to finish. I have dwelt on books far too much this time, but reading is for me a substitute for many things, like communication with the outside world or discussions with friends. The brains of most people work best when they freely relate to others, with their friends. The solution of complex problems often depends upon the intensity of the work of one's brain. For me, reading is proof against the atrophy of the brain. Thus, a tennis player will play against a wall when there's no partner.

If this time I don't write anything about Natasha it's only because she is like air for me, the air with which I breathe and which I don't have to talk about all the time.

What does my tireless traveller do now? Whom does she meet now? Where does she stay and when is she planning to return home? At what kibbutz did she have her rest? Was it near Tiberias? All of my former questions concerning Natulya are still in effect. And my concern for you, Mama, for your health, is in effect too.

Okay, I'm finishing. Best regards to all our relatives and friends everywhere. I'd like to hear more about them. Love to all of you and to my dear Avital.

Tolya

PS There was a medical commission from Kazan today. Clearly, my condition is vegetative neurosis, some changes in the myocardial function but, as I was told, nothing dangerous. For the strengthening of the myocardium a potassium preparation was recommended, after some interval of course, since during the past months I've been taking it in large amounts. They recommended that I move and walk as much as possible.

Ida Milgrom received this letter on 10 May 1983. Reading it, she was shaken by his description of his ill-health: he, who was only just thirty-five years old. On 31 May 1983 she wrote to Andropov: 'For over six years my son Anatoly Shcharansky has been in prison. On January 14 he ceased a 110-day hunger strike. I learned from his letter, received on May 10, that three months after ending his fast his health has deteriorated catastrophically. In practical terms he's bedridden. Many times I asked for the hospitalisation of my son. But all my petitions were refused.'

Ida Milgrom added: 'I am afraid that my son's heart disease, caused by nervous stress during his imprisonment, could endanger his life in the most tragic way. Therefore I continue to ask for his hospitalisation. I hope that at a hospital it would be possible to improve his serious condition.' Her letter ended: 'I am a mother, and the life of my son is so dear to me that I cannot accept the total refusal of all my petitions. Therefore, I ask you, Yury Vladimirovich, to give evidence of your humanity. Please intervene, using your personal authority, to save my son's life.'

Ida Milgrom received no reply. Nor was Shcharansky allowed to leave his cell for the prison hospital.

*　　　　*　　　　*

Avital Shcharansky took no rest. That summer she was in Britain, Spain, the United States and Switzerland. It was in the second week of June, while in Geneva, that she spoke on the telephone to Shcharansky's mother in Moscow, and learnt that in a letter which had reached Moscow on 9 June 1983 Shcharansky wrote of considerable difficulties in writing owing to swellings in his hands and feet. Avital at once sought the advice of an American cardiologist, Professor Allan Ross of the George Washington University Medical Center. The advice Ross gave was sombre: the symptoms described in Shcharansky's various letters were those of a potentially dangerous, even fatal, heart condition. He was in urgent need of hospital care. From Jerusalem, two distinguished Israeli cardiologists appealed direct to Moscow to allow Shcharansky medical treatment in hospital.

On 12 June 1983, Shcharansky's mother travelled the five hundred miles from Moscow to Kazan to intercede with the prison authorities for her son to be sent to hospital. Her journey was in vain. Four days later one of Avital's many friends in the West drafted an appeal to Andropov to allow Shcharansky to go to hospital. 'Shcharansky is your prisoner,' the appeal ended. 'His sentence, though severe, is not a death sentence. We appeal to you therefore to give him the benefit of your medical science, and allow him to live.'

Those with access to the inner counsels of leading men were told, in mid-July, that diplomatic pressure behind the scenes might well secure a breakthrough. As the final phase of the Madrid Conference came to an end, the senior American negotiator submitted to the Soviet delegate a list of more than fifty refuseniks and dissidents whose release was considered imperative by the United States, if the Conference were to end in agreement. The top name on the list was that of Shcharansky.

At the same time, Avital Shcharansky, who had flown to Madrid, then to Washington, was assured that the United States would sign no document at Madrid unless Shcharansky were to be released.

All seemed set for the end of Shcharansky's torment. But in Madrid, the Soviet delegate suddenly informed his American opposite number that Shcharansky's release was conditional upon the prisoner signing a letter, asking to be released 'on the grounds of ill-health'. The Americans assured the Soviets that such a letter would be written by the prisoner in Chistopol, and arranged for Shcharansky's brother Leonid to come to the American Embassy in Moscow, where he was asked to go to Chistopol to persuade his brother to sign.

Not only Leonid, but others, realised that this letter would be a trap. 'It is important to note', two former Prisoners of Zion, Hillel Butman and Iosif Mendelevich, wrote from Jerusalem to the State Department in Washington, 'that all appeals for release sent to the Praesidium of the Supreme Soviet of the USSR – no matter how they are formulated – are treated by the Soviet authorities as appeals for clemency, and hence an admission of guilt on the part of the prisoner.' Any such signature by the prisoner, Butman and Mendelevich stressed, would as a result 'be an admission of guilt for acting on behalf of the United States Intelligence services, which is a lie.'

29

'Truly to Become
a Free Person'

On 5 July 1983 Ida Milgrom and her son Leonid returned once more to Chistopol, and were allowed to meet with Shcharansky. Three days later, on her return to Moscow, Ida Milgrom telephoned to Avital in Jerusalem to report on the meeting. They had been allowed to speak only through a glass screen.

During the meeting Shcharansky explained, as a background to his hunger strike, that his connection with the outside world had been severed when the censor had begun returning all his longer letters. Out of necessity he began writing short letters, one page or less, but these were also returned if there was any mention of his Avital. He was also forbidden to write to her directly. After many complaints, the State Prosecutor arrived at the prison, to be told by the Prison Commandant that Shcharansky had no right to send letters outside the borders of the Soviet Union. The Prosecutor disagreed, affirmed in the presence of both Shcharansky and the Commandant that the prisoner did have the legal right to send letters outside the Soviet Union. It was the continued confiscation of his letters after the State Prosecutor's statement that led Shcharansky to begin his hunger strike against his isolation.

Speaking of his hunger strike, Shcharansky told his mother and brother that the worst part of it was the force-feeding by the jailers. They had tied him up, beat him when he was nearly unconscious and then prised open his mouth, causing wounds and lacerations in his throat. Because, in his condition, these wounds did not heal, they caused him unbearable pain.

Shcharansky commented that this was the most trying period of his life; he had not expected such treatment. To revive himself from his state of near unconsciousness, he would try to turn the radio on full volume. During this period, the Commandant-General of prisons would come from the city of Kazan and 'scream that in the Soviet Union there was no such thing as hunger strikes' and that if Shcharansky refused to eat he would be punished and confined in solitary confinement. As a result, he did indeed spend most of his hunger strike in solitary confinement, in conditions where he was unable to stand upright. It was at this time that the authorities had informed his mother that his letters were being confiscated because he was trying to reveal secret information in code. They also cut out nine of the eleven lines he had written in the note to his mother at the end of his hunger strike. At their meeting Shcharansky told his mother that the erased lines explained the reasons for his hunger strike. He was 'astonished', he said, that since his hunger strike his letters were not being censored, despite the fact that they were twenty to thirty pages long and that Avital's name was mentioned many times. If this was permissible after the strike, he remarked, it was not clear why it had been forbidden for a year and a half.

Five months after his hunger strike, Shcharansky could still only get to his feet from a reclining position. Throughout his meeting with his mother, he kept his hand close to his heart. On 14 January 1983 he had weighed only 35 kilograms (77 pounds) with a height of 1.60 metres (5 feet 3 inches). At the time of the meeting with his mother six months later he weighed 55 kilograms (121 pounds). He told his mother than in his opinion the authorities deliberately prepared for the meeting by making him 'presentable'. Beforehand he was simply not 'presentable'.

Shcharansky told his mother that he had been in 'hot-house' conditions for the last few months. He had been given especially good food, and although the work quota he normally would have been expected to meet was sewing eight sacks daily, he was sewing only one sack daily without being punished. He was convinced, however, that as soon as his mother returned home, his treatment would worsen. At the end of February, he told his mother, he had begun a second hunger strike that had further worsened his physical condition. That strike had been on behalf of another prisoner.

Shcharansky told his mother that a KGB representative who had come to see him had said that his behaviour in prison was 'very important' because this would enable the authorities to arrange a meeting between him and his mother. The possibility of such a meeting depended on 'proper' behaviour in prison. When

Shcharansky had asked for the definition of 'proper' behaviour, the KGB agent replied that this meant 'no deviation from the prison regime'. Shcharansky had replied that he had never deviated from the prison regime. It was the prison authorities that had been violating the rules of conduct set down for Soviet prisons.

Ida Milgrom and Leonid then asked Shcharansky to appeal to the Supreme Soviet to release him on grounds of his severe medical condition. But he stopped them in the middle of their plea, to say that this was not a matter for discussion. Everything that had been done to him for the past six years, he said, 'has been illegal'. He added, 'At my trial it was announced that I had nothing to say to judges who in two hours' time would read a sentence that had been prepared well in advance. I will not say one word, but every day that I am in prison is a continuation of the illegal situation that began with my trial. So on what basis should I appeal?' Shcharansky added: 'Any appeal would be inappropriate. I will not turn to them with any requests. I strongly urge you to find a way to convey to those people who are active politically and in public life, to all my good friends, to those who are working and fighting on my behalf, to those who believe in my cause, those who insist on my innocence, give them my warm thanks. Write to them that I can make no appeal to the Soviet authorities, but the absence of such an appeal will not have a negative effect on any decision regarding my release. Any positive decision will not depend on letters. This is totally clear to me.'

Ida Milgrom and Leonid then tried to tell him that before they received the denial of their appeal, Ida Milgrom had tried to reach him in order to persuade him in the name of the family to appeal for his release. Shcharansky cut them short with the words: 'Understand. This does not depend on one refusal or another. This is something I will not do. I am an innocent victim and this is well known to everyone, especially to those who "framed" me. Therefore I have nothing to say to them.'

If his letters were not received for another three months, Shcharansky told his mother and brother that he would begin a hunger strike again. He also intended to send the next monthly letter that he was allowed to write, in July, to Avital in Jerusalem.

Shcharansky's monthly letters now reached his mother without interruption. But in his hunger-strike struggle to be allowed to write to her, he had damaged his health severely.

From the moment of Shcharansky's arrest in March 1977, the

Soviet authorities had tried their utmost to get him to admit that he had been a spy. In court, in July 1978, he had declared this accusation to be 'absurd'. For the next five years, as a prisoner, in conditions of appalling hardship, he had refused to confess to espionage: to the crime he had not committed. Now he had even refused to be asked to be released for health reasons, realising that such a request, even if followed by his release, could be used by the authorities to imply that his arrest and imprisonment were legitimate.

For the Soviet authorities, the principal purpose of his mother's visit in July 1983 was to pass on to him their promises to release him if he would write a letter stating that he was ill and therefore wished to be released. He refused to do this, and in his first letter to his mother after her visit he cited Galileo as an example of someone who had taken the other course, denouncing his theories to save his life, only to retract his denunciation on his death-bed.

Shcharansky could not agree that Galileo's decision was the right one. The truth existed and had to be told. His letter of July 1983 read in full:

My dear loved ones,

Just now, I wanted to write about my impressions of our recent visit, but I decided to review the copy of the letter that I sent to Avital which included my vivid impressions recorded only two or three days after our meeting.

I noticed how much more accurate my impressions about my mood were then, and all this is understandable, because now, those very vivid sensations appear pale in retrospect. Life has returned to its routine pattern.

However, since you are undoubtedly interested in understanding the dynamics of my feelings and my emotional state, and not just the dynamics of events transpiring around me – the latter portion of my life here, concerning events, translates only into a static formula – I will therefore allow myself to quote from portions of my letter to Avital in which I write about our meeting.

When I wrote in my letter to Avital about my mood after our visit, I was somehow reminded about the illness that deep-sea divers suffer from – the bends – when they rise too quickly from the depths of the sea to the surface. Divers emerge out of the depths very slowly, taking breaks at spaced intervals so that their bodies can adapt to new conditions, and so that the

TRULY TO BECOME A FREE PERSON'

amount of oxygen in the blood can slowly return to its normal level. Otherwise, all the additional gases located within the diver's bloodstream, under intense pressure when he submerges, will be forced out in a sudden burst of energy, causing his blood to boil and leading to the diver's sudden death.

Something analogous occurs when you return after a tour of the depths of the outside world limited to only two hours. First I saw Leonid, and then I saw Mama, who has really aged. I heard their first words, and immediately – not only with my ears and eyes, but with all my blood – I began to take in the air that you breathe in, there on the outside.

Following this, for several days, I returned to my routine pattern of life. The images that I had of our meeting chaotically blended together within myself, then slowly took leave of me and returned to become distinct parts within me, existing apart from myself, like facts about the outside world which one can read about in a letter or a newspaper.

As usual, it was difficult to speak at our meeting. Everything got mixed up in my mind. Questions jumped up from this chaotic mixture in an impulsive manner. And each question was accompanied by a difficult thought: Was it worth 'wasting' precious minutes of this two-hour-long visit whose 'price' was a year and a half of life?

> I said: 'I will take heed to my ways,
> That I sin not with my tongue;
> I will keep a curb upon my mouth,
> While the wicked is before me.'
> I was dumb with silence, I held my peace,
> Had no comfort,
> And my pain was held in check.
> (Psalms 29:2–3)

In the letter to Avital, I turned to the content itself of our conversation during the visit, and I explained my response to your questions.

I then recalled one well-known figure, who came to my mind in those days at Lefortovo prison. I believe that I wrote previously about this subject. I am referring to the story of Galileo Galilei, the scientific genius who, in an extraordinary manner, advanced the accomplishments of the scientific world. And at the end of his life, he uttered the eternal words: 'And yet it moves!'

Of course, there are historians today who believe that
Galileo Galilei never did say those words. That is not important
at the moment. At Lefortovo, I was reminded of him frequently.

There are some verses, taken from the work of Anna
Akhmatova which refer to a state of 'despair laced with fear
which becomes unbearable'. And yet, when one is found in a
state where it almost 'becomes unbearable', one's memory, in
its role as alter-ego, against one's very will, brings forth
convincing examples from history and whispers forth: 'Are
words really that important to you, more so than the fact that it
moves?'

The authority of that great scientist pressed upon me no less
than the arguments of my inquisitors. In the end, I stood up to
debate with him as well, so that surprisingly I and Galileo
Galilei, ended up standing on opposite sides of the fence. He is
one of the few recognised giants in history, who, incidentally,
discovered the law of the inertia of movement. Yet, did the
world acclaim with which he was acknowledged not multiply
many times over all those – in many different times and
different places – who cited the great name of Galileo in order to
justify the place of 'despair laced with fear' with the saying, 'it is
not important that which I say, it is important that it
moves'? . . .

In addition to Newton's law on the universal gravity of
objects, there is also a law of the universal gravity of souls, of
the bond between them, and the influence of one soul on the
other. And it operates in this manner, so that with each word
that we speak, and with each step that we take, we touch other
souls and have an impact upon them. So why should I put this
sin on my soul? If I have already succeeded once in tearing the
spider's web spun by the uncontrollable forces of life; breaking
with the difficult two-faced approach called for by this intoler-
able situation; closing the gap between thought and word; how
is it now possible to take even one step backwards towards the
previous state?

All this is sufficient: enough talk about the visit, enough
peeking at the copy of the letter written to Avital, and enough
plagiarising of myself.

Best regards to all of our friends. I will be able to pen my next
letter only on September 5th.

Tolya

Ida Milgrom had written to the Supreme Soviet on 14 July 1983 to ask for the release of her son on medical grounds. On August 26 she received a reply, from one of the Deputies of the Russian Republic. The question of a 'pardon' had been considered, he wrote, but it had been rejected. The original sentence would stand. In vain did Ida Milgrom reply that she had not asked for a pardon, but for his release on medical grounds. Shcharansky's subsequent letters to her showed just how ill he had become:

August 1983

The gnawing heart pains are characterised by two traits – they are both 'steady' and 'constant'. Thanks to each of them, I have practically become adjusted to these pains.

The pains become more severe when I lie down on the left side of my body, even for a few minutes, after morning exercises, after light running, and as usual, the arrhythmia begins again. The allergy has not returned. I continue to drink calcium. . . . my teeth need repairs. My head hurts, and I have to take Askaphen for this pain.

September 1983

This time, the truth is that I can only repeat again all that I have said in my previous letters. The sole change is that in August, as opposed to other months, I haven't made any progress.

My heart, as usual, hurts constantly, and the pains increase, as I said in past letters. I can't increase my physical exercises, and I must admit that my plan to improve my health by the end of the summer remains unfulfilled.

Two weeks ago, I sent an appeal to the medical department of the Tatar Republic's Ministry of Internal Affairs, in which I emphasised that I utilised all the medical possibilities in Chistopol, and now I am appealing for a full medical check-up and proper treatment in a hospital setting.

In 1983 the Jewish New Year 5744 fell on September 7. That day, Shcharansky wrote to his mother from Chistopol of an event which had taken place five days earlier:

Shana tova for 5744; may you have a happy year!

My dear and loved ones! Do you know what amazing events are 'taking place' in the meritorious city of Chistopol? The rivers flow upstream, mountains float free, our planet has circled the sun twice in an opposite direction and then, the wonder of two years ago repeated itself: on the 24th of Elul of the year 5743 dating from the creation of the world, I, Natan Sharon, received a postcard directly from my wife Avital in the holy city of Jerusalem.

On Natalia's face I see not only weariness, but a pure emotion that has further deepened and clarified our relationship. My dear child, I bless you for the New Year 5744, the year of our jubilee – ten years since our first meeting. I don't mention our blessings, for they're known to us without words, but I do ask you for one thing – save your strength, for my sake, for ours, for the sake of our family.

In a book that I read lately, it says that in ancient times Semites relied on the past: 'Looking forward, he saw the past; the future was behind him'. Forward, to the past! I would like to be reading Natalia's letters of two, three, four years ago. I want to hear her voice as I could up to seven years ago, to be with her as we were nine years ago, I want . . . enough! I don't want to continue towards the past, and anyhow, I'm a Semite, though not an ancient one. So I face the future, keeping the past in a knapsack, and I cross raging rivers and high mountains towards my present with Natalia.

The tenth anniversary of Shcharansky's first meeting with Avital would fall on 13 October 1983. In his letter of September 7 he wrote to her:

My dear 'old lady', our big anniversary is approaching. I ask the Almighty for one thing only – to watch over you for me, your mind and your heart for all of us. As Samson's power was in his hair, so is mine in you, my Avital.

Several days ago, two thick tomes appeared at one of my neighbours': a book of Psalms from Kiev. This is a rare volume from the fourteenth-century original, with commentaries. The main thing is that it includes the Slavic Church version of the Psalms with the aid of which I can try to understand the incomprehensible part of my own book of Psalms.

One of us remembered that precisely with such a book of Psalms 'guesses' were made in ancient times. So once again, with a defence of armour so as not to appear ridiculous to each other, but still not so tough as to be deaf to the voice of our ancestors who believed in luck and destiny, we too began 'guessing'. One had to read out the name, number of the page, and the line. I took numbers from Natalia's birthday. In 'my' line were the words: 'The wicked watches the righteous and seeks to slay him. The Lord will not abandon him to his power' (Psalms 37:32–3). [The verse ends, 'or condemn him when he is brought to trial'.]

Several hours earlier, I received the postcard from Natalia in which she writes, 'In Chistopol, too, there is One who guards us at all times and places.'

I strongly embrace you and kiss all of you and my dearest Avital. Next Year in Jerusalem! Again, blessings for the New Year.

★   ★   ★

The use of Shcharansky by the Soviet propaganda machine as a warning to others never ceased: nor did the reiteration of his guilt, in both domestic and overseas statements. On 13 September 1983 a Moscow Radio broadcast, in English, to North America, spoke of Shcharansky as one guilty not only of espionage but also of forgery.

On 15 September 1983 Shcharansky reached the half-way mark of his sentence. At a rally in Jerusalem, Avital appealed for his release. His health was impaired, and he should be set free. It was now more than nine years since she had seen him. At her side, former Prisoner of Zion Iosif Mendelevich gave a graphic description of the harshness of life in Chistopol.

In October 1983 Shcharansky's monthly letter was again dominated by health problems:

Following my hunger strike, for the first seven to eight months, my health improved slightly; but for me in the last two to three months there has been absolutely no improvement. In the last few weeks, my chest pains have been even more bothersome. In any event, I'm not doing any special exercises; I'm not running; but I'm trying to find an appropriate regimen to maintain my health and to avoid further deterioration. The response to my appeal for hospitalisation about which I wrote to you in my last letter was 'the medical commission will check you in October.' The commission comes every six months, and based on past experiences, I have no reason for any special hopes.

In the meantime, I was given ten injections of vitamin B6. Two weeks later, I was given two additional medications without any positive results. Because of that, I again requested

glucose to be administered intravenously because once before
these injections helped me when I was in the prison hospital.
Last winter when I asked for these injections, I was told that the
injections must be administered in a hospital, and they recommended that I take the medication instead. Now, finally, after I
had tried all the medications to no avail, they responded
affirmatively to my request. Today I received the first injection
of a series of ten (glucose, intravenous, 20 ml each). If this
doesn't help, I really don't know what I can do. . . .

In the last three weeks, I've suffered three attacks of painful,
throbbing headaches. . . . I am continuing to write this letter
from yesterday because after the injection, I was left feeling
very lethargic and unable to concentrate. . . .

Again, I had to stop writing because I received a second
injection which left me weakened, and with a heavy head. . . .

The medical commission came. They listened to my heartbeat, and checked my blood pressure. I told them in full detail
about all my symptoms. Tomorrow I hope to have the results.

I have the feeling that the glucose injections are helping me.
For the first time in months, the pains are receding somewhat.
The last two nights I slept better than usual because, prior to
that time, I had to worry about finding a position that was not
especially painful. Too bad they didn't give me these injections
earlier.

The medical commission didn't reach any new conclusion:
the diagnosis is as before. According to them, the heart muscle is
weakened. Once again, new medications have been given to me.

On 14 October 1983 Iosif Begun was sentenced to seven years in
prison and labour camp, to be followed by five years' Siberian exile.
He was fifty-one years old. There were now twenty-five Prisoners
of Zion in prison, labour camp or internal exile, among them Felix
Kochubievsky, a distant relative of the Boris Kochubievsky, who
had been sentenced to three years' labour camp in 1969 and who
was already in Israel. Osip Lokshin and Vladimir Tsukerman were
serving three years in labour camp, Stanislav Zubko four years, Lev
Elbert of Kiev, and Alexander Panarev and Yury Tarnopolsky of
Kharkov, three years. Evgeni Lein of Leningrad was serving a year
in Siberia 'working for the national economy'. Dr Victor
Brailovsky, one of the leaders of the international scientific seminar
of 1976, was serving a four-year sentence of internal exile, at
Beineu, a remote village in desert Kazakhstan.

On 25 November 1983 Shcharansky, in his prison cell, lit the first candles for the Festival of Chanukkah. As he lit them, he told his mother in his letter of December 1, he thought of Avital lighting her candles at the same time, in Jerusalem. This, he wrote, 'linked them together'. He had also received telegrams for Chanukkah, he said, from two of his friends inside the Soviet Union. But his health was bad, his heart hurt, and he had been refused permission to go into hospital.

Even when in pain or severe discomfort, Shcharansky's optimism and good humour never left him. On 10 February 1984 he began another letter in his prison cell with both Hebrew and Arabic greetings:

My dear ones!

Shalom! How are you? Salam Aleikum! (After all, I have to start practising a bit the second official state language of the State of Israel.)

I promised to send you a letter on February 20 and one to Natasha – on March 1. Today it is only the 10th and I am already writing to you. I want so much to prolong the feeling of contact with you that has not left me this year since the moment of our meeting.

I therefore decided that I will write to you slowly, for ten days, and then – for another ten days – to Natasha while replying in the course of this period to any other letters I might receive. Perhaps I felt like starting to write to you today because February 10 is a special date, and I celebrated it early in the morning by drinking a few gulps of especially strong green tea. I remember the stormy events of seven years ago and I compare my experience with that acquired later.

However, my plan was almost stifled at the outset: I just tuned myself towards communicating with you when news from outside broke into my world and removed me from that wave: they reported on the radio the death of the Secretary-General. 'It seems that fate has not willed it that I should write a letter today,' I thought and put it aside.

An hour has gone by and I am going back to it. This is much more pleasant and useful than to engage in senseless reflections and deliberations on what will happen now. Such activity has long since stopped attracting me and I even find it annoying: it is as if a man 'voluntarily' gives himself up to the play of forces beyond his control, while trying to guess where the next wave will bring him. Will it be to the shore? Or, at least, to some sort of island?

After all, the situation one finds oneself in here also provides one with a wonderful opportunity to become the real master of one's destiny, and to feel these great privileges that a man is granted by the feeling of inner freedom and independence from the chaos outside.

The American sociologist Alvin Toffler talked in his book *Future Shock* about the gigantic and constantly increasing tempo of life, about the avalanche of progress which is now brought down upon civilisation, and how, by crushing and breaking up everything on its way, it leaves society without traditions, and people – without roots.

True, his next book, *The Third Wave*, about which I read in the magazines *USA*, *Canada* and others, seems to be a more optimistic one.

The pace of life cannot, of course, be stopped, but I do think that if man cannot attain spiritual independence from this race for the future, or perhaps from his own self, a catastrophe is imminent.

I suddenly noticed that there was no direct connection between this last paragraph on Toffler and the preceding one. True, there was a gap in the line of thought – the thoughts are running quicker than the 'Parker'. In addition, I've received some 'doping' in that parcel. True, I missed a link in the chain of thought, but after all, this is not a school composition 'on a given subject'. Therefore, the letter really looks more like our conversations. In any case, I am trying not to press the throat of my pen too hard: let it write freely.

Sabbath starts soon. I observe it now in the following way: I read parts of Solomon's Proverbs and of some other wise books, excerpts from which I had copied when I had, for a short time, the possibility of reading the Bible. I then filled a whole thick notebook with these writings. Your parcel will, of course, also come in handy at the Sabbath table.

And where, I wonder, is my wife observing this Sabbath? At Uncle Syoma's? In Los Angeles? Or, perhaps, with our Canadian relatives? I can imagine how sick she must be of travelling! I also think that if I were with her there would have been nothing that could induce her to travel. Would not it be nice to lie down somewhere on the beach in Eilat, to go for a swim in the Red Sea! That would be something. And in the meantime – Shabbat Shalom.

It is now the morning of February 12. Let me tell you about the letters I've received during the last two weeks.

It seems that I've already written about the letter from mother (in my last letter) where she told me about the postcards received from some students from Jerusalem and expressed her regret that I might not be able to read them. A friend of mine said that perhaps one or two of them might still reach me. There are some people who are just 'super-optimists'. I am, of course, doing everything I can to see that the optimists should defeat the sceptics. However, as of January 26 I received another four letters from mother, two from Ida Nudel and a greetings card from Lev Petrovich [Ovsishcher].

Ida is so clever! Once a week she sends me a letter, usually containing translations (probably her own) of stories or perhaps a novel by Elie Wiesel (her first letter was confiscated) about Hassidism and its founder, the 'Besht', *The Story of the Master of the Good Name*. I find it immensely interesting. Mother, please write to Ida as soon as possible, thank her very much for me, and ask her to continue!

If the other letters containing the 'story' reach me, then she will send me the first one again. She writes practically nothing about herself, referring to her first letter which I did not get. Perhaps news about Ida's life would reach me more quickly in mother's letters? In her last letter mother included some information about her conversation with Dina, about Natasha's travels (without details and with a promise to include them in the future). I am waiting.

Before writing about my health, let me have a look at my last letter. Everything I wrote about my heart is still true today. The last issue of the *Zdorovie [Health]* magazine – just don't think I take it seriously – had an article describing osteochondrosis, all the symptoms of which reminded me of those of an infarction. Having read the article I realised instantly, in accordance with the prognosis of Jerome K. Jerome, that I am indeed suffering from osteochondrosis (see: *Three Men in a Boat*). However, if I treat this article seriously it explains a few things. If we assume that I am suffering from osteochondrosis it becomes clear why the chest pains increase following a long period of sitting down, after the use of the left arm and following pressure on that arm; it also becomes clear why I often find it easier to walk than to sit. There are, at the same time, other symptoms: the inability to lie down on my left side, the restrictions I am forced to impose on intensive movement, all this in addition to the electrocardiogram which had shown that the diagnosis – weakening of the cardiac muscle – was still correct.

It would have been all the more important to check the diagnosis and to test the assumption about osteochondrosis by an X-ray of the chest. It was not, however, so simple to do this. My eyes, in the meantime, are more or less satisfactory now.

It seems that lack of vitamins finds its expression now in something else – I've started having chills. Any little draught, any slight change in temperature, can immediately cause a chill which lasts a while. The quantity of warm underwear on me has somehow been increasing lately. I discovered that three tablets of Sulfodemisin help to remove the shivering, but then the next morning I feel weak and feel strong chest pains. I understand, however, that what I need is not to swallow medicine but to get stronger physically. I've therefore started doing some anti-osteochondrosis exercises, some exercises for the heart and some for the eyes. So, you see, I don't have that much time left over for writing letters!

While I lie on my back thinking of nothing, it seems that I could lie like that for a hundred years. The question is: is it worth it?

Beset though he was by ill-health, Shcharansky did not allow his thoughts to become oppressed by pain and medication. In a letter to his mother of 6 May 1984 he revealed his innermost reflections on how and why he was able to maintain his strength of will and his beliefs in the face of a whole system designed to break him. The greater the pressure upon him, the greater his reserves. As he wrote to his mother:

It is most difficult to break through, to remove the barriers that separate one's thoughts, one's words and one's deeds from each other – that is, truly to become a free person.

I'm speaking, of course, of my own personal experiences, and recall how difficult it was for me to break through the first barrier; now it seems humorous even to refer to it as a barrier, in comparison to all the other difficulties that followed, such as my trial, etc.

I'm referring to the subject which has preoccupied me for the past several years: what essentially is there to prevent a person from truly being himself? It seems that first and foremost it is fear: fear of the unknown, fear of losing something, even when the magnitude of loss in many cases carries no great significance. To lose one's life or health, to have one's salary lowered, or to experience a dwindling of affection towards you by another, all operate in the same manner. It's clear that if you succeed once in overcoming fear you acquire some experience and become in a sense immunised, albeit not entirely, as I've learned.

When one again has something to lose, the fear is renewed because of that potential loss, and one must again overcome that fear. Little by little, one must become detached from the slave concealed deep within; this is a task for one's entire life.

What then can – and does – help a person overcome fear? Are there specific ingredients that can definitely help towards this end? In 1978, the answer to that question seemed clearer to me than ever before. However, with the passage of time, this clarity has blurred.

At that point, I had just undergone a most difficult period in my life, particularly those few weeks when I had quickly to prepare myself – not to rid myself entirely of this fear, as if that were possible – but to adapt myself to the prevailing circumstances with all possible speed.

I had to adapt so that at the very least my throat would not constrict and my heart would not be pierced, even under the constant badgering of my jailers as to the fatal severity of the verdict which awaited me; to adapt so that my head would remain clear and my words would emerge well thought out and balanced.

Then, to the surprise of my interrogator, in order to hasten the process of this adaptation, I myself began to initiate conversations in this vein so that my ear would lose its sensitivity to those dreaded words and become accustomed to their sound, so that my ear would become 'callous' through this process, just as the sole of one's foot gradually becomes calloused as one walks on the beach's sharp pebbles at the beginning of each bathing season.

For many months, day after day, I was preoccupied with those dreadful mental gymnastics, all the while faithfully repeating to my inner self hundreds of times that white is white and black is black. And so, gradually my memory proceeded to take me back to my past. I recalled each one of my friends and all of them together, and many other things, all with the purpose

of achieving the one goal which remained clearly before my
eyes: to keep myself fixed in that same constellation of relation-
ships of which I was part in previous years.

I was compelled to summon up everything within me to
achieve this objective – all that was stored within my soul and
within easy reach: pictures from my past, thoughts concerning
history and tradition, the Hebrew language and books that I
read, all that remained in my memory from my preoccupation
with mathematics and chess, even visits to the theatre, and, of
course, the ability to laugh – not at jokes or clever plays on
words, but as if I were a spectator viewing the world from the
sidelines, without undue melodramatics, discovering many
interesting things, both comical and absurd at the same time.

All these devices were employed not for the purpose of
struggling against some external force, but rather as a struggle
that I had to conduct within myself, or, more correctly, with
my fear. All told, I recall those days with satisfaction, albeit
with a certain sense of astonishment and even some disappointment which I find difficult to admit to: why did it take so much
for me to continue being myself? Any way I look at it, the
conclusion at the time seemed perfectly clear. There are things
which can help a person under any circumstances of life: a
person's closeness to his family, tradition and faith, as well as
love, literature, science, and one's sense of humour. These
things, when brought down to a level of utter simplicity, help
to enlighten and to purify man's actions as well as the motiva-
tions behind his actions.

However, it may happen – though fortunately not very often
– that at times one is struck by terror, a terrifying fear of man's
image: not the image of any specific human being, but the
image of man as God's handiwork.

How frantically then do the tricks of one's mind and imagination operate, immersing themselves totally in the task of self-
justification, not just to appease others, but rather to placate
oneself, compelling oneself to believe in delusions that are
either self-produced, or perhaps that were conjured up at a
moment's notice.

Under such circumstances, one's love for family and for
those dearest to one's heart can serve to arouse and intensify the
desire to be united with them at the earliest possible moment;
yet, at the same time, such sentimental ties can result in one's
evasion of personal responsibilities.

The accumulation of such data may lead one to observe that 'it would be a shame for all this good to be lost', while one's sense of humour can offer a pragmatically based philosophical approach used to justify selection of a new value base.

While reviewing this entire process, it suddenly dawns upon me that there is nothing that a person cannot convince himself of, provided his desire is deep enough. One is moved to concur with the words of Ivan Karamazov: '. . . Man's breadth is too great. I would rather see him narrowed.' Upon reviewing such thoughts, one again begins to wonder: where then are those absolute values? Where are the absolute parameters which are capable of delivering unambiguous proof of man's spiritual endurance? It appears that, just as in the case of the two-faced Roman god Janus, there are two faces or sides to each issue, and each can serve either as your friend or your foe.

Clearly faith and culture, intelligence, a sense of humour, cannot in and of themselves bequeath to man the spiritual endurance necessary for confronting the most difficult tests of life.

It seems that the source of such spiritual strength is similar to that found in the children's fable about the cauldron of boiling water. One person immerses himself and emerges younger than when he entered. Another immerses in the same water and there meets his death. This is problematic – and I have no solution to this problem. To find a suitable answer to this question is like finding an answer to the question of what is man's soul and what is his spirit: this then becomes a question of faith, which cannot be approached on the basis of rational considerations.

I'll mention here only one thing: in Psalms and in the Book of Proverbs one frequently encounters the phrase 'fear of the Lord'. I'm sure that these words must have a different connotation in the original and I would have liked to quote from the original source; however, I do not want to impose upon the censor. When I read the Book of Psalms for the first time I understood these words to mean fear of God's retribution in payment for the transgressions we have committed.

Yet, the more I continued to read, the more difficult it became to connect the literal meaning of these words and the message which called out to me from the text.

What does King Solomon mean when he states, 'The fear of the Lord is the beginning of knowledge' (Proverbs 1:7), or King

David by his saying, 'The counsel of the Lord is with them that fear Him and his covenant, to make them know it' (Psalms 25:14)? (Incidentally, these words complete the verse engraved on the tombstone over my father's grave.) It is possible to fill tens, if not hundreds of pages with quotations such as these.

In the course of time, one begins to understand that fear of God is a result of an inner stirring brought about by the lofty Divine vision, by a feeling of submission and respect for God's essence, and especially by the instinctive, subconscious fear of man to expose himself as being unsuited for this lofty role and as being unworthy of being chosen for this task with his meagre talents.

It is possible that this feeling (*yirat shamayim* in Hebrew) is the critical prerequisite for man's achieving inner peace and thus also the prerequisite for man's acquiring spiritual endurance. It is possible that fear of God is the one factor capable of conquering human fear, and thus, all that remains for us is to repeat the words of King Solomon, 'The fear of the Lord is the beginning of knowledge.'

And if you ask me: from where does this fear of God come? Was it bequeathed to us from Heaven, or did it evolve in man as a result of some historical process? I would then note that essentially this is a question concerning the authenticity of religion, for which there is no answer today, nor will there be one tomorrow, although well I know how much blood and sweat were spilled over this question and how significant it is for so many people.

I must confess that in my case this question does not exist; that is, for me, knowing that there is no answer to it, I am not actively searching for its source. Is it really important for us to know from where this religious feeling stems – whether it was man himself who succeeded in overcoming his natural physical instincts, or whether man was created with such sensitivities already implanted within his heart? What is significant for me is that I feel a closeness to God in a most tangible manner. I sense its essence and domination over me.

'This feeling of closeness to God', Shcharansky added, 'permeates all of my actions and has far-reaching effects on my entire life.'

On 4 June 1984, within a month of having written this letter, Shcharansky was awarded an Honorary Doctorate of Humane Letters at Yeshiva University in New York. Avital, who received it for him, told those present: 'Having known nothing of the God of Israel, Anatoly has been educated to his Jewishness in a lonely cell in Chistopol prison, where locked alone with the Psalms of David, he found expression for his innermost feelings in the outpourings of the King of Israel thousands of years ago.' Only one part of her husband's struggle was being fought in Chistopol prison, Avital declared, and she went on to explain: 'Each of us here must fight the same fight, must work for the same goals in his personal and communal life: a strengthened Jewish commitment to Torah and to the God who has shown us the beginnings of our redemption; a strengthened human concern for basic human dignities.'

30

From the Urals to Jerusalem

The rumours which had been so persistent in 1983, that Shcharansky would be released that year, proved false. He remained in Chistopol prison. Nor did 1984 bring him any nearer to his Avital. On 26 October 1984 his three-year additional prison sentence at Chistopol came to an end. Four weeks later, on November 18, Ida Milgrom received a telegram from him, telling her that he had 'reached the old place' five days earlier, and that he was 'not feeling bad'. From this telegram she realised that he had left Chistopol prison, and was back at a labour camp in the Perm camp zone.

While Shcharansky began once more the life of a prisoner in labour camp, official pressures against the Jewish emigration mounted. The number of exit visas granted in 1983 had fallen to 1314. In 1984 they fell further, to 896, the lowest since the 1960s. There was also a substantial increase in the number of activists being arrested, tried and sentenced: in the twelve months following Shcharansky's transfer from Chistopol to Perm, fourteen Jews were sent to prison or labour camp for their part in the Jewish movement.

Shcharansky himself was not forgotten, however, amid the pressures of these new arrests, trials and sentences. 'Releasing Anatoly Shcharansky', a New York Times editorial declared on 30 January 1985, 'would light a candle.' His case, and those of other human rights activists and Jewish prisoners, 'discredit Soviet law and mock Soviet pretensions of strength. So does the refusal to permit emigration. Soviet society survived the annual departure of tens of thousands of Jews over recent years; why make criminals of others who want to leave, letting only 900 emigrate in 1984?'

On 1 February 1985, two days after this leading article was

published, yet another Jewish activist, the Hebrew teacher Alexander Kholmiansky, was sentenced in the Estonian Republic to eighteen months in labour camp. On February 4, in Odessa, Mark Nepomniashchy received a three-year sentence.

Yet, despite these sentences, the Jewish spirit refused to be cowed or crushed. One of the most remarkable documents to come from Moscow in 1985 was an appeal to the new General Secretary of the Communist Party, Mikhail Gorbachev, sent on March 7 and signed by twenty-three refuseniks, on behalf of Ida Milgrom who, at the age of seventy-seven, still fought fearlessly for her son, with all the Shcharansky pluck and optimism. Among the signatories of that letter were two women whose husbands were in labour camp; but they were not afraid to sign. 'We ask you to demonstrate a humane attitude,' their letter ended, 'and to release Anatoly Shcharansky!'

In the United States, Joseph Smukler, who had met Shcharansky a decade earlier, told the *Philadelphia Inquirer* on 13 March 1985 that the continued incarceration of Shcharansky was 'a tragic miscarriage of justice. It is an attempt to crush the Jewish movement in the Soviet Union. As far as what he was charged with is concerned, Shcharansky had no more to do with the CIA than I had. Nothing.'

Joseph Smukler had been one of those mentioned in Lipavsky's article of March 1977 as a CIA agent. 'It was a fine fiction,' Smukler commented, and he added: 'If I ever meet up again with Lipavsky, I'll certainly tell him that. But, so far as I know, Lipavsky has been among the "missing" for the last eight years.'

Shcharansky's friends in Moscow had not and would not forget him. In an interview given to a British television team from the 'Panorama' programme, broadcast on 25 March 1985, Professor Lerner described him as 'a hero of the Jewish emigration movement on such a scale as heroes in the Bible.'

Ida Milgrom now made preparations for her next visit to the Urals. She also awaited her next monthly letter, as allowed by Soviet law. But neither the visit nor a monthly letter were to be allowed. On 28 April 1985 Shcharansky wrote to his mother and brother from labour camp:

My dear ones,

Except for facts I can write nothing. The facts are: don't come to see me – all meetings of '85 have been cancelled, all letters I've written to you in March and April confiscated, and all letters you sent me in the last two months also confiscated.

From now on I'll be able to write only once in two months, so the next letter you will probably receive in August.

I ask Avital and mother to remain calm as I do.

Regards to everyone,

Yours,

Tolya

This letter reached Ida Milgrom in Moscow on May 13. That same day in Kiev, yet another Jewish activist, Anatoly Virshubsky, was sentenced to labour camp: he was given a two-year sentence. Three weeks later, on June 7, in Kharkov, Evgeny Aizenberg was sentenced to two and a half years.

Crushing the Jewish movement seemed still, in 1985, to be as urgent a task for the Soviet authorities as it had been in 1977. The Jewish world remained determined to signal, however, to the Soviet authorities that the Jews of Russia were not forgotten. 'And to the Jews of Soviet Russia', Israel's Ambassador to the United Nations, Benjamin Netanyahu, had declared on 5 May 1985, 'we say: you are not alone. You have not been abandoned. We will go on fighting for your rights. We will go on demanding your freedom. We shall not relent. We will not grow tired.'

The trials continued. On 19 June 1985 Evgeny Koifman was arrested, and later sentenced to one year's 'work for the national economy'. On 8 August 1985 Roald Zelichenok, a Hebrew teacher from Leningrad, was sentenced to three years in labour camp. A week later, in Moscow, Vladimir Brodsky was sentenced to three years. Then, in the third week of October 1985, Shcharansky's friend of Moscow days, Leonid Volvovsky, was brought to trial in the city of Gorky, in which he had been confined. Among the accusations against Volvovsky was that he had known both Shcharansky and Iosif Begun. On October 24, the third and final day of the trial, the Judge asked Volvovsky if he wished to seek the 'pardon' of the court. He replied that he would seek 'God's forgiveness' for the Judge, the Public Prosecutor and all those who had participated in his 'groundless conviction'.

Volvovsky's courage in the courtroom, and his refusal to denounce his wish to live in Israel, not only reminded many observers of Shcharansky's courage, but was a part of the courage of the whole Jewish emigration movement. To show solidarity with a man many had not known, Jews travelled from Moscow and Leningrad to be present outside the courtroom, and to support Volvovsky's wife Mila.

Volvovsky was sentenced to three years in labour camp. His sentence was announced three weeks before the Geneva Summit between President Reagan and Chairman Gorbachev, while the Soviet Foreign Minister, Edward Shevarnadze, was in New York for the fortieth anniversary celebrations of the United Nations.

★   ★   ★

In the months leading up to the Geneva Summit, rumours again abounded that Shcharansky would be released, as a 'gesture' to Soviet–American detente. His release was also said to be high on the President's priorities.

Even as the Geneva Summit was being prepared, Shcharansky's right to send even one letter every two months was in jeopardy. In a letter to his mother on 5 October 1985, he had written of how he had been forced to fight with the labour camp authorities for 'each line' in every letter he tried to send. During October he had protested yet again against the Camp Commandant's refusal to let him see any of the letters sent to him from his mother and his friends. In response to his protest Shcharansky was sentenced on October 14 to six months in the labour camp prison.

In the West, as among the refuseniks, attention now focused on the forthcoming summit meeting between President Reagan and Chairman Gorbachev. The refuseniks, wrote Elie Wiesel in the *New York Times* on 22 October 1985, 'are our heroes. They place their hope on us, on our involvement. There are so many. Ida Nudel, Vladimir Slepak, Anatoly Shcharansky . . . the list could go on and on.' Elie Wiesel went on to ask: 'Is Mr Gorbachev capable of making a gesture? Will he make it? Should he do so, the refuseniks' hope in us may be justified, and our hope in him as well.'

In London and Washington, Shcharansky's name, with Sakharov's, was frequently mentioned as an imminent beneficiary of the new detente. Those who had campaigned for Shcharansky's release, however, felt a deep sense of frustration at the thought of yet another false dawn.

On 1 November 1985 Michael Wyschogrod, an Orthodox Rabbi and a survivor of the Holocaust, who had met Shcharansky in Moscow in 1976, wrote in an American Jewish journal: 'Anatoly Shcharansky has now been in prison over eight years and we have accepted it. Of course, we have not liked it. There have been rallies and advertisements, the US and other governments have been influenced to raise the matter at meetings with Soviet officials and so on. But Shcharansky is still rotting in prison. And as things look now, we will not do very much more no matter how long he rots in Soviet prisons.' Rabbi Wyschogrod added: 'I find this situation unacceptable. I do not know how to get Shcharansky out of prison. But I do know that it is our duty to try harder, until it hurts.'

On 1 November 1985 the West German newspaper *Bild* reported that Gorbachev would 'give a signal' for the 'exchange of Sakharov and Shcharansky if the summit meeting 'comes off well'. Two and a half months later, according to a report in the *International Herald Tribune* by Warren Getler, 'Western diplomatic sources have confirmed that high-level talks took place before the Geneva meeting regarding the possible exchange of East-bloc agents for Mr Sakharov, Mr Shcharansky and several others seeking to leave the Soviet Union.'

On the eve of the Geneva Summit every Jewish organisation, as well as many Western parliamentarians, Senators and Congressmen, urged that Shcharansky's release should be a part of any new detente between the Soviet Union and the United States. In New York, Avital stood in silent protest outside the Soviet Mission to the United Nations, then flew to Geneva where, joined by hundreds of Soviet Jewry activists, including former Prisoner of Zion Iosif Mendelevich, she again drew the attention of the world's journalists to her husband's continued incarceration.

The Geneva Summit began on 18 November 1985. It passed with Shcharansky still, after eight and a half years, a prisoner. Nor was any other prisoner given his freedom.

On the first day of the Geneva Summit, Avital Shcharansky, who had already written to both Reagan and Gorbachev, sent a personal appeal to Gorbachev's wife Raisa:

Mrs Raisa Gorbachev

I write to you now as you accompany your husband the General Secretary to the Geneva Summit, because I have been denied unjustly the accompaniment of Anatoly Shcharansky, my husband, for more than eleven years. I send this letter to you, a wife and mother, because I am being deprived without reason of my right to be a wife and mother, to build a home. I turn to you as a woman in the hope that if you have any influence on your husband's decisions your basic human compassion will bring you to ask him to set my husband Anatoly free.

Perhaps in your heart you will be able to sense the suffering I have undergone knowing that the man I love most dearly is behind bars in Chistopol prison or labouring with a serious heart condition in a labour camp in the Urals. The love you feel for your own husband, Mrs Gorbachev, should guide you in understanding the sadness of separation, the constant fear, mingled with the sense of pride and admiration, that my love for Anatoly brings to me. If your love for the General Secretary means sharing with him the joys of children and grandchildren, of planning and living a life together, then you must know, Mrs Gorbachev, that these joys are all denied to me. My husband Anatoly will not come home this evening, we will not discuss together our children's progress at school or what toys to buy them, we will not consider an excursion together. Why should I not be allowed these simple pleasures, because my husband proudly declared that he is a Jew, that his home is in the Jewish Homeland?

Mrs Gorbachev, please do not dismiss my appeal as power politics or international relations that are not of your concern. The benign influence of wives and mothers throughout time shows that women have influenced their husbands not to ignore the human element, that a woman's voice and heart should temper the decisions of husbands involved with tactics and strategic ploys.

Mrs Gorbachev, hear the voice of a woman who suffers unjustly. Let your own voice be heard.

Sincerely,
Avital Shcharansky

The struggle on behalf of Shcharansky thus continued, both in the Soviet Union and among his friends in the West: among hundreds who had met him and among thousands who had not. It was a struggle not only for Shcharansky, but for all the Prisoners of Zion, for all Jews who suffer in prison, labour camp or Siberian exile for their desire to live in Israel: for prisoners like Iosif Begun and Leonid Volvovsky, who were among Shcharansky's contemporaries, and for the new generation of activists imprisoned since Shcharansky's trial, among them Yuly Edelshtein and Iosif Berenshtein from Moscow, Zakhar Zunshain from Riga and Roald Zelichenok from Leningrad – four of the thirteen Jewish prisoners sentenced in 1984 and 1985.

'In my travels throughout the world,' Avital Shcharansky wrote to me on 3 January 1986, 'I have seen interest in Anatoly. I've asked people why. They explain: "There is truth in his struggle, in what he represents."'

'What is this truth then,' Avital went on to ask, 'that stops the breath of every Jew when he talks about Shcharansky or that raises the heads of non-Jews to listen to his incredible story? The truth is the truth of our people – a nation which after two thousand years, after a terrible Holocaust, has shaken off the chains of exile and silence, to renew and gather-in and return home.'

The continuing protest on behalf of Soviet Jewry, Avital Shcharansky added, 'testifies to the size and validity of the struggle. Even in solitary confinement, Anatoly is not sitting in a vacuum.' The spirit of the return of the exiles 'speaks to us', she declared, 'through the struggle and suffering of Anatoly in prison, of Ida Nudel in exile and of Slepak, Volvovsky and their many colleagues. This message transmitted from the prisoners in the persons of young Jews in Russia has led them to study Talmud today while yearning to return to our Land.'

No day passed, during the first month of 1986, without some reference to Shcharansky in the Western press, or his name being noticed; on 15 January 1986 a former visitor to Moscow, Jonathan Wootliff, wrote from New York: 'Whilst walking past the UN last week – only three blocks from our apartment – I noticed an impressive flight of steps, directly opposite the complex, named after Shcharansky. I was moved to see this.' Wootliff added: 'Alas, Shcharansky remains in the USSR, but he is certainly acknowledged as a great hero. Those steps will remain long after he leaves the USSR, we hope.'

On 20 January 1986, while still being held in the labour camp prison at Perm, Shcharansky reached his thirty-eighth birthday. 'Will he be living in Jerusalem, with his Avital, before he is forty?' I wrote on that day, in the final draft of this book. And I added, 'That is a question which only the Soviet leader can answer. But it is one which concerns men and women throughout the world.'

*   *   *

On 21 January 1986, the day after Shcharansky's birthday, the Frankfurt correspondent of the *International Herald Tribune*, Warren Getler, reported that the United States and the Soviet Union had

'resumed secret talks about the release to the West' of both
Sakharov and Shcharansky. Getler gave as his source 'a highly
placed West German chancellery official' and went on to report that
the official, who 'is close to' the German Chancellor Helmut Kohl,
had said on the previous day that 'the talks about release were very
close to success before the Geneva summit'. The official, who asked
not to be identified, added: 'The fact they have now resumed, after
being dropped suddenly prior to the summit, indicates that the
Soviets are interested in improving the chemistry' between
President Reagan and Mikhail Gorbachev. 'Since the summit,' the
official continued, 'the Soviets seem much more aware of the
importance of such a gesture than before,' and he commented that
an East German lawyer, Wolfgang Vogel, was playing an 'active
role' in the negotiations, which involved 'among several options'
an exchange 'of East-bloc agents held in the West for Mr Sakharov
and Mr Shcharansky, and, possibly, a number of Western agents
imprisoned in the East'.

United States officials in Washington and Bonn had declined to
comment on these rumours of an exchange. In Jerusalem, Avital
expressed her scepticism about the surge of rumours. She had been
disappointed too often in the past when similar rumours proved to
be without foundation. Only a month earlier she had asked that
Margaret Thatcher put forward the idea of just such an exchange.
She and her husband had now been apart for more than four
thousand days.

Unknown in the West, or to Shcharansky's mother and brother
in Moscow, on 22 January 1986 he was moved from labour camp to
Moscow and held there in prison. He did not know what the move
portended; only, as he later recalled, that it followed a sudden and
'enormous' improvement in his labour-camp diet, during which he
gained ten kilograms in weight.

During the move, the labour-camp guards took away
Shcharansky's book of Psalms. 'I said I would not leave without the
Psalms that had helped me so much,' he later recalled. 'I lay down in
the snow and said, "Not another step."'

The guards scrutinised the book, then returned it.

While in prison in Moscow, Shcharansky read a Soviet
newspaper report of a speech by Mikhail Gorbachev stating how
much things had changed for the better in the Soviet Union.
Shcharansky later commented: 'I wanted to write him a letter.
"How can you speak about civilised methods of behaviour?"' After

all, even in Gorbachev's short period of power he had spent 128 days in an isolation cell. Since his arrest on 15 March 1977 he had spent 3255 days in prison and labour camp.

Unaware of Shcharansky's move to Moscow, and unwilling as always to relax her efforts even for a day, Avital continued to seek public support on her husband's behalf, speaking on the morning of 28 January 1986 to a group of Jews from Philadelphia, who had come to Israel on a Young Leadership Mission. Later that morning she and Enid Wurtman reminisced about the tape-recorded message which Enid had brought from Shcharansky more than a decade before. 'With laughter in her voice', Enid wrote to me that night, 'she said, "Soon we'll sit down with Anatoly in Jerusalem and share all our recollections".' Enid Wurtman added: 'She is always so full of hope, so full of optimism.'

The rumours about Shcharansky's imminent release persisted, as diplomatic activity intensified between Jerusalem and Washington, Bonn and East Berlin. 'Dissident May Be Freed in Swap' was the headline in *The Times* on 3 February 1986, where Frank Johnson, Bonn correspondent, reported a claim in the West German newspaper *Bild* that Shcharansky was 'about to be released' in exchange for 'an unspecified, but large, number of captured Eastern bloc agents being held in Western prisons'. According to that morning's issue of *Bild*, 'the exchange will probably take place in the next few days'.

Contacted that day in Moscow by Western journalists, Leonid Shcharansky commented: 'There have been rumours before and I hoped for Anatoly's release, but I did not really believe it would happen. This time I believe it will.'

Leonid Shcharansky also told the journalists who spoke to him on February 3 that he had just received a letter from labour camp, in which his brother reported that he was being 'treated better', was receiving medical attention, and had been allowed 'more time for reading, walking and resting.'

Throughout the evening of February 3 those who maintained regular telephone contact with Moscow passed on the news of the rumours of Shcharansky's possible release. It was at nine o'clock that evening that one of those calls was made to the apartment at which Vladimir Slepak was having supper with a group of refusenik friends and Western visitors. 'They were as delighted for Shcharansky as they would have been for themselves,' one of those visitors recalled.

That same evening, Professor Lerner told Western reporters: 'If

Anatoly is freed, there will be a great festival among all his friends, relatives and fellow refuseniks.' Lerner went on to warn, however, that Shcharansky's release, if it took place, 'does not mean we would follow him. Shcharansky is a special case, a separate problem, and we have seen no sign of improvement in the general area of Jewish emigration.' Similar concerns were expressed by Professor Meiman, Shcharansky's Jewish successor on the now disbanded Helsinki Watchdog group. 'I am very glad for Anatoly and his family,' Meiman declared, 'but this has no meaning for the general question of the observance of human rights in the Soviet Union.'

The worries among refuseniks that Shcharansky's release might not benefit them were swamped in the intensification of speculation. By the beginning of the second week of February it became clear from reports in Washington that the rumours of his imminent release might indeed be true.

On the morning of 11 February 1986, as the Western world awaited the release of Shcharansky, hundreds of television reporters gathered at the Glienicke Bridge linking Potsdam, in East Germany, with West Berlin. Shcharansky awoke that morning in a Moscow prison, not knowing what was in prospect. 'I was sitting in the cell', he recalled three days later 'and reading, by the way, the German writer Schiller. I was suddenly taken from this cell. They took off all my clothes, prison clothes, and brought me civilian ones.' Shcharansky's account continued:

> Then I was taken to the airport and put in the aeroplane, accompanied by four KGB men. And our direction was West, judging from the sun. That's why I presumed that something especially pleasant was going on. I was very excited. Then, when about two hours passed and it seemed it can't be the Urals, it must be the border of the Soviet Union, I started demanding from them to explain. Finally one of the KGB men came and said he was authorised to tell me the Supreme Soviet of the Soviet Union has deprived me of the Soviet citizenship due to my very bad behaviour, undermining the honour of being a Soviet citizen.
>
> Then I answered. I said that first of all, I am deeply satisfied that thirteen years after I asked to deprive me of the Soviet citizenship, my demand is already met.

The aeroplane landed at East Berlin airport. His KGB escort still refused to tell Shcharansky where he was. Then he saw the letters

DDR; he was in the German Democratic Republic. 'It was a little disappointing,' he recalled. But, as the unexplained journey continued to the East German side of the Glienicke Bridge, the KGB escort told Shcharansky 'to walk in a straight line' directly across the bridge to the car of the United States Ambassador to Bonn. 'You know I *never* make an agreement with the KGB,' he replied. 'If you tell me to go directly, I will go in a zig-zag.'

Thus it was that, after a week of intense diplomatic activity and public anticipation, television viewers throughout the Western world watched as Shcharansky took his first steps to freedom. 'For every Jew', he commented, 'the word Berlin evokes mixed feelings. But for me, at this time, it is the most wonderful place.'

Shcharansky, who was not a spy, was exchanged for spies, but, at American insistence, was brought out first and alone. The exchange brought him first from snow-bound Moscow to Berlin, then to Frankfurt where he was reunited with his Avital with the words, 'I'm sorry I'm late,' and finally, in the warmth of a Mediterranean evening, to Israel.

Reaching Israel, Shcharansky was met and embraced at the aircraft by the Israeli Prime Minister, Shimon Peres, and, with Avital at his side, looked out at an ecstatic, singing crowd. A few moments later he spoke to the hundreds of well-wishers, including many Western journalists and former refusenik friends of his Moscow days. With characteristic humour he began: 'I say that I am very glad to have an opportunity to speak to the audience in which my criminal contacts are represented so widely.' Shcharansky went on:

> But at the same time I feel it's very difficult for me to speak now, and it's not only because my Hebrew is still, as you understand, very weak, but also because there are such moments in our life which are simply impossible to describe them and such feelings which it is simply impossible to express them in any language.
>
> I know too little about what happened in the world during these years, but I know very well how dangerous were initial plans of KGB after my arrest and I know very well how strong was their *hatred* and I know very well how firm was their determination never to let this day come.
>
> In this happiest day of our life I am not going to forget those whom I left in the camps, in prisons, who are still in exile or who still continue their struggle for the right to emigrate and for their human rights.

In a telephone call from Ben Gurion airport to President Reagan, Shcharansky told the President: 'First of all I know how great was your role in this greatest event of my and my wife's life, that fact that I could join my people today in Israel, and of course we are both very deeply grateful to you for this. Second, as you know well, I was never an American spy.'

From Moscow, Mila Volvovsky, whose husband, a leading fighter for Jewish rights, was in labour camp in the early months of a three-year sentence, telegraphed to Jerusalem: 'YOUR HEROISM TOLYA GAVE US STRENGTH TO LIVE DURING THESE LONG YEARS. OUR HAPPINESS TODAY IS ENDLESS.'

In Moscow, Alexander Lerner told Western journalists: 'It is the happiest day of my life', while Ida Milgrom, now aged seventy-eight, who had last seen her son more than a year earlier, told Western reporters: 'Anatoly is free. Lord God above, Anatoly is free. I used to read it only on appeals: "Free Anatoly Shcharansky." I am at peace. He will be in his own country with his wife.'

*   *   *

That night in Jerusalem, Shcharansky was carried on the shoulders of an excited crowd milling in front of the Western, or 'Wailing', Wall. There, clasping the book of Psalms which he had always refused to give up while in labour camp, he gave thanks for his deliverance, a solemn moment seen by millions of television viewers throughout the Western world. Then, as he returned with Avital to their apartment in Jerusalem, the city in which she had waited for him for more than eleven years, the vast crowd broke into song: the Jewish and Israeli anthem 'Hatikvah' – Hope; the anthem that had been sung by his friends in July 1978 outside the Moscow courthouse on learning that he had received a thirteen-year sentence.

*   *   *

Within a few hours of Shcharansky reaching his promised land, his qualities, of which his friends and Avital had never been in any doubt, became clear to a wider world. Eight and a half years in prison and labour camp had not diminished his sense of humour or blunted his concern for others. 'I am first of all concerned with the people who belong to the same Jewish movement as I do,' he told his first press conference in Jerusalem. 'At the same time, I cannot forget the prisoners with whom I spent so many hard years and who continue suffering. It is my obligation now to remind people in the West of the fate of people like Andrei Sakharov.'

There were 'so many people' who had helped bring him and Avital together, Shcharansky added: 'We must help these people to help other people.' As well as fighting for prisoners like Iosif Begun and former prisoners like Vladimir Slepak and Ida Nudel, he would, he said, be learning Arabic, in order, as he had earlier explained in one of his letters from prison, to be able to live in a land where Jew and Arab must live side by side in harmony. It was his hope 'that as many Jews as possible will come to live here, and that one day we may have peace in this country.' Learning Arabic was a part of this vision.

Shcharansky's sentiments caught the imagination of tens of thousands of people, who could not but be attracted to the man whom the *Jewish Chronicle* described as having stepped off the aeroplane 'his spirit uncrushed, his mind clear and his vision unclouded'; a man who had shown 'a sense of humour, a lightness of spirit, a shining intelligence, an unshakable resistance to oppression'.

★   ★   ★

In 1973, when Shcharansky first applied for an exit visa, his aim was clear, summed up in the age-old Jewish prayer, 'Next Year in Jerusalem'. That was also what he hoped for in 1975 and 1976, when he mobilised his whole personal strength in the struggle for his fellow Russian Jews who wished likewise to be reunited with their people in Israel. It was what he hoped for in 1977, when the Soviet authorities set in train the plan to crush the Jewish activist movement through the terrible accusation of espionage, an accusation as fearful as it was false, reviving the worst memories of the 'Doctors' Plot' accusation of Stalin's final year. 'Next Year in Jerusalem' was what he hoped for, too, throughout more than fifteen months of imprisonment without trial, and at the trial itself, when, from his mouth, those words were heard in a hostile Soviet courtroom, spoken with such courage and faith, the ancient prayer of two thousand years of hope to return home in the end; and spoken in Hebrew, the language of the Jewish national revival, as he faced a thirteen-year sentence. That hope had remained strong in every one of his letters from prison and labour camp. 'He says it every day, with all his soul': such were Avital Shcharansky's words on 6 January 1986, as she looked back over eleven years of separation, could not see how or when that separation would end, but was made strong by his strength, by his faith, and urged me to try to convey that strength and faith in these pages.

Ten years ago, in sending a message to the West about the Soviet cancellation of the Soviet–American Trade Agreement, on which the refuseniks had placed their hopes, Shcharansky and his friends declared: 'Like the Jewish people at all times we are firmly withstanding the blows of fate. We firmly believe in the idea of ingathering of exiles and we believe in the support of all honest men, Jews and non-Jews, in their strength, influence and abilities to find new methods of struggle for our rights.'

This belief in the in-gathering of the exiles was not destroyed by Shcharansky's unjust sentence, neither for him, nor for hundreds of thousands of other Soviet Jews. Nor can it ever be destroyed. His release on 11 February 1986 was and will remain a beacon of light to them, as well as a call to the Western world not to relinquish its efforts on behalf of those who remain: prisoners, former prisoners, and refuseniks. Shcharansky's struggle focused world attention on their plight; his dramatic arrival in Jerusalem raised their hopes at what is still, for them, a desperate time. 'Everything is deeply frozen, I would say,' was the comment of one activist who spoke to me from Moscow on 12 February 1986, 'except for one event which took place yesterday. We are very glad.' Among Jews everywhere, and among free men, that gladness was universal. So too was the determination to help the remaining prisoners, the former prisoners still refused their exit visas, the ten thousand and more refuseniks, including those in refusal as Shcharansky had been for more than a decade, and all other Soviet Jews who wished to do so, to achieve their Passover prayer and national dream: 'Next Year in Jerusalem'.

Appendices, Bibliography, Maps and Index

Appendix 1

Prisoners of Zion on 12 February 1986

Rabbi Moshe Abramov
Arrested: 19 December 1983
Charge: Malicious hooliganism
Date of trial: 23 January 1984
Sentence: 3 years' labour camp

Evgeny Aizenberg
Arrested: 19 March 1985
Charge: Spreading false information and
                       defaming the Soviet Union
Date of trial: 6 June 1985
Sentence: $2\frac{1}{2}$ years' labour camp, reduced
                       on appeal to 1 year

Iosif Begun
Arrested: 6 November 1982
Charge: Anti-Soviet agitation and
                       propaganda
Date of trial: 14 October 1983
Sentence: 12 years – 3 prison, 4 labour
                       camp, 5 internal exile

Iosif Berenshtein
Arrested: 12 November 1984
Charge: Resisting the authorities
Date of trial: 10 December 1984
Sentence: 4 years' labour camp

Vladimir Brodsky
Arrested: 16 May 1985
Charge: Malicious hooliganism
Date of trial: 15 August 1985
Sentence: 3 years' labour camp

Yuly Edelshtein
Arrested: 4 September 1984
Charge: Trafficking in drugs
Date of trial: 20 December 1984
Sentence: 3 years' labour camp

Nadezhda Fradkova
Arrested: May 1984
Charge: Parisitism
Date of trial: 18 December 1984
Sentence: 2 years' labour camp

Evgeny Koifman
Arrested: 19 June 1985
Charge: Possession of drugs
Date of trial: 17 September 1985
Sentence: $2\frac{1}{2}$ years' service to national
                             economy

Yakov Levin
Arrested: 10 August 1984
Charge: Dissemination of anti-Soviet
                             propaganda
Date of trial: 19 November 1984
Sentence: 3 years' labour camp

Vladimir Livshits
Arrested: 8 January 1986
Charge:
Date of trial:
Sentence:

Mark Nepomniashchy
Arrested:	12 October 1984
Charge:	Defaming the Soviet State
Date of trial:	31 January 1985
Sentence:	3 years' labour camp

Lev Shefer
Arrested:	21 September 1981
Charge:	Anti-Soviet propaganda
Date of trial:	6 April 1982
Sentence:	5 years' prison, strict regime

Yury Tarnopolsky
Arrested:	15 March 1983
Charge:	Defaming the Soviet State
Date of trial:	30 June 1983
Sentence:	3 years' labour camp

Anatoly (Natan) Virshubsky
Arrested:	19 February 1985
Charge:	Misappropriation of State or public property by theft
Date of trial:	7 May 1985
Sentence:	2 years' labour camp

Leonid (Ari) Volvovsky
Arrested:	25 June 1985
Charge:	Anti-Soviet agitation and propaganda
Date of trial:	22 October 1985
Sentence:	3 years' labour camp

Alexander Yakir
Arrested:	19 June 1984
Charge:	Refusal of military service
Date of trial:	2 August 1984
Sentence:	2 years' labour camp

Roald (Alec) Zelichenok
   Arrested: 10 June 1985
   Charge: Anti-Soviet slander
   Date of trial: 8 August 1985
   Sentence: 3 years' labour camp

Zakhar Zunshain
   Arrested: 4 March 1984
   Charge: Defaming the Soviet State
   Date of trial: 22 June 1984
   Sentence: 3 years' labour camp

Appendix 2

Former Prisoners of Zion Still Refused Exit Visas as of 12 February 1986

	Arrested	Completed Sentence
Victor Brailovsky	1980	1984
Boris Chernobilsky	1981	1982
Lev Elbert	1983	1984
Kim Fridman	1981	1982
Gregory Geishis	1980	1982
Gregory Goldshtein	1978	1979
Boris Kalendarev	1979	1981
Boris Kanyevsky	1982	1985
Alexander Kholmiansky	1984	1986
Vladimir Kislik	1981	1984
Felix Kochubievsky	1982	1985
Evgeny Lein	1981	1982
Osip Lokshin	1981	1984
Ida Nudel	1978	1982
Mark Ocheretyansky	1983	1985
Alexander Panarev	1983	1984
Alexander Paritsky	1981	1984
Dmitri Shchiglik	1980	1981
Simon Shnirman	1983	1986
Victor Shtilbans	1970	1971
Vladimir Slepak	1978	1982
Vladimir Tsukerman	1981	1984
Alexander Vilig	1979	1980
Stanislav Zubko	1981	1985

Appendix 3

Annual Emigration of Soviet Jews, 1951 to 1985

Year	Number	Year	Number
1951	186	1969	3,011
1952	56	1970	1,044
1953	39	1971	13,033
1954	26	1972	31,681
1955	123	1973	34,733
1956	460	1974	20,767
1957	1,314	1975	13,363
1958	720	1976	14,261
1959	1,353	1977	16,737
1960	1,917	1978	28,864
1961	216	1979	51,320
1962	184	1980	21,471
1963	304	1981	9,475
1964	530	1982	2,638
1965	887	1983	1,314
1966	2,027	1984	896
1967	1,416	1985	1,140
1968	230		

Bibliography
of works consulted

Section 1: Books and pamphlets

Ludmila Alexeeva, *History of Dissent in the USSR*, New York, 1984 (Russian).

Amnesty International, *Prisoners of Conscience in the USSR: Their Treatment and Conditions*, London, 1975.

Mark Azbel, *Refusenik*, London, 1982.

Salo W. Baron, *The Russian Jew under Tsars and Soviets*, New York, 1964 (second edition, enlarged and revised, 1976).

Cilly Brandstatter (editor), *Yosif Begun, The Struggle for Jewish Culture in the USSR, A Collection of Documents*, Jerusalem, 1979.

Hillel Butman, *The Long Stopover: Leningrad–Jerusalem*, Jerusalem, 1981 (Russian), Jerusalem, 1982 (Hebrew).

Hillel Butman, *It's Time To Keep Silent, It's Time to Speak*, Jerusalem, 1984 (Russian), Jerusalem, 1985 (Hebrew).

Commission on Security and Cooperation in Europe, Congress of the United States, *Reports of Helsinki Accord Monitors in the Soviet Union*, volumes 1–3, 1976–8.

Irwin Cotler, *The Shcharansky Appeal: Petition to the Procurator-General of the USSR from Avital Shcharansky, on behalf of herself and her husband, Anatoly Shcharansky, by her attorney Professor Irwin Cotler*, presented on 30 August 1978.

Evidence Submitted to the Ad Hoc Commission on Justice for Anatoly Shcharansky, Washington DC, 20 October 1977.

George P. Fletcher, *The Current Legal Posture of the Shcharansky Case*, Los Angeles, 1979.

Robert O. Freedman (editor), *Soviet Jewry in the Decisive Decade, 1971–80*, Durham, North Carolina, 1984.

Lev Gendin, *My Visit to the Gulag Archipelago*, Cleveland, Ohio, 1974.

Martin Gilbert, *The Jews of Russia: Their History in Maps and Photographs*, London, 1976 (second edition, dedicated to Anatoly Shcharansky, Vladimir Slepak and Ida Nudel, Jerusalem, 1979).

Yehoshua Gilboa, *The Black Years of Soviet Jewry*, Boston, 1971.

S. J. Goldsmith (editor), *Vladimir Slepak: A Favourite Son of Soviet Jewry*, London, no date.

Alan G. Howard, *The Case of Dr Mikhail Shtern*, London, 5 June 1975.

Jacob Ingerman (editor), *Jews and the Jewish People: Petitions, Letters and Appeals from Soviet Jews*, Jerusalem, 1976.

Israel Women for Ida Nudel, *Our Ida Nudel, Testimonies of Former Prisoners and Refuseniks*, Tel Aviv, 1980.

Z. Jeremiah, *Mark Nashpits, The Story of a Refusenik Dentist*, Manchester, 1981.

Dina Kaminskaya, *Final Judgement, My Life as a Soviet Defence Lawyer*, London, 1982.

Felix Kandel, *The Gates of our Exodus*, Jerusalem, 1980 (Russian), Tel Aviv, 1981 (Hebrew).

Felix Kandel, *My Son Anatoly Shcharansky*, Tel Aviv, 1977.

Felix Kandel and Jerome E. Singer, *People Without a Present, The Prestins, The Plight of a Refusenik Family*, Tel Aviv, 1980.

Lionel Kochan (editor), *The Jews in Soviet Russia since 1917*, London, 1970.

William Korey, *Human Rights and the Helsinki Accord: Focus on U.S. Policy*, New York, 1983.

William Korey, *The Soviet Cage*, New York, 1973.

Edward Kuznetsov, *Prison Diaries*, New York, 1975.

Iosif Mendelevich, *Operation Wedding*, Jerusalem, 1985 (Hebrew).

William W. Orbach, *The American Movement to Aid Soviet Jews*, Amherst, Massachusetts, 1979.

Benjamin Pinkus, *The Soviet Government and the Jews, 1948–1967, A documented study*, Cambridge, 1984.

David Prital (editor), *In Search of Self: The Soviet Jewish Intelligentsia and the Exodus*, Jerusalem, 1982.

Peter Reddaway (editor), *Uncensored Russia, the Human Rights Movement in the Soviet Union*, London, 1972.

Louis Rosenblum (editor), *The White Book of Exodus (January–June 1972)*, Cleveland, Ohio, 1973.

Joshua Rubenstein, *Soviet Dissidents, Their Struggle for Human Rights*, London, 1981.

Avtandil Rukhadze, *Jews in the USSR, Figures, Facts, Comment*, Moscow, 1982.

Leonard Schroeter, *The Last Exodus*, New York, 1974.

Avital Shcharansky (with Ilana Ben-Josef), *Next Year in Jerusalem*, London, 1980.

Colin Shindler, *Exit Visa: Detente, Human Rights and the Jewish emigration movement in the USSR*, London, 1978.

Dr Jerome E. Singer, *The Case of Yosif Begun, Analysis and Documents*, Tel Aviv, 1979.

August Stern (editor), *The USSR vs. Dr Mikhail Stern*, New York, 1977.

Student Struggle for Soviet Jewry, *The Jews of Ilyinka*, New York, 1976.

Student Struggle for Soviet Jewry, *Gulag Diary: life in Perm camp no. 35*, New York, 1977.

Student Struggle for Soviet Jewry, *Shcharansky's Last Letter*, New York, 1977.

Student Struggle for Soviet Jewry, *Letters from Chistopol*, volumes 1–4, New York, 1979–84.

Student Struggle for Soviet Jewry, *Vladimir Prison: Joseph Mendelevich's Inside Story of Life in the Gulag*, New York, 1984.

Union of Councils for Soviet Jews and Student Struggle for Soviet Jewry, *The Labyrinth: How to Apply to Leave Russia for Israel*, New York, 1976.

Union of Councils for Soviet Jews and Student Struggle for Soviet Jewry, *'Next Year in Jerusalem': The Trial of Anatoly Shcharansky*, New York, 1978.

Alexander Voronel and Viktor Yakhot (editors), *I Am A Jew, Essays on Jewish Identity in the Soviet Union*, New York, 1973.

Working Group on the Internment of Dissenters in Mental Hospitals, *The Political Abuse of Psychiatry in the Soviet Union*, London, 1977.

World Conference on Soviet Jewry, *Soviet Jewry and the Implementation of the Helsinki Final Act, Report*, London, 1977.

World Conference on Soviet Jewry, *The Position of Soviet Jewry 1977–1980: Report on the Implementation of the Helsinki Final Act since the Belgrade Follow-up Conference*, Surrey, England, 1980.

World Conference on Soviet Jewry, *The Position of Soviet Jewry, Human Rights and the Helsinki Accords, 1985*, London, 1985.

World Union of Jewish Students, *Leningrad 1970: The Protocols of the Leningrad Trial*, London, 1970.

Michael Yudkin and Joan Dale (editors), *The Excluded from Science, The Story of Soviet Refusenik Scientists*, London, 1983.

Section 2: Articles

Bella S. Abzug, 'The Labyrinth: How to Apply to Leave Russia for Israel', *Congressional Record*, 2 July 1976.

Associated Press, 'Soviet Jews' Symposium Cut Short by Police', *New York Times*, 23 December 1976.

Associated Press, 'Soviet Releases Jews Held 4 Days to Thwart Vigil', *New York Times*, 26 December 1976.

Zeev Ben-Shlomo, 'Intimidation Soviet aim', *Jewish Chronicle*, 21 July 1978.

Zeev Ben-Shlomo, 'Shcharansky release hint', *Jewish Chronicle*, 25 February 1983.

Patricia Blake, 'Visit with a Survivor', *Time*, 24 February 1986.

Barbara Boxer, 'Anatoly Shcharansky's Day in an American Court', *Congressional Record*, Washington DC, 27 January 1983.

Barbara Boxer, 'A Nobel Peace Prize Nomination', *Congressional Record*, Washington DC, 2 February 1983.

Peter Brod, 'Soviet–Israeli Relations 1948–56: from Courtship to Crisis', in Robert S. Wistrich (editor), *The Left Against Zion: Communism, Israel and the Middle East*, London, 1979.

William M. Brodhead, 'Anatoly Shcharansky', *Congressional Record*, Washington DC, 8 June 1977.

Miriam Chinsky, 'Avital Continuing Her Quest', *Canadian Jewish News*, 13 November 1980.

Fred Coleman, 'Life in the Gulag', *Newsweek*, 13 November 1978.

Douglas Davis, 'Avital's Ordeal', *Jerusalem Post Magazine*, 2 March 1979.

Helen Davis, 'Avital's lonely ordeal', *Israel Scene*, January 1981.

Helen Davis, 'Waiting for Anatoly', *Jerusalem Post*, 4 July 1984.

Alan Dershowitz, 'Shcharansky's Innocence', *Washington Post*, 4 August 1978.

Robert F. Drinan, 'Soviet Union Charges Leading Jewish Activist with High Treason', *Congressional Record*, Washington DC, 2 June 1977.

Robert F. Drinan, 'An Appeal to President Reagan on Behalf of Anatoly Shcharansky', *Outcry: Newsletter of the Bay Area Council on Soviet Jewry*, San Francisco, February–March 1981.

Robert F. Drinan, 'Shcharansky: a giant in chains', *Denver Post*, 13 March 1981.

Joshua Eilberg, 'Orphans of the Exodus from the Soviet Union', *Congressional Record*, Washington DC, 16 March, 1976.

Joshua Eilberg, 'A Desperate Appeal for Help', *Congressional Record*, Washington DC, 21 September 1976.

Rowland Evans and Robert Nowak, 'Testing Carter with the Shcharansky Case', *Washington Post*, 9 June 1978.

Millicent Fenwick, 'Monitoring the Helsinki Accord', *Congressional Record*, Washington DC, 23 March 1976.

Millicent Fenwick, 'Anatoly Shcharansky Charged with Treason in USSR', *Congressional Record*, Washington DC, 1 June 1977.

Suzanne Garment, 'Mr Shcharansky Will Soon Be Halfway Home', *Wall Street Journal*, 9 September 1983.

Warren Getler, 'US Reported in Secret Talks on Soviet Dissidents', *International Herald Tribune*, 21 January 1986.

Martin Gilbert, 'Birthday greetings', *Jerusalem Post*, 20 January 1984.

Bernard Gwertzman, 'US "Deeply Concerned" Over Soviet Jewry Activist', *New York Times*, 3 June 1977.

Bernard Gwertzman, 'Carter Denies CIA Engaged Soviet Jew', *New York Times*, 14 June 1977.

Bernard Gwertzman, US Academy Acted to Aid Shcharansky', *New York Times*, 25 December 1977.

Bernard Gwertzman, 'Javits and Visiting Soviet Officials Clash Over the Shcharansky Case', *New York Times*, 27 January 1978.

Sarah Honig, 'An Effort at Intimidation', *Jerusalem Post*, 4 February 1977.

Sarah Honig, 'Dissident's case could lead to show-trial', *Jerusalem Post*, 17 March 1977.

Frank Johnson, 'Dissident May Be Freed in Swop', *The Times*, 3 February 1986.

Laurie Johnston, 'Wife Denies Soviet Dissident is Spy', *New York Times*, 20 October 1977.

William Korey, 'The Story of the Jackson Amendment', *Midstream*, volume 21, number 3, March 1975.

William Korey, 'The Struggle Over the Jackson Amendment', *American Jewish Year Book*, 1976, pages 160–70.

William Korey, 'The Soviet Dreyfus Case: Awaiting the Shcharansky Verdict', *New Leader*, 10 April 1978.

William Korey, 'American Reaction to the Shcharansky Case', *American Jewish Year Book*, 1980, pages 118–29.

Edward Kuznetsov, 'The Shcharansky lesson', *Jerusalem Post*, 29 March 1981.

Anthony Lewis, 'Andropov Could Send a Human Rights Signal', *International Herald Tribune*, 19 November 1982.

Emanuel Litvinoff (editor), 'The Yom Kippur War: Jews in USSR rally to Israel', *Jews in Eastern Europe*, volume 6, number 1, London, May 1974.

Emanuel Litvinoff (editor), 'Why the Soviet Union Cancelled the Trade Agreement', *Insight: Soviet Jews*, volume 1, number 1, London, March 1975.

Emanuel Litvinoff (editor), 'Jewish Prisoners: Their Life in Labour Camps', *Insight: Soviet Jews*, volume 1, number 4, London, June 1975.

Emanuel Litvinoff (editor), 'The Struggle For Liberation', *Insight: Soviet Jews*, volume 2, number 2, London, February 1976.

Phyllis Z. Miller, 'Local Couple Sees Soviet Harassment', *Jewish Exponent*, Philadelphia, 21 December 1973.

Peter Osnos, 'Soviets to Charge Treason', *Washington Post*, 2 June 1977.

Peter Osnos, 'Memories of Moscow: The Spy Brought Roses', *Washington Post*, 10 March 1978.

Claiborne Pell, 'Anatoly Shcharansky', *Congressional Record*, Washington DC, 6 June 1977.

Shimon Peres, 'Israel 25 Years hence', *Jerusalem Post*, 11 May 1973.

Joyce Purnick, 'Kremlin tactic splits husbands and wives', *New York Post*, 24 March 1977.

Peter Reddaway, 'Russian Jews fear spy trials "Dreyfus-style" and fresh persecution', *The Times*, 16 March 1977.

Vitaly Rubin, 'A Third Life', diary extracts, *Narod i Zemliya*, number 3, 1985, pages 152–75 (Russian).

Jonathan Schenker, 'The Shcharansky Commission', *Congress Monthly: A Journal of Opinion and Jewish Affairs*, volume 44, number 8, November 1977.

Serge Schmemann, 'Shcharansky is Reported Back in Prison', *New York Times*, 8 January 1982.

Serge Schmemann, 'The Prison Fast by Shcharansky: Is It Over?', *New York Times*, 30 January 1983.

Serge Schmemann, 'Harried Soviet Rights Unit Disbands', *New York Times*, 9 September 1982.

Avital Shcharansky, 'Human Rights: What's The Use of Talking?', *Wall Street Journal*, 12 August 1983.

Avital Shcharansky, 'Free My Husband, My People', *Wall Street Journal*, 18 November 1985.

David K. Shipler, 'Moscow Jews Say They Were Beaten After a Visa Sit-In', *New York Times*, 20 October 1976.

David K. Shipler, 'Jews Are Promised High Soviet Parley', *New York Times*, 21 October 1976.

David K. Shipler, 'Two Moscow Jews Face Charge of "Hooliganism" After Protests', *New York Times*, 4 November 1976.

David K. Shipler, '2 Moscow Jews Who Faced Prison Up to 5 Years for Protests Are Released as First Offenders and Family Men', *New York Times*, 16 November 1976.

David K. Shipler, 'Uzbek Jew, Deprived of Passport, Gets 3 Years for Not Having One', *New York Times*, 13 January 1977.

David K. Shipler, 'Soviet Links Dissidents to CIA; Arrests Expected', *New York Times*, 5 March 1977.

David K. Shipler, 'Soviet Charges a Key Jewish Human-Rights Activist With Treason', *New York Times*, 2 June 1977.

David K. Shipler, 'Soviet Will Begin Trial Monday For Activist Defended by Carter', *New York Times*, 8 July 1978.

David K. Shipler, 'Mother of Dissident Says She Got No Trial Notice', *New York Times*, 9 July 1978.

David K. Shipler, 'Portents of Soviet Dissident's Trial', *New York Times*, 10 July 1978.

David K. Shipler, 'Shcharansky Link to Reporters Cited', *New York Times*, 13 July 1978.

David K. Shipler, 'Shcharansky Given 13 Years in Prison And Labour Camps', *New York Times*, 15 July 1978.

David K. Shipler, 'Shcharansky Trial Breaks New Ground', *New York Times*, 17 July 1978.

David K. Shipler, 'Crisis for Russia's Dissidents', *New York Times Magazine*, 23 July 1978.

David K. Shipler, 'Shcharansky Case: an Emigré's Version', *New York Times*, 17 December 1979.

David K. Shipler, 'Soviet Jew Accuses KGB of Threats', *International Herald Tribune*, 2 February 1984.

Shmuel Shnitzer, '1984 is not coming', *Maariv*, 31 December 1983.

Seth M. Siegel, 'The Shcharanskys' Story', *Midstream*, December 1980.

Judy Siegel-Itzkovich, 'Free Man in a Soviet Cell', *Jerusalem Post*, 5 November 1982.

Jerome E. Singer and Isaac Elkind, 'The Case of Ida Nudel', *Israel Yearbook on Human Rights*, volume 9, Tel Aviv, 1979.

Aaron Sittner, 'New Soviet anti-Jewish drive worst in 25 years, Allon says', *Jerusalem Post*, 17 March 1977.

Stan Solomon, 'Shcharansky's relatives still have hope for future', *Toronto Globe*, 29 September 1979.

Betty Steck, 'Shcharansky's Friends Tell of His Humanity', *Jewish Exponent*, 25 November 1977.

Philip Taubman, 'Eased Labour Camp Conditions Reported in Letter by Shcharansky', *New York Times*, 4 February 1986.

Telford Taylor, 'Trials and Tribulations in Soviet Courts', *New York Times*, 26 June 1975.

Edward Teller, 'How Andropov could quickly make himself look good', *Christian Science Monitor*, 30 December 1982.

Harold Ticktin, 'A Tribute to Vitaly Rubin, Former Refusenik, Teacher and Scholar', *Congress Monthly, A Journal of Opinion and Jewish Affairs*, June 1982, page 13.

Martin Tolchin, 'President Deplores the Russian Trials as Blow to Liberty', *New York Times*, 13 July 1978.

Robert C. Toth, 'Dilemma of a Soviet Daughter', *Washington Post*, 7 April 1976.

Robert C. Toth, 'Soviet Jews warn of "pogrom"', *Los Angeles Times*, 26 January 1977.

Robert C. Toth, 'Portrait of Dissident-Turned-Betrayer, He Came Well Recommended', *Los Angeles Times*, 8 March 1977.

Robert C. Toth, 'All Shcharansky Wanted Was to Leave', *Los Angeles Times*, 27 June 1977.

Robert C. Toth, 'US Virtually Rules Out Swap for Soviet Dissident', *Los Angeles Times*, 11 May 1978.

Christopher Walker, 'Lonely anniversary for Shcharanskys', *The Times*, 5 July 1984.

Christopher Walker, 'Shcharansky's Mother Weeps for Joy', *The Times*, 12 February 1986.

Craig R. Whitney, 'Soviet Rebuff US on Shcharansky', *New York Times*, 23 December 1977.

Elie Wiesel, 'Appeal for Refuseniks', *New York Times*, 22 October 1985.

Edgar Williams, 'Local lawyer intertwined in crusade by refusenik', *Philadelphia Enquirer*, 13 March 1985.
Christopher S. Wren, 'Soviet Frees Dr Shtern, Object of Western Drive', *New York Times*, 16 March 1977.
Michael Wyschogrod, 'After fifteen years – my world', *Sh'ma, a journal of Jewish responsibility*, 1 November 1985.

Section 3: Journals and magazines

Canadian Committee for Soviet Jewry (Toronto)
Chicago Action for Soviet Jewry (Chicago)
Committee of Concerned Scientists Inc, Action Alert Exit Visa (London)
Greater New York Conference on Soviet Jewry, Freedom Line (New York)
Greater New York Conference on Soviet Jewry, Newsline (New York)
Greater New York Conference on Soviet Jewry, Freedom Wire (New York)
Greater New York Conference on Soviet Jewry, Lifelines (New York)
Helsinki Agreement Watchdog Committee on behalf of Soviet Jews: Soviet Jewish Prisoners of Conscience (London)
Insight: Soviet Jews (London)
Institute of Jewish Affairs Research Report (London)
Israel Public Council for Soviet Jewry, Soviet Jewish Refusenik (Tel Aviv)
Jews in Eastern Europe, A Periodical Survey of Events (London)
Jews in the USSR (London)
Long Island Committee for Soviet Jewry, Report (Long Island)
Medical Mobilization for Soviet Jewry (Waltham, Massachusetts)
National Conference on Soviet Jewry, News Bulletin (New York)
National Conference on Soviet Jewry, News Release (New York)
National Conference on Soviet Jewry, Press Service (New York)
National Council for Soviet Jewry, From the Chairman's Desk (London)
New York Medical Committee on Soviet Jewry (New York)
News from Student Struggle for Soviet Jewry (New York)
Outcry: Newsletter of the Bay Area Council on Soviet Jewry (San Francisco)
Philadelphia Student Struggle for Soviet Jewry, Action Newsletter (Philadelphia)
Refusenik: Information from Chicago Action for Soviet Jewry (Chicago)
Scientists Committee of the Israel Public Council for Soviet Jewry, News Bulletin (Tel Aviv)
Soviet Jewish Affairs, A Journal on Jewish Problems in the USSR and Eastern Europe (London)
Union of Councils for Soviet Jews, Action Alert (Washington DC)
Union of Councils for Soviet Jews, Alert (Washington DC)
Union of Councils for Soviet Jews, News Release (Washington DC)
Union of Councils for Soviet Jews Quarterly Report (Washington DC)
Washington Committee for Soviet Jewry, Action Advisory (Washington DC)

Washington Committee for Soviet Jewry, News Release (Washington DC)
Washington Committee for Soviet Jewry, The Vigil (Washington DC)
Women's Campaign for Soviet Jewry, 35s Circular (London)

Section 4: Films

'A Calculated Risk', Granada Television, 14 June 1976.
'Traders of Souls', Moscow Television, 22 January 1977.
'The Man Who Went Too Far', Granada Television, 23 May 1977.
'Russian Justice', Granada Television, 17 July 1978.
'A Difficult Prisoner', Granada Television, 24 January 1983.
'Jewish Pawns in Russia's Game', Panorama, BBC Television, 25 March
    1985.
'The One That Got Away', Granada Television, 17 February 1986.

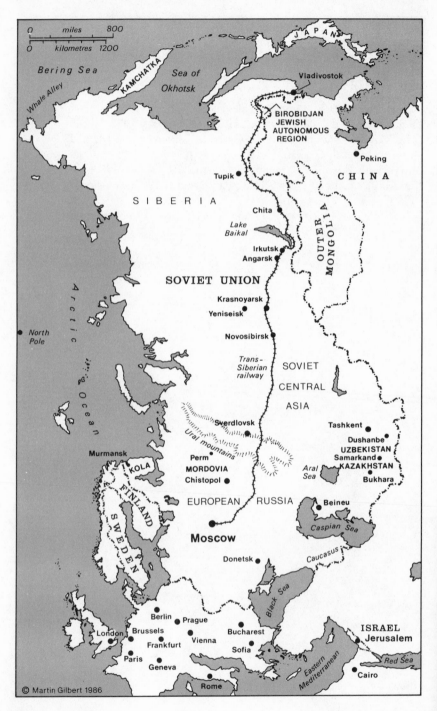

© Martin Gilbert 1986

Index

compiled by the author

Abramov: a witness, 244

Abramov, Moshe: a prisoner, 423

Abramovich, Pavel: signs appeals, 35, 83, 86, 114, 115, 191, 202; a refusenik since 1971, 100, 317; raid on home of, 106

Academy of Sciences (Moscow): 18, 44, 88

'A Calculated Risk': shown, 130; and the interrogation and trial of Shcharansky, 198–9, 209, 213, 233, 246–7, 251, 253–4, 271

Action Committee of Newcomers from the Soviet Union (Tel Aviv): 23

Adamsky, Piotr: a prosecution witness, 242, 261

Ad Hoc Commission on Justice for Anatoly Shcharansky (1977): 218

'A Difficult Prisoner': television film (1983), 361

Afghanistan: a protest concerning, 333

Agursky, Mikhail: at a seminar, 37; signs appeals, 59; receives exit visa, 73

Ahad Ha'am: a lecture on, 150–1

Ahs, Iosif: detained, 134; demonstrates, 138; thrown into a ditch, 142; charged with 'malicious hooliganism', 144–5; released, 146; signs an appeal, 152; 'what will happen?', 180; signs further appeals, 184, 189, 191; questioned, 205, 206–7

Ahs, Mikhaela: her appeal for help, 146; photograph of, plate 18

Aizenberg, Evgeny: sentenced (1985), 407; a prisoner, 423

Akhmatova, Anna: Shcharansky reads poems by, 366, 390

Akiva, Rabbi: 325

Albania: 86

Albert, Carl: in Moscow (1975), 90

Alexandrovich, Ruth: sentenced (1971), 19; appeals for Shcharansky (1982), 355

Alexeeva, Ludmila: and the Helsinki Watchdog group, 124–5, 128, 146, 150, 155, 193; signs an appeal for two Jews, 146; Shcharansky a tutor to, 148; her

apartment searched, 156; an appeal on behalf of, 157; receives an exit visa, 190; an accusation against, 256; mentioned, 310; book by, 431; photograph of, with Shcharansky, plate 35

Alik: a soldier on duty, 338, 343

Allon, Yigal: his protest, 152

Alshansky, Lieutenant-Colonel Nahum: signs a telegram to Israel (1967), 29

American Jewish Conference on Soviet Jewry: 11, 21

American Jewry: Shcharansky's lecture on, 87

Amnesty International: 118

Amnesty International (Moscow group): 77

Anatoly Shcharansky Justice Garden, the: 224

Andropov, Yury: a warning to, 358; a warning from, 361; Ida Milgrom protests to, 382; an appeal to, 382–3; dies, 395

Angarsk: refuseniks in, 60

Anti-Semitism: 2, 5, 10, 12, 16, 56, 67, 80, 96, 106, 107, 123, 142, 166, 176, 178, 181, 202, 229, 233, 236, 247, 253, 257, 258, 268, 270

appeals, protests and messages from Soviet Jews to the West: on 6 August 1969, 17; May 1972, 22; 7 October 1973, 28–9, 29; 26 November 1973, 35; 18 November 1974, 58–61; early 1975, 67; 3 February 1975, 68–9; 6 June 1975, 79; June 1975, 79–82; 15 June 1975, 83; July 1975, 85–6; 18 September 1975, 94–5; October 1975, 95–6; late 1975, 96; 13 January 1976, 106–7; 21 January 1976, 107; 2 February 1976, 107–9; 12 February 1976, 108–9; 17 February 1976; 112; 12 March 1976, 114; March 1976, 115; 30 March 1976, 115; 29 March 1976, 116–7; 24 April 1976, 118–9; 2 May 1976, 123–4; 17 September 1976, 133; 15 October 1976, 136; 4 November 1976, 146; 24 November 1976, 151–2; early 1977, 155–6; 12 January 1977, 156;

20 January 1977, 158–9; February 1977, 166; 28 February 1977, 166–7; 13 March 1977, 183; 13 March 1977, 184–5; 15 March 1977, 187; 30 March 1977, 189–90; 18 April 1977, 190–1; 22 April 1977, 191–2; 17 May 1977, 197–8; 25 May 1977, 198; 8 July 1977, 200–1; 15 July 1977, 202; July 1977, 203; 27 July 1977, 204–5; 17 December 1977, 222; 24 December 1977, 222; 15 March 1978, 226; cited in the trial of Shcharansky, 237–8, 245, 246, 247, 248, 249–53, 257, 269, 269–70; renewed, 17 November 1978, 287; 7 March 1985, 406

Arabic: Shcharansky learns, 364, 374; a greeting in, 395; and Shcharansky's vision, 417

Aristophanes: 'conversations with', 380

Arkhipova Street Synagogue (Moscow): Jews gather outside, 4, 16, 29–30, 80, 174, 180; one of Shcharansky's visits to, 46; an incident outside, 80; and the Jewish New Year in 1975, 92; and the Jews of Ilyinka, 126; and the Rejoicing of the Law in 1976, 137, 140; and Shcharansky's trial, 246; photograph of, plate 15

Artificial Intelligence: Shcharansky reads, 313, 320

Askhinsky, Lev: article by, 379

Associated Press: 114, 248

Association of American Law Schools: a protest at, 222–3

Athens: and a 'traitor', 380

Atlanta (Georgia): a protest in, 222–3

'Avital': a Hebrew name, chosen, 30

Azbel, Professor David: accusations against, 168, 169, 170, 171, 193

Azbel, Professor Mark: arrested, 46; warned, 74–5; meets Senators, 85; signs appeals, 86, 94, 108, 117, 123, 146, 156, 184, 191, 197; and Jewish knowledge, 87; a refusenik since 1972, 101; arrested, 106; meets Soviet officials, 109; and a Public Action group, 146; and a press conference, 152–3; an accusation against, 171; interrogated, 193, 194; receives his exit visa, 205; book by, 431

Babel, Isaak: 26–7

Babi Yar: meeting at (1968), 16; Jews assaulted at (1974), 53–4; wreaths forbidden at (1976), 134–5

Baku: 2, 55

Baltic Sea: 50

Baltimore Sun: letter from Moscow to, 68–9; a journalist from, in Moscow, 185

Baptists: and Shcharansky, 201

BBC, the: 'hostile', 235, 271; broadcasts an account of a visit to Chistopol prison, 291

Beer Sheva (Beersheba): Avital

Shcharansky studying in, 134

Begin, Menachem: and President Sadat, 220

Begun, Alla: greetings from, 306–7

Begun, Ina Shlemova: dedication to, xiii; photograph of, plate 44

Begun, Dr Iosif: dedication to, xiii; and *Jews in the USSR*, 75, 87; signs appeals, 94, 106–7, 123, 155, 167; a refusenik since 1971, 100; raids on home of, 106, 151; detained, 134; denounced, 163; protests, 165; arrested, 167, 183; held in prison, 189; sentenced (1977), 199; Shcharansky asks about (1979), 297; sentenced again (1983), 394, 423; a friend of, sentenced (1985), 407; Shcharansky to fight for (1986), 417; photograph of, plate 43

Begun, Vladimir: attacks Old Testament (1974), 67; his book cited, 236; his book not allowed as evidence, 268

Beilin, Iosif: favours demonstrations, 27; recalls Shcharansky, 28; signs appeals, 35, 82, 106–7, 108, 109, 117, 119, 123, 151, 155, 159, 189, 191, 202, 204; meets Western visitors, 38, 99; detained, 53; his journey, 55; recalls a demonstration (1975), 69–70; threats against, 81; and a Passover service (1976), 117; a pall bearer, 119; detained (1976), 134; 'singing in the candlelight', 142; demonstrates, 144; testifies for Shcharansky (1976), 148; not arrested, 189; and 'the hell of hatred', 220; receives his exit visa, 226; in Israel, 228; photographs of, plates 18, 20, 26, 27

Beilina, Dina: protests (1972), 23; seeks publicity for prisoners, 27; signs a message of solidarity, 29; signs further appeals, 35, 59, 63, 82, 86, 96, 106–7, 107, 108, 117, 119, 123, 136, 146, 155, 159, 167, 184, 189, 191, 191–2, 198, 202, 203, 204, 222, 269; recalls the life of a refusenik, 36–7; meets Western visitors, 38; telephone calls with, 39; and an appeal against a sentence, 71–2; and the search for a spokesman, 73; and the arrest of Malkin, 79; meets Senators, 85; and the Roitburd trial, 89; and Shcharansky's character, 94, 147, 189, 203; and the preparation of lists of refuseniks, 99–102, 128, 205–6, 234, 258, 260; helps compile a letter, 112; and a Passover service, 117; and the death of Davidovich, 118–9; and Israel Independence Day (1976), 123; and an American petition, 126; works with Shcharansky, 133, 143, 149; 'singing in the candlelight', 142; testifies for Shcharansky (1976), 148; and the 'main goal', 151; and a new prisoner (1977), 157; and Shcharansky's lodging place in Moscow (1977), 160; her apartment searched, 172; dictates a statement (1977), 183; not arrested, 189; and the interrogation of Shcharansky, 194, 207; and Boris Shcharansky, 195–6; and Shcharansky's defence, 200, 203, 209–10, 220–1, 223; and an attack on Shcharansky, 219; receives her exit visa, 226; in Israel, 228; reflections of, 276, 287; Ida Milgrom speaks to, 397; photographs of, plates 20, 26

Beilis Trial: recalled, 183, 184

Beineu (Kazakhstan): an exile in, 394

Belgrade: Helsinki review conference in, 134, 204, 217

Bellow, Saul: 87

Beltsy: refuseniks in, 101

Bendery (Soviet Moldavia): 17, 81; refuseniks in, 101

Ben Gurion airport (Israel): 132, 146

Ben Gurion, David: dies, 31

Ben-Josef, Ariel: 284, 310

Ben-Josef, Chanka: 310

Ben-Josef, Ilana: 284, 310, 428

Ben-Josef, Jonathan: 310

Ben-Shlomo, Zeev: and the aim of the Shcharansky trial, 280; articles by, 433

Berenshtein, Iosif: a prisoner, 410–11, 423

Beria, Lavrenti: his successors, 278

Berlin: Lev Ovsishcher reaches (1945), 43; Shcharansky passes through (1986), 415

Berlinguer, Enrico: an appeal to, 357

Bialik, Chaim Nahman: in Odessa, 1

Bible, the: quoted by Shcharansky, 64; Shcharansky studies, 76; extracts from, copied, 396; and a modern hero on the scale of, 406

Bild: an exchange mentioned in, 409; and an exchange said to be imminent, 413

Birobidjan: not one Yiddish school in, 236

Bitov, Andrei: an article by, 379

Black Sea: 50

'Black Years', the (1948–53): cited by Shcharansky, 265

Bogomolny, Benjamin: signs appeals, 123, 159; an appeal on behalf of, 128

Bonn: rumours in, 412; the United States Ambassador to, meets Shcharansky (in Berlin), 415

Bonner, Elena: protests (1970), 18; at a demonstration (1974), 44; a human rights activist, 77; signs appeals, 119, 150, 200; and the charge against Shcharansky, 199; her children allowed to leave, 205; signs a protest, 279; Shcharansky asks about, 297; greetings from, 309; greetings to, 325; internal banishment of (1980), 333; signs the final Helsinki Watchdog group report (1982), 357; a letter from, 373; photograph of, with Shcharansky, plate 34

Books by Mail: and a textbook in Arabic, 364; and a book by James Joyce, 374

Bordnik, A.: his home searched, 252

Boxer, Congresswoman Barbara: nominates Shcharansky, 358–9; articles by, 434

Brailovsky, Dr Victor: signs appeals, 35, 86, 108, 112, 117, 119, 123, 146, 156, 184, 191, 197; arrested, 46, 106; meets Senators and Congressmen, 85, 89, 99; and Jewish knowledge, 87; a refusenik since 1972, 101; meets Soviet officials, 109; interrogated, 193–4; defends Shcharansky, 203; lies concerning, 216; sentenced, 394; released, but refused an exit visa, 427

Brezhnev, Leonid: 58, 61, 86, 94, 152; congressmen protest to, 165; refuseniks protest to, 205; Ida Milgrom's appeals to, 228, 334–5; an appeal to, ignored, 238; 'anti-Soviet slander' of, 239–40; cited in Shcharansky's trial, 257; and President Carter, 290, 291; Shcharansky's letter to (1981), 350–1; President Pertini appeals to (1982), 357; a warning to his successor, 358

Britain: 4, 39; 'friends' in, 304; Avital Shcharansky visits, 382

Brodhead, Congressman William: 157; article by, 434

Brodsky, Vladimir: sentenced (1985), 407; a prisoner, 424

Brooklyn: a telegram from Moscow to, 137

Brussels: Soviet Jewry Conference in (1971), 18–19; further meeting in (1975), 95–6; second Conference in (1976), 112

Brzezinski, Dr Z.: 244

Buber, Martin: protests, 10–11

Buckley, Senator James: in Moscow (1975), 85

Buiko, Valery: in Riga, 55

Bukhara: a journey to, 55

Bukovsky, Vladimir: his lawyer harassed, 154

Bulgakov, Mikhail: 182, 183

Bulgaria: 114

Burton, Congressman Philip: appeals, 187

Butman, Hillel: sentenced (1971), 19; a protest on behalf of, 62; at Vladimir prison, 81, 282, 283; released, 286; in Jerusalem, 311; appeals on behalf of Shcharansky (1982), 355; rejects an 'admission of guilt' (1983), 383; books by, 431

Bychkov: Ida Milgrom's protest to (1982), 355–7

Caine, Professor Burton: his concern, 222–3

California: a Rabbi from, in Moscow

(1976), 141–2

Canada: 24, 39, 86; Ukrainians in, 154; Avital Shcharansky's letters from, 284, 285; Shcharansky's Uncle Noah in, 299–300; 'relatives and friends' in, 304, 396

Canadian Committee for Soviet Jewry: 313

capitalism: criticised in Shcharansky's trial, 255

Carlson, William: in Moscow, 181

Carter, Governor (later President) Jimmy: Jews appeal to, 133, 188; a telegram of support from, 145; an appeal to from senators and congressmen, 187; Sakharov appeals to, 188; and human rights, 190–1; rebutts the charge against Shcharansky, 200, 224, 244, 248, 279; Ida Milgrom's letter to (1978), 275; and Brezhnev, 290, 291

Carter, Rosalyn: an appeal to, 146

Case, Senator Clifford: 91, 124

Caucasus, the: an incident in, 12; a journey to, 55; refuseniks in, 101; a prisoner in, 118; a tribe from, dispersed, 155

Central Committee of the Communist Party of the Soviet Union: an appeal to (1973), 35; and a demonstration (1974), 43; and further demonstrations (1975–7), 106, 109–11, 131, 144; and Shcharansky's trial, 246

Central Intelligence Agency (CIA): accusations concerning, 114, 162, 171, 172, 173, 179, 193, 195, 199, 200, 209, 211, 214, 250, 260, 279, 292, 406; and Dr Lipavsky, 225–6, 233, 245, 250

Central Telegraph Building (Moscow): *Hatikvah* sung in (1976), 141

Cervantes: 'conversations with', 380

Chanukkah festival: in 1975, 104, 105; in 1979, 318, 324; in 1980, 347–8; in 1982, 367; in 1983, 395

Chekhov: 'practically nothing' of, in the prison library, 380

Chernobilsky, Boris: demonstrates, 138; and the KGB, 143; detained, 144–5; released, 146; defence of, 150; signs appeals, 152, 184; his apartment searched, 172; still refused an exit visa, 427

Chernobilsky, Elena: her appeal for help, 146; photograph of, plate 18

Chernovtsy: refuseniks in, 101

chess: Shcharansky an avid player of, 9, 25, 32, 120, 178; in Chistopol prison, 292, 319

Chile: and a possible exchange, 225

Chinsky, Miriam: interviews Avital Shcharansky, 327

Chistopol prison: Shcharansky moved to, 283; Shcharansky's letters from, 283–4, 284–5, 285–6; Leonid Shcharansky and

Ida Milgrom's visits to, 288–90, 341, 343, 358, 359–60; Shcharansky punished in, 290, 291, 353; Hebrew songs in, 292, 333; book store of, 308; Shcharansky meets a fellow Prisoner of Zion in, 326–7; news of the death of Boris Shcharansky reaches, 329–30; Shcharansky returned to (1981), 349; conditions in, 351; fears for Shcharansky in, 352; Psalms in, 363; letters from and to, 376–7; 'the meritorious city', 391; and 'One who guards us', 393; Shcharansky returns to Perm from (1984), 405; photograph of, plate 50

Chita: 78, 103

Chlenov, Micka: a Hebrew teacher, 30, 302; Shcharansky's 'warm feelings' towards, 302–3

Christian Science Monitor: 359

Christie, Agatha: read in Hebrew, 215

Christmas Day: a protest on (1970), 18

Chronicle Press (Khronika Press), the: cited, 271

Church, Senator Frank: 218

Churchill, Randolph: his book discussed, 144

Churchill, Winston: his book discussed, 144

Chusovskaya station (Urals): 335, 337

Cleveland (Ohio): a visitor to Moscow from, 71

Coalition for a Democratic Majority: 224

College of Advocates (Moscow): 200, 209

Columbia University (New York): 11, 218, 259–60

Communist Party of the Soviet Union: 2, 43, 77; its newspaper, links Shcharansky with an alleged spy, 277

Communist Party Congress (25th): (Moscow, 1976), 107; Soviet Jews appeal to, 114, 115, 246

Communist Party Congress (26th): (Moscow, 1981) and religion, 350–1

Conference on Security and Co-operation in Europe: 24, 82, 86

Congressional Record: 56

Congressional Wives Committee for Soviet Jewry: 224, 226

conscription trap, the: 60, 68, 69, 79, 81, 92, 95, 104, 123, 131, 155, 237–8

Constructive Mathematical Logic From the Classical Point of View: Shcharansky reads, 308–9

Contemporary Judaism and Zionism: 10

Corinth: at war with Athens, 380

'cosmopolitanism', campaign against: 8, 10

Cotler, Professor Irwin: and Shcharansky's trial, 239–40; his legal expertise at Avital Shcharansky's disposal, 281; his appeal, 281–2; Shcharansky's greetings to, 318;

presents case for Shcharansky, 361;
publishes 'The Shcharansky Appeal', 431
Crimea, the: 130
Crimean Tatars: 130
Czechoslovakia: and Israel, 6

Damascus: 29
Damocles, Sword of: 185
Daniels, June: in Moscow (1975), 90;
photographs of, admired, 295, 317
Daniels, Roy: a photograph of, admired,
295
Dante: 380; and gluttony, 373
David, King: 'lives and exists', 333; and the
'millennia', 366; and 'fear' of the Lord,
401–2
Davidov, Vladimir: detained, 53; his
journey, 55; signs appeals, 59; receives
exit visa, 73
Davidovich, Maria: receives her exit visa,
119; and the interrogation and trial of
Shcharansky, 214, 254
Davidovich, Sonya: a witness, 242–3, 254
Davidovich, Colonel Yefim: signs
telegrams and appeals, 29, 63, 67, 82, 86,
96, 109; Shcharansky visits, 56, 57;
demoted, 81; threats against, 81; meets
Senators, 85; protests, 96; listed, 101; an
appeal on behalf of, 116–7; dies, 118; his
case referred to, 128; and Lipavsky, 175;
and Shcharansky's interrogation and
trial, 206, 251
Day of Atonement: see index entry for Yom
Kippur
D'Cuellar, Perez: an appeal to, 360
Declaration of Independence (1776): 239
'Defence of Soviet Jews': an alleged code
name, 255
Derbent: 55, 59; refuseniks in, 101, 110; a
witness from, 244, 257
Dershowitz, Professor Alan: 218, 281;
presents case for Shcharansky, 361;
article by, 434
destiny: 'who we are', 105; chosen 'quite
consciously', 375; 'to become the real
master of', 396
Dishler, Bernard: in Moscow (1977), 174
Dnieper, River: and 'a rare bird', 316
'Doctors' Plot', the (of 1953): 8; recalled,
172, 183, 184, 265, 417
Documentary Film Centre (Moscow): 96
Dodd, Senator Christopher: in Moscow
(1975), 77
Domodedovo airport (Moscow): 288
Donbass region: 9
Donetsk: Shcharansky born in, 1; Boris
Shcharansky in, 2; Shcharansky's
childhood in, 5–6, 6–10, 11; a letter and a
postcard from, 378
Don Quixote:'towers...over his author', 380

Dostoevsky: 'practically nothing' of, in
prison library, 380; and Brothers
Karamazov, 401
Dreyfus case: recalled, 183, 184, 202, 265,
279–80
Drinan, Congressman Robert F.: in
Moscow (1975), 88–90; an appeal to, 175;
and appeal from, 187; calls for
Shcharansky's release, 190, 287; articles
by, 434
Drucker, Solomon Ilyich: his ethnographic
handbook, 375
Dubliners: Shcharansky reads (in English),
374
Dubnov, Simon: book by, confiscated, 106
Dubrovskaya, Silva: appointed, 225; her
services not accepted, 231, 232
Dushanbe: refuseniks questioned in, 205
Dutch Parliament: and Shcharansky, 358
Dymshits, Mark: sentenced (1970), 18;
protests on behalf of, 20, 108; released
(1979), 291; appeals on behalf of
Shcharansky (1982), 355

East Germany: Shcharansky released
through, 414
economic crimes: accusations of (1952–63),
8, 10
Edelshtein, Yuly: a prisoner, 410–11, 424
Egypt: 6, 13, 28
Ehrenkranz, Rabbi Joseph: in Moscow,
117; photograph of, plate 28
Eichmann, Adolf: 165
Eilat: 'nice to lie down' on beach at, 396
Eilberg, Gladys: 284
Eilberg, Congressman Joshua: in Moscow
(1975), 77; an appeal to (1976), 119; an
appeal from (1977), 187; Shcharansky
mentions (1978), 284; articles by, 434
Elbert, Lev: a prisoner, 394; released, but
refused an exit visa, 427
Elinson, Chana: a letter from, 305
Elistratov, Victor (Vitya): a letter from,
confiscated, 300; photograph of, plate 18
Elkind, Isaak: demonstrates, 144; detained,
144–5; Shcharansky's appeal on behalf of,
147; defends Shcharansky, 218; writes
about Ida Nudel, 437; photograph of,
plate 18
Ellenstein, Jean: comments on
Shcharansky's trial, 280
Entebbe (Uganda): hijack rescue at, 132,
139, 203
Eskimos: an 'endangered' civilisation, 302
Essas, Ilya: demonstrates, 71; signs appeals,
83, 86, 109, 114, 119; police raid home
of, 106
Estonian Soviet Republic: 34
Ethnogenesis: Shcharansky reads, 374
Everest, Mount: 365

Exodus (from Egypt): 39–40, 76, 117

Faculty of Applied Mathematics (Moscow): 31

Fain, Professor Benjamin: a refusenik, 59–60; demonstrates, 71; and *Jews in the USSR*, 75; meets Senators, 85; signs appeals, 86, 94, 114, 115, 117, 146, 191, 197, 202, 204; demonstrates, 143; and a Public Action group, 146; his home searched, 151; and a press conference, 152–3; interrogated, 193, 194, 195; receives his exit visa, 205; photograph of, plate 17

Fascell, Congressman Dante: 91; refused a visa, 152; an appeal to, 175

Feldman, Alexander: sentenced (1973), 35, 60; pressure on behalf of, urged (1976), 118; a prisoner, 155; reaches Israel (1977), 205

Fenwick, Congresswoman Millicent: in Moscow (1975), 90–1; her Helsinki monitoring bill, 91, 115–6, 124; Shcharansky writes to, 128–9; 'regards' to, 134; an appeal from, 187; articles by, 434

Filatov, A.N.: sentenced to death (1978), 277, 278, 279

Financial Times: 185

Finkelstein, Eitan: signs appeals, 107, 117, 119, 136, 156, 159, 184, 191, 202, 204, 278–9; a pall bearer, 119; criticised, 125; and an American petition, 125–6; and the Lithuanian Helsinki Watchdog group, 146–7, 154; interrogated, 206

Fish, Congressman Hamilton: in Moscow (1975), 77

Fishman, Rabbi Jacob: and Shcharansky's wedding, 238

Fletcher, George P.: in Moscow (1979), 286

Ford (a criminologist): cited, 263

Ford, President Gerald R.: Jewish activists write to, 58–61, 133; signs Trade Reform Act, 63; and the Helsinki Accords, 86; Shcharansky's telegram to, 132, 239

Fradkova, Nadezhda: a prisoner, 424

Frankfurt: a reunion at (1986), 415

Freidman, Mark: refused an exit visa, 80

French Communist Party: appeal to (1976), 107, 206, 246, 247, 251; an appeal by the leader of (1982), 358

Fridman, Kim: released, but refused an exit visa, 427

Friedman, Ilana: 27, 75

Friendly, Alfred: in Moscow, 114, 218

Furman, Lev: a refusenik, 101; signs an appeal, 159; a greeting card from, 309–10

Future Shock: Shcharansky reads, 396

Galanskov, Yury: dies, 245

Galileo Galilei: Shcharansky's debate with, 388, 389–90

Galkin, Investigator: 'shouted and raged', 339; and Shcharansky's hunger strike, 359, 360

Gardner, Professor Martin: his book on mathematical logic, 215, 340

Gayduk (a prisoner): at Vladimir prison, 282

Geishis, Grigory: released, but refused an exit visa, 427

Gelad, Alius: an accusation against, 215

Genesis: quoted, 64

Geneva: Avital Shcharansky in (1977), 185, 187; talks in, not cancelled (1978), 228; Summit conference in (1985), 408–9, 412

Georgia, Soviet Republic of: an appeal from Jews in (1969), 17; Jews from, filmed (1977), 163

German Democratic Republic: a 'disappointing' destination, 414–5

Germans: seek repatriation, 19–20, 131, 190, 254

Germany: 24, 413–4

Getler, Warren: and a 'possible exchange', 409, 411–12

Ginsburg, Alexander: and the Helsinki Watchdog group, 124, 155, 156, 157; an accusation against, 160; arrested 165; in prison, 189; his trial, 228, 240, 245; accusations against, 251, 252, 256, 262, 263, 271; 'honest, brave and courageous; 267; sentenced, 277, 279, 280; released and exchanged (1979), 327

Giscard d'Estaing, Valéry: appeals to, 201, 202

Glienicke Bridge (East Germany): an exchange at (1986), 414–5; photograph of, plate 52

Gogol, Nikolai: quoted, 316

Golan Heights: 28–9

Gold, Eugene: and Dr Lipavsky, 225

Goldfarb, Alexander (Alex): a spokesman, 27, 42; arrested, 46; receives exit visa, 73, 74; and Avital Shcharansky, 125; appeals on Shcharansky's behalf, 188; his departure from Moscow airport photographed, plate 16

Goldin, Ovsei: and a prayer group broken up, 61

Goldstein, Gregory: signs appeals, 109, 117, 156, 159, 184, 191, 202, 204–5; released, but refused an exit visa, 427

Goldstein, Isai: signs appeals, 109, 117, 156, 159, 184, 191, 202, 204–5, 278–9; and an American petition, 125–6

Goldstein, Shirley: in Moscow (1975), 91, 94

Golgotha: 278

Gomulka, Wladyslaw: his 'variant', 15

Goodman, Jerry: 21

Gorbachev, Mikhail: an appeal to (1985), 406; and the Geneva Summit (1985), 408–9, 412; and 'civilised methods of behaviour' (1986), 412–13

Gorbachev, Raisa: Avital Shcharansky's appeal to, 409–10

Gorbunov, Investigator: 219

Gorky: Sakharov banished to, 333; Sakharov appeals on Shcharansky's behalf from, 357; a trial in (1985), 407

Gorky Street (Moscow): 21; a demonstration in (1976), 143–4; Shcharansky stays at apartment on (1977), 179; Slepak unmolested in apartment on, 188

Granada Television: films by, 130, 131, 161, 198, 271, 361

Great Soviet Encyclopaedia: Shcharansky's reference to, 312

Great Synagogue (Odessa): Shcharansky's father hears speakers in, 1

Greater New York Conference on Soviet Jewry: 188, 352; journals of, 434

Greenberg, Jack: and a legal hearing, 218

Gromyko, Andrei: and arms talks, 248

Gumilyev: a book by, 374–5

Haggadah (Passover narrative): 39–40, 117; and learning Hebrew in prison, 333

Hassidism: a novel about, 397

'Hatikvah' (Jewish anthem): sung near Moscow (1976), 123; sung in the Moscow Central Telegraph Building (1976), 141; sung outside a Moscow courthouse (1978), 276; sung at the Western ('Wailing') Wall (1986), 416

Havdalah service (at end of Sabbath): 141–2

Hebrew: songs sung in (1969), 16; a teacher of sentenced (1971), 19; speakers of listed (1972), 24; a note written in (1973), 29; lessons in, 29–30; teachers of, celebrate Passover (1974), 40; teachers of, arrested, 46; Avital studies in Israel, 51, 57, 72; a student of, on the train from Istra (1975), 78; books in, confiscated, 80, 151; study of, forbidden in prison, 81; study of, in Moscow, 87, 93, 140–1, 178; spoken by Muscovites and their Israeli visitors, 97, 98; teachers of, in Leningrad, 101; a possible telegram in, 103; language tapes in, 104; pressure against study of, 113; protest on behalf of study of, 114; reading in, 117; a telegram in, sent from Moscow, 137; study of, in Kishinev, 149–50; teachers of, sentenced, 199, 407; a book in, by Agatha Christie, 215; translations into, in prison, 216; no possibility to study, 235, 258; in Derbent, 244; mentioned at the trial of

Shcharansky, 256; messages in, in Vladimir prison, 282; songs in, in prison, 283, 292; 'new words' in, in prison, 296–7; further study of, in prison, 332, 333, 365–6; and Israel, 375; a greeting in, 395; 'stored within my soul', 400; and moments 'impossible to express . . . in any language', 415

Hebrew language classes: 14, 30, 38, 42, 68, 87

Helsinki: international talks at (1972–3), 24–5, 151

Helsinki Agreement (Helsinki Accords): 85, 86, 90, 93, 94, 95, 99; Shcharansky's hopes for, 105; refuseniks appeal to, 107, 151, 158; and reunification of families, 111, 115; and the death of Davidovich, 119; 'empty words' of, 124; and the Helsinki Watchdog group, 124, 126–7, 129, 132–3, 150, 153–4; a 'counter-attack' on, 134; and a Lithuanian Watchdog group, 146–7; 'abuses' of, denounced, 163, 193; defended, 204; cited by a Soviet official, 224; and Shcharansky's trial, 245, 252

Helsinki Final Act: ratified (1975), 94, 95; comes into force (1976), 115; and the refuseniks, 127, 134, 150, 204; and the American public, 255; contradicted, 279; 'an affront to', 368

Helsinki Monitoring Commission (Washington DC): 91, 115–6; 124, 129, 134; an appeal to, 146; cited in Shcharansky's trial, 271

Helsinki review conference (Belgrade): 134, 204, 217

Helsinki review conference (Madrid): 345, 360–1

Helsinki Watchdog group (Georgia): a protest by, 278–9

Helsinki Watchdog group (Lithuania): established (November 1976), 146–7, 154, 205, 277; a protest by, 278–9

Helsinki Watchdog group (Moscow): established (12 May 1976), 124, 179; its reports, 126–8, 132–3, 150, 153, 155, 206, 235, 357; a member of, receives his exit visa, 131–2; appeals to, 149–50, 156, 158; its members harassed, 156, 157, 182; its leaders arrested, 165; denounced, 170, 193; Shcharansky the 'inspiration and initiator' of, 190; Shcharansky 'active' on, 192, 197, 201, 247; a member of, sentenced, 199; and Shcharansky's interrogation and trial, 209, 210, 245, 247, 251–3, 272; its head sentenced, 227; another member of brought to trial, 228; a protest by (1978), 278–80; a member of, released and exchanged (1979), 327–8; a condemnation by (1980), 333; its final report (1982), 357; disbanded (1982), 357, 414

Herzl, Theodor: and the Dreyfus trial, 265

Herzog, President Chaim: greets Shcharansky, photograph, plate 58

Hillel, Rabbi: 325

History of the Jews (Cecil Roth): confiscated, 106

Hitler, Adolf: 96, 227, 247

Holland: Avital Shcharansky's visits to, 358

Holland, Darrell: in Moscow, 181

Holocaust, the: cited by Shcharansky, 266; a survivor of, on the 'duty to try harder', 408–9; and 'the truth of our people', 411

Holtzman, Congresswoman Elizabeth: in Moscow (1975), 90

Homer: 'read in a rush', 379

House of Representatives (Washington DC): a resolution in (1972), 23; and the Jackson Amendment (1974), 62; Speaker of, in Moscow (1975), 90; and the Helsinki Monitoring Commission (1976), 115–6

human rights: the Universal Declaration of (1948), 5, 18, 82, 86, 150, 239; and the Helsinki negotiations (1972–3), 24–5, 107; and Sakharov, 89; and the Moscow Helsinki Watchdog group, 124–5, 126–7, 154; and Jewish immigration to Israel, 122, 181–2, 190–1; and Shcharansky, 190, 199, 201, 203–4, 217, 415; and a KGB informer, 196; and Shcharansky's imminent release, 415

'Human Rights': and alleged code name, 255

Humphrey, Senator Hubert: in Moscow (1975), 85

hunger strike: in Leningrad and Moscow (1975), 83

Hunt: a book by, 313, 320

Ilyinka: Jews of, 126, 153, 237, 238, 248, 249, 270, 273

Ilyukhin, Prosecutor: 191

Indestructible Jews: 77–8

Inessa (a prison warden): 282

Inhabitants of the World: Shcharansky reads, 375

Institute of Oil and Gas (Moscow): Shcharansky works at, 31, 36, 238–9; Shcharansky dismissed from (1975), 76–7

Institute of Power (Moscow): 10

Institute of Radio Technology (Ryazan): 17

Institute of Steel and Alloys (Moscow): 60

International Committee for the Release of Anatoly Shcharansky: 190, 221, 287

International Congress on Mathematics (Moscow, 1973): 26

International Herald Tribune: 358, 409, 411–12

International Life: an article in, 296

International Red Cross: 118

International Tribunal of Enquiry (San Francisco): 361

'International Zionism': 'alien', 197

Intourist Hotel (Moscow): 143

Intrator, Genya: a telephone conversation with (1979), 313–4; greetings to, 325

Iowa: a visitor from, 90

Iraq: army of, attacks, 6

Islam (by Mosse): Shcharansky reads, 374

Israel: comes into existence, 3, 4; far from Moscow, 13; threatened, 13–14; victorious (1967), 14–15; invitations from (1968–9), 16–17; former Prisoners of Zion in, 16, 17, 20; 'All I wanted was to live in', 18; call for 'repatriation to' (1971), 19–20; 'his historic homeland', 28; and the October War (1973), 28–9; accusations of espionage for, 28, 62, 136; books about, 33; recollections of Shcharansky in (1977–86), 36, 68, 69, 73; 'collect your wages' in, 38–9; Law of Return of, 51; a letter from Shcharansky published in (1974), 55–6; Radio (Voice of), 78, 99, 145; books on, confiscated, 80; sportsmen from, in Moscow (1975), 96–8; Independence Day of, celebrated in Moscow (1976), 123; information on, wanted, 140; 'cannot remain silent', 152; accusations against, 165, 171–2, 215, 242, 256, 258–9, 262, 263; 'his heart is there', 220; 'in which we take such pride' (Shcharansky at his trial), 266; 'friends' in, 304; 'wonderful landscapes' of, 305; 'amazing' landscapes of, 325; Shcharansky hopes his father's remains can be taken to, 342; a former Prisoner of Zion reaches (1981), 351; the President of, appeals on Shcharansky's behalf, 360; and its common language, 375; its second official language, 395; a Jew refuses to denounce wish to live in, 407; Shcharansky arrives in (1986), 415–6; Shcharansky's vision of, 417; flag of, photographed, plates 49, 58; map of, Shcharansky photographed under, plate 21

Israeli Legation (Moscow): 4, 6, 8, 13, 15

Israeli War of Independence (1948): 162

Istra: 25, 34, 77, 78, 105, 116, 132, 141, 147, 160, 166, 167, 189, 334, 362, 366

Italian Communist Party: an appeal to (1976), 107, 206, 246, 247, 251; an appeal to the leader of (1982), 357

Ivanov, Albert: receives refuseniks, 109–111; not to be a witness, 238

Izvestia: 11, 17, 27, 90, 165; Lipavsky's accusations in (4 March 1977), 167–8, 169–74, 175, 177–8; further accusations in, 172, 193; repercussions of accusations in, 182, 183, 190, 208, 211, 314; and Shcharansky's fate, 209, 220–1; and Shcharansky's trial, 241, 250, 260, 264

Jabotinsky, Vladimir (Zev): in Odessa, 1
Jackson Amendment, the: 41, 54, 59, 61, 62, 63, 68–9, 74, 85, 160; and the interrogation and trial of Shcharansky, 208, 233, 236, 245, 248, 249–50, 257, 259, 263, 269; renewal urged, 287
Jackson, Helen: meets Avital Shcharansky, 224
Jackson, Senator Henry M.: 41, 54, 61, 69, 85; and Shcharansky's trial, 246
Jacob: 64
Jacoby, Maître: 281
Janus: 'your friend or your foe', 401
Javits, Senator Jacob: in Moscow (1975), 79, 85; protests (1977), 224
Jerome, Jerome K.: Shcharansky 'in accordance with', 397
Jerusalem: a former Prisoner of Zion in, 16; a refugee from Germany in, 24; postcards of, 34, 366; Avital in, 49, 50, 65, 75, 86, 88, 286, 332, 334, 345; Shcharansky recalled by his friends in, 73, 120–1; an activist buried in, 119; accusations rebutted from, 179–80, 203–4; President Sadat in, 220; a protest from, 228–9; a telegram from, 332; 'God will help us to meet each other in', 345; appeals from, 355, 382; Shcharansky's uncle travels to, 364; 'dear ones' in, 367; 'Brussels Three' conference in (1983), 368; a letter reaches Chistopol prison from, 392; a rally in (1983), 393; postcards from, reach Moscow, 397; 'Will he be living in . . .', 411; Shcharansky's first press conference in (1986), 416
Jerusalem Post: 28, 180, 351
Jesus: and Pontius Pilate's 'scummish tactics', 278
'Jew': inscribed as a nationality, 2, 20
Jewish Agency (Jerusalem): 196
Jewish Anti-Fascist Committee: 4, 236
Jewish Autonomous Region (Birobidjan): not one Yiddish school in, 236; praised, 257
Jewish Chronicle (London): 280, 364; and Shcharansky's 'spirit uncrushed', 417
Jewish Commerical School (Odessa): 1, 321
Jewish Cultural Symposium (Moscow, 1976): 150–3, 155; an accusation against (1977), 170
Jewish New Year (Rosh Hashana): in 1948, 4; in 1975, 91, 92; in 1976, 137; in 1979, 305, 306, 307, 309, 310; in 1983, 391–2
Jewish Theatre (Moscow): 4
Jews in the USSR: under pressure, 74–5;

privately but openly circulated, 87, 95, 114
'Jews of Silence': decide to break silence, 151
John Paul II, Pope: an appeal to, 357
Johnson, Frank: and rumours of an exchange (1986), 413
Jordan: 13
Josephus Flavius: book by, confiscated, 106
Joyce, James: Shcharansky reads book by, 374
Judaism: condemned 10, 67; the grandson of a teacher of, 21; and Shcharansky, 51; books on, confiscated, 80; a teacher of, signs an appeal, 94; Jews want to be 'free to practice', 181
justice: and 'judicial reprisal', 334

Kaddish (prayer for the dead): in Chistopol prison, 331, 362
Kalendarev, Boris: released, but refused an exit visa, 427
Kalistratova, Sofia: 79, 90; signs a protest, 278–9; 'happy when friends depart', 299; signs the final Helsinki Watchdog group report, 357
Kaluga: a trial at, 228, 240, 245
Kama, River: 288
Kamenetsky, Boris: and Dr Lipavsky, 314
Kaminskaya, Dina: her home searched, 150, 154; expelled, 200; defends Shcharansky, 221; a book by, 432
Kandel, Felix: and *Jews in the USSR*, 75, 87; signs appeals, 83, 94, 115, 151, 156, 167, 184, 198, 202; recalls Shcharansky, 120–1, 178–9, 185; a seminar in apartment of, 139, 151; a poem of protest by, 143; demonstrates, 144; and Shcharansky's arrest, 185–6; defends Shcharansky, 203, 221; books by, 432; photograph of, plate 16
Kanyevsky, Boris: a released prisoner, still refused an exit visa, 427
Kaplan, Fanya: a would-be assassin, 96
Karamazov, Ivan: Shcharansky 'moved' to agree with, 401
Kaunas: refuseniks in, 101; an appeal on behalf of a survivor from, 167
Kazan: 288, 290; an oculist from, 294–5; no letters from, 296, 297; no book from, 308–9; doctors from, 316, 319, 381; Ida Milgrom's protests at, 354, 360; Ida Milgrom's journey to, 382; a visitor from, 386
Kazantsev: Ida Milgrom's meeting with (1982), 355–7
Kennedy, Senator Edward: a telegram of support from, 145
KGB: Avital's recollections of, 32, 37, 38, 40; and a meeting of refuseniks (1974),

42; and Shcharansky's first arrest (1974), 47–8; and Shcharansky's wedding (1974), 48; and an informer (1974), 55, 100; Shcharansky's report on (1974), 55–6, 57; and the Jackson Amendment, 69; Lunts and Shcharansky warned by (1975), 74; warn Professor Lerner, 82; warn Lev Roitburd, 92; film a gathering, 98; arrest activists (1975), 106; and the death of Davidovich (1976), 118–9; and a British television film, 130; Shcharansky's 'conversation' with (1976), 135–6; a discussion with, 143; Shcharansky 'tailed' by (1976–7), 147, 149, 165, 178, 179, 180, 182, 185–6, 202, 218; and Shcharansky's arrest, 185–6, 339; a warning from, 152; not 'to triumph', 153; pressure from, 174; and Dr Lipavsky, 177, 180, 260, 314; and the investigation against Shcharansky (1977–8), 187, 193–4, 199, 207, 213, 233, 260, 261; and the isolation of prisoners, 291–2; and the confiscation of a book of Psalms, 348; and Shcharansky's 'courage', 351; Ida Milgrom summoned to (1983), 361; seek Shcharansky's 'proper' behaviour in prison, 386–7; accompany Shcharansky westward (1986), 414; their 'hatred', 415

Kharkov: a Jew from, sentenced (1974), 60; refuseniks in, 101; refuseniks questioned in, 205–6; an appeal from, 226; a further prisoner from (1985), 407

Khenkin, Kyril: a spokesman, 27

Khnokh, Leib: a prisoner, 155

Khnokh, Vladimir: a letter from, confiscated, 300; regards to, 310

Kholmiansky, Alexander: sentenced (1985), 405–6; released, but refused an exit visa, 427

Khrushchev, Nikita: 11

Kiev: executions in (1952), 8; memorial meeting at (1968), 16; a Jew sentenced in (1973), 35; a journey to (1974), 55; a Jew beaten up in, 60; an incident at the synagogue in, 80; a Jew from, sentenced (1975), 89; refuseniks in, 101, 134; a petition from, 222; a fast in, 226; a book of Psalms from, 392; a further prisoner from (1985), 407

King, Martin Luther: 11, 157

Kishinev: anti–Jewish booklet in (1964), 10; two Jews sentenced in (1970), 17; Jews from, arrested (1974), 53–4; a journey to, 55, 56–7; a Jew imprisoned in, 57, 58; information from, 58; protesters from, 62; refuseniks in, 80; Hebrew classes in, 149–50

Kislik, Vladimir: beaten up, 60; questioned, 206; sentenced (1981), 352; released (1984), but still refused an exit visa, 427

Kissinger, Henry: 54, 61; his 'compromise', 61, 79

Knut: a book by, 295, 297

Koch, Edward: and the 'Shcharansky Steps', 352

Kochubievsky, Boris: sentenced (1968), 16; in Israel, 394

Kochubievsky, Felix: a prisoner, 394; released (1985), but still refused an exit visa, 427

Kogan, Isaak: a refusenik, 101

Kogan, Lev: arrested, 46; in Israel, 119; his photograph, 295–6

Kohl, Chancellor Helmut: and 'talks about release', 412

Koifman, Evgeny: sentenced (1985), 407; a prisoner, 424

Kola Peninsula: 176

Kolchak, Admiral A.V.: 21

Konina (a landlady): 234

Kook, Rabbi Avraham (of Jerusalem): 312

Korey, William: and the Jackson Amendment, 63; and a possible exchange, 227; books by, 432; articles by, 435

Kosharovsky, Inna: demonstrates, 143; signs an appeal, 184

Kosharovsky, Yuly: protests (1970), 20; arrested (1974), 46; signs appeals, 83, 94, 109, 114, 155, 167, 184, 198; teaches Hebrew, 87; a refusenik since 1971, 100–1, 317; arrested (1975), 106; meets Soviet officials (1976), 109, 110; demonstrates (1976), 143, 144; denounced (1977), 163; protests, 165

Kosygin, Alexei: his declaration (of 1966), 13, 14

Krasnodar: a Jew from, in trouble, 60, 104

Krasnoyarsk: a refusenik divided family in, 110; an interrogation in, 221

Krasnoyarsk region: 78

Kremen, Michael: his apartment searched, 172; photograph of, plate 18

Kremlin, the: 51, 143, 160, 287

Krimsky, George: cited in Shcharansky's trial, 248

Krivulin, Alexei: accused of being a 'murderer', 61

Kryakutny (an inventor): 312

Kryzhak, Valery: demonstrates, 26–7; signs appeals, 35

Kukui, Valery: sentenced (1971), 20

Kutuzovsky Prospect (Moscow): a meeting on, 246

Kuznetsov, Edward: sentenced (1970), 18; a protest on behalf of, 20; possible exchange of (1978), 225; released (1979), 291, 310; and the cancellation of labour camp visits, 335; and Shcharansky's

'courage', 351; and an appeal for
Shcharansky (1982), 355; book by, 432;
article by, 435

Ladyzhensky, Andrei: 335, 337
Ladyzhensky, Vitya: 335, 337
Landa, Malva: sentenced (1977), 199; signs
a protest (1978), 278–9; Shcharansky asks
about (1979), 297
Latvian Republic: trial in (1971), 19
Law of Return (of the State of Israel): 51
Lawyers Group of the National Conference
on Soviet Jewry: 28
Lazaris, Esther: a plan from, 188
Leahy, Senator Patrick: visits Moscow
(1975), 90; 'regards' to (1976), 134; and
Avital Shcharansky, 140; appeals on
behalf of Shcharansky (1977), 187
Lebanese Embassy (Moscow): protest near
(in 1972), 24, 27; (in 1974), 42–3, 44
Lefortovo prison (Moscow): 187, 190, 193,
210, 215–16, 219, 220, 221, 224, 339, 366,
379, 381, 389; Shcharansky leaves, 296;
Shcharansky not allowed a visit from his
father to, 331; Shcharansky returned to
(1986), 412; photograph of, plate 38
Lein, Evgeni: a prisoner, 394; released
(1982) but still refused an exit visa, 427
Lenin, Vladimir Ilyich: 21, 96; cited in
Shcharansky's trial, 255; his 'kind and
tender' glance, 336
Lenin Library (Moscow): protests near,
69–70, 222
Leningrad: trial in (1970), 18; second trial in
(1971), 19; protests concerning trials in,
18–19, 39, 62, 83, 106, 222, 282; an
incident at the synagogue in, 80;
telephones disconnected in, 80; hunger
strike in, 83; refuseniks in, 101; an appeal
from, 157–8, 158–9; interrogations in,
205, 206; a petition from, 222; a fast in,
226; a witness from, 245; Jews from,
travel to Gorky to support a prisoner's
wife, 407–8
Lermontov, Mikhail: and Shcharansky's
'favourites', 297
Lerner, Professor Alexander: his seminar,
26, 125; signs a message of solidarity
(1973), 29; at a public protest (1974), 44;
signs letters and appeals (1974–86), 59,
63, 82, 86, 96, 106–7, 107, 108, 117, 123,
136, 146, 151, 155, 156, 159, 184–5, 189,
191, 191–2, 198, 202, 204, 222, 287; and
search for a spokesman, 73; warned, 82;
meets visitors, 89, 99; a refusenik since
1971, 100–1, 317; a poem of, 105; helps
compile a letter, 112; a Passover service
in apartment of, 117; an appeal on behalf
of, 119; criticised, 125; and an American
petition, 125–6; an appeal on behalf of,

128; 'singing in the candlelight', 142;
demonstrates, 143; a statement by, 146;
taken into custody, 152; and a telephone
call, 157; accusations against (1977), 168,
169, 170–2, 193; his apartment searched,
172; rejects accusations, 173–4; and
Lipavsky, 175; fears for, 188;
unmolested, 188–9; defends
Shcharansky, 189–90, 202; further
accusations against, 197, 260; questioned,
220; his daughter in Israel, 272;
Shcharansky asks about, 297, 305, 321;
his portrait of Ida Milgrom, 321; and a
birthday celebration, 329; and 'a hero of
the Jewish emigration movement', 406;
envisages 'a great festival', 413–4; 'the
happiest day of my life', 416;
photographs of, plates 16, 20
Lerner, Judith: signs an appeal, 222;
Shcharansky asks about, 297, 321;
Shcharansky receives letters from, 301,
317, 318; a letter from, confiscated, 312;
her health, 317
Lerner, Sonia: receives her exit visa, 44; in
Israel, 128, 180
Letter to a Young Poet: Shcharansky quotes,
375
letters: not delivered, 80, 93, 133, 181
Levin, Professor Nora: in Moscow (1976),
117–8
Levin, Yakov: a prisoner, 424
Levinson, Sender: sentenced (1975), 81,
107; appeals on behalf of Shcharansky
(1982), 355
Levit, Leonid: refused an exit visa, 80
Levitas, Boris: in danger, 81; refused an exit
visa, 127; filmed, 131
Levitsky, Melvin: in Moscow, 114; an
accusation against, 171, 179, 246
Lewis, Anthony: his warning, 358
L'Humanité: declines an invitation, 238
Liacouras, Peter: his concern, 222–3
Lipavsky, Dr Alexander (Sanya): signs
appeals, 94, 109, 133, 136, 159; helps a
refusenik, 116; and the Jews of Ilyinka,
126; and Shcharansky's lodging place in
Moscow, 160, 167, 234; his accusations
(4 March 1977), 167–72, 173–4, 179–80,
180, 184–5; his life and character, 174–8;
the impact and repercussions of his letter,
188–9, 190, 208; further accusations of (6
May 1977), 193; his letter and
Shcharansky's interrogation and trial,
211; and the Central Intelligence Agency,
225; and Shcharansky's trial, 233, 241,
243, 246–8, 250, 259–61, 263, 264, 270,
271, 274; the 'false testimony' of, 279;
new information concerning, 314; his
'fine fiction' recalled, 406; a photograph
of, plate 32

Literaturnaya Gazeta: 98, 222, 223, 365; and postal deliveries, 377; a 'vehement discussion' in, 379

Livshits, Vladimir: a prisoner, 424; his photograph, taken shortly before his arrest, plate 46

Lod airport (later Ben Gurion airport): 31

Lokshin, Osip: a prisoner, 394; released (1984), but still refused an exit visa, 427

London: film of a protest in, 162; 'displeasure' in, 358; rumours in, 408

Long Island: a Justice Garden in, 224; and a possible exchange, 224–5

Long Island Committee for Soviet Jewry: 188, 224

Lookstein, Audrey: a photograph of, admired, 295

Lookstein, Haskell: a photograph of, admired, 295

Los Angeles: 396

Los Angeles Times: 114, 120, 126, 128, 174, 177, 200, 270

Love Story: and a feeling of 'some kind of tragedy', 45

Lubertsy (near Moscow): 297

Lukanov, Judge: and Shcharansky's trial, 231, 232

Lunts, Dr Alexander: and the wisdom of demonstration, 26; signs letters and appeals, 35, 58, 63, 82, 86, 94, 96, 106–7, 107, 269; and the Jackson Amendment, 41; his journey to the provinces (1974), 55; and the letter to President Ford (1974), 58, 59; protests on behalf of prisoners, 62; 'hard daily work' of, 68; demonstrates (1975), 70; warned, 74; letters of, stopped, 80; threats against, 81; meets Senators and Congressmen, 85, 89, 99; worried about Shcharansky (1975), 90; compiles lists, 100, 101, 205–6, 258, 260; arrested (1975), 106; receives exit visa (1976), 107, 116; active in Israel, 119, 132; criticised, 125; and the Helsinki Watchdog group, 128; Shcharansky's letter to (1976), 135; and Dr Lipavsky's accusations (1977), 180, 193; and Shcharansky's arrest, 187, 188; further accusations against, 196, 197; 'best wishes' to, 325; and a birthday party, 329; photograph of, plate 23

Lunts, Ludmila (Lucy): 55

Luzhniki: Sports Complex (Moscow): Israeli sportsmen at (1975), 97

Lvov: a Jew from, 27; a visitor to, 55; information from, 59, 60–1; refuseniks in, 101

Ma'alot: massacre at (1974), 42–3

McGill, William J.:218

Maccabee, Judah: his revolt recalled, 229

Maccabees: their triumph celebrated, 105

Madrid: Helsinki review conference in, 327, 348, 361, 383

Mager, Jeanette: her plea, 188

Mager, Mikhail: signs an appeal, 189; receives his exit visa, 205

'Magnificent Seven': greetings to, 318

Mai, Arkady: leads seminar, 139; signs appeal, 204

Maikop: an appeal from, 154

Malkin, Anatoly: his journey, 55–6; expelled, 60; and a Hebrew class, 68; vulnerable, 69; demonstrates, 71; arrested (1975), 79; held in prison, 81; his trial, 89–90; sentenced, 91–2, 93, 107; lessons of trial of, 94, 95; Shcharansky's concern for, 97, 147; helps compile lists, 100; appeals on behalf of, 119, 127; questioned, 205; cited in Shcharansky's trial, 272; appeals on behalf of Shcharansky (1982), 355

Malofeev, Colonel: at Chistopol prison, 288

'Mamma Phenya': 7

Manekofsky, Irene: in Moscow, 56–7; Shcharansky writes to, 72, 116, 133–4; accusations against, 170, 197; seeks to alert White House, 187, 188; Shcharansky mentions, 284

Manevich, Girsh: 46–7, 48; not allowed as a witness, 238, 240

Marchais, Georges: his letter of protest, 358; a reply to, 361

Marshall, Robert: cited, 262

Martemyanov, Major: interrogates, 205

Masada (Dead Sea): book about, confiscated, 106

Matthias, Senator: in Moscow (1975), 85

Matveev, Shmuel: imprisoned (1975), 126

Mauriac, François: 10–11

Maxwell: formula of, 303

Meiman, Professor Naum: 'singing in the candlelight', 142; signs appeals, 146, 156, 202, 279, 357; and human rights in the Soviet Union, 414

Meir, Golda: in Moscow (1948), 4; a telegram to (1973), 29; 'the Jews in the Soviet Union will be free!' (1976), 112; and the October War (of 1973), 258; quoted in Shcharansky's trial, 258, 259

Mendelevich, Iosif: in labour camp, 44; protests on behalf of, 62, 108; contacts Shcharansky in prison, 282–3; comments on Shcharansky's character, 286; and a prison visitor, 291; 'reliable information' from, 306; meets Shcharansky in prison, 326–7; and the death of Shcharansky's father, 330–1; songs, in prison, 333; released, and arrives in Israel (1983), 351; at the White House, 352; and an appeal

on behalf of Shcharansky, 355; recalls Shcharansky, 361; rejects an 'admission of guilt', 383; describes prison life, 393; book by, 432
Meskhetians: dispersed, 155
Meyerowitz, Allan: visits Moscow, 50–1
Michener, James: 25
Mikhoels, Solomon: murdered (1948), 4
Milgrom, Ida: her marriage, 2; the birth of her sons, 3; recalls childhood of Lyonya and Tolya, 3–4, 5–6, 6–7, 9, 11; meets Natasha Shtiglits, 33–5; advises Natasha Shtiglits, 46, 47; a telegram to, 141; at Istra, 147; interrogated, 189, 219; and her son's 'crimes', 190, 191, 199; and her son's interrogation, 195, 221; and her son's defence, 200, 209–10, 219–20, 225, 226–7; her appeals on her son's behalf, 201–2, 217, 221–2, 228, 334–5, 355–7, 391; and her son's trial, 231, 232, 240, 241, 275, 276; her son's prison letters and telegrams to, 283–4, 284–5, 285–6, 286–7, 293–313, 314–26, 331–2, 349–50, 352, 359–60, 361–4, 364–8, 371–81, 388–93, 393–403, 405, 406–7, 408; visits her son in prison, 288–90, 352–4, 385–7; speaks to relatives in Canada, 313–4; and her son's health, 326; and her husband's death (1980), 329–30; visits her son in labour camp (1980), 335–45; not allowed to see her son, 358, 359–60; summoned to the KGB (1983), 361; an appeal on behalf of (1985), 406; 'I am at peace' (1986), 416; photographs of, plates 5, 12, 39, 40, 47, 55
Ministry of Communications (Moscow): an apology from, 377
Ministry of the Interior (Moscow): 8, 19, 143, 147
Minsk: a Jew from, 43; a journey to (1974), 55–6, 57, 67; information from, 58, 61, 101; telephones disconnected in, 80; an appeal from Jews in, 158; a visitor to, 175; interrogations in, 205, 206, 210–14; a petition from, 222; a fast in, 226; Shcharansky's 'regards' to refuseniks in, 299
Mishener, Iosif: sentenced (1970), 17; at Vladimir prison (1975), 81, 101; appeals on behalf of Shcharansky (1982), 355
Mitterand, François: an appeal to, 357
Mohammed: 374
Moldavia, Soviet Republic of: 17, 80; an appeal from, 149–50
Montgolfier brothers: 312
Montreal: a telephone call from, 141
Moscow: Shcharansky studies in, 11–12; a protest in (1972), 24; Western journalists in, 27, 68; a message of solidarity from (1973), 29; a press conference in, 37;

Passover celebrated in, 39–40; further protests in, 42–3, 53; help for a family from, 51–2; information from, 59; further protests by Jews in, 62; telephones disconnected in, 80; hunger strike in, 83; Israeli sportsmen in, 96–8, 162; a 'guarantee' to the rulers of, 112; Israel Independence Day celebrated in (1976), 123; a telegram sent in Hebrew from, 137; a series of demonstrations in (1976), 138, 142–5; questions concerning lists of refuseniks reaching, 206, 208; a petition from, 222; a vigil in, 222; an appeal from, 226; Shcharansky's trial in, 231, 240; the Jewish anthem sung in, 276, 416; Sakharov banished from, 333; 'dear ones' in, 367; letters to Chistopol from, 377; Jews from, travel to Gorky to support a prisoner's wife, 407–8; Shcharansky moved back to prison in (1986), 412, 413; Shcharansky flown to Berlin from, 414–5; gladness in, 418
'Moscow Aliyah': alleged group, 194, 195
Moscow, Mayor of: and a demonstration (1974), 43
Moscow Olympics (1980): 327
Moscow Public Action Group (see index entry for Helsinki Watchdog group)
Moses: Pharaoh's reply to, 123–4; and 'moral norms', 374; the Five Books of, Shcharansky studying, 76
Mosse: his book, 374
Mount of Olives (Jerusalem): a burial on (1976), 119
Mozambique: 225
Muhammad Ali: cited in Shcharansky's trial, 262
Munich Olympics (1972): 24, 27
Murmansk: 176
Musinchina, Irina: a witness, 243
My Pushkin: Shcharansky reads, 379

Nahariya (Israel): 50
Napoleon: 'bald ... small', 120
Nasha Strana (Our Country): 213–4
Nashpits, Mark: demonstrates, 70; sentenced (1975), 70–1, 73, 78, 81, 107; in Siberia, 93; signs an appeal, 96; Shcharansky visits, 103–4, 105; telephone of, disconnected, 108; an appeal on behalf of, 119; Shcharansky's questions about, 305, 322; letters from, 307, 321; a photograph of, with Shcharansky in Siberia, plate 30
Nasser, President Gamal Abdul: 13
'Natan': a Hebrew name, chosen, 31
Nathanson, Allyn: 172
National Conference on Soviet Jewry: 21, 23, 28, 41, 56, 88, 124, 125, 156, 170, 188, 196, 200, 218, 224, 225, 352;

publications of, 434

Navon, Yitzhak: appeals on Shcharansky's behalf (1983), 360

Nedelya: 165

Nepomniashchy, Mark: sentenced (1985), 406; a prisoner, 425

Netanya (Israel): 50

Netanyahu, Benjamin: 'you are not alone', 407

New Jerusalem (near Moscow): 25, 34

New Times: Shcharansky reads (1983), 365

New York: conference in (1963), 11; bomb at (1976), 106–7; Day of Solidarity in (1976), 123; 'Shcharansky Steps' in (1981), 352; Shcharansky's uncle travels to Jerusalem from, 364; celebrations in, and a labour camp sentence (1985), 408; Avital Shcharansky's silent protest in (1985), 409

New York Times: 114, 142, 146, 153, 157, 199, 225, 228, 240, 275, 314, 405, 408

News Bulletin: published (1972), 24; publishes an appeal from Moscow (1973), 35; and Shcharansky's appeal in (1975), 75

Newsweek: 218, 281

Newton, Isaac: and gravity, 390

'Next Year in Jerusalem': recited in Moscow (1976), 117; spoken by Shcharansky at his trial (1978), 268; written by Shcharansky in a letter from prison (1983), 393; the 'age-old prayer', 417, 418

Next Year in Jerusalem: published (1979), 326

Niebuhr, Reinhold: protests, 10–11

Nisanova, Lidia: a prisoner, 107, 108; warned, 113; her case recounted, 118

Nixon, President Richard M.: visits Moscow (1972), 23, 26; his second visit to Moscow (1974), 46, 116, 144

Nizhnikov, Abram: his affidavit, 227

Nobel Peace Prize: awarded to Sakharov (1975), 98; Shcharansky nominated for (1982), 358–9

Novikov, Mark Zakharovich: 139

Novosibirsk: refuseniks in, 101, 301–2

Novosty News Agency: declines an invitation, 238

Novoye Vremya: attacks activists, 132; Shcharansky reads, 316

Nudel, Ida: protests (1972), 23; supports demonstrations, 27; helps prisoners, 28, 31–2; solidarity with Israel, 29; telephone calls with, 39; an appeal on behalf of (1975), 75; signs letters and appeals, 82, 86, 96, 107, 108–9, 112, 117, 136, 146, 155, 156, 158–9, 167, 184, 189, 191–2, 198, 204, 222; meets Senators and Congressmen, 85, 89; and Dr Lipavsky,

94, 175; a refusenik since 1971, 100–1; an appeal on behalf of, 119; and an American petition, 125–6; 'singing in the candlelight', 142; demonstrates, 143; a statement by, 146; her apartment searched, 172; defends Shcharansky, 203; questioned, 220; sentenced (1978), 227; rumoured release of (1979), 291; Shcharansky's references to, 297, 305, 307, 323; an Atlas dedicated to (1979), 314, 431; and a photograph of Shcharansky, 326–7; Shcharansky receives letters from, 397; one of 'our heroes', 408; 'struggle and suffering' of, 411; Shcharansky to fight for, 417; still refused an exit visa (February 1986), 427; a book about, 432; photographs of, plates 20, 25, 26, 32

Obidin, V.S.: receives refuseniks, 109–111

Ocheretyansky, Mark: a former prisoner, still refused his exit visa, 427

Odessa: 1, 2, 30, 321; information from, 60; Jews pilloried in, 80; a Jew from, arrested, 85, 92; refuseniks in, 101, 134; an appeal from, 154; interrogations in, 205; tales of, 363–4

Ogonyok: 165

Ohio: visitors from, 181

Old Testament: attacked (1974), 67

Omaha (Nebraska): a visitor from, 91

Omaha Committee for Soviet Jewry: 91

Orlov, Chief Justice A.K.: takes 'a firm stand', 286

Orlov, Yury: Shcharansky a tutor to, 77, 148; and the Helsinki Watchdog group, 124, 125, 128, 150, 155, 156, 157, 182, 192, 193; arrested, 165; an accusation against, 170; in prison, 189, 210, 357; sentenced (1978), 227; President Carter condemns trial of, 248; accusations against, 251, 252, 256, 262, 263, 271; 'honest, brave and courageous', 267

Orlovsky, Henrietta: in Israel, 127–8

Oshmiana (Lithuania): refuseniks in, 101

Osin, Major: a labour camp Chief, 337, 338

Osnos, Peter: in Moscow, 114; an alleged message from, 193; and Dr Lipavsky, 225–6, 248, 259; articles by, 435

OVIR (*see index entry for* Visa Office)

Ovsishcher, Colonel Lev: signs telegrams and appeals, 29, 63, 67, 86, 96, 109, 117, 119, 156, 184, 191, 204–5, 287; detained, 43; hostility around, 67; demoted, 81; threats against, 81; meets Senators, 85; protests, 96; listed, 101; harassed, 108; mentioned in an appeal, 115; and an American petition, 126; interrogated, 210–14; a letter from, 299; a greeting card from, 397; photographs of, plates 20, 47

Palatnik, Raisa: sentenced (1971), 20
Palestine: 1, 4, 30, 104, 165
Panarev, Alexander: a prisoner, 394;
    released (1984) but still refused his exit
    visa, 427
Panchenkova (a witness): 235
Panorama: television programme by
    (1985), 406
Paris: a protest in (1980), 10; Avital
    Shcharansky's visit to (1979), 327
Paritsky, Alexander: sentenced (1981), 352;
    released (1984) but still refused an exit
    visa, 427
Passover: 39–40, 76, 80; Shcharansky's
    hopes for, 116; a celebration of, filmed,
    117; a Jew arrested during, 126;
    Shcharansky's 'best wishes' for, 367
Pentecostalists: an appeal on behalf of, 127;
    a campaigner for, receives exit visa, 159;
    and Shcharansky, 190, 201
Percy, Senator Charles: in Moscow (1975),
    85
Peres, Shimon: on Soviet Jewry (1973), 28;
    greets Shcharansky (1986), 415;
    photograph of, greeting Shcharansky,
    plate 53
Perm: refuseniks in, 60, 101
Perm Region Labour Camp Zone: 241–2,
    262–3; Shcharansky to be transferred to,
    315; Ida Milgrom's visit to her son in,
    335–45, 347; Shcharansky's trial in
    (1981), 349; Shcharansky returns to
    (1984), 404; Shcharansky in prison of
    (1985–6), 411; Shcharansky moved from,
    to Moscow (1986), 412
Pertini, President Sandro: an appeal from,
    357
Petah Tikvah: a founder of, 104
Petrenko, Chief: at Lefortovo prison, 339
Petukhov, Valery: not allowed to be cross-
    examined, 251
Pevzner, Vladimir: questioned, 205
Pharaoh: an appeal to, 71; his reply, 123–4
Philadelphia: visitors to Moscow from, 38,
    62, 90, 115; visitors to Jerusalem from,
    413
Philadelphia Inquirer: 406
Philosophical Issues: Shcharansky reads, 375
Physical–Technical Institute (Moscow): 12,
    16, 25, 35–6, 68
Piatkus, Victoras: heads a Helsinki
    Watchdog group, 154–5; arrested (1977),
    205; sentenced (1978), 277, 279
Piper, Harold D.: in Moscow, 185
Pipes, Professor Richard: in Moscow
    (1975), 87–8; accusations concerning,
    233, 244–5, 268–9; a Party member visits,
    241
Plain Dealer (Cleveland, Ohio): 181
Platonov: a witness, at wrong trial, 245

Plyushch, Leonid: his case cited, 237
Podgorny, President Nikolai: a protest to
    (1970), 20; his congratulatory telegram
    (1976), 239
Podrabinek, Sasha: in Siberia, 307
Poland: 15
Poles: seek repatriation, 19–20
Polhan, Isaak: demonstrates, 26–7
Polsky, Victor: 42, 196
Poltinnikov, Dr Irma: her fate, 301–2
Poltinnikov, Dr Isaac: receives an exit visa,
    301
Poltinnikov, Victoria: her fate, 301–2
Polytechnic Institute (Kiev): 127
Polytechnic Institute (Krasnodar): 104
Ponevezhys (Lithuania): refuseniks in, 101
Ponomarev, Boris: visits Washington DC,
    224
Pontius Pilate: the 'innovator', 278
Popov, Vladimir: his warning, 152
Popova (a secretary): 234, 270
Potsdam: an exchange at (1986), 414
Povarenko, Chief: at Lefortovo prison,
    340
Power Institute (Moscow): 10
Pravda (Moscow): 8, 11, 15; comments on
    Shcharansky's trial (1978), 277–8; and
    parapsychology, 296
Pravda (Ukraine): 8
Pressel, Joseph: in Moscow, 114, 174; an
    accusation against, 246
Prestin, Vladimir: signs appeals, 35, 83, 86,
    112, 114, 115, 119, 146, 156, 184, 191,
    202; a refusenik since 1971, 100; raid on
    home of, 106; an 'old' refusenik, 317
Prisoners of Zion: protests concerning, 62;
    'and then be free', 79; pressures on, 81;
    listed, 101; conditions of, 108; a
    champion of, 108–9; an Atlas locates,
    145; pencils for, 147; a 'salute' from Israel
    for, 152; presented as 'speculators', 163
    245, 358; a document on, not cited, 263;
    some released, to Shcharansky's delight,
    290; Avital Shcharansky appeals for, 334;
    an appeal from, on behalf of
    Shcharansky, 355; growing numbers of
    (1983), 394; the struggle for, 410;
    dedication to, xiii
Promised Land: mocked, 197; Shcharansky
    reaches, 416
Prosecutor-General, the: a protest to
    (1972), 23; and Shcharansky's exit visa,
    25–6; further protests to, 28, 144, 219,
    220–1
Proverbs, book of: Shcharansky reads, 396;
    and 'fear of the Lord', 401
Psalms, book of: sung to Jewish tunes, 38; a
    copy of, in prison, 312, 330, 332, 333; a
    copy of, confiscated, 348, 351;
    Shcharansky reads, 362, 363; referred to,

in a poem, 366; and the Psalm of
Deliverance, 367; 'I will keep a curb on
my mouth', 389; a rare copy of, reaches
Chistopol prison, 392–3; and 'fear of the
Lord', 401–2; and Shcharansky's
'innermost feelings', 403; and a struggle
to keep, 412; reaches Jerusalem, 416
Public Action Group: formed in Moscow
(1976), 146
Purim festival: Shcharansky's hopes for,
116; and 'trips in time' on, 366–7

Rabelais: 'conversations' with, 380
Rabinovich, Matus: and family
reunification, 110
Rachel: 64, 325
Radio Free Europe: 235, 255
Radio Liberty: 235, 255, 271
Radio Minsk: attacks Judaism, 67
Radio Moscow: and the Arab–Israeli war of
1967, 13; and Shcharansky's 'crimes'
(1983), 393
Rakhlenko, Arik: greetings from, 309, 322
Ramm, Dimitri: a refusenik, 60
Rappoport, Allan: 281
Raslin, Saul: accusations by, 214–5; a
'secret' witness, 241, 261, 270, 274
Reagan, President Ronald: and a letter to
Avital Shcharansky, 292; meets Avital
Shcharansky, 352; and the Geneva
Summit (1985), 408–9, 412;
Shcharansky's telephone call to (1986),
416
Red Army, the: 2, 4, 21, 34, 96, 124
Red Sea: dreams of a swim in, 396
Reddaway, Peter: article by, 182, 435; book
by, 432
Rejoicing of the Law: celebrated in
Moscow (1969), 16; in 1976, 137, 138
repatriation: of Jews, Poles and Germans,
19–20
Reuters: report by, 213
Reznik, Anatoly: receives exit visa, 116
Reznikov, L. Ya.: article by, 312
Riabsky: a 'secret' witness, 241; his further
evidence, 244–5, 247, 261, 263, 270, 271,
274
Ribicoff, Senator Abraham: in Moscow
(1975), 85; recalls his visit (1978), 281
Richter, Glenn: a campaigner, 11
Riga: a protest march in (1971), 19; a trial in
(1971), 19; an appeal from (1972), 23; a
journey to (1974), 55, 57; information
from, 60; protesters from, 62; refuseniks
in, 101; an appeal from Jews in, 158;
interrogations in, 205, 206; a prisoner
from, 410
Rilke: poems by, 374; a letter of, 375
Riza Lake: 365
Roitberg, Pyotr: and a Moscow press

conference, 152–3
Roitburd, Lev: threatened, 80, 81; arrested,
85–6; sentenced, 89, 92, 107; 'lessons' of
trial of, 94, 95; prison conditions of, 108;
an appeal on behalf of, 127; questioned,
206; cited in Shcharansky's trial, 272;
appeals on behalf of Shcharansky (1982),
355
Roitburd, Lilia: signs an appeal (1975), 96
Romanov, Captain: Shcharansky's letters
and petitions to, 298, 301, 302, 305, 315;
and Shcharansky's hunger strike, 353
Romans: and the destruction of the
Temple, 47
Rome: 161, 162
Rosenblum, Dr Louis (Lou): in Moscow,
41–2; an accusation against, 197; book
by, 432
Ross, Professor Allan: his sombre advice,
382
Rossiya Hotel (Moscow): 56, 79, 191, 281
Roth, Cecil: book by, confiscated, 106
Rubin, Inessa (Ina): and Shcharansky at a
demonstration, 43; and an appeal against
a sentence, 71; types an appeal, 94; 'ready
to be arrested', 109; to receive exit visa,
129; leaves for Israel, 131; and a Party
member's mistake, 241; and Dr
Lipavsky, 259–60; photograph of, plate
24
Rubin, Professor Vitaly: his seminar, 25,
37, 87, 139; at a protest demonstration,
43; signs appeals, 59, 63, 82, 86, 94, 96,
106–7, 107, 108, 115, 117, 119, 123, 269;
and a demonstration of solidarity, 71;
drafts an appeal, 79, 245; letters to,
stopped, 80; meets Senators and
Congressmen, 85, 99; and Professor
Pipes, 88; a refusenik since 1972, 101;
meets visitors, 105; meets Soviet
officials, 109, 111; helps compile a letter,
112; meetings in apartment of, 118; a pall
bearer, 119; and the Helsinki Watchdog
group, 124, 128, 132, 192; to receive exit
visa, 129, 130; leaves for Israel, 131; in
Israel, 132; accusations against (1977),
168, 169, 170–1, 179–80; speaks to
Shcharansky, 180–1; and Shcharansky's
arrest, 187, 188; and Shcharansky's
defence, 203–4; allegations concerning,
234, 244, 248, 259; and a Party member's
visit, 270; photograph of, plate 20
Rudenko, P.: his home searched, 252
Rudenko, Prosecutor-General Roman: 219,
231, 281–2
Rukhadze, Avtandil: and Shcharansky's
'guilt', 358; book by, 432
Rumbuli: memorial meeting at, 19
Russell, Bertrand: 10–11
Russkaya Literatura: article in, 312

Ryazan: Jews imprisoned in (1970), 17

Sadat, President Anwar: 220
Sakharov, Academician Andrei: protests
    (1970), 18; and a protest letter (1971), 19;
    at a demonstration (1972), 24; his letter to
    Congress (1973), 41; at a further
    demonstration (1974), 44; appeals on
    behalf of Dr Shtern (1974), 62;
    Shcharansky does secretarial work for
    (1975), 77; Congressmen visit (1975), 77;
    and Shcharansky, 88–9, 105; awarded
    Nobel Peace Prize, 98; signs an appeal
    about Davidovich, 119; the trial of a
    friend of, 131; his 'respect' for Jews, 145;
    his appeals on behalf of Shcharansky,
    188, 200–1; cited in Shcharansky's trial,
    246; 'honest, brave and courageous', 267;
    speaks up for Shcharansky's mother, 275,
    276; Shcharansky's reference to (1979),
    305; greetings from, 309; greetings to,
    325; stripped of State honours, 332–3;
    appeals on behalf of Shcharansky (1982),
    357; rumours concerning (1985), 408,
    409; Shcharansky's concern for (1986),
    417; photographs of, with Shcharansky,
    plates 33, 34
'Sakharov Affair', the: an alleged code
    name, 255
Salansky, Professor Naum: appeals on
    behalf of, 166–7, 183
Salman, Moshe: 104
Samarkand: a journey to, 55
Samizdat Archives (Munich): 271
Samoilovich, Deborah: signs letters and
    appeals, 63, 96
Samson: his power, and Shcharansky's, 392
San Francisco: International Tribunal of
    Inquiry in (1983), 361
Saratov: information from, 59; a refusenik
    questioned in, 205
Satter, David: in Moscow, 185
Schiller: Shcharansky reading a book by,
    414
Schnur, Zeesy: a telegram to, 136
Schweitzer, Albert: protests, 10–11
Scientists' Committee of the Israel Public
    Council for Soviet Jewry (Tel Aviv): 24,
    35
Scott, Senator: in Moscow (1975), 85
Second World War: murder of Jews in, 2,
    14, 16, 19, 58, 171; and the Jewish
    Anti-Fascist Committee, 236; a Stalin
    speech at end of, 303
Secret and Open Things: shown in Moscow
    (1975), 96
Security Council (of the United Nations):
    106
Segal, Alan: in Moscow, 131
Segal, Dmitri: his lecture, 25, 37

Segal, Erich: his book, 44
Senate Finance Committee (Washington
    DC): 61
Serpukhov: Jews imprisoned at, 144
Shakespeare: 380
Shakhnovsky, Vladimir (Zev): teaches
    Hebrew in Moscow, 76, 87, 140–1; signs
    appeals, 94, 96, 106–7, 202, 204–5; a
    refusenik since 1972, 101; and an
    American petition, 125–6; demonstrates,
    144; photographs of, plates 16, 18
Shapira, Morey: and Shcharansky's trial,
    227
Sharudillo, Investigator: 193
Shauliai (Lithuania): refuseniks in, 101
'Shcharansky Affair', the: activists in
    Moscow demand an end to (1977), 222
Shcharansky, Anatoly (Tolya, Tolik):
    his childhood and youth, 1–11; a
    student in Moscow, 11–12, 13–15; his
    early friendship with Vladimir Slepak,
    21–2; his friendship with Andrei
    Sakharov, 77, 88–9, 105, 188, 200–1, 267,
    305, 309, 325, 357, 416;
    his character, as seen by others, 22,
    35–6, 52, 57, 86, 94, 120–1, 145, 147,
    178–9, 181, 185, 189, 200–1, 203, 220;
    applies for an exit visa, 25–6; joins a
    group of activists, 27, 31–2, 36–7; meets
    Natalia Shtiglits (Avital), 29–30; attends
    Hebrew lessons, 30, 68; gives a friend
    Hebrew language tapes, 104; improves
    his Hebrew, 215, 216; and Hebrew in
    prison, 235, 258, 282, 283, 292, 296–7,
    302, 332, 333, 365–6, 400;
    becomes a refusenik, 31; lives with
    Avital in Moscow, 32–5, 37–8, 40; and
    the KGB, 32, 37, 40, 47, 48, 56, 57, 74,
    98, 130, 135–6, 143, 147, 149, 165, 178,
    179, 180, 182, 185–6, 202, 213, 218, 233,
    260, 261, 291–2, 348, 351, 386–7, 414,
    415; and a telephonic link with London,
    39;
    signs appeals and messages to the
    West, 35, 59, 68–9, 79, 79–82, 83, 85–6,
    94–5, 95–6, 96, 106–7, 107, 107–9, 108–9,
    112, 114, 115, 117, 118–9, 123–4, 133,
    136, 146, 151–2, 155–6, 156, 158–9, 166,
    166–7, 183, 184–5;
    signs the reports of the Helsinki
    Watchdog group, 126–8, 132–3, 150,
    153, 155;
    and a world of Jewish identity and
    revival, 39–40; early work as a translator-
    spokesman, 42, 71, 73–4, 77; at
    demonstrations, 43, 45, 53, 69–71, 109,
    138, 142–4, 166; marries Avital, 45–8;
    held in detention, 46, 53, 70, 144–5;
    his letters to Avital, 48–9, 49–50, 63–4,
    64, 75–6, 76, 77–8, 78, 86, 97, 103–4,

105, 129–30, 132, 138–41, 182–3, 216, 392–3;

his visitors from the West, 50–1, 56–7, 71, 87, 90, 91, 92, 105, 114, 117–8, 135, 137, 141–2, 174, 181, 185–6;

his journey of enquiry (to Riga and Minsk), 55–7;

his personal letters and individual messages to the West, 70, 72, 91–4, 104, 111–2, 116, 128–9, 133–4, 135–6;

dismissed from his research work (1975), 76–7; his concern for others, 52, 71–2, 79, 91–4, 103, 147, 416; and visiting Senators and Congressmen, 85, 88–9, 90, 91; 'This Year in Jerusalem', 91, 94; his journey to Siberia (1975), 103–4; and destiny, 105, 375, 396; filmed by a British television company (1976), 117, 130–2;

and the struggle for human rights, 122, 124–5, 126–7, 131, 153–4, 181–2, 190–1, 199, 201, 203–4, 217, 415; and the Jews of Ilyinka, 126, 153, 237, 238, 248, 249, 270, 273; and the Entebbe hijack rescue (1976), 132, 139, 203; summons a press conference (1976), 152–3; shown on Moscow television (1977), 163; denounced in Izvestia (1977), 167–8, 169–72; and the enigma of an informer, 174–8;

arrested (15 March 1977), 186; held in prison without trial (March 1977–July 1978), 187–229; tried (10–14 July 1978), 231–275; sentenced (14 July 1978), 275–6;

his letters from prison, 283–4, 284–5, 285–6, 286–7, 293–313, 314–26, 331–2, 349–50, 352, 359–60, 361–4, 364–8, 371–81, 388–93, 393–403, 405, 406–7, 408; his mother's visits to, in prison, 288–90, 352–4, 385–7; his mother's visit to, in labour camp, 335–45; his mother's appeals on his behalf, 201–2, 217, 221–2, 228, 334–5, 355–7, 391;

Avital Shcharansky's campaign on his behalf, 180–1, 187, 188, 198, 214, 218, 221, 224, 226, 248, 281, 327–8, 334, 348, 352, 357–8, 360–1, 382, 409–10, 412, 413;

interrogations of others in an attempt to build up a criminal charge against, 193–5, 199, 205–9, 210–14;

and Jewish history, 229; and 'Jewish nationalism', 236, 265–6; and the 'critical individualism' of, condemned, 255–6; praises the 'honest, brave' human rights activists, 267, 278–80; prison conversations with, 282–3, 288–90, 291, 327, 330–1, 333; and prison solidarity, 291–2; and a labour camp trial, 349;

rumours of release of (in 1978), 224–5; (in 1983), 364, 384; (in 1984), 405; (in 1985), 408–9; (in 1986), 411–12, 413; Atlas dedicated to (1979), 314, 431

'man is freedom', 320; and 'a dear and difficult happiness', 367; 'faith' and 'firmness', 379; 'it would be a pity to die', 380; 'with each step that we take, we touch other souls', 390; 'one must become detached from the slave concealed deep within', 399; 'a being unworthy of being chosen', 402;

Avital Shcharansky's appeal to Raisa Gorbachev on behalf of, 409–10; and the 'chains of exile', 411; release of (1986), 414–5; first day in freedom of, 415–6; and the 'in-gathering of the exiles', 417–8

photographs of, in the Soviet Union, plates 1, 3, 4, 5, 6, 7, 8, 9, 10, 11, 13, 16, 17, 18, 19, 20, 21, 23, 24, 25, 26, 27, 28, 29, 30, 31, 33, 34, 35, 36, 37; in freedom, 52, 53, 54, 56, 57, 58

Shcharansky, Avital (for earlier index entries see Shtiglits, Natalia): Shcharansky's letters and messages from Moscow to, 48–9, 49–50, 50, 63–4, 64, 76–6, 76, 77–8, 78, 86, 97, 103–4, 105, 129–30, 132, 138–41, 182–3, 216; Shcharansky's prison letters and references to, 283–6, 293, 294, 296, 297, 299–300, 301, 303, 304, 305, 306, 307, 309, 311, 312, 316, 317, 318, 320, 321, 322, 323–4, 325–6, 332, 350, 359, 362, 363, 364, 366–7, 371, 375–6, 376, 378, 381, 388, 389, 390, 395, 396, 397, 407; in Israel, 51–2, 88, 90, 101, 125, 286, 317, 334, 415; Shcharansky speaks to his visitors about, 50–1, 57, 105, 138; her telephone conversation with her husband, 72; an appeal from (1975), 75; a Senator's promise to (1975), 85; and the Helsinki Accords, 86; photographs from, reach Moscow, 88; photographs to, reach Jerusalem, 90; in the United States, 104, 325, 348, 352, 409; her husband's work in Moscow, 114; Shcharansky writes about, 104, 116; a message from, reaches Moscow, 118; an appeal on behalf of, 128; 'waiting for me', 130; a taped message to (1976), 138–41; campaigns for her husband (1977–86), 180–1, 187, 188, 198, 214, 218, 221, 224, 226, 248, 281, 327–8, 334, 348, 352, 357–8, 360–1, 382, 409–10, 412, 413; her letters stopped, 181; an attempted telephone call to, 183; a final telephone call from, 185; Shcharansky sees film of, 198–9; her marriage discussed in her husband's trial, 238, 240; Shcharansky seeks 'a life with', 267; Shcharansky 'further than ever from', 268; in Canada, 284; and 'a great injustice', 286; and Congressman Drinan's appeal, 287; Ida Milgrom's letters and messages to, 288–90, 335–45, 355–7, 385–6; President Reagan's letter to, 292; a letter from, reaches Chistopol prison, 317; photographs of, reach Chistopol prison, 317, 321; and Shcharansky's health, 326; her book published, 326, 428; and Boris Shcharansky's death (1980), 329–30; a telegram from, reach Chistopol, 332; her gift confiscated, 348; a letter to, confiscated, 350; meets President Reagan (1981), 352; in Stockholm, in a cage, 357–8; visits Holland, 358; and Margaret Thatcher, 360; in Madrid, 360–1; Shcharansky's letter from Chistopol prison to, 392–3; and her husband's honorary doctorate (1984), 402–3; her letter to Raisa Gorbachev (1985), 409–10; and 'the truth of our people', 411; and Shcharansky's future, 411, 413; reunited with her husband, 415; and her husband's qualities, 416; book by (1980), 432; articles by (1983, 1985), 436; and a photograph of her husband, plate 13; photographs of, plates 14, 41, 51, 54, 57, 58; Shcharansky holds a photograph of, plate 29

Shcharansky, Boris: his education, 1; and the Second World War, 2; his sons' childhood, 5–6, 7; in retirement, 21; at Istra (near Moscow), 25, 147; meets Natasha Shtiglits, 34–5; interrogated, 189; and the charges against his son, 195; a lie concerning, 216; and his son's sentence, 278; Shcharansky's prison letters to, 283, 293, 294, 306, 311, 312, 313; his letters to his son, 299, 305, 309, 317; his ill-health, 310, 314, 321, 323; dies, 329–30; his son's memories and reflections, 331–2, 341–2, 363–4; a photograph of, in his coffin, 344; his grave, 350, 363; photographs of, plates 2, 12; photograph of grave, plate 42

Shcharansky, Leonid (Lyonya): his childhood, 3–4, 5–6, 6–7, 9, 312; and his brother's arrest, 189; at his brother's trial, 231, 232, 240, 241, 247, 250, 253, 260, 268; hears his brother's sentence, 276; his brother's prison letters, 283, 293, 294, 324, 362, 363, 367, 373, 389, 413; visits his brother in prison, 288–90, 331, 353, 383, 385–7; his letters confiscated, 298, 301, 312, 316–7; his letters and postcards to his brother, 309, 378; visits his brother in labour camp, 335–45; a photograph of, 362; 'lucky', 363; and rumours of his brother's release, 413; photographs of, plates 4, 39, 49

Shcharansky, Raya: 189, 276; and Shcharansky's prison letters, 283, 297, 304, 306, 309, 322, 367; her specially baked strudel, 339; her culinary 'insistence', 341

Shcharansky, Sasha: Shcharansky's references to (in his prison letters), 297, 304, 311, 313, 317, 320, 322, 325, 367

Shcharansky, Shamai: 1–2, 30–1, 75, 86, 363, 396

'Shcharansky Steps', the (New York): named (1981), 352; a visitor 'moved' by (1985), 411

Shchelekhov, General Nikolai: meets activists, 143, 246; Ida Milgrom's protest to, 354

Shchiglik, Dmitri: greetings from, 306–7; a former prisoner, still refused his exit visa, 427; photograph of, plate 18

Shefer, Lev: a prisoner, 425

'Sheiki': a robot, 320

Sherbourne, Michael: at a protest meeting (1970), 18; his cousin a campaigner for Soviet Jews, 21; his telephone calls to Jewish activists, and to Shcharansky, 39, 59, 67, 82, 94, 107, 115, 136, 150–1, 158, 165, 175, 194, 195; letters and appeals transmitted through, 112–3, 135–6, 172, 183, 197, 198, 204, 223; refused a visa (1976), 152; and Dr Lipavsky, 175; and Shcharansky's arrest (1977), 187; an accusation against, 197; and the charges against Shcharansky, 210, 233

Sherbourne, Muriel: in Moscow, 217–8

Shevarnadze, Edward: in New York, 408

Shinbaum, Myrna: 21; in Moscow, 56; sends photographs to Shcharansky, 88

Shipler, David: in Moscow, 114, 142, 143, 146, 157, 199, 228, 229, 240, 275, 276, 280; in Jerusalem, 314, 329; articles by, 436–7

Shkolnik, Feiga: her protest, 28

Shkolnik, Isak: sentenced (1973), 28

Shnirman, Simon: a former prisoner, still refused his exit visa, 427

Sholem, Professor Gershom: 24, 25

Shraiber, Iosif: questioned, 205

Shtern, Dr Mikhail: arrested (1974), 44; an appeal on behalf of, 62; sentenced (1974), 62–3; a prisoner, 155; released, 185; reaches Holland, 190

Shtiglits, Michael (Misha): imprisoned (1973), 29; reaches Israel (1973), 31; in Israel, 34, 49, 180; in the United States, 180–1; Shcharansky congratulates, 284; photographs of, admired, 295, 317, 324

Shtiglits, Natalia: meets Shcharansky, 29–30; her twenty-third birthday, 32; her life with Shcharansky in Moscow, 32–5, 36, 37–8; celebrates Passover in Moscow (1974), 40; and a demonstration (1974), 43; marries Shcharansky, 45–8 (for future *index entries see* Shcharansky, Avital)

Shtilbans, Victor: a former prisoner, still refused his exit visa, 427

Shudovsky, Noam: accusations against, 170; Shcharansky mentions, 284

Shvartsman family: greetings from, 309

Siberia: rumours of deportations to, 8; exile in, 71, 93; Shcharansky travels to, 103–4; Slepak and Nudel exiled to, 228; 'friends' in, 304

Silnitsky, Alexander: and the 'conscription trap', 60, 81; sentenced (1975), 104, 107; an appeal on behalf of, 127; appeals on behalf of Shcharansky (1982), 355

Simhat Torah: celebrated in Moscow (1969), 16; and in 1976, 137, 140; and in 1979, 317

Simis, Konstantin: his home searched, 150, 154

Sinai Desert: 29

Singer, Lynn: and the campaign for Shcharansky's release, 188, 224

Six Day War (1967): 13–14, 16, 144–5

Skalov, Major: interrogates in Minsk, 210–14

Sklyarsky, Advocate: 200

Slavic Church: and the Psalms, 392-3

Slepak, Alexander: receives exit visa, 228

Slepak, Maria (Masha): 21, 94, 117; an appeal on behalf of, 127–8; signs an appeal, 184; summoned, 220; photographs of, 16, 28, 36

Slepak, Simon: 21, 219

Slepak, Vladimir: his protest (1970), 17; meets Shcharansky, 21; imprisoned (1972), 23; signs a message of solidarity (1973), 29; signs further letters and appeals, 35, 59, 63, 82, 83, 94, 96, 106–7, 107, 108, 112, 117, 119, 123, 136, 151, 156, 159, 167, 184, 184–5, 189, 191, 191–2, 198, 202, 204, 222; telephone calls to, 39, 157; visitors to, 42, 105; a leader, 87; and visiting Israeli sportsmen, 97–8; number three on list of refuseniks, 100; meets Soviet officials, 109; compiles a letter, 112; and emigration prospects, 115; his friendship with Shcharansky, 116–7; and a Passover service (1976), 117; a pall bearer, 119; appeal on behalf of, 119; criticised, 125; and an American petition, 126; and the Jews of Ilyinka, 126; and the Helsinki Watchdog group, 130, 150, 182; and the dissidents, 130–1; no action taken against, 131; telegrams not delivered to, 133; demonstrates (1976), 138, 144; and the KGB, 143, 149; detained, 144, 145; denounced (1977), 162–3, 172; protests, 165; Shcharansky stays with, 166, 179, 182, 185; his apartment searched, 172; prevented from

entering an apartment, 174; and Dr Lipavsky, 175, 176, 177; his aim, 181; and Shcharansky's arrest, 185–6, 189–90, 331; fears for, 188; accusations against, 196, 197; 'an enemy of the people', 219; questioned, 220; protests, 223; sentenced (1978), 228; Shcharansky's references to (1979), 297, 305, 307; an Atlas dedicated to (1979), 314, 431; in internal exile, 357; one of 'our heroes', 408; 'struggle and suffering' of, 411; 'delighted' for Shcharansky, 413; Shcharansky to fight for, 417; one of twenty-four former prisoners, still refused an exit visa, 427; photographs of, plates 16, 18, 20, 23, 27, 28, 37

Slinin, Alexander: sentenced (1974), 60, 61; visited, 175

Smith, Chesterfield: 218

Smukler, Connie: in Moscow (1975), 90; Shcharansky's postcard to (1975), 104; revisits Moscow (1976), 135, 137–42; recalls Dr Lipavsky, 177; a photograph of, admired, 295; photographed, plate 25

Smukler, Joseph (Joe): 104; an accusation against, 170, 177–8; a photograph of, admired, 295; and a 'tragic miscarriage of justice', 406

Socrates: hurries 'as though to help me', 380; 'immensity of', 381

Sokiriansky, Alexander: sentenced, 119

Sokolov, Colonel: Ida Milgrom's interview with (1982), 354; 'on holiday', 355

'Soldier of Zionism': Shcharansky denounced as, 163, 198

Solomon, Debbie: Ida Milgrom speaks to, 314; greetings to, 325

Solomon, King: and Shcharansky's reading, 396; and 'fear of the Lord', 401, 402

Solomon, Stan: a relative, 313

Solonin, Pavel Nikolaevich: and the trial of Shcharansky, 231; his closing speech, 254–64

Solovchenko, Investigator: 193-4

'Solzhenitsyn': an alleged code name, 255

Sophocles: 'conversations with', 380

Soviet–American Trade Agreement (October 1972): and the Jackson Amendment, 41; cancelled, 63, 417

Soviet Committee on Human Rights: 18, 19, 44

Soviet Embassy (London): a protest outside (1970), 18, 39; a letter of protest delivered to (1977), 187; Avital Shcharansky's hunger strike outside (1977), 198

Soviet Embassy (Washington DC): 140, 164

Soviet Ethnography: an article in, 302

Soviet Legation (Tel Aviv): 8

Soviet Mission to the United Nations (New York): 11; Avital Shcharansky's protest at, 409

Soviet Union: and the Jewish State, 1, 4, 5, 6, 8; and the Second World War, 2; and the Six Day War, 13–15; and exit visas for Jews (1967–8), 15–16; Western links with activists in, 38, 39, 41–2, 50–1, 56–7, 71, 87, 90, 92, 117–8, 135, 137, 141–2, 166–7, 174, 181, 214–5; and the Jackson Amendment, 54, 59, 61–3, 68–9, 74, 160; and drops in Jewish emigration, 59, 369; and the Stevenson Amendment, 62; and the Conference on Security and Co-operation in Europe, 24, 82, 86; and an alleged plan to put 'pressure' on, 86; Israeli sportsmen visit, 96–8; refuseniks in, listed, 99–102; Shcharansky's journey to a distant region of, 103–4; repressions in (for refuseniks), 113–4; establishment of a human rights 'Watchdog group' in, 124; Helsinki Agreement signed and ratified by, 86, 93, 94, 115–6; 'Thousands of Jews continue to be kept back in', 204; Shcharansky charged with doing 'considerable material harm' to, 233; Jewish question said to be 'solved in', 257; visit to a labour camp in, 335–45; 'at war against religion', 348; 'drastic cutback' in emigration from, 368; Jewish emigration activists, prisoners in, 422–5; statistics of Jewish emigration from, 425; former prisoners in, still refused exit visas, 426

Sovietische Heimland: attacks Jewish activists (1976), 125

Sovietskaya Hotel (Moscow): an alleged 'illegal' meeting in, 164, 233, 268

Sovietskaya Kultura: 53, 165

Sovietskaya Rossiya: a heart exercise system in, 372; a clipping from, 373

Spain: Avital Shcharansky visits, 382

Spanish Civil War, the: 27

Stalin, Iosif: 1, 5, 8, 96, 227, 229, 236, 265, 417; and 'tiny screws', 303

Stalingrad, battle of: 43

Stanford University: a robot at, 320

Star of David: to be worn with pride, 35, 142, 143, 144; and protest banners, 227, 228; demonstration with, photograph of, plate 22; on Boris Shcharansky's grave, photograph of, plate 42

Steers, Congressman Newton: 157

Stern, Jane: 49, 284; photographs of, 295, 317; greetings to, 318

Stern, Jerry: 49, 284, 317, 318

Stern, Michael: greetings to, 318

Stevenson, Senator Adlai: his amendment (1974), 62

Stevenson Amendment, the: 62, 63

Stockholm: a cage protest in, 357–8

Strategic Arms Limitation Talks: and Shcharansky, 287, 291

Student Struggle for Soviet Jewry: 11, 226, 352; publications of, 433

Succoth, festival: (Moscow, 1975), 97

Suez Canal: 28

Sukhachevskaya, Dr: a witness, 241, 242

Sulakadzev ('The Immortal'): a swindler, 312

Superfin, Gabriel (Garik): Shcharansky asks about, 297

Superfin, Roman: Shcharansky's regards to, 297

Supreme Court (Moscow): protest outside (1970), 18

Supreme Soviet (Moscow): protest outside (1971), 19; letter of protest to (1971), 19; a further protest in (1974), 62, 69; Shcharansky describes a demonstration near (1975), 71; unpublished decree of, 74; ratifies Helsinki Final Act, 94; further demonstration near (1975), 106; a series of demonstrations at (1976), 138, 142–5; a further demonstration at (1977), 166; extends period of detention, 221, 223–4; strips Sakharov of his State honours, 332–3; seeks 'an admission of guilt', 383; rejects a 'pardon', 391; deprives Shcharansky of Soviet citizenship (1986), 414

Suslensky, Yakov: sentenced (1970), 17; at Vladimir prison (1975), 81, 101; appeals on behalf of Shcharansky (1982), 355

Sverdlovsk: a Jew from, brought to trial, 20; a journey to, 55; information from, 60; an appeal on behalf of two Jews from, 155–6

Sweden: 18, 214

Switzerland: Avital Shcharansky in, 183, 187, 382

Syria: 6, 13, 28

Tallinn: Shcharansky and Avital travel to, 34, 324, 366

Talmud, the: study of, 411

Tarasov, V.: 'We hate you', 126

Taratuta, Aba: 83, 101; signs appeals, 112, 159, 167, 202, 204–5

Taratuta, Ida: 83

Tarnopolsky, Yury: a prisoner, 394, 425

Tashkent: 176, 177

Tass: a condemnation from (1971), 19; an editor at, 21; a denunciation from (1976), 117; a possible announcement in, 181; and a 'humane' act, 185; and Michael Sherbourne, 194; and a 'criminal', 221; and 'noisy propaganda campaigns', 364

Tat language (Judaeo-Tat): 244

Tatar Republic: a prison in, 283; and an

ancient civilisation, 302; officials of, and
Shcharansky's health, 307, 391
Tbilisi: refuseniks in, 101
Tekoah, Joseph: an appeal to (1969), 17
Tel Aviv: 4, 8; a clothes cutter from, in
Moscow (1975), 97; a former Prisoner of
Zion reaches (1981), 351
telephones: disconnected, 80–1, 93, 108,
133
Teller, Professor Edward: and 'a martyr',
359
Temple of Jerusalem: destruction of, 47
Ten Commandments: and the Helsinki
Accords, 86
Tesker, Geulah: born, 143
Tesker, Rimma: and 'redemption', 143
Tesker, Zakhar: signs appeals, 35, 184;
arrested, 46, 53; his journey, 55; his case
raised, 110; demonstrates, 138; beaten,
142; his daughter born, 143; photograph
of, plate 18
Thatcher, Margaret: urges 'a humanitarian
gesture', 360; and 'a dark shadow', 368;
and a possible exchange, 412; photograph
of, with Avital Shcharansky, plate 51
The Art of Programming (Knut):
Shcharansky reads, 295
The Creeping Counter-Revolution (Begun);
cited, 236; not allowed as evidence, 268
The Gates of our Exodus (Kandel):
recollections in, 178–9
The Jews of Russia: Their History in Maps and
Photographs (Gilbert): published (1976),
145; re-issued in Jerusalem (1979), 314
The Little Frog Who Travelled A Lot:
Shcharansky's reference to, 311
'The Man Who Went Too Far': and Avital
Shcharansky's campaign, 198
The Master and Margarita (Bulgakov): and
the KGB, 182, 183
The Protocols of the Learned Elders of Zion:
cited, 236
The Six Day War (Randolph and Winston
Churchill): discussed, 144
The Source (Michener): 25, 77–8
The Story of the Master of the Good Name
(Wiesel): 'immensely interesting', 397
The Third Wave (Toffler): Shcharansky
reads, 396
The Times: 143, 182, 187, 413
The Way of Jews in the Red Army: cited, 243
'Thirty-Fives': campaign for Soviet Jews,
20–1
'This Year in Jerusalem': Shcharansky's
message (1975), 91, 94; and in 1976, 137
Thompson, Robert: and a possible
exchange, 224–5
Three Men in a Boat (Jerome): 397
Tiberias: 49, 381
Ticktin, Harold: in Moscow, 71

Time: 281
Tiraspol: information from, 60, 80;
refuseniks in, 101
Toffler, Alvin: his books, 396
Tomilino: a prayer house closed down at,
61
Torah: Shcharansky studying (1975), 76
Toronto: 144; Shcharansky's relatives in,
313–4; Avital Shcharansky's visit to, 327
Torwald, Rune: and a protest in Sweden,
214
Toth, Jenny: photographed, 295
Toth, Robert: in Moscow, 114, 120, 126,
128, 166, 174, 175–7, 178, 226;
questioned, 200; and Shcharansky's trial,
233, 234, 238, 243, 248, 251, 260, 270;
articles by, 437
'Traders of Souls': shown on Moscow
television (1977), 161–2; shown a second
time, 180; mentioned, 198; protests
against, referred to, 206, 212, 247, 253
Transjordan: 6
Trifonov, Edward: and Shcharansky's
'main aim', 69; helps compile a letter,
112; a photograph of, plate 31
Trotsky, Lev (Leon Bronstein): 96
Trud: 53
Tsibulnik, Assistant Prosecutor-General:
Jews protest to, 223–4
Tsipin, Leonid: detained, 53; his journey to
Kiev (1974), 55; and a Hebrew class, 68;
at a demonstration (1975), 70; helps
compile lists, 100; denounces his former
fellow-activists (1977), 196–7, 208; a
'secret' witness, 241; his further
testimony, 245–6, 247, 256, 259, 261,
263, 270, 271; the 'false testimony' of,
279; photograph of, plate 18
Tsitlionok, Boris: signs appeals, 35, 96;
arrested, 46, 53; his journey, 55;
demonstrates, 69–70; sentenced (1975),
70–1, 73, 78, 81, 107; in Siberia, 93; a
refusenik since 1971, 101; Shcharansky's
visit to, 103–4, 105; denounced, 163;
interrogated, 221; Shcharansky's
questions about, 305, 307; a note from,
321, 322; appeals on behalf of
Shcharansky (1982), 355
Tsukerman, Vladimir: a prisoner, 394;
released (1984) but still refused his exit
visa, 427
Tsvetaeva, Marina: Shcharansky reads a
book by, 379
Tufeld, Igor: a refusenik, 145; photograph
of, plate 18
Tula: refuseniks in, 101
Tupik: Shcharansky travels to, 103, 105;
'telephone cut' in, 108
Tverdokhlebov, Andrei: a human rights
activist, 77; sentenced (1976), 131; cited

in Shcharansky's trial, 272
Two Bundles of Letters (a novel): 374
Tykhyi, M.: his home searched, 252

Uganda: hijack rescue in (1976), 132, 139
Ukraine, the: 80; political prisoners in, 154;
'repression' in, 154–5, 252
Ulanovsky, Lev: a student, 22, 31; applies
for an exit visa, 35–6; and the Jackson
Amendment, 42; refused an exit visa, 80,
115; hears Shcharansky lecture, 87; and
Sakharov, 89; and American visitors, 91;
signs appeals, 94, 95, 109, 117, 151, 269;
and the compilation of lists of refuseniks,
99–100, 101; an appeal on behalf of, 128;
and 'a question of priorities', 151; and the
KGB, 153; defends Shcharansky, 202–3;
lies concerning, 216; helps prepare a
report (1979), 287; Shcharansky's
question about, 305; greetings from, 309;
receives his exit visa (1979), 314;
photograph of, plate 16
Union of Councils for Soviet Jews: 21, 23,
56, 124, 125, 156, 157, 189, 197, 226, 227;
publications of, 433; journals of, 438
Unità: declines an invitation, 238
United Arab Republic: 25
United Nations, the: 1, 4, 6, 11, 17, 157;
Jews protest at bomb at (1976), 106–7; an
'absurd' vote in, 123; appeals to, 188,
360; Israel condemned by, 259; an appeal
by Israel's Ambassador to (1985), 407;
celebrations at, and a labour camp
sentence, 408; protest, outside Soviet
Mission to, 409; 'impressive steps'
opposite, 411
United Nations Human Rights
Commission: 17
United Press International: reports a
possible exchange, 224–5
United States, the: and the Second World
War, 4; and the Helsinki Accords, 24–5,
86; visitors to the refuseniks from, 38, 39,
41–2, 50–1, 56–7, 71, 87, 90, 92, 117–8,
135, 137, 141–2, 174, 181, 214–5; and the
Trade Reform Act, 41, 61, 63, 69, 249,
417; protests from, 61; bicentennial of,
132; successful 'pressure' of, 146; the
campaign for Shcharansky in, 180–1,
188, 218, 222–3; criticised in
Shcharansky's trial, 263; 'friends' in, 304;
Avital Shcharansky's visits to, 104,
323–4, 348, 382; opinion in, concerning
Shcharansky and his wife, 358
United States Congress: Sakharov's letter
to (1973), 41; Soviet Jews appeal to
(1976), 108–9; (1977), 156, 191; a letter of
denunciation addressed to (1977), 169,
172; letters to, referred to, 212, 256; a
special debate in (1978), 226; and

Shcharansky's trial, 233, 271
United States Congressmen: in Moscow,
77; Shcharansky talks to, 78, 268
United States Embassy (Moscow): an
appeal handed in to (1975), 79;
accusations concerning (1977), 169, 249,
274; and Shcharansky's possible release
(1983), 383
United States Senate: passes Jackson
Amendment, 61–2; letters to, referred to,
212
United States Trade Reform Act (1972): 41,
61, 63, 69, 249, 417
Universal Declaration of Human Rights: 5,
18, 82, 86, 150, 239
Ural mountains: 410, 414
USA Magazine: Shcharansky reads (1983),
365, 396
Ussishkin, Menachem: in Odessa, 1
Ustinov, Marshal: an appeal to, 155
Uzbekistan: a prisoner from, 157; Dr
Lipavsky in, 314

Valerian, Richard: in Moscow, 71
Vance, Cyrus R.: in Moscow, 188; cancels
two missions, 228; Avital Shcharansky
appeals to, 248
Vanik, Congressman Charles A.: 41, 99
Vechirni Kiev: accusations in, 214, 270
Verein, Lieutenant-Colonel Andrei: 26, 31
Viechernyaya Moskva: endorses a film, 165;
reveals an informer, 196, 208
Vienna: 2, 48, 161, 162
Vilig, Alexander: a former prisoner, still
refused his exit visa, 427
Vilnius: refuseniks in, 101; interrogations
in, 205; a Jewish history book published
in, 324
Vinarov, Yakov: sentenced (1975), 89, 107,
108; an appeal on behalf of, 127; reaches
Israel (1977), 205; referred to in
Shcharansky's trial, 272; appeals on
behalf of Shcharansky (1982), 355
Vinnitsa: 28, 44; refuseniks in, 101
Virgil: 'read in a rush', 379; 'conversations
with', 380
Virshubsky, Anatoly: sentenced (1985),
407; a prisoner, 425
Visa Office (OVIR, Department of Visas
and Registration): 19, 26, 46, 60, 63, 64,
80–1, 99–101, 110, 113, 134, 140, 143,
156, 158, 246, 253
Vitebsk: 43
Vladimir prison: Jewish prisoners in, 81;
conditions in, 241, 262–3, 351;
Shcharansky in, 282–3; Shcharansky's
departure from, 289–90
Vladimirov, Viktor: attacks Shcharansky,
218–9
Vladivostok: Summit conference at, 58, 61

Vogel, Wolfgang: and a possible exchange, 412

Voice of America (radio station): 85, 132, 235

Voice of Israel (radio station): 78, 99; Sakharov's message to, 145

Volga cars: 37, 40

Volga, River: 288

Volodin, V.I.: and 'dangerous crimes', 190, 219; and a photograph, 295

Volokolamsk: a visit to, 34, 320, 366

Volvovsky, Leonid: signs appeals, 114, 123, 155, 167; demonstrates (1976), 144; his home searched, 151; defends Shcharansky (1977), 206; and Shcharansky's trial, 233; tried and sentenced (1985), 407–8; 'struggle and suffering of', 411; a prisoner, 416, 425; photograph of, plate 26

Volvovsky, Ludmila (Mila): a gesture of solidarity for, 407–8; a telegram to Shcharansky from, 416; photograph of, plate 44

Voronel, Professor Alexander: 22, 26, 53; arrested, 46; signs appeals, 59; and *Jews in the USSR*, 75; book by, 433

Voronina, Lidia: a refusenik, 116; signs her first appeal, 116–7; signs other appeals, 123; her apartment searched, 155; receives an exit visa, 159; and an attack on Shcharansky, 219; articles by, 235

Vudka, Yury: sentenced (1970), 17

Waldheim, Kurt: a plea to, 188

Wall Street Journal: 188, 357

Warsaw Cinema (Moscow): 45

Washington Committee for Soviet Jewry: 145

Washington DC: a resolution in (1972), 23; and Shcharansky's possible release (1983), 383; rumours in (1985), 408; no comment in, 412

Washington Post: 114, 193, 225, 248, 259; an open letter in (1979), 287

Weisman, Inez: accused, 197

Weiss, Rabbi Avi: and Shcharansky's hunger strike, 357; and American opinion, 358

West Berlin: 414

Western Europe: visitors from, 39

Western Jewry: 'we feel their support', 131

Western Wall ('Wailing Wall'): Shcharansky reaches, 416; photograph of Shcharansky at, plate 56

Western World: duty of, 357; a call to, 418

Whale Alley: discovered, 302

White House (Washington DC): 187, 200; Avital Shcharansky's visit to, 352

White Russia (Byelorussia): 80

Wiesel, Elie: a novel by, 397; and 'our heroes', 408

Wilson, Harold: in Helsinki, 86

Winston, Frank: in Moscow, 71

Wootliff, Jonathan: and 'a great hero', 411

World Psychiatric Association: a condemnation by, 273

Wurtman, Enid: a message to, 104; visits Avital Shcharansky, 125; in Moscow (1976), 135, 137–42; in Jerusalem (1980), 329; reports Avital Shcharansky's hope and optimism (1986), 413; photographs of (in Moscow), plates 25, 26

Wurtman, Stuart: 104, 189, 329

Wyschogrod, Rabbi Michael: 'our duty to try harder', 408–9

Xenophon: and criminal codes, 380

Yagoda, Henry: his successors, 278

Yakir, Alexander: a prisoner, 425

Yakir, Rimma: a postcard from, 305, 366; a letter from, confiscated, 373

Yamit (Sinai): Avital Shcharansky visits, 304, 317

Yarim-Agaev, Yury: 25–6

Yates, Congressman Sidney: in Moscow (1975), 90, 129; regards to, 134; an 'illegal' meeting with, denounced, 164

Yeniseisk: Shcharansky travels to, 103–4, 105

Yershkovich, Anatoly: 15

Yershkovich, Luba: 15, 22, 218–9

Yeshiva University (New York): Shcharansky's honorary doctorate at, 402–3

Yevseev: his article, 296

Yezhov, Nikolai: his successors, 278

Yiddish: songs sung in (1969), 16; a story told in (1974), 43; the Exodus recited in (1976), 117; no possibility to study in, 235; and a book on ethnography, 375

Yom Kippur: fasting on (1979), 291; Shcharansky's hunger strike begins on (1982), 355

Yom Kippur War (1973): 258

Young, Congressman Andrew: 157, 188

Zagorsk: Jews imprisoned at, 144

Zakharov (a janitor): 234, 260

Zalmanson, Vulf: a prisoner, 108

Zaplyaeva (a typist): and the charge against Shcharansky, 260–1

Zavurov, Amner: sentenced (1977), 157, 183; his father summoned, 174; and Dr Lipavsky, 175, 177

Zavurov, Amnon: a threat against, 174

Zavurov, Boris: summoned by KGB, 174

Zdorovie (Health): an article in, 397

Zelichenok, Roald (Alec): sentenced (1985), 407, 410–11; a prisoner, 426; his

photograph, plate 45
Zen Buddhist: 'legs crossed', 324
Zionism: hostility to, 1, 6, 10, 21, 90, 107,
123, 191; defence of, 20, 236, 265;
'agents' of, 136, 162–3, 164, 196–7,
233–4, 256, 257, 258, 275; a lecture on,
151; denounced in a film, 161–5;
denounced by *Izvestia*, 165; a 'victim' of,
242

Zlotver, Dina: an appeal concerning, 155–6
Zlotver, Isaak: an appeal concerning, 155–6
Znaniye Cinema (Leningrad): 96
Zubko, Stanislav: a prisoner, 394; released
(1985), but still refused his exit visa, 427
Zunshain, Zakhar: a prisoner, 410–11, 426
Zvezdny Gorodok: a commuter to, 176